Manuscripts from Mannheim, ca. 1730–1778

QUELLEN UND STUDIEN ZUR GESCHICHTE DER MANNHEIMER HOFKAPELLE

Herausgegeben von der Forschungsstelle
Mannheimer Hofkapelle
der Heidelberger Akademie der Wissenschaften
unter Leitung von Silke Leopold

Band 9

PETER LANG
Frankfurt am Main · Berlin · Bern · Bruxelles · New York · Oxford · Wien

Eugene K. Wolf
In collaboration with Jean K. Wolf and Paul Corneilson

Manuscripts from Mannheim, ca. 1730-1778

A Study in the Methodology
of Musical Source Research

PETER LANG
Europäischer Verlag der Wissenschaften

Die Deutsche Bibliothek - CIP-Einheitsaufnahme
Wolf, Eugene K.:

Manuscripts from Mannheim, ca. 1730–1778 ; a study in the methodology of musical source research / Eugene K. Wolf. - Frankfurt am Main ; Berlin ; Bern ; Bruxelles ; New York ; Oxford ; Wien : Lang, 2002
 (Quellen und Studien zur Geschichte der Mannheimer Hofkapelle ; Band 9)
 ISBN 3-631-39726-7

This book has been published
with the generous assistance
of the American Musicological Society
and the School of Arts and Sciences
of the University of Pennsylvania.

ISSN 0929-9747
ISBN 3-631-39726-7
US-ISBN 0-8204-6005-2

© Peter Lang GmbH
Europäischer Verlag der Wissenschaften
Frankfurt am Main 2002
All rights reserved.

All parts of this publication are protected by copyright. Any utilisation outside the strict limits of the copyright law, without the permission of the publisher, is forbidden and liable to prosecution. This applies in particular to reproductions, translations, microfilming, and storage and processing in electronic retrieval systems.

Printed in Germany 1 2 3 4 6 7

www.peterlang.de

For
Robert Münster

and the Entire Staff of the
Bayerische Staatsbibliothek, Munich

Past, Present, and Future

Contents

Preface	11
Abbreviations	16
Library Sigla	17
List of Figures	19
List of Tables	20

1. Introduction   23

The Electoral Court at Mannheim, 1720–1778	23
Music in the Life of the Court	27
Dissolution of the Court and Removal to Munich (1778)	34
A Question of Survival: Manuscripts from Mannheim	35
Manuscript Types	38
Autograph scores	38
Copies from the Mannheim court collection	39
Loss of the collection	41
Copyists' scores of operas and related works	44
Copies for external use	44
Relationship of manuscript types and Appendix A, sections I–VI	45

2. Codicological Evidence: Methods for the Study of Eighteenth-Century Music Manuscripts   47

Initial Examination of the Manuscript	50
Paper and Watermarks	55
The recording and reproduction of watermarks	57
Paper in the Mannheim manuscripts	63
Staving	65
Staff-liners and staff-lining in the eighteenth century	68
Analytical specifications for staving	73
Procedures for the analysis of staving	79
The use of rastrology: an example	81
The lining of paper at Mannheim	87
Handwriting and Copyists	88
Copyists in the Mannheim manuscripts	94
Chronological considerations	102

3. The "Core" Manuscripts (App. A/I/1–24)   105

    Manuscripts of the Jesuitenkirche in Mannheim   105
    Autograph Scores by Carlo Grua   107
    Ballets Copied by Sigismund Falgera   108
    Autograph Manuscripts of Mozart   109

4. Sacred and Dramatic Music of Ignaz Holzbauer (App. A/II/1–21)   113

    The Holzbauer Masses at the Bayerische Staatsbibliothek   113
    Autograph Scores   123

5. Orchestral Music of Christian Cannabich in Munich (App. A/III/1–73, M1–7). In collaboration with Jean K. Wolf.   127

    Types of Parts: Original, Duplicate, Added, Replacement   129
        Original parts   129
        Duplicate parts   133
        Added parts   135
        Replacement parts and sets   135
    Chronological Groups   136
        Group 1 (Cannabich 2–15, M1–4, M5 [?])   137
        Group 2 (Cannabich 16–38, M6 [?])   142
        Group 3 (Cannabich 39–55, M7)   150
        Group 4 (Cannabich 56–61)   153
        Group 5 (Cannabich 62–73)   156

6. Autographs of Grua, Richter, and Mozart without Explicit Indication of Provenance (App. A/IV/1–11)   159

    Two Masses of Carlo Grua   159
    Autograph Scores and Parts by Franz Xaver Richter   160
    Oboe Parts by Mozart to K. 175   162

7. Music of Georg Joseph Vogler in Darmstadt and Offenbach (App. A/V/1–43)   163

8. **Other Manuscripts from Mannheim, I: Operas and Related Works from Appendix A/VI. By Paul Corneilson and Eugene K. Wolf.**   173

    Opera at Mannheim and Its Manuscript Tradition   174
    The Manuscripts   175
    The Berlin Catalogue   184
    The Owner of the Collection Identified   194
    Mozart and Count von Sickingen   197
    Appendix: Manuscripts of Mannheim Operas Lost in World War II   199

9. **Other Manuscripts from Mannheim, II: Sacred, Smaller Vocal, and Instrumental Music from Appendix A/VI**   201

    Sacred Music by Holzbauer and Grua in Moravia, Austria, and Germany   201
    The Pretlack Collection (D-B; App. A/VI/39–119)   205
    Other Manuscripts in Berlin (D-B; App. A/VI/13–38)   207
    The Ritschel Manuscripts in Dresden (D-Dsl; App. A/VI/120–38)   208
    Manuscripts from Karlsruhe and Rheda (App. A/VI/146–49, 152)   209
    Regensburg (D-Rtt; App. A/VI/153–91)   210
    Four Manuscripts from Schwerin (now D-SWl, B-Bc)   216
    Mozart's Concerto for Three Pianos, K. 242 (App. A/VI/?202)   217
    Some Manuscripts Probably *Not* from Mannheim   219

Appendix A: Manuscripts from Mannheim   223

    I. Manuscripts Extant at Mannheim or with Explicit Evidence of Mannheim Provenance (the "Core" Manuscripts)   224
    II. Music of Ignaz Holzbauer in the Bayerische Staatsbibliothek, Munich; Autograph Scores   228
    III. Music of Christian Cannabich in the Bayerische Staatsbibliothek   234
        Group 1 (ca. 1755–ca. 1761/62)   234
        Group 2 (ca. 1762–68)   237
        Group 3 (ca. 1769–78)   240
        Group 4 (Munich, ca. 1778–1781/82[?])   243
        Group 5 (Munich, ca. 1781/82[?]–1794)   245
        Miscellaneous Manuscripts (M1–M7)   248
    IV. Autographs of Grua, Richter, and Mozart without Explicit Indication of Provenance   251

V. Music of Georg Joseph Vogler in Darmstadt and Offenbach		254
Dated Manuscripts		254
Undated Manuscripts		258
VI. Other Manuscripts from Mannheim		262

Appendix B: Paper   293

I. Swiss Paper   295
   1. Blum Papers   295
   2. Heusler Papers   303
   3. Miscellaneous Swiss Papers   309
II. German Paper from the Palatinate and Vicinity   309
III. Dutch Paper   312
IV. Alsatian Paper   313
V. Supplement: Paper Used Only in Munich   314

Appendix C: Compound Rastra Used at Mannheim   317

I. Two-Stave Rastra   318
II. Four-Stave Rastra   320
III. Five-Stave Rastra   320
IV. Six-Stave Rastra   325
V. Seven-Stave Rastra   325
VI. Ten-Stave Rastra   325
VII. Twelve-Stave Rastra   332
   Oblong Format   332
   Upright Format   333

Appendix D: Copyists   335

I. Named Copyists   336
II. Principal Copyists   352
III. Other Mannheim Copyists   371

Bibliography   383

Index   395

Preface

The year 1778 marked the demise of one of the most illustrious court societies of the eighteenth century: that of Mannheim, capital of the so-called Electoral Palatinate (*Kurpfalz*) or southwest Rhine region of Germany. In that year, long-standing treaty obligations forced the ruling elector, Carl Theodor, to transfer his court from Mannheim to Munich, where he became ruler of a newly combined Palatinate and Bavaria. The effect upon the renowned musical life of Mannheim was devastating; some two-thirds of the musicians followed the court to Munich, while the remainder stayed behind as pensioners or as members of several musical organizations supported by the elector.

A secondary consequence of the move to Munich was to create a mystery that the present book purports to solve: for until now it had never been determined precisely what happened to the massive musical collection of the Mannheim court. No manuscripts were known to remain in Mannheim, and in Munich the only extensive holdings by Mannheim composers were believed to have been copied there. The obstacle this situation posed for present-day scholars is obvious. With no way of knowing the relationship between extant sources and the Mannheim originals, and with little reliable information regarding such matters as chronology, it was difficult to produce reliable editions of this important body of music or to begin seriously to write its history.

A principal contribution of this book is thus to reveal exactly what happened to the Mannheim performance materials. (Sadly, the vast majority were irretrievably lost, as discussed in chapter 1.) At the same time, the book demonstrates that several large segments of this collection, as well as 45 autograph scores by Mannheim composers, did in fact survive, providing an invaluable foundation for future research. Finally, we have succeeded in identifying over 200 manuscripts that, although not actually part of the Mannheim court library, were definitely copied there, often by official court copyists.

The first goal of this book, then, is to establish the contents of this "newly identified complex of manuscripts from Mannheim" and to outline the evidence for its existence.[1] A second goal is to utilize the tools of manuscript research such as the study of watermarks and handwriting—already the principal basis for estab-

---

[1] The reference is to Eugene K. and Jean K. Wolf, "A Newly Identified Complex of Manuscripts from Mannheim," *Journal of the American Musicological Society* 27 (1974): 379–437, in which these discoveries were first announced. For a more leisurely review of the process leading to these identifications see my article "The Path to *Manuscripts from Mannheim*: A 'Pre-Preface,'" in Ludwig Finscher, Bärbel Pelker, and Rüdiger Thomsen-Fürst, eds., *Mannheim – "Ein Paradies der Tonkünstler"? Kongreßbericht Mannheim 1999*, 171–81 (Frankfurt am Main: Peter Lang, 2002).

lishing the provenance of these sources—to propose approximate dates for most of these sources. These two aims are reflected most concretely in Appendix A of this book, the six sections of which provide a comprehensive *catalogue raisonné* of the over 350 manuscripts identified in this survey as having originated in Mannheim.

While the goals just mentioned will be of greatest interest to specialists, the broader purpose of this book, as emphasized by its subtitle, is to furnish an example of, and detailed introduction to, a basic methodology for the study of music manuscripts from approximately the seventeenth through the mid-nineteenth centuries. The latter aim supplies the rationale for most of chapter 2, which is intended among other things as a kind of handbook of the techniques employed in the modern musicological study of manuscripts. In addition, the book contains many detailed discussions of specific problems that serve to illustrate the methods discussed in chapter 2.

With the exception of the first two chapters, the overall organization of this book follows that of Appendix A. Chapter 1 begins with a consideration of Mannheim as a cultural and musical center, followed by an introductory discussion of the problems presented by the Mannheim manuscripts. Chapter 2 is devoted primarily to the material on methodology just mentioned, with extended sections on the study of paper and watermarks, staving or staff-lining ("rastrology"), and handwriting. These sections also present the main conclusions in each area regarding the characteristics of Mannheim manuscripts (what I shall henceforth refer to, for want of a better word, as their "codicological" characteristics). The remaining chapters then parallel the six sections of Appendix A: chapters 3–7 discuss the works listed in Appendices A/I–V, while chapters 8 and 9 treat, respectively, the large secular dramatic works and the various other works (sacred and smaller vocal works, instrumental music) listed in Appendix A/VI.

Appendix A itself is organized generally according to the strength of evidence for Mannheim provenance of the various sections, the manuscripts of Appendix A/I having direct documentary evidence of their provenance, those of Appendix A/VI only indirect or circumstantial evidence (see the introduction to Appendix A). As the master catalogue of the Mannheim corpus of manuscripts, Appendix A includes all the pertinent details regarding each of the manuscripts and suggests provisional dates for most. It is followed by three other appendices, B–D, that identify and give full information on the papers, staving, and copyists of these manuscripts, in each case referring the reader back to Appendix A.

Bibliographical citations in this book generally follow the principles of the *Chicago Manual of Style*, 14th edition; in this system a colon is used to separate volume and page numbers (e.g., "*JAMS* 2:3" = vol. 2, p. 3 of *JAMS*). Transcriptions of eighteenth-century titles and quotations are intended accurately to reflect the originals, without correction or modernization and without the constant addition of "sic." Translations into English are my own unless otherwise noted.

A word is perhaps in order here about the scholarly stance represented by the present study. Some—many—musicologists will no doubt consider this book an example of rampant positivism (a view that evinces a misunderstanding of that term, incidentally). But my hope would be that those scholars whose interests run to more critical and interpretive approaches would at least recognize the utility for many kinds of studies of having solid control of areas of source research such as authenticity, chronology, and provenance as a foundation or background for their work. (Consider, for example, the currently popular subject of intertextuality, which depends at least initially on just those elements.) In my view, one of the virtues of musicology as it is traditionally conceived is that it encourages us to cross into disciplinary areas we had never expected to visit—and from which we may well gratefully depart as soon as we have solved the relevant problem (perhaps with the help of a primer such as my chapter 2). One might even hope, probably quixotically, that those with other scholarly interests and agendas might grant that interpretation, creativity, and imagination can occasionally characterize even such ostensibly sterile pursuits as the dating of a manuscript or the establishment of a stemma. In any event, I do not myself regard the kind of highly empirical research depicted in this book as inherently more important than, or somehow superior to, the manifold other approaches that are now accepted parts of the pluralistic discipline we call musicology. Indeed, I shall be perfectly happy never again to trace another watermark or measure another set of staves!

A project of the sort depicted in the present book places extraordinary demands upon librarians, requiring as it does the consultation of large numbers of manuscripts, often with meager results. It is thus a particular pleasure to record my gratitude here to the many librarians who have made this study possible. Thanks must go first and foremost to Dr. Robert Münster, former head of the Musiksammlung (now Musikabteilung) of the Bayerische Staatsbibliothek in Munich. From the beginning of this project in the 1960s to the present, he and his colleagues have provided the most generous assistance imaginable, and it is therefore fitting that this book be dedicated to them. Among others on the staff of the Staatsbibliothek over the years I should like to single out Drs. Robert Machold, Renata Wagner, and Helmut Hell (now head of the Musikabteilung of the Staatsbibliothek zu Berlin – Preussischer Kulturbesitz) as well as the present head of the Musikabteilung, Dr. Hartmut Schaefer, all of whom facilitated our work in countless ways.

In addition to the librarians already mentioned, I should like to extend special thanks to the following: Dr. Joachim Jaenecke of the Staatsbibliothek zu Berlin – Preussischer Kulturbesitz; Herr Hugo Angerer, Fürst Thurn und Taxis Hofbibliothek, Regensburg; Dr. Oswald Bill and Frau Irmgard Bröning, Hessische Landes- und Hochschulbibliothek, Darmstadt; de heer Johan Eeckeloo and de heer Julien de Vuyst, Koninklijk Conservatorium/Conservatoire royal de musique, Brussels; Dr. Jiří Sehnal, Moravské muzeum, Brno; Dr. Klaus Häfner, Badische Landesbibliothek,

Karlsruhe; Dr. Hartmut Broszinski, Landesbibliothek und Murhardsche Bibliothek, Kassel; Frau Liselotte Homering and Dr. Grit Arnscheidt, Städtisches Reiss-Museum, Mannheim; Frau Herta Müller, Staatliche Museen, Meiningen; Dr. Albert Ernst, Universitätsbibliothek Munster; Dr. Raimund Jedeck, Landesbibliothek Mecklenburg-Vorpommern, Schwerin; Dr. Frohmut Dangel-Hofmann, Musiksammlung des Grafen Schönborn-Wiesentheid, Wiesentheid; Madame Chantal Husson, Bibliothèque municipale, Châlons-en-Champagne; Chanoine Gérard Grasser and Madame Mireille Brengel, Union Ste Cécile, Strasbourg; Mr. Arthur Searle and Dr. Rupert Ridgewell, The British Library, London; Dr. Sarah J. Adams, Isham Memorial Library of Music, Harvard University, Cambridge, Mass.; and the entire staffs of the New York Public Library and the Library of Congress, Washington, D.C. I am also greatly indebted to Drs. Ortrun Landmann (Dresden) and Gertraut Haberkamp (Munich) of RISM, whose assistance at every stage of this study has been invaluable.

Warm thanks are due to Frau Ute-Margrit André (Offenbach) for permitting me to examine the important manuscripts of the André-Archiv, and to Dr. Axel Beer (Mainz) for his generous assistance in facilitating my work with this outstanding collection. Likewise, Herr Heinz Lindner, formerly archivist of the Jesuitenkirche in Mannheim, graciously permitted us access on several occasions to the small but central music collection of that institution.

More than most, this book is a collaborative effort in both the specific and the general sense. My wife, Jean Kessler Wolf, carried out the initial research on which chapter 5 (on Christian Cannabich) is based, as well as most of the original research in the archives of Munich. Without her indefatigable efforts this book would literally not exist. My other principal collaborator, Dr. Paul Corneilson, now Managing Editor of the C. P. E. Bach edition in Cambridge, Mass., is both co-author of chapter 8 and the source of many valuable suggestions that have contributed immeasurably to this study. Drs. Bärbel Pelker and Rüdiger Thomsen-Fürst of the Forschungsstelle *Mannheimer Hofkapelle* in Heidelberg, under the leadership of Professors Ludwig Finscher and Silke Leopold, have been the source of a veritable trove of new information stemming from their pathbreaking research on Mannheim. Likewise, Frau Brigitte Höft, formerly of the Städtische Musikbücherei in Mannheim, shared with me her extensive knowledge of Mannheim on many occasions. In addition, I want to thank Dr. Margaret G. Grave (New Brunswick, N.J.) for her careful reading of chapter 7 of this book and Dr. Dexter Edge for sending me early drafts of his important new dissertation on Mozart's copyists.

To my colleagues at the University of Pennsylvania I extend my warm appreciation for their unstinting support, particularly Lawrence Bernstein, Eugene Narmour, and Gary Tomlinson and our inimitable music librarian, Marjorie Hassen. My students Mary S. Macklem and Carol Whang provided valuable research assistance on numerous occasions, as did Maria K. Wolf in the realms of copyediting and proofreading. Finally, the influence of Jan LaRue, under whose guidance this study began, will be evident throughout this book, both in its overall approach and in specific technical spheres such as watermarks and handwriting. I am delighted to acknowledge his role as teacher and model.

A major portion of the research for this book was carried out with the support of a fellowship from the John Simon Guggenheim Memorial Foundation, for which I remain deeply appreciative. Additional support was provided by fellowships and grants from the American Council of Learned Societies, the National Endowment for the Humanities, the American Philosophical Society, and the University of Pennsylvania. Thanks are also due to the School of Arts and Sciences of the University of Pennsylvania (Dr. Samuel H. Preston, Dean) for a grant toward publication of this book, as well as to the American Musicological Society for a grant toward production of the illustrations, which were expertly prepared by John A. Wolf of Wolf Biomedical Media, Philadelphia.

Most of the writing of this book was accomplished during a period that many would characterize as difficult. That it has never seemed so is a tribute to my wonderful family—my wife, Jean, and my children, Maria and John. For their unfailing support, encouragement, and love I shall always be grateful.

Abbreviations

Note: For additional bibliographical abbreviations see Library Sigla, below, and the bibliography; for abbreviations relating specifically to watermarks and copyists see Appendices B and D. Full publication data on the bibliographical references below will be found in the bibliography. The abbreviations AC (alto concertante), BC (basso concertante), and so on refer to solo vocal parts of sacred works, while AR, BR, and so on refer to ripieno parts. Finally, lower-case roman numerals refer to movements of a work (i.e., "i" = first movement).

+	Used as superscript with dates (e.g., 1776[+]) to indicate a terminus a quo for a manuscript.
@	at; used in cross-references to refer to footnotes and their associated text
AAA	*Annonces, affiches, et avis divers* (title varies)
AC	alto or contralto concertante
AC	*L'Avant-coureur, feuille hebdomadaire*
Anderson	Emily Anderson, trans., *The Letters of Mozart and His Family*
App.	Appendix
AR	alto or contralto ripieno
aut.	autograph
b.	bass, basso
Bauer-Deutsch	Wilhelm A. Bauer and Otto Erich Deutsch, eds., *Mozart, Briefe und Aufzeichnungen: Gesamtausgabe*
b.c.	basso continuo
BC	basso concertante
bn.	bassoon, fagotto
BP	Bibliothek Pretlack (collection in D-B)
BR	basso ripieno
cb.	contrabass, double bass
cl.	clarinet
DTB	*Denkmäler der Tonkunst in Bayern*
dupl.	duplicate
esp.	especially
fl.	flute
FMPC	Cari Johansson, *French Music Publishers' Catalogues of the Second Half of the Eighteenth Century*
fn(n).	footnote(s)
hn.	horn, corno, corno di caccia
JAMS	*Journal of the American Musicological Society*
Jg.	Jahrgang

KBM	*Kataloge bayerischer Musiksammlungen*
m(m).	measure(s)
MdF	*Mercure de France*
MGG	*Die Musik in Geschichte und Gegenwart*
Mh.	Mannheim
MS(S)	manuscript(s)
mvt.	movement
n(n).	note(s): in references, normally backnotes; in index, footnotes
New Grove	*The New Grove Dictionary of Music and Musicians*
ob.	oboe, hautbois
orig.	original
PA	*The Public Advertiser*
perc.	percussion
repr.	reprint
RISM	*Répertoire International des Sources Musicales*
RRMCE	*Recent Researches in the Music of the Classical Era* (A-R Editions)
SC	soprano concertante
SR	soprano ripieno
TC	tenor(e) concertante
timp.	timpani
TP	title page
TR	tenor(e) ripieno
tr.	trumpet, clarino, tromba
va.	viola
vc.	cello
vn.	violin
WM	watermark

Library Sigla

A-GÖ	Göttweig, Benediktinerstift, Musikarchiv
A-KN	Klosterneuburg, Augustiner-Chorherrenstift, Stiftsbibliothek
A-Wn	Vienna, Österreichische Nationalbibliothek, Musiksammlung
B-Bc	Brussels, Conservatoire royal de musique, Bibliothèque/Koninklijk Conservatorium, Bibliotheek
CZ-Bm	Brno, Moravské zemské muzeum, Oddělení dějin hudby
D-Au(HR)	Augsburg, Universitätsbibliothek, former music collection of the Fürstlich Oettingen-Wallerstein'sche Bibliothek, Schloss Harburg
D-B	Berlin, Staatsbibliothek zu Berlin – Preussischer Kulturbesitz, Musikabteilung
D-BAR	See D-NEhz.

Library Sigla

D-Dl	Dresden, Sächsische Landesbibliothek – Staats- und Universitätsbibliothek, Musikabteilung
D-DO	See D-KA.
D-DS	Darmstadt, Hessische Landes- und Hochschulblbliothek, Musikabteilung
D-FS(Mf)	Freising, Erzbistum München und Freising, Dombibliothek, music collection of the Munich cathedral, the Frauenkirche
D-HR	See D-Au.
D-HV	Hannover, Stadtarchiv, Autografensammlung
D-Kl	Kassel, Landesbibliothek und Murhardsche Bibliothek, Musiksammlung
D-KA	Karlsruhe, Badische Landesbibliothek, Musikabteilung; includes the former music collection of the Fürstlich Fürstenbergische Hofbibliothek, Donaueschingen.
D-Mbs	Munich, Bayerische Staatsbibliothek, Musikabteilung
D-MEIsm	Meiningen, Staatliche Museen, Abteilung Musikgeschichte/Max-Reger-Archiv
D-MHjk	Mannheim, Jesuitenkirche, Archiv
D-MÜu	Münster, Universitäts- und Landesbibliothek, Musiksammlung; includes the music collection of the Fürst zu Bentheim-Tecklenburgische Bibliothek, formerly at Schloss Rheda.
D-NEhz	Neuenstein, Hohenlohe-Zentralarchiv; includes the music collection of the Fürst zu Hohenlohe-Bartensteinsches Archiv.
D-OF	Offenbach am Main, Verlagsarchiv André
D-RH	See D-MÜ.
D-Rtt	Regensburg, Fürst Thurn und Taxis Hofbibliothek
D-SWl	Schwerin, Landesbibliothek Mecklenburg-Vorpommern, Musiksammlung
F-CSM	Châlons-en-Champagne (formerly Châlons-sur-Marne), Bibliothèque municipale, section Patrimoine
F-Pn(c)	Paris, Bibliothèque nationale de France, Département de la musique, ancien fonds du Conservatoire national de musique
F-Susc	Strasbourg, Union Ste Cécile, Bibliothèque musicale; includes the music collection of the Grand Séminaire (Séminaire catholique)
GB-Lbl	London, British Library
I-MOe	Modena, Biblioteca Estense e Universitaria
US-CAhm	Cambridge, Mass., Harvard University, Music Library (including Isham Memorial Library of Music)
US-NYp	New York, N.Y., New York Public Library, Music Division
US-Rs	Rochester, N.Y., Eastman School of Music, Sibley Music Library
US-STu	Palo Alto, Cal., Stanford University, Memorial Library of Music
US-Wc	Washington, D.C., Library of Congress, Music Division

List of Figures

Note: Figures in the main text are referred to by chapter and figure numbers separated by a colon (e.g., "1:2" indicates the second figure in chapter 1). Figures in Appendix D, "Copyists," are referred to by the letter D and a number (e.g., "D:2").

Text

1:1	View of the electoral palace at Mannheim	25
1:2	The *Rittersaal* (Knights' Hall) of the electoral palace at Mannheim	30
1:3	Extract from Traitteur papers	43
2:1a	Division of original sheet of paper, oblong format	53
2:1b	Division of original sheet of paper, upright format	53
2:2	Simple (one-stave) rastrum	70
2:3	Double (two-stave) rastrum	70
2:4	Right half of fold-out plate from Méguin, *Art de la réglure*	72
2:5	Christian Cannabich, Symphony No. 56, flute 1, last page	74
2:6	Specifications for a set of staves ruled with a compound rastrum	75
2:7	Christian Cannabich, Symphony No. 2, violin 1, last page	85
2:8	Ignaz Holzbauer, Cembalo Concerto, title page	86
2:9a	Extract from *Gesellenbrief* (*Lehrbrief*) for Franz Anton Brunner showing signature of Jacob Cramer	98
2:9b	Title page by Mannheim 1	99
4:1	Ignaz Holzbauer, Mass in A, tenor, last page, showing date of 1763	122
8:1	Decorative spines of scores to Gassmann's *L'amore artigiano* and Traetta's *Sofonisba*	182
8:2	Front cover of score to Majo's *Ifigenia in Tauride*	183
8:3–6	Pages 1–4 of Sickingen thematic catalogue	186–189
8:7a	Decorative gilt frame of front and back covers of scores with "Mannheim" bindings	196
8:7b	Coat of arms of Count von Sickingen	196

Appendix D

D:1	Carlo Grua	337
D:2	Franz Xaver Richter	339
D:3	Ignaz Holzbauer	341
D:4	Christian Cannabich, early hand	344
D:5	Christian Cannabich, late hand	345

D:6	Johann Cramer	347
D:7	Georg Joseph Vogler	349
D:8	Fridolin Weber	351
D:9	Mannheim 1 (probably Jacob Cramer)	353
D:10	Mannheim 2 (?Johann Lochner)	355
D:11	Mannheim 3 (?Wilhelm Sepp), early hand	358
D:12	Mannheim 3, late hand	359
D:13	Mannheim 4 (early hand)	361
D:14	Mannheim 5	363
D:15	Mannheim 6	365
D:16	Rtt/Mh. 1 and 3	379
D:17	Rtt/Mh. 1 and 2	380

List of Tables

Note: Tables are referred to by chapter and number separated by a colon (e.g., "2:1" indicates the first figure in chapter 2).

2:1	Manuscripts Ruled with Rastrum 10:28	82
4:1	Manuscripts of Holzbauer Masses in the Bayerische Staatsbibliothek, Munich	118
5:1	Correlation of Rastra and Cannabich Numbers, Group 1	139
5:2	Correlation of Rastra and Copyists, Cannabich Symphonies, Groups 2–3	146
5:3	Correlation of Rastra and Cannabich Numbers, Group 3	151
8:1	Operas and Other Dramatic Works Extant in Manuscripts from Mannheim (to 1780)	176
8:2	Contents of the Sickingen Catalogue	190

Manuscripts from Mannheim

Chapter 1

Introduction

The Electoral Court at Mannheim, 1720–1778

Among the literally hundreds of German courts in the eighteenth century, that of Mannheim was in many ways the most resplendent. The prominence of Mannheim during this period resulted in part from political factors: its ruler, known as the Elector Palatine, was one of the four original secular electors of the Holy Roman Empire[1] and thus occupied an august position within the aristocratic hierarchy. Moreover, the territory over which he reigned, the so-called Electoral Palatinate (*Kurpfalz*) or south-central Rhine region, was of major importance for both its size and its location. The capital of the Palatinate, Mannheim, was strategically situated at the confluence of the Rhine and Neckar rivers, controlling—and profiting from—several of the principal European trade and travel routes. At the same time, the proximity of Mannheim to France assured a continuing French influence at court.

While geopolitical elements such as these gave Mannheim its wealth and power, its most lasting renown derived from its position as one of the leading cultural centers of the Enlightenment. The foundation for this eminence was laid during the reign of Elector Carl Philipp (1661–1742), who came to power in 1716.[2] In Heidelberg, his principal residence from 1718 to 1720, the arch-Catholic elector found himself in frequent dispute with the strong Protestant elements of the town. As a result, he decided to transfer his court in 1720 from Heidelberg to Mannheim, then a town of minor importance in the marshes along the Rhine. There he began a lavish building program, summoning many of the finest architects, sculptors, painters, and craftsmen in Europe to his court. The most important project was the huge

---

[1] The others were the electors of Bohemia, Brandenburg/Prussia, and Saxony. However, during the eighteenth century there were actually nine electors in all: the archbishops of Cologne, Mainz, and Trier and the (secular) rulers of Bavaria, Bohemia, Brandenburg/Prussia, Hannover, the Palatinate or Rhine region, and Saxony. These comprised one college of the imperial diet and were at least nominally responsible for election of the Holy Roman Emperor. This and the following two sections of chapter 1 are adapted from my chapter "The Mannheim Court," in *The Classical Era*, ed. Neal Zaslaw, vol. 5 of *Man and Music*, ed. Stanley Sadie (Englewood Cliffs, N.J.: Prentice Hall, 1989), 213–21, 233–34.

[2] On Carl Philipp see Hans Schmidt, "Karl (III.) Philipp," *Neue deutsche Biographie* 11 (1977): 250–52 (with further references).

electoral palace, the largest of the German Baroque (see fig. 1:1).[3] The first phase of construction was completed by 1737, at which point the elector was able to occupy the palace, and the second by early 1742, when the new opera house in the west wing, designed by the court architect Alessandro Galli da Bibiena, was dedicated.[4]

Carl Philipp possessed a strong interest in music, establishing a tradition that eventually gave Mannheim its most permanent claim to fame.[5] His Kapelle was large for the time, numbering about 50 musicians during most of his reign.[6] It represented an amalgam of musicians from three different sources: first, those brought with him from his previous post in Innsbruck as governor of the Tyrol, Upper Austria, and the Austrian provinces in Swabia; second, musicians who had served his brother and predecessor Johann Wilhelm as Elector Palatine in Düsseldorf; and finally, various new appointees, primarily singers from Italy. His most significant new acquisition was the Bohemian violin virtuoso Johann Stamitz (1717–57), who joined the court orchestra about 1741 and quickly rose to the rank of concertmaster.[7] As there was no opera house until 1742, the principal types of secular music under Carl Philipp seem to have been pastorales, serenatas, cantatas, and the like, as well as the usual orchestral and chamber music. Owing especially to his strong Jesuit affinities, Carl Philipp placed great emphasis on church music, particularly after the death of his daughter Elisabeth in 1728.[8]

---

[3] The electoral palace was almost totally destroyed in World War II but has since been reconstructed. It is today the seat of the University of Mannheim.

[4] The opera house is designated by the letter *b* in fig. 1:1. It had burnt to the ground during the Austrian bombardment of Mannheim in 1795, taking with it much of the music that had been left behind in Mannheim when the court moved to Munich (see below); it was never rebuilt. For information on the opera house see Paul Corneilson, "Die Oper am Kurfürstlichen Hof zu Mannheim," in Ludwig Finscher, ed., *Die Mannheimer Hofkapelle im Zeitalter Carl Theodors* (Mannheim: Palatium Verlag im J & J Verlag, 1992), 113–21; idem, "Reconstructing the Mannheim Court Theatre," *Early Music* 25 (1997): 63–81.

[5] The best treatment of this period is still Friedrich Walter, *Geschichte des Theaters und der Musik am Kurpfälzischen Hofe* (Leipzig: Breitkopf & Härtel, 1898), 71–91.

[6] See the manuscript "Titul- und Nahmen Buch von Ihrer Churfürstlichen Durchleucht zu Pfaltz Gesammten Hofstatt . . . ANNO 1723" (D-Mbs, Handschriftenabteilung, Cod. germ. 1665) and the *Chur-Pfältzischer Staats- und Stands-Calender* for 1734 and 1736 (published in Heidelberg and Mannheim), the only lists to survive from Carl Philipp's reign. The contents of the 1723 and 1734 lists are given in Walter, *Geschichte*, 77–78 and 80–82, respectively. The totals given above include the Intendant but not the trumpets and timpani, which numbered ten and two, respectively, in 1723.

[7] See Eugene K. Wolf, *The Symphonies of Johann Stamitz: A Study in the Formation of the Classic Style* (Utrecht: Bohn, Scheltema & Holkema, 1981), 14.

[8] Eduard Schmitt and Josef Troller, "Mannheim," *MGG* 8 (1960): 1594–95; Jochen Reutter, "Die Kirchenmusik am Mannheimer Hof," in Finscher, ed., *Mannheimer Hofkapelle*, 97–99.

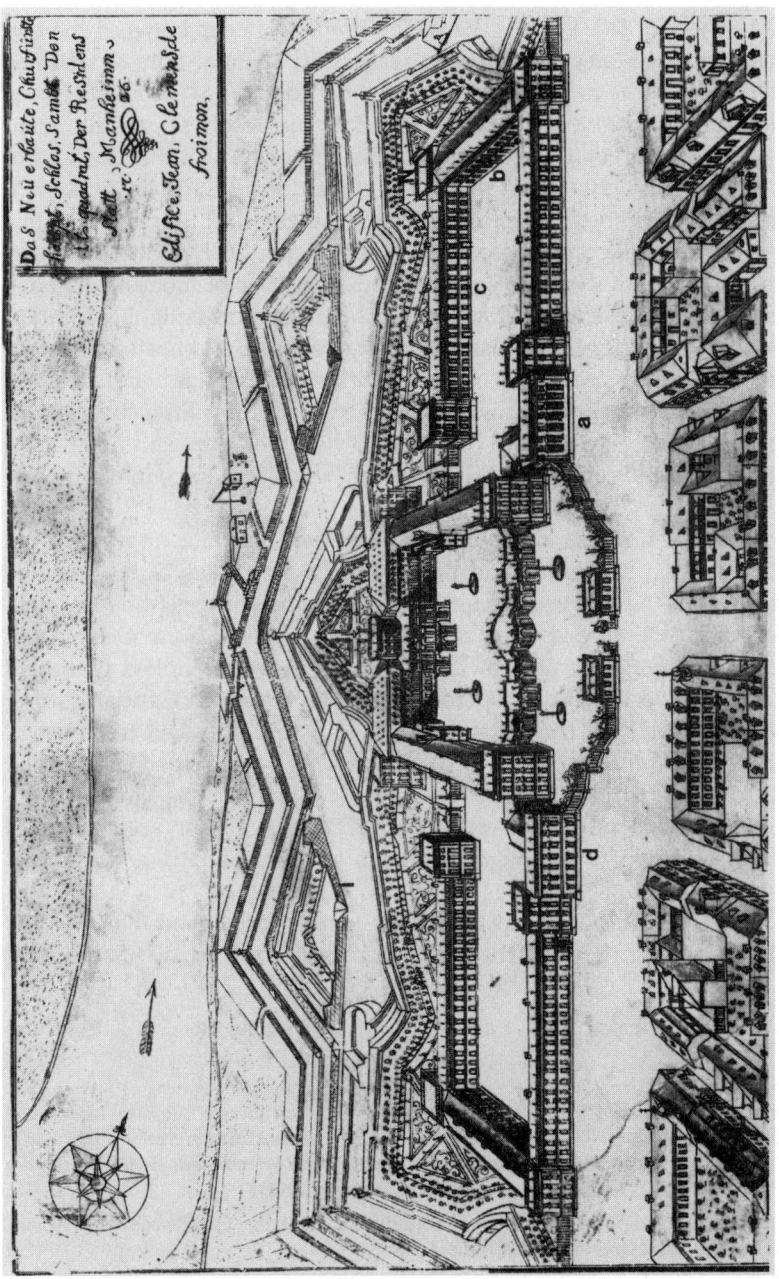

Figure 1:1. View of the electoral palace at Mannheim showing the location of the *Rittersaal* (Knights' Hall) in the central tower, the chapel (*a*), the opera house (*b*), the ball house (*c*), and the library (*d*). Anonymous engraving of 1726, after the drawing by Johann Clemens Froimont. Mannheim, Städtisches Reiss-Museum, Kat. Nr. A 162.

Carl Philipp died on New Year's Eve 1742 and was immediately succeeded by his nephew Carl Theodor (1724–99).[9] The wide difference in age between the two rulers—Carl Philipp was 81 at the time of his death, Carl Theodor only 18 when he assumed power—may serve to symbolize the personal contrast so evident between them. The older elector was the epitome of the Baroque absolutist, an intolerant military man who took Louis XIV as his ideal. By contrast, Carl Theodor was in most respects a typical Enlightenment ruler. Though a devout Catholic who maintained his uncle's powerful ties to the Jesuits, he promulgated, at least in his public pronouncements, a more tolerant approach to other religions. In addition, he was less repressive in the political sphere and fostered a number of modest economic and commercial reforms. His was not, however, the more thoroughgoing Enlightenment approach of Frederick II of Prussia or, later, Joseph II, and few of his initiatives proved substantial or lasting. As Charles Burney wrote after visiting Mannheim in 1772, "The expence and magnificence of the court of this little city are prodigious; the palaces and offices extend over almost half the town; and one half of the inhabitants, who are in office, prey on the other, who seem to be in the utmost indigence."[10]

A more profound Enlightenment influence on Carl Theodor appears in his enthusiasm for science, philosophy, and the arts.[11] In the course of his reign he founded academies for the study of the fine arts (1757), the sciences (the Academia Theodoro-Palatina, 1763), physics and economics (1770), and German language and literature (1775). Establishment of the latter academy was linked with Carl Theodor's influential sponsorship of opera and spoken drama in German during the same period. Similarly, his collections of engravings and drawings (established 1758), naturalia (1765), and especially antiquities (1767) were widely influential. He was also a friendly patron of philosophers and writers such as Voltaire. According to Schubart, who visited Mannheim in 1773, a statue of Voltaire stood outside the electoral library, "as though he were a god presiding over all knowledge."[12]

There can be little question, however, that of all Carl Theodor's interests, music ranked the highest; it was "the chief and most constant of his electoral

---

[9] Quoted from *Dr Burney's Musical Tours in Europe*, ed. Percy A. Scholes (London: Oxford University Press, 1959), 2:30.

[10] On Carl Theodor see Peter Fuchs, "Karl (IV.) Theodor," *Neue deutsche Biographie* 11 (1977): 252–58. Two recent studies of Carl Theodor and his reign are Günther Ebersold, *Rokoko, Reform und Revolution: ein politisches Lebensbild des Kurfürsten Karl Theodor* (Frankfurt am Main: Peter Lang, 1985), and Stefan Mörz, *Aufgeklärter Absolutismus in der Kurpfalz während der Regierungszeit des Kurfürsten Karl Theodor (1742-1777)* (Stuttgart: W. Kohlhammer, 1991).

[11] See Jörg Kreutz, "Aufklärung und französische Hofkultur im Zeitalter Carl Theodors in Mannheim," in Finscher, ed., *Die Mannheimer Hofkapelle*, 1–19.

[12] Carl Friedrich Daniel Schubart, *Leben und Gesinnungen* (Stuttgart: Gebrüder Mäntler, 1791–93), 1:200.

highness's amusements," according to Burney.[13] Like many eighteenth-century rulers, he was a good performer on the flute, and he also played the cello on occasion. The first few years of Carl Theodor's reign seem to have witnessed relatively little overt musical activity, doubtless owing in part to his participation in the War of Austrian Succession (1740–48). But the season of 1747/48 marked the start of an extraordinary series of new opera and ballet productions that extended for thirty years—a time of unbroken peace in the Palatinate—and included important premieres by the foremost composers of Europe.

At about the same date Carl Theodor began to increase the size and improve the quality of the Kapelle, which eventually came to number over 80 members. Appointments during this period brought many of the finest performers and composers in Europe to the Mannheim court, including the composer and bass singer Franz Xaver Richter, the flutist Johann Baptist Wendling, and the oboist Alexander Lebrun (all ca. 1747), the composer and Kapellmeister Ignaz Holzbauer (1753), the cellists Innocenz Danzi and Anton Fils (both 1754), and several notable Bohemian horn players. In addition, Carl Theodor carefully groomed the talented offspring of musicians already at court, often by financing an extended period of study in Italy for them. Such was the case, for example, for several outstanding singers as well as for the violinist Christian Cannabich (1731–98), who succeeded Johann Stamitz as concertmaster after the latter's death in 1757.

Music in the Life of the Court

For those accustomed to the modern tradition of the concert hall, in which music exists primarily as an aesthetic object, the pervasiveness and functional character of music at a large eighteenth-century Catholic court may be surprising. Court life was highly ordered, even ritualistic. Events at every level, from everyday occurrences such as meals to major celebrations spanning several days, were carried out—one is tempted to say choreographed—according to a set plan that remained unchanged for decades. This plan not only specified the order and content of each occasion, but it also stipulated which members of the court were to participate and in what function—a clear reflection of the hierarchy of power on which any monarchy depends. At Mannheim, as at other large courts, the organization of court life was recorded in pocket-sized almanacs or calendars issued annually, which contained a detailed listing of various events throughout the year as well as a roster of court personnel (again hierarchically ordered).[14]

---

[13] *Dr Burney's Musical Tours*, ed. Scholes, 2:36.

[14] At Mannheim these almanacs were issued in both German and French editions, the former with the title *Chur-Pfältzischer Hoff- und Staats-Calender* (the title varies slightly over the years), the latter with the title *Almanach Electoral Palatin*. The best published listing of extant Mannheim almanacs appears in Roland Würtz, *Verzeichnis und Ikonographie der kurpfälzischen Hofmusiker zu Mann-

Chapter 1

Just as the palace at Mannheim provided the visual setting for this daily ritual, with its frescoes by Cosmas Damian Asam and its inner decoration by Nicolas de Pigage, so music provided the aural setting. The ubiquity of music within the life of the court stands out clearly from the following statement by Cosimo Collini, Voltaire's secretary, who visited Mannheim with his master in 1753:

> [The electoral] court was at that time one of the most splendid in Germany. *Fêtes* followed [ceaselessly] upon *fêtes*, and good taste constantly gave them a fresh charm. The hunt, comic opera, French dramas, [and] musical performances by the leading virtuosos of Europe made of the electoral residence [at Mannheim] the most pleasant sojourn imaginable for visitors of distinction or of merit, who in addition received the most heartfelt and flattering reception there.[15]

Collini specifically mentions the two most celebrated elements of musical life at Mannheim: opera and concert. In addition, both the hunts and the dramatic performances to which he referred had important musical components, the latter in the form of incidental music. To these categories we may add the following: music for the river excursions and water pageants popular at court, somewhat similar in function to music for the hunt; music for parades, processions, and military exercises, featuring the elector's corps of twelve trumpeters and two drummers;[16] music for receptions, banquets, and meals (*Tafelmusik*); music for the many court balls; music for ballets and pantomimes, which normally appeared as intermezzos between the acts of operas or as afterpieces in the theatre; smaller vocal works such as serenatas, pastorales, and secular cantatas, either staged or unstaged; chamber music (later referred to as *Kabinettsmusik*) for the private quarters of the elector; and the many forms of sacred music, including both liturgical music and oratorio (see below).

---

heim nebst darstellendem Theaterpersonal 1723–1803 (Wilhelmshaven: Heinrichshofen's Verlag, 1975), 30–32, though many new examples have been found since its publication (e.g., the 1736 issue cited in fn. 6, above; almanacs are now known for every year from 1748 until 1778 but 1753). Würtz includes a reproduction of the title page of the 1760 *Calender* (p. 21). The complete schedule of events from the *Calender* of 1749 is reprinted in Friedrich Walter, "Die Hof- und Kirchenfeste am kurfürstlichen Hof zu Mannheim," *Mannheimer Geschichtsblätter* 14 (1913): 253–59.

[15] "Cette cour était alors une des plus brillante de l'Allemagne. Les fêtes se succédaient, et le bon goût leur donnait un agrément toujours nouveau. La chasse, l'opéra bouffon, les comédies françaises, des concerts exécutés par les premiers virtuoses de l'Europe, faisaient du palais électoral un séjour délicieux pour les étrangers de distinction ou de mérite, qui y trouvaient en outre l'accueil le plus cordial et le plus flatteur." Côme Alexandre [Cosimo Alessandro] Collini, *Mon séjour auprès de Voltaire* (Paris: Léopold Collin, 1807), 106.

[16] The magnificent eighteenth-century trumpets used by the Mannheim trumpet corps are on display in the Musikinstrumentenmuseum of the Munich Stadtmuseum. For a detailed study of them, with several reproductions, see Manfred Hermann Schmid et al., "Trompeten als Zeichen der Representation am Mannheimer Hof," in Ludwig Finscher, Bärbel Pelker, and Jochen Reutter, eds., *Mozart und Mannheim: Kongreßbericht 1991* (Frankfurt am Main: Peter Lang, 1994), 41–64.

The cultural year at Mannheim was divided into three parts. Most important was the autumn and winter "season," extending from early November until Shrove Tuesday and encompassing the varied celebrations of carnival, which at Mannheim began in early January. During a typical week virtually every evening was filled with a performance of one sort or another.[17] Theatrical presentations occurred several times a week; these included French comedies and tragedies or, after dismissal of the French troupe in 1770, works in German. A ballet or pantomime (a harlequinade mimed to music) often followed the principal work, which itself contained incidental music such as an overture and entr'actes. Such performances evidently took place in a theatre in the west wing of the palace, between the court chapel and the opera house.[18]

The second type of large evening event was opera, which occupied a position of special prominence at the electoral court. The opera season began with a gala performance in celebration of the elector's name day, 4 November,[19] and thereafter operas and their associated ballets were staged approximately twice weekly, normally beginning at four or five o'clock (six o'clock when the court was at the summer residence of Schwetzingen). At Mannheim these were *opere serie* until 1769, when the first of numerous full-length Italian comic operas was presented. At Schwetzingen, however, *opera buffa* had formed the mainstay of the theater there from the time of its completion in 1752.

The final main type of evening performance was the "academy" or concert, featuring the incomparable Mannheim orchestra.[20] Academies were generally held twice weekly at six o'clock in the *Rittersaal* (Knights' Hall) in the central tower of the palace (see fig. 1:2). In addition to members of the court, the audiences for all these types of performance—drama, opera, and academy—included noble guests of the elector, visitors to Mannheim (generally admitted to the academies as standees), and invited members of the Mannheim bourgeoisie. Because of the emphasis placed by past scholars on orchestral music at Mannheim, it is worth pointing out that these academies, prestigious and well-known as they were, were not the center of attention during a given week at Mannheim, but almost like respites from the larger-scale, more formal pleasures of opera, drama, and ball. A description by a

---

[17] For a more thorough treatment of the organization of musical life at the Mannheim court see Bärbel Pelker, "Zur Struktur des Musiklebens am Hof Carl Theodors in Mannheim," in Finscher et al., eds., *Mozart und Mannheim*, 29–40, and cf. also her "Theateraufführungen und musikalische Akademien am Hof Carl Theodors in Mannheim: eine Chronik der Jahre 1742–1777," in Finscher, ed., *Die Mannheimer Hofkapelle*, 113–21.

[18] The exact location of this theater within the palace has not to my knowledge been determined.

[19] The opera performance, often a premiere, generally took place the day after, 5 November. The best listing of opera and ballet performances at Mannheim is Pelker, "Chronik," superseding that in Walter, *Geschichte*, 362–68.

[20] See Bärbel Pelker, "Musikalische Akademien am Hof Carl Theodors in Mannheim," in Finscher, ed., *Die Mannheimer Hofkapelle*, 49–58.

Figure 1.2. The *Rittersaal* (Knights' Hall) of the electoral palace at Mannheim, scene of the "academies." Mannheim, Verkehrsverein e. V., photo Robert Häusser.

visitor to Mannheim in 1785, when the court had returned briefly from Munich, shows that—like academies at other courts of the time—members of the court were seated at tables and played cards while the music was playing; the orchestra was placed on risers, probably at the east end of the hall.[21] Hence, these were not concerts in the modern sense, but relatively informal occasions at which music was only one of the attractions, together with cards, conversation, seeing and being seen, and (as we learn from other sources) tea.[22] While it would be going too far to consider the music presented on these occasions as merely background music, it is clear that it did not in general enjoy the concentrated attention of music performed at a public concert to which the audience had paid admission.[23]

There are no surviving listings of the music played at electoral academies, but several extant programs for closely related events allow us to reconstruct a typical evening's fare.[24] First would come a symphony, then several concertos alternating freely with vocal works such as arias and duets. The finale was usually a symphony or a larger vocal ensemble such as a trio or quartet. Maria Anna Mozart's description of the academy at which her son played, to be quoted below as part of her account of the gala days, conforms to this summary as regards the performance of a concerto and final symphony; but on that occasion Mozart, as a visiting virtuoso, also played a sonata and improvised.

The height of pageantry at the Mannheim court came with the so-called galas or gala days, celebrations held in conjunction with major feast-days of the church

---

[21] Gottfried von Rotenstein, *Lustreise in die Rheingegenden, in Briefen an Fr. J. v. Pf.* (Frankfurt and Leipzig, 1791), 102–6 (letter of 11 May 1785), as printed in Friedrich Walter, "Ein Akademiekonzert im Rittersaale des Mannheimer Schlosses 1785," *Mannheimer Geschichtsblätter* 10 (1909): 210–11, and Eugene K. Wolf, "On the Composition of the Mannheim Orchestra, ca. 1740–1778," *Basler Jahrbuch für historische Musikpraxis* 17 (1993): 127–30, the latter article including an English translation.

[22] The informal nature of these academies is confirmed by Mozart's comment about the one at which he performed just after his arrival at Mannheim (cf. Mme Mozart's description of the gala days, to be quoted below): "On both occasions [during the concert] when I played, the elector and electress came up quite close to the clavier" (letter of 8 November 1777, Anderson, 362; Bauer-Deutsch, 2:109).

[23] On the special status of the academy as a listening and social experience see my article "The 'Concert' in Munich under Elector Carl Theodor," in Theodor Göllner and Stephan Hörner, eds., *Mozarts* Idomeneo *und die Musik in München zur Zeit Karl Theodors* (Munich: Verlag der Bayerischen Akademie der Wissenschaften, 2001), 227–30.

[24] See the discussion of program content at Mannheim in Wolf, *Stamitz*, 15 (with further citations). To the programs listed there one should add a printed program from Munich of 8 December 1785, published in facsimile in Heinrich Bihrle, *Die Musikalische Akademie München 1811–1911: Festschrift zur Feier des hundertjährigen Bestehens* (Munich: E. Mühlthaler, 1911), 5, as well as the contents of Mozart's concert at the house of Christian Cannabich on 13 February 1778 (see his letter of 14 February 1778, Bauer-Deutsch, 2:282; Anderson, 482). The latter concert opened with a Cannabich symphony, after which came six works by Mozart: a keyboard concerto, an oboe concerto, an aria sung by Aloysia Weber, another keyboard concerto, another aria for Aloysia, and finally the overture to *Il rè pastore*.

year and the name-days and birthdays of the elector and electress. The name- and birthdays of the Duke and Duchess of Zweibrücken (the duke was Carl Theodor's cousin and heir apparent) were also designated as gala days, as were such occasional events as weddings and major state visits. The most important of these galas would last for several days and include various ceremonies, processions, church services, banquets, receptions, and, in the evening, major dramatic presentations, operas, balls, and academies. The name-day of the elector (4 November) and the birthday of the electress (17 January) were often occasions for an important new operatic production. When Mozart and his mother, Maria Anna, visited Mannheim in 1777/78, they arrived just in time for the name-day celebrations of the elector. In a letter to her husband on 8 November 1777, Mme Mozart provided an unusually detailed description of the different events:

> The gala days are now over. On the first day [Tuesday, 4 November 1777] there was a [church] service at eleven o'clock, during which cannons and rockets were fired off. ... After that there was a splendid banquet and during the evening a magnificent reception. On the second day the grand German opera *Günther von Schwarzburg* [by Ignaz Holzbauer] was performed ... , [along with] a marvelously beautiful ballet. On the third day there was a grand academy at which Wolfgang played a concerto; then, before the final symphony, he improvised and gave them a sonata. He won extraordinary applause from the elector and electress and from all who heard him. On the fourth day there was a gala play, which we went to see with Monsieur and Madame Cannabich.[25]

The way in which pageantry and religion, might and music were woven together in court ritual could hardly be clearer than in the following description, taken from the court almanac for 1755, of the events to take place on the elector's name-day. The power-enhancing stability of such rituals may be seen from the fact that the ceremony parallels almost exactly that described by Mozart's mother 22 years later.

> On the fourth [of November], the feast of St Charles Borromeo, there will be a large gala at court in honor of the high name-day of his electoral highness, our most gracious ruler and lord, lord [sic]. On this high feast-day the entire nobility, ministers, and cavaliers, as well as all [officials of the] law courts, will most graciously be allowed to appear in the electoral apartments to congratulate and kiss the hand [of the elector], after which at about eleven o'clock his electoral highness and the entire court will process between the electoral bodyguard and the Swiss Guard, arranged to the left and right of the palace corridor [*Schloßgang*], to the high mass [in the court chapel], wherein communion will be celebrated and, after the Elevation, a Te Deum laudamus will be performed. During the mass, at the Gloria in excelsis, again at the

---

[25] Anderson, 361; Bauer-Deutsch, 2:108–9. Mozart and his mother arrived in Mannheim on 30 October 1777 and remained there for four and one-half months, finally departing on 14 March 1778.

performance of the Te Deum, and finally at the last sign of the cross, cannons will be fired from the ramparts. Thereafter [there will be] an open banquet, served by the electoral chamberlains.

That evening towards five o'clock an opera will be performed.[26]

While the almanac does not specifically mention music except in the case of the Te Deum and the opera, the mass as a whole would of course have been performed by a full choir, soloists, and orchestra. Moreover, music would have graced the ceremonies in the elector's apartments, and the procession and firing of the cannons would have been accompanied by the trumpet and drum corps.

The passage just quoted, and especially the (to us) bizarre combination of high mass and cannon blasts, may serve as a reminder that the function of music at court was not merely to provide entertainment and aesthetic delight (important as these were), any more than the function of religion was merely to induce piety. These and other elements of court ritual served as well to symbolize, embellish, and indeed enhance the power of the ruler. As has been noted in another context, "Political symbols and rituals were not metaphors of power; they were the means and ends of power itself."[27]

The next major division of the year was Lent, during which all theatrical performance, including opera and ballet, was proscribed. Orchestral concerts still occurred, however, and it is likely that performances of smaller vocal works such as pastorales, cantatas, and serenatas helped to fill the gap. The culmination of

---

[26] "Den 4. St. Carolus Boromæus ist große Galla bey Hof wegen Sr Churfürstl. Durchleucht unsers Gnädigsten Landes-Fürsten und Herrn, Herrn hohen Nahmens-Tag. An welchem hohen Fest gesambter Noblesse, Ministris, und Cavaliers, nebst allen Dicasterien in Dero grossen Apartement zur Gratulation und Handkuß sich einzufinden Gnädigst erlaubt[,] nach welchem Se. Churfürstl. Durchleucht mit samtlichen [sic] Hof-Staat durch die in dem Schloß-Gang lincks und rechts arrangirte sowohl Leibs- als Schweitzer-Garde sich gegen 11. Uhr zu dem hohen Ambt erheben, wobey das Hochwürdigste Gut ausgesetzet, und nach der Elevation das Te Deum laudamus angestimmet wird. Wehrendem hohen Ambt, werden bey dem Gloria in Excelsis, sodann bey Anstimmung des Te Deum, und endlich bey dem letzten heiligen Seegen die Canonen von denen Wällen gelöst, sodann offentliche Tafel, zu welcher die Churfürstl. Cammer-Herren die Speisen tragen. Abends gegen 5. Uhr wird Opera gehalten." *Chur-Pfältzischer Hoff- und Staats-Calender, auf das Jahr . . . MDCCLV* (Mannheim, 1755), entry for 4 November. Which opera was performed on this occasion is not known.

[27] Lynn A. Hunt, *Politics, Culture, and Class in the French Revolution* (Berkeley: University of California Press, 1984), 54; see also Clifford Geertz, "Centers, Kings, and Charisma: Reflections on the Symbolics of Power," in his *Local Knowledge: Further Essays in Interpretive Anthropology* (New York: Basic Books, 1983), 121–46 (with further citations). For a consideration of this point as it relates to music see Albert Dunning, "Official Court Music: Means and Symbol of Might," in *Société internationale de musicologie: Actes du XIIIe congrès, Strasbourg, 1982* (Strasbourg: Association des publications près des Universités de Strasbourg, 1986), 1:17–21, and other papers in the same roundtable. The symbolic aspects of ritual and ceremony have been the subject of numerous studies by anthropologists in recent decades, most notably Victor Turner and Geertz, as well as by historians of court ceremony.

Lent from the musical standpoint was the performance on Good Friday of a major oratorio, often newly composed for the occasion. Held at nine o'clock in the evening in the court chapel, this performance represented the climax of elaborate Holy Week rituals involving the entire court. For instance, the description of the ceremonies for Maundy Thursday requires one and one-half pages in the court almanac; the rites include a complex evocation of the Last Supper in the Rittersaal, during which the elector, taking the part of Christ (!), washes the feet of twelve old men in the presence of the court.[28]

The third part of the cultural year was the summer and early fall (through October), when the elector and his retinue occupied the nearby summer palace of Schwetzingen, the electress her palace at Oggersheim. During this period Schwetzingen, which boasted a lovely small opera house (still extant, today the site of the Schwetzingen Festival), an outdoor theatre in the form of a Greek temple, and renowned gardens, resembled "a magical island, where everything sounded and sang," according to Schubart.[29]

Dissolution of the Court and Removal to Munich (1778)

The glittering era of electoral Mannheim came to a jarring halt in 1778 with the reluctant transfer of the court and most of its personnel to Munich. On 30 December 1777—while Mozart was still in Mannheim, incidentally—elector Maximilian III Joseph of Bavaria died without issue. According to long-standing treaty obligations that could not be abrogated, he was succeeded by Carl Theodor, and Bavaria and the Palatinate were united (as "Pfalzbayern") with Munich as its capital.

In order to cushion the blow, Carl Theodor gave his musicians the choice of remaining in Mannheim at full salary or following the court to Munich, where the Kapellen of the two courts were to be amalgamated under the leadership of Cannabich and Joseph Toeschi.[30] About two-thirds chose Munich, while the remainder

---

[28] See the transcription from the 1749 almanac in Walter, "Hof- und Kirchenfeste," 256.

[29] Carl Friedrich Daniel Schubart, *Ideen zu einer Ästhetik der Tonkunst* (Vienna: J. V. Degen, 1806; written 1784–85). In his *Leben und Gesinnungen*, 1:208–9 and 218–19, Schubart describes two encounters with Carl Theodor at Schwetzingen in 1773, at the first of which the elector played a flute concerto in the bathhouse accompanied by the violinists Joseph and Johann Toeschi and the cellist Innocenz Danzi.

[30] A full transcription of the rescript of 23 June 1778 announcing the policies regarding the move appears in Walter, *Geschichte*, 354–56; the document itself was destroyed in World War II. The principal extant document concerning the transfer is the large "Status" of 6 August 1778, Bayerisches Hauptstaatsarchiv, HR I, Fasz. 457/Nr. 13. It should be noted that not all the assignments to Mannheim or Munich given in this source turned out to be correct; Vogler, for instance, is listed as transferring to Munich but eventually decided to remain behind. See also the list of musicians scheduled to go to Munich in the "Abschrift / Künftiger Besoldungs Status" reproduced in Her-

stayed behind, either as pensioners or as members of the new Nationaltheater (completed in 1777) and a Concert des Amateurs directed by Ignaz Fränzl, both endowed by the elector. With the final removal of the court to Munich in August and September of 1778, Mannheim's brief golden age ended almost as abruptly as it had begun.

A Question of Survival: Manuscripts from Mannheim

As early as 1898 the importance of electoral Mannheim as a musical center was announced by the local historian Friedrich Walter.[31] His pioneering work led quickly to the well-known publications of Hugo Riemann in the series *Denkmäler der Tonkunst in Bayern* (1902–15),[32] whose chauvinistic and often overblown claims sparked various equally chauvinistic publications in what is sometimes referred to as the "Denkmälerstreit."[33] Countless more specialized studies have, of course, appeared since then. Yet from the beginning a formidable obstacle to research on music at Mannheim has been the apparently complete disappearance of the music used in performance by the electoral Kapelle. Next to autograph sources, of which only a handful from Mannheim were known to have survived, such materials would represent the most reliable extant versions of works by Mannheim composers. Regrettably, though, the small group of manuscripts known to have remained in Mannheim was destroyed in World War II.[34] Moreover, except for a

---

mann Jung, "Mannheim nach 1777," in Finscher, ed., *Die Mannheimer Hofkapelle*, 200–201; though it bears the same date as the "Status," there are several differences in the listings of the two documents.

[31] Walter, *Geschichte*. This publication was followed a year later by Walter's fundamental *Archiv und Bibliothek des Grossh. Hof- und Nationaltheaters in Mannheim 1779–1839*, vol. 1: *Das Theater-Archiv*, vol. 2: *Die Theater-Bibliothek* (Leipzig: S. Hirzel, 1899). Walter's pathbreaking efforts have been overshadowed by the publications of Riemann, though the latter would have been impossible without Walter's tireless, meticulous, and still valuable research.

[32] Hugo Riemann, ed., *Sinfonien der pfalzbayerischen Schule (Mannheimer Symphoniker)*, DTB, Jg. III/1, VII/2, VIII/2 (Leipzig: Breitkopf & Härtel, 1902–7).

[33] See Alf Thoor, "Hugo Riemann, Mannheimskolan och 'Denkmälerstriden,'" *Svensk Tidskrift för Musikforskning* 34 (1952): 5–27.

[34] These manuscripts were in the music collection of the Theaterbibliothek of the Mannheim Nationaltheater, a catalogue of which appears in Walter, *Archiv und Bibliothek*, 2:161–96. Because the manuscripts are lost, it is impossible to know for certain whether they were actually copied at the court. Some of the most likely candidates from the realm of opera are listed in the appendix to chapter 8 (q.v.). Other possibilities include a manuscript of Ignaz Holzbauer's oratorio *Betulia liberata* (Walter, *Archiv und Bibliothek*, 2:176) and two sets of entr'actes and a symphony in E by Christian Cannabich (ibid., 2:190, 193). In addition, surviving inventories of the Theaterbibliothek show that music from Schloß Ehreshoven bought at auction in 1924/25 included the score of a "Deutsche Messe (Lobamt)" by Holzbauer that was supposedly an autograph. (Information on these inventories was kindly provided by Dr. Bärbel Pelker of the Forschungsstelle *Mannheimer*

group of works by Christian Cannabich and Ignaz Holzbauer (none, however, with any indication of provenance), the libraries and archives of Munich, to which the court transferred in 1778, numbered very few works by Mannheim composers among their holdings.

What was obviously needed was an attempt to determine whether any manuscripts from Mannheim might still exist in addition to the small body of autograph scores that was already known—a project that, obvious as it was, seemed never seriously to have been proposed. In order to meet this need, my wife (Jean K. Wolf) and myself, in conjunction with research on Christian Cannabich and Johann Stamitz in 1966/67, carried out an extensive documentary examination of music and archival materials relating to Mannheim in the Bayerische Staatsbibliothek and various archives in Munich, as well as of selected manuscripts in Regensburg, Berlin, and a few other centers with important collections of music by Mannheim composers.

This project, the results of which were reported in 1974,[35] succeeded in isolating a corpus of about 125 manuscripts traceable directly to Mannheim. These included seven hitherto unknown manuscripts still extant in Mannheim, additional autograph scores, several other manuscripts with colophons indicating their provenance, most of the Holzbauer and Cannabich manuscripts in Munich, and thirty manuscripts in other collections that could be shown to have originated at the electoral court.

The years since publication of the 1974 article have brought both significant refinement in its methods and conclusions and a large number of additions to its catalogue of Mannheim manuscripts—advances that provide the principal *raison d'être* for the present book. Study of the handwriting and watermarks of these sources has been carried out in far more detail and with greater methodological sophistication. Even more important has been the development and application of rastrology, the study of musical staving.[36] Coupled with the identification of many new Mannheim manuscripts (see below), these refinements have made possible a hitherto unattainable precision in the determination of provenance and date for these manuscripts. Some of the results of this research include (1) the removal of

---

Hofkapelle in Heidelberg.) Finally, a manuscript of Vogler's famous *Messiah* performance of 1777, owned by Max Seiffert (see his article "Die Mannheimer 'Messias'-Aufführung 1777," *Jahrbuch der Musikbibliothek Peters* 23 [1916]: 64), has been missing since World War II, as confirmed in a letter of 28 December 1981 from Dr. Walther Siegmund-Schultze of the Georg-Friedrich-Händel-Gesellschaft in Halle.

[35] Eugene K. and Jean K. Wolf, "A Newly Identified Complex of Manuscripts from Mannheim," *JAMS* 27 (1974): 379–437.

[36] See Jean K. and Eugene K. Wolf, "Rastrology and Its Use in Eighteenth-Century Manuscript Studies," in *Studies in Musical Sources and Style: Essays in Honor of Jan LaRue*, ed. Eugene K. Wolf and Edward H. Roesner (Madison, Wisc.: A-R Editions, 1990), 237–95 (with further citations).

several manuscripts from the original list of Mannheim sources;[37] (2) the ability to distinguish and date multiple layers of additions to the Holzbauer and Cannabich manuscripts in Munich and elsewhere;[38] (3) a clearer sense of which copyists were active in Mannheim and which in Munich (or both) and when;[39] and (4) determination of the probable point within the numbered series of Cannabich symphonies at which the move to Munich took place.[40] More broadly, the entire notion that an extensive corpus of Mannheim manuscripts still existed, though it seems never seriously to have been questioned, had in 1974 admittedly depended upon a complex web of mostly circumstantial evidence; it can now be treated as simple fact.

Likewise, the corpus itself has been greatly augmented, especially by the identification of several important new groups of manuscripts that were copied at Mannheim. These include (1) a substantial body of works by Abbé Georg Joseph Vogler that had been left in Darmstadt after his death there in 1814;[41] (2) 21 widely scattered manuscripts of operas and related secular vocal works;[42] (3) a series of over 80 opera arias, overtures, and other vocal works, principally from the 1750s and 1760s, in the Pretlack collection of the Staatsbibliothek zu Berlin – Preussischer Kulturbesitz;[43] and (4) 19 manuscripts of sacred music, including an oratorio and five masses, by the tragically short-lived Mannheim composer Johannes Ritschel (1739–66) in the Sächsische Landesbibliothek in Dresden.[44]

---

[37] Most notably the manuscripts given in the 1974 *JAMS* article as App. A/II/15 and A/III/28–29, which are not from Mannheim but almost certainly from Munich.

[38] See chaps. 4 and 5, respectively.

[39] For example, some of the parts for the Cannabich symphonies in Munich by the copyists labeled in the 1974 article as Munich (ex-Mannheim) C and D (which we now designate as Mannheim 3 and 4) can now be shown to have been written in Munich; these copyists were unquestionably active in both centers, traveling with the court to Munich in 1778. See the section "Handwriting and Copyists" of chap. 2, also Appendix D.

[40] See the section "Group 4" in chap. 5. As a result, App. A/II/66–73 in the 1974 article (now numbered App. A/III/56–62) were not "possibly" but "definitely" copied in Munich.

[41] About half of these manuscripts still remain in Darmstadt (D-DS), while the other half, almost all autographs, were bought at auction after Vogler's death by Johann André; the latter manuscripts are still in the André archive in Offenbach (D-OF). The Vogler manuscripts are discussed in chapter 7 and catalogued in Appendix A/V.

[42] Identification of these sources was first reported in Paul Corneilson and Eugene K. Wolf, "Newly Identified Manuscripts of Operas and Related Works from Mannheim," *JAMS* 47 (1994): 244–74, a revised version of which appears as chapter 8 of the present book; they are listed by library location in Appendix A/VI. In addition, six important manuscripts were identified that, although not actually copied at the court, can be shown to have been used there or were at least in its possession at one time (see below, @ fnn. 61–62, also chap. 8 [incl. table 8:1]).

[43] See App. A/VI/39–119 and the section "The Pretlack Collection" in chap. 9.

[44] See App. A/VI/120–38 and the section "The Ritschel Manuscripts in Dresden" in chap. 9.

Chapter 1

Manuscript Types

Autograph scores. We may distinguish several different types or categories of manuscript within the Mannheim complex. The first consists of autograph or holograph scores.[45] A total of 45 by Mannheim composers has now been located: six by Carlo Grua (App. A/I/8–13, treated in chapter 3); five by Ignaz Holzbauer (App. A/II/17–21, treated in chapter 4);[46] two by Franz Xaver Richter (App. A/IV/3 and 10a, treated in chapter 6); and thirty-two by Georg Joseph Vogler (see Appendix A/V; treated in chapter 7). In addition, three partially autograph scores are extant, one by Johannes Ritschel (App. A/I/1) and two by Vogler (App. A/V/2a and 14), as well as the scores to an inserted aria by Vogler (see App. A/V/21) and two copied by, but not necessarily composed by, Holzbauer (App. A/VI/151). Comparable to these scores are the eight extant autographs of Mozart written while he was a visitor at Mannheim in 1777/78 (see below).

The normal practice at Mannheim was for composers to retain their original scores, as seen in Mozart's statement to his father regarding the score of *Idomeneo*: "It was always the custom in Mannheim . . . that the original score should be returned to [the Kapellmeister; in this case the composer]."[47] Likewise, after Holzbauer's death his widow was left with a huge group of works which must have consisted in large measure of his autograph scores; he would surely not, for example, have owned the parts to 21 masses, 12 operas, and 205 symphonies and concertos![48] And finally, Vogler clearly took his Mannheim scores with him when he left, many of which remain to this day in Darmstadt, where he died. It seems likely in the case of the autograph scores by Carlo Grua in Munich that they survived only because they were passed down to his son Franz Paul, who was Kapellmeister there. In given instances, of course, autograph scores my have been used *faute de mieux* as conductor/continuo scores for large-scale works; such scores might therefore have ended up (perhaps inadvertently) in the court collection, as may some scores upon the death of their composers.

---

[45] For purposes of this study the distinction between autograph (signed) and holograph (unsigned) manuscripts has little relevance and will not be maintained here; the mere presence of a signature on a manuscript indisputably in the hand of a given composer is trivial for studies of provenance and date, though it may be important for authentication of a work or in setting the market value of the manuscript.

[46] One of these (App. A/II/19) is, however, an aria that has been removed from the original score (App. A/II/18) and should perhaps be counted together with it.

[47] Anderson, 690; Bauer-Deutsch, 3:60 (letter of 16 December 1780).

[48] See the note appended to Holzbauer's autobiography, "Kurzer Lebensbegrif des Herrn Ignaz Holzbauer, kurpfälzischen Kapellmeisters," printed originally in *Pfälzisches Museum* 1/5 (Mannheim, 1783): 460–77 and reprinted, inter alia, in Walter, *Geschichte*, 356–61 (the note is on p. 361).

As already mentioned, another group of autograph scores prepared at Mannheim are those of Mozart, who during his four-month stay there in 1777/78 composed a rather spare number of works. Of these, autograph scores to eight have come down to us (App. A/I/17–24; see chap. 3).[49] Because Mozart wrote on music paper obtained at the court,[50] these manuscripts provide us with useful information for purposes of dating.

Copies from the Mannheim court collection. Of at least equal importance to autograph scores from Mannheim, and certainly more interesting and challenging from the documentary standpoint, are those manuscripts—almost all sets of parts—that can be shown to have belonged originally to the performance materials used at Mannheim. With certain possible exceptions, these are found today only in the Bayerische Staatsbibliothek and the Frauenkirche in Munich (the latter collection now in D-FS), in the Hessische Landes- und Hochschulbibliothek in Darmstadt (sets of parts from the Vogler materials mentioned above), and probably in the Jesuitenkirche in Mannheim. These *fonds* will be discussed in detail in chapters 3–5 and 7. In addition, certain of the manuscripts cited in footnote 34, above, were possibly also from the court collection, but they were lost in the destruction of the Mannheim Theaterbibliothek in World War II.

Manuscripts from the court library have obvious textual importance in that they were actually prepared for and used by the electoral Kapelle. They are thus the approximate equivalent of authentic copies. In a large number of cases, in fact, the extant manuscripts contain one or more parts copied by the composer, showing that he participated in preparation of the manuscript.[51] Manuscripts of this category are not only interesting intrinsically—they are, after all, the parts from which the famous Mannheim Kapelle played—but also, as already implied, because they are nearly as reliable as autograph scores.

---

[49] Another autograph by Mozart written at Mannheim is App. A/IV/11, a set of oboe parts to the piano concerto K. 175.

[50] See his letters of 7 February and 24 March 1778 (Bauer-Deutsch, 2:266, 328; Anderson, 470, 518), in which Mozart states that Fridolin Weber had supplied him with music paper. The paper found in Mozart's autographs written at Mannheim turns out precisely to match that in other court manuscripts of the period (see the discussion of Mozart's autographs in chap. 3).

[51] Examples of the category of *autograph parts* are the string parts to App. A/IV/2 and all of A/VI/144, by Grua; a large number of individual parts and additions by Cannabich to App. A/III/2–55 from his Mannheim period (he only copies full manuscripts after the court arrived in Munich and was subjected to severe cost-cutting measures); most of the parts (some shared with a second copyist) to A/IV/4–9 and 10b, by Richter; and the three voice parts to A/V/28, the horn parts to A/V/29, and the flute, trumpet, and timpani parts to A/V/30, by Vogler. In this regard it is also worth mentioning the partially autograph violin parts in Regensburg to A/VI/168, a symphony by Holzbauer, and the parts, possibly autographs of Innocenz Danzi and Anton Fils, to the cello concertos A/VI/21–22; it is unlikely that any of these three manuscripts belonged to the Mannheim court collection, however.

Owing especially to the loss of most of the archival material from Mannheim, we know little about the material conditions relating to the court collection there. Manuscripts of theatrical works and ballets were almost certainly stored in the theater; not only was that the usual (and logical) practice, but as we shall see, that is where they were—unfortunately—being housed in 1795. It is probable that the other secular instrumental music (symphonies, concertos, chamber music, etc.) was stored there as well, among other reasons because some of this music was required on occasion for use in the theater (as overtures, entr'actes, etc.). Much later, at least—in 1860—it was the practice of the Munich *Hofmusikintendanz* to keep all the music together in the theater (see below); possibly they were continuing a Mannheim tradition.

Sacred music at Mannheim seems likely to have been housed separately, perhaps in or near the court chapel or (less likely) the Seminarium musicum next to the Jesuitenkirche. Aside from being plausible on its face, this hypothesis would explain why certain manuscripts survived to the present day in the collection of the Jesuitenkirche (App. A/I/1-7). Manuscripts from this and other collections show that church music at Mannheim was generally provided with blue or beige wrappers of local paper and that it was classified by letters ("Litt. G," "Litt. K," etc.) indicating the liturgical function of the work (mass, offertory, Te Deum, etc.). The original wrappers of the only secular instrumental works definitely to have survived from the court collection, the Cannabich manuscripts in Munich, were regrettably replaced with newer covers in the nineteenth century, and thus we do not know their precise characteristics. Performing parts to the sacred music are upright in format (i.e., in folio format), whereas parts to everything else were nearly always in oblong format (i.e., quarto format; see chap. 2).

Throughout most of Carl Theodor's reign the court provided salaried part-time positions for several official copyists (see Appendix D and also the section "Handwriting and Copyists" in the next chapter). These were typically ripieno violists and timpanists who presumably had fewer performing commitments and did not have to devote much time to maintaining their performing skills. Copyists were also recruited on a piece-work basis from among the local musicians. The Mozart letters reveal that private individuals could have works copied by the local copyists but that this was very expensive—24 kreuzer per bifolio, versus 6 kreuzer in Salzburg.[52] Lined music paper and possibly also quills and ink ("Schreibmateri-

---

[52] Letter of 29 November 1777 (Bauer-Deutsch, 2:155; Anderson, 397. See also his comment that "copying here [in Mannheim] costs much too much" in his next letter, of 3 December (Bauer-Deutsch, 2:162; Anderson, 402). Much earlier, in 1754, the cost of copying a bifolio at Mannheim was 10 kreuzer; see the letter of F. X. Pokorny printed in Ludwig Schiedermair, "Die Blütezeit der Öttingen-Wallerstein'schen Hofkapelle," *Sammelbände der Internationalen Musikgesellschaft* 9 (1907/8): 119. The price to have a bifolio copied in Vienna was typically seven to nine kreuzer; see, e.g., the advertisements of Simon Haschke quoted in Hannelore Gericke, *Der Wiener Musikalienhandel von 1700 bis 1778* (Graz and Cologne: Hermann Böhlaus Nachfolger, 1960), 104-5 (from the period 1767-71; nine kreuzer per bifolio).

alen"; see below) were provided by the court from a central depot. One of the few extant documents from Mannheim detailing operating expenses lists 253 gulden for this purpose in 1776.[53] A later "Pro Memoria" of 23 November 1778 from Count Joseph Anton von Seeau, *Hofmusikintendant* in Munich, depicts a depot for writing materials ("Schreib Materialen Magazin") where composers of both "church and other" music could obtain writing materials against a receipt; he states that at Mannheim the cost of such supplies for the court music had totaled 962 gulden, 3 kreuzer in three years (presumably the three preceding ones).[54]

Loss of the collection. One of the biggest mysteries about the Mannheim performance materials has always been the fate of those manuscripts left behind in Mannheim after the court departed. As we shall see, the music required for use in Munich was transferred there and is represented today by the Holzbauer and Cannabich collections of the Bayerische Staatsbibliothek (see chaps. 4–5 and Appendix A/II–III) and by the three Grua manuscripts of the Frauenkirche collection (App. A/IV/1–2, A/VI/144). What must have been a huge body of material was, however, left behind under the care of the aging Holzbauer, who had remained in Mannheim as nominal Kapellmeister of the musicians there; after his death in 1783 responsibility for this collection was shifted to the management of the Nationaltheater.[55] When required, music was sent from Mannheim to Munich, as we know happened in the case of Holzbauer's masses and his opera *Günther von Schwarzburg* in 1783.[56]

The most likely hypothesis regarding the disappearance of the Mannheim collection had already been presented by Friedrich Walter in 1898:

> Most of the holdings of the Mannheim court opera were left behind [in Mannheim], for they were rendered superfluous by those in Munich. For the scenery [*Dekorationen*] this is certain, for the music probable.... Some of the music and scenery was removed from the opera house, but the remainder... seems to have burned when the Austrians, firing upon French-occupied Mannheim in November of 1795, reduced the wing of the palace containing the opera house completely to ashes.[57]

---

[53] See Walter, *Geschichte*, 340, citing D-Mbs, Handschriftenabteilung, Cod. germ. 2263.

[54] Munich, Bayerisches Hauptstaatsarchiv, HR I, Fasz. 457/Nr. 13. Along with his letter Seeau sent a brief "Pro Nota" of 10 November 1778 provided to him by an official in Mannheim substantiating the figures he gives. Other documents in the same fascicle also deal with the supply of writing materials and its cost (always rising). See also chap. 2, fnn. 71–74 and related discussion.

[55] Walter, *Archiv und Bibliothek*, 1:448, and *Geschichte*, 354 (n. 1 to p. 313), citing an electoral rescript of 9 May 1783 (formerly Mannheim, Theaterarchiv, F XII, 1).

[56] See chap. 4, fn. 9 and related text.

[57] Walter, *Geschichte*, 313. See also his *Archiv und Bibliothek*, 2:162.

Examination of the papers of Theodor von Traitteur (1756–1830), court librarian and historian in Mannheim,[58] revealed a hitherto overlooked bit of information providing the first concrete documentation that at least a portion of the music left in Mannheim was destroyed in 1795. Traitteur obviously planned some sort of publication on music at Mannheim, and in a list he had made of opera performances there we find the following item (see fig. 1:3):

> 1778 Rosamund / poet Wieland Mus Schweizer / decor Quaglio. ball[et] Mus Cannabich.[59]

Just to the right of "Schweizer," running across the fold of the paper from folio 105-v to 106r, Traitteur has appended the following comment in darker ink (see fig. 1:3):

> [*Rosamunde*] ist 1795 in der Belagerung mit so vieler andren / kostbaren alten Musik [und] all des ehemalig / operns mit dem rechten Schlossflügel / verbrant.

> [*Rosamunde*] was burned in 1795 in the siege along with so much other valuable old music [and] all of the former opera house together with the right wing of the palace.

The opera house was completely leveled in the siege of 1795, and Traitteur's notation is the first concrete evidence that a great deal of music was thereby lost. Whether the music destroyed in the bombardment included instrumental music cannot be proven, but the reference to "valuable old music" implies that it was no longer in use, and thus it may well have consisted in part of the older orchestral repertory left behind in 1778. In addition, certain operas and other music utilized by those musicians left in Mannheim after 1778 was no doubt housed in the new Nationaltheater,[60] begun in 1775 and from its opening in 1777 site of most of the major performances in Mannheim. It was possibly some of this music that was lost in the destruction of the Theaterbibliothek in the bombardment of Mannheim in World War II (see above, fn. 34 and related text).

---

[58] On Traitteur, who left substantial materials devoted to music at Mannheim, see August Rosenlehner, "Zur Lebengeschichte des kurpfalzbayrischen Bibliothekars und Hofhistoriographen Karl Theodor von Traitteur (1756–1830), *Mannheimer Geschichtsblätter* 9 (1908): 170–76.

[59] Munich, Geheimes Hausarchiv (Bayerisches Hauptstaatsarchiv, Abt. III), Korr. Akt 882/V B, fol. 105v. The list is entitled "Unter Karl Theodor. / Die Kapellens Musik und die grossen Oper.- / und Hofconcerte. Von 1746 bis 1780." Thanks are due to the director of the Geheimes Hausarchiv for furnishing reproductions of this document and for obtaining permission to publish a part of it as fig. 1:3.

[60] As noted above, responsibility for the collection fell to the *Intendanz* of the Nationaltheater after 1783 (see fn. 55 and related discussion).

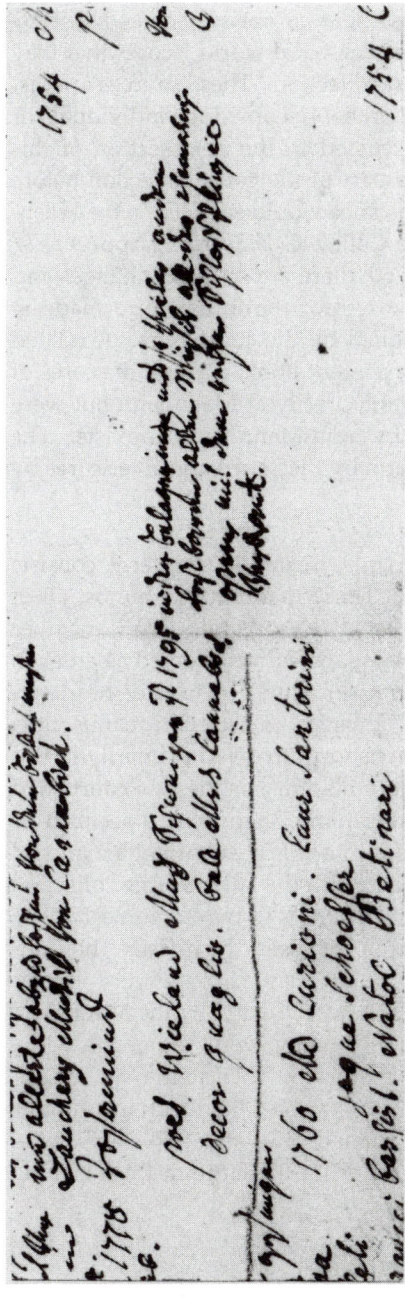

Figure 1:3. Extract from Traitteur papers showing reference to music lost in 1795. Munich, Bayerisches Hauptstaatsarchiv, Abt. III: Geheimes Hausarchiv, Korr. Akt 882/V B, fols. 105v–6r.

Copyists' scores of operas and related works. A special group of manuscripts that does not fit neatly into the categories proposed here comprises scores made by Mannheim copyists of operas and other large secular vocal works, scores that may or may not have originally been part of the court collection. These sources are discussed in detail in chapter 8. While most were probably copied for individuals or as gifts, like a majority of the manuscripts discussed in the next section of this chapter, in certain cases a score may have been part of the court collection before ending up in a different location. An obvious instance would seem to be the Washington score to Niccolò Jommelli and Giuseppe Colla's *Cajo Fabrizio* (App. A/VI/203), which had its premiere in Mannheim in 1760; there are so many changes and serial additions that it is hard to believe this was not the initial copy made at Mannheim from autograph material being supplied by the composers. A related class of manuscripts, not treated in detail in the present book, consists of scores of operas that *were* used or were at least present temporarily at Mannheim but were copied elsewhere, either by their composer or by (non-Mannheim) copyists. The six manuscripts in question include one autograph by Piccinni[61] and five scores by Italian and Viennese copyists.[62]

Copies for external use. A final class of manuscripts, treated in chapter 9, consists of copies made at Mannheim for use elsewhere. These manuscripts, almost all of which are sets of parts rather than scores, are listed in Appendix A/VI, together with those of the previous category. Whether these sources were copied as gifts, on commission, or for sale (surreptitious or otherwise) cannot generally be determined with any certainty. We may speculate, however, that certain manuscripts from Mannheim such as the large group at Regensburg involved primarily gift or presentation copies, or perhaps in some cases commissions, as the two courts had long-standing dynastic connections. On the other hand, there would seem to be little reason for Carl Theodor to have presented a minor Protestant nobleman and military man such as Ludwig Freiherr von Pretlack with the latter's large collection of Mannheim manuscripts (primarily single arias), and we may assume that he merely commissioned their copying or otherwise purchased them (see "The Pretlack Collection" in chap. 9).

Whether such manuscripts were pirated (i.e., copied illicitly by the Mannheim copyists) is again a matter of conjecture; probably many were, given the widespread nature of this practice in the eighteenth century.[63] This claim may be supported by the fact that so many manuscripts owned by non-Mannheim institutions or individuals are lined rather informally with small one- and two-stave rastra (staff-liners), which any copyist would possess, and not the large rastra for lining

---

[61] See table 8:1, no. 12a.

[62] Ibid., nos. 8 (Jommelli), 13a and 14a (Salieri), and 17–18 (Traetta).

[63] See, e.g., Mozart's letter of 15 May 1784 (Bauer-Deutsch, 3:313–14; Anderson, 876–77).

ten and twelve staves at once that were preferred in official court copies. The assumption is that the copyist purchased and lined the paper himself rather than obtaining pre-lined paper from the central depot, thus avoiding embarrassing questions as to its purpose.

Relationship of manuscript types and Appendix A, sections I–VI. As the reader may already have noted, the typology of manuscripts just outlined is only partly congruent with the organization of the manuscripts in Appendix A/I–VI (and thus with their discussion in chapters 3–9). That organization is instead based on a combination of two factors: (1) the strength of evidence for Mannheim provenance (e.g., the manuscripts of Appendix A/I are assigned to Mannheim based on direct documentary evidence, those of Appendix A/VI on circumstantial evidence); and (2) a desire for simplicity and clarity of organization (e.g., division of the manuscripts of Holzbauer, Cannabich, and Vogler into the separate appendices A/II, III, and V, even though most were originally part of the court collection). Hence, autograph scores and manuscript parts from the court collection may appear in any of Appendices A/I through A/V. (Only the category of sources copied for probable use elsewhere shows no overlap; these manuscripts, treated in chapter 9, appear solely in Appendix A/VI, listed together with the scores to large-scale dramatic works discussed in chapter 8.) It is to a discussion of the types of evidence and the methodology that can be brought to bear in studying these manuscripts, and the conclusions that can be drawn about them, that we turn in the next chapter.

Chapter 2

Codicological Evidence:
Methods for the Study of Eighteenth-Century Music Manuscripts

The methodological paradigm for the present study is, or at least was initially, a thoroughly traditional one: first, establishment of an unassailable core group of manuscripts that unquestionably originated at the electoral court in Mannheim; and then, demonstration through comparative studies that other manuscripts ought reasonably to be assigned to Mannheim owing to their high degree of similarity to members of that core group (and, conversely, their lack of congruence with any other known body of manuscripts). In this instance the core group that eventually emerged consisted of 24 manuscripts that have either remained in Mannheim or bear a colophon or other direct evidence of Mannheim provenance. These manuscripts, a detailed *catalogue raisonné* of which appears as Appendix A/I, are discussed in the next chapter; as might be expected, they contain a high proportion of autographs and partial autographs (15 of 24).

The remaining manuscripts are divided into five groups. The first four of these reveal less obvious and direct connections with Mannheim than those of the core group, though some links are still present that support the high degree of physical resemblance to the manuscripts of that group. These four groups are as follows: (1) sacred and dramatic music of Ignaz Holzbauer, now primarily in Munich (D-Mbs; catalogued in Appendix A/II, treated in chapter 4); (2) instrumental works of Christian Cannabich now in Munich (D-Mbs; Appendix A/III, treated in chapter 5); (3) other autograph and partially autograph manuscripts which, though they lack colophons stating explicitly that they originated in Mannheim, can be shown to have done so based on other types of evidence (Appendix A/IV, treated in chapter 6); and (4) sacred music of Georg Joseph Vogler now in Darmstadt and Offenbach (D-DS, D-OF), some of it bearing dates from the Mannheim period and thus clearly written there, the remainder assigned here to Mannheim based on codicological and certain other evidence (Appendix A/V, treated in chapter 7). A final group, the largest by far, is made up of manuscripts in various collections that for the most part can be shown only on codicological grounds to have stemmed from Mannheim (Appendix A/VI; treated in chapters 8–9).

As alluded to at the start of this chapter, the traditional inductive/deductive model just described did not have to be maintained for long in this study. As more and more evidence accrued, both physical and otherwise, it became abundantly clear that the only possible explanation for the genesis of these manuscripts was that they were prepared at Mannheim, and in many cases actually used there, before the departure of the court for Munich in 1778. The applicable paradigm had thus shifted to one far more common in the writing of history than straight syllogistic approaches, one I think of as the "puzzle" or "jigsaw puzzle" paradigm.[1] According to this model, a version of the principle of Occam's razor, there might theoretically be other ways to fit the myriad bits of evidence together, but the simplest by a convincing margin is the one being offered—in this case the Mannheim provenance of these sources. Stated conversely, no other explanation could account for the intricate web of evidence that has come down to us without involving such complexity as to be absurd.

Let us consider a concrete example, namely the origin of the Holzbauer and Cannabich manuscripts of Appendices A/II–III. Here the best alternate explanation to assigning them to Mannheim would be that they were prepared in Munich (their present location) after removal of the court there. But this would require (1) that paper never used otherwise in Munich suddenly appeared there in abundance for the copying of these manuscripts alone; (2) that rastra used to line paper ten years earlier in Mannheim before being abandoned were suddenly taken up again, transferred with the court to Munich; and (3) that several copyists (including Cannabich) whose hands in dated or datable manuscripts evince a clear split between early and late forms, the former associated with Mannheim, the latter with Munich, all abruptly reverted to their earlier hands late in their careers. While none of the above is theoretically impossible, it is simply not credible that all three phenomena would have occurred at once—not to mention the obvious question as to why anyone would have bothered to copy all this music over again, some of it over 25 years old by the time of the Munich transfer. By contrast, all the evidence points consistently, with no significant or unexplainable contradiction, to a much simpler explanation: that the manuscripts were simply transferred from Mannheim to the library of the new court in Munich for use there. (As proof of this view one could at the outset have cited the fact that one of the Holzbauer manuscripts, App. A/II/12, is dated 1763 by its copyist and thus provides direct rather than circumstantial evi-

---

[1] The "puzzle" paradigm is related to what has been called the "explaining how" class of explanations, as opposed to the usual "explaining why" or deductive explanation of cause (the so-called covering- law model); see William Dray, *Laws and Explanations in History* (London: Oxford University Press, 1957), chap. 6, "Explaining Why and Explaining How." Donald Jay Grout characterizes "explaining how" explanations as follows: "A good historical explanation is not one which [necessarily] compels us to accept it as logically entailed by premises but rather one which persuades us . . . to see it as the 'right,' the 'inevitable' way of structuring the given elements"; see his "Current Historiography and Music History," in Harold Powers, ed., *Studies in Music History: Essays for Oliver Strunk* (Princeton, N.J.: Princeton University Press, 1968), 32. In this passage Grout actually goes farther than Dray (whom he does not cite), who only distinguishes between "how-possibly" and "why-necessarily" explanations (pp. 164–69); Grout's is closer to a "how-probably" position. See also Michael Scriven, "Truisms As the Grounds for Historical Explanations," in Patrick Gardiner, ed., *Theories of History* (New York: The Free Press, 1959), 443–75.

dence of its provenance in Mannheim before 1778 [see fig. 4:1]; but that would have made the matter uncharacteristically simple!)

While every scholar working in depth with manuscript material will develop his or her own working methods and preferences, it may be informative at this point to outline the approach that has evolved in the course of the present study. To begin with, I generally distinguish heuristically between (1) an initial phase of study devoted to such obvious bibliographical tasks as transcription of the title page and other textual material, registering the number of parts, recording the format and size of the manuscript, and (if relevant) gaining a preliminary idea of the fascicle structure; and (2) a subsequent, more exhaustive examination of all other relevant physical parameters of the manuscript.

What the latter parameters might be varies to some extent with the type of manuscript under consideration and the goals of one's research. For instance, in the study of scores—not the primary concern of the present project—elements such as the fascicle structure and binding of the manuscript often take on central importance as indications of its history, whereas these elements generally have less significance in a study of manuscript parts, which will probably be much shorter and simpler and will mostly lack bindings. In the present study, dealing with a body of over 350 manuscripts consisting primarily of parts, three parameters have proven of paramount significance: paper type (including watermarks), staving (rastrology), and handwriting (of both copyists and composers). Detailed information about each of these areas of study is found in Appendices B, C, and D, respectively, of the present book.

Until recently, studies of eighteenth-century composers (including my own) have tended to give detailed attention to only the first and last of the categories just mentioned, paper and handwriting.[2] In many cases, however, it is rastrology that provides the most precise information of all, at least when, as we shall see, the papers in question were lined—as at Mannheim and Vienna—with large, multi-nib rastra designed to draw five, ten, and twelve staves at once. Moreover, it is obvious that in comparative studies like this one, in which a primary goal is to determine whether two or more manuscripts have identical origins, the presence of a third class of evidence significantly enlarges the basis for a decision, especially when the evidence of the handwriting or paper is ambiguous. Precisely the same may be said with respect to the determination of chronology.

---

[2] Among scholars who have taken rastrology into account are Alan Tyson in his studies of Mozart's autographs, e.g. his *Mozart: Studies of the Autograph Scores* (Cambridge, Mass.: Harvard University Press, 1987), 9–11 et passim, and Donald Burrows and Martha J. Ronish in *A Catalogue of Handel's Musical Autographs* (Oxford: Clarendon Press, 1994), 325–28. However, as we shall see, the methods employed by these scholars in the area of rastrology are by no means precise enough in many cases to lead to firm conclusions.

Of course, the "triangle" of parameters mentioned is by no means exhaustive. As part of a study of handwriting, for example, ink color can be an important clue in determining whether a given part or passage was added at a later date.[3] A sophisticated technique for the analysis of ink using an isochronous cyclotron has been developed at the Crocker Nuclear Laboratory of the University of California at Davis.[4] This nondestructive technique uses particle-induced X-ray emission (PIXE) to determine the precise atomic content of a given ink. In the study by Bruce Kusko cited in footnote 4, this method was successful in showing that all the annotations, including underlining and other random marks, found in Bach's copy of the so-called Calov bible make use of essentially the same ink and thus are very probably traceable to Bach. Unfortunately, this technique—which incidentally can also be used to analyze the paper of a manuscript and the string used to bind the leaves together—is of limited utility in a study like the present one, as the source must be transported to the laboratory for study.

The following sections of this chapter provide a more detailed explanation of the approach to manuscript study outlined above. The goal is both to describe the methods employed in the present study and to present a basic, practicable set of techniques that may be of use to those interested in pursuing manuscript studies in the future. At the same time, these sections are intended to furnish an introduction to the physical characteristics of a Mannheim manuscript and to present the most important conclusions of the present study in each domain.

Initial Examination of the Manuscript

The call slip has been submitted and, after what often seems an interminable wait, the manuscript has arrived. What to do with it? Most investigators will begin by perusing the title page and then leafing—carefully—through the manuscript to gain some idea of its contents, structure, complexity, and so on. When dealing with typical sets of parts, one may already at this stage wish to begin sorting the parts into groups if any are obvious, for example a clearly original set and later ad-

---

[3] For a recent study of ink color as a means of assigning date see John Arthur, "Some Chronological Problems in Mozart: The Contribution of Ink Studies," in Stanley Sadie, ed., *Wolfgang Amadè Mozart: Essays on His Life and Music* (Oxford: Clarendon Press, 1996), 35–52. The section "Pens and Inks" in Dexter Edge, *Mozart's Viennese Copyists* (Ph.D. diss., University of Southern California, 2001), 179–92, provides a thorough study of eighteenth-century ink. For a comprehensive bibliography on early ink see the extensive website developed by Elmer Eusman and Birgit Reißland, <www.knaw.nl/ecpa/ink/index.html> (information kindly communicated to me by Dexter Edge).

[4] See Bruce Kusko, "Proton Milliprobe Analysis of the Hand-Penned Annotations in Bach's Calov Bible," in *The Calov Bible of J. S. Bach*, ed. Howard H. Cox (Ann Arbor, Mich.: UMI Research Press, 1985), 31–106.

ditions or duplicate parts. This situation is common in the case of manuscripts copied at Mannheim for use at other centers (i.e., most of those in Appendix A/VI). Here the original set will usually have the large format, Swiss papers, and bold, sweeping hands characteristic of Mannheim, while what are clearly duplicate or added parts will generally be smaller, on local paper and by local copyists (as in the Regensburg manuscripts of symphonies by Johann Stamitz to be described briefly below).[5] For more complex manuscripts, however, with additions or differences from part to part that are more difficult to sort out, one will probably want to wait to establish groupings within the manuscript until a more careful study of the watermarks, staving, and handwriting has been carried out.

The next steps in dealing with a manuscript are essentially bibliographical and to a certain extent mechanical. The amount of detail one brings to bear on them depends entirely on the type of project and its goals. In most cases a careful transcription of the title page will be desirable, with placement of the text, overall size of the lettering, and line endings indicated, as such aspects may turn out to be important at a later date. The general principle is never to have to return to a manuscript for information one has failed to record (or has recorded carelessly!) on first examination. Of course, greater leeway may be appropriate if microfilms or photocopies of the source are known to be available. I personally try always to have a camera with me when working in all but the largest libraries; even if one does not photograph the entire manuscript, a film of the title page and selected parts can be very helpful as a backup and when dealing at a later date with the identification of copyists. It is also important to record any seemingly extraneous notations on the title page such as numbers or letters; these may turn out to be librarians' markings from the period that can be helpful in dating. In addition, one will want at some point to comb the manuscript carefully for any added notations in the parts; dates are sometimes placed within the staves or ingeniously woven into decorations at the ends of movements, for example (as in fig. 4:1).

Again depending upon the goals of one's study, it is usually a good idea to register the number of parts present and the precise terminology used for the instruments. Next one might make note of the format (oblong or upright) and take measurements of the parts or score, with indications of any noticeable discrepancies among the different components of the manuscript. Though measuring the dimensions of a manuscript may seem like make-work, knowing the exact size of a manuscript can be useful both in determining the groupings within that manuscript and in comparative studies involving other manuscripts. Measurements, in millimeters (or centimeters and millimeters), should be taken of a typical page or of a range of page sizes; a large, good-quality metric ruler is standard equipment for any manuscript researcher. In recording and reporting such measurements, height always precedes width.

---

[5] See fig. D:17 for a typical title page from the Stamitz manuscripts at Regensburg.

As in most of Catholic Europe, parts for secular music at Mannheim, and most scores, are oblong in format. Their paper consists of one or more bifolios that have been produced by cutting or tearing the original sheet of paper in half horizontally, as shown in figure 2:1a. The resulting manuscripts, especially those used for performance at the electoral court, are usually very large. For instance, the Stamitz manuscripts from Mannheim that are now at Regensburg range from approximately 240 to 270 mm. in height and 350 to 380 mm. in width. (By contrast, the local additions and duplicate parts of the Regensburg Stamitz manuscripts generally measure ca. 220 x 320 mm.)[6] The Cannabich manuscripts at Munich nearly all fall within the same range, but they tend to group near the larger end of the scale, probably because they are mostly later than the Stamitz manuscripts: ca. 260–70 x 370–80 mm. would be typical. The original sheets from which the bifolios of these manuscripts were taken would therefore have conformed to the standard eighteenth-century size known as *Imperial(e)*, the dimensions of which are variously given as ca. 500 to 570 by 740 to 780 mm.

A majority of the manuscripts written for courts other than Mannheim (e.g., most of the manuscripts of Appendix A/VI) tend to be smaller than those actually used at Mannheim (e.g., most of the manuscripts of Appendices II–III), perhaps because the copyists themselves were furnishing the paper or because the manuscripts were to be mailed or otherwise delivered elsewhere.[7] Thus most of the manuscripts in the Pretlack collection now in Berlin, consisting primarily of scores and parts of individual arias (see chap. 9), have dimensions in the range of 225–35 x 305–15 mm. Hence the original sheets from which the paper was taken were of the *Real(e)* size, which measured ca. 440–80 by 610–40 mm. Certain of the Pretlack manuscripts do, however, attain the low to middle dimensions of the Stamitz manuscripts in Regensburg, which date from about the same period.[8] Still others in the Pretlack collection, and many others in various centers, fall between the small and large extremes outlined here.

Parts for sacred music at Mannheim, as elsewhere in Europe, are normally upright in format, possibly because such manuscripts are easier for singers to hold (though the orchestral parts are usually upright in format as well). The paper of

---

[6] The dimensions given are those of a typical folio or leaf of the manuscript, one-half of a bifolio (Ger. *Bogen*) and one quadrant of the original sheet. It was in fact the obvious discrepancy between the large, bold originals and the smaller added parts of the Stamitz symphonies at Regensburg that first caused me to speculate that the original sets might have been from Mannheim: they were clearly imported rather than local, and Mannheim and Regensburg had close ties in the eighteenth century.

[7] Many such manuscripts, notably those at Regensburg, have a vertical crease down the middle, as though they were folded for insertion into an envelope or packet.

[8] E.g., the Holzbauer arias App. A/VI/98–101, the Jommelli arias 112–13, and the Pescetti aria 119 all fall in the range 250–55 x 350–60 mm.

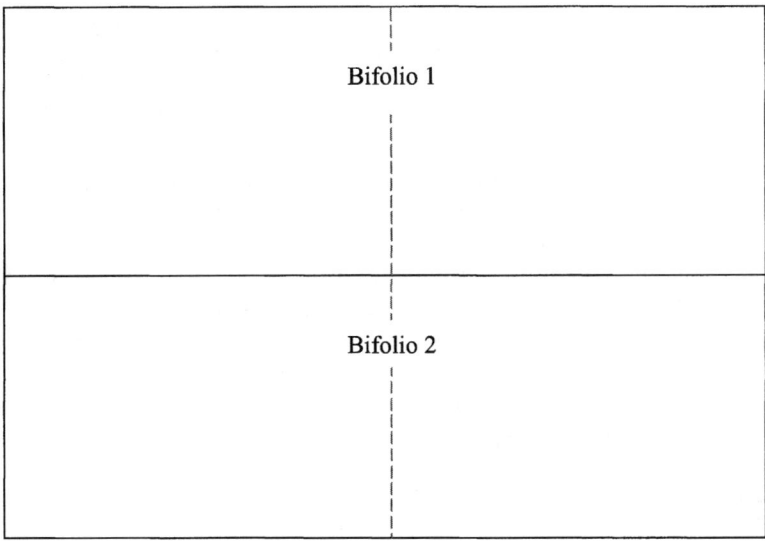

Figure 2:1a. Division of original sheet to produce four oblong folios. The sheet is cut horizontally along the solid line, then folded along the gapped line.

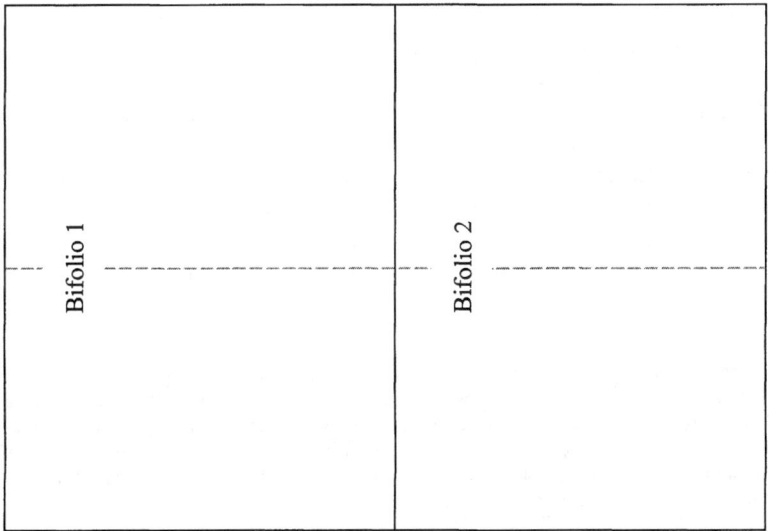

Figure 2:1b. Division of original sheet to produce four upright folios. The sheet is cut along the solid line, then folded along the gapped line.

these parts was prepared by cutting the original sheet vertically (see fig. 2:1b, above).⁹ Many of the sacred parts thus have the same basic dimensions as the larger of the secular parts, but in reverse; just under half of the Holzbauer manuscripts in Munich, for example, measure ca. 360–75 x 265–70 mm., while the remainder are somewhat smaller, ca. 335–45 x 245–65 mm.

Another point for consideration is the type of title page, cover, or, in the case of larger scores, binding. Most Mannheim manuscripts of secular music do not have a separate wrapper on different (usually lesser-quality) paper; either a separate cover containing the title is provided, normally on paper similar to that of the parts, or the title is simply written on the first (blank) page of one of the parts and the other parts inserted within it. To judge by the surviving examples, sacred music at Mannheim was generally provided with a true wrapper, most often of coarse blue "elephant" paper of local manufacture—so called for its size and quality and the rather droll elephant that appears as its watermark (see Knöckel 1 in Appendix B/II).

For full scores of operas or oratorios the binding is often of leather, and a careful study of the decorations, especially any heraldic devices that may be present, can be of great utility. In the present study, for example, it was possible to determine the original ownership (by a Mannheimer) of a group of opera scores scattered in various libraries owing to the inclusion of the owner's coat of arms (see chap. 8, including fig. 8:7b). In addition, the gilt decoration of the binding of these scores resembled that of other bindings from Mannheim, though firm conclusions in this area were difficult to draw owing to the high degree of stylization characteristic of such decorations during this period.

A final concern of this initial stage of research on a manuscript is to make at least a preliminary assessment of the order in which the manuscript was copied and bound—its fascicle structure.¹⁰ For many sets of parts this is a non-issue—the parts are all written on a single folio or bifolio. In other cases the longer parts such as those for the violins may consist of two or more bifolios sewn at the margins, or a bifolio plus a folio sewn so as to leave only a stub where the other folio was re-

---

[9] The two relationships described here between the original sheet of paper and a bifolio of manuscript paper are not the only ones possible. The upright parts characteristic of north German manuscripts (e.g., those of Bach) generally begin with a sheet of paper that is considerably smaller than those described above and simply fold it in half, uncut, along its vertical axis. Even at Mannheim the paper is occasionally cut strangely (especially in early manuscripts), as in some of the Stamitz manuscripts at Regensburg.

[10] For brief discussions of the structure of eighteenth-century manuscripts see, e.g., Douglas Johnson, Alan Tyson, and Robert Winter, *The Beethoven Sketchbooks: History, Reconstruction, Inventory* (Berkeley: University of California Press, 1985), 47–50, 53–54; Georg Feder, *Musikphilologie: eine Einführung in die musikalische Textkritik, Hermeneutik und Editionstechnik* (Darmstadt: Wissenschaftliche Buchgesellschaft, 1987), 47; Burrows and Ronish, *Handel's Musical Autographs*, pp. xxviii–xxix.

moved. Unless something has been added after the original set of parts has been copied, such fascicle structure is normally too mundane to require any comment.

As already stated above, however, in the case of more extended manuscripts—for example, certain large autograph or copyists' scores and some of the huge sets of parts to the Holzbauer masses in Munich, which were altered and revised over many years—the examination of fascicle structure may take on far greater importance. It will therefore generally be carried out in conjunction with more detailed studies of the type discussed in the following sections. Examination of a large, complex manuscript of this type traditionally leads to a detailed listing or diagram of the folios of the manuscript, with nested and interlocking brackets and markings of various kinds to distinguish the various levels of the manuscript.[11] The starting point is provided by the original version, which in the case of large scores was normally copied and bound in gatherings (nested groups) of from three or four to more than a dozen bifolios. Then might come various levels of additions or replacements, extending from smaller or larger paste-overs to added folios or bifolios, the latter indicated by brackets or some other means in the diagram of the fascicle structure. The goal of such diagrams is not simply to catalogue the structure of the manuscript, but to trace its often convolute history in as graphic a manner as possible. Though exhaustive study of this sort does not fall within the province of the present book, I have included the essential information on each manuscript of this type as a basis for what I hope will be more specialized research in this area in the future.

Paper and Watermarks

The paper of a manuscript, identified primarily but not exclusively by its watermarks,[12] furnishes a primary means of establishing provenance and date. While one can justifiably question the value of papyrological evidence under certain circumstances—the paper of an anomalous folio within an autograph manuscript might certainly have been kept for a while by the composer before being used, to cite the standard objection—there can be no doubt of the utility of such evidence in a study of a major court like Mannheim, or in many other types of

---

[11] For typical examples see Tyson, *Mozart: Studies of the Autograph Scores*, 87–88, and various studies of the Beethoven sketchbooks, e.g. Douglas P. Johnson, *Beethoven's Early Sketches in the "Fischhof Miscellany"* (Ann Arbor, Mich.: UMI Research Press, 1988), 1:84–86, 94–96.

[12] An example of the identification of a paper by means other than watermarks is the paper without watermarks labeled "Swiss (no WM)" in Appendix B/I/3; this paper appears in many Mannheim manuscripts in the 1750s and early 1760s (see chaps. 5 and 9). See also David L. Vander Meulen, "The Identification of Paper without Watermarks: The Example of Pope's *Dunciad*," in *Studies in Bibliography* 37 (1984): 58–81.

study.¹³ In the case of Mannheim we are dealing for the most part with large quantities of paper bought on a regular basis by the court for carefully controlled distribution through an official depot, the *Schreibmaterialen Magazin*.¹⁴ That quantities of this paper would have been left lying around for years before being used is unlikely on the face of it. But in any event, the many dated and datable manuscripts from Mannheim disclose a notably consistent succession of papers through the years, indicating a systematic cycle of purchase, distribution, and use. Likewise, the succession of papers correlates closely with the changes in copyists' hands and staving.

As is also true for the study of handwriting, watermark studies in the past have gained a somewhat dubious reputation owing to the sloppy procedures and indiscriminate use of evidence on the part of many practitioners.¹⁵ One common error has been a failure to take full account of the fact that watermarks generally exist in "twin" forms, a result of the process of manufacture with two molds, which are used in alternation.¹⁶ In addition, hand-made paper reveals a distinction between the mold side, with its impressions made by the wires for the chain-lines, laid-lines, and watermarks proper,¹⁷ and the felt side, which is smoother and may

---

[13] The objection that watermarks establish only a terminus a quo in that the paper could have been kept for an extended period has been answered to the satisfaction of most scholars both by traditional watermark studies and in practical applications such as Alan Tyson, *Wolfgang Amadeus Mozart: Neue Ausgabe sämtlicher Werke*, vol. X/33/2: *Wasserzeichen-Katalog* (Kassel: Bärenreiter, 1992); Burrows and Ronish, *Handel's Musical Autographs* (see esp. p. vii); and the present project. These and other studies all show a close correlation between paper type and date.

[14] See chap. 1, fnn. 53–54 and related text.

[15] Frederick Hudson, "The Study of Watermarks As a Research Factor in Undated Manuscripts and Prints: Beta-Radiography with Carbon-14 Sources," in *International Musicological Society: Report of the Eighth Congress, Copenhagen 1972* (Copenhagen: Wilhelm Hansen, 1974), 447, correctly stresses the need for precision in the description and reproduction of watermarks.

[16] See the introduction to Appendix B. The pathbreaking study in this area was Alan H. Stevenson, "Watermarks Are Twins," *Studies in Bibliography: Papers of the Bibliographical Society of the University of Virginia* 4 (1951–52): 57–91. This principle has been espoused in the field of musicology most notably by Alan Tyson; see, e.g., "The Problem of Beethoven's 'First' *Leonore* Overture," *JAMS* 28 (1975): 332–34; *Mozart: Studies of the Autograph Scores*, 1–9; *Wasserzeichen-Katalog*, Textband, pp. vii–ix. But see also the cautionary notes sounded in Jan LaRue, "Watermarks Are Singles, Too: A Miscellany of Research Notes," in *Haydn, Mozart, and Beethoven: Studies in the Music of the Classical Period, Essays in Honour of Alan Tyson*, ed. Sieghard Brandenburg (Oxford: Clarendon Press, 1998), 1–12. For a full description of the production of hand-made paper see Philip Gaskell, *A New Introduction to Bibliography* (Oxford: Oxford University Press, 1972), 57–66.

[17] Chain-lines are produced by the thicker vertical wires spaced some 3–5 cm. apart, laid-lines by the thinner horizontal wires spaced about a millimeter apart. The wires forming the watermarks (the principal watermark, normally on the left half of the original sheet, and the countermark, normally on the right half) were attached to the chain lines with knots of fine wire, which are often apparent in viewing the watermark.

show protrusions rather then indentations.[18] Hence, any careful study of watermarks should always distinguish between the twin forms and should always refer to the form consistently, traditionally from the mold side.[19]

A final flaw in many studies has been a failure to discriminate carefully among the many variant forms that any watermark, even from the same mold, will show.[20] Molds, and their watermarks, were subject to deterioration on a daily basis, and the watermarks will often reveal variations that can be of value in trying to gauge chronology. Obviously, at least in a large and detailed study like the present one, care should be taken not to describe a mark as "the same" or "identical" unless there are literally *no* observable variations. In this domain, as with handwriting, we suffer from a lack of criteria and system for the description and classification of differences.

In addition to watermarks, attention should be given to such characteristics of the paper as size (trimmed or not?), thickness, overall quality and texture, and color. In the latter case, the Swiss papers used at Mannheim are typically a gleaming white or cream, distinguishing them from local German papers with their brown, often splotchy color. An interesting discrepancy is that between the paper Heusler 5 and its later variant Heusler 8, both manufactured in Baden by the famous Basel papermaker Niklaus Heusler (see Appendix B, "Watermarks," for full information on these and all other papers found in the Mannheim complex of manuscripts). The latter paper is found only in manuscripts copied in Munich, though Swiss paper was not generally used there. What is distinctive about it is its strong greenish tinge—a fact that was lost on me in that I am grey-green colorblind, but was most helpful to my wife as a reliable means of initial sorting. While as a practical matter none of the characteristics mentioned except dimension lend themselves to systematic description and classification, they can all be useful in such roles as distinguishing a cover, part, or page added by a copyist at even a slightly a later date.

The recording and reproduction of watermarks. An omnipresent issue in watermark studies is the method one should follow in recording and reproducing watermarks. Ideally, this method would allow absolutely exact reproduction of each mark, so as to permit identification of small differences; it would not be harmful to the manuscript in any way; and it would be both quick and cheap. In addition, any implements required (e.g., light boxes) would be portable, so that, depending on

---

[18] The "felt" side refers to the fact that in the manufacture of hand-made paper the mold, after being dipped into the vat and shaken, was inverted, releasing the (at this point incipient) sheet of paper onto a sheet of felt. As soon as a stack of interleaved paper and felt had accumulated, it was moved to a standing press, where the water was squeezed out of it.

[19] See the extensive discussion of the labeling of watermarks in Appendix B.

[20] See the discussion of watermark irregularities in LaRue, "Watermarks Are Singles," 3–5.

the type of project, they could be used anywhere. Sad to say, none of the methods now in use fulfills all these criteria, but depending again upon the results desired, one or the other can be satisfactory.

The *crème de la crème* of watermark reproduction at present is beta-radiography. In this method a translucent plastic sheet impregnated with Carbon 14 isotopes is placed under darkroom conditions underneath the sheet of paper to be reproduced, with a sheet of X-ray film on top covered by a plate of glass to hold the two firmly in contact.[21] What is superior about this technique is that the radioactive isotopes (which are nondestructive to both manuscript and technician) pass through the ink on the page but register only the relative thicknesses of the paper—in other words, the watermarks and the chain- and laid-lines. The resulting negative can in turn be superimposed on other negatives to identify minor discrepancies between molds, or a positive can be made for reproduction.

Some of the drawbacks of this method will already be clear. It must be carried out under darkroom conditions, and the initial cost of the impregnated sheets is high. In addition, the process can be very slow. These points make ridiculous G. Thomas Tanselle's statement that in the future "the student of paper will need to carry with him a Carbon 14 source."[22] For the time being, at least, beta-radiography is only available through the photographic or reproduction divisions of the largest libraries, and will thus only be satisfactory for certain types of studies. In my case, only a handful of the libraries I have worked in offer this service, and at a price that was prohibitive considering the large number of reproductions required.

Still more high-tech is a method developed by the firm Fotoscientifica of Parma, Italy.[23] This method utilizes a high-definition digital camera to photograph a back-lighted page; the resulting image is then processed using programs that remove all text, notes, staves, and so forth. As with beta-radiography, nothing but the watermark shows. Reportedly planned is a database of watermarks of the Vivaldi manuscripts in Parma and Dresden. Depending upon the details and the way this procedure develops, it could hold considerable promise for the future, especially given the constantly rising quality and falling prices of digital cameras.

---

[21] Much of the information in this section is derived from the excellent survey by David Schoonover, "Techniques of Reproducing Watermarks: A Practical Introduction," in Stephen Spector, ed., *Essays in Paper Analysis* (Washington, D.C.: Folger Books, 1987), 154–67. Schoonover gives a great deal of technical information, including sources of materials, exact procedures to be followed, and the like. For a good earlier treatment of beta-radiography see Hudson, "Beta-Radiography with Carbon-14 Sources," 447–53.

[22] G. Thomas Tanselle, "The Bibliographical Description of Paper," *Studies in Bibliography* 24 (1971): 50.

[23] E-mail <info@fotoscientifica.it>. This method was described at the First International Conference on the History, Function, and Study of Watermarks, held in October 1996 at Virginia Polytechnic Institute and State University, and at the conference "Musica e Mouse" held in Bologna in April 2000. I am grateful to Professor Stephen Shearon of Middle Tennessee State University for informing me of this intriguing new development.

Three other techniques worthy of mention are all variants on backlighted photography of the page. All have the disadvantage of recording all the ink marks on both sides of the page, often making it difficult to discern the watermark. The first is a simple photograph or contact print of a leaf. The second, developed by Robin Alston, uses high-speed duplicating film in what is basically a contact-print method; one of its drawbacks, in addition to that just mentioned, is the necessity to have darkroom conditions available.[24] A third type, developed by Thomas L. Gravell, makes use of DuPont Dylux 503 paper, which is sensitive not to normal light but only to ultraviolet or fluorescent light, thus allowing one to work under normal rather than darkroom conditions.[25] A sheet of Dylux is placed under the paper and a strong fluorescent or UV source is passed over it for a period of several minutes. The image emerges without the necessity of development. A disadvantage of this technique is that the resulting image is opaque and thus cannot be compared directly with other images. Despite their drawbacks, any of these methods might prove useful in certain restricted types of studies.

The traditional way of recording watermarks has, of course, been to make tracings of them on translucent paper. An obstacle to the use of this method is that many libraries now prohibit tracing of their manuscripts on grounds that it can damage them. This is indisputably correct for many practices routinely carried out in the past. For example, use of the large stationary light-boxes found in some libraries to trace sheets of a bound volume runs a high risk of damage either to the volume itself or to one of the sheets, as the volume must be manipulated and the tracing carried out simultaneously. Loosely bound parts, however, do not present this problem. The worst practice of all, one that should never be permitted, is that of tracing against a window, with sunlight serving as the backlight. And needless to say, no tracing should ever be carried out on a manuscript whose paper is fragile or deteriorating.

On the other hand, when the paper is of the robust type found at Mannheim, when scrupulous care is taken by a researcher experienced in working with manuscripts, and when the proper lighting implement and materials are used, tracing presents no more danger to a manuscript than simply examining it in detail. By "proper lighting implement" I mean a portable, low- (or no-) heat light source with a flat surface for carrying out the actual tracing. Several types can be recommended. The first is a variant of a design proposed by Jan LaRue years ago, a home-made wedge-shaped light box constructed of sheet aluminum, with a plexiglass plate on the diagonal side on which the tracing is done.[26] Instead of the in-

---

[24] Robin Alston, "Reproducing Watermarks," *Direction Line* 2 (1976): 1–3.

[25] See Thomas L. Gravell, "A New Method of Reproducing Watermarks for Study," *Restaurator* 2 (1975): 94–104; Gravell and George Miller, *A Catalogue of American Watermarks, 1690–1835* (New York: Garland Publishing, 1979), pp. xiii–xiv. The many reproductions in the latter volume were made using the Dylux process.

[26] See the sketch in Jan LaRue, "Watermarks and Musicology," *Acta musicologica* 33 (1961): 122.

Chapter 2

candescent bulb used by LaRue, which after a few minutes generates enough heat (and smell!) to bring librarians running, I have always used small fluorescent bulbs, the best being the type with a U-shaped element coming from one socket such as the Osram Dulux S 13W/21. These emit very little heat and provide an excellent light source. The advantage of a wedge shape is especially evident in working with large scores, where the light box, not the manuscript, is moved and the narrow part of the wedge can be eased into the binding of the spine for examination of marks that would otherwise be obscured. In constructing such a reader, I place the heavy ballast in a separate small box so as to keep the viewer itself as light and simple as possible.

A commercial version of this type of reader is available that is cheap and can serve nicely with a few modifications. Called the Lite-a-Page 2 Insertable Viewer,[27] it was originally intended for viewing slides in a standard ring binder without having to remove them; but because one surface is flat, it can serve equally well as a light source for tracing watermarks. Several modifications should be made, however, for use as a watermark reader. First, the unit has been designed to do double duty by providing the base of the unit, made (like the top) of milky translucent plastic, with four rows with ridges to hold slides in place for sorting. This sheet should be slid out and replaced with an opaque piece of plastic or aluminum, which can then be backed internally with aluminum foil; these modifications will increase the light output through the top and lessen the risk of damage to the manuscript from the ridges on the original base. For the same reason I recommend covering the entire base of both the home-made and commercial versions of this reader with contact felt, and being certain that no edges are prominent that might snag a page of the manuscript. A more sophisticated (and costly) version of this type of viewer is the Cabin Light Panel, which utilizes an inverter-driven cold cathode fluorescent lamp.[28]

Another type of light, still more sophisticated but also considerably more expensive, is available in two different forms. Each makes use of a thin, flexible sheet that is itself the light source. Only a few millimeters thick at most, these panels omit adequate light and little or no heat, and their thinness means they can easily slip between the pages of even a tightly-bound book.[29] One version is the

---

[27] Available from University Products, Inc., P.O. Box 101, Holyoke, MA 01041-0101 (1-800-628-1912), cat. no. 944-1000. The price in March 2001 was $93.40.

[28] University Products cat. no. 088-0810 (price $459.00 for the 9- by 11¾-inch size).

[29] Jan LaRue seems to have been the first to champion the use of such readers for the study of watermarks. However, early versions of these implements, made from a product with the trademark "Panelescent," were plagued with problems, including light levels that were too low and considerable unreliability.

"Slimlight," designed by Dipl.-Ing. Manfred Mayer of Lieboch, Austria,[30] the other the Fiber Optic Lightsheet.[31] A minor advantage of the latter type is that, thanks to the use of fiber optics, no electrical current comes near the manuscript; the implement can even be used to examine a dampened sheet.

Two objections are commonly raised against tracing as a means of recording watermarks (to which I can add, after all-too-long experience, the tedium of carrying them out). The first is that the process of tracing can damage the surface of the paper. As stated already, this is unlikely with good-quality, sturdy paper of the type used in the Mannheim manuscripts, which will more likely damage you before you damage it. To avoid even the appearance of evil, however, I always use heavy-duty European tracing paper, not the flimsy types common in the United States. If that is not enough, one can place a sheet of transparent plastic between the manuscript and the tracing paper. And of course, one should use pencil rather than pen. By carefully citing all the above precautions, and by patiently explaining the importance of watermarks for one's study—that is, if they *are* central to one's project, not just busy-work being carried out for the sake of completeness or obedience to one's dissertation adviser—one can sometimes negotiate a compromise with recalcitrant librarians. (Whether such negotiation is successful or not, one should always remember the cardinal maxim of scholarly research, taught to me by Jan LaRue: *never* get mad at a librarian.)

An objection of a different sort is that no tracing can ever be precisely accurate. But a carefully done tracing, checked and rechecked against the original, can under most circumstances be accurate enough for most real-world purposes. Anyone who has worked extensively and meticulously with watermark tracings will vouch for the fact that careful tracings of truly identical watermarks—produced from the same mold at virtually the same time—simply "pop" into place when superimposed, much as an image pops into focus on a good camera or enlarger. If one has to move the tracings around a bit to get them to fit, split differences, and so forth, the two marks should not be described as "identical" (except in the sense that the brand and type are the same). In sum, tracing of watermarks will probably remain the workaday solution in most kinds of watermark studies until a better method becomes widely available at a reasonable cost.

Some of the actual procedures in making a usable tracing have already been described or implied above. One should first figure out the composition of the original sheet, in which the principal watermark and a countermark may be on opposite sides, a watermark on one side and no countermark on the other, or a wa-

---

[30] The Slimlight is available through the firm of Anton Glaser Feinpapiergroßhandlung, Postfach 101914, D-70016 Stuttgart (fax +49-711-226 1875, e-mail <Anton-Glaser@t-online.de>). The price in March 2001 was DM 1190,– including a multi-voltage power supply.

[31] Marketed in the United States by University Products (see fn. 27, above; price in March 2001 $1899.95).

termark in the center (to cite the three most common placements). In folio format (see fig. 2:1b above) there will be little difficulty in viewing the watermark unless it is centrally placed, and thus possibly obscured by the binding or cut in half (or both); but in oblong format (see fig. 2:1a) the marks will likely have been cut in half and will have to be reconstructed via the tracing. Here one hopes that the manuscript has not been trimmed. If it has not, in a loose (unbound) set of parts one or more of the original sheets can often be temporarily reassembled by fitting the edges together.

The next step is to determine whether watermark twins are present, always proceeding from the mold side of the paper.[32] In the high-quality Swiss papers used at Mannheim, the mold side can usually be identified by holding the sheet diagonally to the light source so as to create shadows and expose the indentations made by the chain-lines and watermarks; the felt side will be smoother and more regular. However, inferior local papers can present a distinct challenge in this regard.[33]

As already stated, the actual tracing should always be done from the mold side of the paper. In addition to recording the watermarks per se, care should be taken to show the placement of the chain-lines, particularly the points at which the watermark is attached to them, as this can change as the watermark works loose or becomes damaged. After the tracing has been made it should be carefully labeled, not only the manuscript and part from which it came (including the precise page), but exactly where in the original sheet it would have fallen. Useful adjuncts to tracing may be to measure the outer vertical and horizontal dimensions of the marks or any other prominent distances; Alan Tyson's whimsically named "selenometry" is a version of this idea, measurement of the ubiquitous three crescent moons in Italian papers providing at least a preliminary means of classifying them.[34]

---

[32] For a different and somewhat more detailed description of the process described here see Tyson, "*Leonore* Overture," 332–34. Tyson errs in stating (p. 332, no. 3) that twins when viewed from the mold side are nearly always either approximate duplicates of each other (what I label the variation type) or mirror images. A third significant type, which I call the transposition type, simply transposes each image to the opposite page without mirroring it: the first mold's A : B (A on the left folio, B on the right) becomes the second mold's B : A, in both cases viewed from the mold side. This is by far the most common arrangement in the Swiss papers preferred at Mannheim (see the full discussion of watermark typology and naming in the introduction to Appendix B). Cf. also Burrows and Ronish, *Handel's Musical Autographs*, pp. xxvii–xxviii; the authors provide illustrations of the three types enumerated here, labeling them "identical," "mirror," and "fraternal" twins, the latter my transposition type.

[33] As noted in LaRue, "Watermarks Are Singles," 7–8.

[34] On "selenometry" see, inter alia, Tyson, *Mozart: Studies of the Autograph Scores*, p. 8. LaRue, "Watermarks Are Singles," 11, favors using vertical measurements alone, as these tend to vary most significantly. In recording and labeling watermarks he gives these measurements in parentheses after a brief description of the mark. In Appendix B I have chosen instead simply to provide a reproduction of a metric ruler along with the tracings.

Finally, having painstakingly recorded the characteristics of a given paper, one must attempt to identify it. This often long (and, alas, often fruitless) bibliographical process may involve tools ranging from the monumental volumes produced by the Paper Publications Society (Hilversum), which generally deal with the watermarks of a geographical area (see, e.g., the study of Basel papermakers cited in fn. 36, below), to the lists of watermarks often found in studies of specific repertories (collections, a single composer's *œuvre*, etc.). At least when the results have been published as separate studies, online bibliographical databases such as RLIN (the Research Libraries Information Network) can be of considerable assistance in locating relevant studies, which are often highly specialized and produced in minuscule printings. One should also keep in mind that the principal research library or RISM center in a region may have systematically collected works dealing with watermarks of the area. In our case the collections and files of the Bayerische Staatsbibliothek and the western German RISM center in Munich proved to be invaluable. A final resource, especially for research on German watermarks, is the Papierhistorishche Sammlungen of the Deutsches Buch- und Schriftmuseum in Leipzig.[35]

Paper in the Mannheim manuscripts. Let us turn now from methodology to results. A principal conclusion of this study, one heretofore unsuspected, has been that the great majority of the paper used at Mannheim was Swiss, from the mills of the Heusler and Blum families (and probably one or two others) in and near Basel (see Appendix B/I for a full listing of these papers).[36] That the Mannheim court should favor Swiss paper is not, however, surprising considering its abundance and superlative quality when compared with the local product. According to the paper historian Albert Jaffé, "Although four papermills now [late eighteenth century] existed in the Palatinate, their owners could not satisfy the need for paper of either the official ministries or the public. Nor could they silence the complaints of the officials about the quality of the paper, some of which was wholly unusable."[37] Swiss paper could easily be shipped via the Rhine, which flows northward from Basel past Mannheim. It was used at Mannheim not only for music, but for every-

---

[35] Die Deutsche Bibliothek, Deutsches Buch- und Schriftmuseum, Papierhistorische Sammlungen, Deutscher Platz 1, D-04103 Leipzig. See the website <www.ddb.de>.

[36] The most extensive treatment of the famous Basel papermakers is W. Fr. Tschudin, *The Ancient Paper-Mills of Basle and Their Marks* (Hilversum: Paper Publications Society, 1958). Though the Heusler family was from Basel (one of their houses still stands in the St. Albantal district of Basel, where both Heusler and his competitor Blum had mills), a substantial amount of the Heusler paper used at Mannheim was produced not there but just across the border in the margraviate of Baden; see esp. Heusler 5 and 8 in Appendix B, with the Baden coat of arms, and Heusler 7, which includes the location "Cander" (i.e., Kandern, in Baden).

[37] Albert Jaffé, *Die Papierindustrie in den kurpfälzischen Stammlanden unter Kurfürst Carl Theodor* (Schotten: Wilhelm Engel, 1935), 22.

thing from personal letters to official documents and decrees. Even the registers of the Jesuitenkirche in Mannheim are on Basel paper.

Other papers do appear on occasion. Most common are local papers from the Palatinate, generally from the mill of Wolfgang Adam Knöckel in Neustadt/Pfalz (see Appendix B/II, Knöckel 1–2).[38] His papers are found, rather unexpectedly, in one full volume of Stamitz's big Mass in D in Berlin of ca. 1755 (App. A/VI/18) and in manuscripts of the Pretlack collection in Berlin. As already noted, however, Knöckel's most ubiquitous paper is that of the blue "elephant" wrappers of so many sacred and certain other manuscripts. Still less important is Dutch paper—somewhat surprisingly, as its quality was excellent, and Carl Theodor had dynastic and other connections with Holland.[39] The principal examples again occur in the Pretlack collection, a probable indication, together with the use of Palatine paper, that the copyists of these manuscripts were obtaining the paper on their own rather than from court stocks.

Not a single example of Italian paper occurs in an undisputed Mannheim manuscript. Of the only two possible exceptions, the first is the <S CHIARA : cross/shield {fleur-de-lis}> paper of F-Pc, Ms. 20140 (a Richter autograph); this is a borderline case that I have chosen not to include among the Mannheim manuscripts.[40] Despite the Italianate name of the manufacturer, the brownish, rough character of this paper is not characteristic of Italian papers. The second manuscript is F-Pc, Ms. 2199, entitled "Original-Handschrift des Lautenspieler Giovanni Toeschi / Fragment eines Konzertes für Viola d'Amour" (see the reprod. in *MGG* 13:453–54); it was once owned by Aloys Fuchs, who wrote the attribution and title. The watermarks are the common Italian marks <bow-and-arrow/AM : three moons> and <A/HF : three moons>. Because no composer's name appears on the original manuscript, and because Johann Toeschi (1735–1800) was not a lutenist (though he did write for and play viola d'amore, the instrument featured in the concerto), the attribution is somewhat suspect. Even if it is correct, the manuscript could have been written in Munich, where he went in 1778 as Konzertmeister, rather than

---

[38] On paper from the Palatinate see Jaffé, *Papierindustrie*. Earlier, primarily archival, treatments are C. L. Antz, "Die Papiermühlen im Gebiete der Kurpfalz und der heutigen Rheinpfalz," *Mannheimer Geschichtsblätter* 24 (1923): 86–91; Karl Kleeberger, "Urkundliches über die Papiermühle in Mosbach," ibid. 26 (1925): 10–15.

[39] One of Carl Theodor's many titles was Marquis of Bergen op Zoom, and he attended the University of Leiden. The principal study of Dutch paper is W. A. Churchill, *Watermarks in Paper in Holland, England, France, etc., in the XVII and XVIII Centuries and Their Interconnection* (Amsterdam: Hertzberger, 1935). The few Dutch papers found in the Mannheim manuscript complex are listed in Appendix B/III of the present book.

[40] See chap. 6, fn. 11 and related discussion. In naming watermarks in the present study, angle brackets (< >) are used to set off the actual watermark; a solidus (slash) means "over"; a colon separates the principal watermark and the countermark; and curly brackets ({ }) mean "enclosed within." See the full discussion of the labeling of watermarks in the introduction to Appendix B.

Mannheim; Italian paper is fairly common in Munich, being found, for example, in the autograph score to *Idomeneo* and several Cannabich symphonies written there (see App. A/III/58B and 60–61). As for French (in this case Alsatian) paper, it is found in only two full manuscripts and in paste-overs in two other manuscripts.[41]

The results of the present study of watermarks are presented most obviously in Appendices A/I–VI, while the papers themselves are identified and described in Appendix B. In many—but by no means all—cases the careful correlation of changes in the watermark with known dates has succeeded in producing a fairly clear idea of the chronology of the mark or mold(s), a useful tool for dating, especially when combined with other evidence. But even without such confirmation, certain forms of a mold are often so linked with a given chronological period that their presence in an undated manuscript can provide a convincing means of assigning at least an approximate date to the source.

Staving

Perhaps the principal methodological contribution of the present study falls in the realm of rastrology, the study of musical staving. Numerous recent studies of composers' autographs have made use of staving as one type of evidence (see below). The usual approach has been to classify the staving according to the number of staves ruled at a time (i.e., at one pass) and, if more than one staff is involved, the distance from the top line of the top staff to the bottom line of the bottom one (the "total span" or TS, measured in millimeters). No study that I am aware of, however, has yet employed rastrology in a large-scale investigation of parts or of a full repertory, where it can often furnish extraordinarily useful and precise evidence of both provenance and date. At the same time, classification by number of staves and total span alone has proven far too crude a method from which to draw meaningful conclusions, at least about a complex group of manuscripts like that under consideration here, and this study utilizes a much more precise but nonetheless practicable one, described in detail later in this section.

Although rastrological evidence had occasionally been employed by earlier scholars, for example Paul Hirsch in 1929 in an article on Bach's D-minor harpsi-

---

[41] See Appendix B/IV. The two full manuscripts are opera scores by the copyist Mannheim 5, App. A/VI/20 and 196, both from the Sickingen collection (see chap. 8); they are on paper that is probably from Turckheim in Alsace, where the Weyhr or Weyher family was evidently active (see Appendix B/IV, Weyhr 1). Especially because these scores were almost certainly not from the court collection, the copyist undoubtedly obtained the paper independently of the court supplier. The paste-overs are found in Holzbauer's scores to *Betulia liberata* (App. A/II/17, vol. 1, fol. 45r) and *Günther von Schwarzburg* (App. A/II/20, vol. 3, passim); they consist of paper from the mill of Joseph Pasquai (Wasselonne, Alsace).

chord concerto,⁴² its first systematic use came in studies of the manuscripts of J. S. Bach in the 1950s and early 1960s.⁴³ An obvious drawback to these studies was that Bach's papers were lined with what I call "simple" rastra (singular *rastrum*), that is, staff-liners for lining only one stave at a time (see the full discussion in the next section of this chapter). This kind of staving presents two problems for the researcher. First, owing in part to the ease of construction of such rastra (see below), they were ubiquitous—most composers and copyists, and many musicians, must have owned one.⁴⁴ And second, simple rastra furnish a relatively small physical basis for detailed comparison and classification: the only useful specifications are the distance from the top to the bottom line of the staff, the distance of the adjacent lines from each other, and the characteristics of the lines themselves, for example their relative thickness.⁴⁵ As a result, staves lined with two simple rastra can easily be mistaken for staves lined with only one.

For these reasons, studies that have attempted to classify or use the staving of Bach's manuscripts in a comprehensive manner, especially as a means of assigning date, have been less successful than those which apply it to a well-defined smaller body of manuscripts as a means of determining diplomatic groupings or solving a specific problem.⁴⁶ This is not to say that the study of staving in manuscripts lined

---

⁴² Paul Hirsch, "Über die Vorlage zum Klavierkonzert in d-moll," *Bach-Jahrbuch* 26 (1929): 155–56. I am grateful to Arthur Ness and Charlotte A. Kolczynski-Ness for this citation, the earliest known to me on the use of rastrology in the study of eighteenth-century manuscripts. Most of the material on the implements and techniques used to rule music paper and on research methodology in this section of chapter 2 originally appeared in Jean K. and Eugene K. Wolf, "Rastrology and Its Use in Eighteenth-Century Manuscript Studies," in *Studies in Musical Sources and Style: Essays in Honor of Jan LaRue*, ed. Eugene K. Wolf and Edward H. Roesner (Madison, Wisc.: A-R Editions, 1990), 267–87.

⁴³ See the brief survey in Robert L. Marshall, *The Compositional Process of J. S. Bach: A Study of the Autograph Scores of the Vocal Works* (Princeton, N.J.: Princeton University Press, 1972), 1:43, fn. 1, to which should be added the citation given in the previous footnote.

⁴⁴ It is revealing in this regard that a rastrum now owned by the Musikinstrumentenmuseum in Munich (Wolf and Wolf, "Rastrology," Appendix, p. 289, no. 10) was present in the early nineteenth-century case of a violin when the latter came into the possession of the museum (information kindly supplied by Professor Manfred Hermann Schmid, formerly director of the museum and now of the University of Tübingen, who informed me the existence of this rastrum).

⁴⁵ These measurements and how they are made are treated in detail below. Also militating against the usefulness of these measurements in distinguishing simple rastra is their interdependence: the height of the staff, for example, represents merely the sum of the distances between the lines (assuming that all measurements are made from the centers of the lines, as advocated here; see below). Of course, the same is true of certain of the measurements given below for larger, more complex rastra. It might be mentioned at this point that I have not found irregularities at the beginning and end of the staff—e.g., a single line that begins to the left of the four others, protruding into the margin—to be consistent enough, at least in the present repertory, to serve as a reliable criterion for identifying rastra, as will be discussed below (see fn. 64 and related text).

⁴⁶ An example of the former type of study is Christoph Wolff, "Die Rastrierungen in den Originalhandschriften Joh. Seb. Bachs und ihre Bedeutung für die diplomatische Quellenkritik," in *Fest-*

with simple rastra cannot be revealing—I present several examples from the Cannabich manuscripts in chapter 5—but rather that results derived from its comprehensive use (e.g., within the entire body of Bach manuscripts or Handel autographs) must necessarily be treated with caution unless and until it is shown that detailed analysis can distinguish reliably among a large number of simple rastra.

"Compound" or "composite" rastra, those capable of lining from two to sixteen or more staves at once, are less common than simple rastra during the eighteenth century and thus provide a more manageable basis for study. In addition, a set of staves lined with a compound rastrum supplies a much larger body of data with which to work: not only does the number of variables in the complete profile of the rastrum increase geometrically for each additional staff, but one also gains an extremely useful new pair of specifications, the distance from the top line of the top staff to the bottom line of the bottom staff (the aforementioned total span or TS) and the distance between each of the staves (here labeled DS; these measurements are treated in greater detail below). In part for these reasons, the study of manuscripts lined with compound rastra offers greater promise of credible results than that of manuscripts lined with simple rastra. Scholars who have pioneered in this area include Joseph Kerman, Alan Tyson, Richard Kramer, Douglas Johnson, Robert Winter, Donald Burrows, and Martha Ronish in their studies of Beethoven, Mozart, and Handel manuscripts.[47] More recently, the New Haydn Edition has begun to take this type of evidence into account, and Jeffrey Kallberg has employed rastrology as a primary means of assigning dates to Chopin's sketches and autographs, to cite only two examples.[48]

---

schrift für Friedrich Smend zum 70. Geburtstag (Berlin: Merseburger, 1963), 80–92; see Walter Emery's discussion of this article in his review of the Smend Festschrift, *Music and Letters* 45 (1964): 168–70. Nor has Hans Otto Hieckel's unpublished *Katalog der Rastrierungen in den Originalhandschriften J. S. Bachs* (1963; cited after Marshall, *Compositional Process*), commissioned by the Bach-Institut in Göttingen, seemingly had much acceptance. On the establishment of codicological groupings as an initial goal of manuscript studies see the second section of the present chapter and also Eugene K. Wolf, *The Symphonies of Johann Stamitz: A Study in the Formation of the Classic Style* (Utrecht: Bohn, Scheltema & Holkema, 1981), 23–24; cf. also the section "Procedures for the Analysis of Staving," below.

[47] See, e.g., Joseph Kerman, ed., *Ludwig van Beethoven: Autograph Miscellany from circa 1786 to 1799 . . . (the "Kafka Sketchbook")* (facs. ed., London: Trustees of the British Museum, 1970), vol. 1, pp. xxvi–xxviii; Alan Tyson, "A Reconstruction of the Pastoral Symphony Sketchbook (British Museum Add. MS. 31766)," in *Beethoven Studies*, ed. Tyson (New York: W. W. Norton, 1973), 82–83, and *Mozart: Studies of the Autograph Scores*, 9-11 et passim; Richard A. Kramer, *The Sketches for Beethoven's Violin Sonatas, Opus 30: History, Transcription, Analysis* (Ph.D. diss., Princeton University, 1973), 29–57, 82–114 (esp. pp. 36–38, 82–87, 102–4); Johnson et al., *Beethoven Sketchbooks*, 55–58; Johnson, "Fischhof Miscellany," 1:70–293 (esp. 70–82, 227–30), the most comprehensive treatment to date; Donald J. Burrows, "Paper Studies and Handel's Autographs," *Göttinger Händel-Beiträge* 1 (1984): 103–13; Burrows and Ronish, *Handel's Musical Autographs*, pp. xxix–xxxi, 325–28.

[48] See, e.g., Günter Thomas, ed., *Il mondo della luna*, ser. XXV, vol. 7 of *Joseph Haydn Werke* (Munich: G. Henle, 1979–82), 3:605–6, 616; Jeffrey Kallberg, *The Chopin Sources: Variants and Versions in Later Manuscripts and Printed Editions* (Ph.D. diss., University of Chicago, 1982), 375–89.

Chapter 2

Staff-liners and staff-lining in the eighteenth century. The implement used to draw staves in the eighteenth century is known as a *rastrum* (plural *rastra*),[49] from the Latin for rake. Until recently, only a few scholars and museum curators had any idea what these implements were like or how they were constructed; one reads of quills bound together, machines (mostly apocryphal) for lining paper, and the like, without any firm data cited at all. Then, in an extended piece of research published in 1990, Jean K. Wolf was able to construct a substantially complete history of staff- and register-lining in the eighteenth and early nineteenth centuries, from the fabrication of simple rastra for lining one staff at a time to the sophisticated machines of the industrial era.[50] The most essential information for present purposes is as follows, but the reader may wish to consult the 1990 study for further information and for its many additional reproductions.

The essential component of a rastrum was the metal tip or nib, which was easily constructed by scoring and folding a sheet of brass accordion-fashion to produce five narrow V-shaped channels:

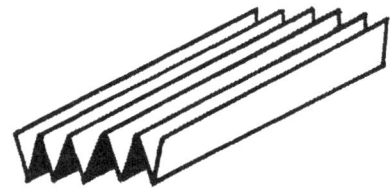

The top of one end was then cut or filed back at a 45-degree angle to make a point:

---

[49] German *Rastral* or *Raster*; French *patte*, meaning paw.

[50] Wolf and Wolf, "Rastrology," 238–67, 288–91, with many additional illustrations. Two new rastra that have come to light since publication of that article are found in the Pinto collection of the Birmingham (England) Museum and Art Gallery. The first is a unique implement for lining plainchant manuscripts. It consists of a turned walnut handle into which are inserted four single folded-brass nibs of the type which, as we shall see in a moment, were generally used in lining registers rather than music paper. The second is a solid brass rastrum like nos. 14–16 in Wolf and Wolf, "Rastrology," Appendix, p. 289; this type, dating from the nineteenth century, is described and illustrated ibid., 249–52. For a discussion and illustrations of these rastra see Edward H. Pinto, *Treen and Other Wooden Bygones: An Encyclopædia and Social History* (London: G. Bell & Sons, 1969), p. 256 and plate 266 (items L and M).

Finally, the point was gently filed to produce slits at the bottom of each channel rather like those of a modern pen-point:

The metal tip was then glued into a recess cut into the end of a wooden handle. As illustrated in figure 2:2, which shows a simple rastrum produced in Winston-Salem, North Carolina, in the early nineteenth century, a brass sheathing was often wrapped around the joint (cf. also the double rastrum pictured in fig. 2:3). As already noted, simple or one-stave rastra like the one in figure 2:2 were undoubtedly owned by many musicians of the eighteenth century,[51] and paper lined with multiple passes of such a rastrum is common throughout Europe during the period. For example, all or nearly all of the Bach manuscripts were lined with one-stave rastra—often with highly irregular results.[52]

The only compound (multi-nib) rastrum known to have come down to us is the implement shown in figure 2:3, made by the Nürnberg coppersmith Georg Lorenz Braun (1647–1719).[53] This handsome double rastrum is comparable in every way to the simple rastrum of figure 2:2 except for the fact that the handle is turned

---

[51] References in the present study to "one-stave" (or "multi-stave") rastra are, of course, elliptical, the meaning being "a rastrum designed to draw one stave (or several) at a time." Other possibilities would be "single-nib," "single-head," etc.

[52] For an informative discussion of Bach's staving see Marshall, *Compositional Process*, 43–47.

[53] We are grateful to Dr. John Henry van der Meer of the Germanisches Nationalmuseum in Nürnberg for providing detailed information about, and photographs of, this important rastrum. Braun's mark, a wild man by a tree, is stamped on the sheathing; see Wolf and Wolf, "Rastrology," 256, fig. 16.

Chapter 2

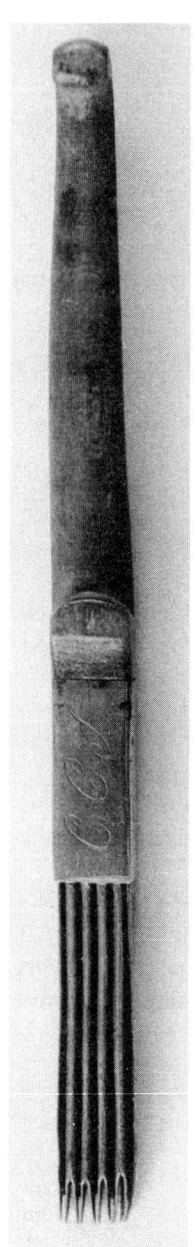 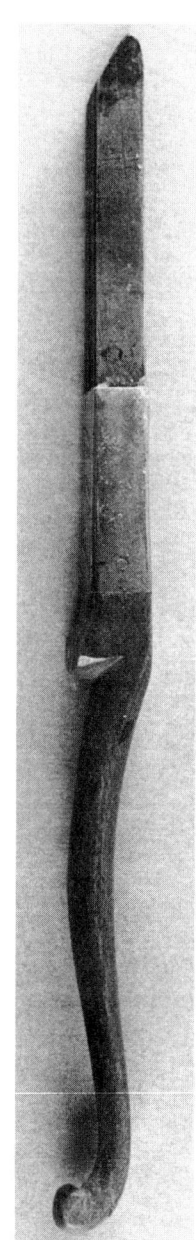

Figure 2:2. Simple (one-stave) rastrum with scrolled handle owned by Christina Caritas Schneider Benzien of Winston-Salem, N.C. (1799–1863), as indicated by the initials "C. C. S." on the sheathing. The rastrum therefore probably antedates 1824, the year of Schneider's marriage. Winston-Salem, N.C., Moravian Music Foundation, Acq. No. 2608.

Figure 2:3. Double (two-stave) rastrum made by Georg Lorenz Braun (1647–1719), a coppersmith and maker of weights in Nürnberg. Here the handle is turned (the usual procedure) rather than scrolled, as in figure 2:2. Nürnberg, Germanisches Nationalmuseum, Rück Sammlung, MIR 1486.

(the more usual type) rather than scrolled and branches into a U shape to hold the two heads.

While no larger rastra capable of lining five, ten, and twelve staves at once are known to exist, we know how they were constructed thanks to a valuable treatise by A. B. Méguin, *Art de la réglure des registres et des papiers de musique*, published in Paris by Augot in 1828.[54] This work includes a large fold-out plate, figures 5–7 of which illustrate the construction of a twelve-nib rastrum for lining a register (see fig. 2:4). The nibs in this case are simple V-shaped pieces of folded brass, cut and filed as described above. These are fitted into notches in one of the pieces of wood making up the handle or base, after which the second piece is glued on top. The smaller protrusion to the left in Méguin's figures 9–10 is an iron guide (shown separately in his fig. 12) that moves along a rail, ensuring evenness. A guide of this sort was not normally used at Mannheim in lining music papers, to judge by the mild waviness of the results in many cases.[55] Such a guide may, however, have been a feature of Viennese rastra, for the papers there are notable for the regularity of their staving.[56]

Although Méguin does not specifically illustrate a compound rastrum for lining music paper, his treatise explains that their construction was the same as for register liners, the only difference being the substitution of five-pointed nibs for the simple nibs used in the latter.[57] The principal problem he notes with the lining of music paper was the difficulty in avoiding blots when two lines run together owing to the close proximity of the individual points. (Such blotting is in fact common in music manuscripts of the period.) To deal with this problem, he states that, when lining music paper, *régleurs* used long, stiff brushes mounted on the side of the ink-well to blot the nibs after inking. Then the paper was lined by drawing the rastrum toward the body, holding it with both hands.

---

[54] See Wolf and Wolf, "Rastrology," 259–64, for a somewhat fuller discussion of Méguin's methods of lining registers (his principal concern) and music papers.

[55] See, e.g., the ten-stave paper reproduced in figs. 2:7–8, below.

[56] While very little research has been done on Viennese staff-lining, there is no evidence I know of for the frequent statement that "machines" for lining music paper were in use there in the eighteenth century (as in Tyson, *Mozart: Studies of the Autograph Scores*, 10, and Johnson et al., *Beethoven Sketchbooks*, 55–56); as a matter of fact, Méguin's treatise specifically states that this was not the case, even as late as 1828 (*Art de la réglure*, 46; see Wolf and Wolf, "Rastrology," 260). The earliest machines for lining paper were, as would be expected given the history of the Industrial Revolution, English and French (Wolf and Wolf, "Rastrology," 257–59, 265–66); as is well known, during the period in question Austria and Germany lagged behind those countries in technological development of this sort. I might note in this connection that a compound rastrum, manipulated by hand, is no more a "machine" in modern English usage than is a pen or hammer (though any of these implements could form *part* of a machine). In my understanding of the word, for a device to be a machine (or "mechanical") requires a decoupling between the operator or agent (the *régleur*, writer, or carpenter) and whatever component—rastrum, pen, hammer—forms the final stage of the device.

[57] Méguin, *Art de la réglure*, 20–27.

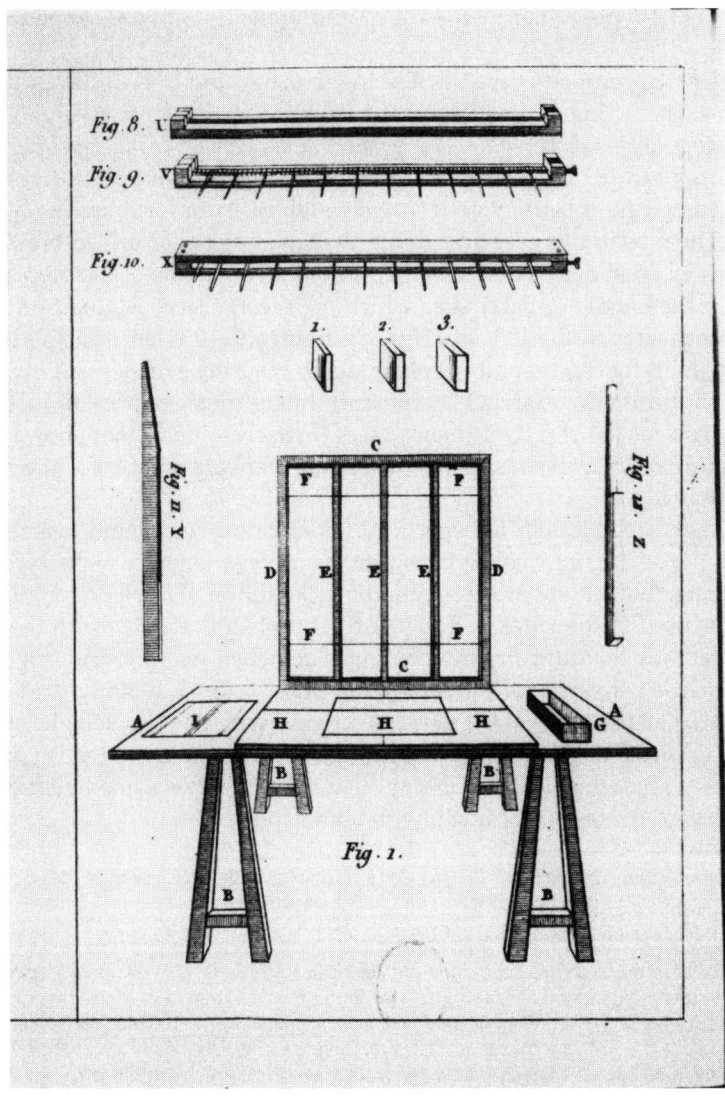

Figure 2:4. Right half of fold-out plate from A. B. Méguin, *Art de la réglure des registres et des papiers de musique* (Paris: Audot, 1828), opposite title page. Méguin's figure 1 shows the worktable with the frame raised at the back. His figures 8–10 show his proprietary adjustable type of rastrum (*outil mobile*) together with three spacers of different size for insertion between the nibs. His figure 11 (to the left) is a single folded-brass nib of the type used to line registers. His figure 12 shows the small metal guide that is inserted at one end of the rastrum (see his figs. 9–10, to the far left of each rastrum); the guide moves along a rail in order to assure straightness of the lines.

Analytical specifications for staving. When I first began to apply rastrology to a study of the presumed Mannheim corpus of manuscripts in the 1970s, I dutifully proceeded in the traditional way, classifying each paper by the type of rastrum that was evidently used to line it (simple or one-stave, five-stave, ten-stave, etc.) and its total span. As we shall see in subsequent chapters, this procedure revealed that the great majority of the manuscripts that we had already demonstrated on other grounds to be part of the Mannheim court collection were ruled using one pass of a ten- or twelve-stave rastrum (sometimes even larger in earlier manuscripts). By contrast, those manuscripts known to be from Munich were mostly lined with smaller one-, two-, and occasionally three-stave rastra.

This information proved especially valuable for the large, extremely complex series of Cannabich symphonies now in Munich, for the first time allowing a reasonably firm determination of the point in the series at which the move to Munich in 1778 took place (see chap. 5). An example from what I consider the first of the Cannabich manuscripts to have been copied in Munich, his Symphony no. 56, appears in figure 2:5: that it was ruled with a one-stave rastrum appears from the fact that the staves are not quite parallel, that they begin and end inconsistently from the vertical standpoint, and that the pattern of irregularities within each staff is precisely the same (e.g., the second and fourth spaces of each staff, always reading downward, are larger than the first and third, and the middle line is slightly heavier).

However, in attempting to classify and (I hoped) date the many ten- and twelve-stave rastra found in the Mannheim manuscripts at Munich, it quickly became apparent that total span alone was wholly insufficient as a means of distinguishing among rastra. On the one hand, many obviously different rastra had the same total span. On the other, the same rastrum might have a total span that varied by several millimeters even within the same manuscript. In part this is because the top and bottom pens—those on the outside of the row—were the ones most subject to abuse.

It therefore became necessary to develop a much more precise taxonomy for staves drawn with a compound rastrum, the principal elements of which—already mentioned in passing above—are illustrated in figure 2:6. For simplicity I have chosen a "field" of three staves—that is, a set of staves drawn with one stroke or "pass" of a three-stave rastrum. Each of the six numbered categories yields a measurement or set of measurements in millimeters, or in certain cases a more qualitative observation. (How these measurements are made is discussed in the next section of this chapter.) It may be noted at this point that the making of careful measurements is unquestionably preferable to the other method that is some-

Chapter 2

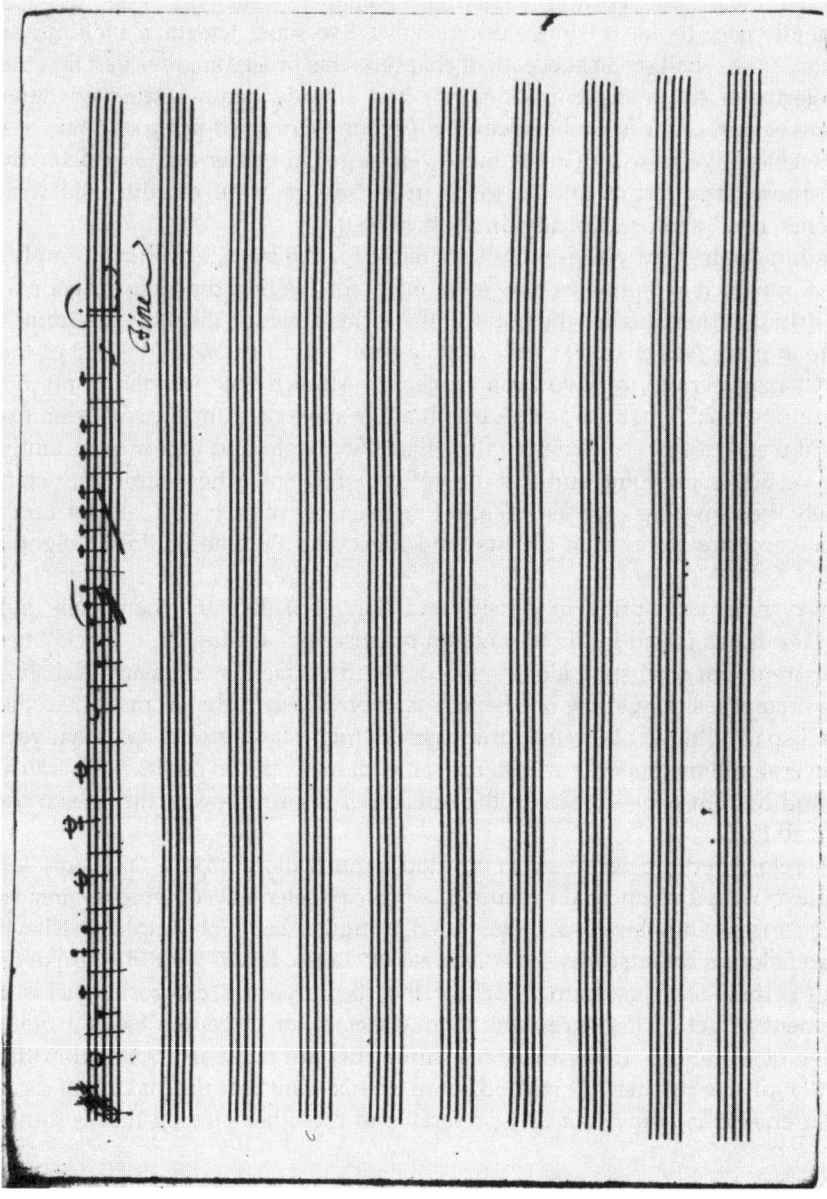

Figure 2.5. Christian Cannabich, Symphony no. 56 (App. A/III/56), flute 1, last page (autograph). Munich, Bayerische Staatsbibliothek, Mus. Ms. 1868.

Codicological Evidence

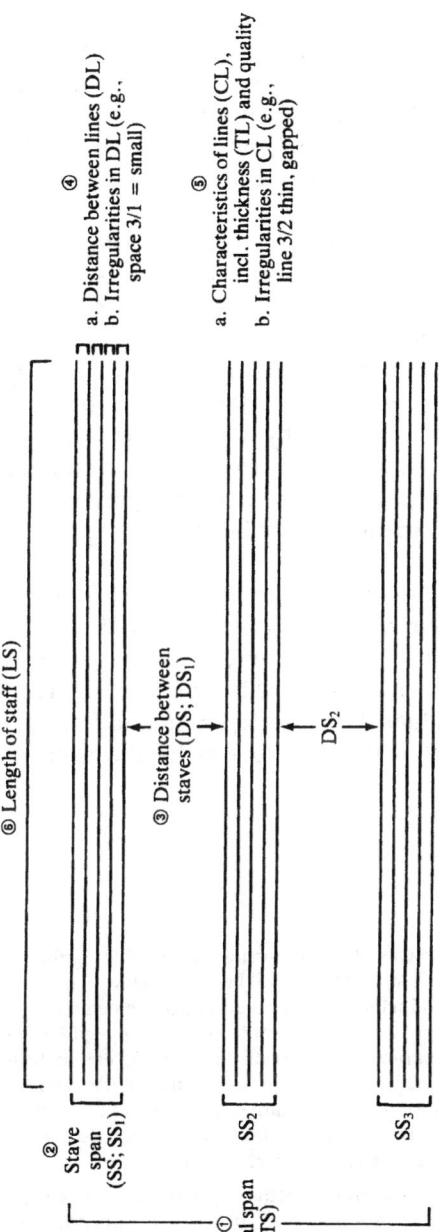

Figure 2:6. Specifications for a set of staves ruled with a compound rastrum.

times used and recommended, namely tracing.[58] Aside from the fact that many libraries now prohibit tracing, numerical results are far easier to compare, classify, order, computerize, and communicate (especially in print, where the problem of reproducing the exact size presents great difficulties). The ease of description by means of measurements is, of course, one of the principal advantages of rastrology over the use of watermarks and handwriting, an advantage that is lost if one relies on tracings. Moreover, if measurements are later needed, they may have to be taken from the tracing, compounding the risk of error.

The first measurement to be taken is the aforementioned one of *total span* (abbreviated TS);[59] under each type of compound rastrum—two-stave, three-stave, five-stave, and so on—total span provides the most convenient initial means of classification. Appendix C, which gives the specifications of all the important compound rastra known to have been used at Mannheim, is organized first by number of staves, then by total span, going from small to large. The individual rastra are designated first by the number of staves, then by their number in the series, separated by a colon: rastra 10:1 and 10:2 are thus the ten-stave rastra with the smallest total spans. Lower-case letters may then be appended to signify variant forms of a single rastrum (e.g., 10:2a, 10:2b; variants are also indicated in Appendix C by a triangle [▶]).

The second item for measurement is the *stave span* (here abbreviated SS),[60] the height of each individual stave. This measurement, though obviously significant for the identification of simple rastra, is less so for compound ones, as it tends to vary less than other parameters. As can be seen under no. 2 in figure 2:6, subscript numbers may be used to specify the individual staves, always counting from the top of the field downward. For example, "$SS_2 = 9.7$" would mean that the height of the second staff of the field was 9.7 mm.

---

[58] As in Feder, *Musikphilologie,* 45. An example of one way of using tracings and publishing the results appears in Thomas, ed., *Haydn: Il mondo della luna,* 3:616. As will be noted below, with a little practice one can produce quite precise and reproducible measurements, measurements that in my experience are much more accurate than tracings. A development to be contemplated for the future is the use of scanners to determine the measurements of a rastrum; it should not be difficult to write a program to find each staff and, given the total span, determine all the relevant measurements from it. Moreover, because it is more often the relative rather than the absolute measurements that are important in comparing rastra, this procedure could be carried out on good Xerographic copies, whether precisely the same size as the original or not.

[59] The system of two-letter abbreviations utilized here is designed both for general efficiency (e.g., in note-taking) and for use as fields in a rastrology database (see fn. 62, below, and Appendix C).

[60] Johnson, *Fischhof Miscellany,* 70–71 et passim, also designates the height of the stave as the "stave span" and uses the abbreviation SS. Both he and Kerman, *Kafka Sketchbook*, vol. 1, p. xxvi, utilize TS and SS measurements in attempting to classify the large rastra used in Beethoven's papers.

Of fundamental importance for compound rastra is the series of measurements of the *distance between the staves* (no. 3 in fig. 2:6, here labeled DS).[61] Subscript numbers may again be used to refer to specific spaces between staves, for example "DS_2" for the distance between staves 2 and 3 (reading downward) in figure 2:6. Owing to the physical makeup of compound rastra, described earlier, these distances vary constantly and substantially within the typical larger rastrum—sometimes by as much as three or four millimeters. Hence, a mere listing of these measurements in order from top to bottom is generally sufficient to identify a given rastrum with confidence. For a ten-stave rastrum, for instance, the total span (TS) plus the nine DS measurements has proven to provide a high level of discrimination among rastra—a kind of numerical fingerprint. These measurements are also quite easy to computerize.[62]

In many cases, especially for smaller rastra producing from one to three staves, it may be helpful to utilize two other descriptive categories. The first of these, no. 4 in figure 2:6, takes account of the spaces within each staff; these spaces may be labeled "DL" (for *distance between lines*) by analogy with no. 3, "DS" (distance between staves). The other category, no. 5, deals with the *characteristics of the lines* themselves (CL), meaning generally their thickness (TL) but also such more subjective aspects as the fact that one line may be discontinuous, a frequent occurrence. The thickness of the lines is itself difficult to measure accurately, and typical comments in this category thus tend to be comparative or relative—for example, "line 8_2 [i.e., staff 8, line 2] = thin, ca. .2 mm. vs. .4 of remainder."

In actual practice, within both categories 4 and 5 a mere examination of each staff for obvious *irregularities* (IR) will often be sufficient to clinch the identification of a larger rastrum. Such irregularities in category 4 would include noticeably larger or smaller spaces, in category 5 noticeably thick or thin lines—irregularities of a type already observed in figure 2:5, above. These irregularities are easy to deal with (and, incidentally, are generally visible on microfilms), whereas truly comprehensive treatment of the spaces and lines within the staves would involve large numbers of painstaking measurements and observations—in the case of a ten-stave rastrum, forty for the spaces, fifty for the lines. Clearly, the returns here are precipitously diminishing, at least for larger rastra. As a matter of fact, these more de-

---

[61] Given the importance (and obviousness) of this set of measurements for compound rastra, it is remarkable to me that the only scholar I know of even to have alluded to it is Donald Burrows, who seems to acknowledge that TS measurements are insufficient for classifying compound rastra ("Paper Studies and Handel's Autographs," 110). However, his later publication, Burrows and Ronish, *Handel*, does not include DS measurements.

[62] It may be of interest that specifications of the rastra catalogued in Appendix C were initially recorded on preprinted index cards (this was well before the advent of portable computers or even personal computers), then entered into dBase 5. The resulting database was eventually transferred to Microsoft Access (in this form it is available for use at the Forschungsstelle *Mannheimer Hofkapelle* in Heidelberg) and subsequently to Microsoft Word for purposes of editing.

tailed measurements can, if required, be made at a later date rather than on the spot if one has either a good Xerox copy of several pages of the manuscript—one that has been carefully compared with the original—or a reliable microfilm and access to a good enlarger or to the right type of microfilm reader.[63]

While on the subject of irregularities within the individual staff, we might consider briefly a class of irregularity that I have *not* found especially helpful in identifying rastra in the present study, namely the point at which the various lines of each staff begin and end in relation to one another.[64] At least in the repertory under consideration here, such irregularities—for instance, a middle line that protrudes into the left margin at the beginning of a staff—have proven too inconsistent to serve as useful distinguishing traits. In figure 2:5 above, for example, lines 2–3 of staff 1 begin to the right of lines 4–5; in staff 2, drawn with the same rastrum, lines 2–3 begin to the left, protruding slightly into the margin. The end of each staff in figure 2:5 might appear at first glance to support the theory of consistent irregularity, as the bottom line stops before the others in the first eight staves, in

---

[63] Xerographic copiers may distort the size of an original to some degree; a relative analysis of the staving based on such a copy is, however, still possible and often very useful, especially when a comparison between original and copy has been feasible. A well-made microfilm and a high-quality enlarger (or certain microfilm readers with adjustable focal length) can produce fairly reliable absolute measurements under carefully controlled conditions. Assuming that such gross measurements as the total span and dimensions of the paper have already been made from the original, one simply adjusts the size of the image by raising or lowering the head of the enlarger (or adjusting the focal length of the reader) until the projected sizes match those of the original. Other measurements can then be taken that should also approximate those of the original. A positive microfilm and (for most enlargers) a high-quality wide-angle lens (ca. 30 mm.) are necessary for this procedure to be successful, and even then it should obviously be regarded as strictly supplementary to direct examination of the manuscript.

[64] Irregularities at the beginning and end of the staff are the principal method of classification proposed in Owen Jander, "Staff-Liner Identification, a Technique for the Age of Microfilm," *JAMS* 20 (1967): 112–16. Tyson, *Mozart: Studies of the Autograph Scores*, cites several useful irregularities of this type in Mozart's autographs (see pp. 99, 119, 165, 243–44), and Dexter Edge has demonstrated the utility of such evidence in dealing with a Mozart fragment in his paper "The Fragmentary Minuet in E-flat, K. *deest*, in the Palácio Nacional da Ajuda in Lisbon," delivered at a study session of the Mozart Society of America, Toronto, 3 November 2000. Kramer, *Sketches*, identifies two sixteen-stave papers used by Beethoven in the period ca. 1799–1805 that have consistent irregularities at the beginnings of the staves (see pp. 83–87 and also 34–42); according to Kramer, the period mentioned shows "a consistency in this respect [the presence of beginning-of-staff irregularities] which is otherwise rare" (p. 83). Johnson, *Fischhof Miscellany*, considers this type of irregularity in some detail but concludes, "Unfortunately, the profiles are distinctive and consistent in only a few paper-types. In some papers the irregularities seem to be completely random. . . . In other papers the . . . pattern is weakly documented, involving only a few of the staves or not all of the folios of the type. Every case must therefore be evaluated on its own merits, and some must remain inconclusive" (pp. 73–74). Johnson's position corresponds closely with my own; at least in a large-scale project, I would recommend recording only those irregularities at the beginning and end of the staff that are consistent within a manuscript. Such observations might logically be included within categories 5 or 6 of fig. 2:6 (CL, LS) or recorded under a separate heading.

several cases quite noticeably; but then in staves 9–10, again drawn with the same rastrum, all the lines end more-or-less evenly. The irregularity seems to lie, not in the rastrum, but in the method of lining; the anonymous *régleur* (perhaps Cannabich himself) probably lifted the rastrum unevenly at the ends of the first eight staves but became more careful as he neared the bottom of the page.

Indeed, our new-found knowledge of how eighteenth-century rastra were constructed shows that consistent irregularities at the beginnings and ends of staves are somewhat unlikely from the physical standpoint. If these rastra had had *flexible* points, like quills or modern nibs, then one or the other prong might well have a different tensile strength than the others, with the result that it might strike and leave the page at a different time and create a consistent irregularity. But as we have seen, the folded-brass head characteristic of eighteenth-century rastra was rigid, allowing no such "give" on the part of the individual points; all have to be aligned evenly with the others for the pen to write at all, a condition achieved by filing all five points at once. Thus the frequent irregularities present at the beginnings and ends of staves seem more often to result from careless manipulation of the pen, as above, or from such factors as uneven ink flow or an uneven paper surface. Incidentally, experimentation with actual rastra tends to confirm these observations.

A final parameter, no. 6 in figure 2:6, is the horizontal *length of the staff* (LS). For most manuscripts this measurement is of only theoretical significance, as it is determined by the size of the paper. However, for printed paper (relatively rare in the eighteenth century) and paper lined by a professional *régleur* it might have some significance.[65] Again, one must use common sense in deciding which measurements are likely to provide the highest return for the time and effort expended recording them. At the bottom of figure 2:6 I have summarized my views regarding the most important features to consider initially when dealing with a repertory like that of the Mannheim complex of manuscripts.

Procedures for the analysis of staving. We may now consider the procedures one might follow in carrying out an actual examination of the staving of a manuscript or group of manuscripts. Any such examination involves two stages: first, determination of the type(s) of staving present, and second, analysis and description of each type, primarily by means of measurements. The goal of the first of these stages is to discover and record the type or types of rastrum used in the manuscript—that is, how the paper was lined. This can usually be accomplished by visual inspection; in sorting out the various groupings within a more complex manu-

---

[65] As Méguin shows in his 1828 treatise (see Wolf and Wolf, "Rastrology," 260–64), professional *régleurs* used forms to hold down the paper and guide the rastrum, and therefore the LS might be more consistent than with free-hand lining like that normally used at Mannheim and other courts.

script, one should keep in mind that groups of pages or parts making use of one rastrum will tend to correspond with groupings based on watermarks, paper types, handwriting, and the like. The principal indicators of the type of rastrum present, all of which we have already used informally in considering figure 2:5 above, are the following:

1. Obviously parallel or non-parallel staves. A page in which all the staves are clearly non-parallel—a frequent occurrence in provincial manuscripts—has been prepared with a simple rastrum; one in which pairs of staves are parallel to each other but not to other pairs, with a double rastrum; and so on.[66]
2. Irregularities involving the beginning and end of the staves. A page in which each staff begins or ends at a different point again indicates use of a simple rastrum; if pairs of staves begin or end in vertical alignment, but the various pairs are not aligned, a double rastrum has been used; and so on. Often mistakes on the part of the liner provide the clearest indication of the staving type: an identical slip at the end of all ten staves on a page, occurring as the liner was lifting the rastrum from the page, obviously identifies it as a ten-stave type.
3. Recurring irregularities within the staves. Patterned recurrences of such inconsistencies as especially large spaces or thick lines, as in figure 2:5, often identify the type of rastrum at a glance. Thus, a noticeably larger space 3 in staves 2 and 7 (only) of a page with ten staves is a clue that the page was lined with two passes of a five-stave rastrum.

One technique that is often helpful is to place one page directly over the other so that the stave beginnings or endings coincide. If both pages have been lined with one pass of the same large rastrum (ten or more staves), the staves will almost leap into place visually. By contrast, discrepancies will generally be readily apparent if two or more passes of a smaller rastrum have occurred or if two different rastra are involved. Two other points to remember are that a page may have been used upside down by the copyist[67] and that two different rastra may have been used to line one page. The most familiar example of the latter practice is the ad hoc addition of staves by a composer or copyist in the bottom margin of pre-lined paper. Less obvious are papers that consistently employ a one-stave rastrum (or one staff of a compound rastrum) to complete a page otherwise lined with a larger one; a fairly common example of this procedure, especially in Italy, is ten-stave paper lined with three passes of a triple rastrum plus one of a single one.

---

[66] Differences in the distances between the staves (DS) other than those resulting from overtly non-parallel staving are not readily distinguishable by the naked eye, doubtless the reason why even major discrepancies in DS were tolerated by *régleurs* and musicians of the eighteenth century.

[67] The possibility that a page has been reversed provides one of the best reasons to computerize the results in a rastrology project; all comparisons among rastra can then easily be carried out in both directions. Of course, for many papers there is no "right side up," as the top and bottom margins are approximately equal. Other (most?) papers, however, are lined with a larger top margin—which is itself often ignored by copyists, who even switch back and forth within the same manuscript.

If the above techniques fail to provide a convincing answer regarding the type of staving in a manuscript—and many manuscripts are ruled so carefully that such will be the case—then measurement of the vertical distances between the staves (DS) will resolve the issue. Measurement of the DS at various points from left to right may, for example, show that two staves that look parallel to the naked eye are not, and thus represent the boundary between two fields. Still more precise is the methodical recording of the DS measurements proceeding vertically down the page. Thus the series DS = 10, 9.5, 10, 9.2, 10, 9.4, etc. (mm.) would indicate the presence of a two-stave rastrum. For larger rastra it is necessary to extend this principle from one page to several: an identical sequence of nine DS measurements on several pages would confirm that one ten-stave rastrum has been utilized.

Once one is certain how the paper has been lined, one can proceed to make and record the measurements discussed above for each rastrum present. For this task I have found a high-quality clear metric ruler sufficient for most purposes,[68] supplemented in difficult or especially critical cases by a loupe or comparator fitted with a reticle containing a metric scale.[69] For the sake of consistency, all vertical measurements should be made at the *center of the staff* and—of critical importance—*from the center of the line*. The latter rule is necessary owing to the constantly varying thicknesses of lines drawn with early rastra; measurement from edge to edge would produce highly variable results. One should try to determine distances within about .2 mm.; surprisingly, with a little experience (and considerable care) one can do so with notable accuracy using only a ruler and the naked eye, as I have found by checking my results with a loupe and when taking the measurements of a manuscript for the second (and third, and fourth) time over a period of years. A loupe allows measurements to about .05 mm., but such precision is rarely necessary merely to establish that one is dealing with the same rastrum. The resulting measurements can be recorded on preprinted index cards or, better, entered directly into one's portable computer.

The use of rastrology: an example. To illustrate the use—and utility—of rastrological information of the sort just described, let us consider a typical example taken from the Mannheim complex of manuscripts. Table 2:1 lists ten manuscripts or portions of manuscripts ruled with the same ten-stave rastrum, identified in Ap-

---

[68] Dexter Edge has suggested to me the use of a good-quality caliper rather than a ruler to take the measurements (personal communication). I have not yet tried this idea, but it seems likely that it would be slower and also pose a greater risk of damage to the manuscript, with no real advantage.

[69] For most papers a 6x loupe provides the proper magnification. A loupe that is ideal for the measurement of most staves is the 6x Edscorp Pocket Comparator No. 30,325 with a Metric Scale Reticle No. 30,323, available from Edmund Scientific Co., Barrington, N.J. 08007. I am grateful to my colleague Lawrence F. Bernstein for his assistance in locating this equipment and for his many valuable suggestions in the preparation of this chapter.

Table 2:1. Manuscripts Ruled with Rastrum 10:28.

No.	Manuscript, Parts	Paper	Copyists	TS, Rastrum	DS
1	App. A/VI/171 (Holzbauer, Cembalo Concerto, D-Rtt; see fig. 2:8)	Heusler 7	Rtt/Mannheim 5	221 (10:28b)	12.25, 13.85, 13.3 13.6, 13.2, 12.95 14-14.05, 13.5-.55, 14.5-.6
2	App. A/III/2 (Cannabich, Symphony no. 2, D-Mbs), vn. 1 (see fig. 2:7), b.; see also no. 4, below.	Swiss (no watermark)	Mannheim 3 (early hand), Cannabich (early hand)	220.5-221 (10:28a)	12.6, 13.8, 13.4 13.5, 13.2, 12.9 14.1-.2, 13.7, 14.75-.9
3	App. A/VI/187 (Toeschi, Symphony G-13, D-Rtt), vns., b.	Swiss (no watermark)	Mannheim 3 (early hand)	221.5-.8 (10:28a)	*Vns.*: 12.7-.8, 13.7, 13.4 13.5-.7, 13.2-.3, 12.7-.85 14.1-.3, 13.2-.6, 14.5-.85 *Bass*: same, but space 1 = 13.2, space 2 = 13.5 (staff 2 lowered)
4	Remaining parts to no. 2, above	Swiss (no watermark)	Mannheim 1	221 (10:28a)	12.75, 13.8, 13.5 13.5, 13.2, 12.85 14.5-.6, 13.2, 14.8-.9
5	App. A/III/11 (Cannabich, Symphony no. 11, D-Mbs)	Swiss (no watermark)	Mannheim 3 (early hand)	221.25-222.5 (10:28c)	13.15, 13.45-.5, 13.4 13.6, 13.3, 12.7-.75 14.3-.5, 13.5, 14.75-.8
6	App. A/VI/152 (Toeschi, Symphony, D-MÜu), strs., bns.	Swiss (no watermark)	Rheda/Mannheim 1	221.2-.5 (10:28c)	13, 13.5, 13.5 (13.2-.3 title page) 13.8, 13.2, 13 14.5-.8, 13.5, 14.8
7	App. A/III/M4 (Cannabich, *Concerto alla Pastorale*, D-Mbs)	Swiss (no watermark)	Mannheim 1	221-221.8 (10:28c)	13-13.05, 13.55-.6, 13.45-.5 13.6, 13.4-.45, 12.75-.85 14.5-.55, 13.35-.4, 14.85
8	App. A/VI/170 (Holzbauer, Flute Concerto, D-Rtt), va.	Heusler 5	Mannheim 1	221.5 (10:28c)	12.9, 13.6, 13.5 13.6, 13.35, 12.75 14.3, 13.4, 14.8-.85
9	App. A/III/12 (Cannabich, Symphony no. 12, D-Mbs), vns.	Heusler 5	Mannheim 1	221.8-222 (10:28c)	13-13.1, 13.5-.55, 13.4-.5 13.6, 13.45-.5, 12.8 14.3-.4, 13.35-.4, 14.8
10	App. A/III/16 (Cannabich, Symphony no. 16, D-Mbs), vn. 1	Heusler 5	Mannheim 1	221.1-222 (10:28c)	13, 13.5-.6, 13.5 13.5-.6, 13.4, 12.7 14.4, 13.35, 14.6-.8

pendix C/VI ("Ten-Stave Rastra") as rastrum 10:28 (q.v.). A word is in order first about the relationship of table 2:1 and the listing in Appendix C. Table 2:1 is merely a more detailed presentation, manuscript by manuscript, of the information furnished in more summary fashion under rastrum 10:28 in Appendix C, together with information from Appendix A concerning the papers and copyists that appear in association with that rastrum (for more precise information on these papers and copyists see Appendices B and D). By contrast, the intent of Appendix C is merely to provide the range of measurements necessary to identify and classify a given rastrum and also to indicate which manuscripts make use of that rastrum. With the latter information in hand, one can then consult Appendix A to determine the precise parts involved, the paper used, and so on (i.e., the type of additional information supplied in table 2:1). More specifically, a glance at Appendix C shows that the ten individual versions of rastrum 10:28 presented in table 2:1 have been reduced to three groups in Appendix C (10:28a–c), in both cases reflecting changes over time in the profile of the rastrum; which form of the rastrum is involved, 10:28a, b, or c, is indicated in parentheses in the "TS, Rastrum" column of table 2:1. However, in table 2:1 the ten different forms are given in what I consider their approximate chronological order, whereas in Appendix C the three groups are ordered entirely by the (increasing) size of their TS, in order to permit easier searching.

Let us return now to table 2:1. Most of the sources given there are easy to identify as Mannheim manuscripts, for they are early members of the Cannabich series in Munich or (in two cases) manuscripts at Regensburg copied by known Mannheim copyists on typical Mannheim papers. The copyists of nos. 1 and 6, however, do not appear in any other manuscripts from Mannheim, and thus we could previously assign these sources only tentatively to Mannheim based on their paper, copying style, and the like. Here rastrology came to the rescue, for as shown in columns 4–5 of table 2:1, the staving of the questionable manuscripts, nos. 1 and 6, closely resembles that of the eight other numbers, which are definitely from Mannheim.

The total span of these manuscripts, given under TS (col. 4), was useful only for preliminary sorting, as it varied by two millimeters; indeed, there are some half-dozen other ten-stave rastra from Mannheim that fall within this range. The distances between the staves, however, immediately differentiated this rastrum from those with a similar total span. These measurements are given under DS in table 2:1 (col. 5). In nos. 1 and 2, for example, the two sequences of DS measurements correspond closely, most falling well within the margin of error for such tiny measurements of about .2–.3 mm. The first space of no. 1, 12.25 mm., is somewhat anomalous, for it is slightly smaller than the first spaces of each of the remaining manuscripts, which range from 12.6 to 13.15 mm. The last space is also slightly smaller, 14.5–.6 as opposed to the more usual 14.6–.9. Such minor variations, especially when isolated, are not significant enough to affect the identification of a rastrum; they were presumably caused by mishandling (perhaps while cleaning the pens) or by small adjustments of the pens within the implement. As a matter of fact, experience shows that fluctuations of this sort tend to occur most often in the first and last of the DS measurements, as here, no doubt because, as already noted, the outer heads of a multi-stave rastrum were the ones most subject to abuse.

A nice example of change within a given rastrum occurs in the next group of parts, no. 3 in table 2:1. Here the DS measurements of the violin and bass parts are the same except for the first two spaces. In the bass part a slight lowering of the second head has produced a somewhat larger space 1, 13.2 mm., and a correspondingly smaller space 2 than the more normal sizes of these spaces in the violin parts. Similar comparisons can be carried out for the remaining manuscripts of table 2:1, in each case showing the close relationship of the staving in contiguous numbers within the list. In sum, a full series of DS measurements is sufficient in this case to demonstrate the relationship of the questionable rastrum no. 1 with nos. 2–4 and of no. 6 with nos. 5 and 7–10, each of the latter parts or sets of parts definitely stemming from Mannheim. One can also use this information for purposes of chronology: because the Cannabich symphonies in question all date from the late 1750s and early 1760s, so likely do the Holzbauer and Toeschi manuscripts.[70]

Examination of the irregularities within each staff provides additional confirmation of the groupings proposed above, again showing the Mannheim provenance and probable date of the questionable manuscripts. As an illustration, figure 2:7 reproduces a page from the violin 1 part of no. 2 in table 2:1, Cannabich's Symphony no. 2. That this page was lined with one pass of a ten-stave rastrum may be apparent from the slight simultaneous wavering of all ten staves in figure 2:7. (As already mentioned, while professional *régleurs* seem often to have followed Méguin in utilizing a guide or straight-edge to prevent wavering, most court *régleurs* obviously used even the largest rastra free-hand.) Here the most marked abnormalities are the larger first space in staff 4 (from the top) and the rather irregular staff 8, with its thicker line 2 and its smaller space 3, the latter surrounded by two larger spaces. As a glance at figure 2:8 will show, these same characteristics recur in the staving of the Holzbauer Cembalo Concerto, no. 1 in table 2:1. In more equivocal cases, or if greater refinement were required, one could make more precise measurements of each of the spaces within the staves (DL measurements) and also describe the lines in more quantitative terms (CL measurements and observations). For present purposes, however, the TS and DS measurements, combined with a cursory visual assessment of the most obvious irregulari-

---

[70] No. 1, the Holzbauer Cembalo Concerto, has what may be the notation "60:" on the title page (see fig. 2:8, below), which if intended as a date would fit perfectly with the chronology implied by the paper, hands, and staving of this manuscript.

Codicological Evidence

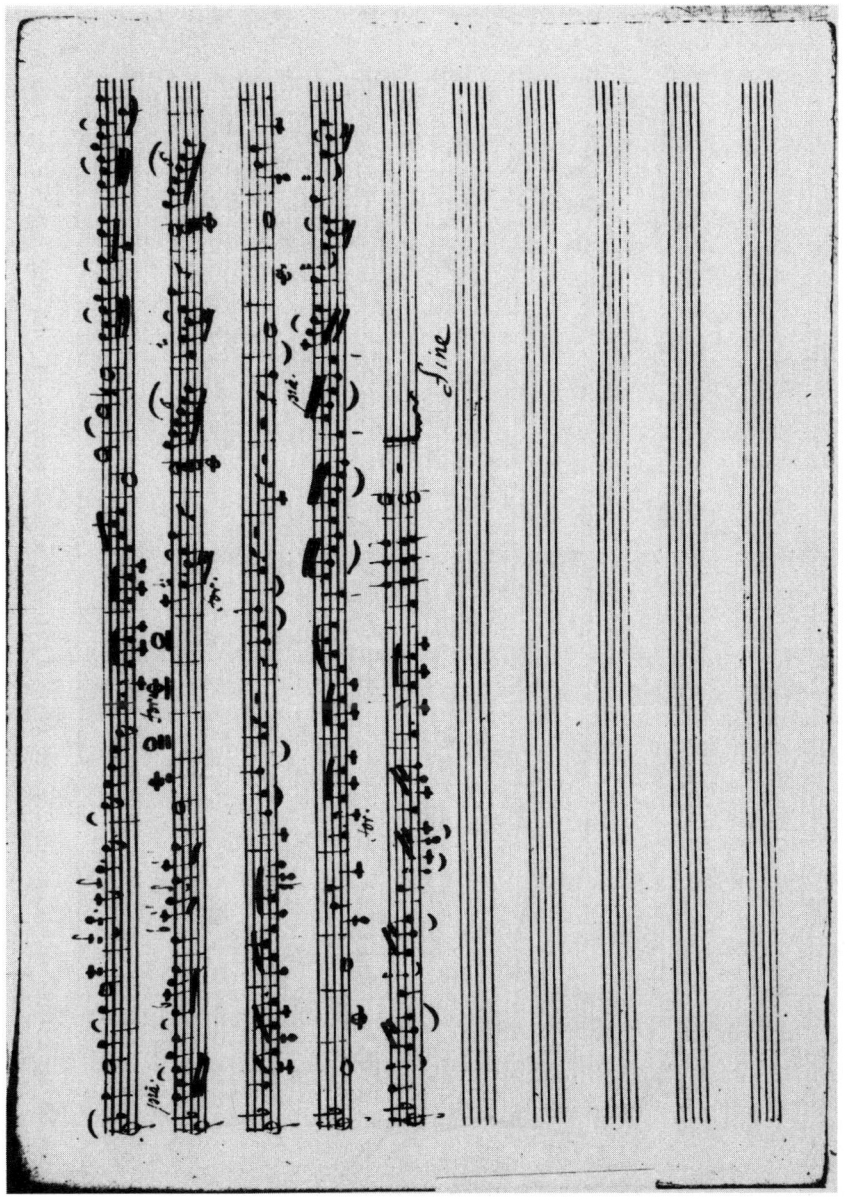

Figure 2.7. Christian Cannabich, Symphony no. 2 (App. A/III/2), violin 1, last page. The copyist is Mannheim 3 at a very early date. Munich, Bayerische Staatsbibliothek, Mus. Ms. 1832.

85

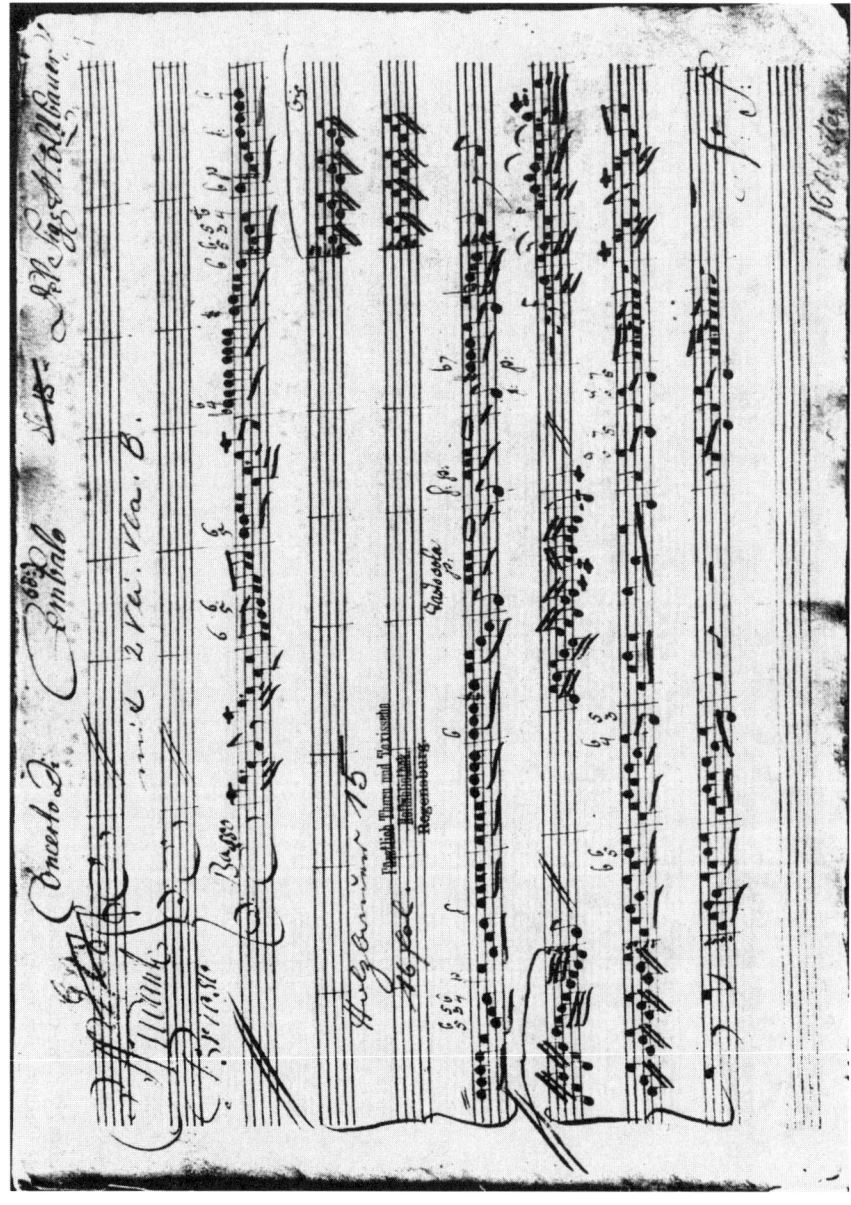

Figure 2:8. Ignaz Holzbauer, Cembalo Concerto (App. A/VI/171), cembalo part, page 1, with title. Regensburg, Fürst Thurn und Taxis Hofbibliothek, Holzbauer 15.

ties, provide more than enough data to show that one rastrum was used to line all these manuscripts.

The lining of paper at Mannheim. There is, of course, one way in which the staving of the paper used in nos. 1 and 6 of table 2:1 might still not have stemmed from Mannheim, even though it were identical with that of every other paper in table 2:1: namely, if all these papers were lined elsewhere than at Mannheim. According to this theory, both Mannheim and the courts of Regensburg and Rheda (in whose collections nos. 1 and 6 appear) might have bought pre-lined paper from the same external source. This would, in fact, have been perfectly normal procedure in a large urban center such as Paris, Vienna, or London, where lined paper was widely available from stationers, *régleurs*, and music shops, as we have seen. But courts like Mannheim obtained their paper directly from the manufacturers; at both Mannheim and Munich the paper was then distributed against receipt from a central depot.[71] At least for the Swiss and German papermakers who were purveyors to the electoral court, there is no evidence whatsoever that they engaged in such specialized services as the lining of music paper. Indeed, I am not aware of any evidence that papermakers of the eighteenth century ever did so.

In the case of Mannheim two documents exist showing that music paper was in fact lined there. The first is an electoral rescript of 1753 stating that the violist "Fränzel" (Ferdinand Rudolph Fränzl [1710–82], father of the famous Mannheim violinist Ignaz Fränzl) was henceforth to be paid the large sum of 100 gulden per year for the lining of music paper at the electoral court.[72] The second is a payment list of 1759 in which Fränzl's annual salary is given as 200 gulden; he is listed as a "Bratcist und Ra[s]trist."[73] As he appears in the court almanacs as a violist until 1778, at which point his salary was still 200 gulden,[74] it is likely that he was responsible for staff-lining at court for the entire period from at least 1753 until departure of the court for Munich in 1778. (He remained behind in Mannheim, as did his son Ignaz.) As still further confirmation, papers from rival manufacturers in

---

[71] See Munich, Bayerisches Hauptstaatsarchiv, HR I, Fasz. 457/Nr. 13, a Pro Memoria of 23 November 1778 to Elector Carl Theodor from the Hofmusikintendant Count Joseph Anton von Seeau, and also Carl Theodor's reply of 27 November 1778 in the same fascicle. Seeau speaks of the court's "Schreib Materialen Magazin," Carl Theodor of the "haupt Schreib Materialen Magazin." Cf. also chap. 1, fnn. 53–54 and related discussion.

[72] Karlsruhe, Badisches Generallandesarchiv, 77/1657, fol. 3, a document detailing how the salary of the recently deceased bassist Georg Anton Hönisch was henceforth to be allocated. Fränzl is to receive the 100 gulden "wegen günstiger rastrirung der Music." This document is cited in Roland Würtz, *Ignaz Fränzl: ein Beitrag zur Musikgeschichte der Stadt Mannheim* (Mainz: B. Schott's Söhne, 1970), 9.

[73] Karlsruhe, Badisches Generallandesarchiv, 77/6193, fol. 51v (from the "Music Staabs Lista" of 28 July 1759, fols. 51–52).

[74] See Munich, Bayerisches Hauptstaatsarchiv, HR I, Fasz. 457/Nr. 13, "Status."

the Mannheim complex are often ruled using the same rastrum—clear proof that they were not lined by the papermaker.

Some manuscripts copied at Mannheim were doubtless ruled, not by a court *Rastrist*, but by their copyists, especially if they were being prepared for other than the official court collection. For instance, most of the manuscripts now found in the large groups of Mannheim manuscripts in the Pretlack collection in Berlin (D-B) and the Hofbibliothek in Regensburg, a majority of which are lined with one- and two-stave rastra, surely fall into this category.[75] In the same way, most of the manuscripts copied for external use by Mannheim 6, including several opera scores and the large group of Ritschel manuscripts in Dresden, are lined with a one-stave rastrum. A different category is the group of magnificent opera scores copied primarily by the copyist Mannheim 5 (see chap. 8), most of which are lined with several different five-stave rastra, using two passes to produce a total of ten staves per page (also a typical Italian and Viennese practice). In this case the copyist probably owned the rastra himself, as the staving produced by each is highly irregular and variable by comparison with that of the "official" court copies and never turns up in manuscripts by any other copyists.

Handwriting and Copyists

At least in the present context, the study of handwriting provides a logical parallel to the study of watermarks and staving, as each of these subjects involves considerations of provenance on the one hand and chronology on the other. In the case of handwriting, "provenance" boils down to the identification of the writer of a manuscript, be it the composer or a copyist. Especially when one is attempting to discriminate among hands that bear a strong family resemblance, such studies will tend to be highly intensive and detailed, seeking small differences that may distinguish one copyist's hand from another's. Chronology is another matter, for here we attempt to associate changes in handwriting style with dated sources, then use the results to establish tentative dates for undated sources.[76] Needless to say, the two areas are closely related, especially in the sense that identification of a given copyist must take account of changes that may have occurred in his copying style over the years. In other words, in each sphere one must always be sensitive to both synchronic and diachronic elements.

---

[75] Tyson, *Mozart: Studies of the Autograph Scores*, 222, points out that, although Mozart preferred what Tyson calls "machine-ruled" (*recte*: professionally lined) paper, ordinarily of ten staves in Salzburg and twelve in Vienna, when such paper was not available he lined his own using a single or occasionally a double rastrum.

[76] See the final section of this chapter, "Chronological Considerations."

No truly scientific method has yet been developed for the study of handwriting, much less musical handwriting. The earliest attempts in this area came from the realm of forensics, namely the use of graphology to determine the authenticity of documents—that is, whether forgery had been committed, not generally a concern of musicologists, or whether a given individual was the source of a disputed document, as in the Lindbergh kidnapping case.[77] Much of the stress in this area naturally fell on such parameters as the chemistry and layering of the ink, determination of erasures, and the like, elements that are of marginal use in musicological projects like the present one. However, many of the basic principles developed in these studies are of fundamental value (and have more often than not been disregarded by musicologists). Nor have the nonmusicological humanistic disciplines progressed very far in devising systematic analytical approaches to calligraphy, though some of their general approaches can be suggestive.[78] But of course their methods deal almost exclusively with text, not with music.

An approach that combines the forensic and the humanistic—at least in the personæ of its two authors—is "graphography," developed by the Swedish musicologist Ingmar Bengtsson and the forensic handwriting expert Ruben Danielson of the Stockholm police force.[79] The purpose was to provide a method of dealing with the large complex of documents and sources relating to the Swedish composer Johan Helmich Roman (1694–1758). Though Bengtsson and Danielson devoted some attention to the classification of musical calligraphy based on elements like the formation of clefs and notes, their most influential contribution has been the concept of the "grapheme" as a tool in analyzing written text. Whereas most studies of handwriting have devoted their principal attention to the formation of individual letters—"writer X makes his capital *A* like this"—Bengtsson and Danielson stressed that the primary unit of analysis should be the partially unconscious

---

[77] For two useful summaries of the forensic approach, with extensive citations, see Peter Jeffery, *The Autograph Manuscripts of Francesco Cavalli* (Ph.D. diss., Princeton University, 1980), 47–61, and Edge, *Mozart's Viennese Copyists*, 225–43. Edge in particular underscores the importance of Albert S. Osborne's classic study *Questioned Documents* (repr. ed., Montclair, N.J.: Patterson Smith Publishing, 1973, of the 2d ed. of 1929; orig. ed., 1910) in establishing a systematic methodology for the analysis of handwriting. I am most grateful to Dr. Edge for sharing with me an early draft of chapter 3 of his dissertation, which provides a much more detailed and comprehensive account of the theory and practice of handwriting analysis than that of the present study. No account need be taken here of the pseudo-science of graphology as ordinarily understood, in which conclusions about personality are drawn from handwriting characteristics. The term as used here refers simply to the scientific study of handwriting.

[78] Jeffery, *Cavalli*, 61–80, provides a review of several such efforts.

[79] Ingmar Bengtsson and Ruben Danielson, *Handstilar och notpikturer i Kungl. Musicaliska Akademiens Roman-Samling* (Uppsala: Almqvist & Wiksells, 1955), chaps. 4–6; see esp. the English summary on pp. 53–59. The typescript of an English translation of these chapters by Per Magnus Wijkman, prepared for Arthur Mendel and Jan LaRue, has been widely circulated. Bengtsson and Danielson proposed the term *graphography* (and its adjective *graphographological* [!]) because of the unsavory connotations of *graphology*.

single stroke or unit, which is not necessarily coterminous with a letter. This they termed a grapheme. On the one hand, graphemes might involve several letters, as when the lower-case letters *c* and *l* are written together in one flourish. On the other, a single letter might contain several graphemes, as in the capital letter *F*. After isolation of the individual graphemes, they may then be classified by their complexity, the speed and fluidity with which they appear to have been written, and so forth. The points of rest that define graphemes are termed minima, the pause with pen lifted from page being the most complete minimum. Graphemes may thus be compared with syllables in speech, minima with the demarcations between syllables.

Bengtsson and Danielson's work is of value heuristically, reminding us that handwriting is a dynamic, partly unconscious effort and that concentration on carefully prepared portions of a text such as title pages may lead to false conclusions.[80] The grapheme idea can be used, for example, both in the traditional sense in analyzing the text of a manuscript ("copyist X always breaks after the *i* of 'Signore,' while copyist Y always bridges over into the *g*") and in detailing precisely how various musical signs such as clefs are written ("X makes his G clefs in one stroke, Y in three"; "X makes his quarter notes by extending the notehead to form the stem, whereas Y always makes the notehead first, then lifts the pen and adds the stem as a second grapheme"). Nonetheless, it must be said that Bengtsson and Danielson's work has not had a strong influence in musicological studies.[81] The primary reason for this is that its only really systematic aspect is a complex system of recording and analyzing graphemes and their grouping; aside from its difficulty of use, this system applies only to extended passages of *written* text, not musical notation. In a broader sense as well, the formation and grouping of graphemes in music is simply one parameter of many that one should examine, not a system as such.

Lacking an accepted method of analyzing and classifying handwriting, most recent studies—including the present one—have relied on the detailed comparison and description of an extended set of scribal characteristics. This method closely parallels what is sometimes called "feature analysis" in the realm of style.[82] It has

---

[80] The idea is comparable to that which forms the basis of one important branch of connoisseurship in painting, which holds that one should examine unconscious, unimportant details such as earlobes rather than more characteristic elements like faces, which are more subject to creative choice and can easily be imitated. For a review of such approaches, especially as they apply to music, see Eugene K. Wolf, "Authenticity and Stylistic Evidence in the Early Symphony: A Conflict in Attribution between Richter and Stamitz," in *A Musical Offering: Essays in Honor of Martin Bernstein*, ed. Edward H. Clinkscale and Claire Brook (New York: Pendragon Press, 1977), 277–78.

[81] See Jeffery, *Cavalli*, 49–51, from a summary of the method on pp. 47–51.

[82] Feature analysis is the principal basis for the related approaches to the use of style in determining authenticity in Marvin Paymer, *The Instrumental Music Attributed to Giovanni Battista Pergolesi: A Study in Authenticity* (Ph.D. diss., City University of New York, 1977), and Scott Fruehwald, *Authenticity Problems in Joseph Haydn's Early Instrumental Works: A Stylistic Investigation* (New York:

been used both for purposes of identification and authentication ("determination of provenance" in the terms used above) and as evidence in attempting to determine chronology. To be successful, such an approach to musical handwriting requires the orderly and objective assessment of a large number of discrete characteristics, ranging from the formation of clefs, notes, rests, and so on to methods of making corrections; the object is to avoid the kind of hasty, impressionistic judgments regarding scribal concordance that have plagued handwriting studies in the past. Recent musicological studies that set high standards in this regard include Wolfgang Horn's of copyists in Dresden and Dexter Edge's of Mozart's Viennese copyists,[83] both of which give extensive attention to methodological concerns.

False identification of a hand often arises because a scholar unfamiliar with a broad range of hands from a given period has mistaken a *family* characteristic for an *idiosyncratic* one.[84] Obviously, if everyone in a group (large or small) makes their T's or treble clefs a certain way, then the presence of T's or treble clefs of that type is worthless as evidence of scribal concordance. A flagrant example of this type of error is Peter Gradenwitz's claim that the score of Johann Stamitz's Mass in D in Berlin (App. A/VI/18) is an autograph.[85] As evidence for this assertion he prints the first two pages of the mass together with the envelope and last page of the only known document in Stamitz's hand, a letter to the Württemberg court in Stuttgart. Referring to the somewhat florid hand of the envelope and of the instrumental designations on page 1 of the score (there is no title page per se), he states,

---

Pendragon Press, 1988). Feature analysis has long been a fundamental component of authentication in painting (see fn. 80, above). As a matter of fact, the use of feature analysis in identifying handwriting is remarkably similar—and at a comparably early stage of development—to that of its use in determining compositional authenticity. In neither case do we yet have a truly systematic, quantitative basis for describing the range of variation between a given feature (whether of a manuscript copy or a composition) and the item or group to which it is being compared. On the theory and literature of authentication see Wolf, "Authenticity and Stylistic Evidence," 275–82; Fruehwald, *Authenticity Problems*, 17–65.

[83] Wolfgang Horn, "Die wichtigsten Schreiber im Umkreis Jan Dismas Zelenkas: Überlegungen zur Methode ihrer Bestimmung und Entwurf einer Gruppierung der Quellen," in *Zelenka-Studien I*, ed. Thomas Kohlhase and Hubert Unverricht, vol. 14 of *Musik des Ostens* (Kassel: Bärenreiter, 1993), 145–47; Edge, *Mozart's Viennese Copyists*, chap. 3, "The Analysis of Manuscript Music and Musical Handwriting."

[84] See Edge, *Mozart's Viennese Copyists*, 229–30 (with further citations). Horn, "Schreiber," 145–47, introduces the notion of the "non-trivial difference" as a means of distinguishing among hands; one can also invert both elements of this formulation and say that "trivial similarity" (similarity of, say, family traits) cannot lead to a reliable judgment as to whether two hands are the same.

[85] Peter Gradenwitz, "The Stamitz Family: Some Errors, Omissions, and Falsifications Corrected," *Notes* 7 (1749/50): 57. Gradenwitz repeats the claim that the Berlin mass is an autograph in "Johann Stamitz als Kirchenkomponist," *Die Musikforschung* 11 (1958): 9–11, now adding that the hand resembles that of a flute concerto by Stamitz in Karlsruhe. The latter would be App. A/VI/147, which is, however, unquestionably by a different copyist than the Berlin mass and may not even be from Mannheim.

"The differences between the handwriting in the text [of the mass] and in the calligraphically adorned names of instruments corresponds to the differences between the text of the letter and the envelope. Partly because of this, it seems probable that the manuscript is in Stamitz' own hand."[86] Yet stylized decoration of this sort is absolutely standard in manuscripts of the eighteenth century and thus provides no basis whatsoever for a claim of concordance. By contrast, even a cursory comparison of discrete characteristics of the handwriting of the letter and mass (e.g., formation of the lower-case letters *c* and *s*, the capital letters *D, F, Q,* and *T*, and the combination "-itz" of "Stamitz") will show that two different hands are involved. That of the mass turns out to belong not to Stamitz but to an anonymous copyist from Mannheim, here labeled Mannheim 21.[87]

There is one type of study in which the analysis of handwriting may involve questions of forgery and thus of forensic analysis, namely the authentication of autograph scores by canonic masters. But at a less rarefied level, studies that attempt to identify and classify copyists seldom have to deal with forgery as such, and comprehensive, careful feature analysis will in fact yield a clear and convincing conclusion in a majority of cases ("These documents were not written by the same person," as in the Stamitz example just cited; "This part is by copyist X"). The difficulty arises, of course, when certain traits of a manuscript correspond to those of other manuscripts, while others are discrepant. Obviously, the explanation for such a situation may be either (1) that the copyist is inconsistent or writing at a quite different time or under different circumstances, or (2) that two different copyists are involved. Unless detailed information is available about the range of variation in a copyist's hand, either intrinsically or over time, the only responsible approach is to be extremely cautious in asserting the identity of the hands in question and scrupulously to inform the reader of the ambiguity. In general, it is far better to label one copyist as though he were two than to claim identity for what in reality are two different hands.

From the methodological standpoint an important point to bear in mind in attempting to determine whether two hands are the same is one emphasized in the forensic literature: that in order to demonstrate convincingly that two hands are identical,

---

[86] Gradenwitz, "Stamitz Family," 57.

[87] See Appendix D. In addition to the Stamitz mass, this copyist appears in a manuscript of a Hasse aria from the Pretlack collection, now in Berlin (App. A/VI/85; see also the section "The Pretlack Collection" in chap. 9); it is hard to imagine the celebrated *Instrumentalmusikdirektor* Stamitz functioning in this rather lowly capacity. Moreover, the mass is not a composing copy but a fair copy, possibly made for the Berlin court, a fact that supports the idea that it was made by a copyist rather than the composer.

There can be no unexplained significant differences between the questioned writing and the authenticated writing. In other words, a handwriting cannot be identified merely on the basis of shared characteristics.[88]

To state the matter differently, in order to show identity between two hands one must determine not only that there are similarities between the two samples that are not merely system characteristics; one must also demonstrate that there are no important *dissimilarities* that cannot reasonably be accounted for by reference to such influences as haste, the dictates of format (as in the Stamitz example cited above), or chronological disparity. Of course, the principal difficulty in applying this rule is determining whether a difference is significant or not. And as Edge points out (p. 235), historians will often have to take a more flexible position than forensic document examiners, leaving the possibility open that two specimens exhibiting unexplained significant differences *may* still be of common authorship.

The practical application of comparative feature analysis of textual material has typically involved a tabular presentation (often, regrettably, with little or no explanation) of how the writer makes each of his or her letters. This should be augmented by a representative sample of important combinations of letters based on the grapheme principle. The same basic approach can be applied to musical calligraphy. For example, I have found the six categories given below to be sufficient to distinguish and identify the hands of most copyists.[89] For quick reference I make tracings of these six elements on 4- by 6-inch (ca. 10 x 15 cm.) heavy-duty tracing paper (see the reproductions in Appendix D). If tracing is not allowed, one can draw imitations of the various forms.

1. All clefs (G, C, F), including several examples of each to illustrate the usual range of variation. The normal left end of the staff should be indicated (i.e., the placement of the clef on the staff). It is worthwhile to attempt to identify the number of graphemes and the direction of motion for each clef.

2. All time signatures.

3. Double bars and repeat signs; any decorations at ends of movements.

4. Quarter and eighth rests.

5. Formation of notes: shape of noteheads, how executed (if possible); stem connection, slant. I like to trace up- and downstem quarters, eighths, and halves, also whole notes, when possible indicating the number, type, and order of strokes for each.

---

[88] Edge, *Mozart's Viennese Copyists*, 229 (Edge's italics). Edge, 233–36, develops this point in some detail, citing Osborn, *Questioned Documents*, 245, 250–51, and Wilson R. Harrison, *Suspect Documents: Their Scientific Examination* (Chicago: Nelson-Hall, 1981 [repr. of the orig. ed. of 1958]), 343.

[89] Cf. the similar list of categories for analysis in Edge, *Mozart's Viennese Copyists*, 263: (1) clefs; (2) time signatures and figures; (3) rests; (4) key signatures and accidentals; (5) noteheads, stems, beams, flags; (6) dynamic marks; (7) textual markings such as tempo and expression marks; (8) articulation marks; and (9) other marks such as braces, double bars, and repeat signs.

Chapter 2

6. Any other distinctive characteristics of note: beaming, lettering (especially of common terms like "Violino Primo" and "Fine"), accidentals, ornaments, dynamics, performance articulations, ornamental flourishes. One should also make note of the overall impression of the handwriting, including slant, spaciousness, shakiness, "weight" (thick vs. thin lines), ink color, and the like.

Because such tracings provide only a kind of thumbnail sketch of the copyist's hand, one should always try to have available a film of the manuscript in question for consultation, or at least samples from the violin, viola, and bass parts. Ideally, the reference tracings would be backed up by a file containing photocopies of at least one page from each of these parts. The logical final step in this initial phase would be to enter the above information into a computer database. However, this is clearly impossible unless one has developed a full descriptive typology for these parameters, one that allows them to be reliably encoded in alphanumeric form. Unfortunately, no such system of classification has yet to my knowledge been devised; it remains a major desideratum in the field of handwriting studies.[90]

For purposes of publication, an index of copyists by tracings, combined with selected reproductions from the copyists' manuscripts, is one standard method, used here in Appendix D. Tracings can either be redrawn or touched up, or they can be scanned in, modified, and enhanced using a graphics editing program such as Adobe Photoshop. Another choice is simply to reproduce several pages of each copyist's manuscripts, possibly superimposed in order to save space.

Copyists in the Mannheim manuscripts. To turn now from theory and method to practice, this study has identified over 50 copyists who contributed substantively to a Mannheim manuscript. These copyists are listed, and the most important of them illustrated, in Appendix D. Of them, ten are found in signed manuscripts or have been identified by comparing their hands with those in other documents they have signed (receipts, etc.). The most important group, however, consists of 21 anonymous copyists found in manuscripts now in the Bayerische Staatsbibliothek in Munich or who appear in two or more present-day collections; these copyists, several of them no doubt official court copyists (see below), are designated here as Mannheim (or Mh.) 1, Mannheim 2, and so forth. A final group of 27 copyists is made up of those with manuscripts in a single collection other than the Bayerische Staatsbibliothek; these are labeled by the present location of the manuscript (using its RISM siglum or another abbreviation) plus a numerical designation as a Mannheim copyist (e.g., DS/Mh. 1 for the first unique Mannheim copyist in the Darmstadt collection).

Many of the Mannheim copyists share a strong family resemblance in copying style, having large, bold hands and utilizing similar clefs, time signatures, double

---

[90] Edge, *Mozart's Viennese Copyists*, 264–94, makes a good start on such a project. Edge is planning a computerized database of typical forms that should help to fill the need expressed above.

bars, and end-of-movement decorations (see the reproductions in Appendix D). Likewise, such aspects as the format of title pages show considerable regularity (see, e.g., fig. D:17). First there appear the title and (often) the gross instrumentation (e.g., "a 11 Stromenti"). This is then followed by the instruments required, each on a separate line; for instrumental works, an incipit (to the bottom right or left); and finally the attribution (normally "del Signore X") at the bottom right. If both incipit and attribution are to the right, the latter may come either above or below the incipit, a variation that may result from the fact that the incipit has been written by one copyist, the text of the title page by another. This was a common division of labor among copyists in the eighteenth century.

As mentioned above and detailed in Appendix D, ten hands can be associated with individuals known by name: those of the composers Carlo Grua, Holzbauer, Richter, Cannabich, Johannes Ritschel, Vogler, and Mozart; the ballet *répétiteur* Sigismund Falgera; the Mannheim musician Fridolin Weber; and the official court copyist Johann Cramer. (The latter worked primarily in Munich after 1778, however.) In addition, two copies of cello concertos in Berlin by the cellist/composers Innocenz Danzi and Anton Fils (App. A/VI/ 21–22) may be autograph parts.[91]

The great majority of the Mannheim manuscripts, however—those of the second and third groups enumerated above—are by anonymous copyists. Nonetheless, it is possible in certain cases to correlate the dates of a copyist's employment at Mannheim (known from almanacs, payment records, and the like) with the dates of manuscripts by a given copyist to produce a tentative identification.

A more concrete bit of evidence that initially seemed promising as a means of associating hands with names is the so-called *Lehrbrief* or *Gesellenbrief* of 29 May 1749, extant in the Reiss-Museum at Mannheim.[92] This splendid document, prepared upon the entry into the trumpeter's guild of Franz Anton Brunner, has signatures and additional text by several of the individuals in the list of court copyists below. However, almost all of this material is written in *Kurrentschrift* (*Deutsche Schrift*) and is thus difficult to compare directly with the normal italic hand employed in music manuscripts. Nonetheless, in the case of the important copyist Jacob Cramer (no. 1 in the list below) there are some similarities between his handwriting in this document and that of Mannheim 1 that support the identification proposed here (see fig. 2:9, below).

The following is a list of all individuals who appear at some point as copyists in the Mannheim almanacs or court records, together with their birth and death dates (if known), information on their employment at Mannheim, and possible

---

[91] See Appendix D/I and the discussion of "Other Manuscripts in Berlin" in chap. 9.

[92] Städtisches Reiss-Museum Mannheim, Sign. A 1749/20; see Friedrich Walter, "Ein Mannheimer Trompeter-Lehrbrief vom Jahr 1749," *Mannheimer Geschichtsblätter* 2 [1901]: 91-92, including a complete transcription.

Chapter 2

identities (i.e., an attempt to associate the hand in question with a name).[93] The order is chronological by the earliest known date of employment as a copyist. I should point out that the descriptions of individuals as copyists in the almanacs is somewhat haphazard and that they begin only in 1754. Until 1775, when the copyists are finally accorded a separate listing, they are designated by the word "Copist(e)" to the right of their normal listing as an instrumentalist (e.g., violist).

1. **Jacob Cramer** (1705–70). Timpanist and (from 1747) violinist 1744–70. Court copyist from at least 1746.[94] In 1760 he took over half the 100-gulden salary of Reinhard (see no. 3, below). He died on 6 October 1770,[95] and his post as copyist, carrying a salary of 250 gulden, passed to his son Johann (no. 5 below).[96] Cramer is probably identical with *Mannheim 1*. In addition to the fact that their dates coincide perfectly, the hand of Mannheim 1 is strikingly similar to that of the younger Cramer (see Appendix D). As is well known, copyists from the same family often share strong resemblances in copying style, the most famous examples being Haydn's copyists Joseph Elssler and his sons Joseph Jr. and Johann; this might well be the case here. Moreover, as already noted, there are certain similarities between Mannheim 1's hand and that of Jacob Cramer in the "Gesellenbrief" for Franz Anton Brunner, specifically the characteristic formation of the upper loops of the letters *b*, *f*, and *h* (cf. figs. 2:9a and b, below).

2. **Johann Lochner** (?–1774). Violist and copyist 1754–74. Lochner evidently died in late 1774, for a rescript of 24 February 1775 states that his copyist's salary of 150 gulden will be paid retroactively from 1 November 1774 to "Ignaz" (*recte*: Joseph) Abelshauser and provides a pension of 100 gulden for his widow and children.[97] Most likely identical with *Mannheim 2*, whose datable copies extend from ca. 1755 to approximately the mid-1770s.

3. **Reinhard.** Dates and given names unknown. Violist and copyist 1755–60. Reinhard had evidently vacated his post by 1 May 1760, for his salary was to be split retroactively from that date between Wilhelm Sepp and Jacob Cramer.[98] Probably identical

---

[93] Regarding another attempt to associate hands with the names of Mannheim copyists, it must be said that the arguments for linking "Lockner" (*recte*: Lochner) and Reinhard (see below, nos. 2–3) with the copyists I now identify as Mannheim 5 and 8, respectively, in Deanna D. Bush, *The Orchestral Masses of Ignaz Holzbauer (1711–1783): Authenticity, Chronology, and Style* (Ph.D. diss., Eastman School of Music, 1982), 77–80, are naïve and unconvincing, lacking any factual basis whatever.

[94] Cramer is given as a copyist and timpanist in a listing of the Kapelle from 1746, Munich, Bayerisches Hauptstaatsarchiv, Abt. III: Geheimes Hausarchiv, Handschrift 206 II, [p. 2]. I am grateful to Dr. Bärbel Pelker for calling this important new document to my attention.

[95] Cramer's death date was recently discovered by Dr. Bärbel Pelker in the *Tauf-, Ehe-, und Totenbuch 1763–1772* at the Katholisches Kirchenamt in Mannheim. I am once again in Dr. Pelker's debt for sending me this information, which is important in showing that Cramer died in late 1770, just after Mannheim 1's last known copies.

[96] Rescript of 30 October 1770, Karlsruhe, Badisches Generallandesarchiv, 77/1668, fols. 3–4.

[97] Ibid., fols. 5–6.

[98] Rescript of 15 August 1760, ibid., fol. 1.

with either *Rtt/Mannheim 1* or *3*, both of whom appear only in manuscripts of ca. 1755–60.

4. **(Johann) Wilhelm Sepp** (ca. 1715–91). Trumpeter, violinist, and (from 1759) violist 1745–78, after which he went to Munich with the court. Functioned as an official copyist from 1760, when with Jacob Cramer he took over half the 100-gulden salary of Reinhard (see the previous entry). Sepp is never, however, actually listed as a copyist in the almanacs and payment lists. Most likely identical with *Mannheim 3*, given his long period of service—paralleling that of the dates of manuscripts in which Mannheim 3 appears—and the fact that he transferred to Munich with the court, as did Mannheim 3, who served as a copyist there for a period after 1778.

5. **Johann Cramer** (1749–1824). Violist and copyist 1770–78; from 1775 copyist only. Traveled with the court to Munich, where he was both a prolific copyist and a timpanist.[99] As stated under no. 1, above, Johann Cramer took over the position and salary vacated on the death of his father, Jacob, in 1770, with a salary of 250 gulden; he first appears in the almanacs in 1771. That he acceded so quickly and at full salary probably means that he had been primed for the post for some time. Cramer's hand, similar to that of Mannheim 1 (probably his father), was identified by Robert Münster.[100]

6. **Andreas Buchsbaum** (or **Buxbaum**; dates unknown). Violist and "Cabinets-" or "Kabinetscopist" 1773–78. Buchsbaum does not appear in the various documents relating to the move to Munich, so he probably died or left the court before that time.

7. **Joseph [Johann? Ignaz?] Abelshauser** (? – 1831). Copyist 1774–78, thereafter listed in Mannheim until 1802 (i.e., he did not transfer with the court to Munich). Replaced Johann Lochner (no. 2, above), with salary retroactive to 1 November 1774.[101] Abelshauser is first listed in the almanacs in 1775 and could be identical with a copyist such as DS/Mh. 3, who is found only in Vogler manuscripts of the 1770s.

Another name sometimes mentioned as a copyist is that of **Caspar Bohrer** (1744–1809), who is listed as a violist and bassist in 1771–78 and as a trumpeter in 1773–74. He went with the court to Munich in 1778. (Roland Würtz confuses Caspar with Johann Philipp Bohrer, a court trumpeter [1744–73], violinist [1748–58],

---

[99] On Johann Cramer see Robert Münster, "Johann Cramer und andere Hofmusik-Kopisten in Mannheim und München zwischen 1770 und 1810," *Die Musikforschung* 22 (1969): 475–77.

[100] Ibid., including a sample of Cramer's hand (opposite p. 476). However, the reproduction of Cramer's hand in Gertraut Haberkamp and Robert Münster, *Die ehemaligen Musikhandschriftensammlungen der Königlichen Hofkapelle und der Kurfürstin Maria Anna in München: thematischer Katalog*, Kataloge bayerischer Musiksammlungen, 9 (Munich: G. Henle, 1982), p. xxxi, is incorrect; the page is by another Munich copyist, probably Joseph Palm (ca. 1755–1803; see *Wolfgang Amadeus Mozart, Idomeneo 1781–1981: Essays, Forschungsberichte, Katalog*, ed. Rudolph Angermüller and Robert Münster, Bayerische Staatsbibliothek, Ausstellungskataloge, 24 [Munich: R. Piper, 1981], 285–86).

[101] Rescript of 24 February 1775, Karlsruhe, Badisches Generallandesarchiv, 77/1668, fol. 5 (the first name is given as "Ignaz" there).

Figure 2.9a. Extract from *Gesellenbrief* (*Lehrbrief*) of 1749 for Franz Anton Brunner showing signature of (Johann) Jacob Cramer, "Hoff und Feldt Paucker," at bottom. Mannheim, Städtisches Reiss-Museum, Sign. A 1749/20.

Figure 2:9b. Title page of Cannabich's Symphony no. 4 (App. A/III/4), copied by Mannheim 1.

and violist [1756, 1759–76 or 77];[102] the latter was probably Caspar's father.) Caspar Bohrer's identification as a copyist arises because in the 1772 *Almanach* the printer has, presumably mistakenly, extended the bracket that in 1771 had heretofore designated only the violists Lochner and Johann Cramer as copyists to include "Gaspar Bohrer," too; otherwise, Bohrer is never labeled as a copyist. If he was in fact a copyist (like many violists), even an unofficial one, he could well be identical with *Mannheim 4*, given the latter's presence in manuscripts beginning in the late 1760s and extending into the Munich period.

While the above associations between names of known copyists and hands found in the manuscripts must be considered tentative, the fact that all but one of the names (that of Abelshauser) can be linked with groups of manuscripts whose dates correlate with the dates of their service as copyists tends to support the identifications as a whole. (See also the discussion below of Mannheim 5–6.) In other words, there is no other way to relate the names and hands that is consistent with the dates known (or assigned here) and the fact that certain copyists moved to Munich while others remained behind in Mannheim. In turn, if these identifications are correct, the dates associated with the names above can now be linked with the hands in question as evidence for chronology.

Two loose ends that cannot be tied up at this point concern the identities of the important copyists Mannheim 5 and 6. The former, Mannheim 5, is the copyist of many large opera scores (especially from the Sickingen collection; see chap. 8) and a few other manuscripts; these extend from the early 1760s (see App. A/VI/203) to as late as 1778 (see App. A/V/21). Therefore, he cannot be either Jacob Cramer or Johann Lochner, who died in 1770 and 1774, respectively. It is perhaps worth noting, too, that Mannheim 5 does not appear a single time in the long series of Cannabich symphonies at Munich, and on only a few occasions in the Holzbauer masses there (though he does collaborate with Holzbauer on the latter's score to *Betulia liberata*, App. A/II/17, probably from 1774). Because his hand occurs relatively rarely in copies of music by the two most important composers at court, and because the biographical data of none of the other official copyists corresponds with his, he may not have been on the court payroll as an official copyist (or at least was not so listed in the almanacs) but merely functioned in that capacity on occasion, leaving him free to accept large-scale private commissions.

Much the same can be said of Mannheim 6, the copyist of many sacred scores and a few operas. Unlike Mannheim 3–4, Mannheim 6 evidently remained behind in Mannheim after the court moved to Munich, as he is the copyist of Holzbauer's dramatic cantata *La morte di Didone* (App. A/VI/27), which had its premiere in Mannheim in July 1779. A Mannheim musician whose biographical data happen to fit the above facts is Ferdinand Fränzl (1710–82), who as stated in the previous section of this chapter was a violist and trumpeter at Mannheim and was evidently

---

[102] Würtz, *Verzeichnis*, 26.

also responsible for the lining of music paper (see fnn. 72–74, above, and related discussion). That violists were often copyists, and that *régleurs* might logically be expected to have taken on copying tasks, might seem to support this identification. However, many of Mannheim 6's copies are lined with single (one-stave) rastra; if he were indeed Fränzl, it is hard to see why he would not have used paper lined with the larger implements available to him as court *régleur*. But more conclusively, Fränzl's hand as found in the "Gesellenbrief" for Brunner does not match that of Mannheim 6.[103]

A final copyist associated with Mannheim is Mozart's post-mortem father-in-law **Fridolin Weber** (1733–79), uncle of Carl Maria von Weber. Though Mozart refers to Weber as a copyist on several occasions, he appears in the court records only as a bass singer (1767–78), after which he went for a year to Munich and then Vienna. A minor triumph of the present study has been to identify Weber's hand, an identification made possible by Bärbel Pelker's discovery of a letter written by him to the elector.[104] The handwriting in this document provides a reasonably convincing match with that of the manuscript A/VI/36, an incomplete set of parts to Mozart's aria "Aer tranquillo" from *Il rè pastore*, K. 208, of 1775. In support of this identification, the Mozart letters contain several references, both indirect and direct, that link this aria with Fridolin Weber and his daughter Aloysia. In the first, from 17 January 1778, Mozart tells his father that he has had four arias copied for the "Princess of Orange" (Princess Caroline von Nassau-Weilburg) by "a certain Herr Weber," whose daughter he goes on to praise (Bauer-Deutsch, 2:226; Anderson, 447; the daughter in question is, of course, Aloysia). These arias are no doubt the same as the four from *Il rè pastore* that a subsequent letter, dated 7 February 1778, says he has given to Aloysia (Bauer-Deutsch, 2:266; Anderson, 470). Finally, Mozart writes that Aloysia has sung "Aer tranquillo" at a concert at Cannabich's house on 12 March 1778 (letter from Paris of 24 March, Bauer-Deutsch, 2:326; Anderson, 517). The same letter again mentions Weber *père* as a copyist, saying that he has copied out *gratis* whatever Mozart needed. In sum, the above passages from the Mozart letters help to confirm the identification of Weber's hand as well as the probability that the parts comprising App. A/VI/36 were those used in the performance at Cannabich's (or, alternatively, the concert Mozart participated in at the residence of Princess Caroline).

---

[103] Fränzl's signature, unlike others in the *Gesellenbrief*, is in italic rather than German script, making possible a reasonable comparison with the italic script of the manuscripts. Particularly characteristic are the idiosyncratic *F*'s and *d*'s of the signature and the *T* of "Trompetter."

[104] Munich, Bayerisches Hauptstaatsarchiv, HR I, Fasz. 473/Nr. 911. The letter (with envelope), dated 27 March 1779, is entirely in Weber's hand. Though the letter is mainly in *Kurrentschrift* (German script), it and the envelope contain enough words in italic script to make possible a detailed comparison with the lettering of the manuscript.

Chapter 2

Chronological considerations. At least until recently, the most extensive and systematic use of feature analysis in the study of musical calligraphy had come in the realm, not of discrimination among hands, but of chronology. Here the principal model has been the work of Georg von Dadelsen in his studies of J. S. Bach's hand.[105] Dadelsen's method, essentially a rather basic form of feature analysis, may perhaps best be introduced by describing a sophisticated recent use thereof that is closer to home, that of Jochen Reutter in his outstanding study of Franz Xaver Richter's sacred music.[106] Reutter isolates a small group of characteristics, not necessarily prominent ones, that change over time in the datable autographs by Richter: (1) the formation of the three types of clefs, (2) the number 4 in time signatures, (3) the flags of down-stem eighth notes, (4) the formation of half and sixteenth notes, (5) the relation of stems and beaming, and (6) the formation of five common letters. The presence or absence of the variant forms can then be used to determine an approximate date for an undated manuscript, though this will naturally be more convincing if it is supported by evidence from other spheres. What will be noticed about Reutter's choice of elements for examination is that it is in no way exhaustive, as it might be if he were attempting to establish a complete profile of Richter's hand for purposes of identification or authentication. All that matters is that a given component change consistently with time; those that do not are useless for this particular purpose.[107]

In the present project, analysis of this type has been profitably carried out on the hands of Cannabich and the copyists Mannheim 3 and 4, though by no means as systematically as in Reutter's study.[108] The results with respect to Cannabich, for whom large numbers of dated and datable sources existed, were especially rewarding. For Mannheim 3 and 4 it was possible to distinguish clearly between early and late hands, the latter characteristic of their late Mannheim and Munich periods. But for the remaining copyists there appeared to be either not enough

---

[105] Georg von Dadelsen, *Beiträge zur Chronologie der Werke Johann Sebastian Bachs*, Tübinger Bach-Studien, 4/5 (Trossingen: Hohner-Verlag, 1958), part 2; see esp. pp. 49–68, on his methodology. See also Yoshitake Kobayashi, *Die Notenschrift Johann Sebastian Bachs: Dokumente seiner Entwicklung*, Neue Bach-Ausgabe, ser. 9, vol. 2 (Kassel: Bärenreiter, 1989), 16–22. Wolfgang Plath employs a related approach in his "Beiträge zur Mozart-Autographie II: Schriftchronologie 1770–1780," *Mozart-Jahrbuch*, 1976/77, pp. 131–73.

[106] Jochen Reutter, *Studien zur Kirchenmusik Franz Xaver Richters (1709–1789)* (Frankfurt am Main: Peter Lang, 1993), 92–110.

[107] The type of careful feature analysis employed by Reutter could obviously be extended to include the identification and classification of copyists in general. As stated earlier, what is needed in this field is a comprehensive but dependable and easily usable typology of each of the relevant parameters (clefs, time signatures, etc.), one that also takes account of chronological changes in a copyist's hand and is computerizable. This should then be combined with a sophisticated application of statistical method and database design.

[108] See Appendix D and also the extended discussion of Mannheim 4's hand in the section "Types of Parts" in chap. 5.

datable material on which to base conclusions or too little observable change in the course of time to warrant a detailed study (seemingly the case for Mannheim 1, 2, 5, and 6). In the latter case I would be delighted if a more intensive study of these copyists in the future were to prove me wrong.

Chapter 3

The "Core" Manuscripts (App. A/I/1–24)

The first group of manuscripts to be considered here consists of 24 manuscripts for which the evidence of Mannheim provenance is direct and unequivocal—normally a colophon or other notation stating that the manuscript was copied at Mannheim (see App. A/I/1–24). These manuscripts fall into four distinct groups: (1) seven sources still located in Mannheim, (2) six autograph scores by the court Kapellmeister Carlo Grua, (3) three ballet scores copied by the Mannheim violinist and ballet *répétiteur* Sigismund Falgera, and (4) eight autographs of Mozart written while he was at Mannheim in 1777/78. Because the evidence that these manuscripts were copied at Mannheim is clear-cut, they provide a basis both for determining the essential physical characteristics of a Mannheim manuscript and for assigning subsequent manuscripts to Mannheim.

Manuscripts of the Jesuitenkirche in Mannheim

Our first group of sources comprises seven manuscripts still found in Mannheim (App. A/I/1–7), a hitherto undocumented collection salvaged from the ruins of the Jesuitenkirche.[1] This important Baroque church was designed by the electoral architect Alessandro Galli da Bibiena and built between 1733 and 1760; it contained frescoes, sculpture, and decoration by some of the leading artisans of Europe, including the Asam brothers of Munich. Originally joined to the palace by a passageway, it was used for occasional ceremonies of the court, though the smaller court chapel in the west wing of the palace was the usual venue for services.[2] It

---

[1] I wish to extend warm thanks to the former archivist of the Jesuitenkirche, Herr Heinz Lindner, for bringing these sources to my wife's and my attention during our initial visit to the archive of the Jesuitenkirche and for his kindness during several subsequent research trips. The Jesuitenkirche, like the electoral palace, was severely damaged in the fire-bombing of Mannheim in 1943–45. It has now been fully reconstructed, though most of the decorative elements were lost. For a photograph of the interior before the war see Jochen Reutter, "Die Kirchenmusik am Mannheimer Hof," in Ludwig Finscher, ed., *Die Mannheimer Hofkapelle im Zeitalter Carl Theodors* (Mannheim: Palatium Verlag im J & J Verlag, 1992), 101.

[2] For example, it was in the chapel that Mozart played the organ during a mass at Mannheim, a performance described in an oft-quoted letter to his father of 13 November 1777 (Bauer-Deutsch, 2:120; Anderson, 370). For those trying to visualize the circumstances of this performance as Mozart so vividly describes them, it should be noted that when the chapel was rebuilt after the bombing of Mannheim in World War II the organ and choir loft were unfortunately moved from

Chapter 3

also maintained a Seminarium Musicum in conjunction with the court and its musicians.

The performing parts to the Jesuitenkirche manuscripts provide our first glimpse of what a typical Mannheim sacred manuscript was like: large, upright in format (the norm for sacred parts throughout Europe), and with covers or wrappers that generally consisted of local Palatine paper—especially blue "elephant" paper, so named for its size and rough quality and usually containing a watermark of an elephant (as in Knöckel 1 paper; see Appendix B/II). Most of these covers do double duty as title pages. But perhaps the greatest initial value of the Jesuitenkirche manuscripts lies in their implication of the importance at Mannheim of Swiss paper from Basel and its environs (see chap. 2). Five of these seven manuscripts, App. A/I/1 and 3–6, employ Swiss paper from mills owned by the Heusler and Blum families for all but the cover sheets (see the "Paper" column of Appendix A and also Appendix B). For the cover sheets, nos. 3 and 5–6 utilize papers from Mosbach and Neustadt (Pfalz), both near Mannheim (no. 3 even contains the initials and coat of arms of Carl Theodor), while that of no. 4 uses similar paper that probably also comes from the Palatinate or nearby.[3] Likewise, all of no. 7 is on German paper, probably from the mill of J. F. Roeder. The unidentified paper of the remaining manuscript in the collection, no. 2, appears to be German as well. The use of local paper for the body of the latter two manuscripts, not just for the covers, doubtless reflects the fact that they derive from the collection of the Jesuitenkirche, not the court; local paper almost never appears in official court manuscripts except as cover sheets or paste-overs.

Information derived from these sources about staving and copyists is of somewhat less utility than one might wish, again because all or most of these manuscripts were associated with the Jesuitenkirche rather than the court. In the case of rastrology this is evident from the appearance of one-stave rastra in all but App. A/I/1, a score (mainly autograph) by the Mannheim vice-Kapellmeister Johannes Ritschel (1739–66), dated 1763, together with four parts. As already discussed in chapter 2, the score, in oblong format, makes use of rastrum 10:10, also found in numerous other manuscripts of just that period—by Cannabich (including his Symphonies no. 14–15), Holzbauer (one manuscript dated 1765), and Ferrari. Of

---

their original position at the front of the church to the rear. For a photograph of the original placement see, inter alia, Reutter, "Kirchenmusik," 100.

[3] The watermark of the cover/title page of App. A/I/4, consisting of a cross over the letters EDPM, is similar to no. 915 in Edward Heawood, *Watermarks, Mainly of the 17th and 18th Centuries* (Hilversum: Paper Publications Society, 1950), and nos. 153 and 309 in Georg Eineder, *The Ancient Paper-Mills of the Former Austro-Hungarian Empire and Their Watermarks* (Hilversum: Paper Publications Society, 1960). Neither scholar specifies a date or provenance. Joachim Jaenecke, *Die Musikbibliothek des Ludwig Freiherrn von Pretlack (1716–1781)* (Wiesbaden: Breitkopf & Härtel, 1973), 73, lists it as no. 15 and gives its provenance as Italy, which is certainly incorrect (among other reasons, the "PM" of EDPM probably stands for "Papiermühle").

the four parts, three are lined with a double (two-stave) rastrum that is otherwise unidentified, one with a simple (one-stave) rastrum.

At least twenty-one copyists occur in these seven manuscripts, sixteen of them in nos. 2–4 alone. Especially among these sixteen, the inconsistent and often amateurish handwriting gives the unmistakable impression that they were not court copyists (or even court musicians) but perhaps members of the Seminarium who had been pressed into service as copyists. However, the copyist of nos. 5–6 is the important court copyist designated here as Mannheim 6 (see Appendix D), whose hand appears in many sacred manuscripts and several operas. And as already mentioned, most of the score of no. 1 is in the hand of Johannes Ritschel.[4]

Autograph Scores by Carlo Grua

Because the music collection of the Bayerische Staatsbibliothek in Munich incorporates the library of the former Munich *Hofmusikintendanz*, one would assume that any music brought from Mannheim to Munich in and after 1778 would be housed there. Yet of the nearly one-thousand manuscripts in the collection of the *Hofmusikintendanz*, only a small number specify their provenance, and only three of these are from Mannheim—autograph scores of sacred music by Carlo Grua, Kapellmeister at Mannheim from about 1733 until his death in 1773 (see App. A/I/8–9, 11).[5] Three other autograph scores of Grua's have also survived, one from the collection of the Frauenkirche in Munich (now D-FS; App. A/I/12)[6] and one each in Kassel and Karlsruhe (App. A/I/10, 13).[7] That so many of Grua's autographs have come down to us doubtless derives from the fact that his son, Franz Paul (1753–1833), went with the court to Munich in 1778, where he later became Kapell-

---

[4] The score of the mass (including the title page) is by Ritschel except for the beginning of the Gloria (by another copyist) and the tempo indication and title at the first of each movement (by a third copyist). A reproduction of the title page of this manuscript appears in Reutter, "Kirchenmusik," 107. Numerous autograph manuscripts by Ritschel from his *Studienjahr* in Bologna are found in I-Bc, allowing us to confirm that this is indeed his handwriting.

[5] Recent research on Grua's exceptionally confused ancestry and genealogy has shown that his name was not Carlo Pietro but Carlo Luigi; the "Pietro" derived from the earlier form of his surname, "Pietragrua." See Andreas Freitäger, "Carlo Luigi Pietragrua d. Ältere (ca. 1665–1726): Studien zur Biographie eines 'Vor-Mannheimer,'" *Musik in Bayern* 44 (1992): 10–11, 30–31. A thematic catalogue of Grua's sacred music appears in Eduard Schmitt, ed., *Kirchenmusik der Mannheimer Schule, 1. Auswahl*, DTB, Neue Folge, 2 (Wiesbaden: Breitkopf & Härtel, 1982), pp. xxxiii–xxxix.

[6] For a brief discussion of the sources for this *Memento Domine David*, which include a set of parts by Mannheim copyists (App. A/VI/144), see the section "Sacred Music by Holzbauer and Grua in Moravia, Austria, and Germany" in chap. 9.

[7] Parts to the Karlsruhe mass, the strings of which are in Grua's hand, are found in the Munich Frauenkirche collection (now D-FS); see App. A/IV/2.

meister; he probably took with him, and thus preserved, at least portions of his father's collection of autograph scores.[8]

As autographs, these sources provide us with a record of Grua's highly idiosyncratic hand (see Appendix D). Equally important, all six are on Swiss paper, from the mills of Heusler and Blum. And finally, the colophons on the last page of each of the scores supply a wide range of precise dates—1733, 1737, I751, 1753, and 1766—thus helping to establish when the various papers and rastra of these manuscripts were in use at Mannheim.

Ballets Copied by Sigismund Falgera

Three other sources stating explicitly that they were copied at Mannheim (or Schwetzingen) are scores to two ballets by Christian Cannabich and one by Joseph Toeschi, formerly in the Fürstl. Fürstenbergische Hofbibliothek in Donaueschingen and now in the Badische Landesbibliothek in Karlsruhe (App. A/I/14–16). These scores were copied and owned by Sigismund Falgera (ca. 1752–90), a violinist and ballet *répétiteur* at Mannheim and later at Munich.[9] The "Mr Bouqueton" mentioned on each of the title pages was the well-known court balletmaster François André Bouqueton.[10]

The two Cannabich manuscripts bear dates of 1769, but the date of the similar colophon at the end of the Toeschi score has been effaced; it may have read 1767 or possibly 1769. No date is otherwise known for the Toeschi ballet, which is entitled *L'enlèvement de Proserpine*.[11] If 1767 is indeed the date of the Falgera score, and if he was indeed born ca. 1752, he would have been only fifteen when he copied it. In

---

[8] Composers at Mannheim had the right to retain their autograph scores; see chap. 1, fnn. 47–48 and related text.

[9] See Munich, Bayerisches Hauptstaatsarchiv, HR I, Fasz. 457/Nr. 13 (1), "Status," a master chart from 1778 specifying which musicians would remain in Mannheim, which would follow the court to Munich, which of the Munich musicians would he retained, and which would be dismissed. Falgera's name appears at the very end of the list of violinists, just before the *Accessisten*. However, his name never appears among the members of the Hofkapelle in any of the almanacs or *Kalender*.

[10] On Bouqueton see Sibylle Dahms, "Ballet Reform in the Eighteenth Century and Ballet at the Court of Mannheim," in *Ballet Music from the Mannheim Court*, ed. Paul Corneilson and Eugene K. Wolf, Part I, Recent Researches in the Music of the Classical Era, 45 (Madison, Wisc.: A-R Editions, 1996), pp. xiii–xv.

[11] A ballet with the same name, but supposedly by Etienne Lauchery and with music by Christian Cannabich, was evidently performed at Kassel in the year 1767; see Rudolf Kloiber, *Die dramatischen Ballette von Christian Cannabich* (Munich: H. Kutzner, 1928), p. 37, no. 11. For a modern edition of the Bouqueton/Toeschi ballet see Paul Cauthen, ed., *Ballet Music from the Mannheim Court*, Part III, Recent Researches in the Music of the Classical Era, 52 (Madison, Wisc.: A-R Editions, 1998). Reproductions of the title page and p. 1 of the Falgera manuscript appear as plates 3–4 of that edition.

any event, it was not copied at the same time as the two Cannabich scores; the staving is different (it employs a one-stave rastrum vs. the ten-stave rastrum, 10:17b, of the other manuscripts), and both the watermarks and Falgera's hand show some variants by comparison with the two Cannabich manuscripts. These differences may provide a modicum of support for the date of 1767.

These three manuscripts furnish us with a sample of Falgera's handwriting (which has not, however, turned up elsewhere). They also provide three more instances, now associated with the late 1760s, of the relatively uncommon use at Mannheim of Heusler 7 paper, a type seen in one of the Jesuitenkirche manuscripts, App. A/I/5. This is especially important because this paper undergoes clearly identifiable changes over the long span of time it occurs at Mannheim (and later Munich for several years); a precise date for one of these forms allows an approximate dating for manuscripts with an identical form (or rather forms, as twins are involved). In addition, two of these scores are bound with the blue "elephant" paper used for that purpose in Mannheim, in this case Knöckel 1, as in two of the Jesuitenkirche manuscripts.

As for the staving of these sources, the rastrum with which the two Cannabich scores were lined, 10:17b, is also found in autograph parts to a Richter psalm that can be assigned on other grounds to almost the same time, 1767–68, just before the composer left Mannheim for Strasbourg (App. A/IV/10b).[12] Association of this rastrum with the dates ?1767–69 allows an approximate dating for a few other sources by Cannabich and Holzbauer, as well.[13] As already noted, the Toeschi score differs from the two others in using a one-stave rastrum, characteristic more of privately prepared than of official court manuscripts.

Autograph Manuscripts by Mozart

On Thursday, 30 October 1777, Wolfgang and Maria Anna Mozart arrived in Mannheim for what turned out to be a disappointing stay of four and one-half months at the electoral court. They reached Mannheim, no doubt intentionally, just in time for the beginning of the so-called gala days in celebration of the nameday of the elector Carl Theodor, 4 November. Mozart was in fact a featured soloist at the academy that traditionally took place toward the beginning of the celebrations, in this case on 6 November, a week after his arrival.[14]

---

[12] See chap. 6, @ fnn. 7–8.

[13] App. A/III/31 and A/VI/16, 192.

[14] For Mozart and his mother's description of this academy see their letter of 8 November 1777 (Bauer-Deutsch, 2:109; Anderson, 361–62). Ironically, the report about this concert by the Saxon envoy at Mannheim, Count Andreas von Riaucour, mentions only that "Prinzessin Marianne" (Maria Anna von Zweibrücken-Birkenfeld) sang two arias; see Bärbel Pelker, "Theateraufführ-

Chapter 3

As is well known, Mozart's compositional output while at Mannheim was rather slim. Of the eight surviving autographs that can be firmly assigned to Mannheim, four (App. A/I/21–24) have a colophon stating they were written there: two concert arias composed for his erstwhile romantic interest Aloysia Weber and for the famous tenor Anton Raaff, dated 24 and 27 February 1778, respectively (K. 294–95); a sonata for keyboard and violin, dated 11 March 1778 (K. 296); and the fragmentary Concerto for Cembalo and Violin (K. 315f/Anh. 56), written not during his principal stay at Mannheim in the winter of 1777/78 but during his brief return trip in late 1778 after his long and, again, disappointing sojourn in Paris.

The other four works, App. A/I/17–20, are the keyboard and violin sonatas K. 301–3 and 305 (K. 293a–d), which Mozart refers to in the familiar letter of 14 February 1778 in which he complains about having to write works on commission for flute, "an instrument [he] cannot bear." He continues, "Hence, as a diversion I compose something else, such as the duets [sonatas] for clavier and violin, or I work at my mass. Now I am settling down seriously to the clavier duets [sonatas for keyboard and violin], so that I can have them engraved."[15] Mozart finished the four works under consideration here while at Mannheim, later completing the set in Paris with K. 304 and 306 (300c and 300l); they were published in 1778 by Sieber.

Of these eight manuscripts I have personally examined four; the remainder, the sonatas K. 301–3 and 305, are reportedly now in a private Swiss collection.[16] However, a detailed description of the latter sources graciously supplied to me by the late Alan Tyson makes clear that from the documentary standpoint they precisely match three of the four I have examined—that is, all but the concerto fragment written on the return trip in late 1778 (App. A/I/24). All use an identical form of the ubiquitous paper Heusler 5, and all were lined with rastrum 12:2a,[17]

---

rungen und musikalische Akademien am Hof Carl Theodors in Mannheim," in Finscher, ed., *Die Mannheimer Hofkapelle*, 257.

[15] Translation after Anderson, 481–82; orig. in Bauer-Deutsch, 2:281.

[16] The Mozarteum in Salzburg owns a microfilm of these manuscripts. Paul Corneilson has consulted this film and kindly sent the following informative report regarding K. 305–6: "The manuscript of K. 305 also includes the beginning of K. 306 as well as the first measure of the recitative 'Basta vincesti' (K. 295a). The present Köchel entry is vague about this; here is the situation: The autograph [of K. 305] is made up of three nested bifolia. The first seven pages preserve a fair copy of K. 305; then Mozart began to copy K. 306 on pages 8 and 9. But when he turned the page, he found the first measure of the recitative to K. 295a upside down on the bottom of page 10. (Apparently, Mozart had begun to write out the aria for Dorothea Wendling but broke off for some reason. When he grabbed some manuscript paper on which to write the violin sonatas, he failed to realize that there was a fragment in the midst of it until he turned the page.) Thus he later had to recopy the entire exposition as well as the rest of K. 306 on another (Parisian) paper."

[17] Though I have not personally examined these sources, the total span reported to me by Alan Tyson precisely matches that of the other four manuscripts, as does the paper, and there is no reason to doubt that the rastra are identical.

otherwise found in several Vogler manuscripts dated 1776–77. Hence, Mozart was making use of court paper obtained from the central depot at Mannheim. Indeed, we can probably identify the precise source of the paper, namely the Mannheim bass singer and sometime copyist Fridolin Weber, father of Aloysia and Constanze: Mozart says in a letter of 7 February 1778 that Weber had given him a supply of music paper as a present.[18] The consistency of the paper and staving of these seven manuscripts supports the view that they all came from the same batch, namely that supplied by Weber, especially as all the works in question postdate his gift to Mozart. By contrast, the fragmentary concerto manuscript of late 1778 is on small Dutch paper lined with one pass of a fourteen-stave rastrum.

To summarize briefly, the manuscripts listed in Appendix A/I reveal a strong preference at Mannheim for Swiss paper from the celebrated manufacturers Heusler and Blum, with local Palatine paper serving primarily as cover sheets. Moreover, as most of these manuscripts are dated or datable, they provide us with an extended series of dates, ranging from 1733 to 1778, for the specific forms of their watermarks and rastra. Finally, though of somewhat less utility, these manuscripts supply samples of the handwriting of one professional Mannheim copyist, Mannheim 6, and of various musicians resident there, most notably Carlo Grua, Johannes Ritschel, and Sigismund Falgera.

---

[18] Mozart's letter asks his father to send him some arias from home for use by Aloysia, saying, "You will find the list of them on the French song which her father [Fridolin] has copied out, the paper of which is part of a present from him; but indeed he has given me much more" (trans. after Anderson, 470; orig. in Bauer-Deutsch, 2:266). No copy of the French song in question is known. For further information on Fridolin Weber, including identification of his hand, see chap. 2, @ fn. 104, and Appendix D/I.

Chapter 4

Sacred and Dramatic Music of Ignaz Holzbauer (App. A/II/1–21)

When Ignaz Holzbauer (1711–83) arrived at Mannheim in 1753 he was already a mature, well-established composer, six years older than his fiery colleague Johann Stamitz. Born and raised in Vienna, his career had begun in the 1730s at the musically active Moravian court of Holešov (Holleschau), after which he again took up residence in Vienna in the 1740s as a theater director. Judging by the large number of sources, many of them unica, extant in Czech collections and in Austria—some three dozen—he must have been extremely active as a composer of symphonies during this time. Indeed, despite the tendency to associate him with Mannheim, he has equal claim to fame as the most prolific early symphonist of the Habsburg Monarchy. Holzbauer left Vienna in 1750 to take up the prestigious position of Kapellmeister to the court of Württemberg, where his principal responsibility was, just as it was to be at Mannheim, the court opera. In 1753 he accepted Carl Theodor's offer to become Kapellmeister at the electoral court.[1] When the court moved to Munich in 1778 he remained behind in Mannheim, dying there five years later.

The Holzbauer Masses at the Bayerische Staatsbibliothek

Although Ignaz Holzbauer is usually thought of as a composer of operas and instrumental works, his output of music for the church was also very substantial.[2] As with the symphonies, a significant portion of it dates from before his Mannheim period.[3] But the largest and most important surviving collection of his sacred music is the group of sixteen masses and an autograph oratorio at the Bayerische

---

[1] Holzbauer was co-Kapellmeister with the older composer Carlo Grua until the latter's death in 1773. Grua was primarily responsible for church music after the arrival of Holzbauer in 1753. On Holzbauer's move from Stuttgart to Mannheim see Eugene K. Wolf, "Driving a Hard Bargain: Johann Stamitz's Correspondence with Stuttgart (1748)," in *Festschrift Christoph-Hellmut Mahling zum 65. Geburtstag*, ed. Axel Beer, Kristina Pfarr, and Wolfgang Ruf (Tutzing: Hans Schneider, 1997), 1555, 1562.

[2] A full thematic catalogue of Holzbauer's sacred music appears in Eduard Schmitt, ed., *Kirchenmusik der Mannheimer Schule, 1. Auswahl*, DTB, Neue Folge, 2 (Wiesbaden: Breitkopf & Härtel, 1982), pp. lxxi–xcii. For a thematic catalogue of the masses see Deanna D. Bush, *The Orchestral Masses of Ignaz Holzbauer (1711–1783): Authenticity, Chronology, and Style* (Ph.D. diss., Eastman School of Music, 1982), 321–412.

[3] On Holzbauer's pre-Mannheim masses see Bush, *Holzbauer*, 198–200, 222–36.

Chapter 4

Staatsbibliothek in Munich, details of which appear in Appendix A/II.[4] Like the Cannabich manuscripts to be considered in the next chapter, these manuscripts can be shown to have formed a part of the original Mannheim court collection (see below). Together with the Cannabich sources, they belonged to the collection of the Munich *Hofmusikintendanz* before its transfer in 1860 to what is today the Bayerische Staatsbibliothek.[5] Probably at the time of this transfer, all but one of the title pages, that of App. A/II/13, were replaced. Similarly unfortunate for the future scholar, the manuscripts were also culled of their duplicate parts, which are listed in pencil in an earlier catalogue of the *Hofmusikintendanz* collection.[6] As would be expected for sacred music, both the vocal and instrumental parts of these manuscripts are in upright format, on paper lined for the most part with twelve staves.

Several types of evidence can be adduced to demonstrate that the Holzbauer manuscripts belonged at one time to the Mannheim collection. First of all, examination of the handwriting of these manuscripts reveals that Holzbauer himself copied portions of two of the Masses—the Kyrie and Gloria of the horns 1–2 *basso* parts in App. A/II/4 and the last two pages of the organ part in A/II/11. Of equal significance, as can be seen in column 6 of Appendix A/II, Holzbauer's hand appears in a large number of additions and alterations in nearly all of the masses: the changes range from substantive revision (App. A/II/5, 7) to the addition of a sin-

---

[4] The score to a seventeenth Holzbauer mass in Munich, Mus. Ms. 2304, was stated in our original article on the Mannheim manuscripts, Eugene K. and Jean K. Wolf, "A Newly Identified Complex of Manuscripts from Mannheim," *JAMS* 27 (1974): 409 (no. 15), to be from Mannheim; it can now be shown on the basis of its watermarks (<shield/A/L>, <4/fleur-de-lis/AST>) to be a local Bavarian production. In addition to the original Mannheim parts for these masses, five of them include vocal scores copied in Munich by Johann Cramer on local papers; these are not listed in Appendix A/II.

[5] Documents concerning this transfer are found in Munich, Bayerisches Hauptstaatsarchiv, Staatstheater Sammlung 13514; see also chap. 5, fn. 2, and Wolf and Wolf, "Complex," p. 398, fn. 50. No indication appears in any of the documents as to how or when the *Hofmusikintendanz* obtained the works. We are greatly indebted to Dr. Robert Münster, former head of the music division of the Bayerische Staatsbibliothek, for his expert and extraordinarily generous assistance at every phase of this project.

[6] This catalogue was discovered in 1971 by Robert Münster. A modern edition of it appears in Gertraut Haberkamp and Robert Münster, eds., *Die ehemaligen Musikhandschriftensammlungen der Königlichen Hofkapelle und der Kurfürstin Maria Anna in München*, Kataloge bayerischer Musiksammlungen, 9 (Munich: G. Henle, 1982); the Holzbauer manuscripts are listed on pp. 82–84. For a discussion of the conclusions one can draw from these pencil notations see Eugene K. Wolf, "On the Composition of the Mannheim Orchestra, ca. 1740–1778," *Basler Jahrbuch für historische Musikpraxis* 17 (1993): 135–36. The Cannabich manuscripts also had their duplicates stripped, probably when they came into the library at the same time as the Holzbauer manuscripts (see the discussion of duplicate parts in the section "Types of Parts" in chap. 5).

gle word to a tempo marking (App. A/II/14).[7] The extensive presence of Holzbauer's hand in these manuscripts provides clear evidence of their Mannheim provenance, for he remained behind in Mannheim when the court moved to Munich in 1778. That one of these masses with extensive emendations by Holzbauer, App. A/II/12, contains a copyist's date of 1763 (see fig. 4:1, below) confirms this view and provides incontrovertible proof that these manuscripts were not copied in Munich after 1778 (the main alternative hypothesis about the origin of these manuscripts, as discussed in chapter 2).

Secondly, Mannheim copyist 6, whose hand appears in two of the Jesuitenkirche manuscripts (App. A/I/5–6), turns up frequently throughout the Holzbauer masses in Munich. Yet his hand does not recur in other manuscripts in Munich, and, as discussed in Appendix D, he can be shown with some certainty to have remained in Mannheim; about a third of the Mannheim Kapelle stayed behind, their salary still paid by the elector. For the other main copyists of these manuscripts, as well—principally Mannheim 1 (probably Jacob Cramer, who died in 1770) and Mannheim 2 (most likely Johann Lochner, who died in 1774)—strong links with Mannheim, and none with Munich, are the rule.

Finally, save for the later vocal scores in Johann Cramer's hand (see fn. 4), these works are copied with only a few exceptions on Swiss paper that is wholly analogous to that of the manuscripts from Mannheim listed in Appendix A/I. Altogether they utilize five such papers, four of which are found among the manuscripts of Appendix A/I. Two types predominate, as in most Mannheim manuscripts of the 1760s and 70s: Heusler 5 and Blum 5. The principal exceptions to the use of Swiss paper in these sources adroitly prove the rule: the additions in Holzbauer's hand pasted into App. A/II/13 are on paper from Mosbach, near Mannheim, and the cover—as already noted, the only original one to remain—is on paper from Neustadt/Pfalz (Knöckel 1, as in two of the Jesuitenkirche manuscripts and two of the ballets copied at Mannheim by Sigismund Falgera; see App. A/I/6–7, 14, 16). In addition, portions of App. A/II/3, those copied by Mannheim 6, are on a Dutch paper occasionally found at Mannheim, from the firm of Pieter van der Ley (Appendix B/III, van der Ley 1).[8] In sum, there can be no question at all that the manuscripts to these sixteen masses originated in Mannheim, and they can therefore be added to those of the "core" group treated in the previous chapter as a basis for future comparisons.

---

[7] Bush, *Holzbauer*, 70–71 provides a list of Holzbauer's additions and corrections to the Munich masses. Her numbering of the manuscripts can be correlated with the call numbers in the Bayerische Staatsbibliothek by using the concordance she provides on pp. 336–38.

[8] Mannheim was not only geographically closer than Munich to Holland, but it was also connected by the Rhine. There were other ties between Mannheim and Holland, as well: as already pointed out in chapter 2, Carl Theodor attended the University of Leiden, and one of his titles was Marquis of Bergen op Zoom. For further information on the Dutch papers found in the Mannheim complex of manuscripts see Appendix B/III.

As it turns out, there is one piece of concrete evidence pointing to a transfer of Holzbauer's music from Mannheim to Munich. According to Friedrich Walter, on 24 August 1783, four months after Holzbauer's death, a rescript was sent to Wolfgang Heribert von Dalberg, Intendant of the Nationaltheater in Mannheim. This document requested the dispatch of, to quote Walter, "Holzbauerscher Messen" and a copy of Holzbauer's opera *Günther von Schwarzburg*; they were to be sent to Count von Seeau in Munich.[9] These and other works had been left in Mannheim under the supervision of the aging Holzbauer, who had remained there as titular Kapellmeister of those musicians who had not moved to Munich. After Holzbauer's death in 1783, responsibility for the collection was transferred to the management of the Mannheim Nationaltheater.[10]

In trying to make sense of these manuscripts and their chronology, one's initial impression is one of daunting complexity. The original sets are often by several copyists, and as already implied, revisions, additions, replacement parts, pasteovers, and corrections are frequent. Despite this complexity, however, careful study of the physical characteristics of the manuscripts, especially their papers and staving, reveals a fairly clear division between the original form of each manuscript and those portions added at one or more later dates. Still more important, the manuscripts fall into three fairly coherent groups that can be assigned at least relative chronological positions. Two of these groups may be further divided into intentionally overlapping subgroups.[11] The following discussion begins by outlining what philosophers would call a *logical* order of these groupings, based on

---

[9] Friedrich Walter, *Archiv und Bibliothek des grossh. Hof- und Nationaltheaters in Mannheim 1779–1839* (Leipzig: S. Hirzel, 1899), 1:448. Unfortunately, it is not possible to determine from Walter's phraseology whether all or merely some of the Holzbauer masses were to be sent to Munich. The issue is further confused by Walter's reference to this rescript in his *Geschichte des Theaters und der Musik am Kurpfälzischen Hofe* (Leipzig: Breitkopf & Härtel, 1898), 354 (n. 1 to p. 313), which states that Dalberg was asked to send *one* Holzbauer mass in addition to the opera. Because the document in question (formerly Mannheim, Theaterarchiv, F XII, 2) was destroyed in World War II, it does not appear that this discrepancy can be resolved with certainty; possibly a search of Walter's *Nachlass*, which is in the Mannheim Stadtarchiv, would clarify the issue. A printed copy of *Günther von Schwarzburg* is in fact extant at the Bayerische Staatsbibliothek; this is presumably the one sent by Dalberg. According to a "Kurzer Lebensbegriff des Herrn Ignaz Holzbauer, kurpfälzischen Kapellmeisters," originally published in *Pfälzisches Museum* 1/5 (1783): 460–77, and reprinted in Walter, *Geschichte*, 356–61, and *Denkmäler deutscher Tonkunst* 8 (1902), pp. v–vii, Holzbauer's widow was in possession of a large number of his works (including 21 masses and a total of 205 symphonies and concertos), which she hoped "ein grosser Fürst" would buy.

[10] Walter, *Archiv und Bibliothek*, 1:448, and *Geschichte*, 354 (n. 1 to p. 313), citing an electoral rescript of 9 May 1783 (formerly Mannheim, Theaterarchiv, F XII, 1).

[11] On the principle of division into flexibly overlapping groups and subgroups as a means of dealing with the chronology of undated works (or here, sources), see Eugene K. Wolf, *The Symphonies of Johann Stamitz: A Study in the Formation of the Classic Style* (Utrecht: Bohn, Scheltema & Holkema, 1981), 76–77. In the present case the order of the manuscripts within each subgroup is *not* intended to be chronological.

shared characteristics, then proceeds to consider to what extent that order can also be deemed *genetic* or chronological.

Table 4:1 presents a somewhat simplified version of the information supplied in Appendix A/II, now arranged according to the groups and subgroups proposed here. The first of these groups shows considerable unity. The papers employed are, like that of both the subsequent groups, mainly Blum 5 and Heusler 5, often used together in the same manuscript.[12] In addition, there occur two earlier Blum papers, Blum 1b and 3; a second Heusler paper, Heusler 7 (the paper of the Falgera ballet scores discussed in the previous chapter, its only appearance among the Holzbauer masses in Munich); and one Dutch paper, van der Ley 1. The copyists are the usual Mannheim scribes 1, 2, and 6,[13] plus one appearance each of Mannheim 7 and 9 and of Johann Cramer, who adds a part at a later date to App. A/II/12.

As regards the staving of these sources, perusal of column 5 of table 4:1 indicates that the original parts to these manuscripts make frequent use of one or another version of rastrum 12:8. At a more detailed level, the concept of logical order is helpful in dividing this group into subgroups. In the first two of these subgroups, the rastra employed for the original parts are interlocking; that is, each contiguous manuscript contains an example of precisely the same rastrum (not just 12:8, for example, but 12:8a). Thus in subgroup 1a the otherwise unique rastrum 6:1 occurs in most of App. A/II/5 and then again in one part of A/II/2. Likewise, in subgroup 1b, rastrum 12:8a—also present in the second manuscript of subgroup 1a, App. A/II/2—is found in the original set of A/II/12 (dated 1763) and in one part of A/II/6. And finally, the remaining parts of the latter manuscript were lined with rastrum 12:8c, which is also found in much of A/II/3, the last work in subgroup 1b. The final two manuscripts in group 1, making up subgroup 1c, are miscellaneous sources included here mainly because they employ papers similar to those of the rest of the group (note especially the presence of Blum 3 in both A/II/16 and 12) and, like A/II/3, one-stave rastra (all different, however); they might also be placed in a separate group entirely. In addition to the parts just discussed, three of the masses of group 1 have parts added at a later date on paper lined with the rastrum 12:10b—in one case copied by Johann Cramer, who would not have begun copying until the late 1760s (he was born in 1749 and would thus have turned eighteen in 1767; his official appointment dates from 1770 [see Appendix D]). This rastrum, also found in group 3 (see below), is clearly later, appearing in several Vogler manuscripts of the mid-to-late 1770s.

Group 2 continues to utilize both Blum 5 and Heusler 5 papers (though the former now predominates); the only departures are the cover and paste-ons of

---

[12] See Appendix B for a full description of the papers mentioned here.

[13] Bush, *Holzbauer*, 131, 363, considers the parts to App. A/II/5 by the copyist designated here as "probably Mannheim 1" to be by a different (new) copyist.

Chapter 4

Table 4:1 Manuscripts of Holzbauer Masses in the Bayerische Staatsbibliothek, Munich

Group 1 (mainly before 1763)

Subgroup 1a

No.[a]	MS	Paper	Staving	Copyists
5	D-Mbs, Mus. Ms. 2293	Blum 1b (most); Heusler 5 (SA/R), Blum 5 (va., b.), latter four parts all added later	2 x 6:1 (most); 12:10b (SA/R, va., b., later)	Mh. 9, prob. Mh. 1 (most); Mh. 6 (SA/R), Mh. 2 (va.), Mh. 8 (b.), all later; Holzbauer (numerous additions and alterations)
2	D-Mbs, Mus. Ms. 2290	Heusler 5 (most); Heusler 7 (hns. alto, added later)	12:8d (most); 2 x 6:1 (BR II); 12:8a (hns. alto, added later)	Mh. 1-2 (most); Mh. 7 (vns. through "Cum sancto spirito"); at least 3 other copyists; Holzbauer (numerous corrections and additions)

Subgroup 1b

12	D-Mbs, Mus. Ms. 2300	Blum 5, Heusler 7, Heusler 5, Blum 3	12:8a (most, orig. set); 12:10b (SR, b. rip, trs., timp., also sinfonia in all parts; all added later)	Mh. 1-2 (orig. set); Johann Cramer (SR); Mh. 5 (added sinfonia, b. rip, trs., timp.); Holzbauer (numerous additions)
6	D-Mbs, Mus. Ms. 2294	Heusler 5, 7	12:8c (most), 12:8a (TR)	Mh. 1
3	D-Mbs, Mus. Ms. 2291	van der Ley 1 (SATB/C, va., obs., hns., org.; all smaller); Heusler 5 (rest)	12 x 1 (van der Ley paper); 12:8c (STB/R, vns., cb./vc., bn.); 12:10b (AR, later)	Mh. 6 (van der Ley parts, AR), Mh. 1 (remaining parts), Holzbauer ("Sinfonia tacet" in Gloria of SR, TR)

Subgroup 1c

10	D-Mbs, Mus. Ms. 2298	Blum 5, Heusler 5	12 x 1 (most); 12:10d (AR, later)	Mh. 6
16	D-Mbs, Mus. Ms. 2306 (2 hns. only)	Blum 5, 3	12 x 1	Mh. 2

118

Music of Ignaz Holzbauer

Group 2 (1760s [ca. 1765?] to early 1770s)

Subgroup 2a

8	D-Mbs, Mus. Ms. 2296	Blum 5	12:7a (most); 12 x 1 (hn. 2)	Mh. 8 (most), Mh. 2 (hn. 2), Holzbauer (numerous corrections)
1	D-Mbs, Mus. Ms. 2289	Blum 5	12:7b (SATB/C, obs., trs., timp., org.); 12:7a (strs., bn.); 1 + 12:7a + 1 (STB/R); 12:10b + 1 (AR, prob. added later	Mh. 1-2
15	D-Mbs, Mus. Ms. 2305	Blum 5 (SATB/R, strs., bn.), Heusler 5 (rest)	12:7b (SATB/R, vn. 2, va.), 12:10b (vn. 1, b., later), 12:7d (bn.); 12 x 1 (remainder)	Mh. 6 (both papers), Mh. 2-3 (Blum paper only), Holzbauer (several additions)
13	D-Mbs, Mus. Ms. 2301	Blum 5, Heusler 5 (most); German, ?J. M. Bach 1 (paste-overs); Knöckel 1 (orig. cover)	12:7d (orig. set); 12:10b (additions by Mh. 6); 12:10a (Kyrie and Gloria of vrns.)	Mh. 2 (orig. set); Mh. 6 (added Kyrie and Gloria of most parts; hns., trs., timp.); Johann Cramer (Kyrie and Gloria of vrns.); Holzbauer (many changes and additions, some cover labels)

Subgroup 2b

4	D-Mbs, Mus. Ms. 2292	Blum 5 (most); Blum 6 (hns. *alto*/trs., added later)	12:7c (most); 12 x 1 (hns. *alto*/trs., later)	Mh. 2; Holzbauer (Kyrie and Gloria of hns. *basso*, numerous minor additions and corrections); Mh. 8 (rest of hns. *basso*)
9	D-Mbs, Mus. Ms. 2297	Blum 5 (most), Heusler 5 (SA/R, vn. 2, later)	12:7c (most), 12:10b (SA/R, vn. 2, later)	Mh. 1-2 (most), Mh. 6 (SA/R, vn. 2, later), Holzbauer (paste-on in ob. 1)

Subgroup 2c

7	D-Mbs, Mus. Ms. 2295	Blum 5, Heusler 5 (most); Heusler 2 (org.)	12:7e (most), 12:10b (vn. 1, b., later); 12 x 1 (org.)	Mh. 2 (most), Mh. 6 (vn. 1, b.); Mh. 1 (org.); Holzbauer (alterations in Kyrie)

119

Chapter 4

Group 3 (ca. 1770–1778)

11	D-Mbs, Mus. Ms. 2299	Blum 5 (Kyrie and Gloria of all parts), Heusler 5 (remainder)	12:10b	Mh. 2, Johann Cramer (Kyrie and Gloria); Holzbauer (last 2 pp. of org., some additions); Mh. 6 (remainder)
14	D-Mbs, Mus. Ms. 2721	Blum 5 (most), Heusler 5 (dupl. vn. 1)	12:10b	Mh. 2 (most), Johann Cramer (vns.), Mh. 6 (dupl. vn. 1), Holzbauer (added word "moderato" in Credo of most parts)

[a] Number in Appendix A/II, taken from the (nineteenth-century) labels on the manuscripts.

A/II/13, on Palatine paper, the added horn *alto* parts of A/II/4, and the organ part of A/II/7, on early Heusler 2 paper. Mannheim 1–2 and 6 again carry out most of the copying, the only new copyists being Mannheim 3 and 8, neither of whom turns up elsewhere in these manuscripts. Once again the interlocking staving of these manuscripts provides the best means of grouping them. In subgroup 2a, rastrum 12:7a appears in the original set of App. A/II/8 and then in about half the parts of A/II/1; rastrum 12:7b appears in most of the remaining parts of the latter manuscript and again in A/II/15; and rastrum 12:7d appears in one part of the latter manuscript and in the original set of A/II/13. Similarly, most parts of the two manuscripts making up subgroup 2b are on paper lined with rastrum 12:7c. Appendix A/II/7 forms a "subgroup" all its own in that it is the only manuscript containing rastrum 12:7e. As in group 1, several of these sources have added parts containing rastrum 12:10b, probably prepared at about the same (later) time as those of group 1.

It is precisely the use of the rastrum just mentioned, 12:10b, together with the presence of Johann Cramer as an integral copyist (i.e., not just a copyist of parts added after the fact) that distinguishes our third and final group. This group of only two manuscripts may also serve to introduce the question of the chronological relationship of the various groups, for it is obviously the latest of the three: not only does it contain Johann Cramer's hand, but as already noted, its lone rastrum, 12:10b, is found in Vogler manuscripts of the mid-to-late 1770s.[14] The manuscripts of this group may therefore be assigned conservatively to the period ca. 1770 to as late as 1777/78.

At the other end of the spectrum, group 1 must certainly be considered the earliest of the three. First, it makes fairly extensive use of two early papers, Blum 1 and 3. Second, App. A/II/12 actually contains a date of 1763, the only one in these manuscripts, interspersed between the abbreviation of the Jesuit motto, "Omnia ad majorem Dei gloriam" (see fig. 4:1). Third, various versions of rastrum 12:8, found in four of these seven manuscripts, appear elsewhere in manuscript parts dated 1753–57.[15] And finally, a manuscript concordant with App. A/II/6, from Oettingen-Wallerstein, may well date from 1754.[16] Hence, we may conservatively assign

---

[14] See the listing in Appendix C. Rastrum 12:10b is also found in a duplicate soprano ripieno part to a Grua mass composed in 1766 (App. A/IV/2); this added part probably dates from the 1770s, too.

[15] See rastra 12:8b and e in Appendix C. Rastrum 12:8a, found in the original parts to App. A/II/12 (dated 1763), the added horn *alto* parts to A/II/2, and the tenor ripieno part to A/II/6, also occurs in the violin 1c part (only) of Grua's mass App. A/IV/1. Though the remaining parts to that manuscript are from 1757, they are on different paper with different staving, and the violin 1c part may therefore well be a later addition (perhaps from the early 1760s). In any event, it is not useful for the dating of rastrum 12:8a.

[16] See chap. 9, fn. 4 and related discussion. The manuscript may actually have been sent to the count of Oettingen-Wallerstein by Holzbauer.

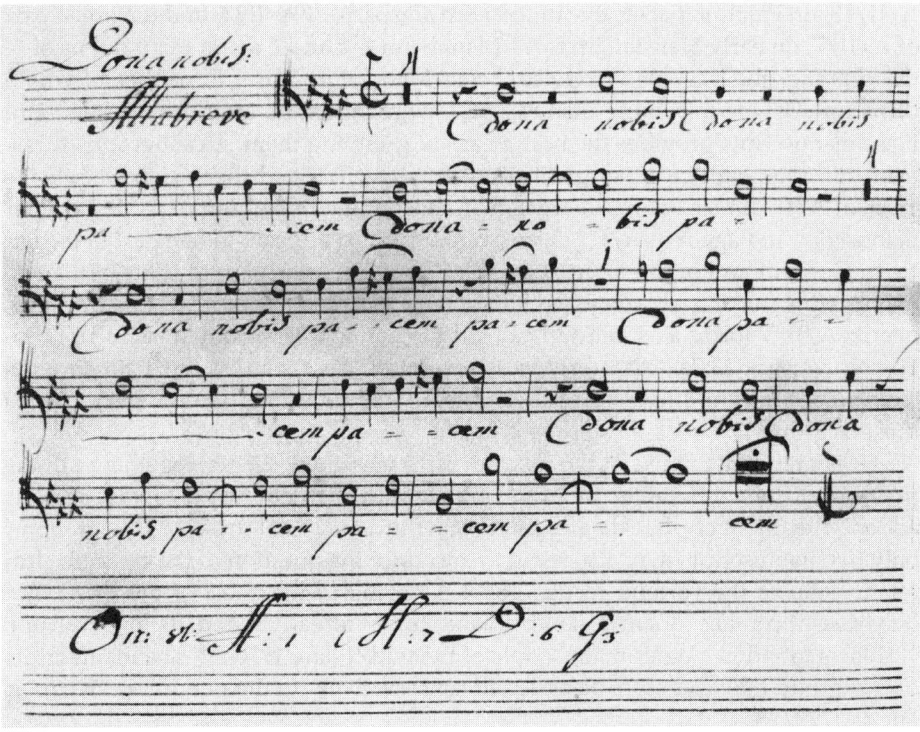

Figure 4:1. Ignaz Holzbauer, Mass in A (App. A/II/12), tenor, last page, showing date of 17 October 1763 ("18: 8b: 1763") interwoven within the abbreviation of the Jesuit motto "Omnia ad majorem Dei gloriam." The copyist is Mannheim 2.

the group as a whole to the years before and after 1760—as early as 1753, the year of Holzbauer's arrival at Mannheim, to at least 1763, the date found in App. A/II/12.

Within this group, it seems likely that subgroup 1a antedates subgroup 1b, given the use in the original set of App. A/II/5 of an early Blum paper. An uncharacteristic, unique rastrum such as 6:1, found in both manuscripts of subgroup 1a, would also be more likely to appear early than late. One more bit of evidence is the fact that the horns *alto* of the second manuscript of subgroup 1a, App. A/II/2, which have clearly been added at a later date, appear on the same paper as the main set of the first two manuscripts in subgroup 1b, indicating that the *original* set of A/II/2 was copied at an earlier date. As regards the remaining two manuscripts, one can say only that the two horn parts that are all that is left of the original source for the mass App. A/II/16 might belong with subgroup 1b owing to its use of Blum 3 paper, also found in App. A/II/12 of 1763.[17]

Although group 2 clearly provides the chronological link between groups 1 and 3, the only direct evidence for its chronology is either unhelpful or somewhat equivocal: (1) the existence of App. A/II/15 in an earlier version in a manuscript in Göttweig monastery dated 1764;[18] (2) the presence in two of these manuscripts of the hand of Mannheim 1, who—if he is indeed Jacob Cramer—died in 1770; and (3) the presence in one of them of the hand of Jacob Cramer's son Johann, who as noted above would not have begun copying until the later 1760s. A somewhat anomalous feature is the presence in the organ part of App. A/II/7 of the early paper Heusler 2; either a small batch of left-over paper has been used, lined with a one-stave rastrum, or an older part has been retained if and when the manuscript was recopied. In sum, group 2 as a whole might date from anywhere in the 1760s through the early 1770s, although most of its manuscripts would seem to fall in the second half of the 1760s.

Autograph Scores

Sources for four other works by Holzbauer remain to be considered in this chapter, all autograph scores from his Mannheim period: the oratorios *Betulia liberata* and *Il giudizio di Salomone* (of which only part 1 survives), the German opera *Günther von Schwarzburg*, and the cantata *Adulatrice corde sonore* (see App. A/II/17–21 for details concerning the papers, staving, and hands involved).[19] The first of these works, *Betulia liberata* (App. A/II/17), presents a fairly unified picture from the codicological standpoint, the main irregularities being the presence of two arias and the B section of a third copied by Mannheim 5, who also copies most of the recitative texts. As usual, Holzbauer has made many corrections and additions, in both his score and the portions by Mannheim 5.

The most interesting aspect here, however, relates to the chronology. Here again paper and especially rastrology provide the firmest evidence. As this score does not bear a date, it has always been associated with the performance of Holz-

---

[17] This accords well with the 1766 date of a manuscript of the Credo of this mass in CZ-Bm (Sign. A.18.944, from the monastery of St. Thomas in Brno); see Schmitt, *Kirchenmusik*, p. lxxvii (under no. 26), and Bush, *Holzbauer*, 376 (referring to her manuscript I35a, p. 333).

[18] See Schmitt, *Kirchenmusik*, p. lxxviii (no. 30 is the earlier version, no. 31 the later, i.e., that found in the Munich source); Bush, *Holzbauer*, 358–60 (A11 is the early version, A11a the later).

[19] Another Mannheim manuscript of a large-scale work by Holzbauer, his "azione dramatica" *La morte di Didone* (Mannheim, Nationaltheater, 6 July 1779; D-B, Mus. ms. 10782), is not included here because it dates from the period after departure of the court for Munich. The score is on Blum 6 paper lined, rather sloppily, with a one-stave rastrum. The copyist is Mannheim 6, who seems therefore to have remained behind in Mannheim.

bauer's *Betulia liberata* that was known to have taken place in 1760.[20] But the specific rastrum (10:25a) that is used to rule folios 5–8, all the recitatives except the first, and all the arias is one that is clearly identified with the early 1770s, not with 1760: it is found in Vogler's ballet *Le Rendez-vous de chasse*, dated 17 May 1772 (App. A/IV/1), and in five Cannabich symphonies that also date from about that time (App. A/II/39–41, 43, and 45).[21] The twelve-stave rastrum used to line the choruses is associated with the 1770s, as well.[22] This manuscript must therefore represent a newly prepared score of the *revised* version of this oratorio that was performed at Mannheim in 1774,[23] not the original form—which was itself probably related to a *Betulia liberata* of Holzbauer's supposedly performed in Stuttgart in 1752 and thus even more out of date.[24]

The other Holzbauer oratorio, *Il giudizio di Salomone*, is dated 1765 in the Vienna score (App. A/II/18), of which only part 1 remains.[25] Unlike *Betulia liberata*, it is all in Holzbauer's hand, and shows much more evidence of revision than does that score. For example, the bifolio making up pages 91–94 is a sewn-in revision of an accompanied recitative that was evidently itself a revision pasted into the original (it is now separated); and a further revision has been pasted onto page 92 of the sewn-in revision. The paper and staving of at least the sewn-in section are helpful in establishing a date for this revision, as the same rastrum, 10:8b, appears in Cannabich's Symphony no. 42, which can be dated ca. 1772 (see App. A/III/42).[26] Several other revisions can also be linked with the 1770s: (1) half a page pasted onto page 104, and the final chorus and its wind parts (pp. 165–74, 176–78), both with

---

[20] See Walter, *Geschichte*, p. 366, no. 107, and also fn. 23 below.

[21] A different form of this rastrum, 10:25c, is found as early as 1766, but the form used in *Betulia liberata* is clearly the later one.

[22] The specific form of this rastrum, 12:2b, occurs only in the added final chorus and a paste-over of Holzbauer's *Il giudizio di Salomone* (App. A/II/18), both probably from the early 1770s; the related form 12:2a is found in numerous manuscripts of the period 1776–78 (see Appendix C).

[23] Walter, *Geschichte*, 186, also p. 367, no. 141. Neither the score nor the 1774 libretto mentioned by Walter is any longer in the Theaterbibliothek collection of the Reiss-Museum in Mannheim; a libretto of the 1760 version is located in the Universitätsbibliothek Heidelberg. Holzbauer's *Betulia liberata* was also known in Vienna, where it was performed at a Lenten academy in 1761; see Daniel Heartz, *Haydn, Mozart and the Viennese School, 1740–1780* (New York: W. W. Norton, 1995), 54, and Howard E. Smither, *A History of the Oratorio*, vol. 3: *The Oratorio in the Classical Era* (Chapel Hill, N.C.: University of North Carolina Press, 1987), 75. The libretto is in B-Bc, a score thereof in A-Wn. Smither points out that the aria forms of the Munich score of *Betulia liberata* (no full da capo arias, a full range of altered da capo types) would be exceptional for a work of 1760 but not of the 1770s, supporting the view presented here that that score must date from 1774.

[24] The 1752 date is taken from Haberkamp and Münster, *Hofkapelle*, 92.

[25] Librettos exist for both a 1765 and a 1766 performance of *Giudizio di Salomone*; see Schmitt, *Kirchenmusik*, p. xci.

[26] The same paper and rastrum are also found in the smaller paste-ons on pp. 147–48. The paper of the paste-on of p. 92 was lined with a five-stave rastrum unique to this study.

the same paper and rastrum as cited above in the revisions to *Betulia liberata* (rastrum 12:2b); and (2) paste-ons between pages 2–3 and on the last page (26) of the sinfonia, lined with a rastrum (10:8b) also found in two insertion arias in Holzbauer's hand in Salieri's *La secchia rapita* of 1774 (see App. A/VI/151). All these revisions may therefore reflect changes made for an as-yet undocumented performance in the early 1770s.

The third Holzbauer autograph in Appendix A/II is easily dispensed with: it is the aria "Non si turba" (App. A/II/19) that had originally appeared on pages 43–66 of the score just discussed, that to Holzbauer's *Giudizio di Salomone* in Vienna. It was itself originally an addition, matching the paper and staving of the sewn-in addition of pages 91–94 described above. It was removed from the score and landed first in the autograph collection of Aloys Fuchs,[27] then in that of Charles Malherbe, whence it came to the Paris Conservatory and finally the Bibliothèque nationale de France.

The most important recent discovery in the field of Mannheim studies was made in 1997 by Dr. Bärbel Pelker of the Forschungsstelle *Mannheimer Hofkapelle* in Heidelberg. While working in the Hohenlohe-Zentralarchiv in Schloß Neuenstein, she noticed a leather-bound three-volume set that turned out to be the autograph score to Holzbauer's German opera *Günther von Schwarzburg* (1777; App. A/II/20, from the collection of Schloß Bartenstein). As the score did not appear in the catalogues of the archive, it had never been studied, even by those who—like myself—had worked in Neuenstein. Although a fair copy of *Günther* by the Mannheim copyist Johann Cramer exists in Berlin (see App. A/VI/26), possession of the original autograph is invaluable both for establishing the text and for tracing the evolution of the work by studying revisions that may be present in the score.

Revisions are indeed numerous in the newly discovered score, all but a few of which are in Holzbauer's hand. These are beautifully reproduced, and are discussed in detail, in the sumptuous facsimile edition that has recently appeared.[28] As this edition includes a detailed discussion of the score, suffice it to say here that two principal papers (Heusler 5 and 7) and two rastra (10:8a and 11a) alternate freely throughout, the main exception being a paste-over in Holzbauer's hand in act 3, scene 5, which was ruled with rastrum 10:6. These papers and rastra are just what one would expect in a Mannheim manuscript of the period 1776–77.

---

[27] The aria is listed in Richard Schaal, "Die Autographen der Wiener Musiksammlung von Aloys Fuchs," *Haydn Yearbook* 6 (1969): 86.

[28] Ignaz Holzbauer, *Günther von Schwarzburg: Singspiel in drei Aufzügen*, ed. Bärbel Pelker, Quellen zur Musikgeschichte in Baden-Württemberg, 1 (Munich: Strube Verlag, 2000). By carefully studying the various revisions the editor has been able to reconstruct the original version, the version performed at the premiere on 5 January 1777, and the version later published by Holzbauer (Mannheim, [1777]). The full score of the final version appears as vol. 1 of the facs. ed., the extensive commentary and the reproductions of the original version, revealed when the paste-overs were removed, in vol. 2.

Chapter 4

A nice, though less spectacular, discovery of the present study was that a little-known Holzbauer cantata in the Pretlack collection now in Berlin was in fact a Holzbauer autograph (see App. A/II/21).[29] Though undated, this manuscript can easily be shown to stem from the mid-1750s, just after Holzbauer's arrival in Mannheim: the paper is similar (but not precisely identical) to that found in Grua's *Memento domine* of 1753 (App. A/I/12), and the rastrum of the ten-stave portion matches that found in a symphony of 1756 by Franz Xaver Pokorny (D-Rtt, "Bernasconi" 4), the paper of which Pokorny very probably obtained in Mannheim while studying there in 1754.[30]

---

[29] The manuscript is catalogued in Joachim Jaenecke, *Die Musikbibliothek des Ludwig Freiherrn von Pretlack (1716–1781)* (Wiesbaden: Breitkopf & Härtel, 1973), 181. For a full discussion of the Mannheim manuscripts in this important collection, which date mainly from the 1750s and 1760s, see chap. 9.

[30] See Pokorny's amusingly illiterate letter of 4 February 1754 to his employer, the prince of Oettingen-Wallerstein, printed in Ludwig Schiedermair, "Die Blütezeit der Öttingen-Wallerstein'schen Hofkapelle," *Sammelbände der Internationalen Musikgesellschaft* 9 (1907/8): 119. Pokorny states that a ream of *Regalpapier* (the *real* size described in chapter 2) cost 32 gulden.

Chapter 5

Orchestral Music of Christian Cannabich in Munich
(App. A/III/1–73, M1–7)

In collaboration with Jean K. Wolf*

The most substantial single collection of manuscripts to be treated in this study consists of orchestral works at the Bayerische Staatsbibliothek by Christian Cannabich (1731–98), Johann Stamitz's successor as concertmaster at Mannheim and from 1778 until his death director of instrumental music in Munich. These manuscripts include parts in oblong quarto format for sixty-three different symphonies, two *symphonies concertantes*, two pastorales, a *Symphonia pastorale*, a *Concerto alla pastorale*, and four other works labeled "concerto." These are listed in Appendix A/III, the symphonies and *symphonies concertantes* in one numbered series, the remaining works in another designated by the letter *M* (for "Miscellaneous").[1] Each of these works with the exception of the clavier concerto (Mus. Ms. 3984, unnumbered in App. A/III because it stems from Munich) has a blue-grey cover on which is pasted a label with a printed catalogue number. These numbers indicate that the Cannabich manuscripts previously belonged to the Bavarian court, for they correlate with the numbers in a handwritten catalogue of material transferred from the Munich *Hofmusikintendanz* to what is today the Bayerische Staatsbibliothek on 11 October 1860.[2] However, as we shall see, the great majority of these manuscripts actually

---

* Portions of this chapter initially appeared in Eugene K. and Jean K. Wolf, "A Newly Identified Complex of Manuscripts from Mannheim," *JAMS* 27 (1974): 387–95. Used with permission. Most of the original research for that article on the Munich archives and on the Cannabich and other works at the Bayerische Staatsbibliothek was carried out by Jean K. Wolf, whose indispensable contributions to the present study I gratefully acknowledge.

[1] Works copied in Munich are included in Appendix A/III both for the sake of completeness and to provide a basis for comparison with the Mannheim portions of the series. Despite the implication to the contrary in Jan LaRue, "Symphonie," *MGG* 12 (1965): 1822, all the symphonies in this group are unquestionably by Christian Cannabich. However, D-Mbs, Mus. Ms. 1826, a cantata catalogued under his name until recently, is by his son Carl (1771–1806). So is the "Ouverture a 15" in C published by Hugo Riemann in DTB, 8/2 (1907), as a work of his father.

[2] The catalogue is entitled "Beilage zum Hofmusik-Intendanz-Bericht vom 4ten August 1860. Loc. III im könig: Hoftheater" and is found in the Bayerisches Hauptstaatsarchiv München, Staatstheater Sammlung 13514. The title indicates that until 1860 the manuscripts were housed in the court theater (presumably the Hof- und Nationaltheater, not the Residenztheater [the so-called Cuvilliés-Theater]). See also Appendix A/III, fn. a.

originated in Mannheim. The circumstances thus parallel almost precisely those of the Holzbauer manuscripts discussed in the previous chapter.

A striking feature of the symphonies and *symphonies concertantes* in this series is that each bears a number in ink on its title page. Except for several omissions and occasional discrepancies, these numbers run consecutively from 2 through 73.[3] In addition, on most of the manuscripts from Cannabich 21 onward the original ink number has been crossed out and replaced by a lower number in brown crayon, an attempt to compensate for the missing numbers.[4] The original ink numbers are given in column 1 of Appendix A/III, and all references to Cannabich's symphonies in the present study employ these rather than the "revised" numbers, generally in the form "Cannabich 2" (= App. A/III/2).

It was originally proposed by Heinrich Hofer, who carried out the first extended study of the Cannabich symphonies, that the title-page numbers denoted the chronological sequence in which the works were written.[5] Hofer was able to validate his theory by demonstrating that nearly half of these symphonies also appeared in printed versions whose dates corresponded approximately to the numerical order of the manuscripts. Many of Hofer's dates can now be fixed more accurately, and a few dated sources unknown to him have also come to light. Moreover, we now have a whole new body of chronological evidence about these manuscripts, adduced through the application of modern techniques of manuscript study. The results in all cases support Hofer's hypothesis.

Another fact cited by Hofer to bolster his theory was the existence in Vienna of what was presumed to be an autograph score of a Cannabich symphony, dated 1794 (four years before the composer's death; App. A/III/73a). This score bears the number "73," the same number found on the orchestral parts in Munich (App. A/III/73b). The work, which lacks a finale in both sources, is therefore Cannabich's last symphony. A second important correlation between score and parts escaped Hofer's attention, however: the handwriting and paper of the two sources

---

[3] Two of the pastorales (M5, M3) and the Concerto alla Pastorale (M4), all relatively early works, bear the numbers 74–76, respectively. Because these numbers are in a different hand than the others and appear to have been added well after the fact, they will be disregarded here.

[4] See Wolf and Wolf, "Complex," 436, for an example of this procedure. On the title page of Cannabich 21, the first symphony of the series with the new numbering, the unknown writer first crosses out "21" and then writes "neu . . . 20," making up for the fact that no. 20 was missing from the series. Four earlier works that are now lacking in the set, nos. 1, 5–6, and 10, were either still present at that time or, more likely, their absence was overlooked or disregarded by the writer.

[5] Heinrich Hofer, *Christian Cannabich: Biographie und vergleichende Analyse seiner Sinfonien* (diss., Munich, 1921), 83–84. Hofer is inconsistent in his use of the ink and crayon numbers to establish chronology, causing unwarranted confusion. As already stated, all references in the present study are to the ink numbers. This has the added advantage of showing where gaps in the numbering occur (presumably because symphonies have been lost).

are identical.⁶ Furthermore, this same hand appears more or less extensively in over two-thirds of the Cannabich manuscripts in Munich. Comparison of the handwriting with that of two letters from Cannabich, written by a scribe but signed by the composer,⁷ shows that it is in fact Cannabich's. This conclusion receives confirmation from the presence of *mano propria* signs attached to several of the signatures in this hand on the manuscripts themselves (e.g., App. A/III/31, 52, 63).⁸ Positive identification of Cannabich's hand establishes for the first time that these manuscripts are a mixture of autograph parts and authentic copies, greatly increasing their significance. It also adds new substance to Hofer's explanation of the title-page numbers, for a comparison of the handwriting establishes that most of the numbers were actually written by Cannabich himself.⁹

Types of Parts: Original, Duplicate, Added, Replacement

Detailed study of the Cannabich sources in Munich reveals them to be exceptionally complex, reflecting a long and convoluted history of production. Most of these manuscripts include portions copied at a minimum of two different times—for example, a set of parts from Mannheim with a new title page copied in Munich—and many of them contain parts that the evidence shows to have been copied at three, four, and even five different times. The challenging task for the scholar faced with such manuscripts is twofold: first, separation of the individual manuscripts into their various codicological groupings or "levels," and then, to the extent possible, association of each level with an approximate chronological period by means of comparative studies. Needless to say, the latter goal is greatly facilitated—not to say made feasible at all—in the Cannabich symphonies by his use of a chronological numbering system.

Original parts. In dealing with sets of parts, one must seek to distinguish between *original* parts and subsequently prepared *duplicate, added,* or *replacement* parts. For

---

[6] See Wolf and Wolf, "Complex," 435–37 (Appendix D, "Christian Cannabich's Handwriting," with additional reproductions); Jean K. Wolf, ed., *The Symphony at Mannheim: Christian Cannabich*, vol. C/III, part 2 of Barry S. Brook and Barbara B. Heyman, eds., *The Symphony, 1720–1840* (New York: Garland Publishing, 1984), 320–21.

[7] Munich, Bayerisches Hauptstaatsarchiv, HR I, Fasz. 464/Nr. 253. The first letter is dated 6 February 1779; the second, though undated, was answered on 31 January 1790 and thus was probably written earlier that month (for purposes of identification, the second letter begins "Euer Churfürstliche Durchleucht haben die höchste Gnade gehabt . . . "). Reproductions of the pertinent signatures appear in Wolf and Wolf, "Complex," 435–36.

[8] See, e.g., Wolf and Wolf, "Complex," 435.

[9] The two numbers from Cannabich 73, clearly in the hand of the composer, are reproduced in Wolf and Wolf, "Complex," 435–36.

the Cannabich symphonies, the "original" parts are those copied shortly after the work was composed, the time of composition being designated relatively by the Cannabich numbers (2–73) and absolutely when other evidence can be brought to bear. It is likely that most of the original parts in the Munich series were copied directly from Cannabich's autograph score, which at Mannheim generally remained in the possession of the composer.[10]

Identification of members of the original set proceeds by a combination of intrinsic and extrinsic (comparative) evidence. Evidence intrinsic to the series ranges from knowledge about what parts are likely to be doubled or require replacement, and what such parts tend to look like, to the construction of an internally consistent hypothesis about the entire series of original parts, one that accounts satisfactorily for the differences that are evident as one proceeds from work to work. In the latter case, as will become more than obvious in the detailed discussion below of the chronological groupings proposed here,[11] the amount of data is so extensive and so complex for the Cannabich symphonies that one could probably fashion an entirely convincing hypothesis based only on evidence internal to the series. To use a metaphor introduced earlier, the puzzle could simply not be made to fit together in any other way.

Fortunately, it is unnecessary in the case of the Cannabich symphonies to rely overly on intrinsic evidence, with its ever-present potential for circularity: as shown in the previous chapters, a good deal of dated and firmly datable material from Mannheim exists, providing a useful basis for comparative chronological studies. Moreover, even undated material can have chronological significance: demonstration that a part by a known Mannheim copyist stems from Munich, for example, places it with virtual certainty in the period after 1778. As it turns out, exhaustive comparative studies to be described in the following section show that there is no reason at all to doubt that the majority of these parts are in fact original; the only major difficulties come in what is labeled here as group 2, in which the complexity of the manuscripts sometimes obscures the distinction between original parts and those prepared later. This conclusion has two important corollaries: (1) that the changing codicological characteristics of the *original* parts correlate with Cannabich's numbering and are chronological, and (2) that, partly as a result, the original parts from the earlier segments of the series unquestionably originated in Mannheim.

Several of the issues just raised, namely the reciprocal relationship between intrinsic and extrinsic evidence and its use in identifying the original parts of a manuscript, may be illustrated by considering a seemingly mundane problem of handwriting. The copyist Mannheim 4 (see Appendix D) is the most important of

---

[10] See chap. 1, fnn. 47–48 and related text.

[11] I divide the Cannabich series into five chronological groups, based primarily on codicological characteristics; see the section "Chronological Groups," below, and also fn. 17.

Cannabich's copyists during the 1770s, appearing in most of the symphonies from number 38 through the Munich copy 58B and two other copies of no. 59 (see below). What is immediately intriguing about this scribe is that he employs, at first glance seemingly at random, two readily identifiable types of treble clef, one consisting of two graphemes, the other of one:

Two-stroke type　　　　　　　　　　　Rounded type

The former type appears consistently in Cannabich 31 (strings only) and all but two symphonies of the series from Cannabich 38 (vn. 1 only) through Cannabich 51, while the latter appears in two parts of the much earlier work Cannabich 21, most of the remainder of Cannabich 38, and in Cannabich 42, 48 (one page only; see fn. 12, below), 53–55, and 58B. Given the importance of Mannheim 4, and also the intricacy of the manuscripts in question, it would obviously be very useful to know the chronological significance, if any, of this particular variation in his handwriting. Yet no dated manuscripts by him have yet been discovered, and thus we turn to other types of proof.

To begin with evidence from the Cannabich series alone, careful examination of the various parameters of the manuscripts shows that the appearance of the rounded type of clef in Cannabich 21, 38, and 42 always occurs in conjunction with precisely the same papers and staving as that found considerably later in the series, in Cannabich 52–55 and 57. (For details, see Appendix A/III and the discussion of group 3, below.) At this point temporal asymmetry, in the form of Cannabich's chronological numbering, comes to our aid. Obviously, only two explanations of the above situation are possible, assuming that Cannabich's numbering is legitimate: either (1) Mannheim 4's parts to Cannabich 21, 38, and 42 were copied at approximately the same (later) time as Cannabich 52–57, probably as replacements for lost or damaged originals, or (2) they were copied earlier, most likely at the time represented by their numbering in the series (i.e., that they are original parts of the original set). But the third possibility, that the parts to Cannabich 53–55 and 58B by Mannheim 4 were copied *earlier* than their numbers might indicate—that is, at the time represented by Cannabich 21, 38, and 42—can be dismissed (again assuming the correctness of the numbering); if we know nothing else, we know that the codicological characteristics cited in Cannabich 52–57, including the use by Mannheim 4 of a rounded clef in his contributions to these manuscripts, were manifest at the (late) date represented by those numbers. They may also have occurred earlier—that is still to be dealt with—but they were definitely present later.

At this stage it should be clear that a decision regarding Cannabich 21, 38, and 42, with their use of a rounded clef in conjunction with paper and staving found in Cannabich 52–57, rests on the likelihood or not that all these elements (handwriting, paper, staving) would have remained precisely the same for a period as extended as that signified by Cannabich 21 through 57. Obviously, that likelihood is small, given that the works in question (21, 38, etc.) are not at all contiguous in the numbering of the symphonies and that these elements changed constantly with time in the demonstrably original parts of the series. It is clearly more reasonable to conclude, at least tentatively, that Mannheim 4's parts to these symphonies are what we shall refer to below as *replacement* parts, prepared at about the same time as Cannabich 52–57, not parts from the original series. Our initial hypothesis would thus be that the two-grapheme clef represents Mannheim 4's early form, present in original parts to most of Cannabich 39–51,[12] while the rounded clef is a later form found in Cannabich 53–55, 58B, and certain replacement parts to earlier symphonies evidently prepared at about the same time.

In support of this view it may be added that, as already mentioned above, Mannheim 4 also employs the rounded form of clef in two copies by him of the still later symphony Cannabich 59, the one in the Fulda collection at the Library of Congress, the other in the library of the count of Schönborn-Wiesentheid (D-WD),[13] thus extending his use of this form still further in the numerical series and demonstrating his overall consistency at this period.

The converse of the above theory would be that Mannheim 4's parts to Cannabich 39–51 (those with the two-grapheme clef) were all copied in Munich *after* the time represented by Cannabich 52–59. While this is obviously unlikely, it is not impossible. Arguing against any such reversal, however, are such intrinsic factors as the clear succession of codicological elements (paper, staving, other hands) in Cannabich 39–51 and their equally clear and logical connection with earlier and later symphonies, together with their total lack of any of the immediately recogniz-

---

[12] The only anomaly occurs in Cannabich 48, in which p. 1 (only) of the first violin part utilizes the rounded clef. The copyist may have begun the manuscript by experimenting with the new clef type, then temporarily abandoned it before taking it up again in Cannabich 53. It may be noted that in speaking of Mannheim 4's *original* parts with two-grapheme clefs I begin with Cannabich 39, not 38. This is because the violin 1 part to Cannabich 38, the only part to this symphony with the two-grapheme clef, is on paper lined with rastrum 10:21, which is otherwise found only later in the series, in Cannabich 48–50. Hence, that part is itself probably a later replacement, not an original part of the series. Likewise, the string parts to Cannabich 31, though still employing the earlier (two-stroke) clef, are definitely later than their apparent position in the series, being associated chronologically with the manuscripts of group 3 (especially Cannabich 39–40; see below).

[13] US-Wc, M 1001.C22P [No. 3] Case; D-WD, Mus. 912. I am grateful to Dr. Frohmut Dangel-Hofmann (Würzburg) for facilitating my study of the latter manuscript, one of a group of four late Cannabich symphonies (nos. 57–59 and 61 [D-WD, Mus. 913, 911–12, and 910, respectively]) copied in Munich.

able traits of the Munich copies (Bavarian papers, use of two- and three-stave rastra, etc.; see below, groups 4–5).

We can also appeal to certain extrinsic evidence, namely the watermarks and staving of other manuscripts definitely from Mannheim. Comparison with those manuscripts shows beyond any doubt that Cannabich 39–51 date from approximately the last decade in Mannheim and that, with a few exceptions, they were copied in order (see group 3, below). In sum, we can consider most of Mannheim 4's contributions to these works (39–51), like his contributions to the later symphonies, original rather than replacement parts. We can even proceed to use his handwriting as chronological evidence, the presence of the two-grapheme clef indicating an earlier date than the rounded form. Incidentally, precisely the same kind of analysis can be applied to the hand of Cannabich himself as well as that of Mannheim 3, and with the same results—that is part of the "extrinsic" evidence cited above. Indeed, for Cannabich the argument is even stronger, for we know the characteristics of his hand all the way through Cannabich 73 in 1794, only four years before his death.

Duplicate parts. Duplicate parts or *Dubletten* are usually violin or bass parts prepared for use by additional stands of players. These were typically copied from a previously prepared part and may date from about the same time as the original set or some time thereafter. In the latter case they may signal an increase in the size of the ensemble, for example addition of a fourth stand of violinists.

At Mannheim, original and duplicate parts were often indicated by the use of roman numerals (I, II, etc.) added after the part title (see figs. D:4 and 11–13); this practice can be observed in manuscripts like those of Vogler in Darmstadt (D-DS) and Grua in the Munich Frauenkirche collection (now D-FS) that have preserved their duplicate parts.[14] Although the Cannabich manuscripts at Munich have not retained their duplicates, which were probably discarded when they came into the possession of the Bayerische Staatsbibliothek (see below), one can frequently recognize that a part was originally a duplicate by the presence of a roman numeral *II* or *III* (sometimes altered to *I* to show its place in the extant set). Even when no roman numerals are present, one can often tentatively identify a part as originally having been a duplicate by the fact that the copyist or paper is different from that of the rest of the manuscript.

In the Cannabich series in Munich, the frequent presence of parts that were initially copied as duplicates—the originals, alas, having later been discarded—is a principal source of the complexity noted earlier in these manuscripts. Whereas the full set of parts might originally have appeared quite straightforward, with, say,

---

[14] For a full discussion of these numbers and their significance with respect to orchestral size see Eugene K. Wolf, "On the Composition of the Mannheim Orchestra, ca. 1740–1780," *Basler Jahrbuch für historische Musikpraxis* 17 (1993): 131–38.

the primary parts by one copyist, duplicate violin parts by a second, and a duplicate bass part by a third, the manuscript as it comes down to us may preserve only the viola and wind parts of the original, the remaining parts being by the two "duplicate" copyists. Indeed, one must be sensitive to this possibility even when no overt indication that parts might originally have been duplicates is present. In general it may be said that identifiable duplicates in the Cannabich manuscripts tend to date from the same time as the original parts, that is, that they were all copied more or less simultaneously as part of a set. In such cases I shall normally refer to the originals and duplicates together as forming part of the "original" series of Cannabich manuscripts, to distinguish the latter from substantially later additions and replacements.

As already stated, full duplicate parts for the Cannabich symphonies in Munich apparently existed into the nineteenth century, for in Cannabich 46 the anonymous individual responsible for altering the original Cannabich numbers in brown crayon has also added the roman numeral *IV* after the part titles of both violin parts, using the same brown crayon (see fig. D:13). In other words, at that time the violin parts in question were the fourth of the set. Just what that time was is unclear, but it was almost certainly after Cannabich 73 of 1794, the number of which has been altered along with those of the rest of the series (rather, those manuscripts from Cannabich 21 on). One's best guess regarding the disposal of the duplicates would be that they were discarded in the previously mentioned process of transferring the manuscripts from the Munich *Hofmusikintendanz* to the Staatsbibliothek in 1860, including the music of Holzbauer discussed in chapter 4. It is worth noting that duplicates are often in somewhat better shape than originals, and someone intent upon condensing the manuscripts who did not know the difference might well have retained them and tossed aside the (more valuable) originals.

In some cases, however, it seems probable that a splitting off of the duplicate parts took place even in the eighteenth century. For example, in Cannabich 12 only the two violin parts, marked "II," are by Mannheim 3 at an early date; the remainder of the manuscript, by the same copyist, is late, probably from the Munich period. What may have happened was that a second manuscript of this symphony was desired, which was produced by taking two duplicate violin parts from Cannabich 12 and recopying the remainder. Similarly, in Cannabich 13 the violins and cello alone (i.e., among the most usual candidates for duplicates) are from the original series, the remainder being later. Here it is especially revealing that the violins originally bore the mark "III," which has then been altered to "I" by erasing the latter two characters; a nineteenth-century librarian in the process of discarding duplicate parts would hardly have bothered. (Support for this statement comes from the fact that the majority of such roman numerals have not been altered.) Alternatively, of course, the remaining parts could have been damaged or lost, but this seems less likely given that so many parts are involved; this is not the common case of an instrumentalist borrowing a part and forgetting to return it.

Added parts. Supplemental parts not present in the original version are fairly frequent in these symphonies. In a minority of cases these are truly new parts, for example the Orchestra II trumpet and timpani parts of Cannabich 44, which were written in Munich, and the very late oboe parts to Cannabich 57, which are not present on the title page. Such parts do not generally alter the basic character of the work, of course. Indeed, the lack of true revision in these symphonies is rather striking.

More common are added parts that merely split a previously dual part into two—a viola or even "Due Viole" part that becomes viola 1 and 2,[15] a bass/cello part that separates the cello. These new parts rarely contain any significantly new material; they are comparable to later duplicates, and may once again represent an expansion in performing forces in the later works.

Replacement parts and sets. The most important category of later additions to these sources comprises the recopying of parts subsequent to the original preparation of the manuscript. Such replacement of parts, already noted on several occasions, may affect anything from title pages alone to entire symphonies. (In the latter case I refer to "replacement sets" rather than parts.)

In many instances the process of replacement is obvious and presents no difficulty, as the new title page or part stands out prominently from the rest of the manuscript. On other occasions, though, only a comprehensive and detailed knowledge of the entire series of manuscripts can permit one to say with any certainty that a given part came into existence at a later date than that indicated by its "Cannabich" number. As already implied in the discussion above of the copyist Mannheim 4, the procedure involves careful comparison of every relevant parameter of the manuscript, especially handwriting, watermarks, and staving; the assumption, which happens to be supported by knowledge of the original series, is naturally that the greater the similarity of these elements between two parts or groups of parts, the more likely those parts are to have been copied at about the same time. It might be pointed out here that the traditional method of making such comparisons, utilizing only handwriting and watermarks, gains greatly in power when combined with rastrology, which is far more precise and objective in showing resemblances. As already noted, the most difficult problems in dealing with potential replacement parts arise in the works of group 2 (Cannabich 16–38); in some of these symphonies the proportion of parts that seem to have been recopied is high enough as to produce uncertainty as to what—if anything—belongs to the original series.

There are several possible explanations for the large percentage of replacement parts and sets in the Cannabich series in Munich. The most obvious is the usual wear and (literally) tear that affect orchestral parts over the years. The nu-

---

[15] See the description of this process in fn. 21, below.

merous new title pages prepared by Cannabich in Munich bear witness to this process; as covers, they are the most likely to be damaged, especially in the course of reshelving. In addition, as every orchestral librarian knows, parts do have a habit of disappearing, often as a result of borrowing by the performers. In the case of the Cannabich series, an aggravating factor in both damage and loss must have been the move to Munich in 1778, which necessitated selecting, packing, and shipping that portion of the music collection required for use there. Parts lost or left behind in the process would then have been recopied from Cannabich's autograph scores or from other parts.

Transfer of the court to Munich may also provide a different kind of explanation for some of these replacements. We have already noted that certain of these manuscripts seem to retain only parts that were originally duplicates, the remainder being newly copied replacements. Going a step farther, there are numerous other examples in this series of substantial and even complete replacement of a manuscript, again as already mentioned. Because many of these fall in the period just before and after the move, it seems reasonable to suggest that the elector may have wished to make some provision for the *Kapelle* left behind in Mannheim, which would have needed a performance library of its own. The musicians remaining in Mannheim had access to the music that was purposely left behind for their use,[16] but Cannabich's music naturally accompanied him to Munich. Thus, some of the replacements could have taken place when portions of the original set of parts were removed to produce a new set for the Mannheimers. This could also have happened in the period after the court arrived in Munich, though here the explanation of damage or loss in transit would appear to be the more probable one in most instances.

None of the above explanations seems sufficient, however, in the case of the manuscripts of group 2, for here the codicological evidence shows that the numerous replacements often occurred long before 1778, as we shall see. As will be discussed in more detail below, one possible explanation for the confused situation might be Cannabich's several sojourns in Paris during precisely this period, after which the rate of replacement declines markedly.

Chronological Groups

The Cannabich symphonies and miscellaneous instrumental works (M1–7) in Munich can be divided for purposes of discussion into five chronological groups.[17]

---

[16] See chap. 1, fnn. 55–60 and related text; chap. 4, fnn. 9–10 and related text.

[17] The groupings proposed here differ somewhat from those in J. Wolf, ed., *The Symphony at Mannheim: Christian Cannabich*, pp. lii–lv, mainly because of the greater stress in the present chapter on classifying and rationalizing the physical evidence presented by the manuscripts. I rely heavily upon that discussion, however, especially for its correlations of physical evidence with bio-bib-

Each of these groups shows relative cohesion from the codicological standpoint, and each can be correlated approximately with events in Cannabich's life and the life of the court. They are:

Group 1: Cannabich 2–15, M1–M4, M5 (?) (ca. 1755–1761/62)
Group 2: Cannabich 16–38, M6 (?) (ca. 1762–68)
Group 3: Cannabich 39–55, M7 (ca. 1769–78)
Group 4: Cannabich 56–61 (first Munich symphonies, fall 1778–ca. 1781/82[?])
Group 5: Cannabich 62–73 (ca. 1781/82[?]–1794)

Group 1 (Cannabich 2–15 [nos. 1, 5–6, 10 missing from series], M1–M4, M5 (?); ca. 1755–1761/62)

The earliest group of Cannabich symphonies, like the latest, presents a relatively uncomplicated picture: it consists predominantly of parts from the original series (or duplicates done at about the same time), plus clearly later additions and replacements made by the important copyist Mannheim 3, very probably in the early Munich period.

Even a superficial glance is enough to identify the original parts within this group of manuscripts. In contrast to the later additions by Mannheim 3, the earlier parts look well-used and rather dirty, their paper has yellowed somewhat, and their ink tends to be light brown (or more faded) rather than the near-black of the additions. As can be seen in Appendix A/III, the principal copyists are the important early copyist Mannheim 1, whom I consider to be Jacob Cramer, and Mannheim 3 in his early phase (see Appendix D). In addition, Mannheim 10 and 11 write most of Cannabich 8 and 14, respectively, in the latter case the only known appearance of this copyist. A second major copyist, Mannheim 2 (Johann Lochner?), furnishes the bass part of Cannabich 4 and (with the exception of the finale of the violin 2 part, by an unknown copyist) both violin parts of Cannabich 8; these were probably originally duplicates, the remainder of the original sets being by a single copyist. This is particularly apparent in Cannabich 8, in which the parts were each originally marked with the roman numeral "II," of which the second digit has been erased to make "I."

The paper of the original portions of these manuscripts relates them unambiguously to the 1750s and early 1760s. Through Cannabich 8 two early types stand

---

liographical material in order to determine date. As with all discussions of periodization, the boundaries chosen here are not absolute but are dependent upon one's goals, and they are to a certain extent arbitrary. In the present instance, a good case can be made for adopting my wife's extension of group 1 to include Cannabich 16–18, as these works show certain affinities with the later manuscripts of group 1, Cannabich 11–15 (see table 5:1, below, and Appendix A/III). Likewise, certain characteristics of group 2 overlap into group 3 (see table 5:2).

out. The first, found all the way through Cannabich 18 (from group 2), is a paper without watermarks that is almost certainly Swiss in origin (see the paper "Swiss [no WM]" in Appendix B/I/3). This paper also occurs among the earliest Johann Stamitz manuscripts in Regensburg, probably dating from the period 1755–60 (see chap. 9). Unusually precise chronological evidence is provided by the sporadic appearances in Cannabich 4 and 7–8 of a second early type, Blum 1, a paper for which a number of dates in the 1750s exist (see Appendix B): the versions of this watermark found in Cannabich 4 and 7–8 come close to those of an anonymous mass of 1757 attributed to Carlo Grua (App. A/IV/1) and to two violin parts added in 1756 to Grua's *Memento domine* of 1753 (App. A/VI/144)—but *not* to the watermarks of the main set of the latter work, which match those of the autograph score of 1753 (App. A/I/12).[18] Watermark evidence thus tends clearly to link Cannabich's earliest symphonies, through number 8, with the mid-to-late 1750s. As we shall see, this conclusion receives support from other quarters as well.

The two most prolific papers of the Cannabich manuscripts, Heusler 5 and Blum 5, appear for the first time in Cannabich 4 and 8, respectively. The second of these papers, produced in Basel between 1756 and 1788 by Hieronymus Blum III (see Appendix B), occurs initially alongside the early Blum paper discussed above, Blum 1. Thereafter the early type disappears, presumably replaced by the more resplendent Blum 5 type. Presence of the latter paper also lends support for a terminus ad quem in the early 1760s for this group of works, as the various forms of this paper in Cannabich 14 resemble those of two masses by Ritschel and Holzbauer, both dated 1763 (App. A/I/1, A/II/12).

With regard to the staving of group 1, the majority of these parts have been lined with a ten-stave rastrum, though paper ruled ten times with a one-stave liner is also common, especially in copies by Mannheim 1. On one occasion a five-stave rastrum appears, used twice to make the usual ten staves.[19] Of the different ten-stave rastra found in the original sets, all occur in multiple copies that show a clear association with chronology (see table 5:1).

With one exception (the horn parts of Cannabich 13),[20] the added and replacement parts of these manuscripts are notably uniform, having been copied by

---

[18] However, the one example of twin B found in Cannabich 4 (bassoon, sheet 1) comes fairly close to the 1753 form, a form also found in a Pokorny symphony dated 1756 in Regensburg (D-Rtt, "Bernasconi" 4); Pokorny was in Mannheim in 1754 and may well have obtained this paper then (see chap. 4, fn. 30). The similarity to the 1753 form may be explained by the earlier chronological position of Cannabich 4 vis-à-vis Cannabich 7–8.

[19] See Cannabich 8. This rastrum turns up later in Cannabich 23–24; all these manuscripts were copied by Mannheim 10, who may have been the owner of the rastrum.

[20] The horn parts of Cannabich 13 are on Blum 5 paper. More significantly, Mannheim 3's hand in these two parts falls chronologically between the early hand of the original series being discussed here and the late one of the other added and replacement parts (in Cannabich 13, the viola, bass/title page, and flutes). Cannabich 13 is thus the only three-level manuscript in group 1, the violin

Table 5:1. Correlation of Rastra and Cannabich Numbers, Group 1.

No.	Rastrum	No. in Appendix A/III	Other manuscripts
1	10:28a	2	
2	10:15	3	App. A/VI/62, aria from Galuppi's *Siroe* (1754)
3	10:26b	4, 7–9	D-Rtt, "Bernasconi" (Pokorny) 5–6, dated 1757 (cf. fn. 18, above); Cannabich M1–3
4	10:28c	11–12	Cannabich 16 (group 2); Cannabich M4
5	10:24a, c–d	13	Cannabich 16, 18, M6 (group 2)
6	10:10	14–15	App. A/I/1, Ritschel mass (1763); App. A/II/18, Holzbauer *Giudizio di Salomone* (1765); Cannabich M5

Mannheim 3 on Heusler 5 paper. They consist mainly of title pages and their associated parts (doubtless replacements for damaged or lost originals), added second viola parts,[21] and—less easily rationalized—single viola and bass parts for two symphonies, Cannabich 8 and 15.

The dating of Mannheim 3's late additions to group 1 may also serve to demonstrate the utility of careful and comprehensive documentary study. From the standpoint of handwriting, the copyist's hand is clearly that of his late contributions to the original series of manuscripts, Cannabich 51–58A: in figure D:12 note the form of the clefs, the inconsistent slant, and the generally crotchety character of the late hand as compared with the early hand of figure D:11. Likewise, the watermarks match those found in Cannabich 49–61. Both these elements link the additions to approximately the second half of the 1770s.

However, the most precise and convincing evidence about the lateness of the added parts derives from a study of their staving. For example, the rastrum 10:29, found in added parts to Cannabich 12–13, appears elsewhere only in the following works: Cannabich 61 (from Munich); Cannabich 30, in parts copied by a known Munich copyist (here labeled Munich 1); and in one part to Vogler's *Deutsche Kirchenmusik* (1777; App. A/IV/24). A second rastrum, 10:27, found in added parts to Cannabich 8 and 12–13, occurs in Cannabich 57 (from Munich) and also in demonstrably late parts to Cannabich 21 by Mannheim 4.[22] Even the one-stave rastra

---

and cello (by Mannheim 1) belonging to the original early phase, the horns to a middle one, and the remaining parts to a late one (very probably Munich; see below).

[21] The process of addition is patent in Cannabich 15–16, in which the copyist (Mannheim 3, late hand) has changed the original designation "Viola" on that part to "Viola Prima" and then added a "Viola Secondo" part. The added parts of Cannabich 15–16 were probably done at the same time, as the new viola part of 16 is copied on the top half of the exact sheet of which the bass/cello part of 15 forms the bottom half.

[22] See the discussion of Mannheim 4's late hand in the previous section of this chapter, and also Appendix D.

of these parts tell the same tale. One is found in Cannabich 15 and then in 56 (from Munich), also in late parts to Cannabich 39. Another appears in Cannabich 7, 9, 12, and 14–16, then in the title page *cum* horn 2 part of Cannabich 30, again definitely copied in Munich. In sum, though one cannot completely rule out the late Mannheim period as the time these parts were recopied, the evidence leans strongly toward the first years of the Munich sojourn (i.e., ca. 1778–80). One can easily imagine a concerted effort to put the collection in order after the long and arduous journey.

Different from the manuscripts discussed to this point is the pair of symphonies Cannabich 12–13.[23] In these sources major portions have been recopied by Mannheim 3 during about the same late period as the added and replacement parts just discussed. But here the parts retained from the original series were *themselves* duplicates: in Cannabich 12 the two violin parts, the first marked "II" to indicate second stand, in Cannabich 13 the two violin and the cello parts, the former marked "III" (in the case of the second violin part, obviously by the original copyist, Mannheim 1). For these manuscripts an explanation such as that advanced in the previous section—for example, purposeful removal of the original primary parts for use elsewhere (perhaps Mannheim after 1778) and recopying of those parts for the Munich series—may be apposite.

Chronological conclusions. The evidence gleaned above from a study of the manuscripts, combined with bio-bibliographical data of various sorts, allows us to draw fairly firm conclusions about the dating of the Cannabich symphonies of group 1. As we have seen, rastra found in Cannabich 3–4 and 7–9 appear elsewhere in manuscripts dated 1754–57, and the watermarks of Cannabich 4 and 7–8 are also found in works of 1756–57. Cannabich is known to have studied with Jommelli in Rome ca. 1750–53, after which he accompanied the latter to Stuttgart; evidently he then went back to Italy (Milan).[24] The date at which he returned to Mannheim to take up permanent residency is not known for certain; at the latest, it would have been upon the death of Johann Stamitz in March 1757. Hence, it seems reasonable to date Cannabich's earliest symphonies from approximately the mid-1750s or slightly later.

At the other end of the spectrum, we have noted watermark and rastrological data that place Cannabich 14–15 as early as 1763. In this case, external bibliographical information provides us with a still more precise and also somewhat earlier dating. As it happens, all the extant symphonies in group 1 were printed in Paris but two, the one-movement works Cannabich. 2 and 11. (These symphonies in-

---

[23] On the added parts to Cannabich 13 see also above, fn. 20.

[24] This information and all subsequent biographical data on Cannabich are taken from J. Wolf, ed., *The Symphony at Mannheim: Christian Cannabich*, pp. xli–xlviii. See also Jean K. Wolf, "(Johann) Christian ... Cannabich," *New Grove*, 2d ed., 2:934–36.

clude a part for organ and thus would group more logically with the miscellaneous sacred *pastorale* works M3–5, to be discussed shortly.) The dates at which the various prints were advertised are strikingly early: Cannabich 3–4 and 9 were already announced in June through August of 1761, and Cannabich 12–16 and 18 in May through August of 1762.[25] In other words, unless there was some sort of delay in printing after the advertisements appeared, Cannabich 9 had already been composed by 1761 (July) and Cannabich 18 by 1762 (August). Hence, a date of 1761/62 seems appropriate for the end of this period (through Cannabich 15). Two related conclusions can be drawn from this dating: that Cannabich was quite prolific as a symphonist in the period after ca. 1755, averaging between two and three symphonies per year, and that he was aggressive in promoting his works in Paris early in his career.

Miscellaneous works (M1–5). Based on the information just presented about the symphonies of group 1, it is a simple matter to place five of the seven unnumbered miscellaneous orchestral works, M1 through M5, within Cannabich's early period or (in the case of M5) possibly slightly later. These manuscripts contain only one later paper (Blum 5), found in M5, a *Pastorale a 12*; the latter manuscript straddles the end of group 1 and the beginning of group 2. The remaining works, M1–4, are all on an early Heusler paper (Heusler 2) and the aforementioned Swiss paper without watermarks found only in group 1 and a few early works from group 2. The copyists are unremarkable except for the appearance in M5 of Mannheim 11, whose only other contribution is the main set of Cannabich 14, again linking M5 with the latter portion of this group. The staving also supports this dating, rastrum 10:10 occurring in Cannabich 14–15 and the Ritschel mass of 1763 (App. A/I/1). Slightly earlier might be the *Concerto alla pastorale* M4, whose rastrum (10:28c) matches that of Cannabich 11–12 and 16, while the use in M1–3 of various forms of 10:26 links those works with the first part of the period.

Both the ease and the confidence with which detailed knowledge of the various parameters of a manuscript allows us to date these works should not go unremarked. Knowing that these are early works allows us to conclude that Cannabich devoted substantial attention early in his career to instrumental music for the church: in addition to the one-movement symphonies with organ mentioned above (Cannabich 2 and 11), three of these miscellaneous works, M3–5, are some sort of pastorale, intended for performance at Christmas services.

---

[25] For details on these publications see the "Comments" column of Appendix A/III and the discussion and thematic catalogue in J. Wolf, ed., *The Symphony at Mannheim: Christian Cannabich*, pp. liii–lv, lxvii–lxix. Cannabich 17 was not printed until 1767, though it must have been composed by 1762, the date at which Cannabich 18 was advertised.

Chapter 5

Group 2 (Cannabich 16–38 [nos. 20, 26, 28, 33 missing from series], M6 (?); ca. 1762–68)

The rather neat and tractable disposition of parts in group 1, with its mostly original sets and easily distinguished later additions, largely collapses in group 2. (Lest the reader lose hope during the necessarily labyrinthian discussion to follow, s/he may wish to know that the subsequent groups return to a more straightforward approach.) The manuscripts of only five symphonies from this period, Cannabich 18, 23–24, 34, and 36, fall both predominantly and unproblematically within the original series (i.e., seem to have been copied at the time represented by their position in the numerical series).[26] The principal later accretions to these works are Cannabich's new title pages, written in Munich, for all but no. 18.

The majority of the extant parts from group 2, however, consist of copies made subsequent to the originals, or in many cases what would have been the originals if any were extant—in other words, copies made at a substantially later date than that signified by the Cannabich number of the symphony. Why this should be so remains unclear, though several possible explanations are presented at the end of this section. Easiest to deal with are those manuscripts (or portions of a manuscript) copied long after the original set, creating a decisive chronological gap. For instance, Cannabich 37 was entirely recopied by a familiar Munich copyist (Munich 1), obviously after the transfer of the court in 1778. In Cannabich 32 only the bass/cello part has been retained from the original set; the remainder is in Cannabich's late hand on paper from the Bavarian mill of Elias Kutter (see Appendix B/V). Similarly, only the flute and horn 2 parts to Cannabich 30 are likely to be original, the rest being by a Munich copyist and by Cannabich (late).[27] Other Munich contributions in this group include (1) the violins and viola of Cannabich 35, by a copyist we label Munich 2; (2) probably the violin 2 and viola parts of Cannabich 21 by Mannheim 4, as they are mostly on the same paper used by Mannheim 3 in his late additions to Cannabich 8 and 12–13 and by the composer himself in Cannabich 57 (all from Munich; rastrum = 10:27); and (3) the many new title pages for these manuscripts, generally on Bavarian paper.

Cannabich 27 poses a slightly more complex problem. Here the violins and bass are by Munich 1 writing on Kutter paper, the remaining parts by a second copyist who does not appear elsewhere in manuscripts known to me.[28] Two bits of

---

[26] For detailed information on these and other manuscripts not specifically discussed in the text see Appendix A/III.

[27] Consideration of the flute and horn 2 parts of Cannabich 30 as originals is based on the resemblance of their watermarks to those of manuscripts from the early 1760s; the staving (10 x 1) is of little assistance.

[28] In addition, the title page/cover of Cannabich 27 is written by a third copyist on thick beige *Packpapier* on the back of a discarded title page for a Haydn symphony dated 1787—an extreme ex-

evidence suggest Munich as the source for this latter group. First, the paper, Blum 6, was used in similar forms in Munich in 1780–82;[29] and second, the use of a two-stave rastrum and the copying style are more characteristic of Munich than of Mannheim.

Similar in approach to the above manuscripts, but more difficult to rationalize, are those in which substantial portions were evidently recopied *before*—sometimes well before—the move to Munich. Cannabich 19 and 25, for example, both disclose a majority of parts copied by Mannheim 3, on paper lined in the first case with a rastrum found primarily in Cannabich 45–52 (10:30a), in the second with a variant of the same rastrum found primarily in Cannabich 51–52 (10:30c). In the same way, most of Cannabich 38, the last symphony of this group, was copied by Mannheim 4 at about the same time as Cannabich 53–55, judging by the presence of his easily identifiable late hand and his use of paper lined with a rastrum identified with that period (10:20b). The first violin part to the same symphony is also by Mannheim 4, copied at a slightly earlier date than the other parts (unlike them, it uses his earlier clef form, for example). Yet as already mentioned in the discussion of this copyist's hand earlier in this chapter, this part may itself be a replacement part, for its staving is otherwise found only in the same copyist's parts to Cannabich 48–50 (rastrum 10:21). If this is true, Cannabich 38 as it now exists preserves *four* different levels of scribal activity: (1) original trumpet and timpani parts by Cannabich and Mannheim 14, on a typical paper of the period (Blum 5) lined with a one-stave rastrum and with penciled verticals to define the margins (this trait will be considered anew below); (2) Mannheim 4's first violin part, with staving linking it to Cannabich 48–50; (3) the same copyist's main set of parts, probably from still later in the Mannheim period, ca. Cannabich 53–55); and (4) Cannabich's new title page from Munich.

Cannabich 29 presents a more obscure picture. In this work the title page and oboe parts by Mannheim 3 are fairly late, the staving relating them to Cannabich

---

ample of late replacement. The same copyist and paper are found on the new title page of Cannabich 2, the earliest extant symphony in the Munich series.

[29] Blum 6 paper appears in portions of acts 1–2 of the original performing score of Mozart's *Idomeneo*, discovered by Robert Münster (D-M, Bayerische Staatsoper, Archiv, St. Th. 265), and in Salieri's *Semiramide* (Munich, 1782; D-Mbs, Mus. Ms. 2523). I am grateful to Dr. Münster for facilitating my study of the Mozart score. The watermark evidence is somewhat less conclusive than one would wish, however, as the same watermark (in variant form) was used in all the scores of works by Johannes Ritschel in Dresden (App. A/VI/120–38), which certainly antedate 1780. It also occurs in a bifolio and aria (the latter now removed; see App. A/II/19) originally inserted in Holzbauer's *Giudizio di Salomone* of 1765 (App. A/II/18); one of the two forms found in those additions comes close to twin A of Cannabich 27. In addition, twin B of Cannabich 27 resembles the watermark of a Fils symphony copied by one Franz Carl Stuckle in 1772 (D-KA [*olim* D-DO], Mus. Ms. 460), which in turn resembles the Mozart and Salieri versions. On the other hand, twin A of Cannabich 27 does not match the mark of a second manuscript of 1772 by the same copyist (ibid., Mus. Ms. 1482, a symphony by Ordonez); since it *does* match that of the Mozart and Salieri manuscripts, Munich still seems the most likely provenance for this portion of Cannabich 27.

39–45 (ca. 1770) and works of 1772 and 1774 (see rastrum 10:25a in Appendix C). The handwriting of Mannheim 3 supports this assignment, as well. Yet the remaining parts, mainly by Mannheim 4 but with horn parts by Mannheim 3, were also copied later than the number 29 would indicate, as evidenced again by the staving (rastrum 10:17a, in this particular variant closest to Cannabich 43) and the fact that Mannheim 4 is present at all—he first appears in the late 1760s at the earliest. Obviously, if the title page and oboe parts by Mannheim 3 were copied at a different, later time than the rest of the manuscript, as implied by the difference in staving and the handwriting in these parts, it was not a great deal later.[30] In any event, it is clear that the entire manuscript represents a later recopying of Cannabich 29; none of the original parts survives.

Such is probably the case for Cannabich 21, as well. This manuscript belongs to a small subgroup, including also Cannabich 30–31 and 34, that makes use of a paper (here for the second horn only) manufactured by Niklaus Heusler in Kandern, a town located near Basel in the former margraviate of Baden (Heusler 7); we have previously encountered this paper in ballet scores copied by Sigismund Falgera from ?1767–1769 (App. A/I/14–16) and in three Holzbauer masses (App. A/II/2, 6, 12). The watermark of the horn 2 part of Cannabich 21 matches that of 34 and the remaining original parts of 30 (flutes, horn 2), and its staving is also that of portions of 34 (rastrum 5:14b).[31] There is no reason to doubt that the violin 1, bass, flute, and horn 1 parts come from the same period in Mannheim as well, their staving (10:25c) also appearing in Cannabich 34, 40, and most of the wind parts of Toeschi's *Mars et Venus* of 1766 (App. A/VI/19). Thus all the parts mentioned seem to be substantially later than their position in the series as number 21 would indicate. Because Cannabich 21 was originally published (in 1766) as an orchestral trio,[32] we may speculate that the present version constitutes a somewhat later arrangement for full orchestra, copied at some point during the period represented by Cannabich 30–40 (ca. 1765–70) and the Toeschi ballet of 1766. As for the remaining parts, Cannabich 21 (and also 30) has already been mentioned as containing more-or-less extensive replacements from the late Mannheim or Munich period.

The most formidable problems in these manuscripts occur in a series of parts, often only one or two within a given work, by the copyists Mannheim 12–14. For these parts the evidence is generally either not very abundant or rather ambiguous—or both. Nonetheless, a congruence of various types of data leads me again

---

[30] Another wrinkle is that the horn parts by Mannheim 3 might have been written at a different time than the main set of parts by Mannheim 4; the principal rastrum, though the same, shows numerous conflicting irregularities (a characteristic of this rastrum in general, making it difficult to use for purposes of dating).

[31] Variant forms of this rastrum occur in one part to Cannabich 32 (rastrum 5:14a) and in Toeschi's *Mars et Venus* of 1766, tending to confirm the dating proposed above.

[32] *Six Sonates en trio qui sont fait pour exécuter à trois ou avec tout l'orquestre . . . nouvellement composées en 1766*, op. 3 (Paris: La Chevardière, 1766; *RISM* C 816), no. 4.

to conclude that all these parts belong to a somewhat later stage of manuscript preparation than that represented by their Cannabich numbers—in other words, that these parts are later replacements rather than members of the original series. One reason this conclusion must be stated somewhat tentatively is that in many of these cases the temporal distance between the original set and the apparently re-copied replacement parts does not appear to be as great as in the previous examples; obviously, the closer the two stages are in time, the more conceivable it is that a given rastrum or paper might have remained in use throughout the intervening period, despite the lack of direct evidence to that effect.

The principal members of this complex comprise various parts by the copyists Mannheim 12–15 to Cannabich 16–19, 31, 34–35, M6, and the later works 40–41 (the latter two symphonies from group 3, included here in order to show continuity). An initial clue that the parts by these copyists might be later than their numbering would imply comes from the chronological distribution of the copies: all but the last of these copyists, Mannheim 15, exhibit a pattern of early appearance in symphonies with Cannabich numbers in the high teens (plus Cannabich 22 for Mannheim 14), after which they reappear beginning only in the thirties (Cannabich 31, etc.; see table 5:2, below). The pattern for Mannheim 13 is especially striking. He first turns up in Cannabich 18, then only in Cannabich 35, 42, 44, and 52. But the gap is even greater than it first appears, for his parts to Cannabich 35 and 42 are obviously considerably later even than their numbers would indicate, making use of staving from Cannabich 51–53 (rastra 10:30c, 10:20a) and watermarks from the late Mannheim and even Munich periods. Mannheim 13's first "real-time" appearance in the series is in the double-orchestra symphony Cannabich 44, from ca. 1773.

That this pattern is not coincidental emerges from a consideration of other parameters of the manuscripts, primarily their staving. Table 5:2 shows all the appearances of the three most important rastra (one an unlabeled simple rastrum that recurs in three of these works) found in this specific complex of parts. In all these cases but 10:30e, the rastra appear first in Cannabich 16–19, then not again until a Cannabich number in the thirties. While a patterning of this sort could conceivably occur coincidentally, a simpler and more plausible explanation would be that the earlier-numbered parts were copied at about the same time as the later.

Various types of evidence may be cited in support of the latter hypothesis. In the first place, all the parts just listed are on the same paper, Blum 5; this fact tends to support the assumption that these parts form a complex copied not too far apart chronologically. Unfortunately, the watermarks of this particular paper are not generally useful for purposes of precise dating. In the present case, fairly close resemblances occur to marks from as early as 1763 and as late as 1774.

A second characteristic linking some of these manuscripts is the use in the third subgroup in table 5:2, those lined with the one-stave rastrum, of penciled verticals at the beginning and often the end of the set of (individually drawn) ten staves; this practice is otherwise rare at Mannheim. Two other places where it does

Table 5:2. Correlation of Rastra and Copyists, Groups 2–3.

No.	Rastrum	No. in Appendix A/III[a]	Copyists
1a	10:30b	17	Mannheim 4 (early hand)
"	10:30b	31	Mannheim 4 (early hand)
"	10:30b	M7 (group 3)	Mannheim 4 (early hand)
1b	10:30d	17	Mannheim 3 (middle hand), 12
"	10:30d	19	Mannheim 14
"	10:30d	31	Mannheim 12
"	10:30d	41 (group 3)	Mannheim 1, 12
1c	10:30e	M7 (group 3)	Cannabich (middle hand), Mannheim 13, 16
2	10:25c	17	Mannheim 12
"		34	Mannheim 15
"		40 (group 3)	Mannheim 14
3	One-stave rastrum, penciled verticals	16	Mannheim 12
"	Same one-stave rastrum, penciled verticals	18	Mannheim 13
"	Same one-stave rastrum, penciled verticals	M6	Mannheim 3, 15

[a] From group 2 unless noted.

occur help to prove the rule: the trumpet and timpani parts to Cannabich 38, by Cannabich and Mannheim 14 (already mentioned in passing), and pages 1–2 of the flute and oboe obbligato parts to the concerto M6 by Mannheim 15. The paper is again Blum 5, but lined with a different one-stave rastrum than that listed in table 5:2. As the latter copyist (Mannheim 15) is found only in Cannabich 34 and M6, we can again show an association with Cannabich 30–40 both for use of this particular paper and format and for the complex of manuscripts as a whole.

As final indicators that these parts all date from the period of Cannabich 30–40, Mannheim 3's hand in Cannabich 17 and 21 resembles his hand in symphonies from that period,[33] and Mannheim 12's hand in Cannabich 16 resembles his hand in Cannabich 41. Incidentally, if the bassoon part for Cannabich 19 by Mannheim 14 was copied at about the same time as Cannabich 30–40, as proposed here, then so, probably, were his and Mannheim 1's violin parts for Cannabich 22. These parts employ a rastrum, 10:32, found elsewhere only on pages 1 and 4 of the bas-

---

[33] It should be recalled that Mannheim 3 is one of the most prolific copyists of the Cannabich series; we have examples of his hand spanning the entire period from Cannabich 2 to 58.

soon part of Cannabich 19; the rastrum of pages 2–3 is that also used in most of Cannabich 41 and elsewhere (10:30d).

For the sake of clarity let us now consider a concrete example of the pattern of distribution just discussed. Cannabich 17 is a manuscript containing contributions by three main copyists, Mannheim 3–4 and 12, plus the bassoon part by Mannheim 1 and also the title page copied by Cannabich in Munich. All the evidence points to the period ca. 1770 for the preparation of all but the latter two items (the bassoon part cannot be dated and could be the only original part in the manuscript) rather than the early 1760s, as implied by its number in the series. (The very next work, Cannabich 18, had already been published in Paris by August 1762.) With respect to the copyists, for instance, Mannheim 4 is inherently later, his first original copies coming in the late 1760s at the earliest, while the hand of Mannheim 3 in this manuscript is that of his middle period. The third copyist, Mannheim 12, turns up elsewhere only in the other work of this pair, Cannabich 16 (violin 2, bass/cello, horn 2/title page), and then again only in Cannabich 31 and 41. The staving of Cannabich 17 is still more explicit: that found in Mannheim 4's parts (rastrum 10:30b) precisely matches that of Cannabich 40, while that of Mannheim 12's viola 1 and Mannheim 3's trumpet and timpani parts (10:30d) precisely matches that of (again) Cannabich 41. Finally, the staving of Mannheim 12's cello/bass, flute, oboe, and horn parts (rastrum 10:25c) is later found in Cannabich 34 and (yet again) 40.

To give another illustration, all of Cannabich 31 would seem to postdate the period at which number 31 should fall, approximately the mid 1760s. Of the wind parts, all by Mannheim 12, the oboes utilize staving found in Cannabich 41 and later additions to 17 and 19, as seen already in table 5:2 (rastrum 10:30d). The horn parts, obviously written at about the same time, employ a different rastrum, 10:17b. As it happens, this precise rastrum is found in three dated or datable manuscripts: the two Falgera ballet scores of 1769 (App. A/I/14–15) and Richter's motet *Super flumina Babylonis*, completed by January 1768 (App. A/IV/10b). Moreover, the watermark of the horn parts, Heusler 7, closely matches that of the 1769 scores—but *not* that of the same paper when it appears in the later horn 2 part of Cannabich 21 and in Cannabich 30 and 34 (i.e., copies from the mid-1760s). The string parts to Cannabich 31, by Mannheim 4, also date from a later period: their staving appears in Cannabich 40 and 44 (rastrum 10:30b), and the watermark is easily identifiable as a late form of Heusler 5. Hence, the entire manuscript, with the exception of Cannabich's still later title page, would seem to date from ca. 1769–70, approximately the period of Cannabich 40–41. Alternatively, the string parts by Mannheim 4 could fall chronologically between Mannheim 12's winds and Cannabich's title page.

There is persuasive circumstantial evidence, then, that the parts to Cannabich 16–19 and 31 by Mannheim copyists 12–14 are considerably later than their Cannabich numbers would indicate, possibly falling between about Cannabich 34 and 41, that is, the period of ca. 1767–73. A more abstract argument can be brought to bear, as well. As the foregoing discussion has shown, these manuscripts belong to a specific source complex. It is striking that none of the four principal copyists of this complex, Mannheim 12–15, *ever* appears in conjunction with demonstrably early staving or on early paper; one can always show that a nominally early form also occurred later in the series. Viewed slightly differently, one would expect that, if these parts were in fact members of the original series and not later copies, they would at *some* point share the paper and staving of the original series of manuscripts; but they do not. Rather, they belong to their own discrete complex.

The one manuscript that seems at first glance to go against these assertions is M6, a *Concerto a 12* for flute, oboe, and bassoon that has already been touched upon several times in passing. This complicated manuscript does in fact mix certain early elements with several of those found in our present (later) complex, namely Mannheim 15's hand, use of the two one-stave rastra with penciled verticals, and so on. But a closer examination reveals that the parts of this manuscript generally fall into the usual two groups, with the contributions by Mannheim 1 and Cannabich (other than the cadenza) associated with earlier paper and staving (rastrum 10:24a–d, found in original parts to Cannabich 13, 16, and 18), the contributions by Mannheim 15 with later (e.g., the two one-stave rastra found in Cannabich 38–39). Yet one copyist does "cross over" from one group to the other, writing on both types of paper: Mannheim 3. Fortunately for our theory, however, his hand is noticeably later in the contrabass/violoncello part, on the (allegedly) later paper. Thus, the dichotomy in his handwriting provides a final bit of support for the claim that the complex in question was copied—or rather recopied—substantially later than the placement of the Cannabich numbers would indicate.

Chronological conclusions. The date of composition of group 2, as opposed to the date at which individual parts were copied, can be determined with some precision owing again to the publication of the majority of these works in Paris. Most telling is the appearance of Cannabich 31–32, the last of Cannabich's symphonies to be printed in Paris, in La Chevardière's op. 4 of 1766 (advertised in October of that year).[34] The staving of about half of Cannabich 34 (rastrum 5:14b) provides a nice confirmation of this date, for it is the same as that of the "violino di repetizione" part of Toeschi's *Mars et Venus*, also of 1766 (App. A/VI/19). A dating of ca. 1766–67 for Cannabich 34, a "Sinfonia concertante" featuring violin, cello, oboes, and bassoons, makes it perhaps the earliest known work in this genre actually to bear the title.[35] The remaining works in this period, Cannabich 35–38, though not pub-

---

[34] Again, see Appendix A/III and the thematic catalogue in J. Wolf, ed., *The Symphony at Mannheim: Christian Cannabich*, for full information on the prints mentioned.

[35] See Barry S. Brook and Jean Gribenski, "Symphonie concertante," *New Grove*, 2d ed., 24:809–10.

lished, would reasonably fall within the next few years. A conservative estimate for the end of the period might therefore be ca. 1768.[36]

The date of no later than 1766 for Cannabich 32 means that Cannabich increased his production of symphonies somewhat during this period: if the first works of group 2, Cannabich 16–18, stem from ca. 1762 (16 and 18 were published in that year), then the composer averaged somewhat over three per year. It is not difficult to find a reason for this accelerated output, namely Cannabich's several trips to Paris during this period, for which he would have needed new compositions. He is known to have journeyed there in 1764 and 1766 (when he met the Mozart family, incidentally), and consistent publication of his works beginning as early as 1760 strongly suggests that he was there even earlier.[37]

Cannabich's Parisian sojourns also supply one possible rationale for the extensive recopying noted in this period. Thus, he might have composed works in Paris that would not be copied in Mannheim until somewhat later; he might have taken along parts from the Mannheim performance library for use in Paris that had to be replaced; or he might have had parts copied for his use in Paris that eventually ended up in the present Munich collection. However that may be, the symphonies of the post-Parisian period show much greater consistency from the codicological standpoint.

Another rationale for at least some of the extensive recopying carried out while still in Mannheim might be the fact that from ca. 1768 Carl Theodor and Elisabeth Auguste maintained separate residences during the long summer season, he at Schwetzingen, she at Oggersheim, both with active musical agendas; it is not out of the question, though it is entirely speculative, to suggest that at this period certain manuscripts might have been split into two to furnish material for the two *Kapellen*, with recopying as necessary of those parts removed from the original. Why this should be so for this period alone is a question that cannot be answered at this time.

---

[36] This estimate also takes into account the very likely date of 1771 or early 1772 that we have for the *symphonie concertante* Cannabich 42 (see group 3, below). If Cannabich 32 dates from 1766 and Cannabich 42 from 1771–72, the composer averaged less than two works per year during this period, again placing Cannabich 38 in about 1768 or 69. Needless to say, we have no proof of how consistent Cannabich's production of symphonies was during this period. It might be pointed out, however, that his rate of production between Cannabich 42 in 1771–72 and Cannabich 55 of ca. 1778 was similar.

[37] Cannabich's first published symphony was La Chevardière's *Simphonie périodique* no. 5 (*RISM* C 821), advertised in June 1760. This work, DTB G-2/Wolf W 8, was no doubt one of the missing numbers 1, 5–6, or (less likely) 10 in the Munich series.

Chapter 5

Group 3 (Cannabich 39–55, M7; ca. 1769–78)

The manuscripts of group 3, encompassing approximately the final decade of the court's residence at Mannheim, display a far more consistent pattern of preparation than those of the preceding group. By contrast with that group, most of these parts belong to the original series of manuscripts, with only scattered examples of later recopying of the type so ubiquitous just before.

The principal characteristic of this group is the near-omnipresence of the copyist Mannheim 4, who appears in all of these symphonies but Cannabich 44 and 52.[38] If all the previous appearances of this copyist involve later replacement parts, as argued in the previous section, then his first copies within the original series occur in Cannabich 39, thus neatly defining the beginning of this period. Other important copyists are Cannabich, Mannheim 3, and Mannheim 13. In addition, Cannabich 40 and 41 bring the last copies by Mannheim 1 (probably Jacob Cramer, who died in 1770) and Mannheim 12 and 14; it was the latter two copyists, it may be recalled, who together with Mannheim 13 figured so prominently in the discussion of subsequent recopying of parts in the previous section. Now they at last appear, like Mannheim 4, as copyists of original (rather than replacement) parts and at the "proper" numerical positions in the series.

The watermarks and staving also show notable consistency throughout this period. Only two papers occur within the manuscripts of the original series: Blum 5 (found for the last time in Cannabich 48 and 54) and Heusler 5. The staving of the original series exhibits great uniformity, as well: with the exception of one part from Cannabich 39, it utilizes ten-stave rastra exclusively. Only four principal rastra occur (all but the last in multiple variants; see table 5:3). As is evident in table 5:3, the various rastra fall into generally coherent patterns of usage. This table also shows that the last of Cannabich's miscellaneous instrumental works, the *Symphonia pastorale* M7, clearly falls within group 3. As one of its copyists, Mannheim 16, otherwise appears only in Cannabich 43 and a copy of Cannabich 42 in Regensburg (App. A/VI/161), M7 probably dates from about the same time as those works, that is, ca. 1771–72.

The relatively small number of subsequent additions and replacements during this period includes numerous new title pages by Cannabich as well as parts by Cannabich and the Munich violinist Sixtus Hirsvogl (ca. 1759–1799) to Cannabich 43–44. The winds and added viola 2 part of Cannabich 39, in Mannheim 3's late hand, are on paper lined with a one-stave rastrum also found in Cannabich 56—here considered the first Munich work—and in the added viola 2 part of Cannabich

---

[38] See the extended discussion of this copyist under "Types of Parts," above.

Table 5:3. Correlation of Rastra and Cannabich Numbers, Group 3.

No.	Rastrum	Number in Appendix A/III (original parts only)
1	10:25a–c	Cannabich 39–41, 43, 45. Rastrum 10:25c also found in App. A/VI/19, Toeschi's *Mars et Venus* (1766);[a] rastrum 10:25a also found in App. A/V/2, Vogler's *Rendez-vous de chasse* (1772), and App. A/II/17, Holzbauer's *Betulia liberata* (1774).
2	10:30a	39, 45–47, 49–52
"	10:30b	40, 44, M7
"	10:30d	41
"	10:30e	M7
"	10:30c	51–52
3[b]	10:20a	42, 52–53
"	10:20b	46, 48, 53–55
4	10:21	48–50

[a] The earliest form of this rastrum, 10:25c, found in the Toeschi ballet of 1766, appears only in the first trumpet part of Cannabich 40, a single folio that may therefore have been kept for a while before being used.

[b] In Cannabich 42, 46, and 48 this staving occurs in what are probably later recopies; see below.

15 by the same copyist;[39] all these parts doubtless come from the Munich period, too. The viola 1 and 2, horn 1, and title page of Cannabich 42, by Mannheim 3 and Cannabich, and the viola part of Cannabich 46 by Mannheim 3, probably also stem from Munich, judging by the lateness of the handwriting (the rastra of these parts are unique and thus of little use for purposes of dating).

The other parts to Cannabich 42, by Mannheim 4, 13, and Cannabich at a somewhat earlier time, belong to a small group of parts that also includes the winds of Cannabich 46, by Mannheim 3, and the cello/bass part of Cannabich 46 and title page/cover of 48, both by the composer. All these are lined with rastrum 10:20, which as shown in table 5:3 is especially characteristic of Cannabich 52–55. Furthermore, it is at precisely this time, in Cannabich 53, that Mannheim 4 begins consistently to use his rounded clef (see the section "Types of Parts," above, and Appendix D); it is this form that occurs throughout his parts to no. 42. Therefore, these parts, and to a lesser extent the relevant portions of nos. 46 and 48, would seem to derive from the late Mannheim period—that is, once again somewhat later than their Cannabich numbers would imply.

Chronological conclusions. The chronological boundaries of this period are established by the probable end of the previous one, ca. 1768, and the move to Munich

---

[39] The procedure is precisely that found in Cannabich 15–16; see fn. 21, above. There seems little question that these additions were all made in Munich at approximately the same time.

Chapter 5

in August and September of 1778, evidently just after Cannabich 55 (see group 4, below). Within these perimeters several dates can be cited that confirm and partly elucidate the chronology of these works. First, table 5:3 has already indicated that a rastrum used in Cannabich 39–45 (10:25) also appears in sources from 1772 and 1774. Second, Cannabich published six of these symphonies, numbers 47–52, as op. 10 with the firm of Johann Michael Götz in Mannheim in 1775.[40] This fits perfectly with the date of no later than August/September 1778 for Cannabich 55, assuming that Cannabich would have had little time for composing in the eight-month period between announcement of the transfer to Munich and the actual move.

Most helpfully of all, we are informed in an article in *Mercure de France* for June 1772 of a "Concert pour les Ecoles gratuites de Dessin, donné au Vauxhal de la Foire St Germain, le 29 Avril 1772" at which

> On a exécuté pour l'ouverture les deux symphonies qui avaient disputé le prix de musique. Ce prix qui est une médaille d'or de la valeur de trois cent liv. a été adjugé à la symphonie concertante de M. Canabitche, musicien de l'Electeur Palatin à Mannheim.[41]

Cannabich wrote eight different works entitled "Symphonie concertante" or its equivalent: Cannabich 34, which we have dated ca. 1766–67 (see group 2); *Sei Sinfonie concertanti o sia quintetti*, op. 7, for two flutes, violin, viola, and cello (*RISM* C 819; Paris: Venier, 1769–70); and Cannabich 42, which must date from somewhere around 1770 based on its position within the chronological sequence and its staving. Of these, the only logical choice is the latter. The earlier *Sinfonia concertante*, Cannabich 34, would have been at least five years old in 1772, and Cannabich would certainly have wanted to submit a recent work for a contest in which the prize was worth 300 livres (about one-fifth of his annual salary). The Venier pieces do not come into question at all, as they are chamber rather than orchestral works and had already been published in Paris several years before. As a result, we can with considerable confidence assign Cannabich 42 to the period 1771–early 1772. This tends also to support a dating of ca. 1769 for the beginning of this period (Cannabich 39).

---

[40] *Six Simphonies*, op. 10, plate number 21 (not in *RISM*); the unique exemplar is I-Bc, TT 22. On the date of this print see Hans Schneider, *Der Musikverleger Johann Michael Götz (1740–1810) und seine kurfürstlich privilegirte Notenfabrique* (Tutzing: Hans Schneider, 1989), 1:65–66 (the latter page with a reproduction of the title page).

[41] *Mercure de France*, June 1772, p. 178. A special second prize, consisting of a medal worth 200 livres, was awarded on the occasion to a symphony of Ernst Eichner.

Group 4 (Cannabich 56–61; fall 1778–ca. 1781/82[?])

Group 4, the first of two from the Munich period, functions as a short transition. After the stability and consistency of the previous period, the manuscripts of this group introduce what can only be described as radical changes in every codicological parameter. The degree of change, coming at what can be shown independently to be the approximate point of the departure from Mannheim (see the previous section), together with the nature of these changes, establishes these manuscripts beyond a reasonable doubt as products of the early Munich period, 1778 to perhaps 1781/82 or later.

What strikes one first about these sources is the shift in copyists. From now on Cannabich himself becomes the principal copyist of his music. Mannheim 3 and 4, who must have accompanied the court to Munich, each appear in only one new manuscript of the series, each for the last time: the first in Cannabich 58A, the second in 58B, a second copy of the same symphony. (However, Mannheim 4 is the copyist of two manuscripts of the next symphony in the series, Cannabich 59, the one originally owned by the episcopal court of Fulda, the other by the count of Schönborn-Wiesentheid.).[42] A third copyist, Mannheim 17, occurs here only in Cannabich 60, writing on two papers associated only with Munich, an Italian paper and Heusler 8 (see below). As this copyist also appears in manuscripts of Vogler from the Mannheim period, his name can be added to those of Mannheim 3–4 and Johann Cramer as a copyist who followed the court to Munich.

The remaining copyists are either demonstrably from Munich or new to the series. The Munich copyists that we number 1–2 and 4 are found in various parts to four of the first five of these works, the exception being 58B (which is all by Mannheim 4). While this consistency of occurrence certainly tends to indicate Munich as the source of the original form of these manuscripts, for Cannabich 56–58A there is not really enough physical evidence to state categorically that the parts by Munich copyists are (or are not) members of the original series. In other words, it is not impossible, at least theoretically, that they are *all* later replacements and thus do not demonstrate Munich provenance for the manuscript as a whole. Nevertheless, it should be observed that not a single one of the twelve previous symphonies in the series (Cannabich 44–55) contained a replacement part by a Munich copyist.

---

[42] See fn. 13, above, and also fn. 49, below. The paper of both manuscripts matches that of Cannabich 58B, the late Heusler 8 type found exclusively in Munich. (On the staving of these manuscripts see fn. 49 and related discussion.) These manuscripts, especially because they are still later than Cannabich 58, provide additional support for the conclusion that Mannheim 4 journeyed with the court to Munich. They also supply a further sample of his late hand, with its distinctive rounded clef. It may be noted here that the title page of Cannabich 58B bears the incorrect number 6 (in the hand of the copyist, not of Cannabich); see App. A/III,/58B, under "Comments."

Two other copyists turn up for the first time in this group. A unique Munich copyist writes the viola 1 part to Cannabich 57, and Munich 5 the clarinet and horn parts to the same work and the violin 2 to Cannabich 58A. Both hands display the typical Munich copying style.[43]

The paper of this group of manuscripts illustrates the transition from Heusler 5, the principal type of the preceding group, to its later version Heusler 8. Both papers are present in Cannabich 56–57, after which the earlier form recurs in only a few parts to Cannabich 60–61. Not a single sheet of Heusler 8 paper has ever been found in a manuscript unquestionably from the Mannheim period; within this repertory it clearly signifies Munich provenance.

The final paper of these manuscripts, a large Italian type with the mark <A/HF/IMPERIAL> opposite a shield containing three stars (Appendix B/V, "A/HF" 1), provides still further evidence of their Munich provenance. On the one hand, no indisputably Italian paper whatever appears among the known Mannheim manuscripts.[44] On the other, it would be logical for Munich to make at least some use of Italian paper, as the Bavarian capital is both closer to Italy than is Mannheim and was the terminus for a major trade route from there. In point of fact, we now know that paper from the same Italian manufacturer as the paper of Cannabich 58B and 60–61 *was* used in Munich at precisely this period (though in the "Real" rather than the "Imperial" size): it is found in the autograph score to Alessio Prati's *Armida* (Munich, 1785)[45] and also, in a different form, in act 3 of the autograph of Mozart's *Idomeneo* of 1780/81.[46] And finally, the same paper can be found in various other

---

[43] See the samples of Munich copyists' hands in Gertraut Haberkamp and Robert Münster, eds., *Die ehemaligen Musikhandschriftensammlungen der Königlichen Hofkapelle und der Kurfürstin Maria Anna in München*, Kataloge bayerischer Musiksammlungen, 9 (Munich: G. Henle, 1982), pp. xxiv–xxxi. Haberkamp and Münster's Kopist I is our Munich 1. In addition, as already noted in chapter 2, fn. 100, the second copyist on p. xxxi is not Johann Cramer but a Munich copyist, probably Joseph Palm.

[44] For the only two possible exceptions see chap. 2, @ fn. 40.

[45] D-Mbs, Mus. Ms. 2481. The other paper of this manuscript is Heusler 7, which for a while after 1778 was common in Munich alongside Heusler 8 (both were manufactured in Kandern, north of Basel in the margraviate of Baden).

[46] D-B, Mus. ms. autogr. Mozart KV 366³, fols. 52–55. Here the countermark is not a shield enclosing three stars, but rather three moons. (The brief appearance of this paper in the autograph of *Idomeneo* was evidently overlooked by Alan Tyson in his monumental study *Wolfgang Amadeus Mozart: Neue Ausgabe sämtlicher Werke*, vol. X/33/2: *Wasserzeichen-Katalog* [Kassel: Bärenreiter, 1992].) It is also possible that Mozart obtained this paper in Salzburg rather than Munich: in the form with the shield as countermark it occurs, for example, in numerous Michael Haydn autographs beginning in 1782; see Charles H. Sherman, *The Masses of Johann Michael Haydn: A Critical Survey of Sources* (Ph.D. diss., University of Michigan, 1967), 110, 115, 120, and idem and T. Donley Thomas, *Johann Michael Haydn (1737–1806): A Chronological Thematic Catalogue of His Works* (Stuyvesant, N.Y.: Pendragon Press, 1993), pp. 281–82 (figs. 33–34) and 304 (fig. 67). However, the paper just before it in the score to *Idomeneo* is clearly from Munich (Heusler 7, fols. 46–51; see the previous footnote), and as already stated, the form is different from that in the Salzburg (but also the Munich!) manuscripts. In any event, to judge by the papers in the Michael Haydn and

Bavarian manuscripts.⁴⁷ In conjunction with the other data presented here, connection of this paper with Munich provides convincing evidence for the Bavarian provenance of this entire group of manuscripts.

The most definitive evidence of all, however, comes from the realm of staving. As one may recall, the original parts to every symphony from Cannabich 40 through 55 had employed ten-stave rastra without exception, and only four of them, at that. The transformation after Cannabich 55 is striking. Most of the parts to Cannabich 56, for example, are ruled using a simple one-stave rastrum (see fig. 2:5)—possibly Cannabich's own, as it was he who copied the parts (itself a significant departure). It is easy to imagine the loss, damage, or delayed arrival of the Mannheim multi-nib rastra as a result of the move,⁴⁸ necessitating use of the less sophisticated type that was available everywhere. Though the rastrum in question recurs in no other parts from this group, it was used to rule added parts for Cannabich 15 (viola 2) and 39, the former part linking it decisively with Munich. The bass/cello part of Cannabich 15, obviously copied at the same time by the same copyist, Mannheim 3, utilizes a second one-stave rastrum that also reappears in Cannabich's title page/horn 1 part to Cannabich 30, again definitely from Munich.

Cannabich 56 also introduces a second innovation in the realm of staving: use of a two-stave rastrum. This practice never occurs in earlier parts of the original series, being found only in later replacement parts and sets. (Two-stave rastra are, though, common in parts copied at Mannheim for other courts, probably owing to the copyists' use of their own rastra.) Yet beginning with Cannabich 56 nearly all the Cannabich symphonies employ this type of staving—still further indication that the Munich period begins here. A highly anomalous arrangement (at least for Mannheim) makes its appearance in Cannabich 58B and 60–61.⁴⁹ For both the Italian and Heusler 8 papers of these manuscripts the paper has first been ruled with three passes of a three-stave rastrum, after which a tenth stave has been added at the bottom—often rather ineptly—with a different one-stave liner. I know of no other examples of this disposition from Mannheim, the only vaguely comparable

---

also the Mozart (both Leopold and Wolfgang) manuscripts, Italian paper was the standard choice in Salzburg, which was closely linked geographically with Bavaria.

[47] See, e.g., Robert Münster et al., *Thematischer Katalog der Musikhandschriften der Benediktinerabtei Frauenwörth und der Pfarrkirchen Indersdorf, Wasserburg am Inn und Bad Tölz*, Kataloge bayerischer Musiksammlungen, 2 (Munich: G. Henle, 1975), p. 176, no. 179; p. 179, no. 258.

[48] Another possibility is that the rastra remained behind in Mannheim with Ferdinand Fränzl, who as we have seen served as a *régleur* for the court (see chap. 2, fnn. 72–74 and related text).

[49] This staving, 3 x 3 + 1, also appears in the Washington and Wiesentheid manuscripts of Cannabich 59 by Mannheim 4 discussed above (see fn. 42 and related text). The staving of the Washington manuscript and of all but the horn 1 part of the Wiesentheid manuscript is the same, but it does not appear to match that of any of the Cannabich manuscripts from Munich. The staving of the horn 1 part of the Wiesentheid manuscript is, however, found in the bassoon part of Cannabich 57.

one being much earlier, the 1 + 3 x 5 staving of Stamitz's Mass in D of ca. 1755 (App. A/VI/18). Finally, a small number of parts from this period do employ ten-stave rastra, but ones unfamiliar from earlier works in the series; two of the three, 10:27 and 10:29, are also found in replacement parts copied in Munich, the latter in conjunction with the hand of Munich copyist 1 (see Cannabich 30).[50]

Group 5 (Cannabich 62–73; ca. 1781/82[?]–1794)

The manuscripts of Cannabich's final period can be characterized in a single paragraph. Only two copyists now appear regularly, the composer and (less often) Sixtus Hirsvogl. The only other hands are those of Munich 5 and a second Munich copyist in the first two works of this group, Cannabich 62–63. Hirsvogl always writes on south-German paper, while Cannabich employs the standard Munich Heusler paper, Heusler 8, and the same south-German types as Hirsvogl. Finally, all the paper of these manuscripts has been lined with two-stave rastra. These characteristics have allowed us to assign many of the additions and replacements found in earlier works in the series to this period; one gets the impression that Cannabich, approaching old age, made a systematic review of his entire corpus of manuscripts.

Chronological conclusions. Perhaps surprisingly, there is much less evidence regarding the dating of the Munich works than the Mannheim ones. Only the termini are clear: fall 1778 for the beginning of group 4, and 1794, the date on the (incomplete) autograph score of Cannabich 73, for the end of group 5. Cannabich therefore produced eighteen symphonies during this sixteen-year period, somewhat less than in Mannheim; but we have almost no information regarding the chronological disposition of the works during this time.[51] We can perhaps assume that little compositional activity took place for a time after the move, and hence a reasonable date for the beginning of group 5 (i.e., the end of group 4) might be ca. 1781/82, allowing some three or four years for the production of the six works of group 4. Cannabich's reduced output during this period finds a ready explanation in the increased responsibilities resulting from the move to Munich—reorganizing

---

[50] The dating of this period is discussed under "Chronological Conclusions" in the next section.

[51] For the one (not very helpful) exception, providing a terminus ad quem of ca. 1789 for Cannabich 64, see the listing of that symphony in Appendix A/III (under "Comments"). Also not useful for purposes of dating is Cannabich's letter to the elector of January 1790 (see fn. 7, above), written some two years after (Joseph) Toeschi's death. Cannabich requests an increase in his salary on the grounds that it is now he alone who is responsible for composing all the symphonies. Though this is an exaggeration, the elector granted him a raise of fifty *Reichsthaler* (see J. Wolf, *The Symphony at Mannheim: Christian Cannabich*, p. xlviii).

and amalgamating the two court *Kapellen*, establishing the Concert des Amateurs—
and in the straitened circumstances of the court during his later years.[52]

---

[52] See J. Wolf, *The Symphony at Mannheim: Christian Cannabich*, p. xlviii. On the electoral academies and the various concert series in Munich during this period see my article "The 'Concert' in Munich under Elector Carl Theodor," in Theodor Göllner and Stephan Hörner, eds., *Mozarts Idomeneo und die Musik in München zur Zeit Karl Theodors* (Munich: Verlag der Bayerischen Akademie der Wissenschaften, 2001), 223–36.

Chapter 6

Autographs of Grua, Richter, and Mozart without Explicit Indication of Provenance (App. A/IV/1–11)

Chapter 6 considers the small, somewhat miscellaneous group of manuscripts listed in Appendix A/IV. These are all autographs and partial autographs or, in one case, an authentic copy that contains such detailed corrections and emendations by the composer, Carlo Grua, that it might as well have been. Unlike most of the autographs included in Appendix A/I, however (see chap. 3), these manuscripts do not contain a colophon or other inscription giving their provenance as Mannheim. Thus the evidence that they were copied there is less direct, though in most cases equally compelling.

Two Masses of Carlo Grua

In 1976, while working at the Bayerische Staatsbibliothek in Munich, I was graciously given permission to comb through the entire collection of the Frauenkirche, the great Munich cathedral, before it was catalogued, filmed, and transferred to the Dombibliothek in Freising. One result was the discovery of an anonymous set of parts to a mass in E♭, dated 1757, that the paper, staving, and handwriting clearly showed to be of Mannheim provenance (App. A/IV/1). Immediately apparent was the fact that this manuscript contained extremely extensive corrections in the highly idiosyncratic hand of Carlo Grua (see Appendix D for samples of his handwriting). Furthermore, the paper, staving, and copyists linked this manuscript closely with a set of parts to a *Memento Domine* by Grua in the same collection (App. A/VI/144, dated 1753 and 1756). It thus seemed likely that, although no score to this work was known, it was in fact by Grua. After examining the mass in question, the late Dr. Eduard Schmitt, an authority on Mannheim sacred music, seconded my opinion and included it as a genuine work of Grua in his 1982 catalogue of Mannheim church music.[1]

In a second mass in the same collection, a set of parts that this time is specifically attributed to Grua (App. A/IV/2), the composer actually copied the string parts himself, as well as making his usual detailed (not to say finicky) corrections. This manuscript can almost certainly be assigned to the year 1766, the date of the

---

[1] Eduard Schmitt, ed., *Kirchenmusik der Mannheimer Schule, 1. Auswahl*, DTB, Neue Folge, 2 (Wiesbaden: Breitkopf & Härtel, 1982), pp. xxxiii–xxxiv (no. I.4).

autograph score now in Karlsruhe (D-KA; App. A/I/13, dated 4 June 1766), among other reasons because the paper of Grua's string parts is precisely the same as that of his score. It could not, in any event, postdate 1773, the year of Grua's death.

These two manuscripts are of interest for the study of performance practice at Mannheim in that, unlike the manuscripts at the Bayerische Staatsbibliothek, they have not been stripped of their duplicate parts. The first manuscript, for example (A/IV/1, the anonymous mass), originally had two first and two second violin parts, the first of each pair dated 1757; to these a third part has been added, probably shortly thereafter (the new first violin part is by a different copyist, Mannheim 2, and on different paper than the rest of the manuscript). This situation almost precisely matches that of the Grua *Memento Domine* (App. A/VI/144) in the same collection: the original set of parts for that work, from 1753,[2] had two firsts and two seconds, to which a third part has later been added that is dated 1757. The manuscript of the second mass (App. A/IV/2), from 1766 (see above), was copied from the start with three first and three second violin parts, confirming that this was the norm for the late 1750s and the 1760s at Mannheim. In earlier sacred music at Mannheim two firsts and two seconds seem to have been the more common complement.[3]

Autograph Scores and Parts by Franz Xaver Richter

The composer and bass singer Franz Xaver Richter (1709–89) was at Mannheim from about 1747 until he left in 1769 to assume the position of *maître de chapelle* at the cathedral of Strasbourg. He was already fairly well known as a composer when he took up his position at Mannheim, having held positions at Ettal and Kempten (among other centers) and having already published twelve symphonies in Paris ca. 1744. Despite his extensive instrumental output, however, Richter's extant autographs from the Mannheim period are all in the realm of church music; they are listed in Appendix IV rather than earlier because none bears a colophon indicating its provenance. In addition, unlike the Holzbauer and Cannabich manuscripts discussed in the two previous chapters, none of these manuscripts formed a part of the former Munich *Hofmusikintendanz* collection.

Little need be said about these manuscripts here, for a richly detailed study making use of the most up-to-date techniques of documentary investigation has

---

[2] See the discussion of A/VI/144 in the second section of chap. 9. While the parts are again undated, the watermark of the original set is exactly the same as that of Grua's autograph score of 1753 (App. A/I/12).

[3] For a full discussion of the question of the number of duplicate parts normally utilized at Mannheim see Eugene K. Wolf, "On the Composition of the Mannheim Orchestra, ca. 1740–1780," *Basler Jahrbuch für historische Musikpraxis* 17 (1993): 131–38.

been published by Jochen Reutter.[4] Reutter isolated nine manuscripts, each mostly in Richter's hand, that a combination of external evidence, watermarks, and a sophisticated analysis of Richter's hand[5] was able to demonstrate stemmed from Mannheim.

The earliest of these sources, the autograph score to Richter's oratorio *Della deposizione dalla croce* (App. A/IV/3), was first performed in April 1748; a date of 1747 or early 1748 for the manuscript is thus reasonable and accords well with the use of Blum 1 paper.[6]

For the latest of these works, the psalm setting *Super flumina Babylonis* (App. A/IV/10), the evidence is of an entirely different sort. Reutter shows that a contest was held in Paris for the best setting of this psalm text, to which Richter submitted an entry.[7] Though he did not win, his work was subsequently performed at the Concert spirituel in 1769; the score at Brussels (App. A/IV/10a) even bears the names of the performers.[8] Because the contest was announced in *Mercure de France* in August 1767 (p. 205) and the works had to be submitted by 1 February 1768, the score, and very likely the parts (App. A/IV/10b), may be assigned with some certainty to late 1767 or early 1768. I can add one bit of confirmation for this dating from the realm of rastrology, as the upper string parts of this manuscript make use of rastrum 10:17b, also found in two ballet scores copied by Sigismund Falgera in 1769 (App. A/I/14–15).[9] For the remainder of these works Reutter is able to propose approximate dates, based primarily on handwriting, of ca. 1755–60 (App. A/IV/4), 1760–65 (A/IV/5–8),[10] and 1765–69 (A/IV/9).

Mention should also be made here of one Richter autograph probably from this period that I have chosen not to include, his *Messa à 4: voci concert:* in F-Pc, Ms. 20140 (olim D. 11761; Reutter A 34). Though Reutter dates it ca. 1755–60 based on Richter's handwriting, its watermark and staving are wholly uncharacteristic of Mannheim, and it may have been written elsewhere.[11] Another autograph by

---

[4] Jochen Reutter, *Studien zur Kirchenmusik Franz Xaver Richters (1709–1789)* (Frankfurt am Main: Peter Lang, 1993). See also my review of this work in *Notes* 51 (1994): 127–31.

[5] On Reutter's methodology see the section on handwriting in chap. 2, above, @ fn. 106.

[6] Reutter, *Studien*, 1:33, 2:418–19.

[7] Reutter, *Studien*, 1:47–48, citing Constant Pierre, *Histoire du Concert spirituel 1725–1790* (Paris: Société française de musicologie, Heugel, 1975), 140–41 (q.v.).

[8] Reutter, *Studien*, 1:48, 2:361.

[9] Cf. chap. 3, @ fn. 12. The remainder of these manuscripts are lined with one-stave rastra except for the 1748 oratorio (App. A/IV/3), which uses a unique rastrum of four staves (rastrum 4:1).

[10] App. A/IV/5 has a probable terminus ad quem of ca. 1767, for its "Dona" is contained in Richter's treatise of that date, the *Harmonische Belehrungen*; see Reutter, *Studien*, 2:110, fn. 26.

[11] Reutter, *Studien*, 2:203. The watermark is <S. CHIARA : cross/shield {fleur-de-lis}>, and the paper is somewhat rough, brownish and opaque (see chap. 2, @ fn. 40). The first flyleaf does, however, consist of Heusler 1 paper, probably indicating that the score was bound in Mannheim. The paper of the manuscript was lined with two passes of a five-stave rastrum, unique to this study,

Richter that might have been included here as a Mannheim manuscript is that to his manuscript composition treatise *Harmonische Belehrungen, oder Gründliche Anweisung zu der musicalischen Ton-Kunst, und regulairen Composition* of ca. 1767.[12] This is written on Heusler 7 paper, like most of the music manuscripts, and provides one basis for the establishment of Richter's hand.[13]

Oboe Parts by Mozart to K. 175

A final manuscript to be treated here is Mozart's autograph part for two oboes to his Piano Concerto K. 175.[14] This part has been described in detail in an article by Klaus Hortschansky, who reproduces a page thereof as well as the watermark, that of the paper Heusler 5.[15] Hortschansky associates it with a performance at Cannabich's house on 13 February 1778, about which Mozart wrote the next day, "I played my old concerto in D major, because it is such a favorite here."[16] Not only does the use of Heusler 5 paper for this leaf argue for Mannheim as its source, as Hortschansky noted, but the rastrum involved, 10:6, is also found in one part of Cannabich's Symphony no. 60 in Munich (see App. A/III/60). Perhaps Cannabich even gave Mozart the paper on which to prepare the part. By contrast, the bass part to this concerto, also discussed by Hortschansky, does not seem to have originated in Mannheim, as it is on Auvergnese paper and utilizes a rastrum not otherwise found among the Mannheim manuscripts. This is also the theory favored by Hortschansky, who proposes that the bass part was copied in Paris.[17]

---

with a TS of 93.65–.75 and DS measurements 12.25, 11.4, 12.5–.6, 12.65–.7. Irregularities are: staves 1/1, 4/1 medium small; staves 1/3, 4/2, 5/4 medium large.

[12] B-Bb, Cabinet des manuscrits, Fonds général, II, 6292.

[13] Another, evidently not utilized by Reutter, is the extensive series of documents from Richter's two decades in Strasbourg (including many receipts signed by him). These are located in the Archives du Bas-Rhin (Archives départementales) in Strasbourg, primarily in the fascicles Evéché de Strasbourg, G 3322–58.

[14] The part is presently in the André-Archiv in Offenbach am Main. I am greatly indebted to Frau Ute-Margrit André for her kindness in allowing me to examine this source in person.

[15] Klaus Hortschansky, "Autographe Stimmen zu Mozarts Klavierkonzert KV 175 im Archiv André zu Offenbach," *Mozart-Jahrbuch*, 1989/90 (Kassel, 1990), pp. 37–54; the reproduction appears on p. 50.

[16] Anderson, 482; Bauer-Deutsch, 2:282.

[17] Hortschansky, "KV 175," 42.

Chapter 7

Music of Georg Joseph Vogler (App. A/V/1–43)

Born and educated in Würzburg, Georg Joseph Vogler (1749–1814; "Abbé" or "Abt" Vogler) was appointed almoner to the Mannheim court in 1770.[1] At that time his interests were clearly centered as much on music as on churchly concerns, and he proceeded to produce three large secular works, the Singspiel *Der Kaufmann von Smyrna* (1771) and two ballets (1771–72), before being sent to Italy by the elector for an extended period of musical study in the years 1773–75. Upon his return he was appointed second Kapellmeister (28 February 1776) as well as spiritual counselor to the elector (6 August 1776),[2] and thereafter he seems to have devoted himself mainly to sacred music, theory, and musical pedagogy. When the court moved to Munich in 1778 Vogler was initially listed among those who would follow it there,[3] but in the end he remained in Mannheim at least temporarily, departing by 1780 for periods of residency in several other centers. In 1807 he was appointed Kapellmeister to the court of Hessen-Darmstadt, where he remained until his death in 1814.

Fortunately for posterity (and the present study), when Vogler came to Darmstadt he brought with him a large body of his music from the Mannheim period, both scores (mainly autograph) and parts. These now survive in two principal collections. The first, in the Hessische Landes- und Hochschulbibliothek (D-DS), has long been known. The second, however, has only recently come to light: it is in

---

[1] The classic study of Vogler's life is Karl Emil von Schafhäutl, *Abt Georg Joseph Vogler: sein Leben, Charakter und musikalisches System, seine Werke, seine Schule, Bildnisse &c.* (Augsburg: M. Huttler, 1888), 3–73. For more recent treatments see Floyd K. Grave and Margaret G. Grave, *In Praise of Harmony: The Teachings of Abbé Georg Joseph Vogler* (Lincoln, Neb.: University of Nebraska Press, 1987), 1–8, and Bärbel Pelker and Rüdiger Thomsen-Fürst, *Georg Joseph Vogler (1749–1814): Materialen zu Leben und Werk* (Frankfurt am Main: Peter Lang; in press). The former study provides an exhaustive, up-to-date discussion of Vogler's theories, the latter a comprehensive listing of his works. Warm thanks are due to Margaret G. Grave (New Brunswick, N.J.) for her many valuable suggestions regarding the present chapter.

[2] Friedrich Walter, *Geschichte des Theaters und der Musik am kurpfälzischen Hofe* (Leipzig: Breitkopf & Härtel, 1898), 190–91. However, Walter gives the former date incorrectly as 1777; the decree naming Vogler as second Kapellmeister is clearly dated 1776 (Karlsruhe, Badisches Generallandesarchiv, HR 77/1656).

[3] See Munich, Bayerisches Hauptstaatsarchiv, HR I, Fasz. 457/Nr. 13, the "Status" of 6 August 1778 detailing the reorganization of the Mannheim and Munich *Kapellen*.

the André archive in Offenbach (D-OF).⁴ Some of the Darmstadt material, most notably the secular works, was very probably part of the Darmstadt court collection at Vogler's death, or at least reverted to it. All or most of the André manuscripts, however, were purchased at auction from Vogler's estate by the firm of Johann André after the composer's death.⁵ Most of the latter manuscripts can be found listed in the printed catalogue of the auction, which is entitled *Verzeichniß der von dem . . . verstorbenen Grossherzoglich Hessischen geistlichen Geheimenrathe, Abt G. J. Vogler nachgelassenen . . . Werke* (Darmstadt, 1814).⁶ Some of the manuscripts now in Darmstadt also appear in the *Verzeichniß*, having been bought by the court at auction.⁷

Of the large collections of Vogler's music in Darmstadt and Offenbach, I assign a total of 43 manuscripts to the Mannheim period—21 now in Darmstadt, 22 in Offenbach. Appendix A/V provides a listing of these manuscripts. The first 21 bear dates (or in one case can be firmly dated based on other direct evidence);⁸

---

⁴ I am most grateful to Dr. Bärbel Pelker for informing me of the existence of the Vogler material in the André archive and for generously sharing her extensive notes on it with me. I am equally grateful to Frau Ute-Margrit André for graciously permitting me to examine the materials of the archive on very short notice, and to Dr. Axel Beer of the University of Mainz, who together with Frau André is in the process of completely reorganizing the archive, for his invaluable assistance in my study of these manuscripts, again on extremely short notice.

⁵ See Joachim Veit, *Der junge Carl Maria von Weber: Untersuchungen zum Einfluß Franz Danzis und Abbé Georg Joseph Voglers* (Mainz: Schott, 1990), 113–14. Veit cites the protocol of the auction (Darmstadt, Hessisches Staatsarchiv, G 28 Darmstadt F 2871/8), which specifies the purchasers of the various items, including Grand Duke Ludewig I of Hesse and Johann André.

⁶ I wish to thank Margaret Grave for supplying me with a copy of this important document. The title page indicates that Vogler's manuscript and printed works would be auctioned off on 29 September 1814 (he died on 6 May 1814). The listing of works is quite detailed, supplying key, instrumentation, format (autograph score, copyist's score, or parts), and date (if present); it thus allows precise identification of many of the works still extant in Darmstadt and Offenbach. A reproduction of the title page and p. 14 of the *Verzeichniß* appears in Joachim Veit and Frank Ziegler, *Carl Maria von Weber in Darmstadt* (Tutzing: Hans Schneider, 1997), 51–52.

⁷ Veit, *Der junge Carl Maria von Weber*, 114. The clearest example is the sequence of smaller church works listed as nos. 76–80 in the *Verzeichniß*, all of which appear in the Darmstadt collection (see App. A/V/29, 26, 31, 28, 30); they would appear to have been bought as a group (again unless they simply reverted to the court in some fashion). As already alluded to briefly, the secular works in the Darmstadt collection—the ballet *Le Rendez-vous de chasse* and the original manuscript to the revised version of the opera *Der Kaufmann von Smyrna* (App. A/V/2 and 21)—do not appear in the catalogue; they were either part of the court collection originally or (less likely) were obtained exclusive of the auction. The same is true of the score and parts of *Die Auferstehung Jesu* (App. A/V/20), which likewise does not appear in the *Verzeichniß*.

⁸ The reference is to App. A/V/20, Vogler's aforementioned German oratorio *Die Auferstehung Jesu*. Though the Darmstadt manuscript of this work bears no date, a score thereof in the Stiftelsen Musikkulturens Främjande in Stockholm (S-Smf), labeled an autograph by the RISM cataloguer, is dated 30 March 1777 (information kindly supplied by Margaret Grave; I have not been able to examine this source, which if it is indeed an autograph should be included in Appendix A/V). Both the codicological evidence and the fact that the names of six of the Mannheim performers are given on the parts, one of whom did not go to Munich (see Appendix A/V, fn. f),

these are given in chronological order in Appendix A/V. Thereafter come the Darmstadt sources, listed in numerical order based on their call numbers, and those from Offenbach, given in alphabetical order because call numbers have not yet been assigned. Dates for some of these manuscripts are supplied in the *Verzeichniß* and recorded in Appendix A/V, though these must be treated with a modicum of caution (see below).

The manuscripts without dates present a special problem in that Vogler remained for a few years in Mannheim after 1778 and continued to compose sacred music there: because he might well have employed the same papers and even copyists during this period as before, it can obviously be difficult to distinguish an undated manuscript from 1778 or earlier from one written a short time later. In general, as has been the practice throughout this study, I have tried to err on the side of caution, excluding those manuscripts for which the evidence is not at least relatively convincing.

An example of the difficulties involved when dealing with Vogler's undated works is the pair of manuscripts D-DS, Mus. ms. 1132 and 1155 (App. A/V/32–33), settings by Vogler of the Sanctus and Credo, respectively. Both are sets of parts on a paper ubiquitous in Mannheim, Heusler 5. The two large rastra used, 10:20c and 31, are found in other Vogler manuscripts of the late Mannheim period (and in two variant forms, 10:20a–b, in Cannabich's Symphonies no. 42–55). By way of contrast, about half of each manuscript is lined, not with the large ten-stave rastra just mentioned, but with simple one-stave rastra; these would be the only appearances of such rastra among the many Vogler manuscript parts that definitely antedate 1778. Nor do any of the decidedly amateurish hands in these manuscripts appear among sources that are demonstrably from Mannheim before 1778. Based on that evidence alone, one might tentatively assign these sources to the period ca. 1778–80, after the departure of the court for Munich. But there is one additional piece of evidence, namely the fact that the auction *Verzeichniß* gives dates of 1776 and 1775, respectively, for these manuscripts (nos. 48, 32). There is no way to know with certainty, however, just how reliable these dates are. The listings in the *Verzeichniß* are for the parts alone (i.e., no score seems to have been extant at the time of the auction), which in their present state contain no dates; perhaps the dates appeared on the original title pages, both of which are missing. In sum, the dating of these sources in the *Verzeichniß* seems to me to tip the balance toward inclusion of them within the Mannheim period; but in fact the evidence is by no means conclusive.

A somewhat similar problem confronts the researcher working with the huge set of scores and parts at Darmstadt of Vogler's *Deutsche Kirchenmusik* of 1777 (App. A/V/24; Mus. ms. 1091a–f). Here the only item that really comes into question as a manuscript from Mannheim is the "Orgel und Bass" part, actually a short score containing all the essential musical material (Mus. ms. 1091f); other portions

---

place the Darmstadt manuscript unquestionably within the Mannheim period, that is, before 1778.

of the set, though they utilize Blum papers, are quite uncharacteristic of Mannheim as regards their staving and handwriting (viz. the full score 1091b, not an autograph, and the parts 1091d–e; the parts are also much smaller than most genuine Mannheim parts). The short score, however, is in Vogler's hand with the exception of the label on the cover and the title on the first page of music, both of which have been added in a different hand. As the cover label bears the date 1777 ("Deutsche Kirchen=Music. 1777"), and as the paper is the standard Mannheim type Heusler 5, one could certainly consider the short score a good candidate for inclusion among the Mannheim manuscripts from before 1778.

On the other hand, the staving was done with a rastrum associated only with the later Munich period, 10:29, found in Cannabich's Symphony no. 61 and several late additions to other of his symphonies. Moreover, the copyist who wrote the label of the short score is found in the full score of the work, Mus. ms. 1091b, which is certainly later and probably local. (One should recall that Vogler did not arrive in Darmstadt until 1807, and thus some of the manuscripts there may have been copied independently of him, that is, in the period before his arrival.)

Here some knowledge of the context is of assistance. In a booklet published together with a score of the *Deutsche Kirchenmusik* in 1808, Vogler tells us that he originally composed the work in 1777 for voices and organ alone, without additional accompaniment.[9] It was in this form that the work was published in 1778 (RISM A/I/9, V 2373). Thereafter, for a performance in Heidelberg in December of 1778—after the court had departed for Munich, it should be noted—he added an accompaniment for orchestra that he describes as optional.[10] Finally, in 1807 Vogler composed an entirely new accompaniment for orchestra, one he takes pains to describe as essential ("wesentlich"), by comparison with what he calls the old-fashioned style of the original accompaniment.[11] I have therefore tentatively concluded that the short score does indeed date from 1777, as stated on the label.

Once again, though, one cannot completely exclude an alternate explanation, the one supported by the staving: that the short score represents, not the original organ accompaniment, but a transcription or even draft of the optional accompaniment made after 1777, presumably in preparation for the Heidelberg performance of late 1778. According to this explanation, the date on the label—which one will recall was added after the fact—would refer merely to the date of the original composition of the work or merely repeat a date from the original manuscript. With respect to the remainder of the Darmstadt material, it would seem to incorporate the 1778 version based on the watermarks and handwriting; it certainly does not appear to date from as late as 1807. However, a complete resolution of

---

[9] *Utile Dulci: A. Voglers belehrende musikalische Herausgaben* (Munich: Senefelder & Gleissner, 1808), 3. Again I express my gratitude to Margaret Grave for information on this important source.

[10] Ibid., 4.

[11] Ibid., 4–7.

this and the other problems presented by the *Deutsche Kirchenmusik* must await further research—which I shall gladly leave to the Vogler experts.

Of the Vogler manuscripts in Darmstadt that are *definitely* from Mannheim, most include both score and parts, the former usually, but not always, a Vogler autograph. Some scores are collective projects, such as that of App. A/V/2, the ballet *Rendez-vous de chasse*: here a copyist prepares the way by writing the clefs and main melodic line through folio 39, after which Vogler fills in the remaining parts and then writes all of folios 41 to the end.[12] The parts to the Darmstadt manuscripts, together with the Grua manuscripts of the Frauenkirche in Munich discussed in chapter 6, provide our best examples of what a set of parts for a piece of sacred music at Mannheim was like: for many of them preserve their original covers and numberings, and the duplicate parts have been retained, allowing us to estimate the number of players who would have been present.[13] The parts to three of these works contain the names of the Mannheim performers for whom they were intended, an obvious indication that they originated at the electoral court (see App. A/V/9, 20, 28). In contrast to the Darmstadt manuscripts, almost all of the Mannheim manuscripts in the André collection are scores (all but one an autograph), even though parts to the same works are listed in the *Verzeichniß*.[14] The latter were evidently discarded at some point, presumably because they were not considered of use to a publisher such as André.

As regards format, most of the autograph scores are on large oblong paper lined with a twelve-stave rastrum; exceptions are the small original score to *Der Kaufmann von Smyrna* (App. A/V/1) and seven large upright scores lined with 16 to 20 passes of a one-stave rastrum (App. A/V/9, 16, 23, and 37, the last two of these written by a copyist, and the double-chorus works 11–13). A peculiar practice of Vogler's in two of the sources bears mention: he writes a first work on only the *recto* sides of the folio, then turns the manuscript over and writes a second work on the *versi*, now proceeding back to front (see App. A/V/16, containing a Credo and an Agnus, and A/V/40, containing a Kyrie and a Sanctus). It is not clear what Vogler perceived the advantage of this arrangement to be, unless it is to allow for increased time for the ink to dry before writing on the overleaf. The parts follow the norm for Mannheim manuscripts, upright format for sacred music, oblong for secular.

---

[12] See Floyd K. Grave, ed., *Ballet Music from the Mannheim Court, Part I*, Recent Researches in the Music of the Classical Era, 45 (Madison, Wisc.: A-R Editions, 1996), plates 3–4. This volume includes a full score of the ballet in question together with extensive introductory material.

[13] For a full discussion of this subject see Eugene K. Wolf, "On the Composition of the Mannheim Orchestra, ca. 1740–1780," *Basler Jahrbuch für historische Musikpraxis* 17 (1993): 131–38.

[14] The André collection also includes some as-yet unidentified miscellaneous parts and numerous fragments, one or the other of which may well be from Mannheim; I have not included these in Appendix A/V. Indeed, to some extent my entire listing of the André manuscripts should be considered provisional, as the archive is still in the process of reorganization and systematization.

The papers of the Vogler manuscripts are almost exclusively the standard ones used at Mannheim in the 1770s, Heusler 5 and 7 and (less often) Blum 5. Likewise, the larger rastra preferred here are found in numerous contemporaneous manuscripts from Mannheim of works by other composers. The Vogler manuscripts are thus very useful in that so many contain dates or can be assigned with confidence to the period 1775–78. The scores mostly make use of twelve-stave rastra, exceptions being a few with ten staves and the aforementioned ones in upright format lined with multiple passes of a simple rastrum. The parts to the two secular works included here also employ ten staves, whereas the parts to the sacred music utilize a handful of large twelve-stave rastra.

The non-autograph portions of these manuscripts make relatively little use of the standard court copyists; of the latter, Mannheim 6 and Johann Cramer are the most common. Instead, Vogler prefers five copyists found only in these manuscripts, here labeled Darmstadt/Mannheim (DS/Mh.) 1–5, and a sixth, Mannheim 17, who otherwise appears in just one other known source, Cannabich's Symphony no. 60 (a Munich work; see App. A/III/60). Several of these manuscripts include as many as seven of these and other copyists, giving the distinct impression that at least some were students of Vogler's pressed into service as copyists (see esp. App. A/V/17, 19).[15]

The only other work of this group to require extended comment in this chapter is the first of the secular works mentioned above, the Singspiel *Der Kaufmann von Smyrna* (App. A/V/1 and 21). As already stated, Vogler made his public compositional debut at Mannheim in 1771 with a setting of this work, the libretto of which was an adaptation by the Mannheim book dealer and writer Christian Friedrich Schwan. According to Sonneck, it played at the Schauspielhaus auf dem Fruchtmarkt, a temporary wooden structure.[16] The exact date of the first performance is not known, but it was probably late summer of 1771, as the preface to the libretto is dated 22 July 1771[17] and the autograph score in the André archive August 1771 (see below).

Two authentic scores to Vogler's Singspiel are now known: the newly discovered autograph of the original version, from 1771 (App. A/V/1), and the Darmstadt score by the prolific court copyist Mannheim 5 (App. A/V/21), which incor-

---

[15] Vogler established a music school at Mannheim, the "Mannheimer Tonschule"; either that or the Seminarium musicum might have provided the students in question. Other of these copyists might, of course, have been colleagues of Vogler's. On Mannheim 5's appearance as the copyist of the Darmstadt score of Vogler's *Der Kaufmann von Smyrna* (App. A/V/21) see below.

[16] Oscar George Theodore Sonneck, *Catalogue of Opera Librettos Printed before 1800*, vol. 1: *Title Catalogue* (Washington, D.C.: Government Printing Office, 1914), 669. Sonneck does not give a source for this statement.

[17] A facsimile of the 1771 libretto appears in Thomas Bauman, ed., *German Opera 1770–1800: A Collection of Facsimiles of Printed and Manuscript Full Scores*, vol. 21 (New York: Garland Publishing, 1986).

porates an added aria for soprano, "O süsses Band der Liebe," in Vogler's hand.[18] The second of these scores would appear to be that of a revised version known to date from ca. 1777–78 (see below), as it bears the date 1778. However, this date appears only on the label on the front of the score, not in the manuscript itself, and one might therefore doubt its reliability—or, to pose the question more positively, one might want at least to see whether the evidence supported this date, at the same time taking the opportunity to review the physical characteristics of the source.

As a matter of fact, the evidence for the later dating of this manuscript is not as clear as one might wish. The paper of the main score is all of the Heusler 7 type. Its watermarks come closest to those of the Darmstadt score of J. C. Bach's *Lucio Silla* of 1775 (App. A/VI/142), but none is an exact match. The rastrum in question, 10:1, provides little real help: it appears elsewhere in works from 1770, 1772 (twice), 1774 (twice), and 1777/78, all but the last copied for the most part by the same copyist as the Vogler score, Mannheim 5 (see App. A/VI/195, 20, 140–41, 143, and 36, respectively).[19] This copyist otherwise appears in dated manuscripts only between 1760 and 1774, and were it not for the present manuscript, he would thus be one of the two most likely candidates (with Mannheim 2) to have been the official court copyist Johann Lochner, who entered the elector's service in 1757 and died in 1774 (see Appendix D). If this copyist were in fact Lochner, the explanation for the present state of the score would have to be that the main portion dates from no later than 1774, to which Vogler has added the aria "O süsses Band der Liebe" sometime thereafter. Indeed, in his *Betrachtungen der Mannheimer Tonschule* Vogler tells us that he composed this aria "after the libretto had already been printed," for the Mannheim soprano Barbara Strasser.[20] Hence, the score as it now stands would have to represent a slightly revised version, from no later than 1774, that was subsequently performed in an as-yet not fully documented staging of the work in 1778, to which the date on the title page would seem to refer.

---

[18] A facsimile of the Darmstadt score to *Der Kaufmann von Smyrna* is printed in Bauman, *German Opera*, vol. 8 (1986). The extensive set of parts included with this score is not from Mannheim; it is presumably local.

[19] The last of these manuscripts, App. A/VI/36, is an incomplete set of parts to the aria "Aer tranquillo" from Mozart's *Il rè pastore*, K. 208, composed in 1775. Recent identification of the copyist of this manuscript as Fridolin Weber, Mozart's post-mortem father-in-law (see chap. 2, @ fn. 104), allows us to assign the date of 1777/78, when the composer was in Mannheim, to this manuscript.

[20] The quotation comes from the title of Vogler's discussion of this and a second aria added later, "O welch' Entzücken," which reads, "Von den zwei brillanten Arien, die nachdem erst eingeschaltet worden, als schon der Text gedrukt war" (*Betrachtungen der Mannheimer Tonschule*, vol. 3 ([Mannheim:] n.p., 1780/81; repr. ed., Hildesheim: Georg Olms, 1974), repr. ed., p. 198 (orig. ed., p. 184). Both arias are printed in the *Gegenstände der Betrachtungen* (vol. 4 of the repr. ed.; pp. 447–51). The reference to Barbara Strasser is on p. 199 of the repr. ed. (orig. ed., p. 185). The second of the arias, written for Aloysia Weber, does not appear in the Darmstadt score, and neither of the arias is found in the 1771 libretto (the only one to my knowledge that has survived).

However, several elements render this version of events suspect. In the first place, of course, the fact that the manuscript bears the date 1778 does carry some weight. Secondly, the title page attributes the work to "Herren Capellen Meister" Vogler, in Mannheim 5's hand and on the same paper as the rest of the score. Thus, unless the title *Kapellmeister* is being used loosely—unlikely in this case, among other reasons because the writer was a long-active court copyist who would have been thoroughly familiar with the titles of his superiors—the manuscript must postdate 1776, when Vogler became vice-Kapellmeister. And thirdly, the evidence of the watermarks does lean slightly toward the later date, especially as the score could have been prepared well before the performance in 1778—that is, in 1777 or even earlier.

The latter assertion receives confirmation from a report from Mannheim of April 1778 found by Friedrich Walter in a Berlin periodical. It states,

> Herr Vogler has newly composed *Der Kaufmann von Smyrna*. The role of Kaled could not have been handled better—even his enemies admit as much—but the other arias are all too difficult and would fit better in a [full-scale] opera [i.e., as opposed to a Singspiel].[21]

This quotation provides our only evidence, other than the date on the score, for a performance of this work in 1778, and because it was published in April of that year, it supports a dating of ca. 1777–early 1778 for the revision and the Darmstadt score.

There remains only the problem of the added aria: for if, as Vogler says, this was composed for Barbara Strasser "after the libretto had already been printed," why would it appear as an *addition* to a score written ca. 1777/78? One answer would be that he wrote the aria for Strasser in the period *before* 1778, then chose to retain it in the new version without recopying it.[22] A second would be that he wrote the aria *after* preparation of the score; this view would assume that his reference in the *Betrachtungen* to a libretto being printed referred to a (now lost) libretto for the 1778 performance.

That the Darmstadt score of *Kaufmann von Smyrna* represented the revised version just referred to was neatly confirmed by the discovery of the autograph of

---

[21] "Herr Vogler hat den Kaufmann von Smyrna neu komponiert. Die Rolle von Kaled ist ihm unverbesserlich geraten, das sagen selbst seine Feinde, die andern Arien sind aber alle zu schwer und schicken sich eher für eine grosse Oper." From the *Berliner Litteratur- und Theaterzeitung* 1 (1778): 389f., as quoted and cited in Walter, *Geschichte*, 275, 352n.

[22] The rastrum of the added aria, 10:22, is unique and is thus of no help in determining the aria's date. The watermark of the paper, Heusler 5, is closest to several examples from 1776. In any event, as Barbara Strasser was only appointed at court in 1773 (at least, that is the year her name begins to appear in the almanacs), the aria would have to date from that year or later. But Vogler was in Italy in 1773–75, and therefore it is probably even later, as also indicated by the watermarks.

the original version of 1771 in the André archive in Offenbach. This small score, on Dutch paper from the firm of J. Honig & Zoon(en), contains dates of February and August 1771, the former at the end of the duet "Ich bleibe hier," the latter at the very end. Unfortunately, it is missing the first one or two bifolios, including the title page. Future study of this valuable new source will indicate to what extent the original was revised for the performance in 1778; at least to judge by a cursory examination, it was hardly "neu komponiert" in any comprehensive way.

Chapter 8

Other Manuscripts from Mannheim, I:
Operas and Related Works from Appendix A/VI

By Paul Corneilson and Eugene K. Wolf*

Chapter 8 is the first of two devoted to the over 200 manuscripts listed in Appendix A/VI.[1] These are sources in collections all over Europe and America for which the overt connection with Mannheim is least strong: they are not autographs by composers from Mannheim, they do not have colophons indicating they were copied there, they are not still found in Mannheim or Munich, and so forth. Nonetheless, in all but a few cases there can be no question that these manuscripts originated at the electoral court, and for a majority of them an approximate date can be assigned based on codicological evidence. All the manuscripts treated in this chapter are scores. While certain of these sources may at one time have been a part of the Mannheim court collection, most of them must have been obtained as gifts or by trade or purchase by other courts or individuals for use elsewhere.

The present chapter deals with the large-scale secular dramatic works catalogued in Appendix A/VI, while chapter 9 treats the remainder. For reasons that will become obvious, chapter 8 also discusses six scores that, while not actually copied in Mannheim, can be shown to have been known and even used there. Because they are not Mannheim copies, these manuscripts do not appear in Appendix A/VI, though several large-scale insertions in them written by Mannheim copyists do. In addition, Appendix A/VI admits one manuscript from the period after the court departed in 1778, Holzbauer's "azione dramatica" *La morte di Didone* of 1779 (App. A/VI/27).

---

* This chapter is revised and adapted from Paul Corneilson and Eugene K. Wolf, "Newly Identified Manuscripts of Operas and Related Works from Mannheim," *JAMS* 47 (1992): 244–74. Three works included in that study are discussed elsewhere in this book rather than in the present chapter: App. A/II/21, a cantata by Holzbauer (see chap. 4); App. A/V/1 and 21, Vogler's *Der Kaufmann von Smyrna* (see chap. 7); and App. A/VI/ 28, another Holzbauer cantata (see chap. 9).

[1] The original listing of these works in Appendix A/III of Eugene K. and Jean K.Wolf, "A Newly Identified Complex of Manuscripts from Mannheim," *JAMS* 27 (1974): 418–20, included just 30 manuscripts, only one of them of an opera.

Chapter 8

Opera at Mannheim and Its Manuscript Tradition

Long renowned for its instrumental music and the quality of its orchestra, Mannheim merits equal attention for its achievements in the realm of opera.[2] In the third quarter of the eighteenth century it was fully the peer of such courts as Dresden, Munich, Stuttgart, Berlin, and Vienna in both serious and comic opera. Important works by Niccolò Jommelli, Tommaso Traetta, Gian Francesco de Majo, and Johann Christian Bach, along with those of the Kapellmeister Ignaz Holzbauer, were commissioned by the court and had their premieres at Mannheim during this period. Likewise, the most recent operas of popular composers like Baldassare Galuppi, Niccolò Piccinni, and Antonio Salieri were standard fare at the magnificent theater of the Mannheim palace or at the smaller opera house of the summer residence at Schwetzingen.

Carl Theodor, his consort Elisabeth Auguste, and his deputies remained constantly alert to the latest operatic styles and trends. Commissions were often generated, and scores obtained, through the intervention of the elector's network of envoys in various European centers. This process is well documented for Jommelli's important opera *Artaserse* (Rome, 1749, produced at Mannheim in 1751), a copy of which was procured for the court by the palatine envoy in Rome.[3] A similar procedure doubtless produced the score referred to in a sardonic anecdote related by Karl August von Hardenberg, who passed through Mannheim in October and November 1772:

> "We have received an excellent opera from Italy," [General Pagnozzi, the court intendant] said once to [Christian] Cannabich. – "How so, Herr General? Have you

---

[2] For recent discussions of opera at Mannheim see Paul E. Corneilson, *Opera at Mannheim, 1770–1778* (Ph.D. diss., University of North Carolina at Chapel Hill, 1992), which includes a catalogue of all known opera libretti from Mannheim, with transcriptions of titles, full cast lists, and other relevant information; idem, "Die Oper am Kurfürstlichen Hof zu Mannheim," in *Die Mannheimer Hofkapelle im Zeitalter Carl Theodors*, ed. Ludwig Finscher (Mannheim: Palatium Verlag im J & J Verlag, 1992), 113–29; Sabine Henze, "Opera seria am kurpfälzischen Hofe," in *Mannheim und Italien: zur Vorgeschichte der Mannheimer*, Beiträge zur mittelrheinischen Musikgeschichte, 25, ed. Roland Würtz (Mainz: Schott, 1984), 78–96; Marita McClymonds, "Mattia Verazi and the Opera at Mannheim, Stuttgart, and Ludwigsburg," *Studies in Music from the University of Western Ontario* 7 (1982): 99–136. The foundation for study of opera at Mannheim was laid by Friedrich Walter, *Geschichte des Theaters und der Musik am kurpfälzischen Hofe* (Leipzig: Breitkopf & Härtel, 1898).

[3] See Adolf Sandberger, "Aus der Korrespondenz des pfalzbayerischen Kurfürsten Karl Theodor mit seinem römischen Ministerresidenten," in *Adolf Sandberger: Ausgewählte Aufsätze*, vol. 1 (Munich: Drei Masken Verlag, 1921), 218–20 (originally published in the Kretzschmar Festschrift of 1918).

already heard it?" – "No," [Pagnozzi replied,] "but [it is on] beautiful paper, and the notes are quite black and well written, and for piano and forte!"[4]

Given the level and quality of operatic activity at Mannheim, the destruction of the elector's large music collection in 1795 (see chap. 1) represents an incalculable loss to scholars, all the more so since those few manuscripts from the court that seem to have remained in Mannheim as part of the collection of the Nationaltheater were burned in World War II.[5] The study of opera at Mannheim has thus always lacked the kind of solid basis for research that survival of the music collection of a court ordinarily provides. One of the most gratifying results of the present study has therefore been to identify 27 manuscripts (mostly complete scores) of operas and other secular dramatic works that were copied in or closely associated with Mannheim, thus offsetting to some extent the loss of the original collection.[6] The present chapter discusses these manuscripts as documents, describes their interrelationship, and outlines several of the sometimes surprising ramifications of this research.

The Manuscripts

A provisional listing of the 27 manuscripts treated in this chapter appears in table 8:1—provisional in that it is obviously impossible for us to have examined all of the relevant opera and related scores of the period. In addition to eighteen manuscripts of fifteen operas, table 8:1 includes manuscripts of one "azione dramatica" (no. 7), one serenata (no. 3), and one dramatic cantata or "azione teatrale" (no. 2, J. C. Bach's *Amor vincitore*) that is known to have been staged at Schwetzingen in

---

[4] "Wir haben eine herrliche Oper aus Italien bekommen, sagt [General Pagnozzi] einmahl zu Cannabich. — Wie so, H. General? haben Sie sie schon gehört? — Nein aber schön Papier und die Noten recht schwarz und gut geschrieben, u. fürs Piano und forte!" Printed in Karl Obser, "Aufzeichnungen des Staatskanzlers Fürsten von Hardenberg über seinen Aufenthalt am Oberrhein im Jahre 1772," *Zeitschrift für die Geschichte des Oberrheins*, Neue Folge, 22 (1907): 166. Hardenberg prefaces the anecdote by saying that "General Pagnozzi, directeur des spectacles, n'y entend pas goute" (to which one is tempted to reply, "Plus ça change . . . ").

[5] These manuscripts are among those listed in Friedrich Walter, *Archiv und Bibliothek des Grossh. Hof- und Nationaltheaters in Mannheim, 1779–1839* (Leipzig: S. Hirzel, 1899), vol. 2: *Die Theater-Bibliothek*. Most of the archive and library of the Nationaltheater was lost in World War II, including all the music manuscripts. The appendix to the present chapter provides a list of these and other manuscripts of operas associated with Mannheim that were burned during the war, some of which undoubtedly stemmed from the electoral court.

[6] For a brief narrative of the process leading to the identification of these sources see Corneilson and Wolf, "Newly Identified Manuscripts," 246–49.

Table 8:1. Operas and Other Dramatic Works Extant in Manuscripts from Mannheim (to 1780).

No.	Composer	Work	Manuscripts
1	Bach, Johann Christian	*Temistocle* (5 November 1772; premiere)	(*a*) D-B, Mus. ms. Bach P 388 (App. A/VI/20). "Mannheim" binding. (*b*) D-Dlb, Mus. 3374-F-1 (App. A/VI/139).[a]
2	Bach, Johann Christian	*Amor vincitore* (cantata, "azione teatrale"; Schwetzingen, August 1774)	D-DS, Mus. ms. 82 (App. A/VI/143)
3	Bach, Johann Christian	*Endimione* (serenata, 1774[?]).[b]	D-DS, Mus. ms. 57 (App. A/VI/141)
4	Bach, Johann Christian	*Lucio Silla* (5 November 1775;[c] premiere)	D-DS, Mus. ms. 60 (App. A/VI/142)[d]
5	Gassmann, Florian Leopold	*L'amore artigiano* (Schwetzingen, May 1772)	D-B, Mus. ms. 7130 (App. A/VI/24). "Mannheim" binding; see fig. 8:1.
6	Holzbauer, Ignaz	*Günther von Schwarzburg* (5 January 1777; premiere)	(*a*) D-NEhz, Musikalien Bartenstein, Bü 111/4 (aut. score; App. A/IV/20).[e] (*b*) D-B, Mus. ms. 10780 (App. A/VI/26).
7	Holzbauer, Ignaz	*La morte di Didone* ("azione dramatica"; Mannheim, Nationaltheater, 6 July 1779; premiere)	D-B, Mus. ms. 10781 (App. A/VI/27)[f]
8	Jommelli, Niccolò	*Artaserse* (17 January 1751)	D-B, Mus. ms. 11245. The score itself, dated 1750 (one year after the Rome premiere), is probably of Roman provenance, but in vols. 2 and 3 the title "L'Artaserse" has been added in the unmistakable hand of Ignaz Holzbauer. In addition, the flyleaves of each volume are on Basel papers common at Mannheim.
9	Jommelli, Niccolò, and Giuseppe Colla	*Cajo Fabrizio* (5 November 1760; premiere)	(*a*) US-Wc, M 1500.J72 C35 (App. A/VI/203). "Mannheim" binding; see fig. 8:7b. (*b*) US-Rs, M 1500.J759 C (App. A/VI/201); identified by Paul Cauthen.
10	Majo, Gian Francesco de	*Ifigenia in Tauride* (5 November 1764; premiere)	(*a*) D-B, Mus. ms. 13396 (App. A/VI/31). "Mannheim" binding; see fig. 8:2. (*b*) D-B, Mus. ms. 13396/1 (App. A/VI/32). Not a complete score but a selection of arias and other numbers, here in one volume (cf. next entry).
11	Majo, Gian Francesco de	*Alessandro nell'Indie* (5 November 1766; premiere)	D-B, Mus. ms. 13400 (App. A/VI/33). Like no. 10b, a selection of arias and other numbers, here bound by act into three volumes.

No.	Composer	Work	Manuscripts
12	Piccinni, Niccolò	*Catone in Utica* (5 November 1770; premiere)g	(*a*) D-Mbs, Mus. Ms. 2426. Aut. score by Piccinni, but with numerous insertions and paste-ons by known Mannheim copyists on Mannheim papers, including an insertion aria by Sacchini (App. A/VI/150).h (*b*) GB-Lbl, Add. 30792–94 (App. A/VI/197).i
13	Salieri, Antonio	*La fiera di Venezia* (22 November 1772)	(*a*) D-Mbs, Mus. Ms. 2524. Score probably Viennese, but with numerous corrections in the hand of Ignaz Holzbauer. (*b*) B-Bc, no. 2336 (App. A/VI/5). (*c*) D-Dlb, Mus. 3796-F-3 (App. A/VI/140).
14	Salieri, Antonio	*La secchia rapita* (5 November 1774)	(*a*) D-Mbs, Mus. Ms. 2525. Score probably Viennese, but with numerous corrections and additions by Holzbauer, including two insertion arias on Mannheim paper (see App. A/VI/151). (*b*) GB-Lbl, Add. 16119 (App. A/VI/196). "Mannheim" binding.j
15	Schweitzer, Anton	*Alceste* (13 August 1775)	US-CAhm, Mus 800.21.605 (cage) (App. A/VI/200). Unbound vocal score, voice parts and continuo only. Italian trans. of original German (see discussion in text).
16	Traetta, Tommaso	*Sofonisba* (5 November 1762; premiere)	(*a*) D-B, Mus. ms. 22001 (App. A/VI/37). "Mannheim" binding; see fig. 8:1. (*b*) US-Wc, M 1500.T76 S5 (App. A/VI/204). Slightly revised version with date of 1763 on title page.
17	Traetta, Tommaso	*Ippolito ed Aricia* (Parma, 9 May 1759)	D-B, Mus. ms. 21995.k Score very probably of Italian origin, but with "Mannheim" binding and flyleaves on Heusler 7 paper. Also listed together with the above manuscripts in a thematic catalogue associated with Mannheim to be discussed below.
18	Traetta, Tommaso	*I Tindaridi* (i.e., *Tintaridi*; Parma, April 1760)	D-B, Mus. ms. 22003; identified by Joachim Jaenecke. Score very probably of Italian origin, but with "Mannheim" binding and flyleaves on Heusler <NH> paper. Also listed together with the above manuscripts in a thematic catalogue associated with Mannheim to be discussed below.

---

[a] The facsimile of *Temistocle* in vol. 7 of *The Collected Works of Johann Christian Bach*, ed. Ernest Warburton (New York: Garland Publishing, 1988), provides an unfortunately typical example of what can happen in the absence of thorough knowledge of the source tradition: this edition reproduces act 2 from a local Darmstadt copy (D-DS, Mus. ms. 62) rather than from one of the extant Mann-

heim manuscripts (nos. 1a–b; acts 1 and 3 are autographs). We might note at this point that we do not consider the manuscript of *Temistocle* at Yale (New Haven, Ct., Yale University, Beinecke Library, Music Library Collection, Misc. Ms. 140) to be from Mannheim: it is on French paper, rare at Mannheim (see Appendix B/IV); it is ruled with a simple rastrum (12 x 1); and none of the copyists is familiar to us. Nor is the other of the Darmstadt manuscripts of this opera, Mus. ms. 63, a Mannheim copy.

b The date of the first performance of Bach's *Endimione* at Mannheim is not clear. A copy of the libretto (Mannheim, n.d.) in the Theatersammlung of the Reiss-Museum in Mannheim (Sign. T 222) has the handwritten notation "februar 1774[.] Vorher oggersheim [summer residence of the electress] 1770." According to Richard Maunder, introduction to *Endimione*, vol. 14 of *The Collected Works of Johann Christian Bach* (New York: Garland Publishing, 1985), p. vii, when the work was first performed in London in April 1772 the Mannheim flutist Johann Baptist Wendling was a featured member of the orchestra. Maunder speculates that Wendling may have taken the score of *Endimione* back to Mannheim and arranged for a performance there before the premiere of *Temistocle* in November 1772, a theory for which, however, no documentary evidence exists. To complicate matters, Count Andreas von Riaucour, Saxon envoy at the Mannheim court, reports on preparations for a gala performance of *Endimione* on 24 July 1773, but gives the composer as Jommelli (Staatsarchiv Dresden [formerly Sächsisches Hauptstaatsarchiv], Geheimes Kabinett, Loc. 2627, Bd. XXVI, report of 20 July 1773; see Corneilson, *Opera at Mannheim*, 381). As a matter of fact, Jommelli did add a new scene for the Mannheim performance of Bach's *Endimione*, the text for which was provided by the Mannheim librettist Mattia Verazi; hence, Riaucour either mistakenly neglected to mention Bach's name in addition to Jommelli's or (less plausibly) the Oggersheim performance was of Jommelli's *own* full setting of *Endimione*, which dates from 1759. In any event, the 1770 date for an Oggersheim performance of Bach's *Endimione* is an unlikely one.

c On this date see Paul Corneilson, "The Case of J. C. Bach's *Lucio Silla*," *Journal of Musicology* 12 (1994): 206–18.

d A facsimile of this manuscript appears in *The Collected Works of Johann Christian Bach*, vol. 8, ed. Ernest Warburton (1986).

e A facsimile of this manuscript, ed. Bärbel Pelker, has appeared in the series *Quellen zur Musikgeschichte in Baden-Württemberg*, vol. 1 (Munich: Strube-Verlag, 2000).

f A revised German version of this work dating from 1780, entitled *Tod der Dido*, is preserved in the manuscript US-Wc, M 1500.H77 T5. The score does not, however, stem from Mannheim; its most likely provenance would perhaps be Vienna.

g *Catone in Utica* received its first performance at Mannheim, though it was evidently not commissioned originally by the court; see Reinhard Strohm, *Die italienische Oper im 18. Jahrhundert* (Wilhelmshaven: Heinrichshofen, 1979), 339–40; Corneilson, "Opera at Mannheim," 104–8. Cf. also fn. 9, below.

h Reinhard Strohm was the first to note that this score contained additions by Mannheim copyists; see Howard Mayer Brown, ed., *Italian Opera, 1640–1770*, vol. 50 (New York: Garland Publishing, 1978), preface (unpag.), n. 5.

i Facsimile in Brown, *Italian Opera*, vol. 50.

j We are grateful to Arthur Searle, former Curator of Music Manuscripts of the British Library, for sending a detailed description of the binding of this manuscript, which allowed us to link it with the other seven manuscripts in this group. We have since examined the manuscript in person and confirmed this conclusion.

k Facsimile in Brown, *Italian Opera*, vol. 78 (1982), ed. Eric Weimer.

1774.⁷ (For full information on the papers, staving, and copyists of these sources see Appendix A/VI.) It also includes the six manuscripts mentioned above that were not actually copied at Mannheim (nos. 8, 12a, 13a, 14a, 17, and 18). Unless otherwise indicated, all dates are those of the first performance at Mannheim. All these works originate from the period before departure of the court for Munich in 1778 except, as already mentioned, Holzbauer's *La morte di Didone* of July 1779 (no. 7), which nonetheless still clearly represents the traditions of court opera at Mannheim (and the score to which is by Mannheim 6, who must therefore have remained there after 1778). The phrase "'Mannheim' binding" in table 8:1 refers to the similar leather bindings with gilt lettering and decoration shared by eight magnificent one-volume scores that were probably bound in Mannheim (see the discussion of the third group of manuscripts below). We might also point out that table 8:1 corrects a great deal of inexcusable misinformation in the secondary literature regarding such matters as dates, library locations, and call numbers for these works.⁸

The 27 manuscripts listed in table 8:1 fall into three fairly distinct groups. The first and largest consists of the more-or-less normal Mannheim manuscripts 1b, 2–4, 6a–b, 7, 9b, 10b, 11, 12b, 13b–c, 15, and 16b. These have been copied for the most part on standard Mannheim papers by known court copyists, primarily Mannheim 1 and 5–6. The staving of these manuscripts is noteworthy in that small one-, two-, and also five-stave rastra are more commonly used in them than in the "official" court copies now located in Munich and elsewhere, which mainly employ large ten- and (for the choruses) twelve-stave rastra; this may indicate that the paper of the opera manuscripts was lined by the individual copyists. In turn, the obvious conclusion to be drawn is that in many cases the copyists were acting on their own in preparing the scores, whether with or without the knowledge of the elector (not to put too fine a point on it).

The next group of manuscripts, consisting of nos. 8, 12a, 13a, and 14a in table 8:1, was not actually copied in Mannheim. However, as already noted, each of these manuscripts contains additions showing that they were used at, or were at least at one time in the possession of, the electoral court. For example, the autograph score of Piccinni's *Catone in Utica* (no. 12a) has numerous paste-ins and insertions by Mannheim copyists, indicating that it was utilized in preparing the

---

[7] The event, at which Gluck was present, is described in Johann Christian von Mannlich, *Rokoko und Revolution: Lebenserinnerungen*, ed. Friedrich Matthaesius (Stuttgart: K. F. Koehler, 1966), 187–88.

[8] Errors common in the work-lists of *The New Grove Dictionary of Opera*, for example, include the continued listing as extant of works destroyed in World War II (see the appendix to the present chapter) and the confusion of works in the former Deutsche Staatsbibliothek with those in the Staatsbibliothek zu Berlin – Preussischer Kulturbesitz and vice versa—the latter errors now happily without consequence, as the collections have been reunited.

performance on 5 November 1770, as part of the elector's name-day celebrations.[9] Similarly, the two copies, probably Viennese, of comic operas by Antonio Salieri (nos. 13a and 14a) were probably provided by the composer for the same purpose, as they have many corrections and additions (including in the latter opera two insertion arias) in the hand of Ignaz Holzbauer.[10]

For the remaining manuscript in this group, that to Jommelli's *Artaserse* (no. 8), the disposition of evidence is a bit different. The score itself is probably of Roman provenance.[11] But the second and third volumes of the manuscript each have the title written on page 1 in Holzbauer's hand, and the flyleaves of all the volumes are on typical Mannheim papers. The title page of the manuscript bears the date 1750, one year before the Mannheim performance of the work and one year after its premiere; as mentioned earlier (see fn. 3 and related discussion), it was in that year that the electoral court obtained a copy of the score, supposedly an autograph, from the composer in Rome.[12]

Certainly the most intriguing of these sources from the methodological and historical standpoints are the eight manuscripts of our third group, consisting of nos. 1a, 5, 9a, 10a, 14b, 16a, 17, and 18. With the exception of no. 9a, the Washington manuscript of Jommelli's *Cajo Fabrizio*, and no. 14b, the London manuscript of Salieri's *La secchia rapita*, all these scores are now in Berlin. The first six of these eight sources are strikingly similar—large one-volume scores by Mannheim 5. The remaining two (nos. 17–18), like the manuscripts of the previous group, were not actually copied at Mannheim but are very probably Italian.

Of the six sources copied at Mannheim, the only real anomaly is the score to *Cajo Fabrizio*. Whereas the other five manuscripts are copied straight through, without revisions or insertions, the Jommelli score presents a far more complicated picture: detailed examination of the fascicle structure, staving, ink color, and the

---

[9] The score of *Catone in Utica* may well have been brought to Mannheim by the tenor Anton Raaff, who returned there from Naples that summer. One of the insertions is an aria by Antonio Sacchini, a favorite of the electress (fols. 79–88, copied by Mannheim 6; see App. A/VI/150). On the circumstances surrounding the Mannheim premiere of this opera see Corneilson, "Opera at Mannheim," 104–8. Cf. also table 8:1, fn. g.

[10] Interestingly, though, another insertion aria in no. 14a (vol. 1, fols. 82r–87v) is in the hand of Sixtus Hirsvogl, a Munich oboist and copyist who was never in Mannheim, showing that the score was used in Munich after 1778, as well.

[11] Helmut Hell, *Die neapolitanische Opernsinfonie in der ersten Hälfte des 18. Jahrhunderts* (Tutzing: Hans Schneider, 1971), 433. There are actually three copyists (not just one) in both the Jommelli and Pergolesi manuscripts mentioned by Hell, one of whom appears in both scores.

[12] Sandberger, "Aus der Korrespondenz des pfalzbayerischen Kurfürsten Karl Theodor," 218–20. See also Cheryl R. Sprague, *A Comparison of Five Musical Settings of Metastasio's Artaserse* (Ph.D. diss., University of California, Los Angeles, 1979), 185–95. We might note at this point that nos. 17–18 in table 8:1, which could logically belong to the present (second) group because they were copied elsewhere (in this case probably Italy), will be discussed as part of our third and final group for reasons that will soon become obvious.

like shows that the manuscript was compiled over at least a somewhat extended period of time, with frequent additions and revisions.[13] The score even includes an optional ending for the second act that is not present in either the libretto or the Eastman score (no. 9b), which follows the libretto closely.[14] These comments are not, however, intended to suggest that, as is frequently the case, the manuscript has accrued revisions and additions over a period of years and from many different sources; the copyist and paper (though not the staving and ink color) are the same throughout. More likely would be a period of months, perhaps as Jommelli—and also Giuseppe Colla, who as indicated in the libretto composed five of the seven arias in act 1 and the first two in act 2—provided fresh material to the court. That Colla was involved at all implies that an element of haste may have been present.

The two remaining works in this group, nos. 17–18, are by Tommaso Traetta. Judging by the copying style and paper of these manuscripts, they are very likely Italian in origin, whereas both manuscripts of the other work by Traetta in table 8:1, no. 16, are definitely Mannheim copies. They also differ from no. 16 in that no performance of either is known to have taken place at Mannheim, and they contain no additions or annotations by known Mannheimers, as had the second group of manuscripts discussed above.

What, then, is the nature of the connection linking nos. 17–18 with the other six scores in this alleged grouping? The most obvious bond between all these manuscripts will be immediately apparent to anyone consulting them: their sumptuous leather bindings, with splendid gilt lettering and decoration on their spines, discreetly highlighted in red (see fig. 8:1). In addition, most of the scores have a decorative frame on both covers containing the abbreviation "N°," but with a blank where the number would go (see figs. 8:2 and 7a, below); the intent on the part of the binder was clearly to leave the actual numbering to the collector.[15] Though the bindings do not all seem to have been done at the same time, they are quite similar in overall style and unquestionably came from the same workshop. As the majority of the scores were known to have been copied in Mannheim, it seemed reasonable to us to suppose that they might have been bound there as well.

---

[13] We thank Paul Cauthen of the University of Cincinnati for making available to us an unpublished essay of his on *Cajo Fabrizio* that includes a detailed study of the physical characteristics of the Washington score.

[14] Also present in the Washington score alone is an alternate setting of the aria "Quando avvien" (act 1, scene 4), by Tommaso Traetta; the first, presumably original, version is by Colla.

[15] In the case of the Washington score the abbreviation "N°" has been obliterated and a coat of arms added within the frame, identification of which has allowed us to determine the owner of these manuscripts; see fig. 8:7b and fn. 35, below. The authors express their appreciation to Dr. Helmut Hell of the Staatsbibliothek zu Berlin – Preussischer Kulturbesitz for permission to reproduce figs. 8:1–7a and to Dr. James W. Pruett, formerly of the Library of Congress, for permission to reproduce fig. 8:7b.

Chapter 8

Figure 8:1. Decorative spines of scores to Gassmann's *L'amore artigiano* and Traetta's *Sofonisba* (App. A/VI/24, 37). Staatsbibliothek zu Berlin – Preussischer Kulturbesitz, Mus. ms. 7130 and 22001.

Figure 8:2. Front cover of score to Majo's *Ifigenia in Tauride* (App. A/VI/31). Staatsbibliothek zu Berlin – Preussischer Kulturbesitz, Mus. ms. 13396. See also figure 8:7a.

In order to test this hypothesis we took several tacks. One was to attempt to ascertain whether additional examples of this binding existed in Berlin; after all, it might be a normal binding from the *Prussian* court. We therefore asked Dr. Joachim Jaenecke of the Staatsbibliothek zu Berlin, an authority on eighteenth-century manuscripts, whether he might be willing to scan the shelves of the manuscript collection there—one of the largest in the world, containing thousands of volumes—to see whether similar bindings might be present. He generously agreed to take on this daunting task, and was able to discover one—but only one—additional source: that to Traetta's *I Tintaridi* (table 8:1, no. 18). This manuscript turned out to be a pair with the manuscript of the same composer's *Ippolito ed Aricia*, no. 17, sharing one of its copyists and one of its papers. Thereafter we were able to determine that the copies of Jommelli's *Cajo Fabrizio* in Washington and Salieri's *La secchia rapita* in London also had the same binding, further evidence that we were not dealing with a collection originally assembled and bound in Berlin.

The next step was obvious: to see whether we could determine what a binding from the court bindery in Mannheim actually looked like. Though most of the famous library of Carl Theodor has been dispersed or destroyed, enough volumes still exist in the library of the Städtisches Reiss-Museum in Mannheim to show a clear similarity between the volumes bound at court and those of this group of manuscripts.[16] The similarities include both basic design and the use of decorative motifs such as flowers, foliage, circles, and stars. However, no *precisely* equivalent binding was found, and the overall similarity of much eighteenth-century gilt decoration and lettering makes it hazardous to draw absolute conclusions on this basis alone. It was thus fortunate for our hypothesis that an additional element of the binding—the flyleaves—supported the attribution to Mannheim, for the latter make use of Swiss papers that were standard there, as well as of a similar marbleized paper as facing for the inside of the covers.

The Berlin Catalogue

Our initial thought was that the Berlin scores might have been copied at Mannheim as gifts for Frederick II, but again the existence in Washington and London of manuscripts that had obviously come from the same original collection (nos. 9a and 14b) seemed to rule this out.[17] Then, while going through the old card catalogue at the former Deutsche Staatsbibliothek in Berlin, Paul Corneilson came upon a refer-

---

[16] We are grateful to Liselotte Homering and Dr. Grit Arnscheidt of the Reiss-Museum Mannheim and to Brigitte Höft, formerly of the Städtische Musikbücherei in Mannheim, for facilitating our examination of these volumes and for many other kindnesses.

[17] The London score was owned by Domenico Dragonetti, who left it to the British Museum upon his death in 1846.

ence to an eighteenth-century thematic catalogue in that collection that listed several Mannheim operas.[18] This catalogue, virtually unknown in the scholarly literature, turned out to contain detailed listings, with extensive incipits, for two oratorios, one psalm setting,[19] and fourteen operas,[20] a majority of which had in fact received performances—often premieres—at Mannheim.

From the physical standpoint, the Berlin catalogue has no title page, date, or indication of origin. The most likely provenance would be France, as the compiler of the catalogue uses the French *page* in various forms on pages 1–4 and frequently adds comments in French like "Parties Detachés" (*sic*; see figs. 8:3–4).[21] The watermark of the catalogue, <D & C BLAUW> with a fleur-de-lis as countermark, is that of a Dutch firm whose papers are fairly common in France. The catalogue is paginated in the hand of the copyist and is evidently incomplete, breaking off with page 32 after the incipit for the first aria of act 2 of Gluck's *Alceste*.[22]

Table 8:2 gives the contents of the Berlin catalogue. We have retained the orthography of the titles in the catalogue. Unless otherwise specified, the dates supplied are those of the first performance at Mannheim. As can be seen in table 8:2, the catalogue is organized by composer, with two oratorios and two operas by Ignaz Holzbauer first, followed by operas (and the one sacred work) by non-Mannheimers. Incipits, both textual and musical, are given for arias, ensembles, and obbligato recitatives, while choruses have only textual incipits (see, e.g., the middle of figs. 8:4 and 6). Purely instrumental numbers as well as simple recitatives are not indicated in any way. Within each work, the copyist provides his own numbering of the various items to the left of the incipit, and the page number of the score on which each item begins to the right.

This is a rather unusual collection of works, to say the least. The one common denominator would seem to be Mannheim: most of the works in the catalogue are known to have been performed there, and many were actually commissioned by

---

[18] Now D-B, Mus. ms. theor. Kat. 860. The catalogue is listed in Barry S. Brook and Richard Viano, *Thematic Catalogues in Music: An Annotated Bibliography* (2d ed., Stuyvesant, N.Y.: Pendragon Press, 1997), pp. 38–39, no. 110.

[19] The psalm setting is Jommelli's *Salmo L*, with Italian text by Saverio Mattei. It has been crossed out in the catalogue (p. 15) and will be disregarded in the remainder of this chapter.

[20] One of the operas, Gluck's *Le feste d'Apollo* (Parma, 1769), consists of a prologue and three independent acts, the last a revised version of his *Orfeo ed Euridice* of 1762; see below. The page numbers given in the catalogue indicate that the four parts of the work were through-paginated, i.e., that the score containing them was probably in one volume, like the other extant manuscripts from the collection.

[21] "Parties Detachés," pp. 4 (fig. 8:4), 31; "Parties Separés," "Fin," p. 15; "Suitte de Nitetti," top of p. 4 (fig. 8:4). In addition, the copyist uses a form of the C clef that is common in French manuscripts (see figs. 8:3–6).

[22] The compiler of the catalogue neglects to indicate the beginning of act 2, however. That the catalogue is in fact incomplete will be shown in the discussion below of no. 15, Schweitzer's *Alceste*.

Figure 8:3. Page 1 of Sickingen thematic catalogue. Staatsbibliothek zu Berlin – Preussischer Kulturbesitz, Mus. ms. theor. Kat. 860.

Other Manuscripts, I: Operas and Related Works

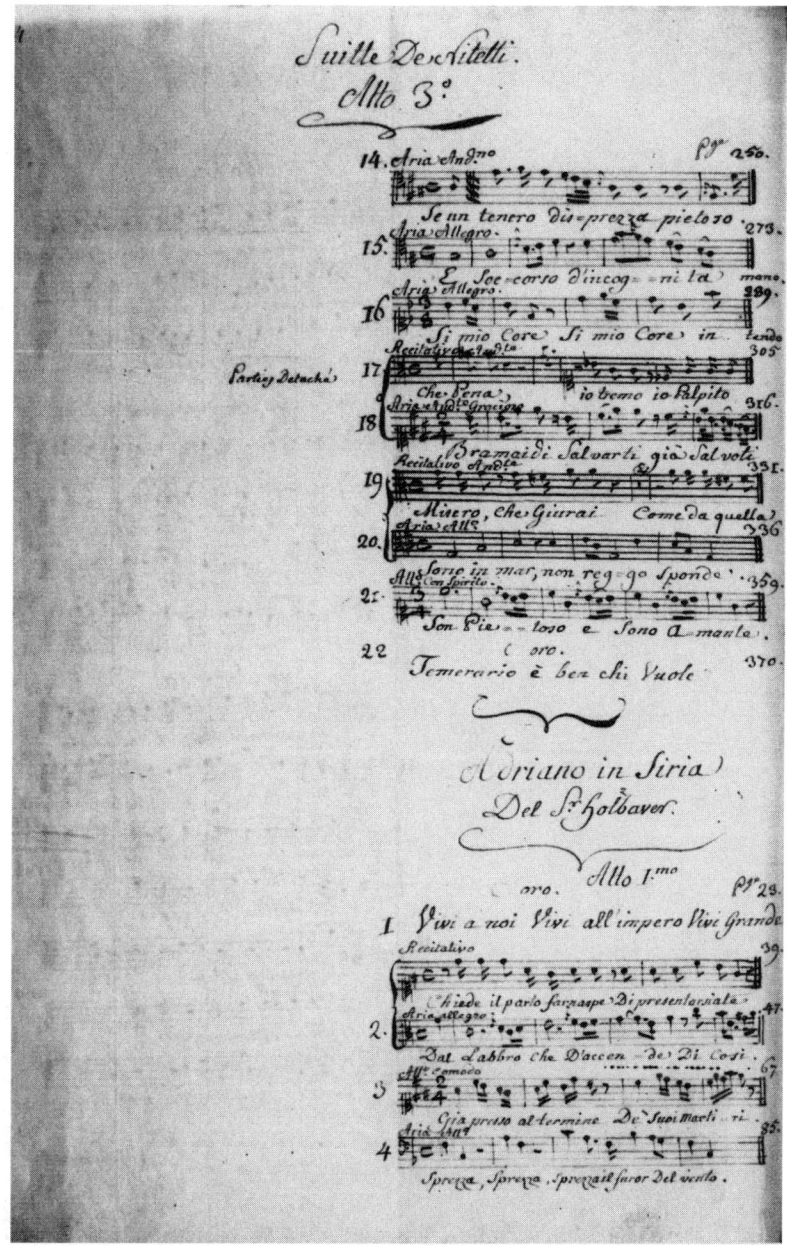

Figure 8:4. Page 4 of Sickingen thematic catalogue, with incipits from act 1 of Holzbauer's lost opera *Adriano in Siria* (Mannheim, 1768).

Figure 8:5. Page 5 of Sickingen catalogue.

Other Manuscripts, I: Operas and Related Works

Figure 8:6. Page 6 of Sickingen catalogue.

189

Table 8:2. Contents of an Eighteenth-Century Thematic Catalogue (D-B, Mus. ms. theor. Kat. 860; the "Sickingen" Catalogue).

No.	Composer	Work	Pages in catalogue	Comments
1	Ignaz Holzbauer	*Il giudicio [giudizio] di Salomone* (1765)	1	See fig. 8:3.
2	Ignaz Holzbauer	*Bertulia [Betulia] liberata* (1760, rev. 1774)	1–2	See fig. 8:3.
3	Ignaz Holzbauer	*La Nitetti [Nitteti]* (1758)	3–4	
4	Ignaz Holzbauer	*Adriano in Siria* (1768)	4–6	See figs. 8:4–6.
5	Tommaso Traetta ("Trajetta")	*Sofonisba* (1762)	6–8	See fig. 8:6.
6	Tommaso Traetta ("Trajetta")	*Ippolito ed Aricia* (Parma, 1759)	8–10	
7	Tommaso Traetta ("Trajetta")	*Tindaridi [Tintaridi]* (Parma, 1760)	11–13	
8	Niccolò Jommelli	*Cajo Fabrizio* (1760)	14–15	Five other arias for this opera by Giuseppe Colla and one by Traetta are listed separately under the rubric "Supplemento in cajo E Fabrizio" on p. 21.
(9)	Niccolò Jommelli	*Salmo L* ("Pietà, pietà Signore")	15	Crossed out in catalogue.
10	Antonio Salieri	*La fiera di Venezia* (1772)	15–17	
11	Antonio Salieri	*La secchia rapita* (1774)	17–19	
12	Gian Francesco de Majo	*Ifigenia in Tauride* (1764)	19–21	
13	Florian Leopold Gassmann	*L'amore artigiano* (1772)	22–23	
14	Niccolò Piccinni	*Catone in Utica* (1770)	24–25	
15	Niccolò Piccinni	*Le contadine bizzar[r]e* (Rome, 1763)	25–27	
16a	Christoph Willibald Gluck	*Prologo d'Appollo* (Parma, 1769)	28	Numbers 16a–d are the four parts of Gluck's *Le feste d'Apollo*.
16b	Christoph Willibald Gluck	*Atto di Bauci* (Parma, 1769)	28–29	
16c	Christoph Willibald Gluck	*Atto d'Aristeo* (Parma, 1769)	29–30	
16d	Christoph Willibald Gluck	*Atto d'Orfeo* (Parma, 1769)	30–31	Orig. version, *Orfeo ed Euridice*, Vienna, 1762.
17	Christoph Willibald Gluck	*Alceste* (1767, Italian version)	32	Act 1 and first aria of act 2 only, after which the catalogue breaks off.
[18]	Anton Schweitzer	*Alceste* (1775)	[35]	Probable listing in original catalogue; see discussion in text.

the court. Indeed, as the observant reader may have noticed, every opera in the catalogue with the exception of Piccinni's *Le contadine bizzarre* and those by Holzbauer and Gluck have already appeared in the list of extant manuscripts from Mannheim given in table 8:1.[23] But the connection is even closer than that: for not only do seven of the eight scores that have what we have labeled "Mannheim" bindings appear in the catalogue (as nos. 5–8 and 11–13; the exception is J. C. Bach's *Temistocle*), but the extremely detailed paginations given therein match precisely, in every case, with those of the manuscripts themselves. Even the rather haphazard spelling of the scores is generally preserved in the catalogue—"Trajetta" for Traetta, "Tindaridi" for *Tintaridi*, and so on.[24] In short, there can be no question that the scores with "Mannheim" bindings were once actually a part of the collection recorded so meticulously in the Berlin catalogue.

As for the other works in the catalogue, the only two with no demonstrable connection to Mannheim are Piccinni's *Le contadine bizzarre* (no. 15) and Gluck's *Le feste d'Apollo*, which as mentioned earlier consists of a prologue with three independent acts, the last a revised version, without division into acts, of his *Orfeo ed Euridice* of 1762 (nos. 16a–d).[25] As regards the other Gluck opera on the list, *Alceste*, no connection with Mannheim had ever been documented until recently, when an examination by Paul Corneilson of the official correspondence of Count Andreas von Riaucour, the Saxon envoy at the court of Mannheim, turned up the following report, dated Mannheim, 25 July 1769:

---

[23] Autograph scores of the two Holzbauer oratorios in the catalogue have survived in Vienna and Munich (App. A/II/17–18), but the paginations show that these were not the manuscripts listed in the catalogue. The score of Holzbauer's *Nitteti* in Regensburg (Bischöfliche Zentralbibliothek, Proske-Musikbibliothek) is neither an autograph nor (in our opinion) a Mannheim manuscript. We have not examined the score of this opera in Lisbon.

[24] Likewise worth noting is that the converse relationship between the catalogue listings and the scores with "Mannheim" bindings also holds, for none of the other manuscripts, those with conventional bindings, matches the listings in the catalogue.

[25] Until World War II the Joachimsthal'sches Gymnasium in Berlin owned manuscripts of the prologue and first two acts of Gluck's *Le feste d'Apollo* (see Robert Eitner, *Biographisch-bibliographisches Quellen-Lexikon der Musiker und Musikgelehrten* [Leipzig: Breitkopf & Härtel, 1898–1904], 4:284), raising the possibility that they, like the six manuscripts with "Mannheim" bindings in the Staatsbibliothek in Berlin, might stem from the collection listed in the catalogue. However, the call numbers in the Gymnasium library are given by Eitner as 108–10, and hence, evidently unlike the score to *Feste d'Apollo* indexed in the catalogue, they seem to have been separate volumes. Nor does Eitner list a manuscript for act 3, the *Atto d'Orfeo*. That the Joachimsthal manuscripts were in separate volumes and lacked the final act is confirmed by two nineteenth-century copies made from them, the one in the Bibliothèque du Conservatoire royal in Brussels (MSM 12.841, dated 1866), the other in the Schweizerisches Literaturarchiv of the Schweizerische Landesbibliothek in Bern (ML Hs 25): both copies, in the same hand, were originally in three separately paginated volumes and lack the *Atto d'Orfeo*. In addition, they show numerous discrepancies in orthography and wording with the listing in the catalogue.

Chapter 8

Last Saturday [22 July 1769], during a rehearsal at court in the presence of the elector and his entire court of the first act of the opera *Alceste*, composed by Gluck, which is to be given at the theater of Mannheim during the next carnival season, there was a violent storm accompanied by thunderbolts, which struck in several places without causing any damage other than to kill one of the horses of the equerry of his electoral highness and to injure another.[26]

Though no performance of *Alceste* seems actually to have taken place—the principal opera for the carnival season of 1770 was Galuppi's *L'amante di tutte*—one was clearly planned, even to the extent of mounting a public rehearsal.

For the two other works in the catalogue that are not known to have been performed at Mannheim, Traetta's *Ippolito ed Aricia* and *I Tintaridi* (nos. 6–7), the bindings of their scores in Berlin establish a firm link with Mannheim. It may be recalled that the third work by Traetta in the catalogue, his *Sofonisba* (no. 5), was commissioned by the elector and received its premiere in Mannheim in 1762; the scores for the two earlier operas may have been obtained by the court as part of the negotiations for that commission.

But for *Ippolito ed Aricia*, at least, there exists a further association with Mannheim, though one of a murkier sort: for on 5 November 1759, just six months after the premiere of the Traetta opera in Parma, Ignaz Holzbauer produced his own *Ippolito ed Aricia* on a libretto that is virtually identical to that of the Traetta setting. However, as only that libretto survives, one cannot know to what extent the Holzbauer version is modeled on—or indeed pirated from—the Traetta original, though the short time between the two productions certainly encourages speculation along those lines.[27]

The inclusion in the catalogue of the four works by Holzbauer has particular importance because the music of one of the operas listed, *Adriano in Siria*, has been lost. Besides documenting the existence of this work, the incipits given in figures

---

[26] "Samedi passé, pendant qu'on faisoit répéter à la Cour en présence de Monseigneur l'Electeur et de toutte sa Cour le premier acte de l'opéra d'Alceste composé par Gluck, qu'on donnera sur le Théâtre à Mannheim pendant le carnaval prochain, il y eut un violent orage accompagné de tonnerre, lequel tomba en plusieurs endroits sans faire d'autre mal que de tuer un des chevaux des écuries de S. A. E. et d'en blesser un autre." Dresden, Staatsarchiv, Geheimes Kabinett, Loc. 2626, Bd. XXII, report of 25 July 1769; see Corneilson, "Opera at Mannheim," 372–73.

[27] The possibility that Holzbauer used at least some of Traetta's music is suggested by Daniel Heartz in his article on the composer in *New Grove*, 1st ed., 19:111. Holzbauer was in Milan during carnival of 1759 and could easily have passed through Parma on his way back to Mannheim, possibly even attending a performance of *Ippolito ed Aricia*. For a fuller treatment of the entire subject see Corneilson, "Opera at Mannheim," 91–93. Klaus Hortschansky, "Ignaz Holzbauers *Ippolito ed Aricia* (1759): zur Einführung der Tragédie lyrique in Mannheim," in *Aufklärungen: Studien zur deutsch-französischen Musikgeschichte im 18. Jahrhundert*, vol. 2, ed. Wolfgang Birtel and Christoph-Hellmut Mahling (Heidelberg: Carl Winter, 1986), 105–16, seems blissfully oblivious to all the issues just raised, and he also gets the date of the Parma premiere wrong (it was 9 May 1759).

8:4–6 may enable someone to identify one of the surviving anonymous settings of the text as Holzbauer's. In addition, though naturally limited in the amount of information they can supply about formal aspects of the work, the incipits preserve most of the tempo markings, along with the time and key signatures, and convey a sense of the character of each number.

The most striking omission in the catalogue is J. C. Bach, at least four of whose works are known to have been performed at Mannheim—two of them operas commissioned by the court.[28] (As will be recalled, all these are extant in copies from Mannheim, nos. 1–4 in table 8:1.) Most notably, the catalogue fails to include Bach's *Temistocle*, the "Mannheim" binding of which links it decisively with the other works in the catalogue. The problem does not seem to be one of date, for *Temistocle* (1772) comes well before the latest work in the catalogue, Salieri's *La secchia rapita* of November 1774. (*Lucio Silla*, however, *is* later, receiving its first performance in November 1775.)[29] The most likely explanation is that *Temistocle* appeared on one of the missing final pages of the catalogue, which as noted earlier breaks off in the middle of Gluck's *Alceste*.

That the catalogue is in fact incomplete, originally containing at least four additional pages, emerges from a consideration of App. A/VI/200, an unbound vocal score of Anton Schweitzer's *Alceste* with the text in Italian rather than the original German. An added notation on the first page of the manuscript refers to the latter characteristic, saying, "ápart Traduit En Allemand a La Table P.^{ge} 36." This notation suggested to us that it might well be referring to a missing page of the catalogue, which breaks off after page 32; each of the listings in the catalogue is, after all, a kind of "table." And indeed this seems to be the case: for a careful examination of the handwriting reveals that the writer of the notation is also the copyist of both the catalogue and the added page numbers in App. A/VI/200 and other manuscripts in the collection. Less clear is the rationale for the translation into Italian; the many performances of *Alceste* at Mannheim in 1775 and 1776 were all in German, as seen also in the reference to the work on page 1 of the score cited above. One notes, however, that all the works in the catalogue are in Italian, and the owner of the collection may have commissioned or otherwise obtained the translation based on personal preference.

However that may be, the surviving evidence allows us tentatively to sketch the likely history of the collection: the manuscripts were copied for or otherwise obtained by a patron with strong ties to the Mannheim court; at least eight of the

---

[28] A fifth work of Bach's that may well have been performed at Mannheim, and was certainly known there, was his cantata *La tempesta*, printed in Vogler's *Betrachtungen der Mannheimer Tonschule*, vol. 1 ([Mannheim:] n.p., 1778), *Gegenstände*, Erste Lieferung (July), plates X–XVI, and Zweite Lieferung (August), plates VII–XVI; repr. ed. (Hildesheim: Georg Olms, 1974), 4:22–28, 35–44.

[29] See Corneilson, "J. C. Bach's *Lucio Silla*."

volumes were bound for him, probably in Mannheim; they were catalogued either for him or (less likely) after his death, possibly in France; and they were eventually sold or otherwise disposed of, the largest segment ending up in Berlin.

The Owner of the Collection Identified

But who was the original owner of this collection? It would not appear to have been Carl Theodor himself, for we know that the court's library of older music, left in Mannheim after 1778, was destroyed in 1795. Ignaz Holzbauer might seem a logical choice because his works appear first, but the catalogue contains only a small portion of his dramatic *œuvre*, and the lavish bindings of the manuscripts would seem to rule out even a high-ranking court musician like him (or, another alternative, Abbé Vogler).[30] In any case, none of the foregoing possibilities squares well with the likely provenance of the Berlin thematic catalogue—possibly French, but almost certainly not Mannheim.

A more intriguing candidate as owner of the collection is Count Carl Heinrich Joseph von Sickingen (1737–91), privy councillor to Carl Theodor and his envoy in Paris from the late 1760s until his death.[31] First of all, Count von Sickingen—a great lover of music and theater as well as a renowned chemist—would have had access to and interest in the works represented in this collection. Second, his presence in Paris provides a perfect explanation for a note to "Monsieur L'Envoyé de Palatin" from the (Parisian) "Duchesse de Cossé" inserted in the Washington score to Jommelli's *Cajo Fabrizio*.[32] This note says,

---

[30] It is worth noting in this connection that neither of these composers' extant autograph scores have this type of binding. Vogler *did* own a copy of at least one of J. C. Bach's Mannheim operas, namely *Lucio Silla*—the one he loaned to Mozart in 1777, soon after the latter's arrival in Mannheim; see Mozart's letter of 13 November 1777 in Bauer-Deutsch, 2:120, and Anderson, 370. This is certainly the copy still present in Darmstadt (table 8:1, no. 4), where Vogler died and much of his *Nachlaß* remained.

[31] On Sickingen see B. Lepsius, "Sickingen, Karl Heinrich Joseph Reichsgraf von S.," *Allgemeine deutsche Biographie* 34 (Leipzig: Duncker & Humblot, 1892): 158–60; Peter Clive, *Mozart and His Circle: A Biographical Dictionary* (New Haven: Yale University Press, 1993), 140–41. Sickingen first appears in the personnel listings of the *Chur-Pfältzischer Hoff- und Staats-Calender* (p. 64) and the *Almanach électoral palatin* (p. 49) in 1769; as these were prepared during the previous year, his appointment probably dates from 1768. (He is already mentioned as a privy councillor to the elector by Riaucour in summer of 1768; Staatsarchiv Dresden, Geheimes Kabinett, Loc. 2626, Bd. XXI.) His position is given in the almanacs as privy councillor and minister plenipotentiary in Paris. Through 1775 his title is "Freyherr" or "Baron," after which it becomes "Graf" or "Comte." Thanks are due to Brigitte Höft for kindly sending information on the 1769 *Calender* and *Almanach*.

[32] The duchesse de Cossé was probably Adélaïde-Diane-Hortense-Délie Mancini de Nevers (b. 1742), who in February 1760 married Louis-Hercule-Timoléon, duc de Cossé and (from 1780) duc de Brissac (1734–92). See "Cossé, Louis-Hercule-Timoléon de," in [François-Alexandre Aubert]

Mad^e La Duchesse de Cossé prie Monsieur L'Envoyé de Palatin de lui faire L'honneur de venir souper chez elle Dimanche prochain 23 du présent[.]

Ce 21. 8bre [probably 1768 or 1774.]³³

Third, von Sickingen's connection with Paris accords well with our tentative designation of the catalogue as French. And fourth, Sickingen was in fact the owner of a substantial collection of opera scores, as we learn from Mozart's letter to his father from Paris on 29 May 1778:

> Yesterday I went for the second time to see Count von Sickingen, the electoral palatine envoy (for I had already dined there once with Wendling and Raaff), who, I do not know if I have already written you this, is a charming man, a passionate amateur, and a true connoisseur of music. There I spent eight hours quite alone with him. We were at the keyboard morning and afternoon until ten o'clock in the evening; all kinds of music [were] played—[and also] praised, admired, reviewed, discussed, and criticized. He has nearly thirty scores of operas.³⁴

The decisive bit of evidence linking this collection with Count von Sickingen, however, is provided by the same score that contained the note to the palatine envoy, namely the Washington manuscript of Jommelli's *Cajo Fabrizio*: for the coat of arms found on the front and back covers of that volume features the small shield with five balls or spheres forming a cross of St. Andrew (i.e., in the form of an X) that had been the Sickingen family's heraldic device since the tenth century (see fig. 8:7b).³⁵ Thus is established beyond a shadow of a doubt not only the provenance

---

de La Che[s]naye-Desbois et [——] Badier, *Dictionnaire de la noblesse* 6 (3d ed., Paris: [Schlesinger frères], 1865): 245 (the date of L.-H.-T. de Cossé's succession to the dukedom should be changed from 1759 to 1757); M. Prevost, "Cossé (Louis-Hercule-Timoléon), VIIIe duc de Brissac," *Dictionnaire de biographie française* 9 (1961): 769–70.

³³ During the period in question, 23 October fell on a Sunday only in the years 1763, 1768, 1774, and 1785. Of these, 1763 is too early (see fn. 31, above) and 1785 probably too late: Sickingen became a count in 1775, and a second, undated note inserted in the score still refers to him as a baron. That note reads, "Mercredi[.] — Vous me l'avés permis[,] monsieur le baron, mais je vous demande pardon, et vous rend mille et mille graces. — J'ose encore vous prier de me rappeler au souvenir de Mr de Carbari [?], et de le prier de ne pas oublier <u>le bonheur des sots</u> n[']allés pas confondre ni lui non plus." The notes are in two different hands.

³⁴ Bauer-Deutsch, 2:368: "Gestern war ich das 2:^{te} mahl bey H: graf v: Sückingen khurf: Pfälzischen gesandten, denn ich hab schon einmahl mit H: wendling und Raaff dort gespeist welcher, ich weis nicht ob ich es schon geschrieben habe, ein charmanter herr, Paßionirter liebhaber, und wahrer kenner der Musique ist. da habe ich, ganz allein bey ihm, 8 stunde zugebracht. da waren wir vormittag und nachmittag bis 10 uhr abends immer beym clavier; allerley Musique durchgemacht — belobet, bewundert, Recensirt, raisonirt und criticirt. er hat so beyläufig gegen 30 Spartiti von opern." Engl. trans. after Anderson, 544.

³⁵ See, inter alia, *J. Siebmacher's grosses Wappenbuch*, vol. 24: *Die Wappen des Adels in Baden, Elsaß-Lothringen und Luxemburg* (repr. ed., Neustadt an der Aisch: Bauer & Raspe, 1974; orig. ed. Nürn-

Figure 8:7a. Decorative gilt frame appearing on front and back covers of scores with "Mannheim" bindings (cf. fig. 8:2). Staatsbibliothek zu Berlin – Preussischer Kulturbesitz, Mus. ms. 13396 (Majo's *Ifigenia in Tauride*, App. A/VI/31).

Figure 8:7b. Coat of arms of Count von Sickingen, added to gilt frame of the type shown in figure 8:7a. Washington, D.C., Library of Congress, M 1500.J72 C35 (Jommelli's *Cajo Fabrizio*, App. A/VI/203), back cover.

of these manuscripts and the others listed in the Berlin catalogue but also a hitherto unsuspected link with Mozart.

Mozart and Count von Sickingen

Mozart's relationship with Count von Sickingen, so vividly described in the letter quoted above, seems to have been one of the few bright spots of his six-month sojourn in Paris in 1778. On 24 March of that year, one day after his arrival in Paris, Mozart wrote to his father that the next day he would call on "electoral palatine minister von Sickingen, who is a great connoisseur and passionate amateur of music."[36] After the day-long visit of 28 May described above, Mozart spent increasingly more time with the count: on 12 June, Maria Anna mentions Wolfgang's frequent lunches with him and Anton Raaff, and on the same day Wolfgang reports that he has been to the count's house six times, staying from one o'clock until ten.[37] Mozart also previewed his "Paris" Symphony for Sickingen and Raaff.[38] Later, the count tried to find Mozart a position at Mannheim or at Mainz, where he had a brother.[39] Finally, it was he who intervened when Baron von Grimm ordered Mozart to leave Paris. Mozart wanted to stay a few extra days in order to check the engraver's proofs of his six violin sonatas K. 301–6, and Sickingen offered him a place to stay; but when Mozart informed Grimm of his intentions, the proud baron apparently threatened to become Mozart's worst enemy if he left his house but did not leave Paris.[40]

In closing, we should like to express the hope that discovery of the relationship between the eight manuscripts with "Mannheim" bindings, the thematic catalogue in Berlin, and Count von Sickingen in Paris will lead to the identification of addi-

---

berg: Bauer & Raspe, 1878), 37–38 and plate 23; Ernst Heinrich Kneschke, ed., *Neues allgemeines deutsches Adels-Lexikon*, vol. 8 (Leipzig: Friedrich Voigt, 1868), 485. On the covers of the Jommelli manuscript the shield with five balls appears as the breast-plate of an imperial eagle holding a sword in one claw and a scepter in the other (see fig. 8:7b); other versions of the family crest feature a swan. Though the entire coat of arms is in gilt here, in colored representations the five balls are silver. As illustrated in fig. 8:7, the Sickingen coat of arms on the Jommelli score has been added within the pre-existent floral frame after erasure of the abbreviation "N°" (without a number thereafter) found in the other manuscripts of his collection; cf. fn. 15, above.

[36] Bauer-Deutsch, 2:326: " . . . khur-Pfälzische[r] Minister H: v: Sückingen[,] welcher ein grosser kenner und Paßionirter liebhaber von der Musick ist."

[37] Ibid., 375.

[38] Ibid., 378.

[39] See Wolfgang's letters of 18, 29, and 31 July and Leopold's of 29 August, ibid., 407, 419, 426, 452–53.

[40] See letters of 3, 19, and 26 October, ibid., 490, 497, 503.

tional manuscripts belonging to his collection; Mozart mentions "nearly thirty" scores, whereas the catalogue contains little more than half that number.[41] But whatever the exact extent of Sickingen's collection, we now have a far more concrete sense of precisely which operas Mozart may have come to know as a result of his friendship with the count.

The presence in the Berlin catalogue (and thus in Sickingen's collection) of Gluck's *Alceste* is especially suggestive in this regard. In the first place, it now appears highly probable that this score was the source—and perhaps also the model—for Mozart's setting of the scena from *Alceste* "Popoli di Tessaglia! / Io, non chiedo, eterni Dei" (K. 316), written for Aloysia Weber while he was in Paris.[42] And second, though many writers have noted similarities between Gluck's *Alceste* and Mozart's *Idomeneo*, no one had previously been able to document Mozart's knowledge of either the Italian or French version of Gluck's opera prior to 1781.[43] We can now say with some certainty that he came in contact with the Italian version in Paris in 1778.

A similar conclusion may be drawn about the influence of the Sickingen collection as a whole: for the knowledge that Mozart had the opportunity to familiarize himself with so many of the central works of the Mannheim tradition while in Paris, in addition to the performances he attended and scores he examined during his long stay at the electoral court in 1777/78, lends even greater weight to the

---

[41] Mozart's account, though he may of course have exaggerated the number of scores in the count's collection, confirms the view that the catalogue is incomplete as it stands. The works in the Berlin catalogue for which matching scores have not yet been identified are, again, Holzbauer's *Il giudizio di Salomone, Betulia liberata, Nitteti,* and *Adriano in Siria* (nos. 1–4); Salieri's *Fiera di Venezia* (no. 10); Piccinni's *Catone in Utica* and *Contadine bizzarre* (nos. 14–15); the four parts of Gluck's *Feste d'Apollo* (nos. 16a–d); and his *Alceste* (no. 17). Mannheim copies of the two Holzbauer oratorios, of Salieri's *Fiera di Venezia*, and of Piccinni's *Catone in Utica* are extant, but none has the characteristic "Mannheim" bindings, together with paginations matching those in the Berlin catalogue, that identify a manuscript as part of Count von Sickingen's collection.

[42] Mozart refers to this aria in a letter from Paris to Aloysia, dated 30 July 1778, as follows: " . . . e con quella occasione avrà anche il Popoli di Teßaglia, ch'è già mezzo Terminato – se lei ne sarà si contenta – comme lo son io – potrò chiamarmi felice; – intanto, sinchè avrò la sodisfazione di sapere di lei steßa l'incontro che avrà avuta questa scena *apreßo di lei* s'intende, perchè siccome l'hò fatta *solamente* per lei – così non desidero altra Lode che la sua; – intanto dunque non poßo dir altro, che, Trà le mie composizioni di questo genere – devo confeßare che questa scena è la megliore ch'hò fatto in vita mia." (" . . . and at that time [completion of the engraving of his sonatas] you shall also have the [scena] *Popoli di Tessaglia,* which is already half finished—if you are as pleased with it as I am, I shall be delighted. Meanwhile, until I shall have the satisfaction of hearing from you yourself what *you* think of this scena [*—you,*] of course, because, as I have composed it *only* for you, I desire no other praise than yours—I can only say that of all my compositions of this kind, I must confess that this scena is the best I have ever composed.") Bauer-Deutsch, 2:420; Engl. trans. after Anderson, 581.

[43] John Platoff, "Writing about Influences: *Idomeneo,* a Case Study," in *Explorations in Music, the Arts, and Ideas: Essays in Honor of Leonard B. Meyer,* ed. Eugene Narmour and Ruth A. Solie (Stuyvesant, N.Y.: Pendragon Press, 1988), 43–65, provides a summary of the secondary literature.

importance of Mannheim in the genesis of *Idomeneo*.[44] Clearly, if Mozart were to write an opera for a court, it would have been in his best interest, as Leopold frequently advised, to study its tastes as fully as possible and adapt his style accordingly so as to win a favorable reception. The broadening of a context for Mozart's music is thus one of the unexpected rewards of the reconstruction of an opera repertory at Mannheim—and of the painstaking documentary study that provides its basis.

Appendix: Manuscripts of Mannheim Operas Lost in World War II

The following is a list of scores to operas produced in Mannheim that were destroyed in World War II (see also the nonoperatic manuscripts listed in chap. 1, fn. 34). Because the manuscripts are lost, it is impossible to know for certain whether they were actually copied at the court, though in the case of certain manuscripts formerly in the Theaterbibliothek of the Mannheim Nationaltheater, that presumption would be strong (see the catalogue of this collection in Walter, *Archiv und Bibliothek*, 2:161–96). Many of the sources in the Theaterbibliothek evidently came originally from the Seyler troupe, which played periodically at Mannheim from 1777 and was resident company of the Nationaltheater in 1778/79; see the summary of the document "Verzeichnis der Seilerischen Theater Musikalien" in Walter, *Archiv und Bibliothek*, 2:163, and cf. also ibid., 260–63. Another group of manuscripts formerly in the Theaterbibliothek was bought in 1924/25 when the collection of Schloss Ehreshoven was auctioned off (information kindly supplied by Dr. Bärbel Pelker). Finally, manuscripts formerly in Darmstadt (D-DS) have been identified through the pre-war card catalogue there. Some or all of these were no doubt brought to Darmstadt by Abbé Vogler, who died there in 1814 (see fn. 30, above). The dates given below are those of the first performance at Mannheim.

1. Galuppi, Baldassare. *Il filosofo di campagna* (1756, revived 1771). D-DS.
2. Galuppi, Baldassare. *Le nozze* (1757). Mannheim, Theaterbibliothek (Walter, *Archiv und Bibliothek*, 2:175).
3. Gassmann, Florian Leopold. *L'amore artigiano* (1772). D-DS; transcription in US-Wc, M 1500.G24 A5.
4. Holzbauer, Ignaz. *Adriano in Siria* (1768). Mannheim, Theaterbibliothek (from Schloss Ehreshoven).
5. [Majo, Gian Francesco de.] *Alessandro [nell'Indie]* (1766). Mannheim, Theaterbibliothek (acts 1–2 only, anon.; Walter, *Archiv und Bibliothek*, 2:166, and see also his *Geschichte*, 136–37).

---

[44] See Daniel Heartz, "The Genesis of Mozart's *Idomeneo*," *The Musical Quarterly* 55 (1969): 1–19; Corneilson, "Opera at Mannheim," chap. 8 et passim. *Idomeneo* was, of course, written for Carl Theodor's court after it transferred from Mannheim to Munich in 1778.

6. Piccinni, Niccolò. *La buona figliuola* (1769). Mannheim, Theaterbibliothek (Walter, *Archiv und Bibliothek*, 2:168). Also German version, *Das gute Mädchen* (ibid., 173).
7. Piccinni, Niccolò. *Catone in Utica* (1770). D-DS. Also a second copy, Mannheim, Theaterbibliothek (from Schloss Ehreshoven).
8. Sacchini, Antonio. *L'isola d'amore* (1772). D-DS (with annotation "Mannheim 1772"); transcription in US-Wc, M 1500.S12 I6.
9. Schweitzer, Anton. *Rosamunde* (Mannheim, Nationaltheater, 1780; originally scheduled for production in 1778). Mannheim, Theaterbibliothek (Walter, *Archiv und Bibliothek*, 2:176).
10. Traetta, Tommaso. *Sofonisba* (1762). D-DS. Also a second copy, Mannheim, Theaterbibliothek (from Schloss Ehreshoven).

Chapter 9

Other Manuscripts from Mannheim, II: Sacred, Smaller Vocal, and Instrumental Works from Appendix A/VI

Having considered the large-scale dramatic works of Appendix A/VI in the previous chapter, we turn now to the much more extensive group that remains, comprising individual sources for sacred music, non-dramatic secular vocal music, and instrumental music. The vocal music treated here ranges from major sacred works such as masses by Holzbauer and Johann Stamitz to a large number of individual arias copied separately from their operas (presumably for performance in the chamber), while the instrumental music includes symphonies, concertos, and chamber works by the foremost composers at Mannheim. Unlike the manuscripts of the previous chapter, most of these sources are still associated directly or indirectly with the institution—church, monastery, court—that was their original owner in the eighteenth century. Such manuscripts might have come into the possession of their owners as gifts (often in expectation of a quid pro quo), as a result of a commission (perhaps by an agent or visitor at Mannheim, perhaps through the mediation of a traveling Mannheim virtuoso), or by purchase from one of the Mannheim court musicians or copyists (doubtless on occasion involving piracy).

That the majority of these manuscripts still form a part of their original collections allows us to organize the following discussion geographically rather than topically, as in the previous chapter. Exceptions are certain manuscripts in Berlin that cannot be linked with a given patron, and also the Stanford manuscript of Mozart's Concerto for Three Pianos, K. 242 (App. A/VI/?202), treated in the penultimate section of this chapter.

Sacred Music by Holzbauer and Grua in Moravia, Austria, and Germany

The large number of masses from Holzbauer's Mannheim period still found in Czech and Austrian collections suggests that, like Johann Stamitz,[1] he maintained connections with that area after departing for Stuttgart and Mannheim.[2] That the

---

[1] See Eugene K. Wolf, *The Symphonies of Johann Stamitz: A Study in the Formation of the Classic Style* (Utrecht: Bohn, Scheltema & Holkema, 1981), 16, 58–61.

[2] Further evidence that Holzbauer retained his ties with Vienna is the performance there in 1761 of his oratorio *Betulia liberata* (Mannheim, 1760; libretto in B-Bc). See chap. 4, fn. 23.

collections of the former monasteries of St. Thomas and Staré Brno in Brno (now CZ-Bm) include a large number of sacred works by Holzbauer, among them five manuscripts copied in Mannheim (App. A/VI/6–10), probably reflects the fact that his first position was in Moravia, at the court of Count Rottal in Holešov.[3] Similarly, the two Mannheim manuscripts in the monastery of Klosterneuburg, near Vienna (App. A/VI/1–2), as well as the large collection of Holzbauer sacred works in Göttweig monastery (none, however, copied in Mannheim), no doubt resulted from the composer's continued contacts with his native land.

Two other clumps of Holzbauer masses illustrate the extensive circulation of his sacred music in Germany. The first consists of five masses in the collection of the counts (later princes) of Oettingen-Wallerstein (now at D-Au), two of which may well have been sent by Holzbauer as gifts in 1754.[4] These are the two that are definitely from Mannheim (App. A/VI/11–12), being copied by Mannheim 2 on Blum 3 paper; use of the latter paper indicates a fairly early date. Three other masses by Holzbauer in this collection are similar in appearance and utilize a typical Mannheim paper, Heusler 7.[5] Nonetheless, I have chosen to exclude them because (1) the cover sheets of two of them, containing the titles, are on thick beige *Packpapier* rather than the blue elephant paper favored for this purpose at Mannheim; (2) the paper is lined with six passes of a two-stave rastrum, an uncharacteristic procedure for a Mannheim manuscript; and (3) the copyist is otherwise unknown to me. None of this can be considered truly conclusive, however.

Another group of Holzbauer masses, together with one by Johann Stamitz, is now located in the Biblioteca Estense in Modena (I-MOe). However, as Deanna Bush has pointed out with regard to the seven sources there that are attributed to Holzbauer, these manuscripts were originally part of the collection of the elec-

---

[3] On these and other Holzbauer masses in the Austro-Bohemian realm see Deanna D. Bush, *The Orchestral Masses of Ignaz Holzbauer (1711–1783): Authenticity, Chronology, and Style* (Ph.D. diss., Eastman School of Music, 1982), 80, 198, 222–36, 333-35, et passim. Thematic catalogues of Holzbauer's masses may be found in Eduard Schmitt, ed., *Kirchenmusik der Mannheimer Schule, 1. Auswahl*, DTB, Neue Folge, 2 (Wiesbaden: Breitkopf & Härtel, 1982), pp. lxxi–lxxx, and Bush, *Holzbauer*, 321–412.

[4] See Fritz Zobeley, "Aus Alt-Mannheimer Musikerbriefen," *Neue Mannheimer Zeitung*, 9 May 1931, p. [3]. Zobeley prints one full letter of Holzbauer, dated 21 December 1754, and briefly describes a second, dated 28 March 1763. (The originals of these letters have been inaccessible to scholars in recent years, and thus I am especially grateful to Dr. Bärbel Pelker for the above citation.) According to the letter of 1754, Holzbauer sent some of his music to Oettingen-Wallerstein (of unspecified genre, however), and the letter of 1763 states that he sent music paper. For a full catalogue of the Oettingen-Wallerstein collection, with extensive introductory material, see Gertraut Haberkamp and Volker von Volckamer, *Thematischer Katalog der Musikhandschriften der Fürstlich Oettingen-Wallerstein'schen Bibliothek Schloß Harburg*, Kataloge bayerischer Musiksammlungen, 3 (Munich: G. Henle, 1976).

[5] See D-Au (HR), III, 4½ , 2°, 105, 110, 114. The second organ part of no. 105, by the local copyist J. S. A. Link on IAH paper (from the nearby mill of J. A. Hilser), probably belonged originally to the manuscript III, 4½ , 2°, 1079, another copy of the same mass, this time entirely by Link.

tor/archbishop of Cologne at Bonn, having been transferred to Modena at some point between 1784 and 1832.[6] Three of the seven manuscripts consist of a score and parts, both in oblong format; Bush identified two of the scores as being from Mannheim, Mus. F. 587 and 591 (App. A/VI/198–99), for they are copied by Mannheim 5 on Heusler 6 paper.[7] To that information I can add that the staving also supports this conclusion, as it was done with rastrum 10:1, characteristic of Mannheim 5's manuscripts from the first half of the 1770s.[8]

In addition to these two manuscripts, Bush tentatively identified a third score, that to Mus. F. 588, as being from Mannheim based on its use of the same paper as the other two, Heusler 6.[9] However, the handwriting of that score is wholly unlike that of any other Mannheim copyist.[10] If Bush had examined the parts to these three sources she would have found that the copyist in question is in fact local (i.e., from Bonn): for in them he appears intermingled with several other copyists that are clearly so.[11] To be sure, all write on Heusler 6 paper, but the staving is not characteristic of Mannheim, and that paper is found all up and down the Rhine. What is intriguing is that the two scores that *are* from Mannheim are on the same paper (but with *Mannheim* staving) as the local parts; this is either sheer coinci-

---

[6] Bush, *Holzbauer*, 78, citing Domenico Fava, *La Biblioteca Estense nel suo sviluppo storico* (Modena: Vincenzi, 1925), 212–14. Among other problems with this citation, Bush gives the initial date at which the transfer of the manuscripts from Bonn to Modena might have occurred as "1780" owing to her incorrect dating of the start of the reign of Maximilian Franz of Cologne, who ruled from 1784 until his death in 1801. Moreover, Fava does *not* write that Max Franz "sent the holdings of the electoral court of Cologne to his brother Ferdinand [of Austria, governor of Lombardy; Bush, *loc. cit.*]"; and if that were indeed true, the terminal date for the transfer would obviously have to be 1801, not 1832. Further, although Bush notes that two of these manuscripts bear the names of musicians in the Bonn/Cologne orchestra (see pp. 361–62, 399), she neglects to cite a source for this information; it is no doubt Max Braubach, "Die Mitglieder der Hofmusik unter den vier letzten Kurfürsten von Köln," in *Colloquium amicorum: Joseph Schmidt-Görg zum 70. Geburtstag*, ed. Siegfried Kross and Hans Schmidt (Bonn: Verlag des Beethovenhauses, 1967), 26–63. Bush considers two of these masses, Mus. F. 589–90, to be of doubtful authenticity.

[7] Bush, *Holzbauer*, 78. These are the masses she numbers A27 and A13.

[8] Bush, *Holzbauer*, 78 and 203, states that these manuscripts must antedate 1761, the year of the Cologne elector Clemens August's death; I know of no evidence at all to support this claim, and she supplies none. According to my dating, they would certainly have been copied under the reign of the next elector, Beethoven's erstwhile patron Maximilian Friedrich (b. 1708, r. 1761–84).

[9] Ibid., 338, 388 (no. 102), as indicated by the presence of a gapped underline; this is Bush's mass A26.

[10] See ibid., 178, for a sample of this hand.

[11] For example, the copyist of the main set of parts to F. 591 is clearly local, appearing on German <W : J A HILSER> paper, never found at Mannheim. To this set the copyist of the score to F. 588 adds two replacement parts at a later date, on Heusler paper but again with a non-Mannheim rastrum. This copyist also copies the parts to a score of Johann Stamitz's Mass in D (Schmitt I.2), Mus. F. 1096, which is by another of the local copyists and which has the attribution in French, something I have never seen at Mannheim. Again the paper is Heusler 6, and the rastra are not from Mannheim.

dence, or the paper was supplied to Mannheim 5 by the court at Bonn, which he then lined himself or had lined at Mannheim.[12]

Mention may also be made here of a *Memento Domine* by Carlo Grua and a mass by Holzbauer found in the collection of the Munich Cathedral, the Frauenkirche (now D-FS; App. A/VI/144–45). The former source, comprising the parts to Grua's autograph manuscript of 1753 of the same work (App. A/I/12; see chap. 3), has already been cited in chapter 6 for its parallels with an anonymous manuscript of a mass of 1757 in the same collection that we can now attribute to Grua, App. A/IV/1. The original set of parts to A/VI/144 bears no date, but the watermark is exactly the same as that of the autograph score, and there can be little question that the parts were copied soon after completion of the score, that is, in 1753. The original set, which has two first and two second violin parts, is by a copyist unique to the Frauenkirche manuscripts, though his hand is clearly in the Mannheim style. But a second copyist, here labeled Mannheim 7, is one that does appear elsewhere in manuscripts from Mannheim, in the anonymous mass of 1757 just cited (App. A/IV/1) and in a Holzbauer mass at the Bayerische Staatsbibliothek (App. A/II/2); in A/VI/144 he supplies a third part for both the first and second violins, dated 1756 at the end of each—three years later than the other parts. In addition to what this tells us about performance practice at Mannheim, it is noteworthy that the watermark, nominally the same as that of the autograph score and the original set of parts, now shows obvious variants—the result of three years of wear and tear on the mold.

The other relevant manuscript in the Frauenkirche collection, that to Holzbauer's Mass in C, Schmitt I.5/Bush A1 (App. A/VI/145), is by three copyists unique to this study; their rather unformed hands lead one to believe they might have been students at the Seminarium or Vogler's "Tonschule," or at least other nonprofessionals. That the manuscript is from Mannheim is unquestionable, though, given (1) its use of Blum 5 and Heusler 5 and 7 papers, (2) its blue cover on Knöckel paper, and (3) the staving of the organ, trumpet, and timpani parts, which are lined with rastrum 12:10d. The latter characteristic allows us to date this manuscript with some precision, for this rastrum is found in several Vogler manuscripts, one of which is dated 1776 (App. A/V/17).

---

[12] With only one exception, all nine manuscripts ruled with the rastrum in question, 10:1, were copied by Mannheim 5. The exception, App. A/VI/36, is by a copyist who can now be identified with some certainty as Fridolin Weber (see chap. 2, @ fn. 104). Hence, the rastrum may have been Mannheim 5's personal possession, especially as it is a bit smaller than the typical "official" rastrum.

The Pretlack Collection (D-B; App. A/VI/39–119)

The largest extant collection of Mannheim manuscripts, at least in terms of the number of individual sources, is that of the Staatsbibliothek zu Berlin – Preussischer Kulturbesitz (D-B). The music division of this library now unites the postwar collections of the former Deutsche Staatsbibliothek in East Berlin (which housed the so-called Königliche Hausbibliothek, to be discussed in the next section) and the Staatsbibliothek Preussischer Kulturbesitz in West Berlin (which housed the remaining manuscripts considered here, including many of the opera scores discussed in the previous chapter). The earliest and largest collection of Mannheim manuscripts in the Staatsbibliothek is that assembled by Johann Ludwig Freiherr von Pretlack (1716–81), "General-Feldmarschall-Leutnant" and commander of the dragoon regiment of the duke of Württemberg. The Pretlack family estates were located in (among other places) Darmstadt, Fränkisch-Crumbach, Babenhausen, and Burg Echzell, and it was in the attic of the latter castle that a trunk was found in 1968 containing a collection of well over 1,000 manuscripts from the eighteenth century. Acquired by the Staatsbibliothek Preussischer Kulturbesitz in 1969, the collection was catalogued and exhaustively analyzed by Joachim Jaenecke, whose comprehensive indexes of the copyists and papers of the collection greatly simplified the task of the present study.[13]

A glance at the list of Pretlack manuscripts in Appendix A/VI (nos. 39–119) will show the extent of this collection. Though the total number of 81 manuscripts is in a sense inflated, since many of them are single arias from the same opera and might well be considered a single "source,"[14] this is nonetheless a sizable collection. Even more important, it dates almost entirely from the late 1740s and the 1750s, as can be seen by scanning the dates of the operas from which individual arias are taken. (Though these dates technically only provide a terminus a quo for the copies, there is no reason to suppose that Pretlack consistently obtained manuscripts of opera arias from the nearby Mannheim court long after the operas had been performed, a conclusion supported by the physical characteristics of the

---

[13] Joachim Jaenecke, *Die Musikbibliothek des Ludwig Freiherrn von Pretlack (1716–1781)* (Wiesbaden: Breitkopf & Härtel, 1973). Without the detailed listings of copyists and especially papers in this book, it would have been necessary either to order all the manuscripts of the collection to see whether they might be from Mannheim, or else to make a "reasonable" selection, which would have missed many of the manuscripts identified here as being from Mannheim. More intensive work on the copyists identified by Jaenecke has naturally led to refinements in his listings; in particular, he assigns numerous manuscripts to a single copyist that in fact involve two (see my Appendix D).

[14] The number reduces to something like thirty-eight if arias from a single work are grouped together.

manuscripts. Joachim Jaenecke also concluded that the collection dated for the most part from the period 1745–60.)[15] Most of these operas were performed at Mannheim in the period from 1749 to 1754, after which we find selections from only one opera from 1757 (App. A/VI/87–95), one from 1760 (App. A/VI/108–9), and one from much later, 1768 (App. A/VI/86).

The close connection with Mannheim receives confirmation from two local covers that had originally enclosed two sets of the Pretlack arias. The first of these, for the manuscripts now catalogued as N. Mus. BP 208–226 (including the Mannheim manuscripts App. A/VI/47–56 together with local copies of the remaining arias), reads "Antigona / Opera del Sig^{re} Galuppi / 1753."[16] What is significant is that this is the date of the *Mannheim* production (on 17 January), not the original production in Rome in 1751. Similarly, the cover to N. Mus. BP 406–427 (App. A/VI/63–84)[17] bears the date of 1750 for Hasse's *Demofoonte*, again the date of the Mannheim performance (18 January), not of the premiere in Dresden in 1748.

As already stated, the paper, staving, and copyists of these manuscripts confirm the early date of the Pretlack manuscripts (and in turn have their early dating confirmed by being present in the collection). The most common paper is Heusler 6, which was used throughout most of the Mannheim period; but following close behind are the early Blum papers 1 and 3. Other Swiss papers found in these manuscripts are also indicative of a date in the 1750s: in several manuscripts Heusler 3 paper, with a watermark consisting simply of a fleur-de-lis opposite the letters NH; in App. A/VI/106 (vn. 1 only) Heusler 4 paper; and in App. A/VI/85 and 88 the Swiss paper without watermarks found in the Regensburg manuscripts of symphonies by Johann Stamitz and in early symphonies of Christian Cannabich (see Appendix B/I/3). Similarly, in App. A/VI/58, 66–67, and 76 we find some of the few examples of the use of Palatine paper in the body of a manuscript (here Knöckel 2), also found in the score to Johann Stamitz's Mass in D of ca. 1755 (App. A/VI/18, part 1; part 2 is on Blum 1 and 3 papers, also common in the Pretlack manuscripts, as just mentioned). Several Dutch papers appear, too, as do a few examples of Heusler 5 and 7.

Most of the copyists of the Pretlack collection are unique to it, and most of the staving is done with one-stave rastra or with unique compound rastra. But a few of the exceptions to both these generalizations again prove useful for purposes of dating. Thus, of the three five-stave rastra found in these manuscripts, rastrum 5:18, the most common, also appears in a Grua *Messa breve* of 1751 (App. A/I/11,

---

[15] Jaenecke, *Pretlack*, 42.

[16] Ibid., 140. Jaenecke misreads the title as "Antigono," another opera by Galuppi (1746), and thus mistakenly includes N. Mus. 207 as part of the set; it is not even clear that the attribution to Galuppi and the added title "Antigono" on that aria are correct. In addition, he misreads the subsequent titles of the set, N. Mus. 208–226, as *Antigono* rather than *Antigona*, the correct title.

[17] See Jaenecke, *Pretlack*, 171.

again on Blum 3 paper); and the copyist Mannheim 21 is found both in an aria of 1752, App. A/VI/85, and (once again) in Stamitz's Mass in D. In sum, the evidence points strongly to the dating proposed above for these manuscripts: ca. 1746–60 (with one exception, from 1768), but with the majority stemming from a still narrower period, ca. 1749–54.

Other Manuscripts in Berlin (D-B; App. A/VI/13–38)

The other individual collection of the Staatsbibliothek zu Berlin that contains manuscripts from Mannheim is that known as the Königliche Hausbibliothek.[18] This famous collection combines the music collections of the various palaces of Frederick II (and to a lesser extent other kings of Prussia), primarily those in Berlin, Charlottenburg, and Potsdam ("Sans Souci"). While Frederick has gained a reputation as a conservative, this collection in fact contains some of the most up-to-date music of the time, including Mannheim manuscripts of ballets by Cannabich (App. A/VI/13, from 1768–69) and Toeschi (App. A/VI/19, from 1766),[19] two symphonies each by Cannabich and Holzbauer (App. A/VI/14–17), and Johann Stamitz's Mass in D (App. A/VI/18). As already alluded to, the latter work was composed by 1755, when it is known to have been performed in Paris,[20] and both the paper and handwriting of the score support a date of about that time for the Berlin exemplar. As it is not an autograph but a fair copy, made by a copyist (Mannheim 21),[21] it was possibly a purchase by one of Frederick's agents or a gift to him on the part of Stamitz or the Elector Palatine.

We have already dealt with the most important of the remaining Berlin manuscripts in the previous chapter: the large opera scores, especially those from the Sickingen collection. Among the sources not yet treated, comprising a miscellaneous group of arias and other vocal and instrumental music, the most interesting are perhaps two cello concertos by the principal cellists at Mannheim, Innocenz Danzi (ca. 1730–98) and Anton Fils (1733–60; App. A/VI/21–22). Given the passion for cello music of Friedrich Wilhelm II, Frederick II's successor as king of Prussia, these might owe their presence in Berlin to him rather than his uncle. Nonetheless, the staving of these manuscripts clearly links them with the period between the

---

[18] See Georg Thouret, *Katalog der Musiksammlung aus der Königlichen Hausbibliothek im Schloße zu Berlin* (Leipzig: Breitkopf & Härtel, 1895), for a full (but nonthematic) catalogue of the collection.

[19] For an edition of the Toeschi ballet, with several reproductions taken from the Berlin manuscript, see *Ballet Music from the Mannheim Court*, Part II, ed. Nicole Baker, Recent Researches in the Music of the Classical Era, 47 (Madison, Wisc.: A-R Editions, 1997).

[20] On the mass see Wolf, *Stamitz*, 17, 21 (n. 60); Peter Gradenwitz, *Johann Stamitz: Leben – Umwelt – Werke* (Wilhelmshaven: Heinrichshofen's Verlag, 1984), 131–33.

[21] See chap. 2, fnn. 85–87 and related text.

arrival of both cellists at Mannheim in 1754 and the death of Fils in 1760: the rastrum of the Danzi, 10:19, is also found in two arias from Holzbauer's *Issipile* of 1754 in the Pretlack collection (App. A/VI/100–101), and that of the orchestral parts to the Fils, 10:15, appears in one of Cannabich's earliest symphonies, no. 3 (App. A/III/3, from the late 1750s), and in an aria from Galuppi's *Siroe* of 1754 (again in the Pretlack collection; App. A/VI/62). Given the early dates of these manuscripts, plus the fact that the Danzi is in an Italianate hand, it would not be out of the question for one or both to be autographs, though we have no documented samples of either of these composers' hands.[22]

The Ritschel Manuscripts in Dresden (D-Dl; App. A/VI/120–38)

In addition to possessing Mannheim copies of J. C. Bach's *Temistocle* and Salieri's *La fiera di Venezia*, already discussed in chapter 8, the superb collection of the Sächsische Landesbibliothek in Dresden (D-Dl) houses, somewhat unexpectedly, a collection of nineteen sacred works by the talented but short-lived composer Johannes Ritschel (1739–66). Like so many Mannheim musicians of his generation, he came from a family long associated with the court: his father and uncle had served elector Carl Philipp while he was still in Innsbruck, following him to Heidelberg and then Mannheim. Ritschel *fils* is first listed in the almanacs as a violinist in 1757, and in October of 1757 he was awarded a three-year period of study with Padre Martini in Bologna. Through 1763 he continues to be listed as a violinist, but in that year he was promoted to Vice-Kapellmeister; he died three years later at the age of 26.

The Dresden manuscripts, consisting of five masses, an oratorio of 1763, and thirteen smaller works, preserve nearly all of Ritschel's *œuvre*; were it not for them he would be little more than a name on a list. The collection is exceptionally unified and was obviously all copied at approximately the same time. It is entirely by one copyist (Mannheim 6, the principal copyist of sacred music at Mannheim), who writes on Blum 6 paper lined with ten to twelve passes of the same one-stave rastrum—probably his own. The only variation is the presence of two different cover papers, grayish-brown Knöckel elephant paper and one other similar paper.

Why these works should be in Dresden is a mystery. A possible explanation might relate to the presence there of a bass singer by the name of Franz Ritschel (spelled Ritzshel, Rietzschel, Ritzel, etc.), listed as a member of the Katholische

---

[22] The "certain" attribution of the handwriting of a mass in Darmstadt (D-DS, Mus. ms. 547) to Fils by Hubert Unverricht is anything but that; see his article "Johann Anton Fils (1733–1760): zur Herkunft und Bedeutung des Komponisten," in Hermann Holzbauer, ed., *Johann Anton Fils (1733–1760): ein Eichstätter Komponist der Mannheimer Klassik* (Tutzing: Hans Schneider, 1983), 18–19 (see also p. 88, no. 101, and the reprod. on p. 89). The manuscript bears none of the characteristics whatever of either a Mannheim manuscript or a composing score.

Kirchenmusik in 1733 and the Hofkapelle in 1735–39;[23] some sort of family connection may conceivably have been involved. As the manuscripts all date from the same period, and include the oratorio *Gioas* of 1763, they may reasonably be assigned to the period from 1763 to the late 1760s. Possibly they were ordered by the court at Dresden after the composer's untimely death in 1766.

Manuscripts from Karlsruhe and Rheda (App. A/VI/146–49, 152)

The Badische Landesbibliothek in Karlsruhe (D-KA) houses a large collection of music manuscripts from the eighteenth century, including the music library of the Fürstenberg family (until recently in Donaueschingen) and that of the former margraviate of Baden-Durlach. Among the clearly identifiable local copies in the latter collection, copies that include virtually the entire output of the prolific Kapellmeister Johann Melchior Molter, a quartet of flute concertos stands out for their large oblong format, use of fine Swiss paper, and professional-quality staving (App. A/VI/146–49). Though the two copyists involved have not otherwise been identified, the papers are those often found in early Mannheim manuscripts. More decisively, study of the staving shows that three of the four manuscripts have been lined with rastrum 10:19, which also appears in Danzi's cello concerto in Berlin and in two arias in the Pretlack collection from Holzbauer's *Issipile* of 1754 (App. A/VI/21, 100–101), in each case on the same paper as the Karlsruhe manuscripts. As three of the four composers represented are from Mannheim (Holzbauer, Johann Baptist Wendling, and Johann Stamitz), and the fourth, Wenceslaus Wodiczka (d. 1774), is from a court with the closest possible associations, Munich, these manuscripts may be assigned tentatively to Mannheim and dated in approximately the second half of the 1750s. The one caveat is that neither of the copyists has been identified, and one cannot rule out the possibility that they are not from Mannheim but are writing on lined paper obtained there.

Almost exactly the same situation, and leading to the same conclusion, characterizes App. A/VI/152, a Toeschi symphony from the northern German court of Bentheim-Tecklenburg, formerly at Schloss Rheda and now on permanent loan to the Universitätsbibliothek Münster (D-MÜu): the copyist resembles a Mannheimer but is otherwise unknown, the paper is the Swiss type without watermark common in early Mannheim manuscripts, and the staving (with rastrum 10:28c) is also found in two Cannabich symphonies in Munich of ca. 1760 (App. A/III/11–12)—which also make use of the same watermark-less paper as the Rheda source.

---

[23] Information kindly supplied by Dr. Ortrun Landmann of RISM in Dresden, to whom I am grateful for manifold other kindnesses, as well. This could not have been the same Franz Ritschel (d. 1763) who was Johannes Ritschel's father; the latter was an organist, appearing in Mannheim court almanacs in 1734 and 1736, almost exactly the time of the Dresden listings.

Chapter 9

Regensburg (D-Rtt; App. A/VI/153–91)

With the possible exception of the Cannabich manuscripts in Munich, the most important extant collection of instrumental music from Mannheim is that of the princes of Thurn und Taxis in Regensburg (D-Rtt).[24] This court maintained very close relations with Mannheim during the eighteenth century. Among other connections, Countess Violanta Therese von Thurn und Taxis (d. 1734) was the third wife of Carl Philipp (d. 1742), Carl Theodor's uncle and predecessor as Elector Palatine. The huge eighteenth-century music collection of the Thurn und Taxis family includes, alongside many local copies of music by Mannheim composers, manuscripts from Mannheim of ten symphonies by Johann Stamitz; seven symphonies, a *symphonie concertante*, and a ballet by Cannabich; eight symphonies attributed to Toeschi; three symphonies and two concertos by Holzbauer (including two holograph parts); three oboe concertos by the Mannheim violinist and *Hof-Fourier* (quartermaster) Gerhard Heymann; two flute concertos by Anton Fils; and a symphony and an oboe concerto by "Ritschel(l)" (probably Johannes Ritschel).

In many ways the most important of these manuscripts are the ten Stamitz symphonies. Immediately apparent to anyone glancing over these manuscripts is the discrepancy between the Mannheim originals and the duplicate and replacement parts added by local copyists.[25] The former are on the large Swiss papers preferred at Mannheim (ca. 24–27 x 35–38 cm.), while the Regensburg copyists consistently employ smaller south German paper (ca. 22 x 32 cm.), even for parts inserted within the larger originals. The following listing of the Swiss papers in the ten Stamitz manuscripts shows that these fall into three relatively distinct groups.[26]

---

[24] For a comprehensive thematic catalogue of the Thurn und Taxis collection see Gertraut Haberkamp and Hugo Angerer, eds., *Die Musikhandschriften der Fürst Thurn und Taxis Hofbibliothek Regensburg: thematischer Katalog*, Kataloge bayerischer Musiksammlungen, 6 (Munich: G. Henle, 1981). The present section is a revised version of material published earlier in Wolf, *Stamitz*, 42–45.

[25] As already mentioned in chapter 2, it was the disparity at Regensburg between the obviously imported main sets and the local additions that first prompted me to entertain the idea that the former might be traceable to Mannheim.

[26] This listing generally duplicates the information presented in Appendix A/VI, but in a somewhat different and slightly more detailed form. Information about the watermarks mentioned appears in Appendix B. The frequency of the term *probably* in the list results from two facts: that neither of the most common papers in these manuscripts, Blum 2 and Heusler 2, has a countermark (i.e., the folio opposite the folio containing the watermark is blank) and that the "Swiss paper without watermarks" described below is therefore easily confused with one of those blank sheets.

Swiss Papers in the Stamitz Manuscripts at Regensburg

Group 1

App. A/VI/175 (DTB/Wolf F-4): ob. 1, probably va., Blum 2; ob. 2, hns., Heusler 2 (remainder of manuscript local). The Swiss paper of this manuscript and portions of others in the list below were cut so that the chain-lines run horizontally across the page rather than vertically, the more normal method. For this reason, the watermarks are positioned rather strangely in many instances.

App. A/VI/176 (DTB/Wolf G-3): hn. 1, probably Blum 2; hn. 2, Heusler 2;[27] remainder of manuscript Swiss paper without watermarks (see below).

App. A/VI/178 (DTB/Wolf G-7): vns., Swiss paper without watermarks; ob. 1, probably b., Blum 2; hn. 1, ob. 2, probably va. and hn. 2, Heusler 2.

App. A/VI/179 (DTB/Wolf D-8): vns., obs., Heusler 2; remainder of main set Swiss paper without watermarks.

App. A/VI/183 (DTB/Wolf E♭-6a): vns., Swiss paper without watermarks; obs., Heusler 2; hn. 2, probably hn. 1, Blum 2; va., b., probably Blum 2 or Heusler 2.

Group 2

App. A/VI/177, 180, 181 (DTB/Wolf G-4, D-11, D-12): Swiss paper without watermarks.

Group 3

App. A/VI/174 (DTB/Wolf F-3): all but hn. 2, Blum 3; hn. 2, paper of unknown origin (watermark = shield enclosing fleur-de-lis; probably Dutch).

App. A/VI/182 (DTB/Wolf D-15): vns., Heusler 7, the only appearance of this paper among these ten manuscripts; remainder of manuscript Blum 3.

The manuscripts of group 1 are probably the earliest of the ten. Blum 2 paper was evidently manufactured mainly during the first half of the century.[28] It appears in no other Mannheim manuscripts known to me and may have been replaced by the Blum 1 or 3 forms, both of which came into use at Mannheim during the 1750s. The second paper, Heusler 2, also indicates a relatively early date for Mannheim: it occurs in an early Cannabich concerto (App. A/III/M1) and also in one part from a Holzbauer mass in Munich (App. A/II/7), both in forms similar to

---

[27] Though no watermark is present in either of the horn parts, the paper of the first horn is similar to the Blum 2 paper of the preceding and following manuscripts, while that of the second horn is definitely the same as that of the second oboe and first horn parts of the following manuscript, App. A/VI/178.

[28] W. Fr. Tschudin, *The Ancient Paper-Mills of Basle and Their Marks* (Hilversum: Paper Publications Society, 1958), 151, records a date of 1709 for this mark (his no. 196).

those found here. The final paper in group 1 is that referred to above as "Swiss paper without watermarks" (see the paper "Swiss [no WM]" in Appendix B/I/3). Found in portions of group 1 and all of group 2, this paper occurs especially in Cannabich's early symphonies 2 through 21, which date from the late 1750s and early 1760s (see chap. 5 and Appendix A/III). The distinctive aspect of this paper is its complete lack of watermarks; comparison of its chain-lines, thickness, color, size, and the like show that it is not simply one of the standard papers with the watermark trimmed away but rather a type in its own right, one clearly related to the other Swiss papers found in Mannheim manuscripts of the period.

Unfortunately, although we know approximately how *late* these papers were used at Mannheim, implying a terminus ad quem of the early 1760s for this group, we have no solid evidence as to how *early* they came into use there—certainly none that would justify a conclusion that these manuscripts antedate Stamitz's death in 1757 (though this could be the case). Indeed, one of these works, App. A/VI/183 (DTB/Wolf E♭-6a), must be considered among Stamitz's latest based on its style.[29] The other nine symphonies transmitted by these manuscripts are all considered here to be "middle-period" works of ca. 1745/48 to ca. 1752/54 except App. A/VI/176, an advanced early symphony of ca. 1745–48. Hence, there seems to be no correlation between the above groupings and the apparent date of composition.

Group 2 differs from group 1 mainly in having been written entirely on the watermark-less paper just discussed. Relative to group 1, with its characteristic use of Blum 2 and Heusler 2 paper, this group is probably slightly later in date.

Group 3 represents a clear departure from the two previous ones and also finds us in a somewhat better position to determine a date. The first of the papers encountered here, Blum 3, occurs as early as 1751 at Mannheim (in App. A/I/11, a mass by Grua). However, the mold for one twin of this watermark precisely matches that of a watermark found in a later Mannheim manuscript of a mass by Holzbauer, dated 1763 (App. A/II/12). The other paper found in this group, Heusler 7, is common at Mannheim from the mid-1750s on. It happens to fit closely with the watermark of a Pokorny symphony at Regensburg, Pokorny 69, dated 1761,[30] and it also resembles the watermark of App. A/VI/171, a Holzbauer cembalo concerto that probably dates from about 1760 (see below). Yet it is at least equally close to the watermark of another Pokorny symphony at Regensburg, dated 1754 (Pokorny 159). Nonetheless, the preponderance of the evidence suggests a tentative date of the early or mid 1760s for this group.

---

[29] See Wolf, *Stamitz*, 295–98, 310–11, et passim.

[30] Pokorny was in Mannheim in 1754 and probably brought back a stock of paper with him (see chap. 4, fn. 30 and related text, also fn. 50, below). He seems to have continued to obtain paper from Mannheim on occasion, as some of his later autograph manuscripts now in Regensburg contain papers common at Mannheim that contrast strikingly with the local types used at the Thurn und Taxis court (or that of Oettingen-Wallerstein, where Pokorny was employed until 1767).

For once, staving is of little use in analyzing these manuscripts; like most of the other Mannheim sources in Regensburg, they are lined with unique one- and two-stave rastra, possibly by the individual copyists involved. The only exception is App. A/VI/182, from group 3, the violin parts of which are lined with two ten-stave rastra that are, alas, unique. The presence of such rastra does at least tend to show that group 3 is the latest.

Consideration of the handwriting of these manuscripts also supports the view that group 3 is the latest. Excluding local additions, the ten manuscripts are the work of three copyists unique to the Regensburg manuscripts (see Appendix D). The first of these, Rtt/Mh. 1, is the principal copyist, appearing in every manuscript and serving as the sole copyist of App. A/VI/175 (group 1) and all the manuscripts in group 2. The florid hand of Rtt/Mh. 2 makes its appearance only on title pages, a frequent division of labor in eighteenth-century sources. In App. A/VI/174, 178, and 183 he provides the title page except for the incipit, which copyist 1 has supplied; but in App. A/VI/179 he copies the incipit as well, furnishing us with a brief sample of his musical calligraphy (see fig. D:17). This copyist thus appears in three of the five manuscripts from group 1, in none from group 2, and in one from group 3 (App. A/VI/174). A final copyist, Rtt/Mh. 3, is found only in App. A/VI/182, where he completes the viola part begun by Rtt/Mh. 1 (see fig. D:16) and copies the rest of the main set with the exception of the bass part by Rtt/Mh. 1. The mixture of several hands in these manuscripts gives the clear impression of an organized team of copyists.

Though none of these three copyists has been found in other collections, substantiation of their association with Mannheim emerges from a comparison with the Cannabich and Toeschi manuscripts in Regensburg. Appendix A/VI/153 and 155 (Cannabich) and App. A/VI/184 and 189 (Toeschi) clearly stem from Mannheim: they adopt the obligatory Swiss paper, in this case Heusler 5 and 7 (the latter also found in App. A/VI/182, from group 3 of the Stamitz symphonies), and they include title pages and other portions by one of the most important Mannheim copyists, Mannheim 3. However, the *principal* copyist of these manuscripts proves to be none other than the copyist of most of the Stamitz symphony App. A/VI/182, Rtt/Mh. 3. Likewise, in App. A/VI/191, another Toeschi symphony, Mannheim 3 copies most of the set, Rtt/Mh. 3 the horn parts. The collaboration of these two copyists thus establishes a solid connection between Mannheim and the Stamitz symphonies in Regensburg.

Why the three Regensburg/Mannheim copyists should fail to appear elsewhere, especially within the full series of Cannabich symphonies in Munich, may relate to chronology: Stamitz died in 1757, at a time when Cannabich's and Toeschi's careers were just getting under way. At Regensburg the first of the pair of Cannabich symphonies in which Rtt/Mh. 3 occurs, App. A/VI/153, is in fact among the earliest of the Cannabich symphonies in Munich, no. 3. (The other, App. A/VI/155, is lacking in the Munich series.) Likewise, the two Toeschi symphonies bearing this copyist's hand, App. A/VI/184 and 189, are considered here to date from the early 1760s (see below). Therefore, the other two copyists of the Regensburg Stamitz manuscripts, Rtt/Mh. 1–2, may well antedate those of the Cannabich manuscripts, with only Rtt/Mh. 3 overlapping with them in these four works. This would also reaffirm our placement of group 3 later than the other Stamitz symphonies in Regensburg, in approximately the early to mid 1760s.

Discovery that the ten Stamitz manuscripts can be traced to Mannheim is of considerable musical significance, for the versions embodied in them differ markedly in many cases from more widely circulated ones. For example, the Regensburg account of E♭-6 (App. A/VI/183) departs strikingly from the version printed in Paris (Huberty, op. 5, no. 1) in every movement: the first is substantially recomposed, now featuring horn parts of great difficulty in the recapitulation;[31] a brief eight-bar transition now replaces the protracted slow movement of the print; the minuet is altered, and a new trio again brings forward the horns; and the finale is even more drastically recast than the first movement, shortening the printed version by two-thirds. The Regensburg (ex-Mannheim) manuscripts deviate from the readings transmitted by Stamitz's Parisian prints in two other important respects: they supply minuets and trios for two works published with only three movements (App. A/VI/176–77, G-3 and G-4), and they provide wind parts for three symphonies printed with reduced scoring (App. A/VI/176, 179, and 180 [G-3, D-8, and D-11], the latter two manuscripts providing a pair of trumpets plus timpani in addition to horns and oboes). Thus exhaustive documentary work proves once again to lead to genuine musical results.

With one or two exceptions, the Mannheim manuscripts of symphonies by Christian Cannabich at Regensburg seem to be relatively early. Those corresponding to Cannabich's numbered works in Munich have the numbers 3, 9, and 14–15, from ca. 1755–63, while three others not present in Munich, App. A/VI/ 155–56 and 158, could fall within the unnumbered slots—primarily early in the series—1, 5–6, 10, 20, 26, 28, or 33, dating to ca. 1766 (see chap. 5). The principal exception to this early dating is App. A/VI/161, the *Simphonia concertante* (Cannabich 42) of no later than 1772. Regensburg also possesses the only known source for a ballet attributed to Cannabich, *Les fêtes du seraïlles* (App. A/VI/162). Though no documentation whatever exists for this work other than this source, the likelihood of its authenticity is enhanced by the fact that it clearly came from Mannheim, being copied in part by Mannheim 3 and 14 on Blum 3 and Heusler 6 papers.

The seven Mannheim manuscripts of authentic symphonies by Joseph Toeschi at Regensburg pose a minor enigma from the chronological standpoint.[32] Like many of the other Mannheim manuscripts at Regensburg, four of them, App.

---

[31] See Wolf, *Stamitz*, 295–98, including example 12:1.

[32] An eighth symphony, App. A/VI/186, is actually a well-known work by Richter. On the date of this manuscript see below.

A/VI/187 and 189–91, may be assigned to the late 1750s or early 1760s; all were published in Paris by 1762/63.³³ The other three manuscripts, however (App. A/VI/184–85 and 188), were all issued considerably later, in the period 1768/69– 1773. On the assumption that Toeschi, like Cannabich, published his works fairly promptly, we would normally be inclined to date these three manuscripts from approximately that time.

Yet the first of these symphonies, App. A/VI/184, published in 1768/69, clearly belongs with the earlier group of four manuscripts: the paper and staving match not only that of App. A/VI/189–91, all published in 1762, but that of A/VI/153 as well, a manuscript of one of Cannabich's earliest symphonies, no. 3 (published 1761). Equally telling, the rather complex disposition of the copyists is almost the same as in A/VI/189 and 153. I therefore consider it warranted to group App. A/VI/184 with the other early Toeschi and Cannabich manuscripts and say that the time lag between date of composition and date of publication appears here to have been greater than usual.

The two remaining Toeschi symphonies, App. A/VI/185 and 188 (published in 1771 and 1773, respectively), parallel many of the other Regensburg sources in making use of Blum 3 paper (here copied by Mannheim 2), already seen in the two latest Stamitz manuscripts at Regensburg and in Cannabich's ballet *Fêtes du serailles*. Our provisional dating of the latter work in the late 1760s or early 1770s, based mainly on the presence of the copyist Mannheim 14, correlates well with that of the later Toeschi prints. Likewise, the two Ritschel works utilizing this paper (App. A/VI/172–73) would surely not have antedated Johannes Ritschel's return to Mannheim from Italy in 1763—assuming, of course, that the Ritschel in question was indeed Johannes.³⁴ On the other hand, the viola part and part of the violin 2 to App. A/VI/186 (the Richter symphony falsely attributed to Toeschi, again on Blum 3 paper) is by Rtt/Mh. 1, the principal copyist of the Regensburg Stamitz manuscripts—most or all of which are certainly earlier than most or all of the supposedly later group of Toeschi manuscripts. As rastrology is of little use here in determining chronology, a date for all the manuscripts on Blum 3 paper of anywhere in the 1760s to the early 1770s is possible, with the mid-to-late 1760s somewhat more likely in most cases.

Of the other Mannheim manuscripts at Regensburg, two that are noteworthy are of works by Holzbauer—the first, App. A/VI/168, only because it has two hol-

---

³³ The chronological numbering of Toeschi's symphonies ("Münster" numbers) and the dates for his publications cited here and in Appendix A/VI are taken from the "Chronologisches Verzeichnis der gedruckten Sinfonien" in Robert Münster, *Die Sinfonien Toeschis: ein Beitrag zur Geschichte der Mannheimer Sinfonie* (diss., Munich, 1956), 362ff.

³⁴ For two other uses of Blum 3 paper from the mid-to-late 1760s see App. A/VI/192–93, symphonies in Schwerin by Holzbauer and Toeschi (see the discussion of these manuscripts in the next section of this chapter).

ograph violin parts by the composer (the second violin only partially by him). The second manuscript, the cembalo concerto App. A/VI/171, has what may be the inscription "60:" at the top of page 1 of the cembalo part, which also serves as the title page (see fig. 2:8). If so, this could represent a date of 1760, which happens to accord well with its use of rastrum 10:28, found in Cannabich 2, 11–12, and 16 (ca. 1755–64), though not in precisely the same form (see Appendix C).

Four Manuscripts from Schwerin (now D-SWl, B-Bc)

The north-German duchy of Mecklenburg-Schwerin might seem an unlikely place to find manuscripts from the court of Mannheim, but this musically lively court fostered extensive contacts with important centers throughout Europe during the second half of the eighteenth century. One result is the presence in the former music collection of the dukes of Mecklenburg-Schwerin (now D-SWl)[35] of manuscripts of one symphony each by Holzbauer and Toeschi, both very probably from the 1760s (App. A/VI/192–93). Two other Mannheim manuscripts, symphonies by Holzbauer, were formerly owned by the Schwerin collector and erstwhile court organist Johann Jacob Heinrich Westphal (1756–1825; see App. A/VI/3–4).[36] These were sold between 1829 and 1839 to François-Joseph Fétis, and they eventually came into the collection of the Conservatoire royal de musique in Brussels when Fétis's library was bought by the state in 1871.[37]

The two Holzbauer symphonies in Brussels are straightforward copies of the usual sort by Mannheim 1, on Blum 3 paper lined with a one-stave rastrum. Both the paper and copyist would place these manuscripts before 1770. The Toeschi manuscript in Schwerin is of a work published in Paris in 1769, DTB D 3/Münster 41. Its copyist, again writing on Blum 3 paper, would seem to be a very young Johann Cramer (b. 1749; see Appendix D).[38]

More complex is the remaining Holzbauer symphony, App. A/VI/192, which shows a process of revision comparable to that of several of the Holzbauer masses in Munich. In addition to boasting a title page in the hand of the composer, the manuscript comprises at least two distinct levels. The first, consisting of the violin

---

[35] Otto Kade, *Die Musikalien-Sammlung des Grossherzoglich Mecklenburg-Schweriner Fürstenhauses aus den letzten zwei Jahrhunderten* (Schwerin: Sandmeyersche Hofbuchdruckerei, 1893), provides a full thematic catalogue of this collection that remains valuable.

[36] On Westphal see Miriam Terry, "C. P. E. Bach and J. J. H. Westphal—A Clarification," *JAMS* 22 (1969): 106–15.

[37] Ibid., 107, 114–15.

[38] The copyist could also be Mannheim 1, as in the Brussels manuscripts; his hand is similar to Johann Cramer's early hand. As discussed in Appendix D and elsewhere in this book, the probable reason for this is that Mannheim 1 was very likely Johann Cramer's father Jacob (d. 1770), who would have trained him.

2 and bass parts, contains an original second movement in F minor, marked "Andante brioso"; over this has been pasted a new second movement, in B♭, marked merely "Andante." The second level, including the violin 1, viola, and bassoon parts, presents *only* the new second movement, with no trace of the old. The second movement of the oboe parts was originally marked "tacent," and because there was no room for a paste-over, the new second movement is supplied on separate sheets; therefore, the original oboe parts were presumably part of the first level.[39] The horns are tacent in the second movement. The horn 1 part probably belongs to the first level alongside the oboes, as the paper, staving, and copyist are the same as in those parts; the horn 2 part, which bears the title, is definitely part of the second level. In this symphony the interplay of paper and staving between the levels implies a relatively narrow chronological span for the entire manuscript—probably the mid-to-late 1760s, despite the fact that rastrum 10:10, found in the level 2 parts and additions, occurs elsewhere in manuscripts dated slightly earlier, 1763 and 1765 (see Appendix C).

Mozart's Concerto for Three Pianos, K. 242 (App. A/VI/?202)

Mozart's Concerto for Three Pianos, K. 242, was written in Salzburg in February 1776 and also exists in a version for two pianos. The large assortment of parts for this work, now in the Memorial Library of Music at Stanford University (US-STu; App. A/VI/?202), seems something of a mess when first confronted. But as the following list shows, this initially rather inchoate material easily reduces to four distinct groups, as the late Alan Tyson kindly wrote in correspondence with me about this fascinating manuscript.[40]

Grouping of Parts to K. 242 (App. A/VI/?202)

Group 1: parts for cembalo 1 and 2 (only) from the three-piano version, on Heusler 5 paper lined with six passes of a unique two-stave rastrum. Unidentified copyist ("Stanf./?Mh. 1"), with a hand similar to others at Mannheim. The third keyboard part has been lost; or else the cembalo 3 part from group 3, or the autograph, served that purpose.

Group 2: full set of orchestral parts to the three-piano version, by the same copyist, on Blum 5 paper lined with two passes of a five-stave rastrum.

---

[39] However, the staving matches that of the addition, not the remainder of the parts belonging to the first level, so the matter is hardly crystal-clear.

[40] Though the grouping described here is based on that proposed by Tyson, I have reversed his groups 2 and 3 in order to place the related keyboard and orchestral parts together.

Group 3: cembalo 3 (only) and orchestral parts to the three-piano version. The copying chores are divided between two copyists, the first writing the first two movements, the second the finale. These copyists are neither from Salzburg[41] nor Mannheim and appear to be south German; the paper is also a standard south-German one from the mill of Joseph Anton Unold in Wolfegg (Württemberg; this paper is extremely common in Regensburg and Munich, for example). This group was evidently owned at one time by Heinrich Henkel,[42] who correctly notes on page 1 of the cembalo part that it contains autograph corrections by Mozart (as do several other parts). The manuscript is lined with a one-stave rastrum.

Group 4: cembalo 2 part (only) to the *two*-piano version, in a copyist's hand that would seem to be Viennese or at least Austrian. Italian paper (<PS : three moons/REAL>); ten-stave rastrum.

To provide a simple explanation that fits the above data is not without its difficulties. (I shall disregard the single part to the two-piano version here ["group" 4], which could date from Mozart's early Viennese period or perhaps earlier.) We know that Mozart took K. 242 with him on his grand tour of 1777–79, for he played it at a concert in Augsburg on 22 October 1777 and at an "academy" in Mannheim at Cannabich's house on 12 March 1778, just before he left for Paris.[43] The obvious hypothesis would be that the parts from group 3, on Unold paper, were copied in Augsburg for the performance there, presumably from Mozart's score.

As for the parts from groups 1–2, the use in them of the two most common Mannheim papers, Heusler 5 and Blum 5—in forms characteristic of the time, incidentally—and the knowledge that the concerto was in fact played at Mannheim make it tempting to link groups 1–2 with Mannheim. Support for this view comes from the copying style, and it would be equally tempting to speculate that the hand might be that of Fridolin Weber, father of Aloysia and Constanze, who Mozart says "copied out gratis whatever I required [while he was at Mannheim and] supplied me with music paper" (letter of 24 March 1778).[44] However, the

---

[41] See Cliff Eisen, "The Scoring of the Orchestral Bass Part in Mozart's Salzburg Keyboard Concertos: The Evidence of the Authentic Copies," in Neal Zaslaw, ed., *Mozart's Piano Concertos: Text, Context, Interpretation* (Ann Arbor: University of Michigan Press, 1996), p. 422, n. 7.

[42] On Henkel see Eugene K. Wolf, "Fulda, Frankfurt, and the Library of Congress: A Recent Discovery," *JAMS* 24 (1971): 289, and the "Communication," ibid. 25 (1972): 122-23; idem, "The Music Collection of the Hessische Landesbibliothek Fulda and Its Relationship with Collections in Frankfurt, Washington, and Elsewhere," in *Von der Klosterbibliothek zur Landesbibliothek: Beiträge zum zweihundertjährigen Bestehen der Hessischen Landesbibliothek Fulda*, ed. Artur Brall (Stuttgart: Anton Hiersemann, 1978), 362–65, 368–69.

[43] See Mozart's letters of 24 October 1777 (Bauer-Deutsch, 2:84; Anderson, 340) and 24 March 1778 (Bauer-Deutsch, 2:326; Anderson, 517).

[44] Bauer-Deutsch, 2:328; Anderson, 518.

recent identification of Weber's hand rules him out as the copyist of groups 1–2, as the hands are not the same.[45]

What is not easy to explain is the existence of the two sets: if Mozart had already had the manuscript copied in Augsburg, why would it have been recopied in Mannheim? Conceivably he left the Augsburg set there in order to lighten his luggage, either to be reclaimed on the way home or sent back to Leopold; or the Mannheim set was made for someone there and was later brought together with the other material. In any event, though hardly conclusive, the evidence seems to justify a provisional attribution of this manuscript to Mannheim.

Some Manuscripts Probably *Not* from Mannheim

From time to time in the preceding pages we have considered the claim of certain manuscripts to be from Mannheim that did not seem to meet the standards of proof of the "accepted" manuscripts.[46] Five other manuscripts in that category include two concertos from Regensburg (D-Rtt, Haymann 3, Toeschi 22) and three symphonies from Schloss Harburg (D-AUu, III 4½ 4° 563, 729, and 757, by Stamitz, Cannabich, and Toeschi, respectively).[47] In each case the paper is one common at Mannheim, Blum 3 for the Regensburg manuscripts, Heusler 7 and Blum 5 for the Harburg ones. The staving provides no evidence one way or another, being done with a one-stave rastrum, as are many of the Mannheim manuscripts at Regensburg. And as the copyists of the main sets are otherwise found in no other Mannheim manuscripts, and do not especially fit the Mannheim copying style, there is simply not enough reason to claim Mannheim provenance for them.[48] The most one can hope for in the future would be to find concordant sources for these hands that allow us to identify them with a specific center—or at least definitively exclude them from Mannheim.

---

[45] See chap. 2, fn. 104 and related text.

[46] See, e.g., the manuscripts discussed in chap. 2, @ fn. 40; in table 8:1, fn. a (the Yale manuscript of J. C. Bach's *Temistocle*); in chap. 8, fn. 23 (the score to Holzbauer's *Nitteti* in the Proske-Bibliothek in Regensburg); and in fnn. 5 and 9–11 and related text of the present chapter (Holzbauer masses in the Harburg collection at D-Au and in I-MOe). Four other manuscripts not from Mannheim are D-DS, Mus. ms. 216 and 218–19, ballets by Christian Cannabich, and 217, his melodrama *Electra* (1781; Munich copy).

[47] In Wolf, *Stamitz*, 431, I called the first of the Harburg manuscripts, that of Stamitz's symphony DTB/Wolf E♭-5b, a "possible" Mannheim manuscript (see also ibid., 46). For a sample of the copyist's hand see ibid., 466.

[48] Precisely the same constellation of evidence characterizes D-Mbs, Mus. Ms. 1279, an aria attributed to Mozart, "Perche t'arresti" (K. C. 701 [Anh. 187]). The use in this manuscript of Heusler 7 paper is simply not enough to attribute the manuscript to Mannheim when the copyist is unknown and the staving 10 x 1.

Chapter 9

To some extent that is what can be done for another manuscript, part of a collection that has recently come to light in the Bibliothèque municipale of Châlons-en-Champagne (*olim* Châlons-sur-Marne; F-CSM).[49] One of the many valuable early sources in that collection, Ms. 1494, no. 291, is a "Trio da camera . . . Del: Sig: Antoni Fils."[50] The three original parts, by an unidentified copyist unique to this manuscript, are on Heusler 6 paper that must have come originally from Mannheim, as it was lined with rastrum 10:15, found in several Mannheim manuscripts of the late 1750s—Cannabich 3 in Munich (App. A/III/3), Fils's cello concerto in Berlin (App. A/VI/22), and an aria from Galuppi's *Siroe* of 1754 in the Pretlack collection (App. A/VI/62). Based on this information alone, one would be inclined to assign the manuscript to Mannheim.

Indeed, this identification would seem to be supported by the fact that in another manuscript in the collection, a trio sonata by Domenico Ferrari (Ms. 1494, no. 333), a second Mannheim rastrum occurs, 10:10; this rastrum is found in a Ritschel autograph of 1763 (App. A/I/1), Cannabich's Symphonies no. 14–15 (App. A/III/14-15), and Holzbauer's *Betulia liberata* of 1765 (App. A/II/17). But the opposite is true. For unlike the copyist of the Fils piece, the copyist of this manuscript is *not* unique to it, being also found in a trio sonata attributed to Jommelli and two early symphonies by Stamitz and Holzbauer (Ms. 1494, nos. 275, 403, 441). *Those manuscripts are copied on coarse, opaque German paper and are upright in format*, clearly connecting this copyist, and thus the entire complex, to a smaller German court—probably one in close contact with Mannheim, given the use of Mannheim paper and the presence among its manuscripts of several rare Mannheim works.[51] (This would also explain the presence of the Ferrari piece, which so far as I know has no association with Mannheim.) The French owner, one of the principal copyists of the collection, actually refers to the provenance of the manuscript (though inconclusively) in a note on the duplicate first violin part, saying, "J'ai copié ce 1er violon par duplicata sur le manuscrit qui m'apartient et m'a été envoyé d'Allemagne" (!). As a matter of fact, that same owner/copyist *did* have

---

[49] This collection is one of those catalogued in François-Pierre Goy and Marc Desmet, *Catalogue des fonds musicaux anciens conservés en Champagne-Ardenne, 1500–1800* (Paris: Minkoff, 2000). See also the brief description of the collection in Goy, "Bilan de l'inventaire des fonds musicaux anciens: Région Champagne-Ardenne," *Revue de musicologie* 81 (1995): 278–79. I am grateful to Dr. Christian Meyer (Strasbourg) of the Centre national de recherche scientifique for alerting me to the existence of this important new *fonds*.

[50] DTB, Jg. XVI, Filtz F-moll 1; published in 1760 as op. 3, no. 4, by La Chevardière in Paris (*RISM* F 792).

[51] We know that paper was for sale at Mannheim to individuals; see Pokorny's letter of 4 February 1754, printed in Ludwig Schiedermair, "Die Blütezeit der Öttingen-Wallerstein'schen Hofkapelle," *Sammelbände der Internationalen Musikgesellschaft* 9 (1907/8): 119. The cost at that time was 25 gulden per ream. In addition, Holzbauer is known to have sent manuscript paper from Mannheim to the Oettingen-Wallerstein court in 1763; see above, fn. 4.

contact with Mannheim, if indirectly: two Richter symphonies in the collection, copied entirely by him on French paper, have the notation "Aporté de Manheim par M. Gargan en 1760" (Ms. 1494, nos. 464, 470). Such notations are, incidentally, frequent in the Châlons collection, providing rare evidence as to how manuscripts circulated in the eighteenth century.

In sum, it is by no means out of the question for the Fils manuscript also to be from Mannheim: it could have been obtained there together with the paper on which the second, local copyist wrote his four manuscripts. But the simpler explanation—that it is likewise a local copy, but on paper bought in Mannheim—would seem the more convincing, unless and until the first copyist can be more firmly associated with Mannheim. Thus, as on so many occasions in this book, careful study of the detailed characteristics of a given manuscript, of its relationship with other manuscripts in the collection of which it is a part, and of possible connections with manuscripts in other collections has led us to a more nuanced and judicious—or at least a more cautious—conclusion.

Appendix A: Manuscripts from Mannheim

Appendix A is a comprehensive *catalogue raisonné* of all the manuscripts considered here to have originated at the Mannheim court. Its six parts are organized as follows (for more on the organization of Appendix A see the final section of chap. 1): first a group of sources still in Mannheim or with clear documentary or other evidence of their Mannheim provenance, normally a colophon referring to Mannheim or the summer palace of Schwetzingen (the "core" manuscripts, Appendix A/I); then manuscripts of works by Ignaz Holzbauer and Christian Cannabich, most of which were originally part of the court collection (Appendices A/II–III); next a miscellaneous group of autograph and partly autograph manuscripts without colophon (Appendix A/IV); then music of Georg Joseph Vogler (Appendix A/V); and finally a large group of "other" manuscripts that fit none of the previous categories (Appendix A/VI). Each of these appendices is paralleled by, and provides the essential basis for, chapters of the text: Appendices A/I–V by chapters 3–7 and Appendix A/VI by chapters 8–9, the latter two chapters treating the operas and a few other large dramatic works on the one hand, the non-operatic sources on the other. All manuscripts are assumed to be sets of parts unless otherwise stated.

In each of the six parts of Appendix A the first columns supply the numbering assigned here, the location of the manuscript using RISM sigla, and a transcription of the title given in the manuscript (in italics) or, when deemed appropriate, a more extensive transcription of the title page (in quotes). Capitalization, misspellings, and so on are preserved to the extent feasible. However, line endings are not normally indicated, and so-called *Faulheitsstriche*, strokes over a letter to indicate that it should be doubled (e.g., $\bar{n} = nn$) have been resolved. In general, the format of the various sources (oblong or upright) has only been indicated when it departs from the norm at Mannheim of oblong autographs and secular parts and upright sacred parts.

Next come three columns listing the paper and watermarks, the staving, and the copyists of each of the manuscripts, referring to Appendices B ("Paper"), C ("Compound Rastra"), and D ("Copyists"). While most references here will be to listings in the latter appendices, an occasional unique watermark, rastrum, or copyist that does not appear in Appendices B–D will be given directly in Appendix A. With respect to the relationship between these appendices, it should be emphasized that Appendix A represents the master catalogue which must always be consulted for details on, for example, precisely which parts contain which papers; Appendices B–D are intended mainly to list, and identify more fully, the various watermarks, rastra, and copyists referred to in Appendix A. (For more on Appendices B–D see the sections of chap. 2 dealing with each of these types of evidence.) A final column, found in all but Appendices A/I and V, provides comments on the manuscript in question, usually a suggestion as to its approximate date.

Regarding the conventions for specifying dates adopted in these appendices, parentheses indicate a date that actually appears in a manuscript, square brackets a firm date that does not. "Ca. 1750–55" means "ca. 1750–ca. 1755," while "ca. 1750–

Appendix A / I

1755" means "about 1750 to precisely 1755." The formulation "1750/51," with a solidus (slash) rather than an en dash, refers to the season spanning those two years (i.e., approximately the second half of 1750 through the first half of 1751). Finally, "1750+" means "1750 or later." Such a date normally refers to an undated manuscript of a work known to have been performed at Mannheim for the first time in that year, as the full citation in Appendix A should make clear; although the evidence indicates that the copy is from about the same time, this cannot be proven beyond a doubt. Dates of opera performances without any mention of place refer to performances at Mannheim or Schwetzingen; references to performances elsewhere will supply the location.

I. Manuscripts Extant at Mannheim or with Explicit Evidence of Mannheim Provenance (the "Core" Manuscripts)

No.	MS, Format	Title, Colophon	Paper	Staving	Copyists
1	D-MHjk (score, mainly aut.; ATB, vc. parts)	"Toni B. Messa a 4° Con Instrumt. Mannheim @ 14 Maggio 1.7.6.3. Ho finito a Schwezing [i.e., Schwetzingen, the summer palace of the elector.] Di Gio: Ritschel" (Schmitt I.6)[a]	Blum 5 (portions of score; parts); Heusler 5 (rest of score)	10:10 (score); 6 x 2 (TS 35.5, DS 16; ATB parts); 14 x 1 (vc.)	Johannes Ritschel (most of score), 2d copyist (Gloria of score), 3d copyist (movement captions of score; vc.); MHjk 1 (ATB parts)
2	D-MHjk (parts)	"Te Deum Laudamus. à 4 Voci. ... Del Sig. Zach. In usum Sem. Mus. ad S. Aloys. [i.e., the Seminarium Musicum of the Jesuitenkirche] Mannh. 1764."	German, "ICH"	12–13 x 1	Orch. parts by 3 copyists, voice parts a 4th; TP either the 1st of these copyists at a different time or a 5th copyist.
3	D-MHjk (parts)	"Stabat Mater à 4. Voc. ... Del Sign. Per[g]olesi [crossed out] Thuma [added above in different hand.] In Usum Seminarii Musici ad D. Aloysium Mannhemii 1766."	Heusler 6; German, ?J. M. Bach 1 (TP)	11 x 1	One copyist (S, TP); 3 other copyists (ATB parts, respectively); MHjk 2 (both org. parts)
4	D-MHjk (parts)	"VII. Psalmi. 4. Voci. ... Del Sig. Starck." At end of timp. part: "O A M D G / E B V M H 1766."	Heusler 6 (parts); German, "EDPM" (TP)	12–13 x 1	MHjk 2 (vn. 2), 7 other copyists (rest of parts, TP)
5	D-MHjk (parts)	"[Vespe]rae mi Vespertini De Dominica ... De Sigr Riegl" (orig. TP, damaged; also a newer TP, "Rigel")	Heusler 7; German, Knöckel 1 (TP)	12–13 x 1	Mh. 6, incl. new TP at somewhat later date

224

The "Core" Manuscripts

No.	MS, Format	Title, Colophon	Paper	Staving	Copyists
6	D-MHjk (parts)	"Vesperae de Dominica . . . Del Sig. Hoffstätter"	Blum 4; German, Knöckel 1 (TP)	12 x 1	Mh. 6
7	D-MHjk (score, upright format)	"Missa Ex D. Del Sign^{re} Vogler."	German, ?J. F. Roeder 1	14 x 1	MHjk 1
8	D-Mbs, Mus. Ms. 1981 (aut. score)	"Messa a 4^{tro} a Capella con Istromenti se piace per la quadragesima" (by Carlo Grua; Schmitt I.1). At end of MS: "Finis in N. D. Die vigesima octava Januarii 1733 Manheim. [Later addition:] Carol. Grua."	Heusler 1a (most); Blum (<eagle/shield [Basel crozier]/B>; fols. 9-16); Heusler (<laurel wreath [Basel crozier]: cross/M>; endpapers)	2 x 5:19 (Heusler 1a); 2 x 5:9 (Blum paper)	Carlo Grua (see fig. D:1)
9	D-Mbs, Mus. Ms. 1982 (aut. score)	"Littanie della Beata vergine a 5. con Istromenti. [Later addition:] Carolo Grua" (Schmitt II.6). At end of MS: "Finis in N. D. Manheim 1737 die nona novembris."	Heusler 1b	5 x 2:6	Carlo Grua
10	D-Kl, Ms. mus. Anhang 13 (aut. score)	"Messa Breve a 4^{tro} con Trombel,] Tympani, e VVni. [Added:] et oboe" (by Carlo Grua; Schmitt I.2). At end of MS: "Finis in N. D. Manheim 1751 die tertia junii."	Heusler 5; ?Blum or Heusler 1 (endpapers)	2 x 7:1	Carlo Grua
11	D-Mbs, Mus. Ms. 1987 (aut. score)	"Messa Breve a 4^{tro} con istromenti. [Later addition:] Carolo Grua" (Schmitt I.3). At end of MS: "Finis in N. D. Mannheim 1751 die decima quarta junii."	Blum 3	2 x 5:18	Carlo Grua
12	D-FS (Mf), Mf 596[a] (aut. score; for parts see App. A/VI/144)	"Memento Domine David a 4^{tro} con istromenti" (by Carlo Grua; Schmitt II.2). At end of MS: "Finis in Nomine Domini Manheim 1753 die tertia novembris."	Blum 1	2 x 7:1	Carlo Grua
13	D-KA, Mus. Hs. 1393 (aut. score; for parts see App. A/IV/2)	"Messa Breve a 4^{tro} con istromenti [by Carlo Grua.] Manheim 1766 Die quarta junij" (from label, aut.; Schmitt I.5). At end of MS: "Finis in N. D. Manheim 1766 Die quarta junij."	Blum 3	10:12	Carlo Grua

Appendix A/I

No.	MS, Format	Title, Colophon	Paper	Staving	Copyists
14	D-KA (formerly D-DO), olim Mus. Ms. 240 (score)[b]	"Le Rendes-Vous / Ballet de chasse / Del Sig.e. Cannabich / Apt.et a Falgera / fait a mannheim par M.r Bouqueton / 1769." At end of MS: "Copie a Chevetzingen [i.e., Schwetzingen] l'ane 1769."	Heusler 7; German, Knöckel 1 (cover)	10:17b	Sigismund Falgera
15	D-KA (formerly D-DO), olim Mus. Ms. 241 (score)	"Ceyx est Alcyonne / Ballet heroique / Del Signor Cannbich / fait par M.r Bouqueton, a / Manheim. / Appartient a falgera 1769." At end of MS: "Copie a manheim l'anne [1769; effaced]."	Heusler 7	10:17b	Sigismund Falgera
16	D-KA (formerly D-DO), olim Mus. Ms. 1922 (score)[c]	"L'enlevement de Proserpinne / Ballet heroique / Del Sig.or joseph Toe[s]chi / fait a Mannheim par M.r Bouqueton / apartient a falgera." At end of MS: "Fine del Ballo[.] Copie a Manheim [?1767; effaced] Le 8 Novem."	Heusler 7; German, Knöckel 1 (cover)	10 x 1	Sigismund Falgera
17[d]	Private collection (aut. score)	"Sonata I" for clavier and violin, Mozart, K. 301 (293a)	Heusler 5	12:2a[e]	Mozart
18[d]	Private collection (aut. score)	"Sonata II" for clavier and violin, Mozart, K. 302 (293b)	Heusler 5	12:2a[e]	Mozart
19[d]	Private collection (aut. score)	"Sonata III" for clavier and violin, Mozart, K. 303 (293c)	Heusler 5	12:2a[e]	Mozart
20[d]	Private collection (aut. score)	"Sonata V" for clavier and violin, Mozart, K. 305 (293d). Also includes the opening of K. 306 and the first measure of K. 295a; see chap. 3, fn. 16.	Heusler 5	12:2a[e]	Mozart
21	D-HV, Stadtarchiv, Autografensammlung, Sign. 1585 (aut. score)	"Aria. Non sò d['] onde viene / Recitativ. Alcandro, lo confeso } für Sopran [K. 294]. di Amadeo Wolfgango Mozart.mpa 1778[.] Per la sig.ra Weber. à Manheim. li 24 di feb:ro"	Heusler 5	12:2a	Mozart

226

The "Core" Manuscripts

No.	MS, Format	Title, Colophon	Paper	Staving	Copyists
22	D-B, Mus. ms. autogr. Mozart KV 18, 48, 295, [etc.] (aut. score)	"Aria [K. 295] Per il Sig:^{e} Raff. di Amadeo Wolfgango Mozart$_{mp}$[.] Mannheim li 27 di Feb:^{ro} 1778."	Heusler 5	12:2a	Mozart
23	US-NYp, JOF 73-12 (Herter Collection)	"Sonata [for clavier and violin, K. 296.] Di Wolfgango Amadeo Mozart mp^a[.] li 11 di marzo 1778 à Manheim. pour Mademoiselle Therese [Pierron; torn off.]"	Heusler 5	12:2a	Mozart
24	F-Pn(c), Ms. 246	"Concerto per il Cembalo e Violino [K. 315f/Anh. 56; fragment] di Wolfgango Amadeo Mozart$_{mp}$[.] Mannheim ii 1778" (i.e., exact date left blank; begun between 6 Nov. and 9 Dec. 1778).	Dutch, Rogge 1^f	1 × 14 (TS 161.5)	Mozart

^a "Schmitt" references here and elsewhere in Appendix A are to the thematic catalogue in Eduard Schmitt, *Kirchenmusik der Mannheimer Schule, 1. Auswahl*, DTB, Neue Folge, 2 (Wiesbaden: Breitkopf & Härtel, 1982). For a reprod. of the title page of this manuscript see Jochen Reutter, "Die Kirchenmusik am Mannheimer Hof," in Ludwig Finscher, ed., *Die Mannheimer Hofkapelle im Zeitalter Carl Theodors* (Mannheim: Palatium Verlag im J & J Verlag 1992), 107.

^b A mod. ed. of this ballet, with reprods. from this manuscript, appears in RRMCE, vol. 45 (1996), ed. Floyd K. Grave (see Bibliography).

^c A mod. ed. of this ballet, with reprods. from this manuscript, appears in RRMCE, vol. 52 (1998), ed. Paul Cauthen (see Bibliography).

^d I have not personally examined App. A/I/17-20, which are reportedly in a Swiss private collection. However, the late Alan Tyson kindly provided me with his extensive personal notes on these manuscripts, on which the above information is based.

^e Though I have not studied these manuscripts personally (see fn. d), it is virtually certain that they were lined with rastrum 12:2a based on the total span (reported to me by Alan Tyson) and the use of this rastrum in all other Mozart manuscripts of this period, which are on the same paper.

^f This paper also appears in a second Mozart fragment, that of the Kyrie K. 322/296a (Salzburg, Mozarteum, Sign. KV 296a = 322). As the latter manuscript has no colophon and could obviously have been written after Mozart left Mannheim (the position taken by the editors of K^6), it has been omitted here.

II. Masses of Ignaz Holzbauer in the Bayerische Staatsbibliothek; Autograph Scores

Appendix A/II lists the sixteen sets of parts to Ignaz Holzbauer's masses in the Bayerische Staatsbibliothek, Munich (D-Mbs), and his five extant autograph scores. The manuscripts of the former group, like the Cannabich manuscripts in Appendix A/III, were originally part of the performance materials of the electoral Kapelle, first in Mannheim and then in Munich. For nos. 1–15 of these manuscripts the numbering in column 1 follows that of the labels on the manuscripts, which is not, however, chronological. These numbers obviously provided the basis for assignment of the present call numbers in Munich, which are given in column 2. Column 3 then gives the title of the work (for nos. 1–16 again from the labels) and their sigla in Eduard Schmitt's and Deanna Bush's indices of Holzbauer's masses (see Bibliography). In the Comments column the references to "groups" refer to the chronological groupings of the mass manuscripts proposed in chapter 4 (see esp. table 4:1).

No.	MS, Format	Work	Paper	Staving	Copyists	Comments
1	D-Mbs, Mus. Ms. 2289 (parts)	*Missa* in C (Schmitt I.6, Bush A6)	Blum 5	12:7b (SATB/C, obs., trs, timp., org.); 12:7a (strs, bn.); 1 + 12:7a + 1 (STB/R); 12:10b + 1 (AR)	Mh. 1-2	Group 2a, 1760s (ca. 1765–70?). AR, by Mh. 2, prob. copied later than main set (rastrum 12:10b characteristic of group 3 and Vogler MSS of 1770s; hand varies from that of Mh. 2's other parts).
2	D-Mbs, Mus. Ms. 2290 (parts)	*Missa* in B♭ (Schmitt I.15, Bush A25)	Heusler 5 (most); Heusler 7 (hns. *alto*, added)	12:8d (most); 2 x 6:1 (BR II); 12:8a (hns. *alto*, added)	Mh. 1-2 (most); Mh. 7 (vns. through "Cum sancto spirito"); at least 3 other copyists; Holzbauer (numerous corrections and additions)	Group 1a, ca. 1753–60. Horns *alto*, by Mh. 1, added later. See Bush, 385–86, for further details on this complex MS.
3	D-Mbs, Mus. Ms. 2291 (parts)	*Missa* in E♭ (Schmitt I.19, Bush A14)	van der Ley 1 (SATB/C, va., obs., hns., org.; all smaller); Heusler 5 (rest)	12 x 1 (van der Ley paper); 12:8c (STB/R, vns., cb./vc., bn.); 12:10b (AR)	Mh. 6 (van der Ley parts, AR), Mh. 1 (remaining parts), Holzbauer ("Sinfonia tacet" in Gloria of SR, TR)	Group 1b, mid-1750s–ca. 1765; a copy of this mass exists in A-H, dated 1766 (see Bush, 331 [no. 8], 365–66). AR (Mh. 6) later than main set (rastrum 12:10b; see App. A/II/1, Comments).

228

Music of Ignaz Holzbauer

No.	MS, Format	Work	Paper	Staving	Copyists	Comments
4	D-Mbs, Mus. Ms. 2292 (parts)	Missa in B♭ (Schmitt I.16, Bush A26)	Blum 5 (most); Blum 5 (hns. alto/trs.; added later)	12:7c (most); 12 × 1 (hns. alto/trs.)	Mh. 2; Holzbauer (Kyrie and Gloria of hns. basso numerous minor additions and corrections); Mh. 8 (rest of hns. basso)	Group 2b, late 1760s–early 1770s. Hns. alto/tr. parts added later.
5	D-Mbs, Mus. Ms. 2293 (parts)	Missa in E♭ (Schmitt I.18, Bush A13)	Blum 1b (most), Heusler 5 (SA/R), Blum 5 (va., b.)	2 × 6:1 (most), 12:10b (SA/R, va., b.)	Mh. 9, prob. Mh. 1 (most);[a] Mh. 6 (SA/R), Mh. 2 (va.), Mh. 8 (b.); Holzbauer (numerous additions and alterations)	Group 1a, ca. 1753–no later than 1759 (orig. set on early paper; copy of this mass in the Muzeum české hudby in Prague (dated 1759 [see Bush, 335 (no. 59), 363–64]).[b] SR, AR, va., b. later (rastrum 12:10b; see App. A/II/1, Comments).
6	D-Mbs, Mus. Ms. 2294 (parts)	Missa in e (Schmitt I.21, Bush A15a)	Heusler 5 and 7	12:8c (most), 12:8a (TR)	Mh. 1	Group 1b, mid-1750s–ca. 1765. An earlier version of this mass is found in a MS from Olomouc in CZ-Bm, dated 1744, and in one at Heiligenkreuz monastery (A-HE) dated 1749 [no. 9], 331 [no. 9], 366–67).
7	D-Mbs, Mus. Ms. 2295 (parts)	Missa in D (Schmitt I.36, Bush A7)	Blum 5, Heusler 5 (most); Heusler 2 (org.)	12:7e (most), 12:10b (vn. 1, b.); 12 × 1 (org.)	Mh. 2 (most), Mh. 6 (vn. 1, b.); Mh. 1 (org.); Holzbauer (alterations in Kyrie)	Group 2c, 1760s–early 1770s. Org. part on early paper; vn. 1, cb. later (rastrum 12:10b; see App. A/II/1, Comments).
8	D-Mbs, Mus. Ms. 2296 (parts)	Missa in G (Schmitt I.25, Bush A21)	Blum 5	12:7a (most); 12 × 1 (hn. 2)	Mh. 8 (most), Mh. 2 (hn. 2), Holzbauer (numerous corrections)	Group 2a, 1760s (ca. 1765–70?).
9	D-Mbs, Mus. Ms. 2297 (parts)	Missa Brevis in A minor (Schmitt I.10, Bush A23a)	Blum 5 (most), Heusler 5 (SA/R, vn. 2)	12:7c (most), 12:10b (SA/R, vn. 2)	Mh. 1–2 (most), Mh. 6 (SA/R, vn. 2), Holzbauer (paste-on in ob. 1)	Group 2b, later 1760s–early 1770s. SR, AR, vn. 2 later (rastrum 12:10b; see App. A/II/1, Comments). An earlier version of this mass is found in a MS from Olomouc in CZ-Bm dated 1747 (see Bush, 334 [no. 45], 380–81).

Appendix A/II

No.	MS, Format	Work	Paper	Staving	Copyists	Comments
10	D-Mbs, Mus. Ms. 2298 (parts)	Missa in Bb (Schmitt I.17/2, Bush A27a)	Blum 5, Heusler 5	12 × 1 (most); 12:10d (AR)	Mh. 6	Group 1c, 1753–ca. 1765(?): AR later (rastrum 12:10d, dated elsewhere 1776). An earlier version of this mass is found in a MS from Olomouc in CZ-Bm dated 1746 (see Bush, 334 [no. 40], 388–89, 496–97). For a transcription of the later version see Bush, 521–70.
11	D-Mbs, Mus. Ms. 2299 [I, II] (parts)[c]	Missa in C (Schmitt I.7, Bush A3)	Blum 5 (Kyrie and Gloria of all parts), Heusler 5 (rest)	12:10b	Johann Cramer (vns. of Kyrie and Gloria),[d] Mh. 2 (rest of Kyrie and Gloria); Holzbauer (last 2 pp. of org. [Dona nobis], some additions); Mh. 6 (rest)	Group 3, ca. 1770–1778. Kyrie–Gloria copied separately from Credo–Agnus, then bound together.
12	D-Mbs, Mus. Ms. 2300 (parts)	Missa in A (Schmitt I.37, Bush A22). Dated 1763.	Blum 5, Heusler 7, Heusler 5, Blum 3	12:8a (most, orig. set); 12:10b (SR, b. rip., trs., timp., also sinfonia in all parts)	Mh. 1–2 (orig. set); Johann Cramer (SR), Mh. 5 (added sinfonia, b. rip., trs., timp.); Holzbauer (numerous additions)	Group 1b. Dated 17 October 1763 at end of TR part; see fig. 4:1. SR, b. rip., trs., timp., sinfonia all clearly added later (rastrum 12:10b; see App. A/II/1, Comments; Johann Cramer was only 14 in 1763).
13	D-Mbs, Mus. Ms. 2301 (parts)	Missa in F (Schmitt I.12, Bush A16a)	Blum 5, Heusler 5 (most); German, ?J. M. Bach 1 (paste-overs); German, Knöckel 1 (orig. cover)	12:7d (orig. set); 12:10b (additions by Mh. 6); 12:10a (Kyrie and Gloria of vns.)	Mh. 2 (orig. set); Mh. 6 (added Kyrie and Gloria of most parts; hns., trs., timp.); Johann Cramer (Kyrie and Gloria of vns. [see fig. D-6]); Holzbauer (many changes and additions, some cover labels)	Group 2a, 1760s (ca. 1765–70?). Added portions later (rastrum 12:10a–b found in Vogler MSS ca. 1776; see also App. A/II/1, Comments).
14	D-Mbs, Mus. Ms. 2721 (parts)	Missa Brevissima in F (Schmitt I.13, Bush A17)	Blum 5 (most), Heusler 5 (dupl. vn. 1)	12:10b	Mh. 2 (most), Johann Cramer (vns.), Mh. 6 (dupl. vn. 1), Holzbauer (added word "moderato" in Credo of most parts)	Group 3, ca. 1770–78 (or ca. 1770–74 if Mh. 2 is identical with Johann Lochner, who died in that year).

No.	MS, Format	Work	Paper	Staving	Copyists	Comments
15	D-Mbs, Mus. Ms. 2305 (parts)	*Missa* in D (Schmitt I.31, Bush A11a)	Blum 5 (SATB/R, strs., bn.), Heusler 5 (rest)	12:7b (SATB/R, vn. 2, va.), 12:10b (vn. 1, b.), 12:7d (bn.); 12 x 1 (rest)	Mh. 6 (both papers), Mh. 2-3 (Blum paper only), Holzbauer (several additions)	Group 2a, 1760s (ca. 1765–70?). Vn. 1, b., by Mh. 6, later (rastrum 12:10b; see App. A/II/1, Comments, and cf. App. A/II/7). An earlier version of this mass is found in A-GÖ, dated 1764 (see Bush, 331 [no. 4], 358–59).
16	D-Mbs, Mus. Ms. 2306 (2 hn. parts only)	*Missa* in G (Schmitt I:26, Bush A19). No. 18 on label.	Blum 5 and 3	12 x 1	Mh. 2	Group 1c, 1753–ca. 1765. Full sets of parts to this mass exist in Ebrach (D-EB), dated 1773, and A-GÖ, dated 1774 (see Bush, 336 [no. 66], 331 [no. 5], 375–76).
17	D-Mbs, Mus. Ms. 2288 I, II (score in 2 vols., mainly aut.)	"Betulia Liberata. Oratorio"	Blum 5, Heusler 5; Alsatian, J. Pasquai (<FIN DE / JOS PASQUAI / EN ALSACE / 1742>; paste-over vol. 1, fol. 45r).	10 x 1 (fols. 1-4, 9-12); 10:25a (all recits. but 1st, arias); 12:2b (choruses)	Holzbauer (most); Mh. 5 (vol. 1, fols. 65r-75v, 83v [last 2 mm.]-85v; vol. 2, fols. 56r-65r; text of majority of recits.); 3d copyist (remaining text of recits.)	Although the original performance of *Betulia liberata* took place in 1760, the use here of rastra 10:25a and 12:2b, as well as the specific form of the Heusler 5 watermark, clearly indicates a date in the 1770s. This score is therefore associated with the revival of Holzbauer's oratorio in 1774 (for further information see chap. 4, @ fnn. 20–24).
18	A-Wn, S.A.68.B.35 (Fond Kiesewetter; aut. score)	"Il Giudizio di Salomone. Oratorio[.] 1765," part 1 (part 2 lost)	Blum 5 (most); Heusler 5 (final chorus and added winds, pp. 165-78; p. 104, paste-on); Blum 6 (added bifolio, pp. 91-94, itself including a paste-on)	10:10 (most); 12:5 / 12 x 1 (pp. 83-90, 98-111); 14 x 1 (p. 158-orig. p. 165); 10:7 (pp. 91-94, smaller paste-on pp. 147-48); 12:2b (pp. 165-78; p. 104, paste-on); 2 x 5 (TS 93.5; p. 92, paste-on); 10:8b (paste-on across pp. 2-3; p. 26, paste-on)	Holzbauer	The score as a whole dates from 1765, while most of the revisions can be assigned to the early 1770s based on their paper and staving (see chap. 4).

Appendix A/II

No.	MS, Format	Work	Paper	Staving	Copyists	Comments
19	F-Pn(c), Ms. 2097 (aut. score)	"Non si turba" (aria from *Il Giudizio di Salomone*)	Blum 6; ?Blum or Heusler 1 (but with no fleur-delis as countermark; flyleaves)	10:7	Holzbauer	This aria was removed from the previous MS; it has the page nos. 43-66, which are lacking there. It was once part of the Aloys Fuchs collection (Vienna). The aria was itself an addition made in the early 1770s; it is on the same paper and uses the same rastrum as pp. 91–94 of the previous MS, which are also added.
20	D-NEhz, Musikalien Bartenstein, Bü 111/4 (aut. score, 3 vols.)[e]	"Günther von Schwarzburg / ein Singspiel in drei Aufzügen"	Heusler 5, 7; ?Blum or Heusler 1, also Alsatian, J. Pasquai (<FIN DE / JOS PASQUAI / EN ALSACE / 1742>; endpapers)	10:11a, 10:8a (most); 10:6 (paste-over in vol. 3; facs. ed., 1:649)	Holzbauer, incl. many additions, revisions, paste-overs (see facs. ed., vol. 2; fig. D:3); Johann Cramer (added page in vol. 3, possibly also a small addition in vol. 3; facs. ed., 1:648, 625; copyist identified by Bärbel Pelker); at least one other copyist (brief cadenza in vol. 2; facs. ed., 1: 438)	Though no date appears on the score, the opera received its premiere on 5 January 1777, and this manuscript must therefore date primarily from the previous year, 1776.
21	D-B, N. Mus. BP 467, 13 (aut. score)	"Adulatrici corde sonore" (cantata)	Blum 1a	12:4 (fols. 1-7), 10:23 (fols. 8-17)	Holzbauer	The watermarks and staving of this MS indicate a date from the mid-1750s.

[a] Bush, 131 and 363, considers the copyist designated here as "prob. Mh. 1" to be a different, new copyist.

[b] According to the dating proposed here, the references to "Sigre Giorgetti" in the AC part are probably later additions; the castrato Silvio Giorgetti first appears in the court almanacs in 1767. It should be noted that Bush's date of 1751 for the listing of this mass in the Herzogenburg Catalogue (p. 363) is incorrect; that catalogue was only *begun* in 1751.

c For a mod. ed. of this mass, with extensive introductory material and reprods. of pages by the principal copyists, see Ignaz Holzbauer, *Missa in C*, ed. Jochen Reutter, Musik der Mannheimer Hofkapelle, 1 (Stuttgart: Carus-Verlag, 1995).

d Reutter, ibid., p. xxix, Abb. 2, incorrectly identifies the copyist of p. 1 of the vn. 2 part as "Munich (ex-Mannheim) A" (now labeled Mannheim 1), presumably based on the misidentification in Eugene K. and Jean K. Wolf, "A Newly Identified Complex of Manuscripts from Mannheim," *JAMS* 27 (1974): 409.

e For a sumptuous facs. ed. of the autograph of this opera see Ignaz Holzbauer, *Günther von Schwarzburg: ein Singspiel in drei Aufzügen*, ed. Bärbel Pelker, Quellen zur Musikgeschichte in Baden-Württemberg, 1 (Munich: Strube Verlag, 2000). Because Holzbauer's score is unpaginated, references here are to the facs. ed. Volume 1 of this edition contains the full score of the final version, with the many paste-overs still in place, vol. 2 the critical commentary and reprods. of the material revealed when the the paste-overs were detached.

Appendix A/III

III. Music of Christian Cannabich in the Bayerische Staatsbibliothek, Munich

Appendix A/III, prepared in collaboration with Jean K. Wolf, is devoted primarily to the large collection of manuscript parts of works by Christian Cannabich now in Munich, all originally part of the performance library of the court. Cannabich's lone surviving autograph score, now in Vienna (A-Wn), is also included (see no. 73a below). The symphonies and one concerto are given first, grouped according to the chronology proposed in chapter 5. As fully discussed in that chapter, Cannabich numbered his symphonies chronologically from 1 to 73; these numbers appear in column 1. Numbers 1–55 are considered here to belong to the Mannheim period, the remaining manuscripts to the period after the transfer of the court to Munich in 1778. (The latter manuscripts, though not from Mannheim, are included here for the sake of completeness and also to permit comparison with the Mannheim manuscripts, which include many additions and replacement parts from the Munich period.) In addition to the symphonies, the Bayerische Staatsbibliothek owns seven miscellaneous works from the Mannheim period that Cannabich did not number (the numbers 74–76 on three of these manuscripts are not original with the composer); these are listed after the symphonies as M1–7, the order being approximately chronological.

In column 3, "DTB No." refers to the numbering in Hugo Riemann's index of Cannabich's symphonies in *Denkmäler der Tonkunst in Bayern*, Jg. III/1 and VII/2 (see Bibliography). In column 4, information on the "A/HF," Kutter, and Unold papers, all used only in Munich, will be found in Appendix B/V. In the "Comments" column, "integral" manuscripts are those in which all the parts were compiled at about the same time (normally that indicated by the Cannabich number), in contrast to the many sources, especially from group 2, that combine parts from two or more time periods. In the same column the abbreviations *AAA*, *AC*, *MdF*, and *PA* refer to advertisements, anouncements, and reviews in the eighteenth-century periodicals *Annonces*, *affiches*, *et avis divers*, *Avant-coureur*, and *Mercure de France* (Paris) and the *Public Advertiser* (London), respectively; references to these publications are taken from the thematic catalogue of Cannabich's symphonies and pastorales in Jean K. Wolf, *The Symphony at Mannheim: Christian Cannabich* (see fn. e below). Additionally, *FMPC* refers to Cari Johansson, *French Music Publishers' Catalogues of the Second Half of the Eighteenth Century* (Stockholm: Almqvist & Wiksells, 1955).

Group 1 (ca. 1755–ca. 1761/62)

No.	MS	Work, DTB No.	Paper	Staving	Copyists	Comments
[1]	*Deest*					

No.	MS	Work, DTB No.	Paper	Staving	Copyists	Comments
2	D-Mbs, Mus. Ms. 1832	*Sinfonie* (F-13)	Swiss (no WM); TP prob. Bavarian (thick, no WM visible)	10:28a	Mh. 3 (vn. 1), Cannabich (b.), Mh. 1 (remaining parts), one other (TP; also copies TP of no. 27)	Church symphony in one movement (Adagio–Allegro vivace), with organ. Integral MS with exception of late TP from 1780s or later (see no. 27). See fig. 2:7.
3	D-Mbs, Mus. Ms. 1831	*Sinfonia a 8 Inst.* (C-2)	Swiss (no WM)	10:15	Mh. 3	Integral MS. Advert. 17 Aug. 1761 (*AAA*).
4	D-Mbs, Mus. Ms. 1830	*Sinfonia à: 10 Stromt.* (Eb-2)	Heusler 5, Blum 1	10 x 1, 12 x 1 (most); 10:26b (b., bns. pp. 9-10)	Mh. 1 (most), Mh. 2 (b.)	Integral MS. Advert. June 1761 (*MdF*). See fig. 2:9b.
[5]	Deest					
[6]	Deest (see no. 58)					See no. [58B]. This symphony, numbered 6 in the series (by a copyist, not by Cannabich), is a second MS of no. 58, from group 4 (early Munich period).
7	D-Mbs, Mus. Ms. 1840	*Sinfonia à 8 Stromt.* (E-1)	Blum 1, Heusler 5	10:26b (vns.); 10 x 1 (rest)	Mh. 2 (vn. 1), Mh. 3 (b./TP; late hand), Mh. 1 (rest)	Integral MS with exception of b./TP, which is later, prob. from the early Munich period (see chap. 5; rastrum found in added parts to nos. 9, 12, 14–16, and the late hn. 2/TP of no. 30). Print advert. 5 April 1764 (*PA*), but the symphony itself (and most of the present MS) is earlier, ca. 1760.
8	D-Mbs, Mus. Ms. 1839	*Sinfonia @ 8 Strom.* (G-8)	Blum 1 (vns.), Heusler 5 (va.), Blum 5 (rest)	10:26b (vns.), 10:27 (va.); 2 x 5:12c (rest)	Mh. 2 (vn. 1, vn. 2/iii), 2d copyist (vn. 2/iv), Mh. 3 (late hand; va.), Mh. 10 (rest)	Orig. set by Mh. 10. Vns. originally marked "II," changed to "I." Va. later, prob. from early Munich period. Print advert. 1763–64 (*FMPC*), but the symphony itself (and most of the present MS) is earlier, ca. 1760–61 (cf. the comment to the next entry).

Appendix A/III

No.	MS	Work, DTB No.	Paper	Staving	Copyists	Comments
9	D-Mbs, Mus. Ms. 1838	*Sinfonia à 8 Stromt.* (Bb-2)	Swiss (no WM; most), Heusler 5 (vc., cb.; cl. 2/TP)	10 x 1 (most); 10:26b (vc., cb.)	Mh. 1 (most), Mh. 3 (cl. 2/TP; late hand)	Integral MS with exception of cl. 2/TP, which is later, prob. from early Munich period (see no. 7). Advert. 23 July 1761 (AAA).
[10]	Deest					
11	D-Mbs, Mus. Ms. 1837	*Sinfonia à 15 Stromti* (D-11)	Swiss (no WM)	10:28c	Mh. 3 (see fig. D:11)	Church symphony in one movement (Allegro con spirito), with organ. Integral MS.
12	D-Mbs, Mus. Ms. 1836	*Sinfonia à 8 Stromt.* (D-9)	Swiss (no WM; vns.); prob. Heusler 7 (<shield [fleur]>; ob. 2, hn. 2); Heusler 5 (rest)	10:28c (vns.), 10:29 (va., cb./vc./TP, bns.), 10:27 (hn. 1); 10–12 x 1 (obs., hn. 2)	Mh. 3 (all but vns. late hand)	Only vns. from orig. set; rest later, prob. from early Munich period (see no. 7). Advert. Aug. 1762 (AC). Vn. 1 marked "II."
13	D-Mbs, Mus. Ms. 1835	*Sinfonia à 8 Stromt.* (A-5)	Heusler 5 (2 forms; most), Blum 5 (hns.)	10:24a–b (vns.), 10:29 (va., cb./TP, fl. 2), 10:24c (vc.), 10:27 (fl. 1); 5 x 2:8 (hns.)	Mh. 1 (vns., vc.); Mh. 3 (va., b./TP, fls. late hand; hns. also in late hand but at different, prob. earlier, time)	Only vns., vc. from orig. set, rest later: va., b., fls. prob. from early Munich period, hns. prob. somewhat earlier. Advert. Aug. 1762 (AC). Vns. originally marked "III," changed to "I."
14	D-Mbs, Mus. Ms. 1834	*Sinfonia 11 Stromt.* (C-5)	Blum 5 (most), Heusler 5 (vas.)	10:10 (most); 10 x 1 (vas.)	Mh. 11 (most), Mh. 3 (vas., incl. TP; late hand)	Integral MS with exception of va. [1]/TP and va. 2, which are later, prob. from early Munich period (see no. 7). Advert. 24 June 1762 (AAA).
15	D-Mbs, Mus. Ms. 1850	*Sinfonia à 11 Stromt:* (F-1)	Heusler 5 (2 forms)	10:10 (most); 10 x 1 (va. 2, cb./vc.)	Mh. 1 (most), Mh. 3 (va. 2, cb./vc.; late hand)	Integral MS with exception of added va. 2 and cb./vc, which are prob. from early Munich period (see no. 16). Simple rastrum of va. 2 (only) also found in no. 56 (Munich). Advert. 17 May 1762 (AAA).

Group 2 (ca. 1762–68)

No.	MS	Work, DTB No.	Paper	Staving	Copyists	Comments
16	D-Mbs, Mus. Ms. 1849	*Sinfonia a 8 Stromt.* (G-12)	Swiss (no WM; vn. 1); Blum 5 (vn. 2, cb./vc., hn. 2/TP); Heusler 5 (2 forms: earlier, va. 1, obs., hn. 1; later, va. 2)	10:28c (vn. 1); 10 x 1 (vn. 2, cb./vc., hn. 2/TP; rastrum also found in Cann. 18, M6, 39); 10:24a (va. 1, obs., hn. 1); 10 x 1 (va. 2; different rastrum)	Mh. 3 (vn. 1; va. 2 late hand); Mh. 12 (vn. 2, cb./vc., hn. 2/TP); one other (va. 1, obs., hn. 1)	Only vn. 1 from orig. set. Va. 2 later (prob. early Munich period; on same orig. sheet of paper as va. 2 of no. 15 (q.v.); remainder from ca. 1767–73 (see chap. 5, incl. table 5:2). Advert. Aug. 1762 (AC). Vn. 1 and cb./vc., possibly also vn. 2, originally numbered "II"; altered to "I" in vn. 1. Number and incipit by Cannabich in his middle hand.
17	D-Mbs, Mus. Ms. 1848	*Simphonia a 13 Stromt:* (D-4)	Heusler 5 (vns., va. [2]), Blum 5 (rest of parts); Kutter 1 (TP)	10:30b (vns., va. [2]), 10:30d (va. [1], trs., timp.), 10:25c (vc./cb., fls., obs., hns.), 10 x 1 (bns.), 5 x 2 (TP)	Mh. 4 (vns., va. [2]), Mh. 12 (va. [1], vc./cb., fls., obs., hns.), Mh. 1 (bns.), Mh. 3 (trs., timp.; middle hand), Cannabich (TP; late hand)	Bn. possibly from orig. set, TP from Munich; remainder all from ca. 1767–73 (see chap. 5, incl. table 5:2). Advert. 9 Feb. 1767 (AC).
18	D-Mbs, Mus. Ms. 1847	*Symphonia* (E♭-6)	Swiss (no WM; vns.), Blum 5 (hn. 1, hn. 2/TP), Heusler 5 (rest)	10:24c (vns., va.), 10:24d (cb./vc., ww.); 10 x 1 (hn. 1, hn. 2/TP; rastrum also found in Cann. 16, M6, 39)	Cannabich (vns. [see fig. D:4]), Mh. 13 (hn. 1, hn. 2/TP), Mh. 1 (rest)	All from orig. set except hn. 1 and 2/TP, which date from ca. 1767–73 (see chap. 5). Latter parts prob. from a second MS, as they contain page nos. (25–32); none is present in the rest of the MS. Advert. Aug. 1762 (AC).
19	D-Mbs, Mus. Ms. 1846	*Symphonia à [8] Stromt.* (E♭-5)	Heusler 5 (most), Blum 5 (bns.)	10:30a (most); 10:32 (bns. pp. 1, 4), 10:30d (bns. pp. 2–3)	Mh. 3 (most; middle/late hand), Mh. 14 (bns.)	Most of MS from 1770s, bns. prob. somewhat earlier (see chap. 5, incl. table 5:2). Va. part missing. Advert. 9 Feb. 1767 (AC).

Appendix A/III

No.	MS	Work, DTB No.	Paper	Staving	Copyists	Comments
[20]	Deest (see no. 60)					
21	D-Mbs, Mus. Ms. 1845	Sinfonia. (G-1)	Blum 5 (most), Swiss (no WM; fls.), Heusler 7 (hn. 2); German, ?J. M. Bach (<top of shield : MOS-BACH>; vc./TP)	10:25c (vn. 1, b., fls., hn. 1), 10:27 (vn. 2 pp. 1-2, va.), 10:20b (vn. 2 pp. 3-4); 2 x 5:14b (hn. 2); 10:18 (vc./TP)	Mh. 3 (vn. 1, b.), Mh. 4 (vn. 2, va.), Cannabich (fls., hns.), one other (vc./TP)	Vn. 2, va. prob. from Munich; remainder prob. ca. 1766-70 (see chap. 5). Publ. 1766 as an orchestral trio (RISM C 816); this version prob. a later arrangement for orch. thereof.
22	D-Mbs, Mus. Ms. 1844	Simphonia. (C-3)	Blum 5 (vns., cb./vc., bn.), Kutter 1 (va., obs., hns., TP)	10:32 (vns.); 10 x 1 (cb./vc., bn.); 5 x 2 (va., obs., hns., TP)	Mh. 1 (vn. 1, cb./vc., bn.), Mh. 14 (vn. 2), Cannabich (va., obs., hns., TP; late hand)	Cannabich parts from Munich. Vn. 1 possibly from orig. set (dupl. part); vn. 2, cb./vc, bn. parts later, from ca. 1767-73 (see chap. 5). Publ. 1766 (privilege). Vn. 1 originally marked "III," vn. 2 "II."
23	D-Mbs, Mus. Ms. 1843	Simphonia a 8to Stromt: (Bb-3)	Blum 5 (most); Kutter 1 (hn. 1/TP)	2 x 5:12b (vns., b.); 2 x 5:13 (va., ob. 1 p. 1, hn. 2); 2 x 5:12d (ob. 1 p. 2, ob. 2); 5 x 2 (hn. 1/TP)	Mh. 10 (most), Cannabich (hn. 1/TP; late hand)	All from orig. set but hn. 1/TP, from Munich. Publ. 1766 (privilege).
24	D-Mbs, Mus. Ms. 1842	Simphonia a 10 Strom: (Eb-11)	Blum 5; Kutter 1 (TP)	2 x 5:12b (vn. 1, b., fl. 2, cls. [most]); 2 x 5:13 (vn. 2, pp. 1, 3, etc., va.); 2 x 5:12d (vn. 2, pp. 2, 4, etc.); 2 x 5:12e (fl. 1, hns.); 2 x 5:12a (cl. 1, p. 4); 5 x 2 (TP)	Mh. 10; Cannabich (TP; late hand)	All from orig. set but TP, which is from Munich.
25	D-Mbs, Mus. Ms. 1858	Symphonia á 8 Stromt. (A-2)	Heusler 5 (most), Blum 5 (bn.)	10:30c (most); 10 x 1 (bn.)	Mh. 3 (most; middle/late hand), Mh. 1 (bn.)	Most of MS from later Mannheim period (rastrum found in nos. 51-52).; bn. prob. from orig. set. Ad-vert. 9 Feb. 1767 (AC).
[26]	Deest					

Music of Christian Cannabich

No.	MS	Work, DTB No.	Paper	Staving	Copyists	Comments
27	D-Mbs, Mus. Ms. 1833	Ouverture II (crossed out, Sinfonia added above) in D (D-10)	Kutter 1 (vns., b.); Blum 6 (remaining parts); TP prob. Bavarian (thick, no WM visible; same as TP of no. 2)	5 x 2 (2 forms)	Mun. 3 (vns., b.); Mun. 6 (rest of parts); 3d copyist (TP, 1787; also copies TP of no. 2)	Entire MS from Munich. The orig. title and no. 27 have been crossed out and "Sinfonia" and the number 68 added. As there is already an authentic no. 68 in the series, it is clear that the number 27 is correct. TP from 1787 or later (recycled from TP of Haydn symphony that reads "ist im 10' conc. 1787. wieder gegeben worden," referring to the Munich Liebhaberkonzerte).[a]
[28]	Deest					
29	D-Mbs, Mus. Ms. 1857	Sinfonia à 8: Stromt. (D-2)	Blum 5 (most), Heusler 5 (obs., TP)	10:17a (most), 10:5 (hns. p. 2), 10:25a (obs., TP)	Mh. 4 (most), Mh. 3 (hns.; obs. and TP later hand)	Entire MS from ca. 1770–75; TP and obs. prob. somewhat later than other parts (see chap. 5). Publ. 1766 (privilege).
30	D-Mbs, Mus. Ms. 1856	Sinfonia (F-3)	Heusler 5 (most), Heusler 7 (fls., hn. 2)	10:29 (strs.); 10 x 1 (fls., hn. 2); 10 x 1 (hn. 1/TP; late hand)	Mun. 1 (strs.); 2d copyist (fls., hn. 2); Cannabich (hn. 1/TP; late hand)	Only fl. and hn. 2 parts from orig. set; rest Munich. Advert. 9 Feb. 1767 (AC).
31	D-Mbs, Mus. Ms. 1854	Sinfonia a 8to Stmt: (G-3)	Heusler 5 (strs., TP), Blum 5 (obs.), Heusler 7 (hns.)	10:30b (strs.), 10:30d (obs.), 10:17b (hns.), 10:30c (TP)	Mh. 4 (strs.), Mh. 12 (obs., hns.), Cannabich (TP; late hand)	All but TP ca. 1769–70 (see chap. 5); strs. (Mh. 4) possibly a bit later than winds. TP still later, prob. 2d half of 1770s. Advert. 13 Oct. 1766 (AC).
32	D-Mbs, Mus. Ms. 1855	Simphonia a 10 Strom: (D-3)	Kutter 1 (most), Blum 5 (cb./vc.), Heusler 8 (hn. 2)	5 x 2 (most; late hand); different 5 x 2 (hn. 2); 2 x 5:14a (cb./vc.)	Cannabich (most; late hand), Mh. 3 (cb./vc.)	Only cb./vc. from orig. set; rest Munich. Publ. 1766 (privilege).
[33]	Deest					

Appendix A/III

No.	MS	Work, DTB No.	Paper	Staving	Copyists	Comments
34	D-Mbs, Mus. Ms. 1853	Sinfonia Concertante (orig. TP), Simphonia Concertante (new TP; F-14)	Blum 5, Heusler 7 (incl. vn. 1); Kutter 1 (new TP)	10:25c (Blum paper); 2 x 5:14b (Heusler paper); 5 x 2 (new TP)	Mh. 14 (vn. 1). Mh. 15 (rest of parts, orig. TP), Cannabich (new TP; late hand)	All but new TP from orig. set; new TP Munich.
35	D-Mbs, Mus. Ms. 1852	Symphonia a 15 Stromt. (D-20)	Kutter 1 (vns.), Heusler 8 (va.); Heusler 5 (rest)	5 x 2 (vns.); 5 x 2 (va.); 10:30c (cb./vc., winds), 10:30a (timp./TP)	Mun. 2 (vns., va.), Mh. 13 (cb./vc.), Mh. 3 (winds), Cannabich (timp./TP)	Vns., va. from Munich; rest from late Mannheim period (see chap. 5).
36	D-Mbs, Mus. Ms. 1851	Simphonia a 13 Strom. (G-13)	Blum 5; Kutter 1 (TP)	10 x 1 (most); 11 x 1 (fls.); 5 x 2 (TP)	Mh. 1; Cannabich (TP; late hand)	All but TP from orig. set; TP Munich.
37	D-Mbs, Mus. Ms. 1888	Sinfonia (F-11)	Heusler 8	5 x 2	Mun. 1	All from Munich.
38	D-Mbs, Mus. Ms. 1863	Sinfonia a 8to Strom: (D-14)	Heusler 5 (vn. 1), Blum 5 (remaining parts; 2 different forms); Heusler 7 (TP)	10:21 (vn. 1), 10:20b (most); 10 x 1 (trs., timp.); 5 x 2 (TP)	Mh. 4 (most; vn. 1 early hand, rest late); Cannabich (trs., p. 1 of timp. earlier hand, TP late hand); Mh. 14 (timp. p. 2)	Prob. only tr./timp from orig. set (see chap. 5): vn. 1 prob. from mid-1770s; remaining parts by Mh. 4 prob. somewhat later, ca. 1776–78; TP Munich.

Group 3 (ca. 1769–78)

No.	MS	Work, DTB No.	Paper	Staving	Copyists	Comments
39	D-Mbs, Mus. Ms. 1862	Sinfonia (G-9)	Heusler 5 (most), Blum 5 (b.)	10:25a (portions of vns., va. 1), 10:30a (remainder of vns., va. 1); 10 x 1 (va. 2, winds, TP); 10 x 1 (vc./cb.)	Mh. 4 (vns., va. 1), Mh. 3 (vc./cb.; va. 2, winds = late hand), Cannabich (TP; late hand)	Vns., va. 1, vc./cb. from orig. set; rest Munich. Simple rastrum of va. 2, winds also found in no. 56 and in late va. 2 part of no. 15. Vc./cb. originally marked "III." Mh. 4's parts are his first from an orig. set.

No.	MS	Work, DTB No.	Paper	Staving	Copyists	Comments
40	D-Mbs, Mus. Ms. 1861	Symphonia a 11 Stromt. (D-19)	Heusler 5, Blum 5; Heusler 8 (TP)	10:25a (vns., vc./cb., tr. 2, timp.), 10:30b (vas., ob. 2, hns.), 10:25c (tr. 1), 10 x 1 (ob. 1); 5 x 2 (TP)	Mh. 4 (vns., b.), Mh. 3 (vas., winds), Mh. 14 (trs., timp.; on Blum 5 only), Cannabich (TP; late hand)	TP Munich; rest original. "Vor die accademie" written on TP, indicating that this MS was used in performance at an electoral academy in Munich.
41	D-Mbs, Mus. Ms. 1860	Sinfonia à 10 Stromt (Eb-9)	Blum 5 (most), Heusler 5 (va.)	10:30d (most), 10:25a (va., vc.)	Mh. 12 (vns.), Mh. 4 (va., vc.), Mh. 1 (remainder, incl. TP; his last appearance)	All original. Both vn. parts marked "II"—i.e., the original first-stand parts, presumably by Mh. 4, have been discarded.
42	D-Mbs, Mus. Ms. 1859	Simphonia Concertante (Eb-7)	Heusler 5; Heusler 8 (TP)	10:20a (most), 10:7 (vas.), 10:8a (hn. 1); 5 x 2 (TP)	Mh. 4 (most, incl. vns. prin.), Mh. 13 (vn. 1, b.), Mh. 3 (vas./i), Cannabich (bns.; vas./ii, hn. 1, TP = later hand)	Vas., hn. 1, TP later, prob. from early Munich period. Rest prob. from late Mannheim period (i.e., somewhat later than the no. 42 would imply; see chap. 5, incl. table 5:3). Almost certainly the symphonie concertante performed in Paris on 29 April 1772 (see chap. 5, @ fn. ?40?.
43	D-Mbs, Mus. Ms. 1893	Simphonia a 12. Stromt: (C-11)	Kutter 1 (vns., obs., hns.); Blum 5 (remaining parts); Heusler 8 (TP)	5 x 2 (Kutter parts); 10:17a (va.), 10:9 (vc./cb, trs., timp.), 10:25b (bns.); 5 x 2 (TP)	Cannabich (Kutter parts, TP; va./i-ii, vc./cb, bns., timp.); Mh. 4 (va./iii), Mh. 16 (trs.)	Vns., obs., hns., TP from Munich; rest original. Vc./cb. part originally labeled just "Violoncello"; "et contrabasso" added in different hand (i.e., orig. cb. part discarded or reused).
44	D-Mbs, Mus. Ms. 1892	Symphonia à Due Orghestre (C-10)	Kutter 1 (all vns., vas., orch. II trs., timp.), Blum 5 (portions of bn. parts), Heusler 5 (rest)	5 x 2 (Kutter parts); 10 x 1 (orch. I bns.); 10:30b (rest, incl. TP)	Sixtus Hirsvogl (all vns., vas.), Mh. 13 (most), Mh. 3 (bns.), Cannabich (all trs., timp.; TP)	All Kutter parts Munich; remainder orig. with exception of "Andante tacet" and iii of orch. I trs., timp., which are from the late Mannheim or the Munich periods.

Appendix A/III

No.	MS	Work, DTB No.	Paper	Staving	Copyists	Comments
45	D-Mbs, Mus. Ms. 1891	*Symphonia a 8to Stromt:* (A-6)	Blum 5 (most), Heusler 5 (va.); Heusler 8 (TP)	10:25a (most), 10:30a (va. pp. 1-2); 5 x 2 (TP)	Cannabich (vns., vc./cb., fls.; TP late hand); Mh. 4 (va.), one other (bns., hns.)	All orig. but Munich TP.
46	D-Mbs, Mus. Ms. 1890	*Symphonia 15 Stromt:* (D-17)	Heusler 5 (vns., vas.), Blum 5 (vc./cb., winds); Heusler 8 (TP, timp.)	10:30a (vns.); 10 x 1 (vas.); 10:20b (vc./cb., winds); 5 x 2 (timp., TP)	Mh. 4 (vns. [see fig. D:13]), Mh. 3 (vas., winds), Cannabich (vc./cb.; TP, timp. late hand)	TP, timp. from Munich; vc./cb., winds possibly from late Mannheim period (see chap. 5, incl. table 5:3) or, like remaining parts, original. Vns. marked "IV" (see fig. D:12), indicating that four parts were present at one time.
47	D-Mbs, Mus. Ms. 1889	*Symphonia a 8 Stromt:* (G-11)	Heusler 5	10:30a	Mh. 4 (strs.), Cannabich (winds; TP late hand)	All orig. but TP, which is from Munich. Publ. 1775 as op. 10, no. 2 (Mannheim: Götz).[b]
48	D-Mbs, Mus. Ms. 1899	*Sinfonia a 8to Stromt:* (Bb-4)	Heusler 5 (most), Blum 5 (vc./cb., TP)	10:21; 10:20b (TP)	Mh. 4 (most), Cannabich (vc./cb., TP)	All orig. except TP, which may be somewhat later (see chap. 5, incl. table 5:3). Publ. 1775 as op. 10, no. 3 (Mannheim: Götz).
49	D-Mbs, Mus. Ms. 1898	*Simphonia a 8 Stromt:* (F-5)	Heusler 5; Kutter 1 (hn. 2/TP)	10:21 (strs.), 10:30a (winds except hn. 2); 5 x 2 (hn. 2/TP)	Mh. 4 (most), Cannabich (hn. 2/TP; late hand)	All orig. but hn. 2/TP, which is from Munich. Publ. 1775 as op. 10, no. 4 (Mannheim: Götz).
50	D-Mbs, Mus. Ms. 1897	*Symphonia a 8to Stromt:* (Dm-1)	Heusler 5; Heusler 8 (TP)	10:30a (strs.), 10:21 (winds); 5 x 2 (TP)	Mh. 4; Cannabich (TP; late hand)	All orig. but TP, which is from Munich. TP has pencil notation "rest h[at] [Philipp] Sedlmayr buchhalter." Publ. 1775 as op. 10, no. 5 (Mannheim: Götz).
51	D-Mbs, Mus. Ms. 1896	*Symphonia â 8. Strmet.* (D-6)	Heusler 5	10:30a (strs., obs.), 10:30c (hns., TP)	Mh. 3 (vn. 1/i, TP), Mh. 4 (vn. 2/i, va./i), 3d copyist (b./i), Cannabich (strs./ii-iii, all winds)	All orig. Publ. 1775 as op. 10, no. 1 (Mannheim: Götz).

No.	MS	Work, DTB No.	Paper	Staving	Copyists	Comments
52	D-Mbs, Mus. Ms. 1895	*Symphonia a 8to Stromt.* (E-3)	Heusler 5	10:30c (vns., cb./vc., TP), 10:30a (va., fls.), 10:20a (hns.)	Mh. 13 (vn. 1, va.), Mh. 3 (vn. 2, cb./vc.), Cannabich (TP, winds)	All orig. Publ. 1775 as op. 10, no. 6 (Mannheim: Götz).
53	D-Mbs, Mus. Ms. 1894	*Simphonia a 14. Stro:* (D-18)	Heusler 5 (most); Heusler 8 (timp.), Kutter 1 (TP)	10:20b (vns.), 10:20a (most); 5 x 2 (timp.), 5 x 2 (TP)	Mh. 4 (vns.), Cannabich (rest)	Main portion of MS from late Mannheim period. MS in five stages, all but the 4th copied by Cannabich: (1) i of va., vc., bn.; (2) perhaps slightly later, i of fls., obs., hns., trs.; (3) still later, ii–iii of all the foregoing parts (on same paper, which had been left blank); (4) vns. by Mh. 4, incorporating the mvts. added by Cannabich (these were thus prob. dupl. parts, copied from the lost originals by Cannabich; (5) TP, timp. added in Munich.
54	D-Mbs, Mus. Ms. 1870	*Symphonia a 8to Stromt.* (Eb-8)	Blum 5 (vn. 1, hns.), Heusler 5 (remaining parts); Heusler 8 (TP)	10:20b (parts); 5 x 2 (TP)	Mh. 4 (vn. 1, va., vc./cb., cls.), Cannabich (vn. 2, hns.; TP)	All orig. but TP, which is from Munich. Orig. set ca. 1777–78.
55	D-Mbs, Mus. Ms. 1869	*Simphonia a 14. Strom:* (C-8)	Heusler 5; Kutter 1 (TP)	10:20b (parts); 5 x 2 (TP)	Mh. 4 (vns.), Mh. 3 (remaining parts), Cannabich (TP)	All orig. but TP, which is from Munich. Orig. set ca. 1778 (last MS from Mannheim).

Group 4 (Munich, ca. 1778–ca. 1781/82[?])

No.	MS	Work, DTB No.	Paper	Staving	Copyists	Comments
56	D-Mbs, Mus. Ms. 1868	*Sinfonia a 8to Strom:* (A-3)	Heusler 5 (most), Heusler 8 (va., vc./cb., TP)	10 x 1 (Heusler 5); 5 x 2 (Heusler 8)	Cannabich (most), Mun. 2 (va., vc./cb.)	First orig. set from Munich, ca. 1778 (fall)–79. See fig. 2:5.

Appendix A/III

No.	MS	Work, DTB No.	Paper	Staving	Copyists	Comments
57	D-Mbs, Mus. Ms. 1867	Sinfonia (E♭-10)	Heusler 5 (strs., bns., TP), Heusler 8 (cls., obs., hns.)	10:27 (vns., vc./cb.); 5 x 2 (rest; 3 forms)	Cannabich (most), 2d copyist (Munich; va. 1), Mun. 4 (va. 2), Mun. 5 (cls., hns.)	For a mod. ed. of this symphony, incl. a reprod. of the TP of the present MS, see J. Wolf, 286–318.
58[A]	D-Mbs, Mus. Ms. 1866	Sinfonia (C-6)	Heusler 8	5 x 2 (3 forms)	Mh. 3 (vn. 1 [see fig. D:12], va., cb./vc.), Mun. 5 (vn. 2), Mun. 4 (obs., hns.), Cannabich (TP)	On the numbering of this symphony see the next entry.
[58B]	D-Mbs, Mus. Ms. 1841	Symphonia a 8te Stromt. (C-6)	"A/HF" 1 (most), Heusler 8 (vn. 2)	3 x 3 + 1 (most); 5 x 2 (vc./cb. p. 1)	Mh. 4	This symphony appears in two copies, one numbered 58 (here designated as 58[A], i.e., the previous MS), the other numbered 6 (not by Cannabich but by a copyist, prob. Mh. 4; here labeled [58B]). The higher number is clearly the correct one on codicological grounds. In addition, it was one of a numbered group of symphonies attributed to Cannabich formerly in D-DS (destroyed in World War II); this group comprised Cannabich 56–57, 6/58 (the present work), and 59–61, thus again linking 6/58 with the Munich period.
59	D-Mbs, Mus. Ms. 1865ᶜ	Symphonia a 8ᵗᵒ Strom: (D-13)	Heusler 8	5 x 2 (3 forms)	Mun. 1 (vns., vc./cb.), Cannabich (rest)	

No.	MS	Work, DTB No.	Paper	Staving	Copyists	Comments
60	D-Mbs, Mus. Ms. 1864	*Sinfonia* (orig. TP), *Sinfonia a 8to Stromt:* (new TP, F-12)	"A/HF" 1 (vns., hn. 1, hn. 2/orig. TP), Heusler 8 (vas., vc./cb., ob./cl. 1), Heusler 5 (ob./cl. 2); prob. Bavarian (new TP)	3 × 3 + 1 (vns., hns.); 5 × 2 (vas., vc./cb., ob./cl. 1, hns.); 10:6 (ob./cl. 2)	Mh. 17 (most), Cannabich (vc./cb., obs./cls., new TP)	The orig. TP of this symphony has the number 20 (not in Cannabich's hand), the new TP the number 60. The latter number is obviously correct on codicological grounds and also because this was one of the six symphonies in D-DS mentioned under no. 58B, Comments.
61	D-Mbs, Mus. Ms. 1876	*Simphonia.* (C-7)	Heusler 8 (most), "A/HF" 1 (va. 1), Heusler 5 (va. 2, vc./cb.)	5 × 2 (most); 3 × 3 + 1 (va. 1, bns.); 10:29 (va. 2, vc./cb.); 5 × 2 (different rastrum; TP)	Cannabich	This symphony marks the last appearance in the Cannabich series of both Heusler 5 paper and ten-stave rastra.

Group 5 (from Munich, ca. 1781/82[?]–1794)

No.	MS	Work, DTB No.	Paper	Staving	Copyists	Comments
62	D-Mbs, Mus. Ms. 1875	*Symphonia* (E♭-12)	Heusler 8	5 × 2 (2 forms)	Cannabich (strs. [see fig. D:5], bns., TP incipit and number), Mun. 5 (TP, cls., hns.)	
63	D-Mbs, Mus. Ms. 1874	*Simphonia a 15 Strom:* (D-15)	Kutter 1 (strs.), Heusler 8 (rest, incl. TP)	5 × 2 (3 forms)	Sixtus Hirsvogl (strs.; vn. 1 signed by him), Cannabich (obs., cls., bns.; mvts. i–ii of hns., trs., timp.), one other (iii of hns., trs., timp.)	See DTB, Neue Folge, vol. 11, pp. xxx–xxxi, for reprods. of two pages from this MS, the first bearing Hirsvogl's signature ("Sixt: Hirsvogl scrip.") at the end of the vn. 1 part.

Appendix A/III

No.	MS	Work, DTB No.	Paper	Staving	Copyists	Comments
64	D-Mbs, Mus. Ms. 1873	Simphonia (F-10)	Kutter 1 (vns., cb./vc.), Heusler 8 (rest)	5 × 2 (2 forms)	Sixtus Hirsvogl (vns., cb./vc.), Cannabich (rest)	The vn. and cb./vc. parts by Hirsvogl may originally have been duplicates (see next symphony). Below the attribution on the TP Cannabich has added, "Den 5' Nove[m]bre den 1' Concert des 8' Jahrgangs zum Schluss das 2' Mahl gespielt worden," referring to the Munich Liebhaberkonzerte. These concerts evidently began in late 1782 or early 1783,^{d} and thus the performance in question would have occurred in approximately late 1789, providing a (not very useful) terminus ad quem for this MS.
65	D-Mbs, Mus. Ms. 1872	Symphonia a 10 Strom: (G-10)	Kutter 1 (vns., TP), Heusler 8 (rest)	5 × 2 (3 forms)	Sixtus Hirsvogl (vns.), Cannabich (rest)	The vn. parts by Hirsvogl were originally duplicates, marked "III."
66	D-Mbs, Mus. Ms. 1871	Sinfonia (E-2)	Kutter 1 (most), Heusler 8 (vas.)	5 × 2 (4 forms)	Cannabich	
67	D-Mbs, Mus. Ms. 1887	Symphonia a 10 Strom: (G-14)	Kutter 1 (most), Heusler 8 (2d TP)	5 × 2 (2 forms)	Cannabich	See DTB, Neue Folge, vol. 11, p. xxxi, for a reprod. of p. 1 of the vn. 1 part.
68	D-Mbs, Mus. Ms. 1886	Symphonia a 12 Strom: (Bb-6)	Kutter 1 (most), Heusler 8 (2d TP, obs.)	5 × 2 (2 forms)	Cannabich	Obs. and a 2d TP added later (obs. not mentioned in orig. form of either TP); orig. TP has the added notation "2 Obois," but in a 19th-century hand.

No.	MS	Work, DTB No.	Paper	Staving	Copyists	Comments
[69]	D-Mbs, Mus. Ms. 1885	No TP (Eb-14)	Kutter 1 (strs.), Heusler 8 (winds)	5 x 2 (2 forms)	Cannabich	As the TP is lacking, no Cannabich number is present. However, both the sequence of present-day call numbers (indicating the physical presence of this MS between nos. 68 and 70 upon arrival at the Staatsbibliothek) and the codicological evidence show that 69 is the correct number. Strs. and winds possibly from different times.
70	D-Mbs, Mus. Ms. 1884	Simfonia (D-16)	Heusler 8 (strs.), Kutter 1 (winds), Unold 1 (TP)	5 x 2 (3 forms)	Cannabich	"Vor die Kirch" on TP. Strings and winds possibly from different times.
71	D-Mbs, Mus. Ms. 1883	Symphonia (Eb-13)	Kutter 1 (most), Unold 1 (vn. 2)	5 x 2 (2 forms)	Cannabich	
72	D-Mbs, Mus. Ms. 1882	Simfonia a 12 Strom: (Bb-5)	Unold 1; Kutter 1 (TP)	5 x 2 (2 forms)	Sixtus Hirsvogl (strs.), Cannabich (winds, TP)	
73a	A-Wn, Mus. Hs. 16.811e (aut. score)	Symphonia a 12 Strom: (C-9)	Unold 1	6 x 2	Cannabich (aut. score)	Dated "nel mese di X^{bre} 1794" to left of title. Only the first two movements of this symphony were completed by Cannabich.
73b	D-Mbs, Mus. Ms. 1881f (parts)	Simfonia a 12 Strom: (C-9)	Unold 1; Heusler 8 (TP)	5 x 2 (2 forms)	Cannabich	As in the aut. score (see previous entry), the third movement is lacking.
...	D-Mbs, Mus. Ms. 3984	Concerto Per il Cembalo o fortepiano in F	Kutter 1 (orch. parts), Unold 1 (kbd. part); prob. Bavarian (cadenza to 1st mvt.); Heusler 8 (cadenza to 3d mvt.)	5 x 2 (orch. parts); 2 x 5 (kbd. part); 10 x 1 (cadenza in 1st mvt.); 5 x 2 (cadenza in 3d mvt.)	Cannabich (most), one other copyist (vn. 2, va., b.)	Munich MS (date uncertain).

Appendix A/III

Miscellaneous Manuscripts from Mannheim

No.	MS	Work, DTB No.	Paper	Staving	Copyists	Comments
[M1]	D-Mbs, Mus. Ms. 1827	*Concerto à 8 Strom.* in D	Heusler 2	10:26b (most), 10:26c (vc., ob. 2, hn. 2)	Mh. 1 (most), Mh. 2 (vc.)	From group 1, ca. 1755–60 (rastrum 10:26b found in Cannabich 4, 7–9; early paper; see chap. 5, incl. table 5:1). Not a concerto for soloists but a one-movement orchestral work (Largo–Allegro). prob. originally for use in church.
[M2]	D-Mbs, Mus. Ms. 1828	*Concerto à 7 Strom*[ti] in D for fl.	Swiss (no WM)	10:26d (most); also 3 variant forms of that rastrum, interspersed: 10:26b (vn. 2 p. 1, etc.), 10:26c (va. p. 1, bn. p. 1, etc.), 10:26e (TP)	Mh. 1 (most), Mh. 2 (vn. 2)	From group 1, ca. 1755–60 (see previous MS). In one movement, prob. originally for use in church.
[M3]/75	D-Mbs, Mus. Ms. 1880	*Pastorale a 12 Istromentti* in D (Wolf P2)	Swiss (no WM)	10:26e (most, incl. vn. 2 p. 1, vc., org., most winds, TP); also 2 variant forms of that rastrum, interspersed: 10:26d (vn. 1 p. 1, va., etc.), 10:26c (fls. p. 2, etc.)	Mh. 2	From group 1, ca. 1755–60 (see M1). Number 75 on TP not authentic. In one movement (Largo–Allegro Pastorale), for use in church.
[M4]/76	D-Mbs, Mus. Ms. 1878	*Concerto alla Pastorale à 8 Strom*t: in C for fl., ob., bn., hn.	Swiss (no WM)	10:28c	Mh. 1	From late in group 1, ca. 1760–62 (rastrum 10:28c found in Cannabich 11–12, 16; see chap. 5, incl. table 5:1). Number 76 on TP not authentic. In one movement (Andante alla Pastorale), for use in church.

No.	MS	Work, DTB No.	Paper	Staving	Copyists	Comments
[M5]/ 74	D-Mbs, Mus. Ms. 1879	*Pastorale a 12 Stromt:* in D (Wolf P1)	Blum 5	10:10	Mh. 1 (most), Mh. 11 (b.)	From late in group 1 or early in group 2, ca. 1760–65 (rastrum 10:10 found in Cannabich 14–15, App. A/I/1 [a Ritschel mass dated 1763], and App. A/II/18 [Holzbauer's *Giudizio de Salomone* of 1765]; Mh. 11 otherwise found only in Cannabich 14: see chap. 5, incl. table 5:1). No. 74 on TP not authentic. In one movement (Pastorale un poco Andantino–Allegro), for use in church.
[M6]	D-Mbs, Mus. Ms. 1829	*Concerto a 12 Stromt.* in C for fl, ob, bn.	Heusler 5 (vns., va. 1, bn./vc., org./cb., trs., timp., TP); Blum 5 (va. 2; fl., ob., bn. obbl.; cb./vc., hns., cadenza)	10:24d (TP, most Heusler), 10:24b (va. 1 p. 1), 10:24a (va. 1 p. 3), 10:24c (tr. 2, timp.); 10 x 1 (Blum parts); 10 x 1 (cadenza)	Mh. 3 (vns.; cb./vc. later hand), Mh. 1 (va. 1, org./cb., bn./vc., trs., timp.), Mh. 15 (fl., ob., bn. obbl.; va. 2, hns.), Cannabich (TP; cadenza)	Orig. parts, by Mh. 3, Mh. 1, and Cannabich (TP), all on Heusler paper, from early in group 2 or late in group 1, ca. 1760–65 (rastrum 10:24a–d found in nos. 13, 16, 18); parts on Blum paper later, from late 1760s or early 1770s (e.g., one-stave rastrum also found in nos. 38–39; see chap. 5, incl. table 5:2). In one movement (Allegro assai moderato), for use in church.
[M7]	D-Mbs, Mus. Ms. 1877	*Symphonia Pastorale* in F (Wolf P3)	Heusler 5 (strs.), Blum 5 (rest)	10:30b (strs.), 10:30e (rest)	Mh. 4 (strs.), Cannabich (org., bns., TP), Mh. 16 (fls., hns.), Mh. 13 (obs.)	From early in group 5, ca. 1769–early 1770s (rastrum 10:30b found in nos. 40, 44; see chap. 5, incl. table 5:3). In one movement (Largo–Allegro), for use in church.

[a] Also on the Haydn title page is the ink notation "hat H Eck [Friedrich Egk, 1767–1838] die abgehenden Stimmen" and the pencil notation "rest im Comedien Haus."

[b] Götz's complete op. 10 has been published in a mod. ed. by Allan Badley (Wellington, NZ: Artaria Editions, 1997).

c See DTB, Neue Folge, vol. 11, ed. Stephan Hörner, for reprods. from this manuscript (p. xxx) and from two other concordant manuscripts copied in Munich by Mh. 4 (in D-WD and US-Wc; pp. xxxii–xxxiii). This edition includes mod. eds. of Cannabich's Symphonies no. 59, 63–64, and 67–68.

d On the dating of the Lieberhaberkonzerte see Eugene K. Wolf, "The 'Concert' in Munich under Elector Carl Theodor," in Theodor Göllner and Stephan Hörner, eds., *Mozarts Idomeneo und die Musik in München zur Zeit Karl Theodors* (Munich: Verlag der Bayerischen Akademie der Wissenschaften, 2001), 227–30.

e A complete facsimile of this manuscript may be found in Eugene K. and Jean K. Wolf, *The Symphony at Mannheim: Johann Stamitz, Christian Cannabich*, vol. C/III of *The Symphony, 1720–1840*, ed. Barry S. Brook and Barbara B. Heyman (New York: Garland Publishing, 1984), 321–39.

f For a reprod. of the title page of this manuscript see ibid., 320.

IV. Autographs of Grua, Richter, and Mozart without Explicit Indication of Provenance

Appendix A/IV provides information on various manuscripts that are either wholly or partially in the hands of Carlo Grua, Franz Xaver Richter, and Mozart. Unlike the autographs of Appendix A/I, however, these manuscripts lack colophons or other direct evidence that they originated in Mannheim, though in most cases indirect evidence can be brought to bear (see chap. 6). References to "Reutter" in the "Work" and "Comments" columns below are to Jochen Reutter, *Studien zur Kirchenmusik Franz Xaver Richters* (Frankfurt am Main: Peter Lang, 1993); references to "Schmitt" are to Eduard Schmitt's thematic catalogue of Mannheim sacred music in DTB, Neue Folge, vol. 2 (see Bibliography).

No.	MS, Format	Composer	Work	Paper	Staving	Copyists	Comments
1	D-FS (Mf), Mf 597 (parts)	Anon. [Carlo Grua]	Mass in Eb (Schmitt I.4). Dated 1757.	Blum 1 (most), Heusler 7 (vn. 1c)	12:8e (most), 12:8a (vn. 1c)	Mh. 7 (most), Mh. 2 (vn. 1c). All parts have extensive emendations by Grua.	Dated 1757 at end of vn. 1a and 2a. The hn. parts of this MS are much later (early 19th century, from Munich). The MS contains three vn. 1 and 2 and two va. parts.
2	D-FS (Mf), Mf 598 (parts; see App. A/I/13 for aut. score to this work, dated 1766)	Carlo Grua	*Missa Breve à quattro voci con Inst:* in F (Schmitt I.5)	Blum 5 (orig. voice parts, org.), Heusler 5 (2d SR), Blum 3 (str.), Knöckel 1 (cover)	12:7e (most), 12:10b (2d SR)	Mh. 2 (orig. voice parts, org.), Mh. 6 (2d SR), Grua (strs., numerous corrections)	Almost certainly from 1766, the date of the aut. score in D-KA. The MS contains two SR parts (the second marked "Soprano ripit:"), three vn. 1 and 2, and two va. parts. The 2d SR part is prob. from the 1770s based on its use of rastrum 12:10b.
3	D-MEIsm, Ed 147° K (aut. score)	Richter	*Oratorio Della Deposizione dalla Croce* (Reutter I 7; perf. 12 April 1748)	Blum 1; Blum (<crown/CC: Basel crozier in oval frame/ B>; endpapers)	3 x 4:1	Richter	First performed on Good Friday of 1748 (12 April), i.e., soon after Richter's arrival in Mannheim; see Reutter, 1:33, 86–87, 2:418–19. Reutter, 2:418–26.

251

Appendix A/IV

No.	MS, Format	Composer	Work	Paper	Staving	Copyists	Comments
4	F-Susc, M 1 (parts)	Richter	*Messe de Dimanche* in B minor (Reutter A 34)	Heusler 7	13 x 1	Richter[a]	Dated ca. 1755–60 by Reutter based on the handwriting (1:112, 2:203). MS once owned by "Ph. J. Pfeffinger" according to note on flyleaf. The aut. score to this mass (F-Pc, Ms. 20140), on <S. CHIARA> paper, is not classed here among the Mannheim MSS (see chap. 6, fn. 11 and related text). Reutter, 2:196–203.
5	F-Susc, M 23 (parts)	Richter	*Messe de Dimanche et Fete* in G (Reutter A 20)	Heusler 7	13 x 1	Richter (most, incl. all mvt. headings; also clefs and time signatures of p. 1 of vas., obs.); Strasb./Mh. 1 (rest of vas., obs.)	Dated ca. 1760–65 by Reutter based on the handwriting (1:112, 2:118) and the inclusion of the "Dona" of this mass in Richter's MS treatise *Harmonische Belehrungen* of ca. 1767 (2:110, fn. 26). Reutter, 2:110–18.
6	F-Susc, M 84 (parts)	Richter	*Pastores laeti properate* (motet; Reutter B 34)	Blum 5	11 x 1	Richter (orig. set)	Dated ca. 1760–65 by Reutter based on the handwriting (1:112, 2:259). The two S parts are later, from Strasbourg. Reutter, 2:258–59.
7	F-Susc, M 49 (parts)	Richter	*In exitu* (Psalm 113) and *Magnificat* (Reutter D 4: [5], [11])	Heusler 7	13 x 1	Richter (most, incl. mvt. headings and clefs of p. 1 of vns.); Strasb./Mh. 1 (rest of vns.)	Dated ca. 1760–65 by Reutter based on the handwriting (1:112, 2:308). Reutter, 2:302 (*In exitu*), 306–7 (*Magnificat*), 308 (MS 1.b.1).
8	F-Susc, unnumbered (parts)	Caldara, Richter	*Lauda Jerusalem* (Psalm 147, by Caldara, arr. Richter; Reutter D 4: [10]); *Laudate Dominum* (Reutter D 4: [6])	Heusler 7	13 x 1	Richter	Dated ca. 1760–65 by Reutter based on the handwriting (1:112, 2:309). Reutter, 2:305–6 (*Lauda Jerusalem*), 302–3 (*Laudate Dominum*), 309 (MS 1.c.[1]).

Autographs of Grua, Richter, and Mozart

No.	MS, Format	Composer	Work	Paper	Staving	Copyists	Comments
9	F-Susc, M 63 (S, A of main set)	Richter	Reges terrae congregati sunt (motet; Reutter B 41)	Blum 5	10 x 1	Richter	S and A parts of main set dated ca. 1765–69 by Reutter based on the handwriting (1:112, 2:270); rest of set pre-Mannheim (2:269). Reutter, 2:268–70.
10a	B-Bc, MSM 201 (aut. score)	Richter	Super Flumina Babylonis (Psalm 136; Reutter D 16)	Heusler 7, Blum 5	11 x 1 (two forms)	Richter	Dated by Reutter August 1767–January 1768 based on required submission of work by 1 Feb. 1768 to a contest in Paris announced in August 1767 (see chap. 6, @ fn. 7; Reutter, 1:47–48, 94; 2:361). Performed at the Concert Spirituel, Paris, 29 March 1769; the score bears the names of the soloists in this performance (Reutter, 2:361). Reutter, 2:357–62.
10b	F-Susc, M 51 (parts to previous work)	Richter	Super Flumina Babylonis (Psalm 136; Reutter D 16)	Blum 5 (voice parts), Heusler 7 (instr. parts)	8 x 1 (voice parts); 10 x 1 (winds); 10:17b (vrns., vas., cb./vc., cb./vc./bn.)	Richter	See comments on previous MS, also Reutter, 2:362. In addition to the evidence on dating presented there, rastrum 10:17b is found in two MSS dated 1769 (App. A/I/ 14–15).
11	D-OF, KV 175 (part for 2 obs.)[b]	Mozart	Piano Concerto, K. 175	Heusler 5	10:6	Mozart	Part prob. written for a performance at Cannabich's house on 13 Feb. 1778, at which Mozart played this concerto (see chap. 6, @ fnn. 14–17).

[a] Reutter, 2:203, considers some (unspecified) parts from this manuscript to be in the hand of Strasb./Mh. 1. In my opinion, all the parts but the local "Basse Ripieno" are by Richter.

[b] For a reprod. of the first page of this manuscript see Klaus Hortschansky, "Autographe Stimmen zu Mozarts Klavierkonzert KV 175 im Archiv André zu Offenbach," Mozart-Jahrbuch, 1989–90, p. 50.

Appendix A/V

V. Music of Georg Joseph Vogler in Darmstadt and Offenbach

Appendix A/V lists those manuscripts of music by Georg Joseph Vogler, primarily autographs, that are considered here to date from the Mannheim period (see chap. 7). Those manuscripts that actually bear dates are given first, in chronological order, those without dates second; the Darmstadt (D-DS) manuscripts preceding those in the André archive in Offenbach (D-OF). Because the Offenbach manuscripts have not yet been assigned call numbers, those without dates are given in alphabetical rather than numerical order. Works that are assigned dates only in the *Verzeichniß*, the auction catalogue prepared after Vogler's death (see chap. 7, @ fn. 5), are included here among the undated sources, as the dates do not appear in the manuscripts themselves.

Dated Manuscripts

No.	MS, Format	Work, Date	Paper	Staving	Copyists
1	D-OF (small aut. score, lacking TP and one or more bifolios at beginning)	*Der Kaufmann von Smyrna*, 1st version. Dated 2 Feb. 1771 at end of tenor/bass duet "Ich bleibe hier"; dated Aug. 1771 at end. See no. 21, below, for 2d version.	Dutch, J. Honig & Zoon(en) 1	10 x 1	Vogler
2a	D-DS, Mus. ms. 1123 (score, partly aut.).[a] See also next MS.	*Le Rendez-vous de Chassel,] ou Les Vendanges interrompues par les Chasseurs[.] Ballet Pantomime*. Dated 17 May 1772 at end.	Blum 5	10:25a	Mh. 18 (clefs and main melodic line of fols. 2-39); one or possibly two others (text of fols. 1-12); Vogler (remainder of fols. 2-39; fols. 41-end)

254

No.	MS, Format	Work, Date	Paper	Staving	Copyists
2b	D-DS, Mus. ms. 1124 (vn. part "per il Signore Direttore della Musica" containing main melodic line). See previous MS.	Same	Same	Same	Mh. 18 (most), one other (portions of nos. 16-17); Mh. 3 (pasteons)
3	D-OF (aut. score)	*Credo* in D. Dated Oct. 1775.	Heusler 5	12:3	Vogler
4b	D-OF (aut. score)	*Kyrie / e Christe Fugato / a 4 Voci Concerti e ripieni.* Dated "Mannh. 13 9br. 1775"; perf. dates of 8 Dec. 1775 and 1 Jan. 1776.	Heusler 5	12:2a	Vogler
5b	D-OF (aut. score)	*Gloria in Excelsis a 4 Voci Concerti e Ripieni.* Dated "Mannh. 21 9br. 1775"; same perf. dates as nos. 4, 6-7.	Heusler 5	12:2a	Vogler
6b	D-OF (aut. score)	*Credo a 4 Voci Concerti e Ripieni . . . Sanctus.* Dated 28 Nov. 1775 on flyleaf; same perf. dates as nos. 4-5, 7.	Heusler 5	12:2a	Vogler
7b	D-OF (aut. score)	*Agnus Dei, Dona nobis a 4 Voci Concertate e Ripieni.* Dated "Mannh. 29. 9br 1775"; same perf. dates as nos. 4-6.	Heusler 5	12:2a	Vogler
8	D-OF (aut. score)	*Te Deum Laudamus a 4 Voci.* Dated 31 Dec. 1775.	Heusler 5	12:2a	Vogler

Appendix A/V

No.	MS, Format	Work, Date	Paper	Staving		Copyists
9	D-DS, Mus. ms. 1055 [I] (aut. score; upright format), 1055a (parts)[c]	*Alma Redemptoris ... a due Soprani.* Dated 6 Jan. 1776 on flyleaf of score (prob. a perf. date).	Heusler 5; Dutch, C. & I. Honig 1; flyleaves of score); German, Knöckel 1 (cover of parts)	18 x 1 (score); 12:10b (parts)		Vogler (score); DS/Mh. 1 (main set of parts, incl. org.), Mh. 6 (dupl. vns., one va., all b. parts)
10	D-DS, Mus. ms. 1055 [II] (aut. score, written on *versi* of 1055 [II]); 1055b (parts)	*Crudelis Herodis a due Bassi.* Dated 6 Jan. 1776 on inside of 2d flyleaf (prob. a perf. date).	Same as no. 9.	Same as no. 9, but in the parts line 10/1 of rastrum 12:10b is thick throughout.		Vogler (score); DS/Mh. 1 (main set of parts), DS/Mh. 2 (dupl. vn. parts)
11[d]	D-OF (aut. score)	*Kyrie* for double chorus and double orch. Perf. dates of 2 Feb. and 7 April 1776 on inside of cover.	Blum 6	20 x 1		Vogler
12[d]	D-OF (aut. score). Large upright format.	*Kyrie / Credo et Sanctus* for double chorus and orch. Same perf. dates as nos. 11 and 13.	Heusler 5	18 x 1		Vogler
13[d]	D-OF (aut. score)	*Agnus Dei* for double chorus and double orch. Same perf. dates as nos. 11-12.	Heusler 5	20 x 1		Vogler
14	D-DS, Mus. ms. 1125 (score, mostly aut.)	[*Requiem*]. Perf. dates of 21 Feb. and 1-2 Nov. 1776.	Heusler 5	12:2a		Vogler (most), DS/Mh. 1 (fols. 9r, 10r)
15a	D-DS, Mus. ms. 1103 (aut. score, a cappella version)	*Miserere a quattro Voci senza Stromenti.* Dated 9 March 1776 at end; perf. dates of 13-29 March on inside of cover.	Heusler 5	12:2a		Vogler

Music of Georg Joseph Vogler

No.	MS, Format	Work, Date	Paper	Staving	Copyists
15b	D-DS, Mus. ms. 1103a (score, version with orch.), 1103b-c (parts)e	*Miserere a 4 Voci colli Stromenti a piacere*. See previous MS.	Heusler 5 (score, voice parts, cb./vc. parts, bns.); Blum 6 (vns., vas.)	12:2a (score); 10 x 1 (vns., vas.); 12:10a (remaining parts)	Score by one copyist; parts by Mh. 6 except for additions to TC 1-2 by DS/Mh. 1
16	D-OF (aut. scores; upright format).	*Credo* in B minor, *Agnus Dei* in D, latter written on versi of former. Perf. dates of 14 April and 1 Nov. 1776 on inside of cover.	Heusler 5	18 x 1	Vogler
17	D-DS, Mus. ms. 1096 (aut. score; parts)	*Kyrie* in C. Dated 13 Oct. 1776 at end of score; perf. date of 19 Nov. 1776 on inside of cover.	Heusler 7 (score), Heusler 5 (parts)	12:2a (score), 12:10d (parts)	Vogler (score); parts by at least seven copyists, not professional (possibly students of Vogler)
18	D-OF (aut. score)	*Credo* in C. Dated 19 Nov. 1776 on inside of cover (prob. a perf. date).	Heusler 5	12:2a	Vogler
19	D-DS, Mus. ms. 1095 (parts; org., all voice parts but SR upright format; remaining parts oblong)	*Kyrie* in D. Dated 8 Dec. 1776 on org. part.	Heusler 7 (most voice parts; org.), Heusler 5 (SR, rest of instr. parts)	12:10c (Heusler 7), 12:3 (Heusler 5)	Seven, incl. DS/Mh. 2 (vns. 1d and 2d, va. 2, one vc./cb., org.), DS/Mh. 3 (other vc./cb., SR); some or all possibly students of Vogler
20	D-DS, Mus. ms. 1059 (score), 1059c (T solo), 1059d-e (voice, instr. parts),f all oblong format	*Die Auferstehung Jesu* [1777]g	Heusler 5 (score, portions of T solo and of str. parts); Blum 7 (remainder, incl. all orig. chorus parts)	10:20c (beginning and other portions of score; those portions of T solo and strs. on Heusler paper); 12:2a (most of score); 9–10 x 1 (those portions of T solo and parts on Blum paper)	Score, T solo DS/Mh. 3; main instr. parts DS/Mh. 3-4 and Mh. 17, with final chorus added by Johann Cramer; remainder at least four other copyists, possibly Vogler students

257

Appendix A/V

No.	MS, Format	Work, Date	Paper	Staving	Copyists
21	D-DS, Mus. ms. 1090 (score, partly aut.),[h]	*Der Kaufmann von Smyrna ... von dem Capelmeister Georg Vogler in Mannheim.* 1778. (Title from label on cover.) 2d version. See no. 1 for 1st version.	Heusler 7 (most), Heusler 5 (added aria "O süsses Band der Liebe," no. 3, fols. 38-49)	10:1 (most), 10:22 (added aria, fols. 38-49)	Mh. 5 (most); Vogler (added aria, fols. 38-49, prob. some additions and corrections); 3d copyist (trs., clars., "flautini" of no. 7, fols. 85-102)

Undated Manuscripts

No.	MS, Format	Work, Date	Paper	Staving	Copyists
22	D-DS, Mus. ms. 1053 (score, parts)	*Agnus dei* in G minor	Heusler 5 (score), Blum 5 (parts)	12:3 (score), 12:10a (parts)	DS/Mh. 3 (score); Mh. 6 (voice parts, vc./cb., org.), Johann Cramer (vns., vas.)
23	D-DS, Mus. ms. 1073 (score, parts; both upright format)	*Gloria* in F. Dated 1775 in *Verzeichniß* (no. 27).	Heusler 7, prob. Blum 6, possibly one other (score); Blum 5 (parts); German, Knöckel 1 (cover)	16 x 1 (score), 12:10a (parts)	DS/Mh. 3 (score, fls. p. 2), Mh. 6 (vocal parts, cb./vc., org., hns.), DS/Mh. 4 (vns., vas., solo ob., cl., bn.), 2 others (fls. p. 1, trs., timp.)
24	D-DS, Mus. ms. 1091f (org. and bass, ≅ short score; rest somewhat later, prob. local)	*Deutsche Kirchen=Music.* 1777 (title and date from label, in later hand)	Heusler 5	10:29	Vogler
25	D-DS, Mus. ms. 1099 (aut. score; parts)	*Regina coeli* in C; arrangement as *Laudate Dominum* also written into score, with extra voice parts added as required.	Heusler 5 (most); Blum 5 (extra voice parts for *Laudate Dominum*)	12:2a (score), 12:10b (parts)	Vogler (score); Mh. 6 (voice parts, org.), Johann Cramer (other instr. parts)

Music of Georg Joseph Vogler

No.	MS, Format	Work, Date	Paper	Staving	Copyists
26	D-DS, Mus. ms. 1100 (aut. score; parts)	*Laudate pueri* in E	Heusler 5; German, Knöckel 1 (cover)	12:3	Vogler (score); DS/Mh. 3 (SATB/C, vn. 1d and 2a, va. 1-2, org.), Mh. 17 (vn. 1a-c, 2b-d), DS/Mh. 2 (vc./cb. [3]), 2 others (SATB/R, 2 hns. respectively)
27	D-DS, Mus. ms. 1101 (score), 1101a (voice parts; SC, SR oblong format, remainder upright), 1101b (instr. parts; upright format)	*Magnificat* in C	Heusler 5	12:3 (most of score); 10:20c (rest of score; SC, SR instr. parts); 12:10a (rest of voice parts)	DS/Mh. 3 (most), one other (vn. 1d)
28	D-DS, Mus. ms. 1102 (aut. score; parts, some = oblong format)[j]	*Memento Domine David* in G	Heusler 5 (score, most parts); Heusler 7 (two vn. 1, one vn. 2, cb., all smaller); German, Knöckel 1 (cover)	12:3 (score); 12:10d (T, most instr. parts), 12:2a (vn. 1d, 2b, one cb./vc.); 10:20c, 10:31 (SAB parts)	Vogler (score, SAB parts), DS/Mh. 3 (vn. 2b), DS/Mh. 5 (remainder)
29	D-DS, Mus. ms. 1118 (aut. score; parts)	*Beatus vir* in F	Heusler 5 (score, most parts); Heusler 7 (SATB/R); German, Knöckel 1 (cover)	12:2a (score); 12:10d (SA/solo, SATB/R), 12:10c (remaining parts)	Vogler (score [see fig. D:7], hns.), DS/Mh. 3 (voice parts, vn. 1d and 2c, va.), Mh. 17 (vn. 1a-c, vn.2a-b, vc., b.), two others (vn. 2d; dupl. va., b.)
30	D-DS, Mus. ms. 1119 (aut. score; parts, oblong format)	*In exitu Israel* in C	Heusler 5; German, Knöckel 1 (cover)	12:3	Vogler (score; fls., trs., timp.); DS/Mh. 3 (voice parts, most dupl. vns.; vas.), Mh. 17 (vns. 1a and 2a-b), DS/Mh. 5 (rest of winds)
31	D-DS, Mus. ms. 1128 (aut. score; parts)	*Salmo e Motetto Laudate dominum* in B♭	Heusler 5	10:20c (score), 12:10b (parts)	Vogler (score); Mh. 6 (voice parts [2 of each], vns. 1a and 2a, 2 va. parts, hns.); Johann Cramer (vns. 1b-d, 2b-d); one or possibly two others (2 b. parts)

259

Appendix A/V

No.	MS, Format	Work, Date	Paper	Staving	Copyists
32	D-DS, Mus. ms. 1132 (parts)	Sanctus in C (title from parts; no cover or TP). Dated 1776 in Verzeichniß (no. 48).	Heusler 5	10:20c (one side of paper), 10:31 (other side; all voice parts but AR; vn. 1d, va.); 12 x 1 (AR, remaining instr. parts)	Several non-professionals, possibly students of Vogler (same as no. 33)
33	D-DS, Mus. ms. 1155 (parts; oblong format)	Credo in C (title from parts; no TP). Dated 1775 in Verzeichniß (no. 32).	Heusler 5; a few sheets with <BASEL>, prob. from Blum 5 paper; German, Knöckel 1 (cover)	10:20c (one side of paper), 10:31 (other side; all voice parts but AR, TR; some instr. parts); 10 x 1 (AR, TR, most instr. parts)	Several non-professionals, possibly students of Vogler (same as no. 32)
34	D-OF (aut. score)	Confitebor a 4 Voci / 4 Stromenti	Heusler 5	12:3	Vogler
35	D-OF (aut. score)	Credo in F. Dated 1775 in Verzeichniß (no. 37).	Heusler 5	12:2a	Vogler
36	D-OF (aut. score)	Credo in D minor. Dated 1775 in Verzeichniß (no. 39).	Heusler 5	12:2a	Vogler
37	D-OF (score)	Credo in F. Dated 1775 in Verzeichniß (no. 38).	Heusler 5	20 x 1	All one copyist, prob. DS/Mh. 3j
38	D-OF (aut. score)	Fac ut arde	Heusler 5	12:2a	Vogler
39	D-OF (aut. score)	Gloria	Heusler 5	12:3	Vogler
40	D-OF (aut. scores)	Kyrie, Sanctus in B♭, latter written on versi of former[k]	Heusler 5	12:3	Vogler
41	D-OF (aut. score)	Magnificat] a 4 voci / Stromenti	Heusler 5	12:3	Vogler
42	D-OF (aut. score)	Motetto ("Sancta Maria"). Dated 1776 in Verzeichniß (no. 64).	Heusler 5	12:3	Vogler
43	D-OF (aut. score)	Salve Regina	Heusler 5	12:2a	Vogler

a A mod. ed. of this ballet, with reprods. from the present manuscript, has been published in RRMCE, vol. 45 (1996), ed. Floyd K. Grave (see Bibliography).

b App. A/V/4–7 form a full mass cycle and were performed together at Mannheim.

c The two soprano parts are designated as being for two Mannheim singers, Silvio Giorgetti and Francesco Roncaglio.

d App. A/V/11–13 were probably conceived as part of a mass cycle, presently lacking only the Gloria.

e Mus. ms. 1103b contains a third (bound) score of this work that is probably a somewhat later local copy (Blum 7 paper, very irregular 10 x 1 staving).

f This manuscript contains a large number of duplicate parts—doubled and even tripled voice parts and a total of six first violin parts, four seconds, two viola, and three bass parts. Five of the parts record the names of the performers: Cannabich, Toeschi and Dan[ner] (together on one part), Winter, Bohrer, and Friedel, all well-known Mannheim instrumentalists. Of these, all went to Munich in 1778 with the notable exception of the bassist Joseph Friedel; his inclusion here connects the manuscript decisively with Mannheim.

g Though this manuscript contains no date, the work itself is dated 30 March 1777 in a score at the Stiftelsen Musikkulturens Främjande, Stockholm (S-Smf), labeled an autograph by RISM (information kindly supplied by Margaret G. Grave). As the present manuscript clearly antedates 1778 (see the previous footnote), a date of 1777 for it seems all but certain. I have not personally examined the Stockholm score; if it is indeed an autograph, it should be included in part 1 of the present appendix.

h The parts included with this manuscript are probably local. For a facsimile of the score see Thomas Bauman, ed., *German Opera, 1700–1800*, vol. 8 (New York: Garland Publishing, 1986).

i The tenor part of this manuscript is designated as being for the Mannheim singer Franz Hartig.

j See also App. A/V/23. The *Verzeichniß* incorrectly lists this score as an autograph (no. 38).

k A Sanctus in B♭, dated 1776 in the *Verzeichniß* (no. 47), may be identical with the Sanctus of no. 40. However, it was supposedly a set of parts, not a score (as here), and it has four horn parts (none is present in the André manuscript).

Appendix A/VI

VI. Other Manuscripts from Mannheim

Section VI of Appendix A lists those manuscripts that do not fit within any of the previous categories, that is, those manuscripts for which the evidence of Mannheim provenance is entirely or primarily codicological in nature (see chaps. 8–9). The order is alphabetical by library. In column 2, the phrase "Mannheim binding" refers to the sumptuous leather bindings of the scores in question (see chap. 8, @ fn. 15). In column 4, the sigla provided for sacred music are taken from the thematic catalogues of Eduard Schmitt (Mannheim sacred music) and Deanna Bush (Holzbauer). For instrumental music, sigla in the form "D-8" refer to the indices in DTB, Jg. III/1 and VII/2, and in the case of Johann Stamitz also to that in Eugene K. Wolf, *The Symphonies of Johann Stamitz*; sigla for the symphonies of Christian Cannabich refer to Jean K. Wolf, *The Symphony at Mannheim: Christian Cannabich*; while sigla and dates for the symphonies of Joseph Toeschi refer to the "Chronologisches Verzeichnis" of Robert Münster, *The Symphonies of Joseph Toeschi* (for further details on these references see the Bibliography). Finally, references to "Corneilson/Wolf" in the "Comments" column are to the list of Mannheim manuscripts in Paul Corneilson and Eugene K. Wolf, "Newly Identified Manuscripts of Operas and Related Works from Mannheim," *JAMS* 47 (1994): 250–53, which for the most part corresponds to table 8:1.

No.	MS	Composer	Work, ID	Paper	Staving	Copyists	Comments
1	A-KN, Sign. 644/3	Holzbauer	Mass in B♭ (lacks TP; Schmitt I.16, Bush A26)	?J. J. Heusler 1	12:6	KN/Mh. 1 (voice parts), three others (vn. 1, va., org.)	Benedictus and rest of parts local. Rastrum unique to this and the following MS. The present MS is a copy of the mass found in the MS A/II/4, dated here from the late 1760s–early 1770s.
2	A-KN, Sign. 665/4	Holzbauer	Mass in E♭ (lacks TP; Schmitt I.19, Bush A14)	Blum 4a	12:6 + (2-3) x 1	KN/Mh. 1 (voice parts), Mh. 1 (vns., va.), three others (ob. 1, hn. 1; ob. 2, hn. 2; org.)	Rastrum unique to this and the previous MS. The present MS is a copy of the mass found in the MS A/II/3, dated here from the later 1750s–ca. 1765.

Other Manuscripts from Mannheim

No.	MS	Composer	Work, ID	Paper	Staving	Copyists	Comments
2.5a	B-Bc, MSM 3704 (score)	J. C. Bach	Recitative and aria "Rosanne / Or a dammi" from *Temistocle* (5 Nov. 1772)	Blum 6 (top half of sheets only; but cf. A/VI/ 139, a full score of *Temistocle*)	12 x 1, as in A/VI/139 (see previous column)	All one copyist, ≅ Johann Cramer but with numerous discrepancies	1772+ (date of Mannheim perf.).
3	B-Bc, MSM 7700 (1)	Holzbauer	*Sinfonia à 8 Stromt:* (D-8)	Blum 3 (strs.), Blum 1a (winds)	9-10 x 1	Mh. 1	Between 1753 (the year of Holzbauer's arrival in Mannheim) and the early 1760s based on the WMs (Blum 2 ≡ 1750s, Blum 3 found as late as 1766).
4	B-Bc, MSM 7700 (2)	Holzbauer	*Sinfonia à 8 Stromt:* (E-5)	Blum 3 (vn. 2, va., b.), Blum 1a (winds; vn. 1 local)	9-11 x 1 (same rastrum as previous MS)	Mh. 1	See previous MS.
5	B-Bc, MSM 2336 (score, 3 vols.)	Salieri	*La Fiera di Venezia* (22 Nov. 1772). See also no. 140.	Blum 4b (most), Heusler 6 (larger ensembles, choruses); Blum 5 (some pages of added winds at end of vol. 2)	2 x 5:4a (most); 2 x 5:4b (2d half of no. 5, etc.); 2 x 5:3 (vol. 2, pp. 17-80, added winds, etc., all on Blum paper); 12:1 (Heusler paper)	All Mh. 5 but added winds (2d copyist)	1772+ (date of Mannheim perf.). Table 8:1, no. 13b; Corneilson/Wolf no. 15b.
6	CZ-Bm, A 19.101 (prov. Staré Brno)	Holzbauer	*Missa Brevis in G sol re ut* (Schmitt I.25, Bush A21)	Heusler 7	12 x 1	Mh. 2	App. A/VI/6–10 all stem originally from the monastery of St. Thomas in Brno (information kindly supplied by Dr. Jiří Sehnal). This and the next MS were obviously copied at about the same time, prob. the late 1760s or early 1770s. The Munich (ex-Mannheim) MS of this mass (App. A/II/8) is considered here to date from the 1760s (ca. 1765-70?).

Appendix A/VI

No.	MS	Composer	Work, ID	Paper	Staving	Copyists	Comments
7	CZ-Bm, A 19.102 (prov. Staré Brno)	Holzbauer	Missa Solemnis in F: Fa ut (Schmitt I.12, Bush A16)	Heusler 6	12 x 1 (same rastrum as previous MS)	Mh. 2, one other (obs.)	See comment on previous MS. A variant version of this mass is found in App. A/II/13, dated here in the 1760s (ca. 1765–70?).
8	CZ-Bm, A 20.469 (prov. Staré Brno)	Holzbauer	Mass in Bb (lacks TP; Schmitt I.16, Bush A26)	Blum 7 (most), Blum 5 (hns.)	12:9 (most), 12:7b (hns.)	Mh. 19 (most), Mh. 8 (hns.)	Prob. late 1760s or early 1770s: Mh. 8 found in two MSS of that period (App. A/II/4, 8); rastrum 12:7b found in MSS dated here in the 1760s (ca. 1765–70? App. A/II/1, 15); Blum 7 paper. The Munich (ex-Mannheim) MS of this mass (App. A/II/4) is dated here in the late 1760s to the early 1770s.
9	CZ-Bm, A 20.672 (prov. Staré Brno)	Holzbauer	Missa Solemnis in D (Schmitt I.36, Bush A7)	Heusler 7	12 x 1	Mh. 2	Prob. later 1760s–early 1770s. The Munich (ex-Mannheim) MS of this mass (App. A/II/7) is dated here in the 1760s–early 1770s.
10	CZ-Bm, A 20.810 (prov. Staré Brno)	Holzbauer	Messa con Canoni in b.mi (Schmitt I.29, Bush A12)	Blum 7	12 x 1	Mh. 2 (most), Mh. 8 (SC, AC)	Prob. first half of 1770s or late 1760s: Mh. 8 found in two MSS of that period (App. A/II/4, 8); Blum 7 paper (cf. no. 8 above). The cover, containing the title, is local.
11	D-Au (HR), HR III 4½ 2° 162	Holzbauer	Missa in C (Schmitt I.5, Bush A1)	Blum 3	12 x 1	Mh. 2	This and the next MS were obviously copied at about the same time, possibly in 1754 (see chap. 9, fn. 4 and related text).
12	D-Au (HR), HR III 4½ 2° 952	Holzbauer	Missa In E. minor. (Schmitt I.21, Bush A15a)	Blum 3	12 x 1 (same rastrum as previous MS)	Mh. 2	See previous MS.
13	D-B, KHM 783	Cannabich	Renaud et Armide[,] Ballet Heroique [1768+]b	Blum 5	10 x 1	Mh. 2	Performed as 2d ballet to Holzbauer's Adriano in Siria, 25 Nov. 1768.

264

No.	MS	Composer	Work, ID	Paper	Staving	Copyists	Comments
14	D-B, KHM 808	Cannabich	*Sinfonia a 10 Stromt:* (Cannabich 35, D-20)	Blum 5	10:30d	Mh. 6	Ca. 1767–70: Cannabich 35 dated here ca. 1767–68; rastrum 10:30d also found in Cannabich 41 (ca. 1770).
15	D-B, KHM 810	Cannabich	*Sinfonia Concertante à 16 Stromt:* (Cannabich 42, E♭-7)	Blum 6 (vns. princ.; no bell shows, but the shield is similar to that of Blum 6), Blum 5 (rest)	10 x 1 (vns. prin.); 10:17a (rest)	Mh. 20 (most), one other (vns. prin.)	Ca. 1771–72: Cannabich 42 almost certainly performed 29 April 1772; rastrum 10:17a also found in Cannabich 43 (ca. 1772).
16	D-B, KHM 2379	Holzbauer	*Sinfonia in De la, Sol re* (D-14)	Heusler 5 (most), Blum 5 (hn. 1)	10:17b (in hn. 1, on Blum paper, irregs. of staff 7, spaces 3–4 have been corrected)	Mh. 5	Ca. 1768–70: rastrum 10:17b found in App. A/I/14–15 of 1769 and A/IV/10b of 1767/68.
17	D-B, KHM 2380	Holzbauer	*Sinfonia a 8 Stromt:* (E♭-4)	Heusler 7	5 x 2:1	Mh. 18	Ca. 1772? Mh. 18 appears in App. A/V/1, from 1772, and other MSS of the period.
18	D-B, KHM 5319 (score in two parts; upright format)	J. Stamitz	*Messa* in D	German, Knöckel 2 (Part I); Blum 1 (Part II, outer sheet [pp. 77–78, 135–36]), Blum 3 (rest of Part II)	1 + 3 x 5:16 (Part I); 16 x 1 (beginning of Part II [pp. 77–80]); 1 + (3 x 5:17) (Part II, pp. 81-end)	Mh. 21	Ca. 1755+ (mass performed Paris, 4 Aug. 1755); Mh. 21 also found in an aria from Hasse's *Leucippo*, performed Mannheim 1752 and later (App. A/VI/85).
19	D-B, KHM 5455 ("Violino di Repetitione" in short score, parts)	[Joseph] Toeschi	*Ballo Secondo*[,] *Mars et Venus* [1766+]c	Blum 5	10 x 1 (strs., bns.); 10:25c (remaining winds); 2 x 5:14c (vn. di repet.)	Mh. 1 (all parts; overture and some tempo markings of vn. di rep.); 2d copyist (most of vn. di repet.)d	Performed as 2d ballet to Majo's *Alessandro*, 5. Nov. 1766. The "Violino di Repetitione" part contains all the essential melodic material.

Other Manuscripts from Mannheim

Appendix A/VI

No.	MS	Composer	Work, ID	Paper	Staving	Copyists	Comments
20	D-B, Mus. ms. Bach P 388 (score, "Mannheim" binding)	J. C. Bach	*Temistocle* (5 Nov. 1772; premiere). See also no. 139.	Alsatian, Weyhr 1 (most); Heusler 6 (pp. 127-46, occasionally thereafter); Heusler 5 (flyleaves)	2 x 5:8 (Weyhr paper), 10:1 (Heusler paper)	Mh. 5	1772+ (date of Mannheim perf.). From Sickingen collection. Table 8:1, no. 1a; Corneilson/Wolf no. 1a.
21	D-B, Mus. ms. 4485	Innocenz Danzi	*Concerto . . . Violoncello Obbligato* in G	Blum 1	10:19	Bln./Mh. 2 (unique), Italianate hand; Danzi?	1754 (date of Danzi's arrival in Mannheim)– ca. 1760 (1754-55?): rastrum found in App. A/VI/100–101 and arias from Holzbauer's *Issipile* (1754); early paper. May have been written soon after Danzi's arrival at the electoral court (cf. the next MS).
22	D-B, Mus. ms. 6221/1	Fils	*Concerto à Violoncello Principale* in Bb	Heusler 7	8:1 (vc. prin. fols. 1, 4); 8 x 1 (vc. prin. fols. 2-3); 10:15 (orch. parts)	Bln./Mh. 3 (unique); Fils?	1754 (date of Fils's arrival in Mannheim)– ca. 1760 (date of Fils's death; 1754–55?): rastrum 10:15 found in Cannabich 3 (mid-1750s) and App. A/VI/ 62, an aria from Galuppi's *Siroe* (1754). May have been written soon after Fils's arrival at the electoral court, possibly in conjunction with the previous MS.
23	D-B, Mus. ms. 6222/5	Fils	*Trio per Violoncello obligato, Violino e Basso* (DTB, Jg. XVI, Fils G-7)	Blum 3	5:15 (vc. fols. 1r, 2v); 5:14a and c (rest)	Mh. 3	Prob. early or mid 1760s: rastrum 5:14a found in App. A/III/32 (publ. 1766), rastrum 5:14c in App. A/VI/19 (1766); Blum 3 paper not otherwise found after 1766.
24	D-B, Mus. ms. 7130 (score, "Mannheim" binding)	Gassmann	*L'Amore Artigiano* (Schwetzingen, May 1772)	Heusler 6; Heusler 5 (flyleaves)	2 x 5:7; 2 x 5:10a-d	Mh. 5	1772+ (date of Schwetzingen perf.). From Sickingen collection. Table 8:1, no. 5; Corneilson/Wolf no. 5. A reprod. of the spine of this MS appears in fig. 8:1 and Corneilson/Wolf, 263.

Other Manuscripts from Mannheim

No.	MS	Composer	Work, ID	Paper	Staving	Copyists	Comments
25	D-B, Mus. ms. 10779	Holzbauer	Aria in Soprano, "Numi se giusti" (from Adriano in Siria, ?5 Nov. 1768)	Blum 7, but evidently without the countermark "Basel"	10 x 1	Mh. 20	1768+ (date of Mannheim perf.).
26	D-B, Mus. ms. 10780 (score, 3 vols.)	Holzbauer	Günther von Schwarzburg[.] Ein Singspiel in drei Aufzügen (Mannheim, 5 January 1777; premiere). See also App. A/II/20, the aut. score of this work.	Heusler 5	10:8a (vol. 1, fols. 1-9; all or most of vols. 2-3); 10:11 (all or most of vol. 1, fols. 10-end)	Johann Cramer	1777+ (date of Mannheim perf.). Table 8:1, no. 6; Corneilson/Wolf no. 8.
27	D-B, Mus. ms. 10781 (score)	Holzbauer	La morte di Didone[.] Azione dramatica Da cantarsi (Mannheim, 6 July 1779; premiere)	Blum 7	10 x 1	Mh. 6	1779 (date of Mannheim perf.). Table 8:1, no. 7; Corneilson/Wolf no. 9. A German version of this work from 1780, entitled Tod der Dido, is found in US-Wc, M 1500.H77 T5. The score is not from Mannheim.
28	D-B, Mus. ms. 10782e	Holzbauer	La Tempesta: Cantata di Soprano:	Blum 5	10 x 1	Mh. 1	Prob. 1760s (WMs; Mh. 1 prob. = Jacob Cramer, who died in 1770). Corneilson/Wolf no. 7.
29	D-B, Mus. ms. 10783 (score)	Holzbauer	Aria: "Non è ver" (Issipile, 10 Nov. 1754)	Blum 3	10 x 1	Mh. 1	MS marked "Sig.ra Dousart," i.e, for Maria Anna Dus(s)art, at Mannheim 1748-55. Date: 1754-55 (see col. 4).
30	D-B, Mus. ms. 10783/1	Holzbauer	Aria in Soprano solo, "Voi che di grandi"	Heusler 7	10 x 1	All one copyist (unique).	Neither this text nor the opera from which it was taken has yet been identified.

267

Appendix A/VI

No.	MS	Composer	Work, ID	Paper	Staving	Copyists	Comments
31	D-B, Mus. ms. 13396 (score, "Mannheim" binding)f	G. F. de Majo	*Ifigenia in Tauride* (5 Nov. 1764; premiere)	Heusler 5; Blum 5 (added folio, pp. 150-51)	10:17a (most), 10:2 (added folio, pp. 150-51)	Mh. 5 (see fig. D:14)	1764+ (date of Mh. perf.). From Sickingen collection. This MS could be a somewhat later copy; rastrum 10:17a is otherwise found in MSS from ca. 1770-75. Table 8:1, no. 10a; Corneilson/Wolf no. 12a.
32	D-B, Mus. ms. 13396/1 (score)	G. F. de Majo	*Ifigenia in Tauride* (title from spine; 1764), selections	Heusler 7	10 x 1	Mh. 6 (see fig. D:15)	1764+ (date of Mh. perf.). Table 8:1, no. 10b; Corneilson/Wolf no. 12b.
33	D-B, Mus. ms. 13400 (score, 3 vols.)g	G. F. de Majo	*Alessandro* [nell'Indie] (5 Nov. 1766; premiere), selections	Intersperses Blum 6 (act 1, sc. 2, 4, etc.) and Blum 7 (act 1, sc. 3, 5, 7, etc.)	10 x 1 (three forms)	Blum 6 paper: Bln./Mh.:1 (most), 2d copyist (act 1, sc. 15); Blum 7 paper: Mh. 6	1766+ (date of Mh. perf.). Table 8:1, no. 11; Corneilson/Wolf no. 13.
34	D-B, Mus. ms. 13400/8 (parts for vns., va., obs., hns.)	G. F. de Majo	Aria, "Se il ciel mi divide" (*Alessandro*, 1766)	Blum 7, but evidently without the countermark "Basel" (cf. no. 25)	10 x 1	Mh. 20	1766+ (date of Mh. perf.). The bass part of this MS, containing the title, is local, copied by the compiler of the two previous MSS.
35	D-B, Mus. ms. 13401/1 (score)	G. F. de Majo	Aria, "E specie di follia" (*Ifigenia in Tauride*, 1764)	Prob. German (<D/ROTAL[?] ... in frame : shield? eagle?>)	10 x 1	?Johann Cramer (very early; Cramer was only born in 1749!)	1764 or (more likely) later, given that the copyist seems to be Johann Cramer (see previous column).
36	D-B, Mus. ms. 15142/5 (parts for vn. 1, va., b., obs. only)	Mozart	Soprano Solo *Aer tranquillo e di Sereni* (from *Il rè pastore*, K. 208 [Salzburg, 1775]; no. 3)	Heusler 6	10:1	All by Fridolin Weber except for obs. p. 1, system 3 to end of page, by 2d copyist (takes over after clefs)	1777/78. In Mozart's letter of 7 Feb. 1778 (Bauer-Deutsch, 2:266) he states that he has given four arias from *Il rè pastore* to Aloysia Weber, of which this may well be one (see the full discussion of this MS in chap. 2, @ fn. 104). See fig. D:8.

268

No.	MS	Composer	Work, ID	Paper	Staving	Copyists	Comments
37	D-B, Mus. ms. 22001 (score, "Mannheim" binding)	Traetta	*La Sofonisba* (5 Nov. 1762; premiere). See also no. 204.	Blum 6; Heusler 7 (flyleaves)	2 x 5:20b (overture; p. 45ff., etc.); 2 x 5:20a (pp. 41-44, etc.)	Mh. 5	1762+ (date of Mannheim perf.). From Sickingen collection. Table 8:1, no. 16a; Corneilson/Wolf no. 17a. A re-prod. of the spine of this MS appears in fig. 8:1 and Corneilson/Wolf, 263.
38	D-B, Mus. ms. 30115 (no. 12 in vol. of miscellaneous arias; score)	G. F. de Majo	*Aria*, "Tornò la mia speranza" (*Ifigenia in Tauride*, 1764)	Blum 5	10 x 1	Mh. 1	1764+.
39[h]	D-B, N. Mus. BP 26	"Sig. Amadori" (added in different hand; could refer to performer)	*Aria*, "Contro il destin" (from Metastasio's *Antigono*)	Heusler 6	10 x 1, 12 x 1	Mh. 1	The castrato Giovanni Tedeschi, known as "Amadori," is not known ever to have composed or performed in an *Antigono*. The incipit of this aria does not appear in the RISM database or in the Breitkopf Catalogue, and the aria is not the same as that in the settings of *Antigono* by Gluck, Hasse, or Galuppi available to me.[i]
40-41	D-B, N. Mus. BP 41, 64 (scores plus instr. parts)	[Jommelli]	Two arias from *Caio Mario* (Bologna, 1751)	Blum 1b	2 x 5:18	BP/Mh. 1	1751+ (early 1750s): rastrum 5:18 appears in a Grua MS of 1751 (App. A/I/ 11) and in numerous MSS of the Pretlack collection from operas premiered in 1751 and (in one case) 1749.[j]
42	D-B, N. Mus. BP 65 (score)	Anon.	*Aria*, "Se ardire e speranza" (from *Demofoonte*)	German, Knöckel 2	2 x 5:1	BP/Mh. 2	Prob. 1749–early1750s (see nos. 58–60 and 64–84 [1750+], all lined with rastrum 5:1). This aria is not the same as that in Hasse's setting of 1748, and it only begins similarly to the setting by

Appendix A/VI

No.	MS	Composer	Work, ID	Paper	Staving	Copyists	Comments
(42)							Galuppi in B-Bc, supposedly from the Padua, 1758 version (the orig. version [Madrid, 1749] is evidently lost).
43	D-B, N. Mus. BP 81 (score plus instr. parts)	[Galuppi]	Aria, "Vorrei spiegar l'affano" (Semiramide, Milan, 1749)	Blum 1b	2 x 5:18	BP/Mh. 1	1749-early 1750s (see comment on nos. 40-41 above).
44	D-B, N. Mus. BP 171 (score; upright format)	ptro Chiarini	Aria, "Se al labbro mio non credi"	Heusler 3	15 x 1	Mh. 1 (see fig. D:9)	Aria not yet identified.
45	D-B, N. Mus. BP 174 (instr. parts)	Cocchi	Aria, "Al caro porto" (lacks TP)	Blum 1a (vns.); Dutch, C. & I. Honig 1 (rest of parts)	10-12 x 1	Mh. 1	Aria not yet identified. The voice and dupl. bass parts of this MS are local.
46	D-B, N. Mus. BP 207 (score)	"Galuppi"	Aria à Soprano ... opera Antigono, "Contro il destin non frema"	Heusler 6	2 x 5:2	Mh. 9	Prob. early 1750s (same rastrum as no. 85 [1752+]). Both the attribution to Galuppi and the title Antigono have been added later, and in fact the aria's text is not the same as that in Metastasio's Antigono, Galuppi's setting of which, moreover, makes use of entirely different music. See also chap. 9, fn. 16.
47-56	D-B, N. Mus. BP 210-11, 214-15, 217, 219, 221, 223-25 (voice parts only)	Galuppi	Ten arias from Antigona (17 Jan. 1753)	Blum 3 (most), Blum 1a (dupl. S parts of nos. 47, 55 [BP 210, 224])	10 x 1	Mh. 1	1753+. BP 208-26, including both local copies and the Mannheim MSS listed here, were originally enclosed in a cover giving the Mannheim perf. date of 1753 (not that of the premiere in 1751). See chap. 9, @ fn. 16. In no. 52 (BP 219) only the 1st of the two soprano parts is from Mannheim; the 2d part and the rest of the MS are local.

270

Other Manuscripts from Mannheim

No.	MS	Composer	Work, ID	Paper	Staving	Copyists	Comments
57	D-B, N. Mus. BP 229 (S with b.c., instr. parts)	Galuppi	Aria, "Conservati fedele pensa" (*Artaserse*, Padua, 1751; lacks TP)	Heusler 6	10 x 1	Mh. 1	1751+.
58-60	D-B, N. Mus. BP 230-32 (scores)	Galuppi	Three arias from *Demofoonte* (Madrid, 1749)	Heusler 6 (nos. 58-59 [BP 230-31]); German, Knöckel 2 (no. 58 [BP 232])	2 x 5:1	BP/Mh. 2 (no. 58; no. 59, title "Aria"; no. 60); Mh. 9 (music of no. 59)	1749–early 1750s (same rastrum as nos. 64-84 [1750+]).
61	D-B, N. Mus. BP 234 (score)	"Galuppi"	Aria, "Pupille care, se vi girate"	Blum 1b	2 x 5:18	BP/Mh. 1	Early 1750s (see comment on nos. 40-41). This aria is attributed to Giovanni Battista Pescetti (ca. 1704–1766) in several sources, incl. GB-Lbl, Add. MS 31597 (24), which also happens to contain another Pescetti aria in the Pretlack collection, no. 119 below. That Pescetti was a collaborator with Galuppi may explain the attribution to Galuppi here. Another attribution of this aria to Galuppi, in I-Bc, stating that it comes from *Demetrio*, is weak in that the present text is not by Metastasio, the librettist of Galuppi's *Demetrio*.
62	D-B, N. Mus. BP 237	[Galuppi]	Aria, "Fra dubbi afetti" (*Siroe*, Rome, 1754; lacks TP)	Heusler 5, 7	10:15	BP/Mh. 3	1754+ (1754–late 1750s; rastrum also found in Cannabich 3 from that period).
63	D-B, N. Mus. BP 406	Hasse	*Sinfonia à 4.tro dell'Opera Demofoonte* (17 or 18 Jan. 1750)	Heusler 6	10 x 1	Mh. 1	1750+. The original cover to nos. 63-84 (BP 406-27; see Jaenecke, *Pretlack*, 171) bears the date of the Mannheim perf. 1750, and not that of the premiere (Dresden, 1748).

Appendix A/VI

No.	MS	Composer	Work, ID	Paper	Staving	Copyists	Comments
64-84	D-B, N. Mus. BP 407-27 (scores)	Hasse	Twenty-one arias from *Demofoonte* (18 Jan. 1750)	Heusler 6 (nos. 64-68, 71-78, 80-84 [BP 407-11, 414-21, 423-27]; German, Knöckel 2 (nos. 69-70, 79 [BP 412-13, 422])	2 x 5:1	BP/Mh. 2 (nos. 64, 66-70, 79-84 [BP 407, 409-13, 422-27]; titles only of 71-74, 76-77); Mh. 9 (all of nos. 65, 71-78 [BP 408, 414-21] except for above titles)	1750+ (early 1750s; see previous comment and also nos. 58-60 above).
85	D-B, N. Mus. BP 437	[Hasse]	Aria, "Se agli' occhi" (*Leucippo*, 5 May 1752; lacks TP)	Blum 3	2 x 5:2	Mh. 21 (most), one other (ob. 1)	1752+. The copyist Mh. 21 is also found in Johann Stamitz's Mass in D of ca. 1755 (App. A/VI/18).
86	D-B, N. Mus. BP 454	Holzbauer	Aria in Soprano, "Se non ti maro allato" (*Adriano in Siria*, 5? Nov. 1768)	Heusler 6 (S, vns.), van der Ley 2 (va., b.)	10 x 1 (S, vns.); 12 x 1 (va., b.)	Mh. 1	1768+. One of the rare MSS of the Pretlack collection to postdate ca. 1760.
87-95	D-B, N. Mus. BP 468-76 (voice parts; instr. parts of 84, 86, 89 [BP 468, 470, 473] only)	Holzbauer	Nine arias from *La Clemenza di Tito* (5 Nov. 1757; premiere)	Swiss (no WM; nos. 88, 91 [BP 469, 472]); Heusler 7 (no. 90 [BP 471]); Heusler 6 (nos. 93-95 [BP 474-76]); Blum 1a, Heusler 6 (S, orch. parts respectively of nos. 87, 89, 92)	10 x 1 (voice parts); 9-10 x 1 (instr. parts)	Mh. 1	1757+.

272

Other Manuscripts from Mannheim

No.	MS	Composer	Work, ID	Paper	Staving	Copyists	Comments
96-97	D-B, N. Mus. BP 477-78	Holzbauer	Two arias from *Demetrio*	Heusler 6 (S, vns.), van der Ley 2 (rest of parts)	9-12 x 1	Mh. 1	These two arias, "Dal suo gentil sembiante" and "Non so frenare il pianto," are identified by Jaenecke as being from Metastasio's *Demetrio*. However, no setting by Holzbauer of *Demetrio* has yet been discovered. Alternatively, as suggested to me by Paul Corneilson, they might be insertion arias for Jommelli's *Demetrio* (perf. Mannheim, 4 Nov. 1753, just after Holzbauer's arrival in Mannheim). Based on the WMs (see, e.g., the use of Blum 1a in nos. 98–101), these MSS date from the 1750s (presumably after 1753) or possibly the early 1760s.
98-99	D-B, N. Mus. BP 481-82	Holzbauer	Two arias from *L'isola disabitata* (15 June 1754; premiere)	Blum 1a	10 x 1	Mh. 1	1754+.
100-101	D-B, N. Mus. BP 486-87 (score)	Holzbauer	Two arias from *Issipile* (10 Nov. 1754; premiere)	Blum 3 (no. 100, fols. 1-2, 5-6), Blum 1a (no. 100, fols. 3-4, 7-10; no. 101 all)	10:14 (no. 100, fols. 1-2, 5-6); 10:13 (no. 100, fols. 3-4); 10:19 (no. 100, fols. 7-10; no. 101 all)	Mh. 2 (see fig. D:10)	1754+.
102	D-B, N. Mus. BP 490	Holzbauer	*Aria in Soprano*, "Sentirsi dire dal caro bene" (*Semiramide*)	Heusler 6 (S, vns.), van der Ley 2 (va., b.)	9-11 x 1	Mh. 1	Identified by Jaenecke as being from Metastasio's *Semiramide*, which Holzbauer is not known to have set. Nor is a *Semiramide* known ever to have been performed at Mannheim for which Holzbauer might have written a substitute aria.

Appendix A/VI

No.	MS	Composer	Work, ID	Paper	Staving	Copyists	Comments
103	D-B, N. Mus. BP 492	Holzbauer	Aria in Soprano, "Or adanni d'un ingrata" (Temistocle)	Heusler 6 (S, vns.), van der Ley 2 (rest)	10-12 x 1	Mh. 1	Identified by Jaenecke as being from Metastasio's Temistocle, which Holzbauer is not known to have set. The only Temistocle known to have been performed at Mannheim was that of J. C. Bach; both the late date, 1772, and the circumstances surrounding this opera make it extremely unlikely that this could be a substitute aria for it.
104	D-B, N. Mus. BP 493	Holzbauer	Aria in Soprano, "Vi conosco amate stelle" (Zenobia)	Heusler 6 (S, vns.), van der Ley 2 (va., b.)	9-11 x 1	Mh. 1	Identified by Jaenecke as being from Metastasio's Zenobia, which Holzbauer is not known to have set. Nor is a Zenobia known to have been performed at Mannheim for which Holzbauer might have written a substitute aria.
105	D-B, N. Mus. BP 503	Jommelli	Aria, "Così Leon feroce" (Achille in Sciro, Vienna, 1749)	Dutch, C. & I. Honig or L. van Gerrevink(<IV : fleur-de-lis/ shield (diagonal stripes)>)	10 x 1	Mh. 1	1749+.
106	D-B, N. Mus. BP 505	Jommelli	Sinfonia dell' Opera Artaserse (17 Jan. 1751)	Heusler 4a (vn. 1), Blum 3 (vn. 2, b./TP), Heusler 7 (va., winds)	10 x 1 (vn. 1); 2 x 5:18 (vn. 2, b./TP); 12 x 1 (va.); 9 x 1 (obs.); 5 x 2:14 (hns./trs.)	Mh. 1	1751+ (early 1750s; see comments on nos. 40–41, 115).
107	D-B, N. Mus. BP 507 (vocal score with b.c., upright format; instr. parts)	Jommelli	Duetto for two sopranos, "Tu vuoi ch'io viva" (Artaserse, 17 Jan. 1751)	Heusler 3 (vocal score), Blum 3 (orch. parts)	15 x 1 (score); 10 x 1 (vns.); 12 x 1 (va., b.)	Mh. 1	1751+ (early 1750s; see comments on nos. 40–41, 115).

274

Other Manuscripts from Mannheim

No.	MS	Composer	Work, ID	Paper	Staving	Copyists	Comments
108	D-B, N. Mus. BP 514	Giuseppe Colla	Aria, "Quando avvien che in calma rida" (from *Cajo Fabrizio* of Jommelli and Colla, 5 Nov. 1760)	Heusler 6 (most), Heusler 3 (orig. bass part only)	9-11 x 1	Mh. 1	1760+.
109	D-B, N. Mus. BP 517	Giuseppe Colla	Aria, "Di rea gelosia spiegar" (from *Cajo Fabrizio* of Jommelli and Colla, 5 Nov. 1760)	Heusler 6	10 x 1	Mh. 1	1760+.
110	D-B, N. Mus. BP 517A	[Prob. Francesco Uttini]	*Overtur à 8 In:* (to Jommelli's *Caio Mario*, 2d version, Bologna, 1751)	Blum 1	2 x 5:18	BP/Mh. 1	1751+ (early 1750s; see comment on nos. 40–41). Though circulated as the overture to the Bologna, 1751 version of Jommelli's *Caio Mario*, this piece is not by Jommelli.k It is attributed elsewhere to Francesco Uttini (LaRue 7937–38), who was evidently in Bologna at the time.
111	D-B, N. Mus. BP 519	Jommelli	Aria, "Se perde l'ussignuolo" (*Caio Mario*, Rome, 1746)	Blum 3 (S), Heusler 4 (orch. parts)	10 x 1 (S); 9-11 x 1 (orch. parts)	Mh. 1	Prob. 1751+, date of the Bologna version; see previous comment.
112	D-B, N. Mus. BP 520	[Jommelli]	Aria, "Padre, sposo" (*Caio Mario*, Rome, 1746)	Blum 1	2 x 5:18	BP/Mh. 1	Prob. 1751+ (early 1750s; see comment on nos. 40–41, also the date of the Bologna version [see comment on no. 110]).

Appendix A/VI

No.	MS	Composer	Work, ID	Paper	Staving	Copyists	Comments
113	D-B, N. Mus. BP 520A (score, parts)	[Jommelli]	Aria, "A mille dubbi" (Caio Mario; 2d version, Bologna, 1751)	Blum 1b	2 x 5:18	BP/Mh. 1	1751+. The music of the original version (Rome, 1746) is different.
114	D-B, N. Mus. BP 530	Jommelli	Sinfonia dell' Opera Ifigenia [in Aulide] (4 Nov. 1751)	Blum 3	9-11 x 1	Mh. 1	1751+.
115	D-B, N. Mus. BP 531A (olim 39)	[Jommelli]	Coro [Scena ultima], "Deh tergi omai" (Ifigenia in Aulide, 4 Nov. 1751)	Voice parts Blum 3; instr. parts Dutch? (<backwards 4/CH>)	4 x 2:14 (T [Agamemnon]); 10 x 1 (other voice parts, vns.); 8-9 x 1 (rest of instr. parts)	Mh. 1	1751+ (early 1750s; rastrum 2:13 also appears in no. 106 from that period [q.v.]).
116	D-B, N. Mus. BP 536	Jommelli	Aria, "Rinoverà l'Aprile" (with horn obbligato)	Blum 3	10 x 1	Mh. 1	The text of this virtuoso aria has not yet been traced; possibly it comes from a cantata or serenata, not an opera.
117	D-B, N. Mus. BP 568 (score)	G. F. de Majo	Aria, "Bel piacer saria d'un core" (Semiramide, Naples, 1751)	Heusler 3	10 x 1	Mh. 1	1751+.
118	D-B, N. Mus. BP 572 (score)	G. F. de Majo	Aria, "Fuggi dagl'occhi miei" (Semiramide, Naples, 1751)	Blum 3 (but with no shield as countermark); Heusler 3 (last page, pasted in)	10 x 1	Mh. 1	1751+.

No.	MS	Composer	Work, ID	Paper	Staving	Copyists	Comments
119	D-B, N. Mus. BP 595A (score, parts)	[G. B. Pescetti]	Aria, "Serba l'intatta fedele"	Blum 1b	2 x 5:18	BP/Mh. 1	Early 1750s (see comment on nos. 40–41). Identified as Pescetti by Jaenecke, from the concordant MS GB-Lbl, Add. 31597 (23); cf. no. 61 above.
120	D-DJ, Mus. 3321-D-1 (score)	Johannes Ritschel	*Messa a Quatro Voci* in C (Schmitt I.2)	Blum 6; German, Knöckel 1 (cover)	10 x 1	Mh. 6	1763 (date of *Gioas*, no. 125)–late 1760s (see chap. 9).
121	D-DJ, Mus. 3321-D-2 (score)	Johannes Ritschel	*Messa a Quatro Concertato* in G (Schmitt I.3)	Blum 6; German, Knöckel 1 (cover)	10 x 1	Mh. 6	1763 (date of *Gioas*, no. 125)–late 1760s (see chap. 9).
122	D-DJ, Mus. 3321-D-3 (score)	Johannes Ritschel	*Messa breve à Otto Voci Con Instrumt:* in G minor (Schmitt I.4)	Blum 6; German, Knöckel 1 (cover)	11 x 1	Mh. 6	1763 (date of *Gioas*, no. 125)–late 1760s (see chap. 9).
123	D-DJ, Mus. 3321-D-4 (score)	Johannes Ritschel	*Messa à Quatro Voci* in F (Schmitt I.5)	Blum 6; German, Knöckel 1 (cover)	10 x 1	Mh. 6	1763 (date of *Gioas*, no. 125)–late 1760s (see chap. 9).
124	D-DJ, Mus. 3321-D-5 (score)	Johannes Ritschel	*Messa à Quatro Voci Con Instrumt:* in F (Schmitt I.6)	Blum 6; German, Knöckel 1 (cover)	10 x 1	Mh. 6	1763 (date of *Gioas*, no. 125)–late 1760s (see chap. 9).
125	D-DJ, Mus. 3321-D-6 (score, 2 vols.)	Johannes Ritschel	*Oratorio Di Gioas Rè di Giuda* (1763; Schmitt III)	Blum 6; cover German (<4/IP or IHP>)	10 x 1	Mh. 6	1763+ (1763 [date of 1st perf.]–late 1760s; see chap. 9).
126	D-DJ, Mus. 3321-D-7 (score)	Johannes Ritschel	*Dixit Dominus à Quatro voci* in D (Schmitt II.4)	Blum 6; German, Knöckel 1 (cover)	10 x 1	Mh. 6	1763 (date of *Gioas*, no. 125)–late 1760s (see chap. 9).
127	D-DJ, Mus. 3321-D-8 (score)	Johannes Ritschel	*Miserere à Quatro voci* in G (Schmitt II.6)	Blum 6; German, Knöckel 1 (cover)	12 x 1	Mh. 6	1763 (date of *Gioas*, no. 125)–late 1760s (see chap. 9).

No.	MS	Composer	Work, ID	Paper	Staving	Copyists	Comments
128	D-Dl, Mus. 3321-D-9 (score)	Johannes Ritschel	*Miserere à Quatro voci* in Eb (Schmitt II.5)	Blum 6; German, Knöckel 1 (cover)	12 x 1	Mh. 6	1763 (date of *Gioas*, no. 125)–late 1760s (see chap. 9).
129	D-Dl, Mus. 3321-D-10 (score)	Johannes Ritschel	*Invitatorio della Resuretione Con i Responsorij a 4tro Con Istromenti* in D (Schmitt II.2)	Blum 6; German, Knöckel 1 (cover)	10 x 1	Mh. 6	1763 (date of *Gioas*, no. 125)–late 1760s (see chap. 9).
130	D-Dl, Mus. 3321-D-11 (score)	Johannes Ritschel	*Te Deum Laudamus à Quatro Concertato* in D (Schmitt II.3)	Blum 6; German, Knöckel 1 (cover)	13 x 1	Mh. 6	1763 (date of *Gioas*, no. 125)–late 1760s (see chap. 9).
131	D-Dl, Mus. 3321-E-1 (score)	Johannes Ritschel	*Motetto per il Contr'Alto Solo*, "Agitata sine pace" (Schmitt II.1/1)	Blum 6; German (<4/IP or IHP>; cover)	12 x 1	Mh. 6	1763 (date of *Gioas*, no. 125)–late 1760s (see chap. 9).
132	D-Dl, Mus. 3321-E-2 (score)	Johannes Ritschel	*Motetto Di Tenore Solo*, "Collocata in monte Dei" (Schmitt II.1/2)	Blum 6; German (<4/IP or IHP>; cover)	10 x 1	Mh. 6	1763 (date of *Gioas*, no. 125)–late 1760s (see chap. 9).
133	D-Dl, Mus. 3321-E-3 (score)	Johannes Ritschel	*Motetto di Contr'Alto solo*, "Furiae infernalis" (Schmitt II.1/3)	Blum 6; German, Knöckel 1 (cover)	10 x 1	Mh. 6	1763 (date of *Gioas*, no. 125)–late 1760s (see chap. 9).
134	D-Dl, Mus. 3321-E-4 (score)	Johannes Ritschel	*Motetto per il Basso*, "In procelloso mari" (Schmitt II.1/4)	Blum 6; German (<4/IP or IHP>; cover)	10 x 1	Mh. 6	1763 (date of *Gioas*, no. 125)–late 1760s (see chap. 9).

Other Manuscripts from Mannheim

No.	MS	Composer	Work, ID	Paper	Staving	Copyists	Comments
135	D-Dl, Mus. 3321-E-5 (score)	Johannes Ritschel	Motetto per il Soprano Solo, "Sicut cerva vulnerata" (Schmitt II.1/5)	Blum 6; German (<4/IP or IHP>; cover)	10 x 1	Mh. 6	1763 (date of Gioas, no. 125)—late 1760s (see chap. 9).
136	D-Dl, Mus. 3321-E-6 (score)	Johannes Ritschel	Motetto per il Soprano Solo, "Surge vaga mihi grata" (Schmitt II.1/6)	Blum 6; German (<4/IP or IHP>; cover)	10 x 1	Mh. 6	1763 (date of Gioas, no. 125)—late 1760s (see chap. 9).
137	D-Dl, Mus. 3321-E-7 (score)	Johannes Ritschel	Motetto per il Contr'Alto Solo, "Surgit atra rea procella" (Schmitt II.1/7)	Blum 6; German (<4/IP or IHP>; cover [back only])	10 x 1	Mh. 6	1763 (date of Gioas, no. 125)—late 1760s (see chap. 9).
138	D-Dl, Mus. 3321-E-8 (score)	Johannes Ritschel	Motetto per il Basso Solo, "Tonat coelum ruinas ruinatur" (Schmitt II.1/8)	Blum 6; German (<4/IP or IHP>; cover)	10 x 1	Mh. 6	1763 (date of Gioas, no. 125)—late 1760s (see chap. 9).
139	D-Dl, Mus. 3374F-1 (score, 3 vols.)	J. C. Bach	Temistocle (5 Nov. 1772; premiere). See also nos. 2.5, 20.	Heusler 7 (vols. 1 and 3, 2d half of vol. 2); Blum 6 (1st half of vol. 2)	12 x 1	Dres./Mh. 1 (vol. 1; vol. 3 to last page of sc. 3); Mh. 6 (vol. 2, rest of vol. 3)	1772+. Table 8:1, no. 1b; Corneilson/Wolf no. 1b.
140	D-Dl, Mus. 3796-F-3 (score, 3 vols.)	Salieri	La Fiera di Venezia (22 Nov. 1772). See also no. 5.	Heusler 6	10:1	Mh. 5	1772+. Table 8:1, no. 13c; Corneilson/Wolf no. 15c.

Appendix A/VI

No.	MS	Composer	Work, ID	Paper	Staving	Copyists	Comments
141	D-DS, Mus. ms. 57 (score, 2 vols.)	J. C. Bach	L'Endimione[,] Serenata a 4^{tro} (?1774)	Heusler 6	10:1	Mh. 5 (vol. 1, fols. 1–144r [to "Siritira"]; vol. 2, fols. 31–42v); DS/Mh. 6 (rest)	?1774$^+$. On the date of Endimione see table 8:1, fn. b. Table 8:1, no. 3; Corneilson/Wolf no. 3.
142	D-DS, Mus. ms. 60 (score, 3 vols.)[1]	J. C. Bach	Lucio Silla[,] Drama per Musica (5 Nov. 1775; premiere)	Heusler 7	12 x 1 (overture and all gatherings containing choruses); 10 x 1 (rest)	Mh. 6	1775$^+$. Table 8:1, no. 4; Corneilson/Wolf no. 4.
143	D-DS, Mus. ms. 82 (score)	J. C. Bach	Amor vincitore[,] Cantata a Due Voci Con Cori e Stromenti ...1774 (Aug. 1774)	Heusler 6	10:1	Mh. 5	1774$^+$. Table 8:1, no. 2; Corneilson/Wolf no. 2.
144	D-FS (Mf), Mf 596[b] (parts; see App. A/I/12 for aut. score to this work, dated 1753)	Carlo Grua	Memento Domine David (Schmitt II.2). Dated 1756 at end of added vns. 1c and 2c.	Blum 1 (WM of orig. set of parts matches that of aut. score [1753]; WM of vns. 1c and 2c [1756] differs slightly)	12:8b (orig. set), 12:8e (vns. 1c, 2c)	Mf/Mh. 1 (orig. set), Mh. 7 (vns. 1c, 2c)	Main set = 1753 (date of aut. score), vns. 1c and 2c = 1756.
145	D-FS (Mf), Mf 884	Holzbauer	Missa Ex C à Solennis (Schmitt I.5, Bush A1)	Blum 5 (most); Heusler 7, prob. Blum 3 (va.); Heusler 5 (org., trs., timp.); German, Knöckel 1 (cover)	14–15 x 1 (most); 12:10d (org., trs., timp.)	Mf/Mh. 2 (most); 2d copyist (vn. 2; org. after p. 1, staff 7, m. 4); 3d copyist (beg. of org.)	1770s (rastrum 12:10d also found in App. A/V/17, a Vogler Kyrie of 1776).

No.	MS	Composer	Work, ID	Paper	Staving	Copyists	Comments
146	D-KA, Mus. Hs. 208	Holzbauer	Concerto col Flauto Traverso Principale in A	Blum 1a	10:19	KA/Mh.(?) 1	Prob. 1750s, after Holzbauer's arrival in Mannheim in 1753 (early Blum paper; rastrum 10:19 also found in App. A/VI/100–101, Holzbauer arias from 1754+). This and the next three MSS are less certain to be from Mannheim than usual, as the copyist is unique to them.
147	D-KA, Mus. Hs. 913	Johann Stamitz	Concerto a Flaut Travers Principale [in G] ... del Sign: Stamitz	Heusler 5	9-10 x 1	KA/Mh.(?) 2	1750s, i.e., the same time as nos. 146 and 148–49 (q.v.).
148	D-KA, Mus. Hs. 1001	Johann Baptist Wendling	Concerto à 5 Strom[.,] Flauto Traverso Principale in D	Blum 1a	10:19	KA/Mh.(?) 1	1750s, after Wendling's arrival in Mannheim ca. 1753 (i.e., the same time as nos. 146–47 and 149 [q.v.]).
149	D-KA, Mus. Hs. 1003	Wenzeslaus Woditzka	Concerto à 5 Stromt: [per] Flauto Traversiere [in D] . . . del Sig: Wenze[s]lao Woditzka	Blum 1a	10:19	KA/Mh.(?) 1	1750s, i.e., the same time as nos. 146–48 (q.v.).
150	D-Mbs, Mus. Ms. 2426, vol. 2, fols. 79-88	Sacchini	Aria "Ovunque m'aggiri" inserted in aut. score of Piccinni's Catone in Utica (5 Nov. 1770; premiere)	Blum 5	2 x 5:4a	Mh. 6	1770. See also chap. 8, @ fnn. 9–10.

Appendix A/VI

No.	MS	Composer	Work, ID	Paper	Staving	Copyists	Comments
151	D-Mbs, Mus. Ms. 2525, vol. 1, fols. 47-59; vol. 3, fols. 23-28 (scores)	[Holzbauer?]	(1) Recit. (end) and aria for Culagna, (2) aria for Gherarda inserted in score of Salieri's *La secchia rapita* (5 Nov. 1774)	Heusler 7	10:8b	Holzbauer	1774. The possible attribution to Holzbauer is based mainly on his being the copyist of both insertions. The Salieri score itself (table 8:1, no. 14a) is not an autgraph; it appears to be Viennese, i.e., to have been copied in Vienna for use in Mannheim. See also chap. 8, fn. 10 and related discussion.
152	D-MÜu (RH), Rheda Ms 787	Joseph Toeschi	*Sinfonia* (E♭-9, Münster M 3), strs., bns. (rest local)	Prob. Swiss (no WM)	10:28c	RH/Mh. 1	Late 1750s–early 1760s (rastrum 10:28c also found in Cannabich 11–12, 16).
153	D-Rtt, Christ. Cannabich 10	Cannabich	*Sinfonia à 8 Stromt.* (Cannabich 3, C-2)	Heusler 5	5 x 2:3	Rtt/Mh. 3 (most); Mh. 3 (text only: TP; face page of va., obs.)	Prob. 2d half of 1750s, though conceivably as late as 1765–70; see the very similar MS App. A/VI/184 (Toeschi C-8/Münster 37, a symphony that only appears in print in 1768–69). Cf. also the similar MSS App. A/VI/155, 189.
154	D-Rtt, "Christ. Cannabich" 11	[Holzbauer]	*Sinfonia à 9 Stromt.* (Holzbauer C-7)	Blum 1a (most), Heusler 7 (trs.)	10:26a (vns., va., vc./bn., cb./TP); 10 x 1 (obs.); 10:15 (trs.)	Mh. 1	Prob. 2d half of 1750s (rastra found in Cannabich 3–9 and in MSS dated 1754+ and 1757). The (incorrect) attribution to "Canabich" was added later, probably by an early librarian.
155	D-Rtt, Christ. Cannabich 12	Cannabich	*Sinfonia à 9. Stromt.* (Wolf W-2, D-8)	Heusler 7 (vns., va., bn.), Heusler 5 (b., obs., hns.)	5 x 2:3	Rtt/Mh. 3 (most); Mh. 3 (text only: TP; face page of va., obs., bn.)	Prob. 2d half of 1750s, though possibly later (cf. the very similar MSS App. A/VI/153 [Cannabich 3], 184, 189).
156	D-Rtt, Christ. Cannabich 13	Cannabich	*Sinfonia à 10 Stromt.* (Wolf W-10, G-7)	Blum 3	9–11 x 1	Mh. 1	Mid to late 1760s? (use of Blum 3 paper).

No.	MS	Composer	Work, ID	Paper	Staving	Copyists	Comments
157	D-Rtt, Christ. Cannabich 14	Cannabich	*Sinfonia a 10 Stromt.* (Cannabich 14, C-5)	Heusler 5	5 x 2:4a	Mh. 3	Early 1760s (date of Cannabich symphony; cf. the similar MSS no. 158, 160).
158	D-Rtt, Christ. Cannabich 15	Cannabich	*Sinfonia a 11 Stromt.:* (Wolf W-10, G-7)	Heusler 5 (most), Heusler 7 (hn. 2)	5 x 2:4a (most); 5 x 2:4b (hn. 2)	Mh. 3	Late 1750s or early 1760s (cf. the similar MSS no. 157, 160).
159	D-Rtt, Christ. Cannabich 22	Cannabich	*Sinfonia à 8 Stromt.* (Cannabich 9, Bb-2)	Heusler 5	5 x 2:3	Mh. 3	Late 1750s or early 1760s (date of Cannabich symphony).
160	D-Rtt, Christ. Cannabich 24	Cannabich	*Sinfonia à 11 Stromt.* (Cannabich 15, F-1)	Heusler 5	5 x 2:4a	Mh. 3	Early 1760s (date of Cannabich symphony; cf. the similar MSS no. 157–58).
161	D-Rtt, Christ. Cannabich 25	Cannabich	*Simphonia Concertante* (Cannabich 42, Eb-7)	Blum 5	10 x 1 (vn. 1 prin.); 10:9 (vn. 2 prin., vn. 1, vas., winds); 10:25b (vn. 2 b., bns., TP)	Mh. 16 (parts), Cannabich (TP)	Early 1770s (the work itself dates from no later than 1772; see chap. 5, @ fn. 41).
162	D-Rtt, Christ. Cannabich 34	Cannabich	*Les fetes du serailles* (ballet; no known perf. or date)	Blum 3 (strs.; ob. 2 fols. 2-3), Heusler 6 (rest of winds; perc.)	10 x 1 (strs.); 5 x 2:8 (ob. 2 fols. 2-3); 10:4a (rest, on Heusler 6 paper)	Rtt/Mh. 4 (vns. [most], cb.; winds except obs.; perc.); Mh. 3 (obs.); Mh. 14 (vn. 2 pp. 2-3, vas.)	Date uncertain; possibly from the later 1760s or first half of 1770s based on the appearance of Mh. 14 in MSS of Cannabich from that period, also the use of Blum 3 paper. In addition, rastrum 10:4a may be related to rastrum 10:3a, found also in A/VI/182, assigned here to the early or mid 1760s or possibly later. Although rastrum 2:8 is found elsewhere in the horn parts by Mh. 3 to A/III/13, which

Other Manuscripts from Mannheim

Appendix A/VI

No.	MS	Composer	Work, ID	Paper	Staving	Copyists	Comments
(162)							date from the late Mannheim or early Munich period, the handwriting there is clearly later; possibly the paper of these parts was used well after it was originally ruled.
163	D-Rtt, Fils 18	Fils	*Concerto à 7: Stromt.* in D for flute	Heusler 4b (most), Heusler 7 (fl. princ. fols. 2-3)	5 x 2:11	Mh. 3	2d half of 1750s? The rastrum 2:11 is unique to this and the next MS.
164	D-Rtt, Fils 19	Fils	*Concerto à 7 Stromt.* in C for flute	Heusler 4b	5 x 2:11	Mh. 3	Same as previous MS.
165	D-Rtt, Haymann 1	Johann Gerhard Heymann	*Concerto à 10 Stromt.* in C for oboe	Blum 5 (most), Heusler 7 (b./TP), Blum 3 (va., hns, tr. 2)	5 x 2:5a (most); 5 x 2 (TS 32.1, DS 13.2 [possibly a variant of 2.5a]; vn. 2)	Mh. 3	Mid to late 1760s (use of Blum 3 paper; presence of rastrum 2:5a in the Ritschel concerto of App. A/VI/173, which if by Johannes Ritschel [d. 1766] would date from that period).
166	D-Rtt, Haymann 2	Johann Gerhard Heymann	*Concerto à 5 Stromt.* in F for oboe	Blum 5	10 x 1	Mh. 3	Prob. early to mid 1760s.
167	D-Rtt, Haymann 4	Johann Gerhard Heymann	*Concerto à 5 Stromt.* in C for oboe	Blum 5	5 x 2:5b	Mh. 3	Prob. early to mid 1760s.
168	D-Rtt, Holzbauer 4	Holzbauer	*Sinfonia ex. D:* (D-13)	German, Strasser 1 (vn. 1); Alsatian, Palatine? (<crown/FC/grapes : bishop with staff>; vn. 2); 'J. J. Heusler 1; rest]	5 x 2:2 (vn. 1); x 5 (TS 93.2; vn. 2); 10 x 1 (rest)	Holzbauer (vn. 1, vn. 2/i); 2d copyist (vn. 2/ii-iv); Mh. 1 (rest)	Late 1750s or early 1760s, like most of the Regensburg Mannheim MSS?
169	D-Rtt, Holzbauer 6	Holzbauer	*Sinfonia à 6 Strom:* (G-1)	Blum 3	10 x 1	Mh. 1	Mid to late 1760s? (use of Blum 3 paper).

Other Manuscripts from Mannheim

No.	MS	Composer	Work, ID	Paper	Staving	Copyists	Comments
170	D-Rtt, Holzbauer 13	Holzbauer	Concerto a: 5: Stromt: in G for flute	Swiss (no WM; fl. prin., vns., b.), Heusler 5 (va.)	10 x 1; 10:28c (va.)	Mh. 1	Late 1750s–early 1760s (rastrum 10:28c also found in Cannabich 11–12, 16).
171	D-Rtt, Holzbauer 15	Holzbauer	Concerto Di Cembalo in C	Heusler 7	10:28b	Rtt/Mh. 5	What may be the number "60." (but which could also be read as 68!) on the 1st page of the MS (see fig. 2:8) might possibly represent a date of 1760, about the time implied by other elements of this MS.
172	D-Rtt, Ritschel 1	[Johannes?] Ritschel	Sinfonia à 6 Stromt: . . . Del Sig^{re} Ritschell in C	Blum 3	9-10 x 1	Mh. 1	Prob. mid to late 1760s.
173	D-Rtt, Ritschel 3	[Johannes?] Ritschel	Concerto à 5 Stromt. . . . Del Sig. Ritschel in Bb for oboe	Blum 3	5 x 2:5a	Mh. 3	Prob. mid to late 1760s.
174	D-Rtt, J. Stamitz 1	Johann Stamitz	Synphonia à 8 Stromen (F-3)	Blum 3 (most); ?Dutch (<shield {fleur-de-lis}>; hn. 2)	10 x 1 (same rastrum as no. 178)	Rtt/Mh. 1 (most, incl. TP incipit); Rtt/Mh. 2 (TP text)	Early or mid 1760s (see chap. 9).
175	D-Rtt, J. Stamitz 2	Johann Stamitz	Sinfonia (F-4)	Blum 2 (ob. 1, prob. va.), Heusler 2 (ob. 2, hns.; rest of MS local)	10 x 1 (not same rastrum as previous MS)	Rtt/Mh. 1	1750s.
176	D-Rtt, J. Stamitz 4[a]	Johann Stamitz	Synphonia a 8. (G-3)	Swiss (no WM; most); prob. Blum 2 (hn. 1), Heusler 2 (hn. 2)	5 x 2:10a	Rtt/Mh. 1	1750s.

285

Appendix A/VI

No.	MS	Composer	Work, ID	Paper	Staving	Copyists	Comments
177	D-Rtt, J. Stamitz 5	Johann Stamitz	Symphonia a 8. (G-4)	Swiss (no WM)	5 x 2:10a	Rtt/Mh. 1	Mid to late 1750s.
178	D-Rtt, J. Stamitz 6	Johann Stamitz	Symphonia à 8 Stromen (G-7)	Swiss (no WM; vns.); Blum 2 (ob. 1, prob. b.); Heusler 2 (ob. 2, hn. 1; prob. va., hn. 2)	10 x 1 (same rastrum as no. 174)	Rtt/Mh. 1 (most, incl. TP incipit); Rtt/Mh. 2 (text of TP)	1750s.
179	D-Rtt, J. Stamitz 10	Johann Stamitz	Symphonia à 11 Instr: (D-8)	Heusler 2 (vns., obs., prob. va.); Swiss (no WM; hns., trs., timp.)	5 x 2:9 (vns., va., obs.); 10 x 1 (hns., trs., timp.)	Rtt/Mh. 1 (parts), Rtt/Mh. 2 (TP w. incipit [see fig. D:17])	1750s.
180	D-Rtt, J. Stamitz 11	Johann Stamitz	Symphonia a 11. (D-11)	Swiss (no WM)	5 x 2:10b	Rtt/Mh. 1	Mid to late 1750s.
181	D-Rtt, J. Stamitz 12	Johann Stamitz	Symphonia à 8. (D-12)	Swiss (no WM)	5 x 2:10a	Rtt/Mh. 1	Mid to late 1750s.
182	D-Rtt, J. Stamitz 13	Johann Stamitz	Symphonia. a 11 Stromen: (D-15)	Heusler 7 (vns.), Blum 3 (rest)	10:16 (vn. 1), 10:3a (vn. 2, with TP); 10 x 1 (rest)	Rtt/Mh. 3 (most), Rtt/Mh. 1 (va. through p. 1, staff 4, m. 15; b.)	Early or mid 1760s, possibly later. See fig. D:16 for p. 1 of the va. part.
183	D-Rtt, J. Stamitz 18	Johann Stamitz	Symphonia à 8 Stromen. (Eb-6a)	Swiss (no WM; vns.), Heusler 2 (obs.), Blum 2 (hn. 2, prob. hn. 1); va., b. prob. also Heusler or Blum 2	5 x 2:9 (vns.); 10 x 1 (rest)	Rtt/Mh. 1 (most, incl. TP incipit); Rtt/Mh. 2 (text of TP)	2d half of 1750s.
184	D-Rtt, Toeschi 3	Joseph Toeschi	Sinfonia a 14 Stromenti (C-8; Münster 37 [1768/69])	Heusler 5 (most), Heusler 7 (va./TP, ob. 2)	5 x 2:3 (vn. 1, fl. 2, ob. 2, hn. 1, trs.); 5 x 2:12 (rest)	Rtt/Mh. 3 (most); Mh. 3 (text only: TP, face page of ob. parts)	Prob. late 1750s or 1st half of 1760s based on the codicological evidence, despite the fact that this symphony was published considerably later, in 1768/69 (see chap. 9, @ fn. 33). Cf the similar MSS App. A/VI/153, 155, 189.

Other Manuscripts from Mannheim

No.	MS	Composer	Work, ID	Paper	Staving	Copyists	Comments
185	D-Rtt, Toeschi 6	Joseph Toeschi	Sinfonia a 8 Istromenti (G-7; Münster 42 [1771])	Blum 3	10 x 1, 12 x 1	Mh. 2	Prob. mid to late 1760s (Blum 3 paper, date published [1771]).
186	D-Rtt, Toeschi 7	[Richter]	Sinfonia (Richter G-3)	Blum 3	10 x 1	Rtt/Mh. 3 (vn. 2, p. 1, staves 1-5; obs., hns.); Rtt/Mh. 1 (va., but TP on va. part prob. local; rest of vn. 2)	Mid to late 1760s (Blum paper) or possibly earlier (presence of Rtt/Mh. 1, copyist of most of the Stamitz symphonies in Regensburg; see chap. 9). The misattribution of this fairly well-known Richter symphony to Toeschi was made by what appears to be a local copyist, thus helping to explain the error.
187	D-Rtt, Toeschi 10	Joseph Toeschi	Sinfonia a 8 Stromt. (D-10; Münster 4 [1762/63])	Swiss (no WM; vns., b./TP); Heusler 7 (va., winds)	10:28a (vns., b./TP); 5 x 2:7 (va., winds)	Mh. 3 (most), 2d copyist (vn. 2/i)	Prob. late 1750s or early 1760s.
188	D-Rtt, Toeschi 11	Joseph Toeschi	Sinfonia a 12 Istromenti (D-11; Münster 44 [1773])	Blum 3	10 x 1	Mh. 2	Prob. mid to late 1760s (Blum 3 paper, date published [1773]).
189	D-Rtt, Toeschi 16	Joseph Toeschi	Sinfonia a 8 Stromt. (B♭-2; Münster 8 [1762])	Heusler 5	5 x 2:3	Rtt/Mh. 3 (vns., va., ob. 2, hns.); Mh. 3 (text only: TP; face page of vn. 1; rest local)	Prob. late 1750s or early 1760s. Cf. the similar MSS App. A/VI/153 (Cannabich 3), 155, 184.
190	D-Rtt, Toeschi 18	Joseph Toeschi	Sinfonia à 8: Stromt. (E♭-4; Münster 11 [1762])	Heusler 5 (most), Heusler 7 (obs.)	5 x 2:12 (vns. pp. 1, 4); 5 x 2:3 (rest)	Mh. 3	Prob. late 1750s or early 1760s.

Appendix A/VI

No.	MS	Composer	Work, ID	Paper	Staving	Copyists	Comments
191	D-Rtt, Toeschi 19	Joseph Toeschi	Sinfonia à 8 Stromt. (E♭-2; Münster 6 [1762])	Heusler 7 (most), Heusler 5 (bns.; prob. hns., fl. 2)	5 x 2:3 (most); 5 x 2:12 (bns.)	Mh. 3 (most), Rtt/Mh. 3 (hns.)	Prob. late 1750s or early 1760s.
192	D-SWl, Mus. 2904	Holzbauer	Sinfonia (F-2)	Blum 5 (vns, b., obs., hn. 1); Heusler 7 (vas., bns., hn. 2/TP); Blum 3 (new 2d mvt. in vn. 2, b. [pasted over orig.] and obs. [sep. sheets, inserted loosely])	10:25c (vn. 1); 10:30d (vn. 2, b.); 10:17b (vas., bns.); 10:10 (obs., hn. 1; new 2d mvt. in obs., vn. 2, b.); 10 x 1 (hn. 2)	Mh. 8 (vn. 1); Mh. 2 (vn. 2, b.); Mh. 19 (vas., bns., hn. 2); 4th copyist (obs., hn. 1); 5th copyist (new 2d mvt. in obs., vn. 2, b.); Holzbauer (TP)	This MS shows an extensive process of revision, with a new second movement added (see the section on Schwerin in chap. 9). *Date*: mid to late 1760s based on the clear evidence of the staving (both original and revision).
193	D-SWl, Mus. 5440	Joseph Toeschi	Sinfonia à 8 Stromti (D-3; Münster 41 [1769])	Blum 3	10 x 1	?Johann Cramer (very early) or possibly Mh. 1 (?)	Mid to late 1760s or later (Johann Cramer was only born in 1749).
194	F-Pc, L.73	Cannabich ("Del Sig.e Christiano Cannabich")	Quintetto for 2 fls, vn., va., vc. in F	Heusler 7	10:3b	All one copyist (unique)	Based on the use in this MS of a variant of rastrum 10:3a—found elsewhere only in App. A/VI/182, a Stamitz symphony in Regensburg also on Heusler 7 paper)—this MS can probably be dated to the early or mid 1760s or possibly later.
195	F-Pc, L.2603	Cannabich ("Del Sig.e Christiano Cannabich")	Violino Solo con Basso in A	Blum 5	10:4b	All one copyist (unique)	Based on the use in this MS of a variant of rastrum 10:4a—found elsewhere only in App. A/VI/162, a Cannabich ballet tentatively assigned here to the late 1760s or early 1770s—this MS might also date from that period; otherwise prob. 1760s.

No.	MS	Composer	Work, ID	Paper	Staving	Copyists		Comments
196	GB-Lbl, Add. 16119 (score, "Mannheim" binding)	Salieri	La Secchia Rapita (5 Nov. 1774)	Alsatian, Weyhr 1	2 x 5:5a (p. 62, etc.), 5b (pp. 28–29, etc.), 5c (pp. 55–56, etc.), 5d (pp. 1–17, etc.); 5:6a (pp. 180, 182, etc.), 6b (pp. 181, 183, etc.); 5:11a (pp. 18–27, etc.), 11b (pp. 57, 59, etc.), 11c (p. 38, etc.), 11d (pp. 63–68, etc.); 6 x 2 (pp. 708–23 [final chorus])	Mh. 5		1774+. From Sickingen collection. Table 8:1, no. 14b; Corneilson/Wolf no. 16b.
197	GB-Lbl, Add. 30792-94 (score, 3 vols.)ᵐ	Piccinni	Catone in Utica (5 Nov. 1770; premiere)	Heusler 6	10:1	Mh. 5		1770+. Table 8:1, no. 12b; Corneilson/Wolf no. 14b.
198	I-MOe, Mus. F. 587 (score only)	Holzbauer	Missa non Brevis a 4ᵗʳᵒ voci in G (Schmitt I.25)	Heusler 6	10:1	Mh. 5		1770s (rastrum 10:1 found ca. 1770–78).
199	I-MOe, Mus. F. 591 (score only; Benedictus inserted, also = Mannheim)	Holzbauer	Messa. a 4.° Voci, Con Instrumenti in Eb (Schmitt I.18)	Heusler 6 (all, incl. Benedictus)	10:1 (all, incl. Benedictus)	Mh. 5 (all, incl. Benedictus)		1770s (rastrum 10:1 found ca. 1770–78).

Appendix A/VI

No.	MS	Composer	Work, ID	Paper	Staving	Copyists	Comments
200	US-CAhm, Mus 800. 21.605 (cage) (unbound vocal score, voice parts plus b.c. only)	[Anton Schweitzer]	*Alceste* (numerous perfs. Schwetzingen and Mannheim, 13 Aug. 1775–5 Nov. 1776)	Blum 5 (most), Heusler 7 (last two gatherings)	4 and 5 x 2:13 (most), 10:1 (last two gatherings)	Mh. 5	1775[+]. From Sickingen collection; see the discussion of table 8:2 in chap. 8. Table 8:1, no. 15 (q.v.; not in Corneilson/Wolf).
201	US-Rs, M 1500.J759C (score)	Jommelli, Giuseppe Colla	*Il Cajo Fabrizio* (5 Nov. 1760; premiere). See also no. 203.	Heusler 7	10 x 1	Mh. 6	1760[+]. Table 8:1, no. 9b; Corneilson/Wolf no. 11b.
?202	US-STu, MLM 766 (set of parts for cemb. 1 and 2 and orch., with TP on bass part)[n]	Mozart	*Concerto per il Cembalo Principale Primo ... Terzo* (K. 242; composed Feb. 1776, perf. Mannheim 12 March 1778)[o]	Heusler 5 (cemb. parts), Blum 5 (orch. parts)	6 x 2 (TS 25.6, DS 8, cemb. parts; in addition, a tiny one-stave rastrum is occasionally used to add a staff); 2 x 5:23 (orch. parts)	Stanf./Mh. 1 (*not* Leopold Mozart, as stated on TP)	1777/78, if this MS did indeed originate in Mannheim; though the Mannheim provenance of the MS receives support from the context, no definitive conclusion can be reached in that neither the rastrum nor the copyist is otherwise known.
203	US-Wc, M 1500.J72 C35 (score; "Mannheim" binding, with Sickingen coat of arms)	Jommelli, Giuseppe Colla	*Cajo Fabrizio*[,] Opera (5 Nov. 1760; premiere). See also no. 201.	Blum 6	10:2 (pp. 1–4, etc.); 2 x 5:22 (pp. 5–7, etc.), 5:20a (pp. 46–121, etc.), 5:21 (pp. 122–25, etc.), 5:20b (pp. 222–53; 636-46 [final chorus])	Mh. 5	1760[+]. From Sickingen collection. Table 8:1, no. 9a; Corneilson/Wolf no. 11a. A reprod. of the back cover of this MS, showing the Sickingen coat of arms, appears in fig. 8:7b and Corneilson/Wolf, 271.

No.	MS	Composer	Work, ID	Paper	Staving	Copyists	Comments
204	US-Wc, M 1500.T76 S5 (score, 3 vols.)	Traetta	*Sofonisba. Dramma per Musica da Rappresentarsi alla Corte Elettorale Palatina . . . L'anno 1763* (orig. 5 Nov. 1762; premiere). See also no. 37.	Blum 5	10 x 1	Mh. 1	1763+. Slightly revised version of App. A/VI/ 37, here dated 1763 on TP. Table 8:1, no. 16b; Corneilson/ Wolf no. 17.

a The existence of this manuscript was kindly reported to me by Paul Corneilson. I was only able to examine it shortly before this book went to press, too late to undertake a renumbering of Appendix A/VI.

b For a mod. ed. of this ballet, with reprods. from this manuscript, see RRMCE, vol. 57, ed. Carol G. Marsh (1999; see Bibliography).

c For a mod. ed. of this ballet, with reprods. from this manuscript, see RRMCE, vol. 47, ed. Nicole Baker (1997; see Bibliography).

d Surprisingly, this copyist also appears in the local manuscript D-Rtt Christ. Cannabich 23 (Cannabich 35; obs., clar. 1 only), side by side with several local Regensburg copyists. Hence he must have been at the Thurn und Taxis court at some point, briefly or otherwise.

e For a mod. ed. of this work, with reprods. and a full discussion of the manuscript and its history, see *Ignaz Holzbauer / Franz Beck: Solowerke für Sopran und Orchester*, Musik der Mannheimer Hofkapelle, 2, ed. Bärbel Pelker (Stuttgart: Carus-Verlag, 1999).

f For a mod. ed. of this opera, with reprods. from this manuscript, see RRMCE, vol. 46, ed. Paul Corneilson (1996; see Bibliography). For a reprod. of the front cover of this manuscript see fig. 8:2 and Corneilson/Wolf, 264.

g Act 2, sc. 14 of this manuscript has been inserted in the manuscript; it is not from Mannheim.

h App. A/VI/39–119 are from the collection of Ludwig Freiherr von Pretlack, most of which stems from the period ca. 1745–60 (see chap. 9 and Joachim Jaenecke, *Die Musikbibliothek des Ludwig Freiherrn von Pretlack* (Wiesbaden: Breitkopf & Härtel, 1973), which provided many of the identifications in the following section.

i For this and similar information in the section to follow I am grateful to Mary S. Macklem (University of Pennsylvania) for her expert research on arias of the Pretlack collection.

j These two arias were identified by Paul Cauthen of the University of Cincinnati.

k Helmut Hell, *Die neapolitanische Opernsinfonie in der ersten Hälfte des 18. Jahrhunderts* (Tutzing: Hans Schneider, 1971), 587.

l A facsimile of this manuscript appears in *The Collected Works of J. C. Bach*, vol. 8, ed. Ernest Warburton (New York: Garland Publishing, 1986).

m A facsimile of this manuscript appears in Howard Mayer Brown, *Italian Opera, 1640–1770*, vol. 50 (New York: Garland Publishing, 1978). For a comprehensive study of the opera, including the present source, see Wolfram Enßlin, *Niccolò Piccinni, Catone in Utica: Quellenüberlieferung, Aufführungsgeschichte und Analyse* (Frankfurt am Main: Peter Lang, 1996).

n None of the other portions of MLM 766, including the third piano part, is from Mannheim; see chap. 9, @ fn. 40.

o On these dates see chap. 9, @ fnn. 40–45.

Appendix B

Paper

Appendix B provides information on the most important papers and watermarks in the Mannheim complex of manuscripts, superseding Appendix B of Eugene K. and Jean K. Wolf, "A Newly Identified Complex of Manuscripts from Mannheim," *JAMS* 27 (1974): 379–437. (See also the section "Paper and Watermarks" in chapter 2 of the present book.) Swiss paper, by far the most common, is treated first, followed by local German (primarily Palatine), Dutch, and Alsatian paper. A supplement then lists several Italian and south German papers used only in Munich after the court moved there in 1778. Under each national type the arrangement is alphabetical by manufacturer or, if the manufacturer is unknown, place of manufacture or a monogram present in the watermark. When more than one paper from a given family or firm occurs, these are generally designated by the family name and a number (e.g., Blum 1, Blum 2, etc., for papers produced in mills owned by the Blum family); the order is approximately chronological, though much overlap will inevitably occur.

After the name of the paper there appears a concise listing, in parentheses, of the principal components of each version of the watermark, based freely upon the principles outlined in Jan LaRue, "Abbreviated Description for Watermarks," *Fontes artis musicae* 4 (1957): 27. These abbreviated descriptions or taxonomies are designed to reflect what we know to have been the manufacturing process employed in producing paper during this period, namely that two different molds were normally used in alternation, resulting in papers with two more-or-less distinct sets of watermarks; in order to be accurate, these "twins" must be carefully distinguished one from the other.

The two primary methods for avoiding confusion between twins were propagated in studies of Mozart's and Beethoven's manuscripts by Alan Tyson: (1) always to reproduce a watermark from the *mold* (rather than the felt) side of the paper, which is usually distinguishable by the slight impressions left by the wire of the watermarks and the chain-lines; and (2) always to distinguish carefully between the *principal watermark* (the larger and more distinctive of the two marks, in Swiss papers generally situated on the left half of the original uncut sheet of paper when viewed from the mold side) and the *countermark* on the opposite side, being certain to specify their precise placement in the original sheet. In labeling watermarks in the present study, a single centered colon is used to separate the watermark and countermark of a specific sheet of paper, but *without* any implication as to whether that sheet represents twin A or B, a fact that for various reasons may be impossible to determine with any certainty.

Using these principles, we find that most relationships between twin papers in the Mannheim complex of manuscripts fall into one of three categories:

1. What I call the **transposition type** (*transposition* referring to typographical rather

Appendix B

than musical transposition!). Here the basic forms of the watermark and countermark of twin A remain the same, though with enough variation to show that two different molds are involved; but in twin B they appear on the opposite folio by comparison with twin A:

Twin A   Twin B

E : F   F : E

This relationship, the most common among the Swiss papers utilized at Mannheim, is symbolized in the abbreviated descriptions by a transposition sign between the two components rather than a colon, for example "Papermaker 1 (<E ~ F>)." Note in this example the use of angle brackets to set off actual components of the watermark, rather like specialized quotation marks.

2. The **mirror type**, in which twin B represents a full inversion of twin A—as though the entire sheet had been turned over from right to left:

Twin A   Twin B

E : F   ꟻ : Ǝ

This arrangement, ubiquitous in Italian and Dutch paper of the eighteenth century, is common only in the earliest Swiss papers of the Mannheim complex, after which it is generally replaced by the transposition type. It may be symbolized as follows: "Papermaker 2 (<E ∩ F>)."

3. The **variation type**, in which the components remain in the same position (e.g., the principal watermark remains on the left, the countermark on the right) but, just as in the previous examples, show enough identifiable differences to indicate that two molds have been employed:

Twin A   Twin B

E : F   E : F

This type, rare among the papers favored at Mannheim, may be symbolized "Papermaker 3 (<E :: F>)," indicating that the papermaker was using two versions of a similar mold.

Three final conventions in the description of watermarks are (1) the use of a solidus (slash) between two components to indicate that the second appears below the first; (2) the use of a vertical line (|) between two components to indicate that the second appears to the right of the first; and (3) the use of curly brackets ({ }) around an item to mean that it appears within the previous element, for example a fleur-de-lis within a shield. Thus, the designation "Papermaker 4 (<shield {fleur-de-lis}/4 | cross ~ blank folio>)" would denote a transposition type in which, on the left half of the bifolio, twin A has a shield containing a fleur-de-lis, under which is found the papermaker's mark "4" with a cross to its right; no countermark appears on the right half. By contrast, as indicated by the transposition sign, twin B has a blank folio on the left and an unmirrored variant of the <shield/4|cross> complex on the right.

Within the abbreviated description of the watermark, the makeup of the twins will, as already illustrated, be specified by the use of either a transposition sign, a backwards curved arrow, or a double colon; when these are insufficient to delineate the characteristics of the paper clearly, each twin will receive a separate description, separated by a comma. After the abbreviated description come (1) any relevant comments on the paper in question, especially its provenance and dating; (2) a list of the manuscripts containing that paper, always referring to the full description of the source in Appendix A; (3) citations of selected reproductions of the watermarks in other publications, details of which may be found in the Bibliography; and (4) tracings of at least twin A of the most important watermarks, with the principal mark and the countermark separated by a solid line. Most of the tracings have been redrawn in ink (with the inevitable minor distortions any recopying entails), while those for Blum 1 and 6 consist of enhanced reproductions of our actual pencil tracings.

With respect to (2) above, it must again be emphasized that full information on precisely which parts of the manuscript contain which paper, the dating of the source, and the like do not appear here, in Appendix B, but in Appendix A, the full catalogue of the Mannheim manuscripts. However, the list of manuscripts given in Appendix B does supply any firm dates present in, or convincingly assignable to, the various manuscripts, in order to give an idea of the chronological span during which the paper in question was employed at Mannheim. (On the conventions for dates employed here see the introduction to Appendix A.)

I. Swiss Paper

Paper manufactured by the Blum and Heusler families in Basel and its vicinity was among the finest in Europe. The high quality of their paper, together with the fact that the Rhine flows northward from Basel past Mannheim, doubtless explains why it was the overwhelming choice of the electoral court not only for manuscript documents such as music and registers, but also for printed music, engravings, and books. Information given here about the firms of Blum and Heusler has been derived primarily from W. Fr. Tschudin, *The Ancient Paper-Mills of Basle and Their Marks* (Hilversum: Paper Publications Society, 1958), which is itself partly based on Paul Heitz, *Les filigranes avec la crosse de Bâle* (Strasbourg: J. H. Ed. Heitz, 1904).

1. Blum Papers

The Blum family owned various mills in and around Basel from as early as 1530 until 1788 (Tschudin, 229). For most of that period their house mark was a stylized *B*, often in combination with the famous crozier of Basel (see Blum 1–3 below). However, one of the two last important members of the family, Hieronymus Blum III, preferred the mark <H Blum>;

Appendix B

he operated mills in Basel only in the years 1756–88 (Tschudin, 139), allowing one to assign approximate dates to papers containing that mark (see Blum 4–7 below). Blum papers are second in frequency only to Heusler papers among the Mannheim manuscripts; interestingly, they appear in no manuscripts at all after the move to Munich, whereas Heusler papers continued to find favor there for a time.

In addition to the papers treated below, two other Blum papers should be mentioned that appear only once within the Mannheim manuscripts: (1) the rare paper found in App. A/I/8 of 1733 (<eagle/shield {Basel crozier}/B>; see the similar mark reproduced in Tschudin, 181, no. 315); (2) the paper used for the endpapers of A/IV/3 of 1748 (<crown/CC [first C backwards, as in Coco Chanel's well-known monogram] ∩ ornamental oval frame {Basel crozier}/B>; see the reprod. in Tschudin, 193, no. 340).

Blum 1 (*Blum 1a*: twin A: <B : Basel crozier>, twin B: <Basel crozier [mirrored] : blank folio>; *Blum 1b*: <B ∩ Basel crozier>). NB: the designation "Blum 1" below and in Appendix A means that only twin A is present in the manuscript, that is, that a distinction between Blum 1a and 1b, which share the same principal watermark, is not possible.

Blum 1 and 1a, twin A:

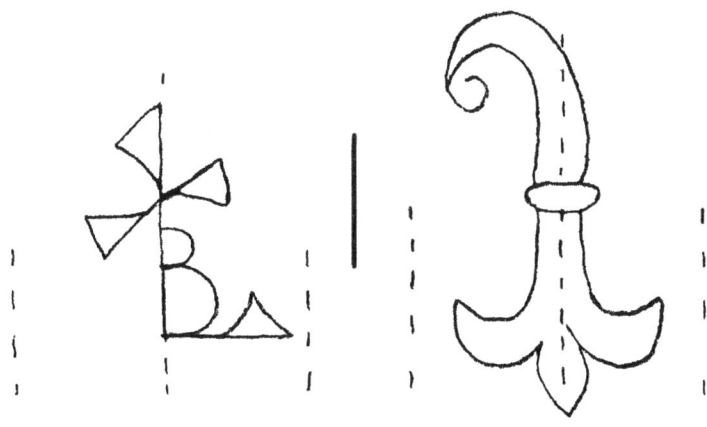

Blum 1a, twin B:

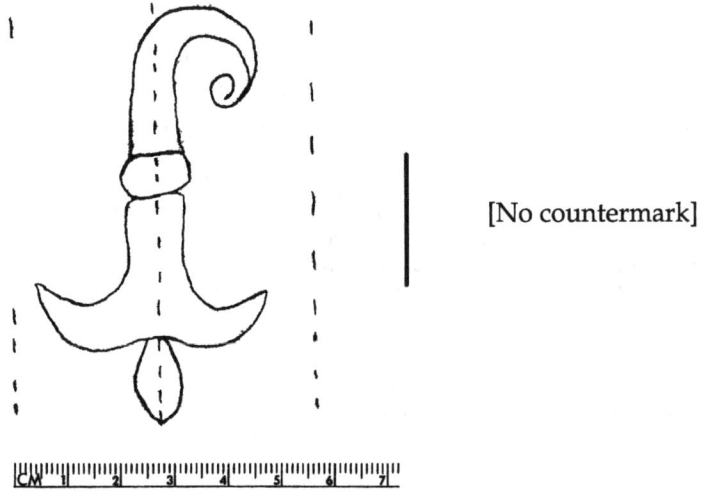

[No countermark]

Blum 1b, twin A: same as twin A of Blum 1 and 1a.

Blum 1b, twin B:

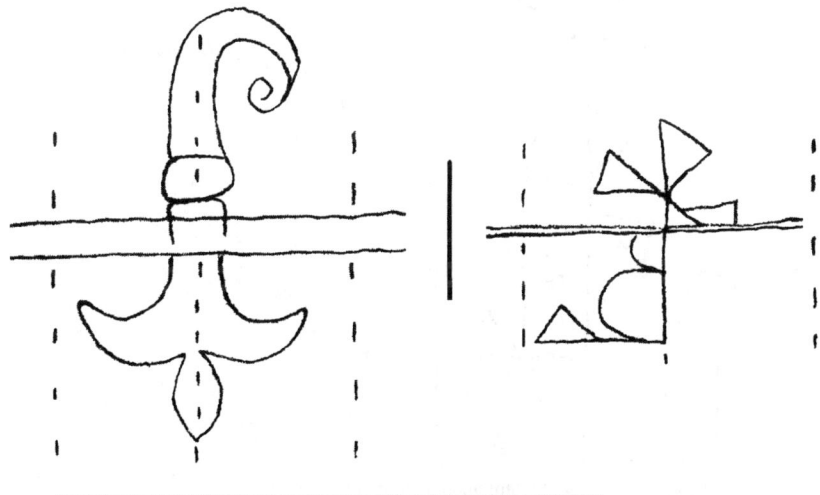

Appendix B

Blum 1 paper presents a more complex picture than usual in that two different forms of twin B occur. As illustrated above, in twin B of what I shall call Blum 1a, a mirrored (i.e., backwards) form of the crozier appears on the left and a blank folio on the right, while in twin B of Blum 1b *all* of twin A appears in mirrored form, with mirrored (backwards) forms of both the crozier on the left and the *B* on the right; possibly the backward *B* mark was simply wired to the previously blank mesh on the right side of the twin B mold of Blum 1a. Blum 1 paper is common in manuscripts at Mannheim from the late 1740s and especially the 1750s.

Found in: Blum 1a: A/I/12 (1753); A/II/21; A/III/4, 7–8; A/IV/3 (1748); A/VI/3–4, 18 [ca. 1755⁺], 21, 45, 47, 55, 87, 89, 92, 98–101 (nos. 87–92 and 98–101 are from Holzbauer operas premiered at Mannheim in 1754–57), 144 (1753, 1756), 146, 148–49, 154. Blum 1b: A/II/5; A/VI/40–41, 43, 61, 113, 119. Blum 1: A/IV/1 (1757); A/VI/110, 112.

Blum 2 (<Basel crozier/B ∩? blank folio>)

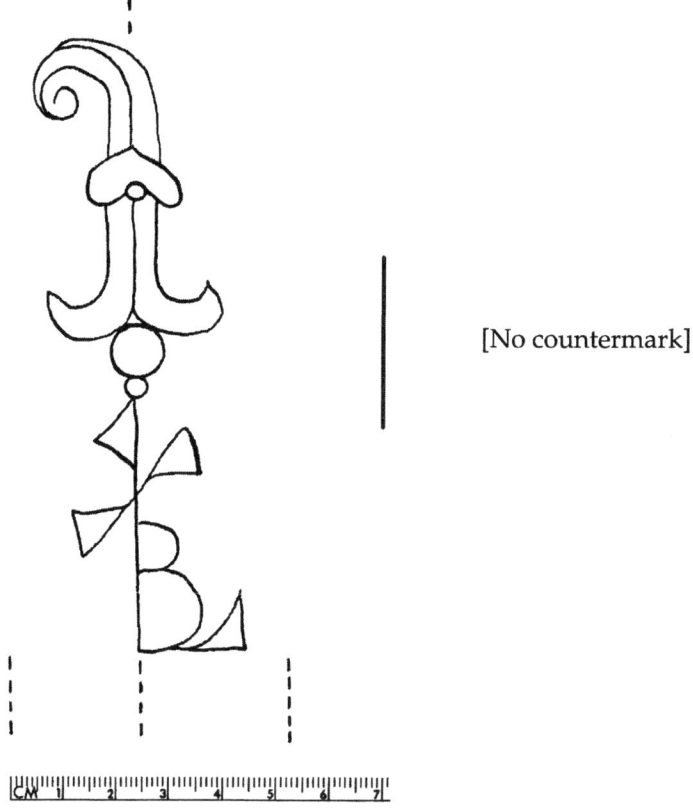

[No countermark]

Blum 2 is found in only four Mannheim manuscripts, all symphonies by Johann Stamitz in Regensburg (D-Rtt). The paper of these manuscripts is cut strangely, along the chain-lines, making it difficult to determine the precise composition of the twins; they are most likely mirrored, as was the case with Blum 1. Like most of the manuscripts making use of the latter paper, these sources can be assigned to the 1750s, though Heitz located an example of this watermark as early as 1709 (see below).

Found in: A/VI/175–76, 178, 183.

Additional reproductions: Tschudin, 151, no. 196, taken from Heitz, *Bâle*, no. 80 (dated 1709; see Tschudin, 130).

Blum 3 (<shield {fleur-de-lis} ~ B>)

Appendix B

In addition to the usual transposed twins of Blum 3, the *B* alone occasionally occurs without a countermark (i.e., <B : blank folio>), as in App. A/VI/118, an aria from Majo's *Semiramide* of 1751, and D-Rtt, "Bernasconi" 4 (dated 1756; the paper of the latter manuscript may well have been obtained in Mannheim by the true composer of this work, Franz Xaver Pokorny, during his stay there in early 1754). Blum 3 is very common in Mannheim manuscripts of the 1750s and first half of the 1760s; dates found range from 1751 to 1766, and it occurs in numerous arias in the Pretlack collection in Berlin from operas of the early 1750s.

Found in: A/I/11 (1751), 13 (1766); A/II/12 (1763); A/IV/2 [1766]; A/VI/3–4, 11–12, 18 [ca. 1755$^+$], 23, 29, 47–56, 85, 100–101, 106–7, 111, 114–16, 118 (<B : blank folio>), 145, 156, 162, 165, 169, 172–74, 182, 185–86, 188, 192–93.

Blum 4 (*Blum 4a*: <shield {fleur-de-lis} ∩ H BLUM>; *Blum 4b*: <somewhat different shield {fleur-de-lis}/beehive ~ H BLUM> [the lettering of the latter is smaller than in Blum 4a]). NB: the designation "Blum 4" below and in Appendix A means that I am uncertain whether the manuscript uses Blum 4a or 4b paper.

The paper designated here as Blum 4 encompasses two different, rare variants of Blum 5, both manufactured by Hieronymus Blum III, as indicated by their countermark, <H BLUM>. The first, Blum 4a, lacks the typical beehive below the shield found in Blum 4b and 5 (the beehive presumably evokes the meaning of *Blume* [flower]). In addition, neither 4a nor 4b includes the word *Basel* found in Blum 5 (and also 7). Blum 4b in particular may thus be related to the later paper Blum 6 (which also lacks the *Basel*) as well as to Blum 5, and indeed the one example of it occurs in a manuscript that must postdate 1772.

Found in: Blum 4a: A/VI/2. Blum 4b: A/VI/5 [1772$^+$]. Blum 4: A/I/6.

Blum 5 (<shield {fleur-de-lis}/beehive/H BLUM ~ BASEL>)

See next page for tracing.

Blum 5, found in some 75 manuscripts, is the second most popular paper within the Mannheim complex, after Heusler 5. It appears throughout the period from ca. 1760 (Cannabich's symphony A/III/8) until the departure of the court in 1778 (Cannabich's symphony A/III/54, considered here to be his penultimate Mannheim work). Despite the longevity and relative stability of this mark, careful comparison, especially of the lettering, can often lead to a more precise dating.

Found in: A/I/1 (1763); A/II/1, 4–5, 7–11, 12 (1763), 13–17, 18 (1765); A/III/8, 13–14, 16–19, 21–25, 29, 31–32, 34, 36, 38–41, 43–46, 48, 54, M5–7; A/IV/2 [1766], 6, 9, 10a–b [1767–68]; A/V/2a (1772), 22–23, 25, 33 [1775]; A/VI/5 [1772$^+$], 8, 13 [1768$^+$], 14–16, 19 [1766$^+$], 28, 31 [1764$^+$], 38 [1764$^+$], 145, 150 [1770$^+$], 161, 165–67, 192, 195, 200 [1775$^+$], ?202 [?1777/78], 204 [1763$^+$].

Blum 5:

Additional reproductions: Tyson, NMA, no. 49; Haberkamp, KBM, vol. 3, p. 262, HR 62.

Appendix B

Blum 6 (<shield {fleur-de-lis}/bell ~ H Blum>)

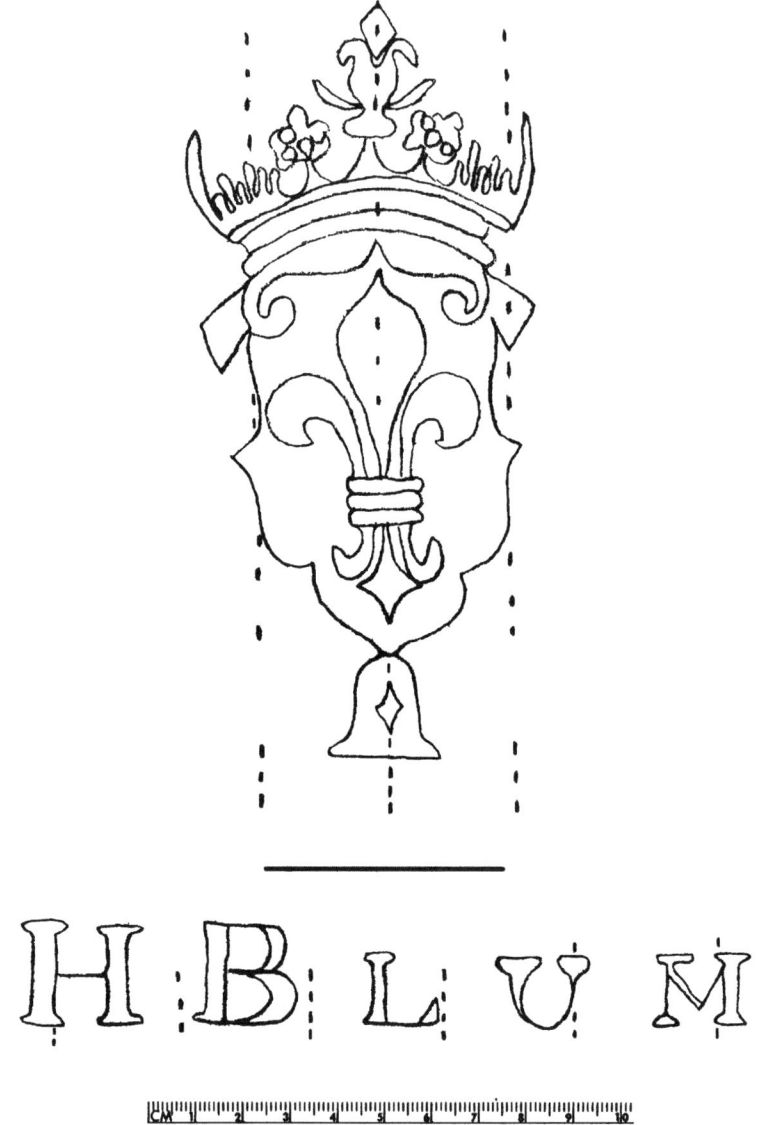

Blum 6 is a common variant of Hieronymus Blum papers, omitting the word *Basel* and combining selected elements of the Blum marks 4–5 and 7. In Blum 6 as well as Blum 7 the beehive of Blum 4b and 5 is replaced by a bell. Blum 6 is found in Mannheim manuscripts from ca. 1760 through the mid-1770s.

Found in: A/II/4, 18–19 (1765); A/III/27; A/V/11 (1776), 15b (1776), 23 (?); A/VI/2.5, 15, 33 [1766⁺], 37 [1762⁺], 120–24, 125 [1763⁺], 126–38, 139 [1772⁺], 203 [1760⁺].

Additional reproductions: Jochen Reutter, *Studien zur Kirchenmusik Franz Xaver Richters* (Frankfurt am Main: Peter Lang, 1993), 1:605.

Blum 7 (<shield {fleur-de-lis}/bell/H BLUM ~ BASEL>)

A fairly common late variant of Blum 5, now with a bell below the shield, as in Blum 6. The <H BLUM> appears in two different positions, the first with the *B* under the bell, the second with the *L* under the bell. Blum 7 occurs in Mannheim manuscripts from the second half of the 1760s through the late 1770s.

Found in: A/V/20 [1777]; A/VI/8, 10, 25, 27 [1779], 33–34 [1766⁺].

2. Heusler Papers

The Heusler family, which included many of Basel's most renowned papermakers, was active for the remarkably extended period of 1519 to 1859 (Tschudin, 223–24). In addition to Basel, from 1735 until 1819 they operated mills in the neighboring margraviate of Baden that were major sources of paper for the Mannheim court; the watermark of these papers often incorporates the Baden coat of arms, with its distinctive pair of simple diagonal stripes (see nos. 5 and 8 below). The Heusler family mark was, somewhat confusingly, an *M* with a cross attached above (see Heusler 1a and 4 and also the paper ?Blum or Heusler 1, below). An *H* for Heusler and a second, vertical crossbar were often added to the original crossbar (see Heusler 2 and 4b, below).

In addition to the papers given below, the flyleaves of A/I/8 (1733) utilize Heusler paper (<Basel crozier in laurel wreath : cross/M>; see the reprod. in *The Nostitz Papers*, ed. E. J. Labarre [Hilversum: Paper Publications Society, 1955], plate 41, no. 186).

Heusler 1 (*Heusler 1a*: <cross/M ∩ blank folio>; *Heusler 1b*: <shield {fleur-de-lis} ∩ N H>)

See next page for tracing of Heusler 1a.

The paper labeled here as Heusler 1 comprises two different, rare papers with dates in the 1730s. The first, Heusler 1a, has the standard Heusler housemark alone (cf. Heusler 4a, below, a somewhat smaller version). The second, Heusler 1b, has as its main watermark the shield enclosing a fleur-de-lis common in Swiss marks and a countermark with the letters *N H* (for Niklaus Heusler) about 2.8 cm. apart. Both papers have mirrored twins. Yet

Appendix B

Heusler 1a:

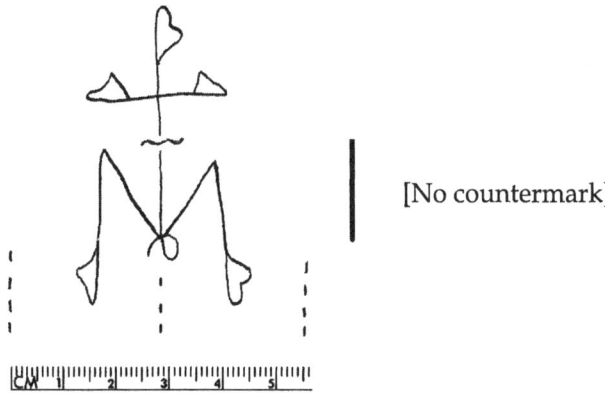

[No countermark]

another version of this paper, combining a shield similar to that of Heusler 1b with the <cross/M> of 1a, is found in the local manuscript D-Rtt, Pokorny 13, dated 17 November 1754; Pokorny probably obtained this paper at Mannheim during his stay there earlier in 1754.

Found in: Heusler 1a: A/I/8 (1733). Heusler 1b: A/I/9 (1737).

Heusler 2 (<blank folio :: cross with vertical crossbar/H/M>)

[No watermark]

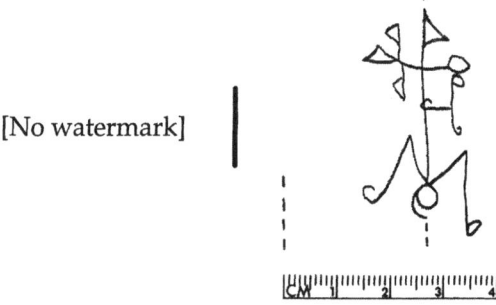

Judging by the Holzbauer and Cannabich examples listed below (A/II/7, A/III/M1), Heusler 2 is evidently a rare example among the Mannheim manuscripts of variation-type twins; that is, twin B is similar to twin A except that in the latter the *M* is more upright rather than tilting to the right, as in the tracing above. (The paper of the Stamitz examples, A/VI/175

304

et seq., is cut along the chain-lines, disallowing easy determination of the original makeup of the sheets. Cf. also Heusler 4b, with a different, considerably larger, version of the H/M complex.) This paper was used at Mannheim in the 1750s.

Found in: A/II/7; A/III/M1; A/VI/175–76, 178–79, 183.

Heusler 3 (<fleur-de-lis : NH>)

A somewhat smaller, better-quality paper reminiscent of post paper. Heusler 3 is found only in manuscripts of the Pretlack collection copied by Mannheim 1, all arias from operas of the period 1751–60. The N and H of the countermark are connected, sharing the middle vertical (as in Heusler 8, but in Heusler 3 with the correct diagonal and without the cross).

Found in: A/VI/44, 107–8, 117–18.

Heusler 4 (*Heusler 4a*: <shield {fleur-de-lis} ~ [∩?] cross/M> [cf. Heusler 1a; the shield of A/VI/106 is considerably larger than that of A/VI/111]; *Heusler 4b*: <different shield {fleur-de-lis} ~ cross with vertical crossbar/H/M [cf. Heusler 2]>)

The two rare, transitional papers included under Heusler 4 each have different shields. Their countermarks, though similar in form to those of Heusler 1a and 2, have become significantly larger: the M of Heusler 4a is ca. 2.2 cm. in height, while those of Heusler 4b are 2.5 cm. (twin A) and 2 cm. (twin B). They both represent late versions of the familiar Heusler house-mark, from the second half of the 1740s and the 1750s (possibly slightly later in the case of Heusler 4b); the papers in which they appear are thus listed separately here.

Found in: Heusler 4a: A/VI/106, 111. Heusler 4b: A/VI/163–64.

Heusler 5 (<Baden shield ~ blank folio>)

See next page for tracing.

Heusler 5 is the most popular paper among the Mannheim manuscripts, being found in 125 manuscripts. As already mentioned, this paper was manufactured in Baden, north of Basel; hence the use of a simplified Baden shield as the watermark. Dates found for it extend as far back as 1751 and as late as the early Munich period, though variants in the shield can often provide evidence as to a more exact date.

Found in: A/I/1 (1763), 10 (1751), 17–20 [1777/78], 21–23 (1778); A/II/2–3, 5–7, 9–11, 12 (1763), 13–15, 17, 18 (1765), 20 [1776/77]; A/III/4, 7–9, 12–19, 25, 29–31, 35, 38–42, 44–57, 60–61, M6–7; A/IV/2 [1766], 11; A/V/3–8 (1775), 9 (1776), 12–19 (1776), 20 [1777], 21

Appendix B

Heusler 5:

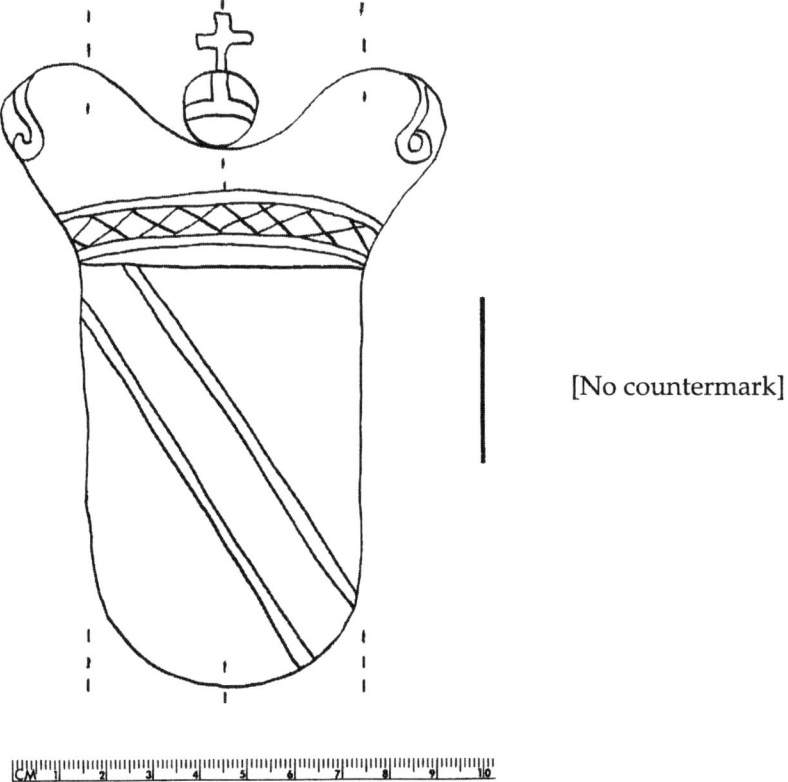

[No countermark]

(1778), 22, 24–43; A/VI/16, 20 [1772⁺], 24 [1772⁺], 26 [1777⁺], 31 [1764⁺], 62, 145, 147, 153, 155, 157–60, 170, 184, 189–91, ?202.

Additional reproductions: Tyson, NMA, no. 43; Haberkamp, KBM, vol. 6, p. 443, Rtt 184.

Heusler 6 (<NIC HEISLER ~ blank folio>)

See next page for tracing.

A period sometimes appears after the abbreviation <NIC>. Heusler 6 paper appears in manuscripts from the early 1750s (in the Pretlack collection) to as late as 1778 (in Mozart's "Paris" Symphony, K. 297).

306

Paper

Heusler 6:

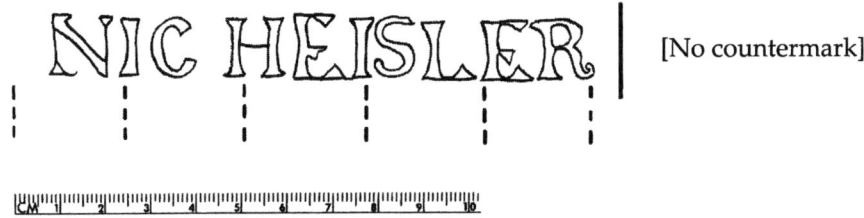 [No countermark]

Found in: A/I/3–4 (both 1766); A/VI/5 [1772⁺], 7, 20 [1772⁺], 24 [1772⁺], 36, 39, 46, 57–60, 63–84, 86–97, 102–4, 108–9, 140 [1772⁺], 141 [?1774⁺], 143 (1774), 162, 197 [1770⁺], 198–99.

Additional reproductions: Tyson, NMA, no. 47.

Heusler 7 (<cross/NH/CANDER ~ shield (fleur-de-lis)>)

Appendix B

Another long-lived Heusler paper, found in Mannheim manuscripts from the 1750s through 1778 and occasionally thereafter in the Munich period, e.g. in Mozart's autograph score to *Idomeneo* (1780/81). Heusler 7 was manufactured at Kandern, in Baden, as indicated by the watermark. There are many variations of this paper, only one of which is reproduced above; these include a C whose top extends further to the right and down, an N with the second vertical doubled, a different shield whose fleur-de-lis has a narrower central petal, and chain-lines that fall in different places in relation to the letters.

Found in: A/I/5, 14–15 (1769), 16 (?1767); A/II/2, 12 (1763); A/III/21, 30–31, 34, 38; A/IV/1 (1757), 4–5, 7–8, 10 [1767/68]; A/V/17 (1776), 19 (1776), 21 (1778), 23, 28–29; A/VI/6, 9, 17, 22, 30, 32 [1764+], 37 [1762+], 87–95, 106, 139 [1772+], 142 [1775+], 145, 151 [1774+], 154–55, 158, 163, 165, 171, 182, 184, 187, 190–92, 194, 201 [1760+].

Additional reproductions: Tyson, NMA, no. 50; Haberkamp, KBM, vol. 3, p. 262, HR 81.

Heusler 8 (Baden shield ∩ cross/NH)

A later version of Heusler 5, to my knowledge only occurring in manuscripts from the Munich period (i.e., after 1778), where it temporarily overlaps with, and then supplants, Heusler 5. The N and H of the countermark are connected, sharing the middle vertical, and the diagonal of the N is incorrect, slanting downward to the left (see the reprod. cited below). The paper generally has a greenish tinge (I am told).

Found in: A/III/32, 35, 37, 40, 42–43, 45–46, 50, 53–54, 56–70, 73b [1794], also Cannabich's keyboard concerto D-Mbs, Mus. Ms. 3984.

Reproductions: Wolf and Wolf, "Complex," 425, no. 7.

?J. J. Heusler 1 (<I ♡ H in cartouche ∩ shield (fleur-de-lis)>)

The shield is similar to those of other Basel papers of the period. However, it varies in size in the two Mannheim manuscripts in which it is found, in one case (A/VI/1) measuring 10.5 cm. vertically, in the second 12.7. I believe this to be a Basel paper, among other reasons because it is present in a local Basel manuscript, CH-Bu, kr II 63 (a symphony by Johann Stamitz). It may stem from a member of the Heusler family identified by Tschudin (pp. 39–40, 224) as Johann Jakob Heusler IV "de Niklaus Heusler," who operated mills in the St. Albantal section of Basel from 1757 until 1788.

Found in: A/VI/1, 168.

3. Miscellaneous Swiss Papers

?Blum or Heusler 1 (<laurel wreath {Basel crozier} ∩ fleur-de-lis>)

This paper is found only on endpapers; it is of better quality than that of the usual music manuscript, close to post paper in thickness and texture. A similar paper, but with the Heusler <cross/M> housemark as a countermark, is used for the flyleaves of A/I/8 (1733).

Found in: A/I/10 (1751); A/II/19, 20 [1776/77].

"Swiss (no WM)"

Numerous manuscripts from Mannheim of the period ca. 1755–65 utilize a paper that resembles the usual Swiss papers in every way (and appears alongside them) but contains no watermarks indicating its origin. Nor does comparison of the chain-lines reveal a clear identification with other known papers. At least within the closed body of Mannheim manuscripts, this paper must be considered a distinct type.

Found in: A/III/2–3, 9, 11–12, 16, 18, 21, M2–4; A/VI/87–95, 152, 168, 170, 174, 176–81, 183, 187.

II. German Paper from the Palatinate and Vicinity

Local paper from the Palatinate and vicinity was generally disdained by the electoral court, at least for music manuscripts. Palatine paper appears somewhat more often in the form of post paper, often incorporating the Palatine coat of arms and the initials CT for Carl Theodor; such paper was often used for paste-overs in the Mannheim manuscripts, e.g. in Holzbauer's autograph scores. The principal use of Palatine paper was, however, for the rough cover pages of the manuscripts (so-called elephant paper; see Knöckel 1 below), though some examples exist of its use as music paper. The information on individual Palatine papermakers given below is taken primarily from Albert Jaffé, *Die Papierindustrie in den kurpfälzischen Stammlanden unter Kurfürst Carl Theodor* (Schotten: Wilhelm Engel, 1935). On another paper possibly from the Palatinate see section IV, Alsatian Paper, below.

?J. M. Bach 1 (<shield with Palatine coat of arms/superimposed C and T [for Carl Theodor] : MOSBACH>)

Appendix B

Johann Michael Bach was a supplier to the electoral court, operating a mill in Mosbach (Pfalz) from 1751 or 1752 until 1796 (Karl Kleeberger, "Urkundliches über die Papiermühle in Mosbach," *Mannheimer Geschichtsblätter* 26 [1925]: 10–15; Jaffé, 17–22). Another paper from Mosbach (<top of shield : MOSBACH>) is found in the cello part of the Cannabich symphony A/III/21.

Found in: A/I/3 (1766); A/II/13.

"EDPM" (<cross/EDPM>; "PM" is a frequent abbreviation for *Papiermühle*)

Found in: A/I/4.

Reproductions: Heawood, plate 141, no. 915; Eineder, nos. 153, 309.

"ICH" (<ICH : W>)

Though the manufacturer of this paper is uncertain, he could be related to Johann Georg or Josef Anton Hilser, who also used a W in their watermarks, evidently for Waldkirch (Breisgau); see Reutter, *Richter*, 1:71.

Found in: A/I/2.

Knöckel 1 (<WAKNST ?~ elephant>; the S and T are superimposed)

This special paper was used only for cover sheets and bindings. It was manufactured by Wolfgang Adam Knöckel, a papermaker in Neustadt (Pfalz) from 1745 until 1780 and a supplier to the Palatine court (Jaffé, 37). It is usually blue, less often beige or greyish-beige (in the latter cases generally quite thick).

Found in: A/I/5–6, 14 (1769), 16 (?1767); A/II/13; A/IV/2 [1766]; A/V/9, 23, 26, 28–30, 33; A/VI/120–33, 145.

Knöckel 2 (<4/WAK : NST>, <backwards 4/WAK : NTS [*sic*; the N and S are both backwards]>)

A second, "normal" register paper from the mill of W. A. Knöckel. It is found on occasion in music manuscripts from the 1750s, most notably Johann Stamitz's Mass in D of ca. 1755 (A/VI/18).

Found in: A/VI/18, 42, 58–60, 64–84.

?J. F. Roeder 1 (<4 : IFR>)

The family of Jobst (or Johann) Friedrich Roeder (also Röder, Roedter, Rödter, etc.) was from Württemberg (see Friedrich von Hössle, *Württembergische Papiergeschichte* [Biberach/Riss: Karl Höhn, 1914], 97, 100–102, 114) but owned mills in the Palatinate as well, including that of J. M. Bach from 1796 (Jaffé, 15, 21–22, 52; Kleeberger, 12–13).

Found in: A/I/7.

Strasser 1 (<SBST in cartouche/WAHLDMICHELBACH>)

Sebastian Strasser was a son-in-law of Johann Michael Bach of Mosbach. As indicated by the watermark of this paper (almost illegible, but identified with the help of Jaffé, 54), Strasser operated a mill in Waldmichelbach.

Found in: A/VI/168.

Appendix B

III. Dutch Paper

It is somewhat surprising that so little paper from the Netherlands appears among the Mannheim manuscripts, given its excellent quality and the close dynastic and even academic ties linking the two areas (one of Carl Theodor's multiple titles was Marquis of Bergen op Zoom, and he attended the University of Leiden). Information on the papermakers below is taken primarily from W. A. Churchill, *Watermarks in Paper in Holland, England, France, etc., in the XVII and XVIII Centuries and Their Interconnection* (Amsterdam: Hertzberger, 1935). For further examples of the use of Dutch paper at Mannheim see Wolf and Wolf, "Complex," 384–85, fn. 16.

C. & I. Honig 1 (<fleur-de-lis : C & IHONIG>)

The important firm of C. & I (Cornelis and Jan Adriaan) Honig operated mills in Zaandyk from 1675 until as late as 1902 (Churchill, 15).

Found in: A/V/9 (1776); A/VI/45. In addition, the paper of A/VI/105 (<IV : fleur-de-lis/shield {diagonal stripes}>) stems from either Honig's firm (see the reprod. in Haberkamp, KBM, vol. 3, p. 260, HR 14) or that of Lubertus or Lucas van Gerrevink (Churchill, 14).

J. Honig & Zoon(en) 1 (<shield/bell/J HONIG & ZOONEN : J HONIG & ZOON)

The firm of Jan Honig and Son(s) owned mills in Zaandyk from 1737 until 1787 (Churchill, 15). This paper is much smaller than that of a typical Mannheim manuscript (one folio = 20 x 24.5 cm.).

Found in: A/V/1 (1771).

Rogge 1 (<A ROGGE ∩ shield {fleur-de-lis}>)

Adriaan Rogge's firm was established at Zaandam in 1704 and remained in existence until 1803 (Churchill, 16). This paper is small (one folio = 21.1 x ca. 28 cm.).

Found in: A/I/24 (1778).

Reproductions: Tyson, NMA, no. 48.

van der Ley 1 (<PL, the *L* in perspective ⌒ blank folio>; two versions, one ca. 2.9 cm. in height, the other ca. 3.5 cm., the former version the only one found among the Mannheim manuscripts)

Pieter van der Ley established one of the first important papermills in Holland at Zaandyk in 1665, and he operated a mill at Wormerveer until 1765 (Churchill, 9, 16). For additional documents containing his papers see Wolf and Wolf, "Complex," 384, fn. 16.

Found in: A/II/3.

Additional reproductions: Tyson, NMA, no. 5 (with twin B, a mirror of twin A); Wolf and Wolf, "Complex," 429.

van der Ley 2 (<fleur-de-lis/VDL ?⌒ IV>; the *V* and *D* are joined, sharing the right diagonal of the *V*)

Found in: A/VI/86, 96–97, 102–4.

IV. Alsatian Paper

Paper that is evidently from the important papermaking region of Alsace occurs in substantive fashion in only two Mannheim manuscripts, both large opera scores copied by Mannheim 5. In addition, post paper from the mill of Joseph Pasquai in Wasselonne (<FIN DE / JOS PASQUAI / EN ALSACE / 1742>) is used for paste-overs in A/II/17 and 20. Another possible use of Alsatian, or at least French, paper is found in the second violin part of A/VI/168 (<crown/FC/grapes : bishop with staff>; see the reprod. in *The Nostitz Papers*, plate 12, no. 556); grapes are a standard French mark. However, the paper could also be from the Palatinate, which was and remains Germany's principal wine-making region.

Weyhr 1 (or Weyher; <shield {fleur-de-lis}/bell : C I W<small>EYHR</small>>)

Tschudin, 239, n. 56 refers to a mill in Turckheim (Alsace) operated by one Louis Weyher; presumably C. I. Weyhr was a member of the same family. The shield is similar to those found in Basel papers like Blum 6–7.

Found in: A/VI/20 [1772$^+$], 196 [1774$^+$].

Appendix B

V. Supplement: Paper Used Only in Munich

The final section of Appendix B lists one Italian and two German papers that were used in Munich but *not* Mannheim; these papers have nonetheless been cited in Appendix A/III because they are found in the Cannabich series in Munich, either in older manuscripts to which parts were added in Munich after the move of 1778 or in new works composed by Cannabich after that date. It may be recalled that the paper Heusler 8 (see above) has already exemplified this category, as it is never known to have been used in Mannheim, only in Munich after 1778.

"A/HF" 1 (<crescent moon/crown/shield {3 stars} ∩ crescent moon/crown/A/HF/ IMPERIAL>)

Paper from this as-yet unidentified Italian firm is found in numerous manuscripts in, or from, Munich (e.g., the autograph to *Idomeneo*), Salzburg (e.g., many Michael Haydn manuscripts), and Vienna (e.g., see Tyson, NMA, nos. 54, 60, 62), usually in the *Real* rather than the present *Imperial* size and with a watermark containing the three moons typical of Italian paper. Hence this paper is definitely associated with southern Germany and Austria rather than Mannheim, the latter still mentioned as a possibility in Wolf and Wolf, "Complex," 429.

Found in: A/III/58B, 60–61.

Reproductions: Heawood, plate 108, fig. 687, and plate 128, fig. 820.

Kutter 1 (<backwards 4/crossbar/ii/backwards C/EK : blank folio>)

Elias Kutter owned three mills near Ravensburg (Württemberg) from 1741 on; he was a supplier to the Bavarian court in Munich (Hössle, *Württembergische Papiergeschichte*, 38). Kutter paper was Cannabich's principal brand after the transfer to Munich.

Found in: A/III/17, 22–24, 27, 32, 34–36, 43–44, 49, 53, 55, 63–72, also Cannabich's keyboard concerto D-Mbs, Mus. Ms. 3984.

Reproductions: Jean K Wolf, *The Orchestral Works of Christian Cannabich: A Documentary Study* (M.A. thesis, New York University, 1968), Appendix D, p. 8.

Paper

Unold 1 (<crown/shield (lion or wolf; varies)/IAV/WOLFEG ~ blank folio>)

Joseph Anton Unold operated mills in Wolfegg from 1740 until his death in 1785 (Hössle, *Württembergische Papiergeschichte*, 50–51).

Found in: A/III/70–72, 73 (1794), also Cannabich's late keyboard concerto D-Mbs, Mus. Ms. 3984.

Reproductions: Münster and Machold, KBM, vol. 1, p. 173, no. 9; J. Wolf, *Cannabich*, Appendix D, p. 9.

Appendix C

Compound Rastra Used at Mannheim

Appendix C supplies full specifications for, and information about, most of the compound rastra (rastra for drawing two or more staves at a time) utilized in lining the paper of the Mannheim complex of manuscripts. A few rastra found only in small portions of a unique manuscript have been omitted. Of course, though couched in terms of the rastra themselves, this is not really a catalogue of the implements per se, no examples of which from the electoral court are known to survive. Rather, it is a catalogue of the manifold *stavings* that resulted from their use, which provide our only evidence of their precise dimensions and other characteristics. The intent is to lay bare the evidence for assertions about provenance and date made in the course of the present study and also to allow identification of rastra used in the preparation of manuscripts not included here.

The overall organization of Appendix C is from small to large: its seven sections progress from rastra intended to line two staves at once to those for lining twelve, and within each section from smaller rastra to larger as measured by the total span (abbreviated TS, the distance from the top line of the top staff to the bottom line of the bottom staff; on these and other measurements see fig. 2:6 and related discussion). The first column of each section gives the label assigned here to each rastrum, the first number representing the number of staves, the second (after a colon) the numerical order. Thus rastrum 10:3 would be the third ten-stave rastrum in our list. ("Ten-stave rastrum" is a circumlocution employed in this study for "rastrum designed to line ten staves at once," i.e., a rastrum with ten heads or nibs; see the full description of the physical characteristics of eighteenth-century rastra in chapter 2.) If several distinct variants of a given rastrum occur, these are designated by lower-case letters preceded by a triangle (▶ 10:3b, ▶ 10:3c, etc.). Column 2 then gives the total span (TS) in millimeters (all measurements in this appendix are in millimeters). As the total span often varies from manuscript to manuscript or even page to page, this will generally be a range of measurements, in which case it is the *first* (smallest) number that determines the position of the rastrum in the list. Variants of a given rastrum are, however, kept together, even if the total span of the variant is significantly larger than that of subsequent rastra in the list (see, e.g., rastrum 2:4b below, the total span of which is larger than that of 2:5a). Hence, in searching for a specific rastrum one should always look well above and below the nominal point in the list at which that rastrum should appear.

The next column (or columns) provides the "DS" measurements, the distances between each of the staves going from the top to the bottom of the page. For ease of use, these are split into multiple columns beginning with Appendix C/III, "Five-Stave Rastra." Here, for instance, the column headed "DS 1–2" gives the measurements between staves 1–2 and 2–3, the next column (DS 3–4) the measurements between staves 3–4 and 4–5. Exceptionally, Appendix C/I (on two-stave rastra) is then followed by two columns giving the "DL" measurements for each of the two staves, the distances between each of the five lines; DL measurements are included in this instance because only one DS measurement is present in a two-stave rastrum, generally too little to identify a rastrum with any confidence. These measurements are merely a more precise method of specifying irregularities in line spacing than that employed here for the larger rastra.

One particular characteristic should be noted with respect to the DS and DL columns. Though, as mentioned, measurements are given from the top to the bottom of the page, copyists frequently used the pages upside down in random fashion. Thus in searching for a given set of DS or DL measurements, *one should always scan the measurements given here both backwards and forwards*. In the present catalogue, when I have found that a paper has actually been used both right side up and upside down by a copyist, I have terminated the list of measurements with a backwards arrow (←) as a special reminder to read the measurements in reverse as well as normal order.

The three final columns are devoted to (1) irregularities that may help to identify a rastrum, (2) manuscripts in which the rastrum appears, and (3) comments, the latter generally about the dating of the rastrum. In the column on irregularities the following abbreviations are employed: "CL" = characteristics of lines (gapped, heavy, light, etc.); "line 2/5" = staff 2, line 5; "1/4" = staff 1, space 4; and "S," "M," and "L" = small, medium, and large, referring to the relative size of the spaces between the lines. As in Appendix B, the next column ("Found In," giving the manuscripts in which the rastrum occurs) is merely a raw list; for details it is necessary to refer to the full catalogue of manuscripts, Appendix A. For convenience, however, dates in the manuscripts are supplied, in parentheses, as well as other firm dates, in brackets. On these and other conventions regarding the dates suggested here see the introduction to Appendix A. Finally, it should be noted that all the manuscripts cited in Appendix C are oblong in format unless otherwise stated, and that in references to the process of lining a page "2 × 5," for example, means that the page has been lined with two passes of a five-stave rastrum (to make ten staves).

I. Two-Stave Rastra

Most of the two-stave (double) rastra in the Mannheim complex of manuscripts are found in Regensburg (D-Rtt) rather than in manuscripts used at the electoral court, suggesting that the rastra may have been owned by the copyists themselves. Two-

Compound Rastra

stave rastra are also the norm in manuscripts written after the move to Munich in 1778; these rastra are not included here. Both the Mannheim and Munich papers are generally lined with five passes of the rastrum (5 × 2 = 10 staves).

Rastrum	TS	DS	DL Staff 1	DL Staff 2	Irregs.	Found In	Comments
2:1	29.7-.8	11.75-.8	2.15, 2.75, 2.3, 2.2	2.4, 2.25, 2.2, 2.3	Line 2/5 often heavy; very wavy staving.	A/VI/17	Prob. early 1770s or late 1760s.
2:2	29.8	11.8	2.25, 2.3, 2.2, 2.35	2.2, 2.3-.35, 2.2, 2.3	Lines 2/2, 2/4 heavy; line 2/3 light.	A/VI/168	Prob. late 1750s or early 1760s.
2:3	30.5-31.1	12.5-.85	2.2-.5, 2.15-.25, 2.2-.3, 2.2-.4	2.15-.2, 2.4-.5, 2.2-.4, 2.25-.5←	Line 2/4 often light.	A/VI/153, 155, 159, 184, 189-91	Late 1750s–early 1760s or possibly later. Light ink color.
2:4a	30.8-31.5	12.7-.85	2.1-.15, 2.1-.2, 2.1-.15, 2.4-.5	2.5, 2.4-.5, 2.35, 2.2-.25		A/VI/157-58, 160	Early 1760s or possibly late 1750s.
▶ 2:4b	32.2	13.6-.75	2.2, 2.25, 2.2, 2.5	2.5, 2.5, 2.4, 2.25		A/VI/158	DL measurements given in reverse order for purposes of comparison. Two heads of rastrum 2:4a spread apart (cf. DS). *Date*: early 1760s or late 1750s.
2:5a	30.8-31.5	12.8-13	2.3-.4, 2.2-.25, 2.3-.5, 2.35-.4	2.25-.3, 2.2-.25, 2.5-.6, 2.1-.15←	Line 2/5 often light.	A/VI/165, 173	Prob. mid to late 1760s.
▶ 2:5b	31	12.8	2.2, 2.15, 2.3, 2.4	2.3, 2.15, 2.4, 2		A/VI/167	Prob. early to mid 1760s, possibly later.
2:6	31.1-.2	12.5-.6	2.25, 2-2.05, 2.25, 2.3	2.3, 2.3, 2.3, 2.15		A/I/9 (1737)	Ca. 1737.
2:7	31.75	13.6	2.2, 2.3, 2.3, 2.6	2.5, 2.35, 1.95, 2		A/VI/187	Prob. late 1750s or early 1760s.
2:8	31.75-.9	13.2-.25	2.4, 2.5, 2.25, 2.3	2.4-.5, 2.45-.5, 2.3-.35, 2.4		A/III/13; A/VI/162	Date unclear; prob. 1760s–early 1770s or later.

Appendix C

Rastrum	TS	DS	DL Staff 1	DL Staff 2	Irregs.	Found In	Comments
2:9	31.8-32	13	2.6-.75, 2.3-.35, 2.3-.4, 2.15-.35	2-2.1, 2.2-.25, 2.3, 2.5-.65		A/VI/179, 183	1750s, esp. 2d half.
2:10a	32-32.1	12.5-.85	2.2-.3, 2.55-.6, 2.5-.75, 2.4-.5	2.15-.35, 2.25-.4, 2.8, 2.15-.2	Line 2/5 often light.	A/VI/176-77, 181	1750s, esp. mid to late.
▶ 2:10b	33	13.1-.15	2.4, 2.5, 2.5, 2.5	2.25, 2.25, 2.75, 2.5	Same.	A/VI/180	Mid to late 1750s.
2:11	32-32.5	13.2-.5	2.3-.5, 2.2-.25, 2.2-.25, 2.5	2.15-.2, 2.3-.5, 2.3-.35, 2.5-.6		A/VI/163-64	Prob. 2d half of 1750s.
2:12	32-32.25	14-14.2	2.2-.35, 2.2-.25, 2.3-.5, 2.15-.2	2.2-.35, 2.2-.25, 2.2, 2.25-.3←		A/VI/184, 190-91	Prob. late 1750s or early 1760s.
2:13	32.5	12.9	2.3, 2.5, 2.8, 2.25	2.5, 2.3-.35, 2.5, 2.6	Line 1/4 heavy, 1/5 light; line 1/1 often very light (varies)	A/VI/200 [1775⁺]	1775⁺
2:14	36.6-37	12.3-.5	2.5, 2.5, 2.55-.6, 2.3-.4	2.25-.4, 2.4-.5, 2.3, 2.4-.5		A/VI/106 [1751⁺], 115 [1751⁺]	Early 1750s.

II. Four-Stave Rastra

Rastrum	TS	DS	Irregs.	Found In	Comments
4:1	62.75-.85	9.75, 10.5-.75, 10.4-.5	1/4 L, 2-3/4 ML; 4/4 S.	A/IV/3 [1748]	12 staves, ruled 3 x 4. *Date*: ca. 1748.

III. Five-Stave Rastra

Ten-stave paper lined with two passes of a five-stave rastrum (2 × 5) is very common in Italian and Viennese music manuscripts, somewhat less so in those from Mannheim, where their most noteworthy appearances are in manuscripts from before

Compound Rastra

ca. 1760 and then mostly in the large opera scores copied by Mannheim 5. In the latter case, the physical instability of the rastra used by Mannheim 5, as evidenced by the extreme variability of their staving, and their appearance only in copies by him, suggests that they belonged to him rather than to the central paper depot at Mannheim, where the "official" paper was lined.

Rastrum	TS	DS 1-2	DS 3-4	Irregs.	Found In	Comments
5:1	85-85.4	11.85-.9, 10.75-.9	12.2-.5, 11.5-.65	1-4/4 ML/L; 1/1 S. Line 1/1 light, often gapped; lines 1/4-5 heavier. Light ink.	A/VI/42, 58-60, 64-84 [1750⁺]	Ca. 1749–early 1750s.
5:2	85.2-.4	10.4-.5, 10.45-.6	9.95-10, 9.9	1/4 L, 2-4/4 ML (A/VI/85); 4-5/4 L, 1-3/4 ML (A/VI/46).	A/VI/46, 85 [1752⁺]	Early to mid 1750s.
5:3	90.2-.3	11.15-.2, 12	11.25-.35, 10.35-.4←	4/4 L; 4/2, 5/3 S/MS.	A/VI/5 [1772⁺]	1772⁺.
5:4a	90.5-91	10.9-11, 11.3-.4	11.15-.2, 10.35-.4	Line 5/1 often heavier.	A/VI/5 [1772⁺], 150	Ca. 1770–72 or later.
▲5:4b	91	10.7, 11.15-.25	11.15-.2, 10.35-.4←	2/4 L; 5/4 S. DL much more irregular than in 5:4a. Line 5/5 often heavier.	A/VI/5 [1772⁺]	1772⁺.
5:5a	90.7-.8	10.9, 11	10.6, 10.1	2/4 L, 5/3-4 ML; 2/2-3 MS. Line 1/4 heavy. See also the Comments column.	A/VI/196 [1774⁺]	Rastrum 5:5 is found only in A/VI/196 (Salieri's *La secchia rapita*, perf. Mannheim, 5 Nov. 1774), copied by Mannheim 5. Like other rastra used by this copyist here and in A/VI/24, 37, and 203 (see esp. 5:6a-b, 5:10a-d, 5:11a-d, and 5:20a-b), this one shows great instability, with many differences in DS and DL within the MS; these rastra may well have been his own. *Date:* 1774⁺.
▲5:5b	90.8	12, 10.8	10.1, 11	2/4 L; 1/1 and 3 MS, 1/2 and 4 ML. Line 5/4 thick.	A/VI/196 [1774⁺]	See comment under 5:5a.

321

Appendix C

Rastrum	TS	DS 1-2	DS 3-4	Irregs.	Found In	Comments
▶ 5:5c	90.9	12, 11	10.3-4 (.75 some exs.), 10.2-.3	1-2/4 L/ML; 1/3 MS. Line 5/4 often heavy.	A/VI/196 [1774+]	See comment under 5:5a.
▶ 5:5d	91.2-.3	12, 11	11.05-.15, 11.3-.5	2/4 L; 1/1 and 3 MS, 1/2 and 4 ML. Lines 3/1, 5/4 often thick.	A/VI/196 [1774+]	See comment under 5:5a.
5:6a	90.7-91	9.25, 11.2	10.5, 11	1/3, 5/4 L/ML; 1/4, 5/2 MS.	A/VI/196 [1774+]	See comment under 5:5a. *Date:* 1774+.
▶ 5:6b	90.7-91	9.25, 12-12.15	9.75, 11	Same.	A/VI/196 [1774+]	Same. This form of the rastrum provides a clear example of staff 3 being lowered, thereby increasing DS 2 and decreasing DS 3.
5:7	91.1-.2	10.5-.6, 10.8-11.2	10-10.2, 10.5	2/4 L; 3/3, 5/2 MS. Line 3/3 often heavy.	A/VI/24 [1772+]	Found only in A/VI/24 (Gassmann's *L'amore artigiano*, perf. Schwetzingen, May 1772), copied by Mannheim 5. See also the comment under 5:5a. *Date:* 1772+.
5:8	91.4-.7	11.85-.9, 12.1	10.2, 11.65-.7	2/4, 3/4 L; 1/3 MS. Staff 5 usually begins and ends to right of others.	A/VI/20 [1772+]	1772+ (date of Mannheim premiere of A/VI/20, J. C. Bach's *Temistocle*).
5:9	91.5-.9	9.8-.9, 9.1-.15	9.4, 9.4-.5←	1/3, 4/2-3 MS.	A/I/8 (1733)	Ca. 1733.
5:10a	91.5	11, 10.85	10.15, 9.75	3/4 L. Line 2/5 often heavy.	A/VI/24 [1772+]	See comments under 5:7 and 5:5a. *Date:* 1772+.
▶ 5:10b	92.1	11.1, 11.6	9.85, 9.9	Same.	A/VI/24 [1772+]	Same.
5:10c	92.2	11.5, 11.4	10.1, 9.75	Same.	A/VI/24 [1772+]	Same.
▶ 5:10d	92.2-.3	11.75, 11.15	10.2, 9.75	Same.	A/VI/24 [1772+]	Same.
5:11a	92	10.4-.5, 11.85	10.2, 10.8	1/3, 5/3-4 L/ML; 1/5, 5/2 MS. Lines 5/3-4 often heavy. Some lines light, gapped.	A/VI/196 [1774+]	See comment under 5:5a. *Date:* 1774+.

Compound Rastra

Rastrum	TS	DS 1-2	DS 3-4	Irregs.	Found In	Comments
▶ 5:11b	92	10.6, 12	9.9-10, 10.5(?).-9	Same, but 5/2 now more regular.	A/VI/196 [1774+]	Same.
▶ 5:11c	92	10.5(?), 12.1	10.2-.25, 10.2-.3	1/3, 5/3-4 ML; 1/4 MS.	A/VI/196 [1774+]	Same.
▶ 5:11d	92	10.5-.6, 12.1-.2	9.85, 10.5-.7	1/3, 5/3-4 ML; 1/4, 5/2 MS. NB: pp. 65, 67 have 1/4 ML, 1/3 MS.	A/VI/196 [1774+]	Same.
5:12a	95.1-.2	12.9, 13	10.8, 11.25	1/4 L, 2/2, 3/4, 5/1 S. Line 1/5 often heavy.	A/III/24	Ca. 1764-65; later form of rastrum 5:12c. Found only in copies by Mannheim 10, whose personal rastrum it may have been.
▶ 5:12b	95.5-96.2	12.5-.9, 13-13.5	10.6-11.3, 11.7-12.2←	2/2, 3/4, 5/1 S. Line 1/5 heavy.	A/III/23-24	Same.
▶ 5:12c	96.8-97	12.9, 13	11.2, 12.7-13.1←	Same.	A/III/8	Prob. late 1750s; earlier form of rastrum 5:12a-b and d-e.
▶ 5:12d	97	13.6-.9, 13	10.2-.4, 12.8-.85←	1/1, 2/2, 3/4 S.	A/III/23-24	Same as 5:12a.
▶ 5:12e	98.5	12.6, 13.4	11.8, 13.5	2/2, 3/4, 5/1 S.	A/III/24	Same as 5:12a.
5:13	95.3-.5	13-13.2, 11.8-.85	11, 12.2-.5←	1/1, 2/2, 3/4 S.	A/III/23-24	Ca. 1764-65. Found only in copies by Mannheim 10, whose personal rastrum it may have been.
5:14a	96.25-.85	13.15-.5, 12-12.25	10.85-11.1, 12.7-.85	2/1 S; DL, CL inconsistent.	A/III/32; A/VI/23	Ca. 1764-66.
▶ 5:14b	96.4-.6	13.1-.2, 12.45-.6	10.75-.85, 12.2-.4	Same.	A/III/21, 34	Ca. 1765-70.
▶ 5:14c	97-97.5	13-13.25, 12.5-.6	10.85-11.3, 12.8-13←	Same.	A/VI/19 [1766+], 23	Ca. 1766 or later.
5:15	96.5	11.9, 12.95-13	11.15-.2, 12.9-13.05	1-5/3, 1/4, 4/4 L/ML; 1/1, 2/2 S/MS.	A/VI/23	Prob. ca. 1766 or later; used alongside rastrum 5:14c (q.v.).
5:16	96.6-.8	12.5-.6, 13	13, 12.2-.3←	1/1 MS.	A/VI/18	MS in upright format; 16 staves, ruled 1 + (3 x 5). *Date*: ca. 1755+.
5:17	96.9-97.1	11.7, 12.35-.4	12.4-.45, 12.45←	1/4, 3/4 ML.	A/VI/18	Same.

Appendix C

Rastrum	TS	DS 1–2	DS 3–4	Irregs.	Found In	Comments
5:18	97.4-.5	12.8-13, 12-12.15	12.55-.7, 12.25-.4	4/4 L/ML; 3/3 MS.	A/I/11 (1751); A/VI/40-41 [1751+], 43, 61, 106 [1751+], 110 [1751+], 112, 113 [1751+], 119	Early 1750s.
5:19	99.5	12.3-.5, 12.8	12.9, 12.5	1/3 L; 1/1 S. Lines 2/2, 2/4 heavier.	A/I/8 (1733)	Ca. 1733.
5:20a	99.6-100.1	13.4-.65, 12.6-.7	13.1-.35, 13.8	Very inconsistent irregs. One group (e.g., A/VI/37, p. 59ff.; A/VI/203, pp. 46-121) = 2/2 L/ML, 3/2 MS, heavier line 2/3; another (e.g., A/VI/37, pp. 41-44; A/VI/203, pp. 310-12) = 3/2 M/ML, heavier line 5/4.	A/VI/37 [1762+], 203 [1760+]	Found only in A/VI/37 (Traetta's *Sofonisba*, premiere Mannheim, 5 Nov. 1774) and A/VI/203 (Jommelli and Colla's *Cajo Fabrizio*, premiere Mannheim, 5 Nov. 1760), both copied by Mannheim 5; see comment under 5:5a. *Date*: ca. 1760–62 or later.
▶ 5:20b	100.2-.5	12.8-.85, 12.6-.65	13.3-.4, 13.75-.85	1-5/4 L/ML; 4/3, 5/2 S. Line 2/1 often heavy.	A/VI/37 [1762+], 203 [1760+]	Same.
5:21	99.8-100	13.2-.35, 12.9-13	13.35-.4, 13.65-.7	1/4 ML; 2/3 MS. Line 5/2 often heavy.	A/VI/203 [1760+]	Found only in A/VI/203, copied by Mannheim 5; see comments under 5:20a and 5:5a. *Date*: ca. 1760.
5:22	101.5-.6	13.1, 12.85-.9	13, 12.8-.85	4-5/3 L/ML; 4/2 MS.	A/VI/203 [1760+]	Same.
5:23	102.65-.75	12.8-.85, 13.35-.5	12.7-.8, 13.35-.4 ←	1-2/4, 4-5/4 L/ML; 2/3 MS. Line 3/4 often heavy, line 3/5 often light; lines often discontinuous.	A/VI/202	All measurements taken from vn. 1 part, which has more regular ruling; those of the TP/b. part are reversed. *Date*: prob. 1777/78; A/VI/202 composed 1776.

Compound Rastra

IV. Six-Stave Rastra

Rastrum	TS	DS 1–3	DS 4–5	Irregs.	Found In	Comments
6:1	133.5	15.3, 15.8, 15.85	14.7, 15.6–7←	1/1-2, 5/4 L; 2/3 S.	A/II/2, 5 (no later than 1759)	Upright format; 12 staves, ruled 2 x 6. *Date:* ca. 1753–60.

V. Seven-Stave Rastra

Rastrum	TS	DS 1–3	DS 4–6	Irregs.	Found In	Comments
7:1	114.1–115	9.1-2, 9.75-.85, 9.25-.3	10.15-.25, 9.2-.3, 9.2-.25	2/4, 3/2 L; 3/1 S.	App. A/I/10 (1751), 12 (1753)	14 staves, ruled 2 x 7. *Date:* ca. 1751–53.

VI. Ten-Stave Rastra

Rastrum	TS	DS 1–3	DS 4–6	DS 7–9	Irregs.	Found In	Comments
10:1	193.5–194.4	12.1-5, 12.2-.4, 11-11.2	12.1-.3, 11.6-.9, 12-12..4	11.9-12.2, 12.8-13.1, 11.8-12.25 ←	1/3, 10/1 L/ML; 7/1 S/MS. Lines 1/5, 8/1-2, or 10/1 often heavy.	A/V/21 (1778); A/VI/ 20 [1772+], 36 [1777/78], 140 [1772+], 141, 143 [1774+], 197 [1770+], 198-99, 200 [1775+]	Ca. 1770–78, esp. 1770–75.
10:2	195	10.8-.85, 10.7-.8, 10.1	10.6-.7, 10.5, 10.6-.8	10.5-.6, 11.5, 10.85-11.1	1/1, 6/2, 7/1 S/MS.	A/VI/31 [1764+], 203 [1760+]	Ca. 1760–64 or later.

Appendix C

Rastrum	TS	DS 1-3	DS 4-6	DS 7-9	Irregs.	Found In	Comments
10:3a	197.5	12.5, 11.5, 12.5	12.2, 13, 11.35	11.15-.2, 13.2, 12.1-.15	1/2-3, 5/4, 7/3 ML; 1/4, 6/4, 7/1-.2, 9/2 MS. Lines 9/5, 10/1 light.	A/VI/182	May be same as, or somehow related to, rastrum 10:4. *Date*: early or mid 1760s or possibly later.
▶ 10:3b	197.6-198	12.35-.4, 11.65-.7, 12.5-.55	11.9-12, 12.85, 11.1-.15	11.1-.15, 12.85, 12	Same.	A/VI/194	Same.
10:4a	198	12.2, 11.6, 12.5	12, 12.8, 11.1	11.05-.1, 12.75-.8, 11.9-12.1	1/3, 5/4 L/ML; 1/2 M; 1/1, 3/1, 6/4 S/MS. Line 5/5 heavy.	A/VI/162	May be same as, or somehow related to, rastrum 10:3. *Date*: uncertain, but prob. 1760s or early 1770s.
▶ 10:4b	198	12, 11.4, 12.45-.5	11.55, 12.65-.7, 10.85-.9	10.9, 13.15, 11.9-12	Similar to 10:4a, but staff 1 = S-L-ML-S. Staves 9-10 discontinuous, esp. line 9/3.	A/VI/195	Same.
10:5	199.1	11.4, 11.7, 12.15	12.5, 11.1, 11.9-12	11.5, 11.6, 11.5-.8	9/1 L; 9/2-4 S.	A/III/29	Ca. 1770-75.
10:6	200.7-201.9	12.2-.25, 12.75-.8, 13.5	12.2-.3, 12-12.2, 12.8-13	12.15-.25, 12.5-.65, 12.5-.55←	7/1, 4 ML; 7/2-3, 9/1 S. Line 10/5 often heavy.	A/II/20; A/III/60; A/IV/11	Used in both Mannheim and Munich. *Date*: late 1770s–early 1780s.
10:7	201.7-202.7	12.45-.6, 12.5-.6, 12.9-13.1	12.6-.7, 12.6-.8, 13-13.2	12.8-.9, 13.1-.3, 12.35-.4←	6/2, 7/4 S.	A/II/18-19; A/III/42	Evidently used in both Mannheim and Munich. *Date*: ca. 1770-80.
10:8a	202-203.5	12.3-.5, 12.6-.8, 12.4-.6	12.3-.5, 12.65-.9, 11.85-12	12.85-13.1, 12.5-.75, 13-13.2←	4/4 L; 9/3 S.	A/II/20; A/III/42; A/VI/26 [1777†]	Ca. 1777, prob. also early Munich period.
▶ 10:8b	202-204	12.5-.8, 12.7-.9, 12.6-.8	12.4-.65, 12.5, 12.6-.9	12.7-.8, 12.8-.9, 13.1-.15	Same.	A/II/18; A/VI/151	1st half of 1770s.

Compound Rastra

Rastrum	TS	DS 1-3	DS 4-6	DS 7-9	Irregs.	Found In	Comments
10:9	202-202.9	11.5-7, 13-13.1, 12.5-.9	11.8-12.2, 12.6-.7, 13	12.8-.85, 12-12.1, 12.8-13←	10/1 L; 8/2, 10/2 S.	A/III/43; A/VI/161	Early 1770s.
10:10	202.2-203.5	11.8-12, 12.7-.8, 11.8-12	11.8-12, 12.5-.7, 13.1-.5	12.8-13.2, 12.2-.5, 12.2-.6←	1/2, 2/4 S; 10/1 L/ML.	A/I/1 (1763); A/II/18 (1765); A/III/14-15, M5/74; A/VI/192	Ca. 1760-65. Rastrum also found in F-CSM, Ms. 1494, no. 333, a trio sonata by Domenico Ferrari; see the final section of chap. 9.
10:11a	202.3-.5	12.4-.5, 12.7-.8, 12.8-.85	12.8-.85, 12.2-.3, 12.35-.4	13.1, 12.35-.5, 12.35-.5←	5/1, 10/1 L; 1/4, 6/3 S.	A/II/20	1776-77.
▶ 10:11b	202.5-.8	12.35-.4, 12.25-.35, 12.8	12.25-.65, 12.25-.4, 12.9-.95	12.8-13, 12.85-.9, 12.4←	Same.	A/VI/26	1776-78.
10:12	202.5-203	11.9, 12.25, 13-13.1	13.25-.35, 12.85-.95, 12.15	12.2, 12.6, 11.9-.95←	1/1 L; 1/3, 10/4 S.	A/I/13 (1766)	Ca. 1766.
10:13	205	12, 12, 12	13, 12.5, 12.2	12.3, 12, 12←	2-3/4, 8/4 L/ML, 4/2 MS.	A/VI/100-101	Mid-1750s.
10:14	206	13, 12, 12.5	12.2, 12.7, 12.5	11.8, 12, 12←	3/3, 6/2, 9/3 L/ML, 3/1, 6/1, 6/3 S.	A/VI/100-101 [1754+]	Mid-1750s.
10:15	206.3-208	12.1-.4, 11.9-12.2, 12.7-13.1	12.1-.4, 11.7-12, 11.8-12.1	12.5-.8, 12.6-13.1, 12-12.4←	4/4, 7/1 L; 4/1, 6/1, 8/4 S.	A/III/3; A/VI/22, 62 [1754+], 154	Ca. 1754-55 or a bit later. Also found in F-CSM, Ms. 1494, no. 291, a trio sonata by Fils; see the last section of chap. 9.
10:16	206.6-.9	12.3, 12.2, 12.9	12.1, 11.85, 11.75-.8	12.75, 13-13.1, 12.3-.4	1-7/4, 8-9/2 L/ML; 6/1, 8/4 MS. Line 7/3 light.	A/VI/182	Early or mid 1760s or possibly later.
10:17a	216.5-217.4	13.7-14, 13.3-.4, 12.5	12.6-.7, 13-13.1, 13.2-.4	12.6-13, 13.2-.25, 12.8-13.1←	7-8/3, 10/2 L (A/III/29, 43); 1-2/4, 10/1 L, 1/3 MS (A/VI/31).	A/III/29, 43; A/VI/15, 31 [1764+]	Ca. 1764-early 1770s. A/VI/15 (Majo's *Ifigenia in Tauride*, premiere Mannheim, 5 Nov. 1764) may of course be a somewhat later copy, with a date more in line with that of the other MSS (i.e., the early

Appendix C

Rastrum	TS	DS 1-3	DS 4-6	DS 7-9	Irregs.	Found In	Comments
(10:17a)							
▶ 10:17b	216.6-217.8	13.6-8, 13.2-4, 12.6-7	12.5-6, 12.9-13.1, 12.5-8	12.5-8, 13-13.3, 12.7-8←	3/3, 7/3 L; 7/2, 7/4 S. Irregs. of 7/3-4 corrected in A/VI/16, hn. 1.	A/I/14-15 (both 1769); A/III/31; A/IV/10b [Aug. 1767-Jan. 1768]; A/VI/16, 192	1770s). Cf. also 10:17b, with firm dates of 1767-69. 1767-69.
10:18	218.2-3	13.6-7, 13.95, 13.3-4	13.6-8, 13.6-65, 13.5	13.9, 13.6-65, 13.85-9	8/2, 10/3 ML; 7/1 MS; otherwise fairly regular. Thin lines.	A/III/21	Prob. ca. 1766-70.
10:19	218.2-219	13.6-9, 13.5-9, 13.7-9	13.5-7, 13.7-14.1, 13.8-14.1	13.3-6, 14.2-4, 13.2-6 (13.9 in A/VI/146, 148-49)←	DL irregs. inconsistent. Line 10/5 generally light.	A/VI/21, 100-101 [1754†], 146, 148-49	Ca. 1754-55 or a bit later.
10:20a	218.6-220	13.5-6, 12.85-9, 12.75-8	12.75-8, 13.2-3, 13.7-14	12.6-7, 14.2-4, 13.7-9	4/2 L; 8/1, 8/4 S.	A/III/42, 52-53	Late Mannheim period, ca. 1775-77 or 78.
▶ 10:20b	218.7-220	13.3-6, 12.8-9, 13.4-5	12.9-13.1, 13.3-5, 13.9-14	12.5-6, 14.1-2, 13.6-9	Same.	A/III/21, 38, 46, 48, 53-55	Late Mannheim period, ca. 1774-78. Possibly reused briefly in Munich.
▶ 10:20c	219.4-220.8	13.5-7, 12.8-13, 13.45-6	13.3-6, 13.3-5, 13.8-14	12.6-8, 14.3-45, 13.8-.85←	Same.	A/V/20 [1777], 27-28, 31-33	Ca. 1775-78. This form of the rastrum appears only in the Vogler MSS.
10:21	219-220.5	13.4-5, 13.2-3, 12.7-13	12.8-13, 14-14.2, 13.3-.5	13.3-.5, 14.25-.3, 14.1-.2	4/2, 7/2 L; 9/4 S.	A/III/38, 48-50	Mid-1770s.
10:22	219.1-220.3	12.65-.75, 12.8-.85, 12.6-.65	12.75, 13.1-.2, 13.7-.75	12.3-4, 13.3-.35, 12.9-.95	2/4 L, 4/4 ML; 9/2 S, 4/3 MS.	A/V/21 (1778)	Ca. 1778.
10:23	219.6-9	13.3-.5, 13.7-9, 13.7-8	13.2-3, 13.7-14, 13.5-.6	13.5-.6, 13.6-9, 14.2-.6	7/2 ML; 7/1 MS; 10/1 S (Pokorny MS	A/II/21	Also found in an aut. MS by Franz Xaver Pokorny dated 1756 (D-Rtt, "Bernasconi" 4),

Compound Rastra

Rastrum	TS	DS 1-3	DS 4-6	DS 7-9	Irregs.	Found In	Comments
(10:23)					only; see Comments).		on paper almost certainly obtained at Mannheim. *Date:* mid-1750s.
10:24a	220-220.5	12.25-.35, 14.2-.4, 13-13.2	13.5, 13.15-.2, 13.1-.2	14.3-.5, 12.1-.3, 13.1-.3	6-7/1 S. Line 10/2 heavy.	A/III/13, 16, M6	Two of the three MSS in which this rastrum occurs (A/III/13, 16) can be dated ca. 1760-61; A/III/M6 is prob. from about the same period or a bit later.
▶10:24b	220.5-221	12.25-.35, 14.45-.5, 13.15-.2	13.5, 13.15-.2, 13.4-.5	14.5-15, 12.25-.35, 13.25-.3	Same.	A/III/13, M6	See comment under 10:24a.
10:24c	221.1-.9	12.25-.65, 13.75-14, 13.35-.5	13.5-.7, 13.25-.3, 12.9-13	14-14.6, 13.2-.7, 14.75-.8	8/3, 10/3 S (A/III/13; 18 va.), M6; 8/1, 10/1 S (A/III/18 vns.).	A/III/13, 18, M6	Ca. 1760-62; see comment under 10:24a.
▶10:24d	221.15-.6	12.4, 13.9-14, 13.35-.4	13.5-.7, 13.15, 13.1-.4	14.5-.6, 12.7-.75, 14.4-.5	7-8/1, 10/1 S/MS. Line 10/2 often heavy.	A/III/18, M6	Same.
10:25a	220-221	13.4-.6, 13.2-.5, 13.5-.8	13, 13.1-.3, 13.5-.7	12.7-.9, 13.9-14.2, 13.8-14←	10/3 L; 10/2 S.	A/II/17; A/III/29, 39-41, 45; A/V/2a (1772)	Ca. 1769-1775.
▶10:25b	220.5-.6	13.5-.55, 13.3-.45, 12.7-.8	13, 13.2-.3, 13.7-.8	12.8-13, 13.75-.8, 13.8-.9	Same.	A/III/43; A/VI/161	Early 1770s.
▶10:25c	220.7-221.2	13.5-.6, 13.4-.5, 12.7-.8	12.9-13.1, 13-13.2, 13.5-.8	12.9-13, 13.8, 13.7-.9←	10/3 L.	A/II/17, 21, 34, 40; A/VI/19 [1766+], 192	Ca. 1766-early 1770s; prob. the earliest form of this rastrum.
10:26a	220.1-.5	13.4-.6, 13.85-.9, 13.8-14.1	13.45-.6, 13.2-.25, 12.6-.7	13.9-14, 13.6-.7, 12.9-13←	1/4, 10/1 L; 10/3 S. Line 1/5 heavy.	A/VI/154	Ca. 1755-60.

Appendix C

Rastrum	TS	DS 1-3	DS 4-6	DS 7-9	Irregs.	Found In	Comments
▶ 10:26b	220.5-221.5	13.2-5, 13.5-8, 13.3-6	13.5-9, 13.1-6, 12.7-13	13.8-14, 13.5-9, 12.8-13.1 (12.3) ←	10/1, 10/4 L/ML; 8/4, 10/3 S. Line 1/5 often heavy.	A/III/4, 7-9, M1-2	Same.
▶ 10:26c	221-221.8	13.3-4, 13.45-65, 13.3-.5	13.6-8, 13.4-5, 12.7-13	13.7-14, 13.2-14, 13.3-.6←	7/2 S.	A/III/M1-3	Same.
▶ 10:26d	221.2-.8	13.4, 13.5-.6, 13.5	13.6-.65, 13.4-5, 13	13.6-.9, 13.7-14, 13.9-14.1←	7/2, 8/4 S.	A/III/M2-3	Same.
▶ 10:26e	221.5-.8	13.35-.4, 13.8-.9, 13.5	13.9-14, 13.5-8, 12.7-.8	13.2-.5, 14.1-.2, 13.8-.9	Same.	A/III/M2-3	DS figures given in reverse order for purposes of comparison. *Date*: ca. 1755-60.
10:27	220.2-222.5	12.7-.9, 12.8-13, 12.7-.9	12.8-13, 13.1-.2, 13.7-.9	12.25-.3(.6), 13.2-.6, 13-13.1	2/4 L; 4/3, 9/2 S.	A/III/8, 12-13, 21, 57	Munich rastrum, or possibly brought from Mannheim. Found mainly in late additions to Cannabich MSS.
10:28a	220.5-221.8	12.6-8 (13.2), 13.7-.8 (13.5), 13.4-.5	13.5-7, 13.2-.3, 12.7-.9	14.1-.6, 13.2-.7, 14.5-.9	7/2 S/MS; 8/1 S (all of A/III/2 but vn. 1, b., in which 8/3 S), A/VI/187; 10/1 S/MS (all of A/III/2 but vn. 1, b.), A/VI/187 (vns.). Line 8/2 often heavier.	A/III/2; A/VI/187	For a more detailed analysis of rastrum 10.28 see table 2:1 and related discussion. In the bass part (only) of A/VI/187, DS 1 = 13.2, DS 2 = 13.5—i.e., staff 2 has been lowered. *Date*: ca. 1755-60 or slightly later (A/III/2 is the earliest extant Cannabich symphony).
▶ 10:28b	221	12.25, 13.85, 13.3	13.6, 13.2, 12.95	14-14.05, 13.5-.55, 14.5-.6	7/2, 8/3 S/ MS. Line 8/2 often heavier.	A/VI/171 (1760?; possible date on MS)	Ca. 1760.
▶ 10:28c	221.1-.9	12.9-13.15, 13.45-.6, 13.2-.5	13.5-.8, 13.2-.5, 12.7-13	14.3-.8, 13.35-.5, 14.6-.85	7/2, 8/1, 10/1 S.	A/III/11-12, 16, M4; A/VI/152, 170	Late 1750s-early 1760s.

Compound Rastra

Rastrum	TS	DS 1-3	DS 4-6	DS 7-9	Irregs.	Found In	Comments
10:29	221.2-222.5	13.3-.5, 13.8-14, 12	12.9-13, 14.1-.3, 12.8-9	12.3-.5, 13.2-.4, 13.2-.25←	4/3, 9/2 S/MS.	A/III/12-13, 30, 61; A/V/24 (1777[?]; date in later hand)	Ca. 1777–early 1780s; rastrum evidently brought from Mannheim to Munich.
10:30a	221.3-223.2	12.7-.8, 13.2-.6, 12.9-13 (13.2)	12.8-13.3, 13.4-.6, 13.2-.5	13.7-14, 13.7-14.3(.5), 13.4-.7←	7/1 S/MS, otherwise fairly regular. Broad tips, fairly wavy staving.	A/III/19, 35, 39, 45-47, 49-52	Ca. 1769–mid-1770s.
▶ 10:30b	222.4-223.4	12.7-.8, 13.5-.7, 13-13.15	13-13.2, 13.5-.7, 13.4-.5	13.8-14, 14.4-.6, 13.35-.4	Same.	A/III/17, 31, 40, 44, M7	Ca. 1767-73.
▶ 10:30c	222.5-223	13-13.05, 13-13.2, 13.15-.25	12.9-13, 13.3-.4, 13.3-.4	13.6-.7, 12.9-13, 14.15-.25	1/2, 2/4 L; 1/1, 2/1-3 S. Broad tips, fairly wavy staving, light ink.	A/III/25, 31, 35, 51-52	Ca. 1769–mid-1770s.
▶ 10:30d	222.7-224	13.4-.6, 13-13.2, 13.2-.65	12.9-13, 13.5-.85, 13.8-14.1	13.2-.5, 14-14.2, 13.5-.75←	7/1 S/MS. Broad tips, fairly wavy staving, light ink.	A/III/17, 19, 31, 41; A/VI/14, 192	Ca. 1767-73.
▶ 10:30e	223.5-224.3	12.8-.85, 13.7-.75, 13.1-.15	13.1-.15, 13.65-75, 14.4	13.2, 14-14.1, 13.65-.7	Same.	A/III/M7	Ca. 1769–early 1770s.
10:31	221.6-223	13.05-.15, 12.5-.6, 13.7-.9	12.7-.9, 13.2-.4, 13.5	12.6-.7, 13.6-.8, 14.4-.8←	4/3 S. Staff 9 smaller than others (SS = 9.1 mm.).	A/V/28, 32-33	Ca. 1775-76.
10:32	223.4-.7	13.65, 13.65-.8, 12.95-13	13.4-.5, 13.7-.75, 13-13.1	14, 13.25-.3, 13.6	3/2, 7/2, 10/4 MS.	A/III/19, 22	Prob. 2d half of 1760s.

Appendix C

VII. Twelve-Stave Rastra

Oblong Format

Rastrum	TS	DS 1-3	DS 4-6	DS 7-9	DS 10-11	Irregs.	Found In	Comments
12:1	198.5	9.7, 9.5, 9.85-.9	10.2-.25, 10.7-.75, 9.5	10.4, 10, 9.8	10.5, 10.65	Very irregular: 5/3, 7/3-4 L; 4/4, 5/2, 7/1, 8/3, 9/1, 9/4 S. Lines 7/4, 11/3 heavy.	A/VI/5 [1772+]	1772+.
12:2a	220.3-223	11(10.85)-11.2, 11.5-.7, 11-11.2	11.15-.3, 11.1-.25, 11.15-.3	11.4-.6, 11-11.3, 11.5-.7	10.8-11, 11.8-12←	8/1 L/ML; 5/2 S/MS.	A/I/17-23; A/V/4-8, 14, 15a-b, 17-18, 20 (all 1775–77); A/V/25, 28-29, 35-36, 38, 43	Ca. 1775-78.
▶ 12:2b	223.7-224.5	11.3-.4, 11.75, 11.15-.4	11.3-.4, 11.15-.3, 11.25-.45	11.7-.8, 11.25-.3, 11.7-.75	11-11.1, 12←	Same.	A/II/17-18	Ca. 1774.
12:3	220.5-222	11.6-.8, 10.7-.8, 10.3-.4	10.8-11, 11.2-.5, 11.7-.8	11.1-.2, 11.7-.8, 11.15-.25	11.2-.4, 10.6-.7←	5/4 generally L; 5/1-2 S/MS. Staff 3 larger than others.	A/V/3 ((1775)), 19 (1776), 22, 26-28, 30, 34, 39-42	Ca. 1775-76.
12:4	223.8-.9	10.8, 10.65-.7, 10.8	10.5, 10.5, 10.5	10.8-.9, 10.6-.7, 10.4-.5	10.85-.9, 10.9-11←	1/1, 4/4 L/ML. Line 3/1 often thicker.	A/II/21	Mid-1750s.
12:5	224.7-.8	10.8, 10.65-.7, 10.15	10.2, 11.4-.5, 11.4-.5	11-11.1, 10.8-.85, 11.1-.15	10.6-.65, 10.5-.55	3/4 L. Lines 1-3/5 often heavy; line 6/3 light, often gapped. Staff 12 small (SS = 7.75 mm.).	A/II/18	Ca. 1765.

Compound Rastra

Upright Format

Rastrum	TS	DS 1-3	DS 4-6	DS 7-9	DS 10-11	Irregs.	Found In	Comments
12:6	253-253.3	12.5/.9, 12.9-13.1, 13	12.1-2, 11.9-12, 13	12.5-13, 12, 12.5	11.9-12.1, 12.2-3	6/4 L; 6/3, 7/3 S.	A/VI/1-2	Date uncertain.
12:7a	282.5-283.3	15.1-2, 15, 14.3(14)	16.7-8, 14.5-.7, 15.8	14-14.1, 14-14.2, 15.8	15.3, 13.8-14.2←	8/4 L; 3/2 S.	A/II/1, 8	1760s (ca. 1765-70?)
▶ 12:7b	283-283.7	14.75-.9, 14.9-15, 14.1-2	16.2, 14-14.15, 17.2/.7	12.8-13, 14-14.1, 16.8	14.1-2, 14.1←	4/3 L; 4/2 S. Line 1/5 often thick.	A/II/1, 15; A/VI/8	1760s (ca. 1765-70?)–early 1770s.
▶ 12:7c	283-284.3	15.1-.25, 14.9-15.1, 14.3	16.9/17.25, 14.4-.5, 15.8	14.6-.7, 14-14.1, 15.5-.7	15.1-.3, 14.3-.4←	8/4 L; 3/2, 8/1 S. App. A/II/9 only: lines 12/2-4 thick, line 12/5 thin.	A/II/4, 9	Late 1760s–early 1770s.
▶ 12:7d	283.2-.8	14.8, 14.85-.9, 14.1-.2	16.2, 14, 17.9-18	12.2, 14, 16.7-.8	14, 14.2-.5←	4/3 L; 4/2 S	A/II/13, 15	1760s (ca. 1765-70?).
▶ 12:7e	283.9-284.1	15.1-.2, 14.9-15.1, 14.3	17.8, 13.7/14.15, 15.8	14.3, 14, 15.5-.6	15.3, 14.2-.3←	3/2 S. Lines 12/2-4 or 3-4 thick, line 12/5 thin.	A/II/7; A/IV/2 [1766]	1760s–early 1770s (ca. 1766?).
12:8a	284.1-285	15.05-15 15.05-15.2, 15.7	15.6-.75, 14.8-.9, 14.7-.85	14.9-15.1, 15.2-.3, 15.5-.6	15.2-.25, 15.7-.85	2/4, 3/1 and 3, 7/3-4 ML; 3/2, 12/4 MS.	A/II/2, 6; A/II/12 (1763); A/IV/1 (1757)	1753-ca. 1765 (ca. 1757-63 only?).
▶ 12:8b	284.5-.8	15.5, 15.25, 15	15.3, 15, 14.65-.7	14.85, 15.3-.4, 15.5	15.2, 15.6←	2/4, 7/4 ML; 3/2, 12/4 MS.	A/VI/144 [1753]	Ca. 1753.
▶ 12:8c	284.8-285.2	15.9-16, 15.1, 15.7	15.7-.75, 14.8, 14.7	15-15.1, 15.4-.5, 15.5-.6	15.2-.25, 15.5-.65	Same as 12:8a.	A/II/3, 6	Later 1750s–ca. 1765.
▶ 12:8d	285.3	15.75 15.3, 15.9	15.75, 15.2, 14.9	15.2, 15.45, 15.6	15.5, 15.7	Same as 12:8a.	A/II/2	1753–ca. 1760.

Appendix C

Rastrum	TS	DS 1-3	DS 4-6	DS 7-9	DS 10-11	Irregs.	Found In	Comments
▶ 12:8e	285.3-.5	16.2, 14.8-15, 15.7-.75	15.4-.55, 14.95-15.2, 14.6-.8	15-15.1, 15.4-.55, 15.7	15.05-.15, 15.6-.65←	Same as 12:8a, but space 3/3 more regular.	A/IV/1 (1757); A/VI/144 (1756)	Ca. 1756-57.
12:9	284.2-.6	15.7, 15.8, 15.5	15.9, 15.3, 15.1	15.7, 15.3, 15.9	15.5, 16.1	DL generally regular. Broad tips.	A/VI/8	Prob. late 1760s or early 1770s.
12:10a	291-292.3	16-16.1, 16.1-.2, 15.4-6	15.7-.85, 15.4-.6, 15.8	15.2-.3, 14.8-15, 15.6-.8	15.75-.9, 15.7-.85←	3/2, 4/2 L/ML; 3/1 S. Line 1/5 thick.	A/II/13; A/V/15b (1776), 22-23, 27	Ca. 1776.
▶ 12:10b	291-293.1	16-16.1, 16-16.2, 15.7-.9	15.7-.9, 15.5-.7, 15.6-.8	15.2-.3, 14.9-15.1, 15.7-.9	15.9(.8)-16, 15.8-.9←	3/2, 4/2 L/ML; 3/1 S/MS.	A/II/1, 3, 5, 7, 9, 11-15; A/IV/2; A/V/9 [1775/76], 25, 31	Mid-1770s.
▶ 12:10c	291.2-291.8	16-16.05, 16-16.15, 15.7-.85	15.85-16, 15.7, 15.7-.9	15.1-.3, 14.75-.85, 15.5-.75	15.75-.85, 15.8	Same.	A/V/19 (1776), 29	Ca. 1776.
▶ 12:10d	292.4-293.2	16-16.1, 16.1-.2, 15.6-.85	15.7-.85, 15.6-.8, 15.85-16	15.5-.65, 14.8-15, 15.7	15.85-16, 15.75-.9←	Same.	A/II/10; A/V/17 (1776), 28-29; A/VI/145	Ca. 1776.

Appendix D

Copyists

Appendix D provides information on the most important copyists active at the Mannheim court. (See also the section "Handwriting and Copyists" of chapter 2, especially the subsection "Copyists in the Mannheim Manuscripts.") The term *copyist* is used here to mean anyone who wrote down music—not only professional copyists but also composers, instrumentalists pressed into service on occasion, and so on.

Appendix D is divided into three sections. The first is devoted to those copyists, usually composers, whose names are known, and who are therefore so cited. The second is devoted to those copyists whose manuscripts are found either among the Mannheim court materials at the Bayerische Staatsbibliothek in Munich (D-Mbs) or in two or more collections; these copyists are labeled Mannheim 1–21. The third section is devoted to copyists whose manuscripts appear in only one collection (other than D-Mbs); these copyists are identified by an abbreviation of the present location of the manuscript plus a numerical designation as a Mannheim copyist (e.g., Rtt/Mh. 1 for the first Mannheim copyist at Regensburg).

Depending on the amount of data available, information is then provided (1) identifying the copyist, (2) listing the works in Appendix A in which his hand appears, and (3) giving the dates at which the manuscripts indicate he was active as a copyist. Tracings are supplied for the most prolific copyists; these consist of our actual pencil tracings (enhanced using Adobe Photoshop) except for those of Mannheim 1–6 and Rtt/Mh. 1 and 3, which have been redrawn in ink. In addition, for the most important copyists, reproductions of a page or two of their hands are provided. Other reproductions containing samples of the various hands are also cited whenever possible.

It is important to note with respect to the second and third of the categories mentioned above that, as in Appendices B and C, this appendix merely extracts and summarizes certain information presented in greater detail in Appendix A. Thus the rubric "Found in," giving the sources in which the copyist in question appears, merely lists the manuscripts in question and any firm dates associated with them; one must always refer to the comprehensive description of that manuscript in Appendix A for details on precisely which portions of the manuscript are in the copyist's hand. Likewise, the heading "Dates of activity as copyist" (with "at Mannheim" understood) simply gives the dates of the earliest and latest manuscripts identified in this survey that contain the copyist's hand, extracted from the full description of the source in Appendix A; it does not furnish an independent assessment based, for example, on biographical data. (For the most important of these copyists, such an assessment will be found in chapter 2 or at another relevant point in the text.)

On the conventions for specifying dates adopted here see the introduction to Appendix A. As before, a free-standing date or one in parentheses is one I consider reliable that actually appears in the manuscript, while a date in (square) brackets is one I consider certain or

Appendix D

virtually certain but does not actually occur there (e.g., an undated set of parts to a dated score that was clearly prepared at the same time as the latter).

I. Named Copyists

The first section of Appendix D treats those copyists who are known by name, principally composers at the electoral court who have left signed autographs or have been otherwise identified. The order is approximately chronological. Three other names also come into consideration but have not been incorporated here for various reasons. The first is that of Johann Toeschi (1735–1800), younger brother of the concertmaster Joseph Toeschi. What seems to be a sketch for a concerto for viola d'amore attributed to him exists in F-Pc, Ms. 2199 (see the reprod. in *MGG*, 1st ed., 13:453–54); my argument for not including this manuscript here is laid out in the section "Paper in the Mannheim Manuscripts" of chapter 2. Secondly, though the hand of Carl Stamitz (1745–1801) is known (see, e.g., the reprod. in *MGG*, 1st ed., 12:1157–58), no manuscripts by him can be shown to stem from his Mannheim period (to 1770). Finally, the copyists Bln./Mh. 2 and 3, found in the manuscripts A/VI/21 and 22 (both cello concertos), could be the composers and cellists Innocenz Danzi and Anton Fils. However, because no documentary evidence exists to support such an attribution, they are relegated to Appendix D/III.

1. Carlo Grua

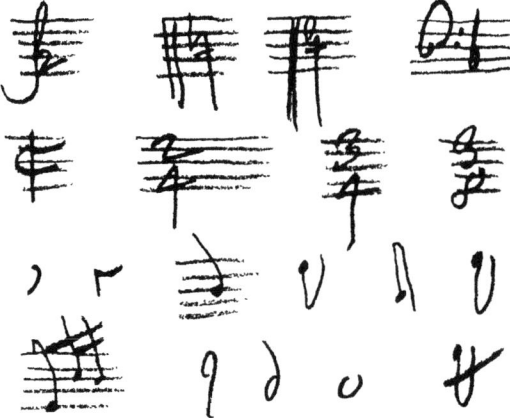

Grua (ca. 1695/1700–1773) was Kapellmeister at Mannheim from at least 1734 until his death. He composed the festival opera *Meride*, the music of which has not survived, for the wedding of Carl Theodor and Elisabeth Augusta on 18 January 1742. From 1751 on he

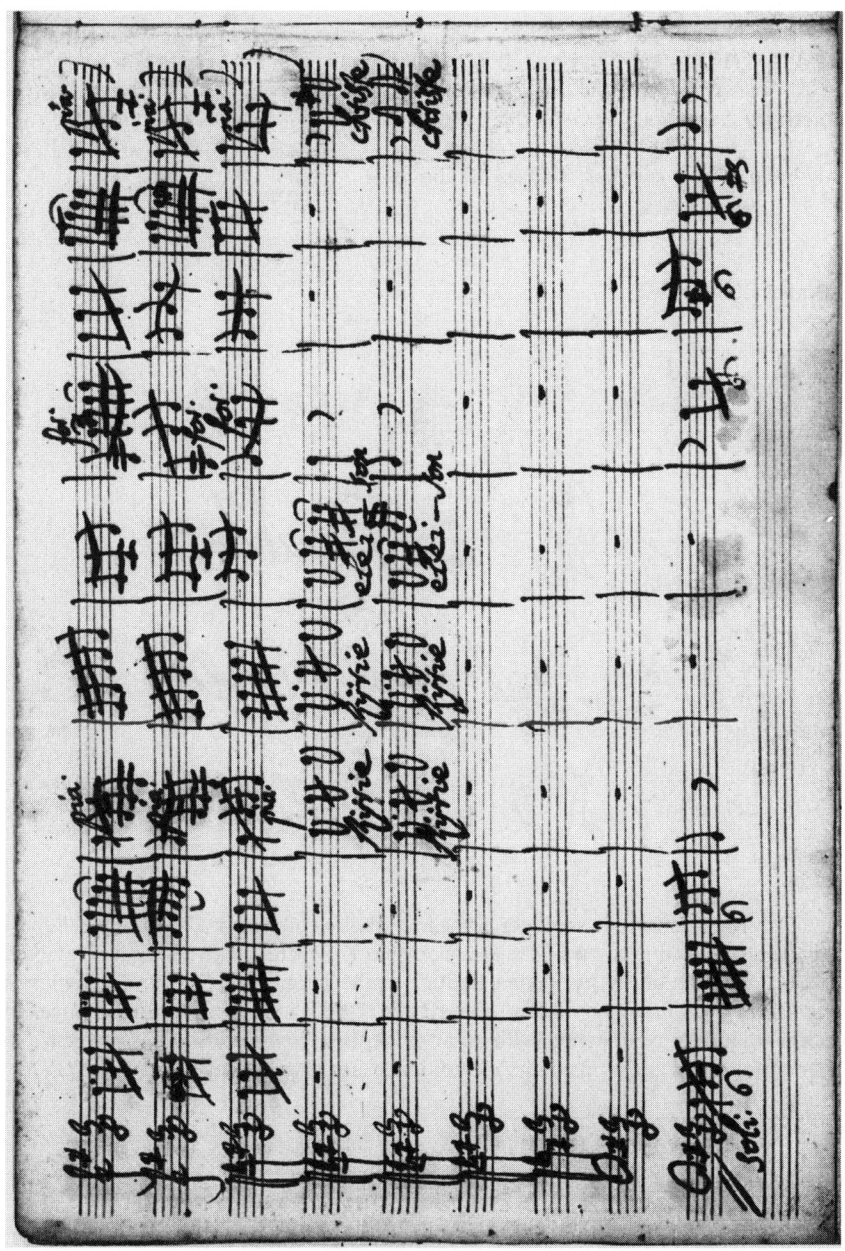

Figure D:1. *Carlo Grua.* First page of autograph score to his *Littanie della beata vergine* (1737; App. A/I/9). Munich, Bayerische Staatsbibliothek, Mus. Ms. 1982.

Appendix D

shared the post of Kapellmeister with Johann Stamitz and later Ignaz Holzbauer, devoting himself primarily to sacred music.

Found in: A/I/8 (1733), 9 (1737), 10–11(1751), 12 (1753), 13 (1766); A/IV/1 (1757), 2 [1766].

Dates of activity as copyist: 1733–66.

Additional handwriting samples: figure D:1, above.

2. Franz Xaver Richter

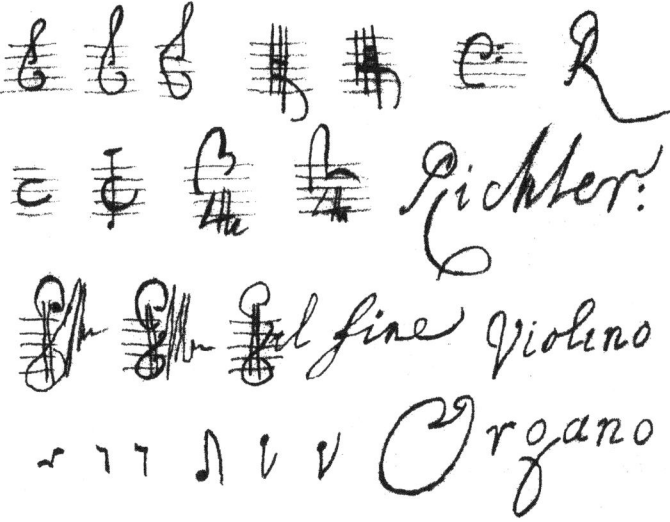

Richter (1709–89) appears as a bass singer at the Mannheim court from 1747 until his departure to take the post of *maître de chapelle* in Strasbourg in 1769. His handwriting has received an admirably thorough study by Jochen Reutter in the latter's *Studien zur Kirchenmusik Franz Xaver Richters* (Frankfurt am Main: Peter Lang, 1993), 1:92–110. Various changes in the composer's hand, in conjunction with other evidence, allow Reutter to assign dates to the undated autographs with considerable confidence (see chap. 6 and Appendix A/IV).

Found in: A/IV/3 [1747/48], 4–9, 10 [1767/68].

Dates of activity as copyist: 1747/48–1767/68.

Additional handwriting samples: figure D:2; Reutter, 1:608–15.

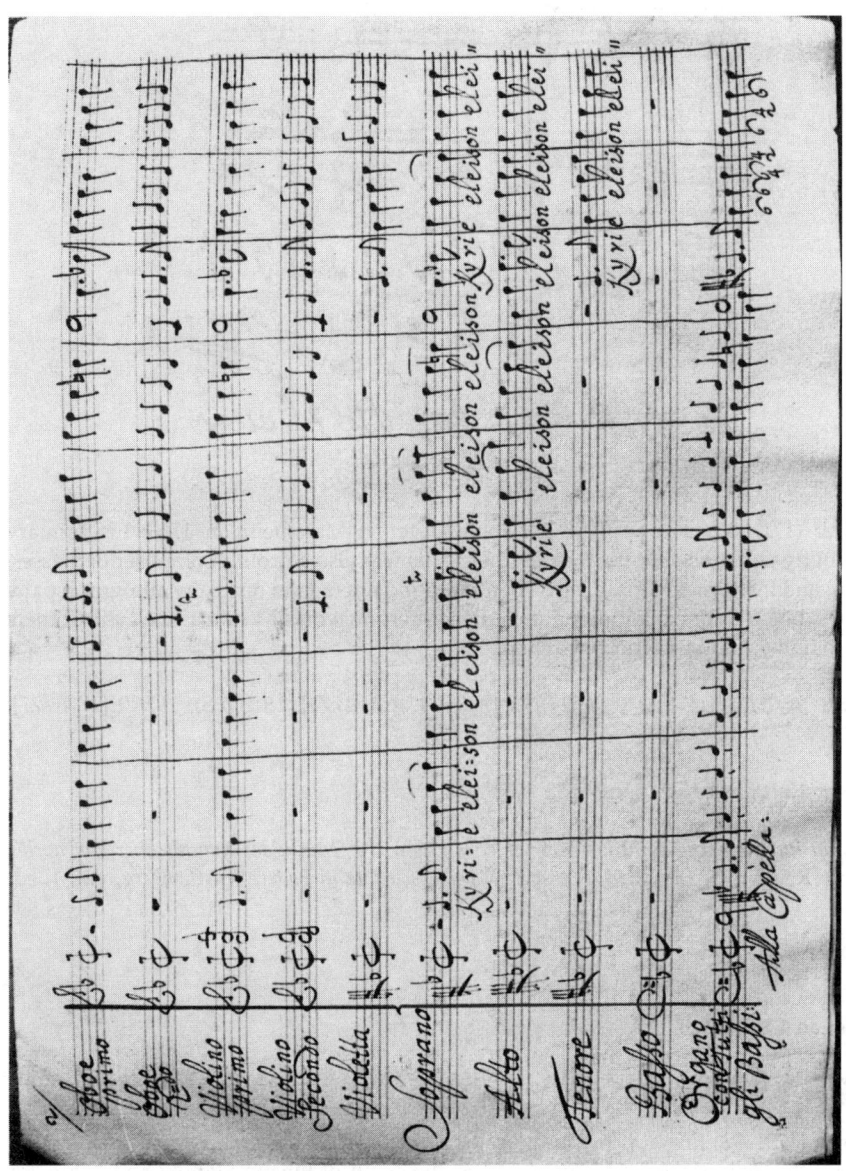

Figure D:2. *Franz Xaver Richter.* First page of autograph score to his *Messa a 15 voci* (ca. 1777–81; Reutter A 4). Strasbourg, Union Ste Cécile, M 25.

Appendix D

3. Ignaz Holzbauer

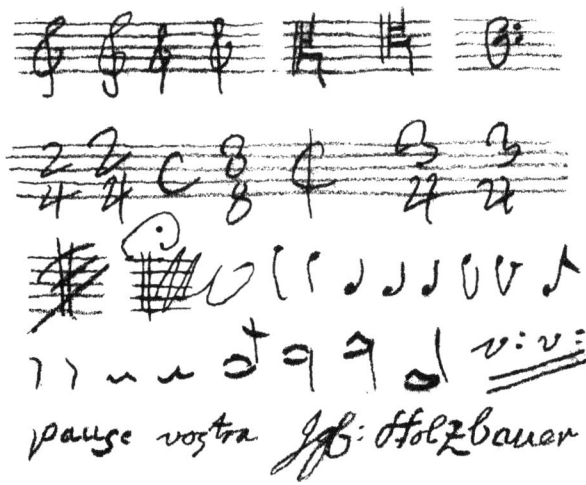

Holzbauer (1711–83) was appointed Kapellmeister at Mannheim in 1753; his primary responsibility was music for the theater, though he was also a prolific composer of masses, oratorios, and instrumental music. His hand is found not only in his many autograph parts and scores, but in frequent additions and emendations to works by him as well as by others that came under his jurisdiction (see chap. 4).

Found in: A/II/2–5, 7–9, 11, 12 (1763), 13–15, 17 [ca. 1774], 18 (1765), 19, 20 [1776/77]; A/VI/151 [1774], 168, 192.

Dates of activity as copyist: ca. 1753–1776/77.

Additional handwriting samples: figure D:3; Bush, 132; *Musik der Mannheimer Hofkapelle*, vol. 1, ed. Reutter, p. xxxvii; *Quellen zur Musikgeschichte in Baden-Württemberg*, vol. 1, ed. Pelker.

4. Christian Cannabich

See page 342 for tracings.

Cannabich (1731–98) first appears in the court records in 1744 as an accessist, then in 1746 as a violinist. He became concertmaster after the death of Johann Stamitz and "Direktor der Instrumentalmusik" in 1774 before traveling with the court to Munich in 1778. His hand, first identified by Jean K. Wolf (Wolf and Wolf, "Complex," 387–88, 435–37), appears initially in his earliest extant symphony, the church symphony A/III/2, then (beginning

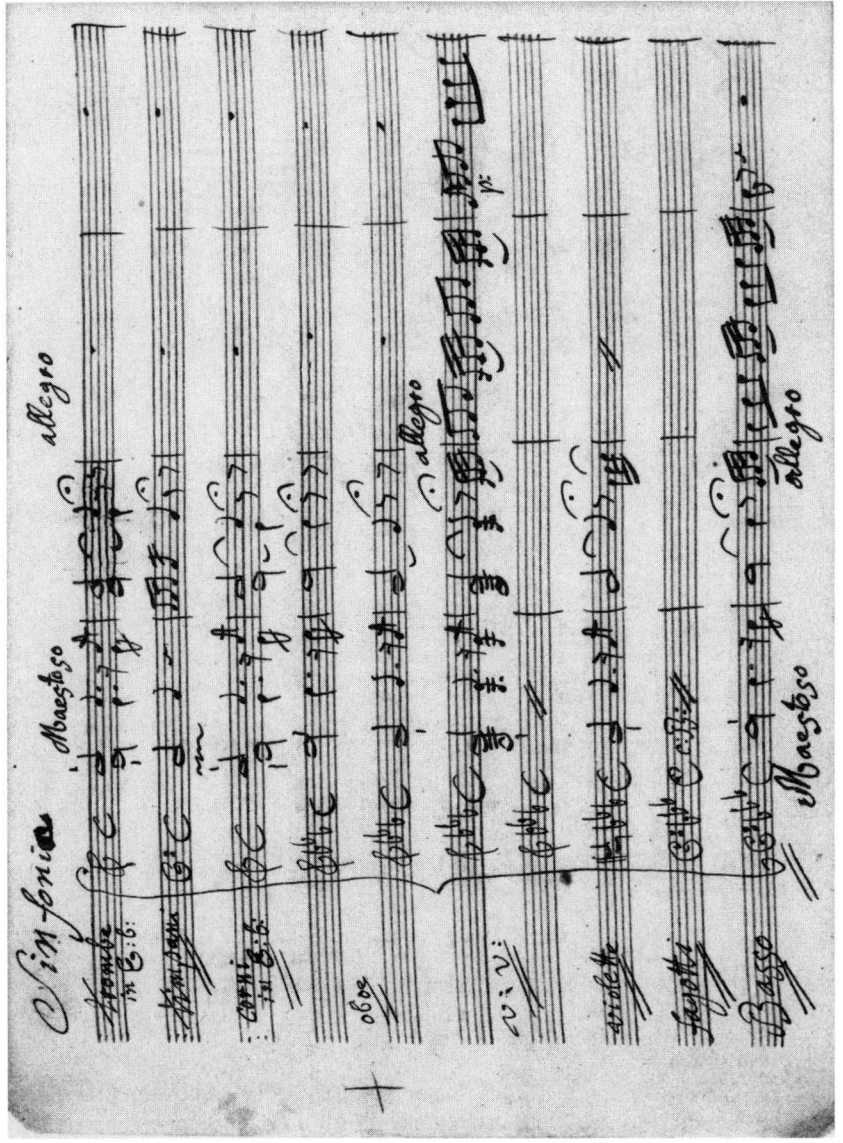

Figure D:3. *Ignaz Holzbauer.* First page of autograph score to his *Günther von Schwarzburg* (1777; App. A/II/20). Neuenstein, Hohenlohe Zentral-Archiv, Musikalien Bartenstein, Bü 111/4.

Appendix D

Cannabich, early hand:

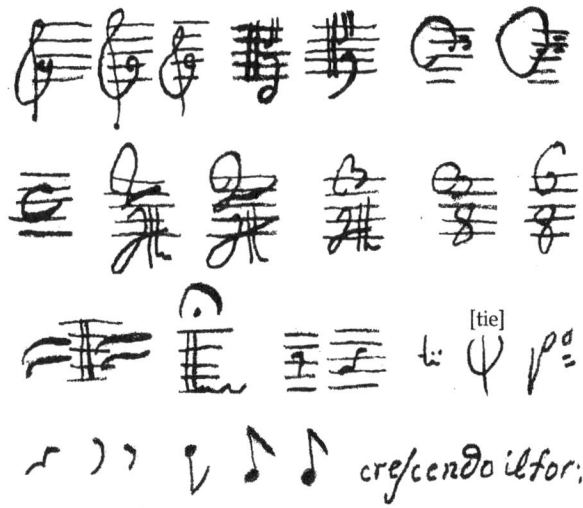

Cannabich, late hand:

in A/III/17) in numerous individual parts, many added after the fact to the preexistent series (see chap. 5 and Appendix A/III). Only in Munich does he become the principal copyist of his manuscripts, presumably as a result of the straitened financial situation there. Cannabich's handwriting shows a fairly clear development in the course of his career, as can be seen in the tracings and figures reproduced here; particularly evident is the shift beginning in A/III/47 (ca. 1772–74) to a simpler, more fully rounded treble clef (i.e., without the hook-like flourish to the right; the earlier clef form continues to occur sporadically thereafter, however) and in the frequent use of one-grapheme white noteheads, resembling a rounded *U*, beginning in A/III/51 (ca. 1774–75).

Found in: A/III/2, 18, 21–24, 30–32, 34–36, 38–40, 42–57, 58A, 59–72, 73a (1794), 73b [1794], M6–7; A/VI/161.

Dates of activity as copyist: ca. 1755–1794.

Additional handwriting samples: figures D:4–5; Wolf and Wolf, "Complex," 435–37; Wolf and Wolf, eds., vol. C/III of *The Symphony, 1720–1840*, pp. 286, 320–39; DTB, Neue Folge, 11, ed. Hörner, p. xxxi. All but the first of these examples are from Cannabich's late period.

5. Johannes Ritschel

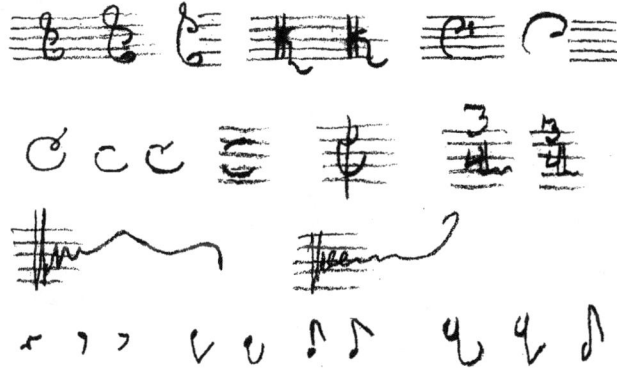

Ritschel (1739–66) is listed as a violinist at court from 1756 until 1763, then as Vice-Kapellmeister from 1764 until his early death two years later at the age of 26. He studied with Padre Martini in Bologna in the period 1758–62; autograph manuscripts from that period now in I-Bc have allowed the identification of his hand.

Found in: A/I/1 (1763).

Dates of activity as copyist: 1763.

Additional handwriting samples: Reutter, "Die Kirchenmusik am Mannheimer Hof," in Finscher, ed., *Die Mannheimer Hofkapelle*, 107–8.

Appendix D

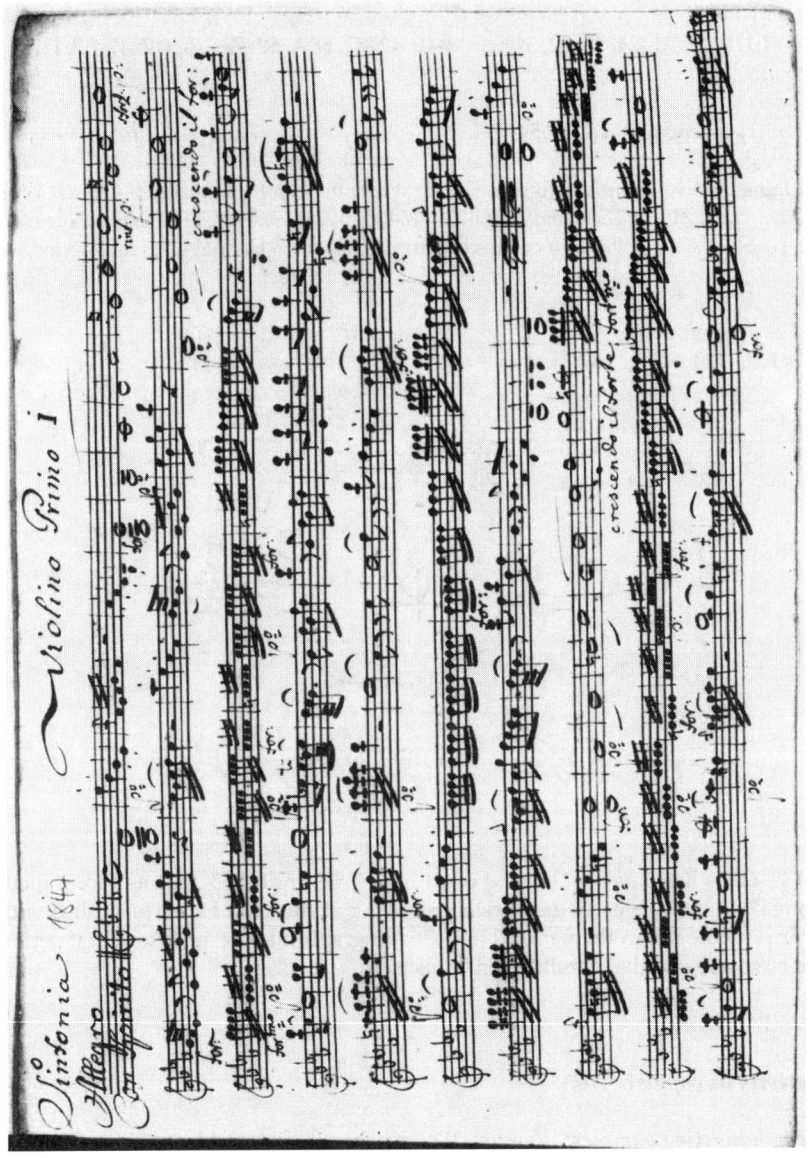

Figure D:4. *Christian Cannabich, early hand.* Violin 1, page 1 of his Symphony no. 18 (ca. 1762; App. A/III/18). Note the roman numeral *I* to the right of "Violino Primo," indicating that this was the first of several violin 1 parts; comparable numbers appear in figures D:11–13. Munich, Bayerische Staatsbibliothek, Mus. Ms. 1847.

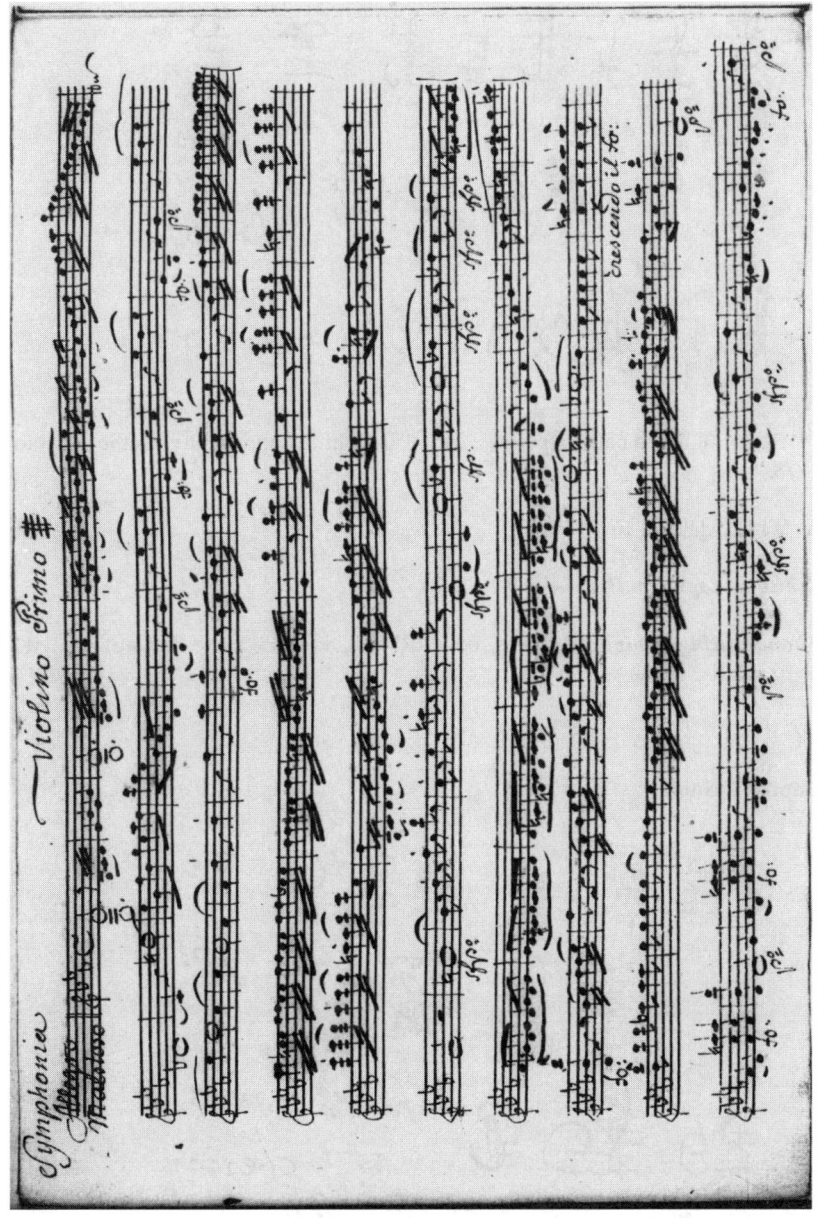

Figure D.5. *Christian Cannabich, late hand.* Violin 1, page 1 of his Symphony no. 62 (ca. 1781/82[?]; App. A/III/62). See also figure 2.5. Munich, Bayerische Staatsbibliothek, Mus. Ms. 1875.

Appendix D

6. Sigismund Falgera (also Falgara)

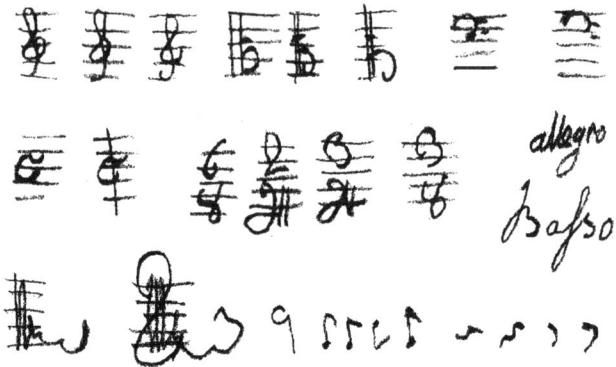

Falgera (ca. 1752–1790) was a ballet *répétiteur* and also violinist who went with the court to Munich in 1778.

Found in: A/I/14–15 (1769), 16 (?1767).

Dates of activity as copyist: ?1767–1769

Additional handwriting samples: Grave, ed., RRMCE, vol. 45, plate 1; Cauthen, ed., RRMCE, vol. 52, plates 3–4.

7. Johann Baptist Cramer

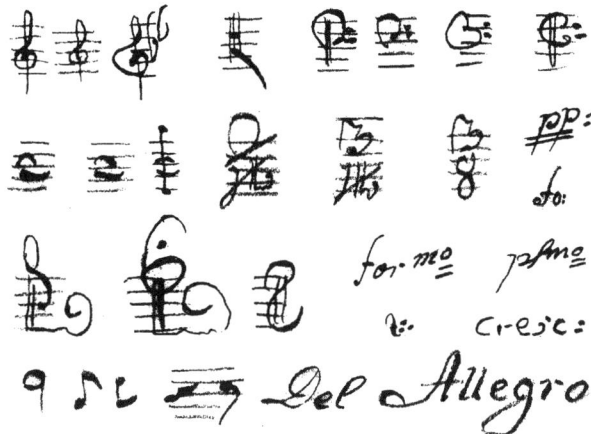

Figure D:6. *Johann Cramer.* Violin 1, page 1 of Ignaz Holzbauer, *Missa* in F (App. A/II/13). Cf. also the similar hand of figure D:9, by Mannheim 1, probably Johann Cramer's father, Jacob. Munich, Bayerische Staatsbibliothek, Mus. Ms. 2301.

Appendix D

Johann Cramer (1749–1824) assumed his father Jacob's position as an official copyist after the latter's death in 1770, though he was probably serving as a copyist at court before then. He is also listed as a violist in the almanacs of 1771–74. He journeyed with the court to Munich in 1778, where he became the elector's main copyist. His hand, similar in many respects to that of Mannheim 1 (probably his father, Jacob; see below), was first identified in Robert Münster, "Johann Cramer und andere Hofmusik-Kopisten in Mannheim und München zwischen 1770 und 1810," Die Musikforschung 22 (1969): 475–77.

Found in: A/II/11–14; A/V/20 [1777], 22, 25, 31; A/VI/2.5 (?), 26 [1776/77], 35 (?), 193 (?).

Dates of activity as copyist: second half of 1760s (at latest 1770)–1777.

Additional handwriting samples: figure D:6, above; Bush, 136–37; Münster, "Cramer," 477; Reutter, "Die Kirchenmusik am Mannheimer Hof," in Finscher, ed., Die Mannheimer Hofkapelle, 110; Reutter, ed., Musik der Mannheimer Hofkapelle, vol. 1, p. xxix (there identified as Munich [ex-Mannheim] A, i.e., Mannheim 1). (NB: the reprod. in Haberkamp and Münster, KBM, 9, p. xxxi, incorrectly identifies the hand as that of Cramer; it is probably that of the Munich copyist Joseph Palm [see chap. 2, fn. 100]).

8. Georg Joseph Vogler

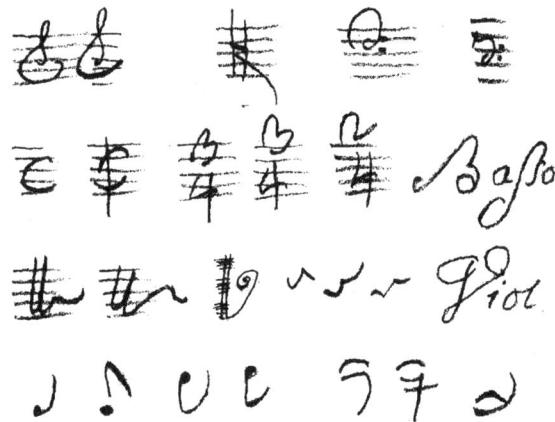

In addition to his musical duties, "Abbé" or "Abt" Vogler (1749–1814) was court chaplain and spiritual counselor to elector Carl Theodor during the 1770s. By February of 1776 he had become second Kapellmeister to Holzbauer, but eventually chose not to accompany the court to Munich in 1778. Vogler's extant manuscripts from his Mannheim period (see chap. 7 and Appendix A/V) include two early secular works, a large body of liturgical music from the period 1775–76, and two large German sacred works from 1777; these comprise both autograph scores and parts.

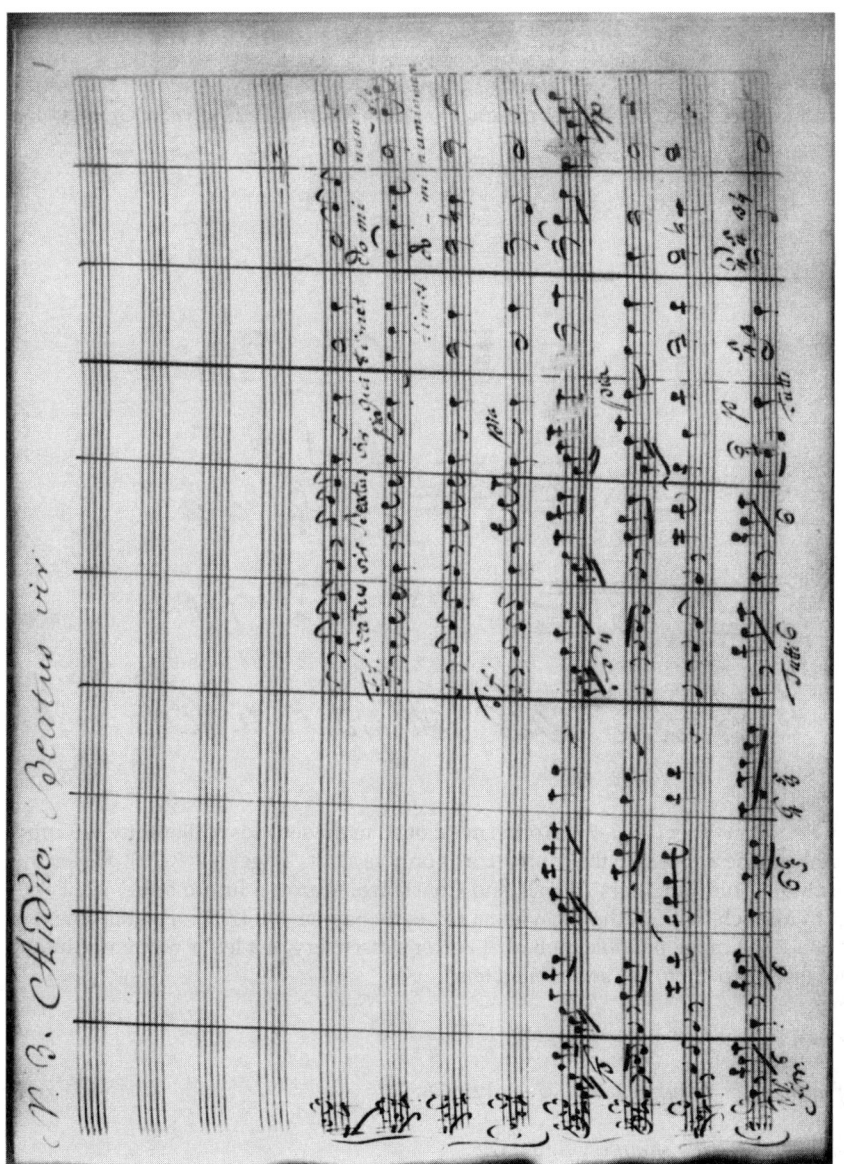

Figure D.7. *Georg Joseph Vogler.* First page of autograph score to his *Beatus vir* (App. A/V/29). Darmstadt, Hessische Landes- und Hochschulbibliothek, Mus. ms. 1118.

Appendix D

Found in: A/V/1 (1771), 2a (1772), 3–14 (1775–76), 15a (1776), 16–19 (1776), 20 [1777], 21, 24 [1777], 25–26, 28–36, 38–43.

Dates of activity as copyist: 1771–77.

Additional handwriting samples: figure D:7, above; Grave, ed., RRMCE, vol. 45, plates 3–4 (music of all but vn. 1, but not textual material or clefs); Bauman, ed., *German Opera*, vol. 8, fols. 38–49.

9. Fridolin Weber

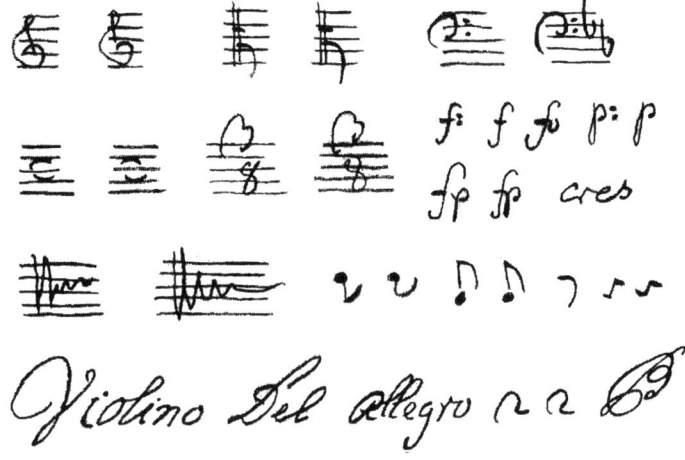

Although Fridolin Weber (1733–79) is often mentioned in the secondary literature as a copyist at Mannheim, he appears in the court records only as a bass singer (1767–78). He and his family, including his daughters Aloysia and Constanze, Mozart's future bride, went with the court to Munich in 1778, then to Vienna (by early September 1779). Establishment of Weber's hand was made possible by Bärbel Pelker's discovery of a letter written by him to the elector (see chap. 2, fn. 104 and related text).

Found in: App. A/VI/36 [late 1777–early 1778].

Dates of activity as copyist: late 1777–early 1778.

Additional handwriting samples: figure D:8.

Copyists

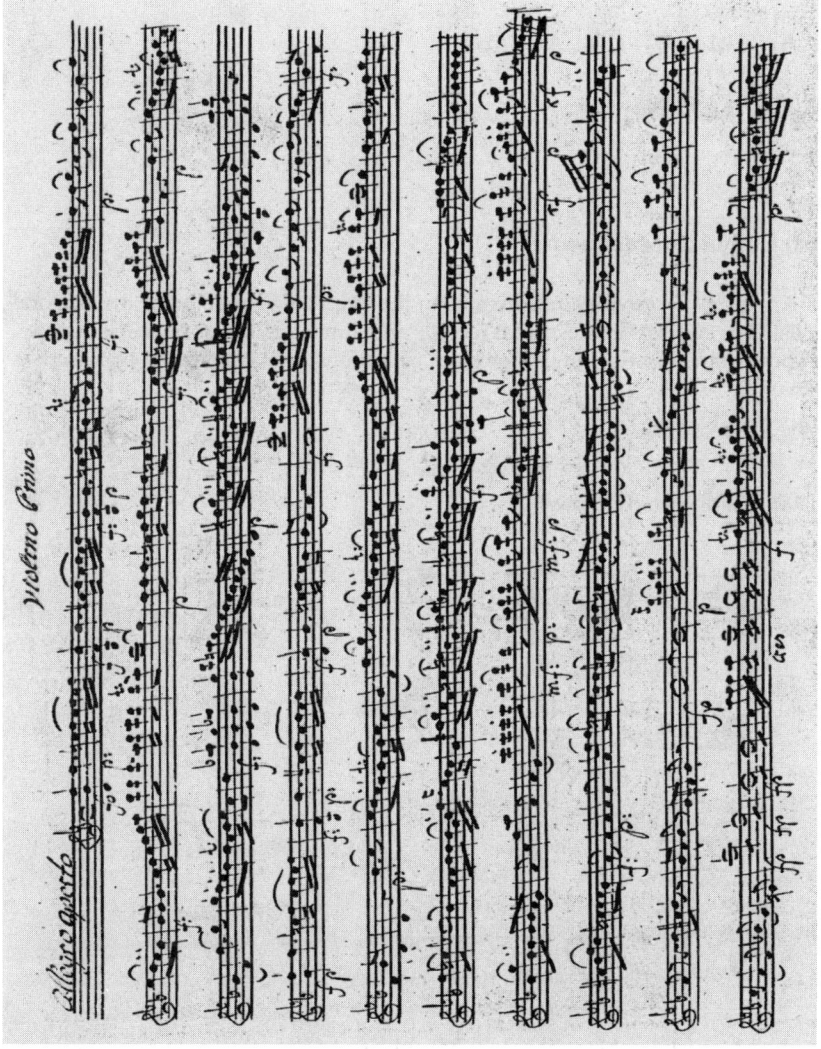

Figure D:8. *Fridolin Weber.* Violin 1, page 1 of Mozart's aria "Aer tranquillo," from *Il rè pastore*, K. 208 (App. A/VI/36, from 1777/78). Berlin, Staatsbibliothek zu Berlin – Preussischer Kulturbesitz, Mus. ms. 15142/5.

Appendix D

10. Wolfgang Amadeus Mozart

The extant autograph manuscripts of Mozart from his sojourn in Mannheim in 1777/78, and a fragment from his return visit in November and December of 1778, are listed in Appendix A/I and (one part for two oboes) A/IV.

Found in: A/I/17–24 (?1777–1778); A/IV/11.

Dates of activity as copyist: ?late 1777–1778.

II. Principal Copyists (Mannheim 1–21)

Section II of Appendix D provides information on the main copyists active at the electoral court, some listed as copyists in the official records and almanacs, others not. These copyists either appear in manuscripts in two or more collections or in Mannheim manuscripts now in D-Mbs.

Mannheim 1 (probably Jacob Cramer)

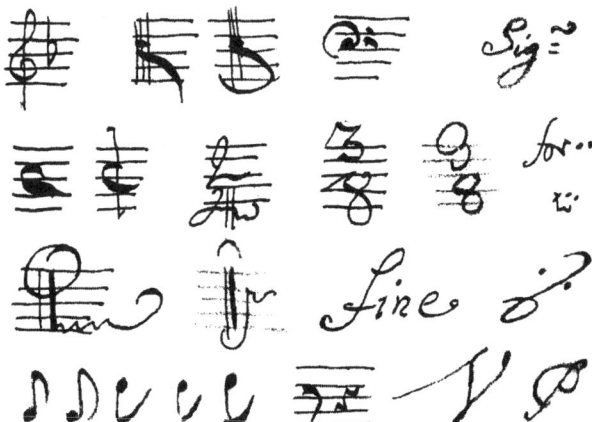

Previously called Munich (ex-Mannheim) A. Mannheim 1 is the most active copyist identified here, at least in terms of number of items copied; his hand is found in a total of 83 manuscripts. He was a principal copyist of the Cannabich symphonies through no. 41, and he appears in many of the Holzbauer masses, a large number of single arias from the 1750s and early 1760s in the Pretlack collection in Berlin, and numerous instrumental works in Regensburg. He also copied the complete score of Traetta's *Sofonisba* of 1763 (A/VI/204).

Figure D:9. *Mannheim 1* (probably Jacob Cramer). First page of Pietro Chiarini, "Se al lab[b]ro mio non credi" (App. A/VI/44). See also figures 2:9a–b. Berlin, Staatsbibliothek zu Berlin – Preussischer Kulturbesitz, N. Mus. BP 171.

Appendix D

Identification: based on the dates at which he was active and the strong similarity of his hand to that of the later Mannheim copyist Johann Cramer (see above), Mannheim 1 can probably be identified as Johann Cramer's father, Jacob (1705–70), the principal court copyist from at least 1746 until his death (see the discussion in the section "Copyists in the Mannheim Manuscripts" of chap. 2).

Found in: A/II/1–3, 5–7, 9, 12 (1763); A/III/2, 4, 7, 9, 13, 15, 17–18, 22, 25, 36, 41, M1–2, M4/76, M5/74, M6; A/VI/3–4, 19, 28–29, 38–39, 44–45, 47–57, 63, 86–99, 102–9, 111, 114–18, 154, 156, 168–70, 172, 193, 204 (1763 or possibly later).

Dates of activity as copyist: ca. 1750 (see A/VI/57, 63, 106–7, 113–15, and 117–18, excerpts from operas with premieres at Mannheim in 1750–51)–ca. 1770 (date assigned here to A/III/41, a Cannabich symphony).

Additional handwriting samples: figure 2:8b; figure D:9, above; Bush, 133–34, 156–57; Pelker, ed., *Musik der Mannheimer Hofkapelle*, vol. 2, pp. xxxix–xliii.

Mannheim 2 (?Johann Lochner)

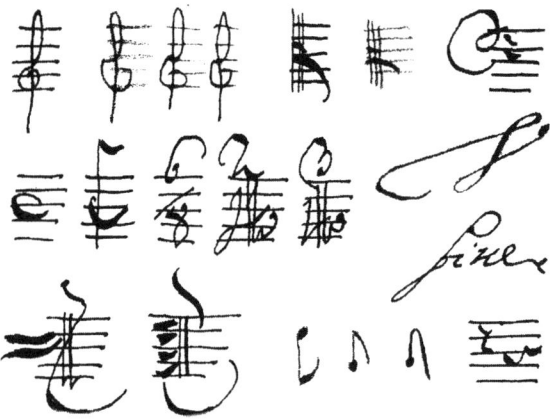

Previously called Munich (ex-Mannheim B). Mannheim 2 was primarily a copyist of sacred music. He is one of the two main scribes of the Holzbauer masses in Munich, and also copied Holzbauer masses for distribution elsewhere. His hand appears in some instrumental music, especially a half-dozen early symphonies of Cannabich in Munich and a few miscellaneous instrumental works in Regensburg, and he is the copyist of the complete manuscript of Cannabich's ballet *Renaud et Armide* of 1768 (A/VI/13).

Identification: most likely the violist and copyist Johann Lochner, who appears in court records from 1754 until his death in late 1774; datable copies by Mannheim 2 extend from

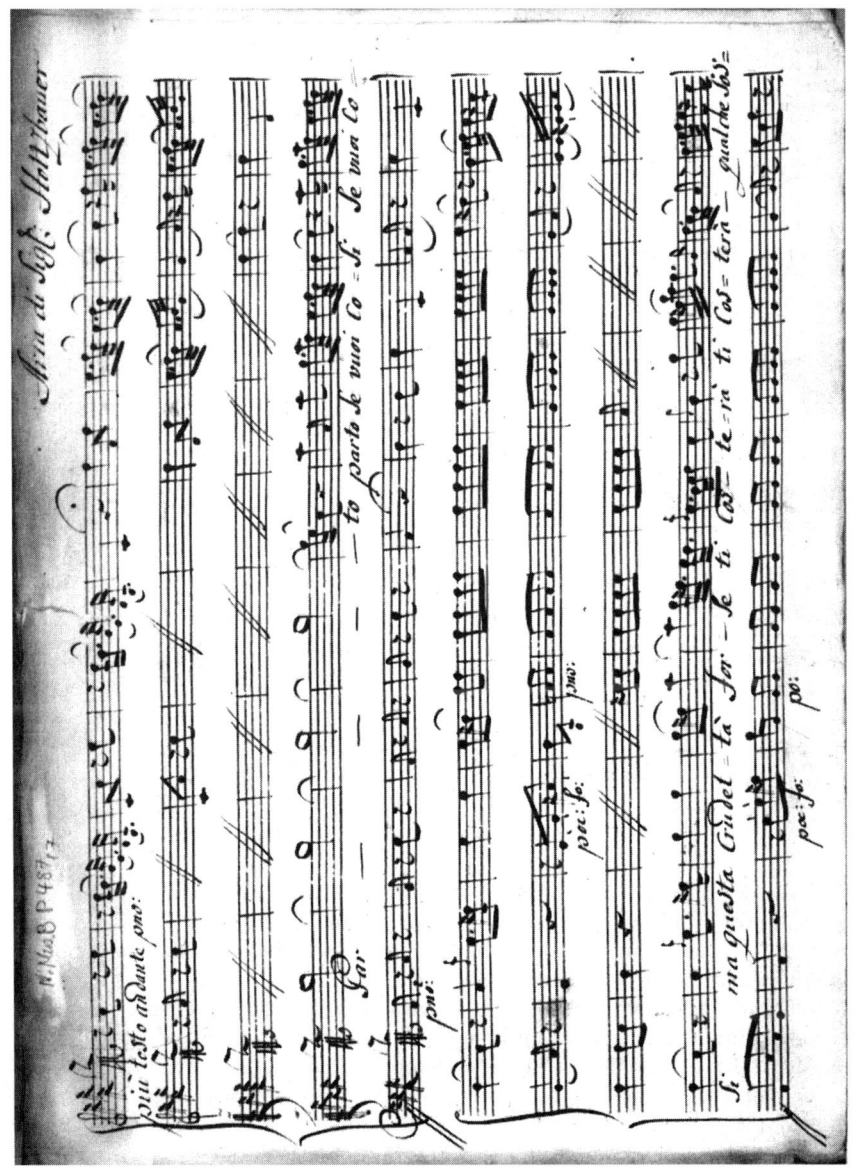

Figure D:10. *Mannheim 2* (?Johann Lochner). First page of Ignaz Holzbauer, "Parto se vuoi così," from *L'isola disabitata* (1754; App. A/VI/101). See also figure 4:1. Berlin, Staatsbibliothek zu Berlin – Preussischer Kulturbesitz, N. Mus. BP 487.

Appendix D

ca. 1755 to the mid-1770s only, almost exactly the dates of Lochner's service (see the discussion in the section "Copyists in the Mannheim Manuscripts" of chap. 2).

Found in: A/II/1–2, 4–5, 7–9, 11, 12 (1763), 13–16; A/III/4, 7–8, M1–2, M3/75; A/IV/1 (1757), 2 [1766]; A/VI/6-7, 9-12, 13 [1768+], 100-101 [1754+], 185, 188, 192.

Dates of activity as copyist: ca. 1753 (earliest Holzbauer masses from Mannheim; App. A/VI/100-101, two arias from Holzbauer's *Issipile* of 1754)–mid-1770s (single parts to A/II/1 and 5, also A/II/14).

Additional handwriting samples: figure D:10, above; Bush, 138–39; Marsh, ed., RRMCE, vol. 57, plates 1–2; Reutter, ed., *Musik der Mannheimer Hofkapelle*, vol. 1, pp. xxx–xxxiv.

Mannheim 3 (?Wilhelm Sepp)

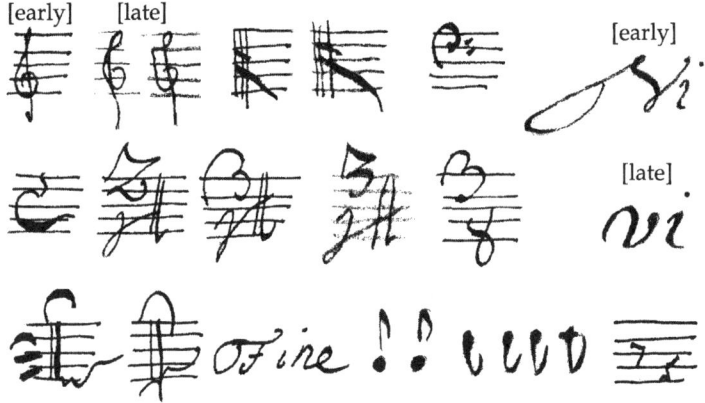

Previously called Munich (ex-Mannheim) C. Mannheim 3 is nearly tied with Mannheim 6 as the second most prolific copyist at the court (after Mannheim 1), with 44 manuscripts to his credit. These span some 25 years, from the mid-1750s to the early Munich period, a slightly longer period than that represented by Mannheim 2. In his later copies his hand changes significantly, as shown in the tracing above and in figures D:11–12; many of these parts are later additions to the Cannabich series of symphonies in Munich (see chap. 5 and Appendix A/III). With only one exception (App. A/II/5), his extant manuscripts are exclusively of instrumental music, most notably in the Cannabich series, where he appears as early as no. 2 and as late as 58A, and in many instrumental works in Regensburg.

Identification: the only copyist at court who fulfills the criteria of length of service and transfer with the court to Munich is evidently Wilhelm Sepp (ca. 1715–91). Sepp appears as an instrumentalist in court records from 1745 onward but is never actually listed in the almanacs as a copyist; however, a rescript of 1760 provides an annual salary for him as a copyist (see the section "Copyists in the Mannheim Manuscripts" of chap. 2).

Found in: A/II/15; A/III/2–3, 7–9, 11–17, 19, 21, 25, 29, 32, 35, 39–40, 42, 44, 46, 51–52, 55, 58A, M6; A/V/2b (paste-ons); A/VI/23, 157–60, 162–67, 173, 187, 190; parts to Cannabich's ballet *Médée et Jason*, D-DS, Mus. ms. 219, very probably from Munich.

Dates of activity as copyist: ca. 1755–ca. 1780 (Cannabich symphonies A/III/2–58A).

Additional handwriting samples: figures D:11–12; Bush, 140; Baker, ed., RRMCE, vol. 47, plate 4 (from *Médée et Jason*, considered here to come from the early Munich period).

Mannheim 4 (Caspar Bohrer?)

Previously called Munich (ex-Mannheim) D. Mannheim 4 presents an interesting case in that he appears exclusively in Cannabich's symphonies of the Munich series, primarily nos. 38–58B (the latter a Munich copy), and in two manuscripts of Cannabich 59 (ca. 1780) in other collections (D-WD, Mus. 912, and US-Wc, M 1001.C22P [No. 3] Case, a manuscript from the Fulda collection). A notable characteristic of his hand is the change in his treble clef from a two-grapheme to a rounded form (see the tracing above), the latter found from Cannabich 53 on and in other manuscripts considered here to date from the same time, the very late Mannheim and early Munich periods (see the extended discussion of this issue in the section "Types of Parts" in chap. 5).

Identification: given the dates of his manuscripts of the Cannabich symphonies, from ca.

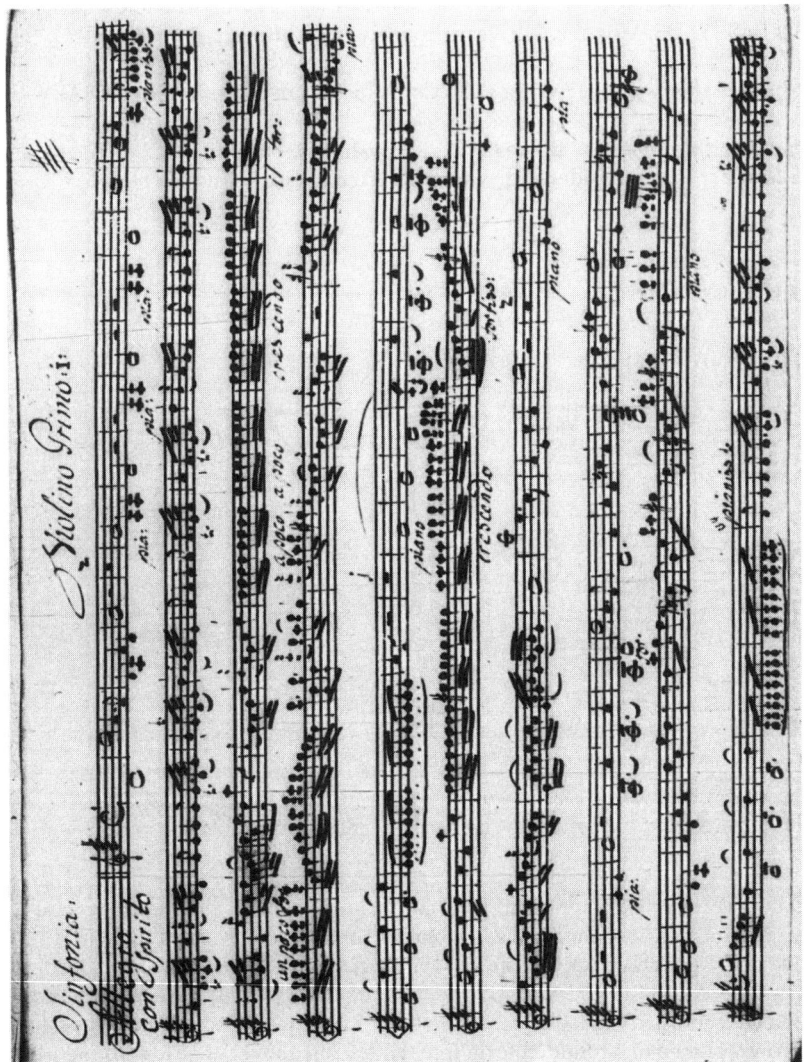

Figure D:11. *Mannheim 3* (?Wilhelm Sepp), *early hand.* Violin 1, page 1 of Christian Cannabich, Symphony no. 11 (ca. 1760; App. A/III/11). See also figure 2:7. The roman numeral *I* to the right of "Violino Primo" indicates that this was the first of several violin 1 parts; similar markings also appear in figures D:4 and D:12–13. Munich, Bayerische Staatsbibliothek, Mus. Ms. 1837.

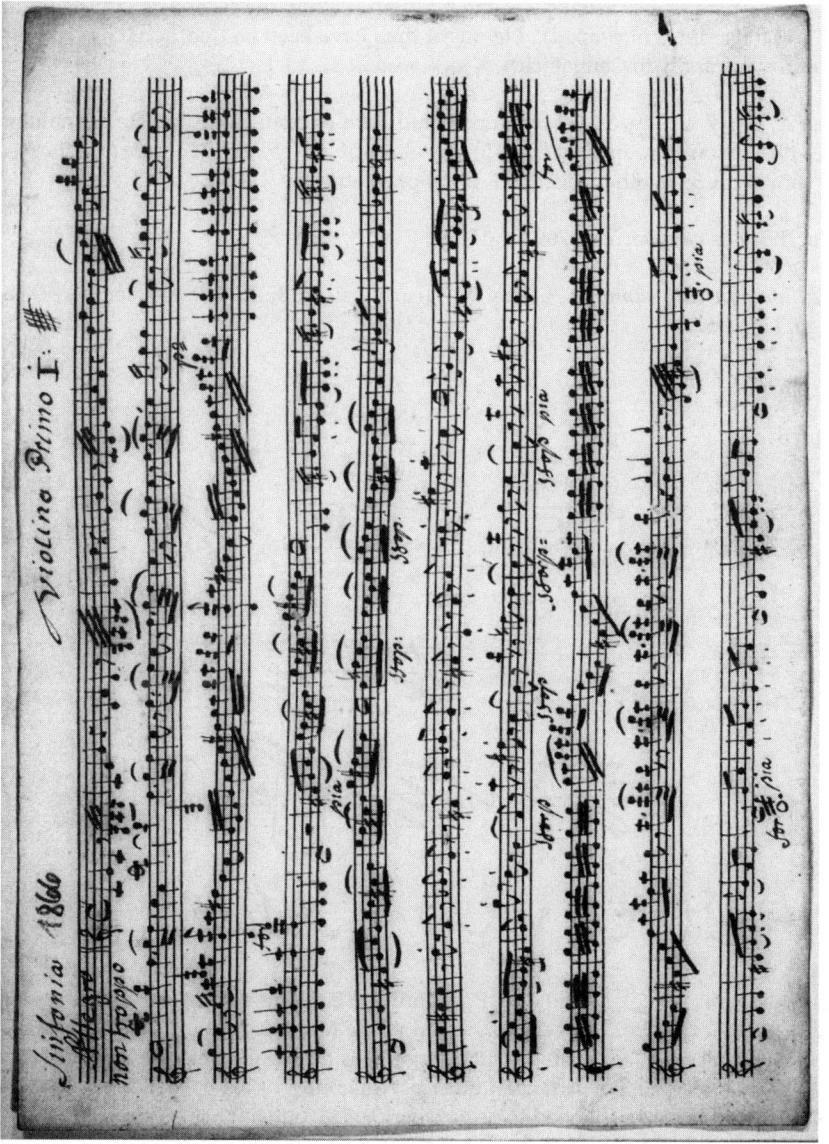

Figure D:12. *Mannheim 3* (?Wilhelm Sepp), *late hand.* Violin 1, page 1 of Christian Cannabich, Symphony no. 58[A] (ca. 1779–80; App. A/III/58[A]). Munich, Bayerische Staatsbibliothek, Mus. Ms. 1866.

Appendix D

1769 to ca. 1780, Mannheim 4 could be identical with Caspar Bohrer (1744–1809); Bohrer is given as a violist and bassist in court records from 1771 until 1778 and, like Mannheim 4, traveled with the court to Munich. However, he is only designated as a copyist in the 1772 *Almanach*, probably by mistake (see the full discussion in the section "Copyists in the Mannheim Manuscripts" in chap. 2). He might thus have been an unofficial copyist with responsibilities primarily to Cannabich.

Found in: A/III/17, 21, 29, 31, 38 (all considered here to stem from the late Mannheim period; see the section "Group 2" of chap. 5), 39–43, 45–51, 53–55, 58B, M7 (note also the two copies by him of no. 59 in other collections mentioned above).

Dates of activity as copyist: ca. 1769–ca. 1780.

Additional handwriting samples: figure D:13 (early hand); Bush, 140; Hörner, ed., DTB, Neue Folge, 11, p. xxxii.

Mannheim 5

Previously called Munich (ex-Mannheim) E. Mannheim 5 is noteworthy as the most important copyist of the large opera scores deriving from the Mannheim court, especially those of the Sickingen collection (see chap. 8). Otherwise he is found in scattered copies of other vocal and (in only one case) instrumental music. While most of his opera scores are from the 1770s, three are of works that had their premieres at Mannheim in 1760–64 (A/VI/203, 37, and 31). It should be noted that the latest manuscript ascribed to him here, A/IV/21 (dated 1778), shows some variations in handwriting by comparison with the earlier scores, for example a one-grapheme common-time signature rather than the two-grapheme signature shown here.

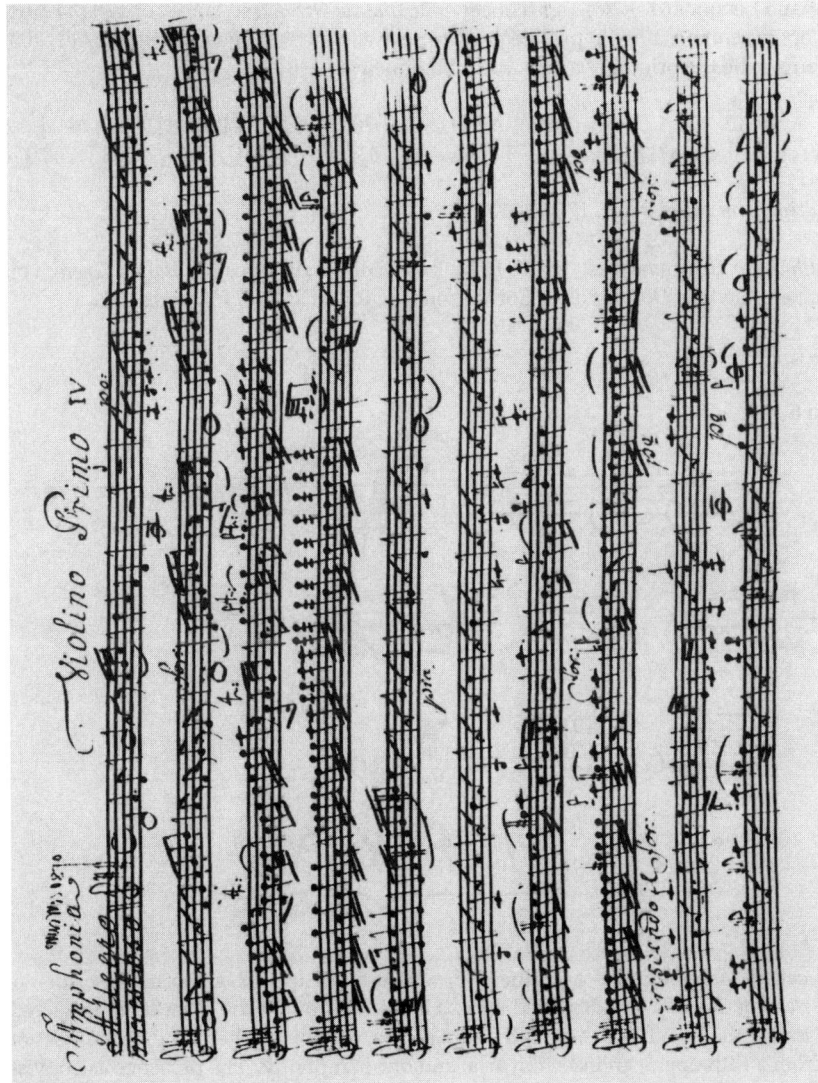

Figure D:13. *Mannheim 4 (early hand).* Violin 1, page 1 of Christian Cannabich, Symphony no. 46 (ca. 1772–75; App. A/III/46). The roman numeral *IV* to the right of "Violino Primo" indicates that at one time there existed four violin 1 parts. Munich, Bayerische Staatsbibliothek, Mus. Ms. 1890.

Appendix D

Identification: uncertain, as there is no remaining official copyist whose biographical data correspond with the data on his manuscripts. For instance, as the copyist of Schweitzer's *Alceste* (A/VI/200; Mannheim, 1775) and of most of the revised version of Vogler's *Kaufmann von Smyrna* (A/V/21; Mannheim, 20 Feb. 1778), he cannot be either Jacob Cramer (d. 1770) or Johann Lochner (d. 1774). It is conceivable that he was a free-lance copyist at court, supplying opera scores mainly to private patrons such as von Sickingen (though A/VI/203, at least, seems to be the original score used at Mannheim).

Found in: A/II/12, 17; A/V/21 (1778); A/VI/5, 16, 20 [1772⁺], 24 [1772⁺], 31 [1764⁺], 37 [1762⁺], 140 [1772⁺], 141 [?1774⁺], 143 [1774⁺], 196 [1774⁺], 197 [1770⁺], 198–99, 203 [1760⁺].

Dates of activity as copyist: ca. 1760–1777/78.

Additional handwriting samples: figure D:14; Bush, 140–41; Brown, ed., *Italian Opera*, vol. 50; Bauman, ed., *German Opera*, vol. 8; Corneilson, ed., RRMCE, vol. 46, plates 1–2.

Mannheim 6

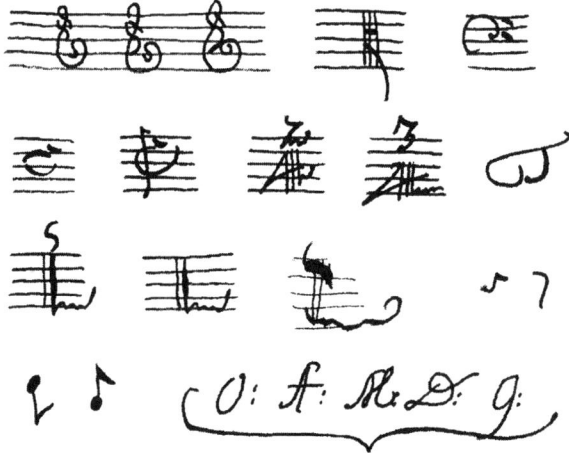

Previously called Mannheim A. Mannheim 6, whose hand appears in 45 manuscripts, is the second most active copyist identified here. He is found by far the most often in sacred music, but is also the copyist of three full opera scores, part of another, an extensive set of selections from a fifth opera, an insertion aria, and one symphony. His presence as copyist of Holzbauer's *La morte di Didone* (App. A/VI/27; Mannheim, 6 July 1779) indicates that he remained in Mannheim after 1778.

Identification: uncertain. Although the biographical data on the violist and *régleur* Ferdinand Fränzl (1710–82, in service to the court from at least 1744) parallels that of Mann-

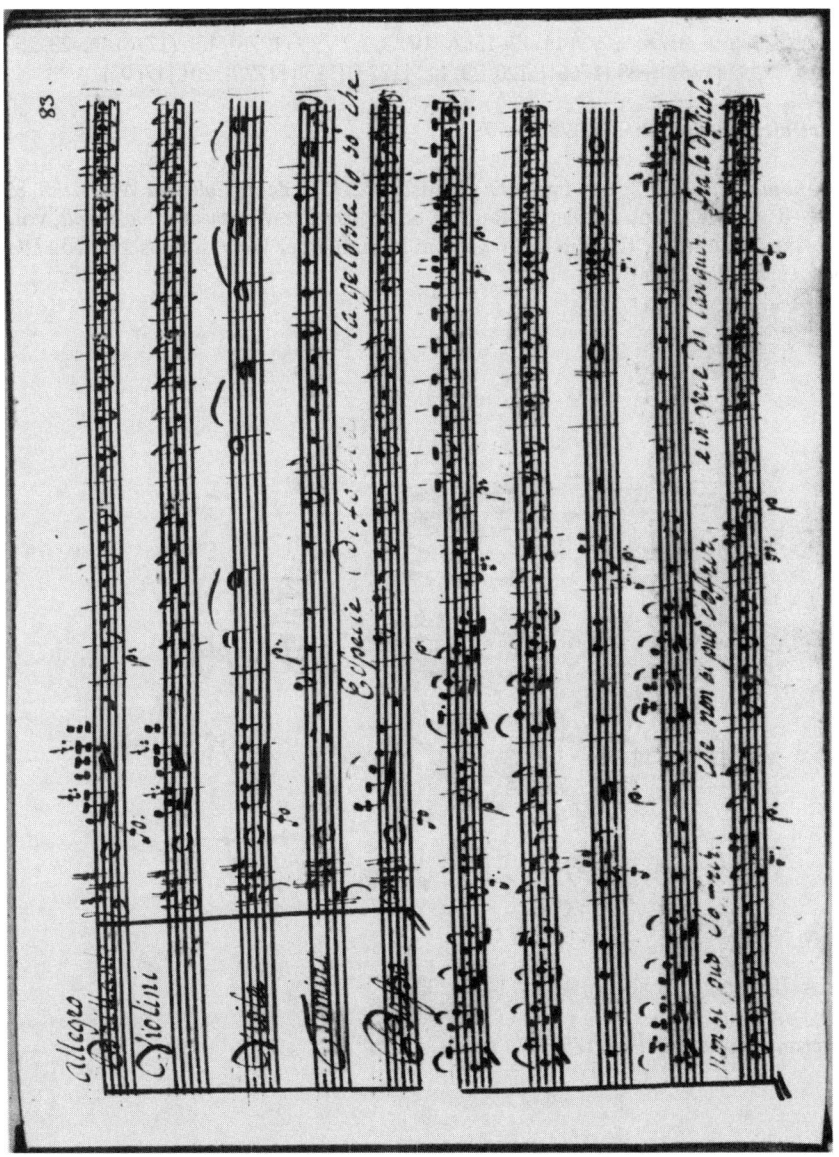

Figure D:14. *Mannheim 5.* First page of Gian Francesco de Majo, aria "È specie di follia," from act 1 of *Ifigenia in Tauride* (1764; App. A/VI/31). Berlin, Staatsbibliothek zu Berlin – Preussischer Kulturbesitz, Mus. ms. 13396.

Appendix D

heim 6, a small handwriting sample of Fränzl's, from the *Gesellenbrief* of 1749, does not appear to match his hand (see the fuller discussion in the section "Copyists in the Mannheim Manuscripts" of chap. 2).

Found in: A/I/5–6; A/II/3, 5, 7, 9–11, 13–15; A/IV/2; A/V/9 (1776), 15b (1776), 22–23, 25, 31; A/VI/14, 27, 32 [1764⁺], 33 [1766⁺], 120–39, 142 [1775⁺], 150 [1770], 201 [1760⁺].

Dates of activity as copyist: late 1750s–1779.

Additional handwriting samples: figure D:15; Bush, 132; J. C. Bach, *Collected Works*, vol. 8; Corneilson, ed., RRMCE, vol. 46, plate 3; Reutter, ed., *Musik der Mannheimer Hofkapelle*, vol. 1, pp. xxxiv–xxxv; Reutter, "Die Kirchenmusik am Mannheimer Hof," in Finscher, ed., *Die Mannheimer Hofkapelle*, 111.

Mannheim 7

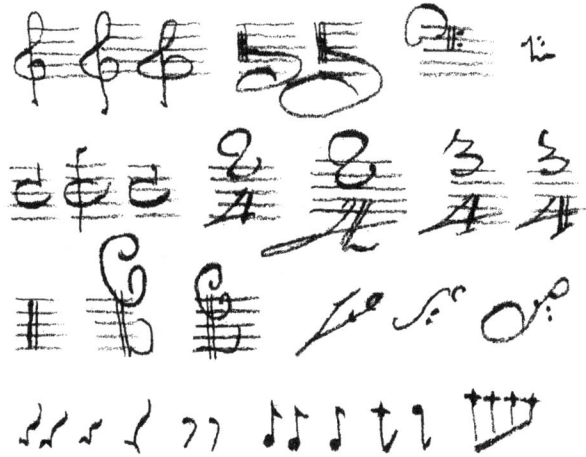

Found in: A/II/2; A/IV/1 (1757); A/VI/144 [1753].

Dates of activity as copyist: ca. 1753–57.

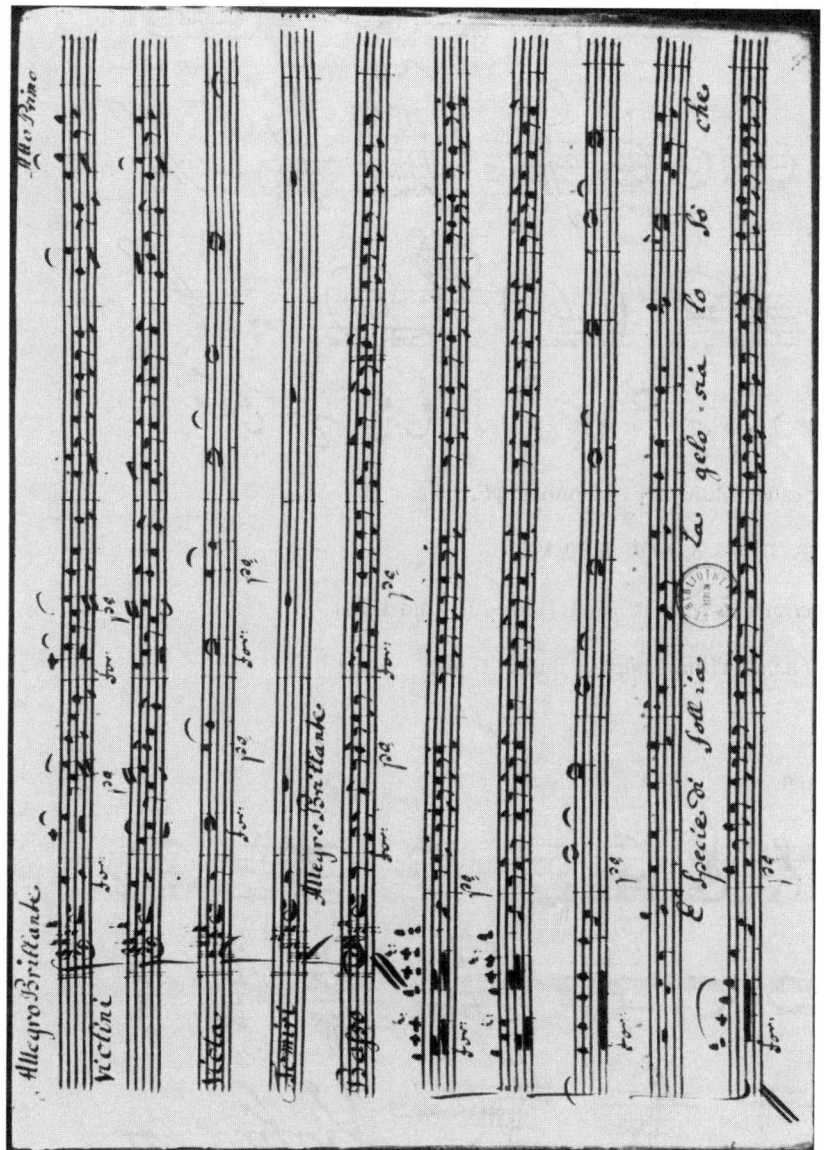

Figure D:15. *Mannheim 6.* First page of Gian Francesco de Majo, aria "È specie di follia" (variant version), from act 1 of *Ifigenia in Tauride* (1764; App. A/VI/32, consisting of selections from the opera). Berlin, Staatsbibliothek zu Berlin – Preussischer Kulturbesitz, Mus. ms. 13396/1.

Appendix D

Mannheim 8

Previously called Munich (ex-Mannheim) F.

Found in: A/II/4–5, 8; A/VI/8, 10, 192.

Dates of activity as copyist: 1760s (1765–70?)–mid-1770s.

Additional handwriting samples: Bush, 141–42.

Mannheim 9

366

Previously called Munich (ex-Mannheim) U. Joachim Jaenecke, *Die Musikbibliothek des Ludwig Freiherrn von Pretlack* (Wiesbaden: Breitkopf & Härtel, 1973), 61 et passim, conflates my two copyists Mannheim 9 and BP/Mh. 2 (q.v.).

Found in: A/II/5; A/VI/46, 58–60, 65, 71–78 [1750⁺]. The A/VI manuscripts all consist of arias from the Pretlack collection.

Dates of activity as copyist: ca. 1750 (arias from Hasse's *Demofoonte* [perf. Mannheim, 18 Jan. 1750])–ca. 1759.

Mannheim 10

Previously called Munich (ex-Mannheim) H.

Found in: A/III/8, 23–24.

Dates of activity as copyist: ca. 1760–66.

Mannheim 11

Previously called Munich (ex-Mannheim) J.

Found in: A/III/14, M5/74.

Dates of activity as copyist: early 1760s.

Mannheim 12

Previously called Munich (ex-Mannheim) K.

Found in: A/III/16–17, 31, 41, all but the last comprising later additions to the Cannabich series (see chap. 5, esp. table 5:2).

Dates of activity as copyist: ca. 1767–73.

Appendix D

Mannheim 13

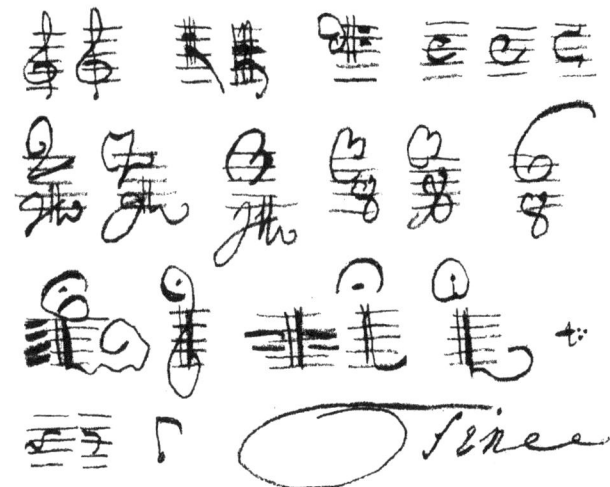

Previously called Munich (ex-Mannheim) M.

Found in: A/III/18, 35 (both considered here to be later additions; see chap. 5, esp. table 5:2), 42, 44, 52, M7.

Dates of activity as copyist: ca. 1767–75.

Mannheim 14

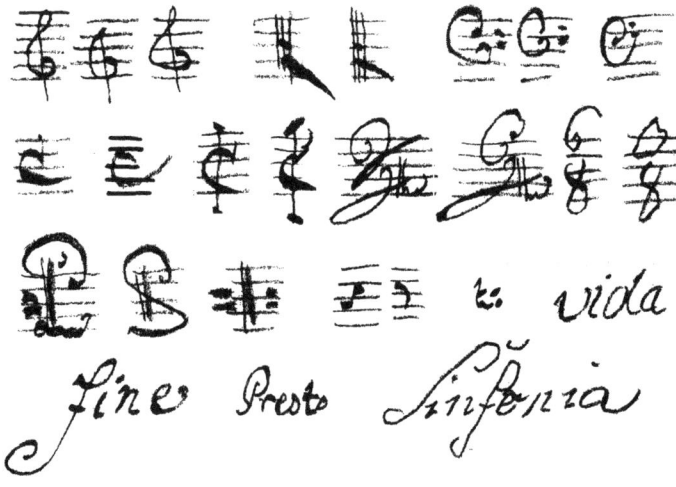

Previously called Munich (ex-Mannheim) N.

Found in: A/III/19, 22 (both considered here to be later additions; see chap. 5, esp. table 5:2), 34, 38, 40; A/VI/162.

Dates of activity as copyist: ca. 1767–73 or later (the date of A/VI/162, a Cannabich ballet, is not known).

Mannheim 15

Previously called Munich (ex-Mannheim) P.

Found in: A/III/34, M6.

Dates of activity as copyist: ca. 1767–early 1770s.

Mannheim 16

Previously called Munich (ex-Mannheim) Q.

Found in: A/III/43, M7; A/VI/161.

Dates of activity as copyist: ca. 1769–mid-1770s or slightly later.

Mannheim 17

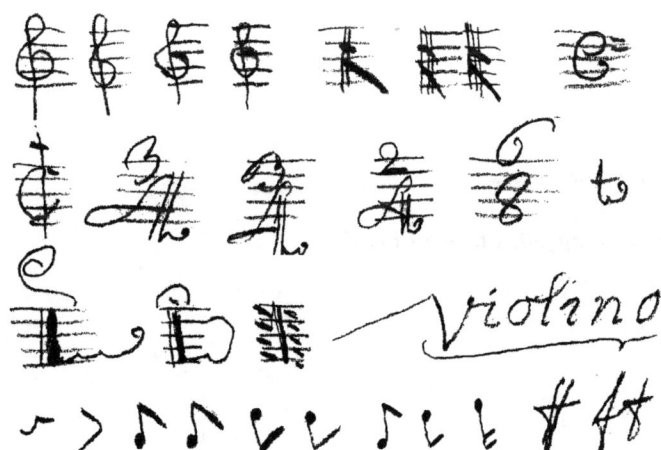

Appendix D

Previously called Munich (ex-Mannheim) T. Mannheim 17 worked in both Mannheim and Munich, appearing in Vogler manuscripts of the late Mannheim period and a Munich manuscript in the Cannabich series, A/III/60.

Found in: A/III/60 (Munich); A/V/20 [1777], 26, 29–30.

Dates of activity as copyist: ca. 1777–80.

Mannheim 18

Found in: A/V/2a–b (1772); A/VI/17.

Dates of activity as copyist: ca. 1772.

Additional handwriting samples: Grave, ed., RRMCE, vol. 45 , plates 3–4 (clefs and vn. 1 only).

Mannheim 19

Found in: A/VI/8, 192.

Dates of activity as copyist: mid 1760s–early 1770s.

Mannheim 20

Found in: A/VI/15, 25, 34.

Dates of activity as copyist: ca. 1766–after 1772.

Mannheim 21

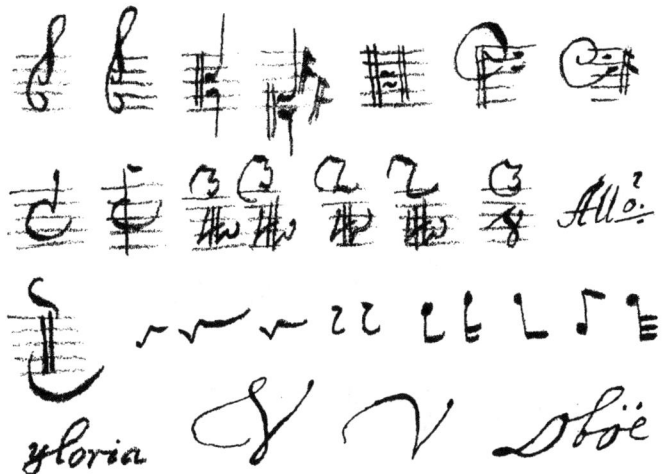

This copyist is designated as K 90 in Jaenecke, *Pretlack*, 63 et passim. However, Jaenecke's "K 90" is actually two different copyists (see App. A/VI/85).

Found in: A/VI/18 [ca. 1755+], 85 [1752+].

Dates of activity as copyist: mid-1750s.

Additional handwriting samples: Gradenwitz, "Stamitz Family," 59.

III. Other Mannheim Copyists

The final section of Appendix D lists 27 Mannheim copyists whose manuscripts are now found in a single library other than the Bayerische Staatsbibliothek in Munich. These copyists are given dual sigla: first an abbreviation specifying the present location of their manuscripts, then a numerical designation as a Mannheim copyist. Thus, "Rtt/Mh. 1" would be the first Mannheim copyist enumerated here whose manuscripts are found only in the Thurn und Taxis library in Regensburg. The library abbreviations chosen are the German RISM sigla (i.e., "Rtt" = D-Rtt), with the following exceptions: "Bln." = D-B; "BP" = Bibliothek Pretlack, the Pretlack collection at D-B, originally from the area of Darmstadt; "Dres." = D-Dlb; "KN" = A-KN; "MHjk" = Mannheim, Jesuitenkirche; "Stanf." = US-ST; "Strasb." = F-Susc. (For further information on these collections and the Mannheim manuscripts they contain see the relevant sections of chaps. 3, 6, and 9.) The order in this section is alphabetical.

Appendix D

1. Bln./Mh. 1

Found in: A/VI/33 [1766⁺].

Dates of activity as copyist: 1766⁺.

2. Bln./Mh. 2 (Innocenz Danzi?)

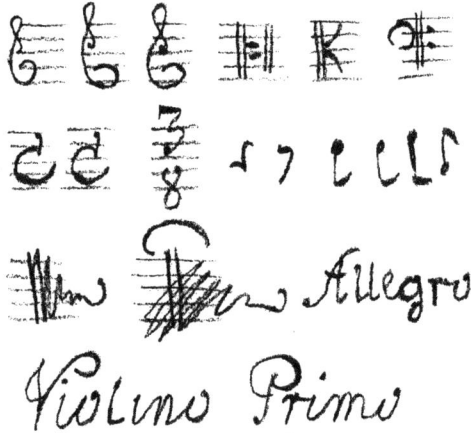

This copyist could be the Mannheim cellist Innocenz Danzi (ca. 1730–1798), who joined the Mannheim Kapelle in the same year as Anton Fils, 1754; the work in question here, A/VI/21, is a cello concerto by him, and the hand is rather Italianate.

Found in: A/VI/21.

Dates of activity as copyist: ca. 1754–60.

3. Bln./Mh. 3 (Anton Fils?)

See next page for tracing.

This copyist could be the Mannheim cellist Anton Fils (1733–60), at Mannheim from 1754 until his death. A/VI/22 is a cello concerto by him.

Found in: A/VI/22.

Dates of activity as copyist: ca. 1754–1760.

Bln./Mh. 3:

4. BP/Mh. 1

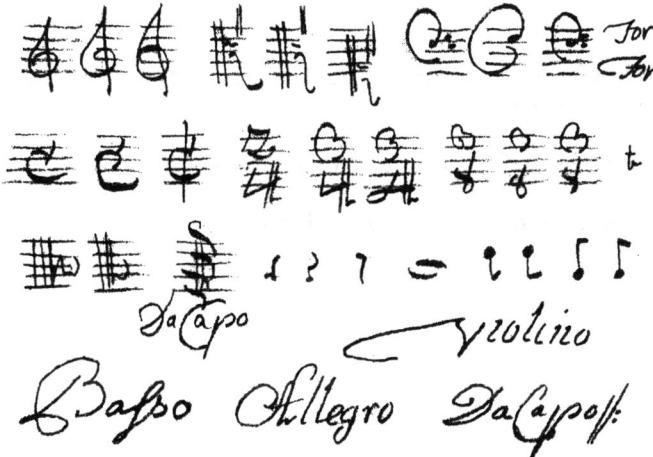

This copyist is K 80 in Jaenecke, *Pretlack*, 62 et passim.

Found in: A/VI/40–41 [1751⁺], 43, 61, 110 [1751⁺], 112, 113 [1751⁺], 119.

Dates of activity as copyist: early 1750s.

Appendix D

5. BP/Mh. 2

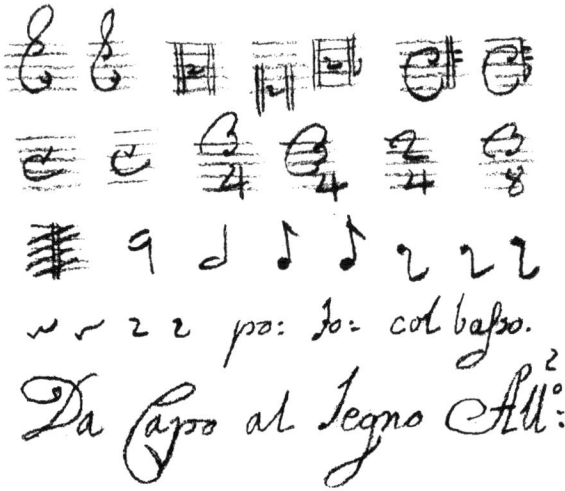

My copyists BP/Mh. 2 and Mannheim 9 (see above) are treated as one copyist, K 25, in Jaenecke, *Pretlack*, 61 et passim.

Found in: A/VI/42, 58–60, 64 [1750+], 66–74 [1750+], 76–77 [1750+].

Dates of activity as copyist: early 1750s or slightly earlier.

6. Dres./Mh. 1

Found in: A/VI/139.

Dates of activity as copyist: 1772+.

7. DS/Mh. 1

Found in: A/V/9–10, 14, 15b (all 1776).

Dates of activity as copyist: 1776.

8. DS/Mh. 2

Found in: A/V/10, 19 (both 1776), 26.

Dates of activity as copyist: ca. 1776.

9. DS/Mh. 3

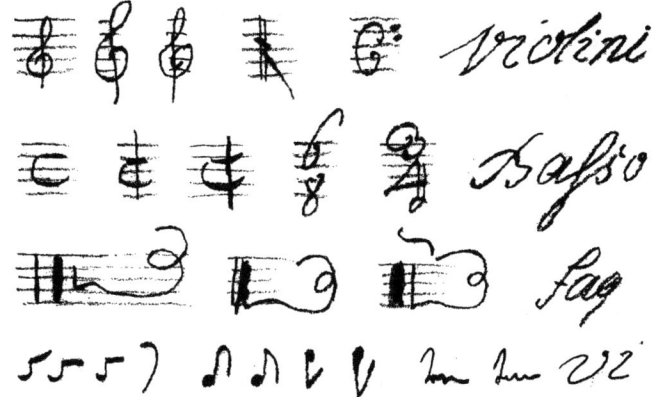

Found in: A/V/19 (1776), 20 [1777], 22–23, 26–30, 37.

Dates of activity as copyist: ca. 1776–77.

10. DS/Mh. 4

Found in: A/V/20 [1777], 23.

Dates of activity as copyist: ca. 1777.

11. DS/Mh. 5

Found in: A/V/28, 30.

Dates of activity as copyist: mid-1770s.

Appendix D

12. DS/Mh. 6

Found in: A/VI/141 [?1774⁺].

Dates of activity as copyist: ?1774⁺.

13. KA/Mh.(?) 1

This copyist and the next are perhaps somewhat less likely to be from Mannheim than the others included in Appendix D.

Found in: A/VI/146, 148–49.

Dates of activity as copyist: ca. 1753–60.

14. KA/Mh.(?) 2

Found in: A/VI/147.

Dates of activity as copyist: ca. 1753–60.

15. KN/Mh. 1

Found in: A/VI/1–2.

Dates of activity as copyist: uncertain, presumably late 1750s–early 1770s.

16. Mf/Mh. 1

Found in: A/VI/144 [1753].

Dates of activity as copyist: ca. 1753.

17. Mf/Mh. 2

Found in: A/VI/145.

Dates of activity as copyist: 1770s.

18. MHjk/Mh. 1

Found in: A/I/1 (1763), 7.

Dates of activity as copyist: 1763–1770s.

19. MHjk/Mh. 2

Found in: A/I/3–4 (1766).

Dates of activity as copyist: ca. 1766.

20. RH/Mh. 1

Found in: A/VI/152.

Dates of activity as copyist: late 1750s–early 1760s.

21. Rtt/Mh. 1

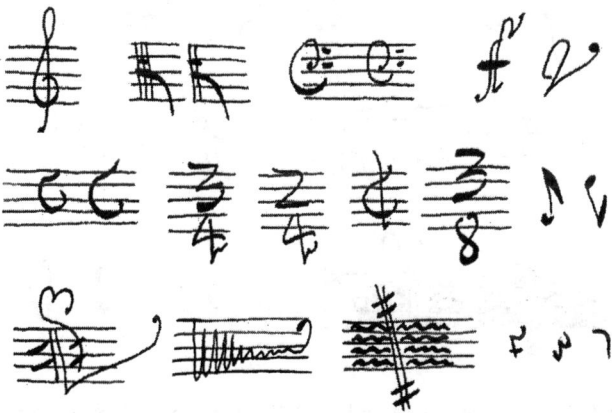

Previously called Regensburg (ex-Mannheim) A. This copyist might be the "Reinhard" listed in the almanacs as a violist and copyist from 1755 to 1760 (see also Rtt/Mh. 3, below, and the section "Copyists in the Mannheim Manuscripts" of chap. 2). As noted in Wolf, *Stamitz*, 61-62 (n. 13), my earlier suggestion in Wolf and Wolf, "Complex," 400–401 that this copyist might be Valentin Roeser cannot be sustained.

Appendix D

Found in: A/VI/174–83, 186.

Dates of activity as copyist: 1750s–early or mid 1760s (1760 if Reinhard).

Additional handwriting samples: figure D:16; Wolf and Wolf, "Complex," 433; Wolf, *Stamitz*, 464 (all these examples are of the same page).

22. Rtt/Mh. 2

Previously called Regensburg (ex-Mannheim) B.

Found in: A/VI/174, 178–79, 183 (title pages only; 179 with incipit).

Dates of activity as copyist: 1750s–early or mid 1760s.

Handwriting samples: figure D:17; Wolf and Wolf, "Complex," 434; Wolf, *Stamitz*, 465 (all of same page).

23. Rtt/Mh. 3

Previously called Regensburg (ex-Mannheim) C. This copyist might be the "Reinhard" listed in the almanacs as a violist and copyist from 1755 to 1760, though the slightly earlier copyist Rtt/Mh. 1 is perhaps a more likely candidate.

Found in: A/VI/153, 155, 182, 184, 186, 189, 191.

Dates of activity as copyist: late 1750s–mid-1760s or later (1760 if Reinhard).

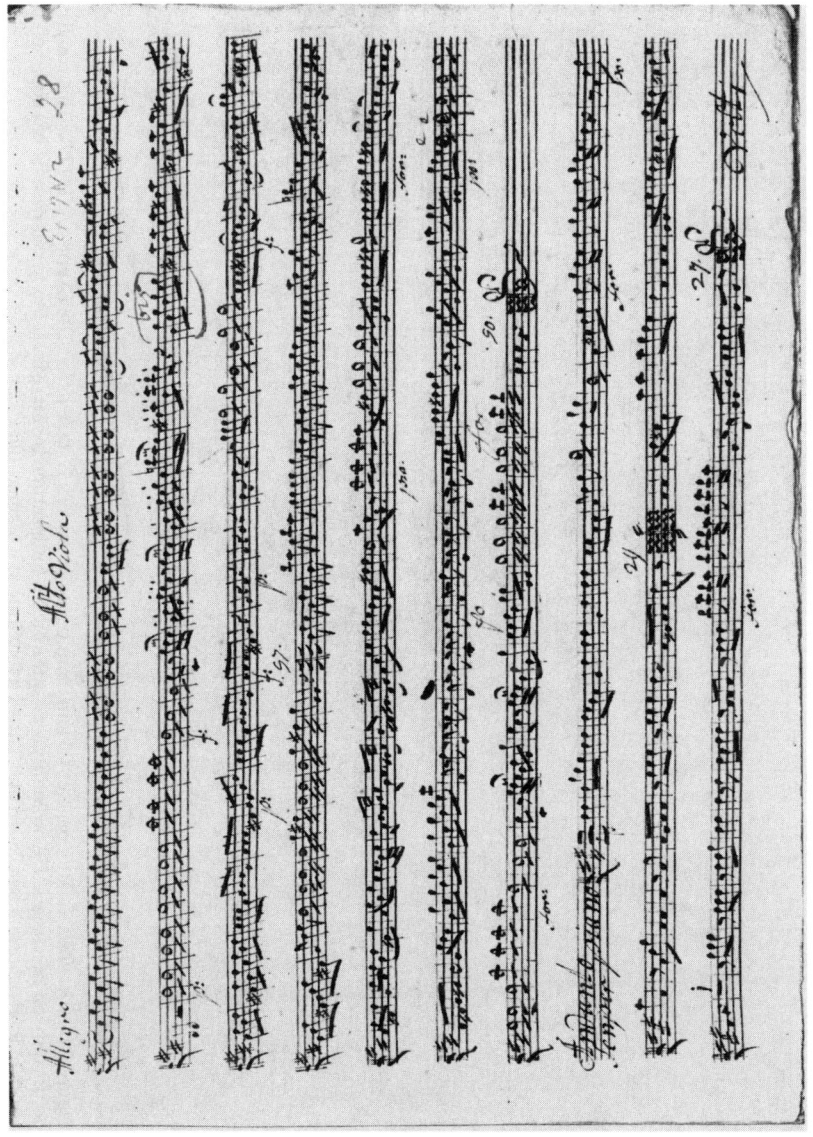

Figure D:16. *Rtt/Mh. 1 and 3.* Viola, page 1, of Johann Stamitz, Symphony in D, DTB/Wolf D-15 (App. A/VI/182). Rtt/Mh. 1 begins the part, continuing through staff 4, measure 15, at which point Rtt/Mh. 3 takes over (e.g., note the difference in slant and beaming and the variant form of the barline at that point). Regensburg, Fürst Thurn und Taxis Hofbibliothek, J. Stamitz 13.

Appendix D

Figure D:17. *Rtt/Mh.* 2. Title page of Johann Stamitz, Symphony in D, DTB/Wolf D-8 (App. A/VI/179). This copyist occurs only on title pages. He ordinarily leaves the incipit for insertion by Rtt/Mh. 1, but in this case he has supplied it himself. Regensburg, Fürst Thurn und Taxis Hofbibliothek, J. Stamitz 10.

Additional handwriting samples: figure D:16, above; Wolf and Wolf, "Complex," 433; Wolf, *Stamitz*, 464 (all of the same page).

24. Rtt/Mh. 4

Found in: A/VI/162.

Dates of activity as copyist: uncertain, possibly late 1760s–early 1770s.

25. Rtt/Mh. 5

Found in: A/VI/171.

Dates of activity as copyist: ca. 1760.

Handwriting samples: figure 2:8

26. Stanf./?Mh. 1

Found in: A/VI/?202.

Dates of activity as copyist: prob. 1778 (A/VI/?202 composed 1776, perf. Mannheim 12 March 1778).

Appendix D

27. Strasb./Mh. 1

Found in: A/IV/5, 7.

Dates of activity as copyist: ca. 1760–65.

Bibliography

Almanach électoral palatin. Mannheim: Nicolas Pierron, later L'Imprimerie électorale; issued yearly from at least 1750 until at least 1776.
Alston, Robin. "Reproducing Watermarks." *Direction Line* 2 (1976): 1–3.
Anderson, Emily, trans. and ed. [**Anderson**]. *The Letters of Mozart and His Family.* 2d ed. by A. Hyatt King and Monica Carolan. London: Macmillan, 1966.
Angermüller, Rudolph, and Robert Münster, eds. *Wolfgang Amadeus Mozart, Idomeneo 1781–1981: Essays, Forschungsberichte, Katalog.* Bayerische Staatsbibliothek, Ausstellungskataloge, 24. Munich: R. Piper, 1981.
Annonces, affiches, et avis divers [*AAA*; title varies]. Paris, 1752–1806.
Antz, C. L. "Die Papiermühlen im Gebiete der Kurpfalz und der heutigen Rheinpfalz." *Mannheimer Geschichtsblätter* 24 (1923): 86–91.
Arthur, John. "Some Chronological Problems in Mozart: The Contribution of Ink Studies." In *Wolfgang Amadè Mozart: Essays on His Life and Music,* ed. Stanley Sadie, 35–52. Oxford: Clarendon Press, 1996.
L'Avant-coureur, feuille hebdomadaire [*AC*]. Paris, 1760–73.
Bach, Johann Christian. *Endimione, Lucio Silla,* and *Temistocle.* Vols. 14, 8, and 7, respectively, of *The Collected Works of J. C. Bach,* ed. Ernest Warburton. Facs. ed. New York: Garland Publishing, 1985, 1986, 1988.
Baker, Nicole, ed. *Ballet Music from the Mannheim Court.* Part II: Carl Joseph Toeschi, *Mars et Vénus*; Christian Cannabich, *Médée et Jason.* Recent Researches in the Music of the Classical Era, 47. Madison, Wisc.: A-R Editions, 1997.
Bauer, Wilhelm A., and Otto Erich Deutsch, eds. [**Bauer-Deutsch**]. *Mozart, Briefe und Aufzeichnungen: Gesamtausgabe.* 7 vols. Kassel: Bärenreiter, 1962–75.
Bauman, Thomas, ed. See Vogler, Georg Joseph.
Beck, Franz. See Pelker, Bärbel, ed.
Bengtsson, Ingmar, and Ruben Danielson. *Handstilar och notpikturer i Kungl. Musicaliska Akademiens Roman-Samling.* Studia musicologica upsaliensia, 3. Uppsala: Almqvist & Wiksells, 1955.
Bihrle, Heinrich. *Die Musikalische Akademie München 1811–1911: Festschrift zur Feier des hundertjährigen Bestehens.* Munich: E. Mühlthaler, 1911.
Braubach, Max. "Die Mitglieder der Hofmusik unter den vier letzten Kurfürsten von Köln." In *Colloquium amicorum: Joseph Schmidt-Görg zum 70. Geburtstag,* ed. Siegfried Kross and Hans Schmidt, 26–63. Bonn: Verlag des Beethovenhauses, 1967.
Brook, Barry S., and Jean Gribenski. "Symphonie concertante." *New Grove,* 2d ed., vol. 24, pp. 807–12.
Brook, Barry S., and Richard Viano. *Thematic Catalogues in Music: An Annotated Bibliography.* 2d ed. Stuyvesant, N.Y.: Pendragon Press, 1997.
Brown, Howard Mayer, ed. See Piccinni, Niccolò; Traetta, Tommaso.
Burney, Charles. *Dr Burney's Musical Tours in Europe.* Ed. Percy A. Scholes. 2 vols. Vol. 2: *An Eighteenth-Century Musical Tour in Central Europe and the Netherlands.* London: Oxford University Press, 1959.

Burrows, Donald J. "Paper Studies and Handel's Autographs." *Göttinger Händel-Beiträge* 1 (1984): 103–13.
Burrows, Donald J., and Martha J. Ronish. *A Catalogue of Handel's Musical Autographs*. Oxford: Clarendon Press, 1994.
Bush, Deanna D. [**Bush**]. *The Orchestral Masses of Ignaz Holzbauer (1711–1783): Authenticity, Chronology, and Style*. Ph.D. diss., Eastman School of Music, 1982.
Cannabich, Christian. *Ausgewählte Sinfonien aus der Münchener Schaffensperiode*, ed. Stephan Hörner. DTB, Neue Folge, 11. Wiesbaden: Breitkopf & Härtel, 1996.

———. *Renaud et Armide* and *Les Mariages Samnites*. Part IV of *Ballet Music from the Mannheim Court*, ed. Marita P. McClymonds, Patrick M. Keady, and Carol G. Marsh. Recent Researches in the Music of the Classical Era, 57. Madison, Wisc.: A-R Editions, 1999.

———. *Symphonies, op. 10, no. 1[–6]*. Ed. Allan Badley. Wellington, NZ: Artaria Editions, 1997.

———. See also Baker, Nicole, ed.; Grave, Floyd K., ed.

Churchill, W. A. *Watermarks in Paper in Holland, England, France, etc., in the XVII and XVIII Centuries and Their Interconnection*. Amsterdam: Hertzberger, 1935.
Chur-Pfältzischer Hoff- und Staats-Calender [title varies]. Mannheim: Churfürstliche Hof(f)-Buchdruckerei, Matthias Oberholzer (from 1749 "Nicolao von Pierron," Spies, etc.); issued yearly from at least 1748 until 1778.
Chur-Pfältzischer Staats- und Stands-Calender. Heidelberg: Jacob Simon, 1734; Mannheim: Johann Friedrich Knoch, 1736.
Clive, Peter. *Mozart and His Circle: A Biographical Dictionary*. New Haven: Yale University Press, 1993.
Collini, Côme Alexandre [Cosimo Alessandro]. *Mon séjour auprès de Voltaire*. Paris: Léopold Collin, 1807.
Corneilson, Paul. "The Case of J. C. Bach's *Lucio Silla*." *Journal of Musicology* 12 (1994): 206–18.

———. "Die Oper am Kurfürstlichen Hof zu Mannheim." In Ludwig Finscher, ed., *Die Mannheimer Hofkapelle im Zeitalter Carl Theodors*, 113–29.

———. *Opera at Mannheim, 1770–1778*. Ph.D. diss., University of North Carolina at Chapel Hill, 1992.

———. "Reconstructing the Mannheim Court Theatre." *Early Music* 25 (1997): 63–81.

Corneilson, Paul, and Eugene K. Wolf [**Corneilson/Wolf**]. "Newly Identified Manuscripts of Operas and Related Works from Mannheim." *JAMS* 47 (1992): 244–74.
Dadelsen, Georg von. *Beiträge zur Chronologie der Werke Johann Sebastian Bachs*. Tübinger Bach-Studien, 4/5. Trossingen: Hohner-Verlag, 1958.
Dahms, Sibylle. "Ballet Reform in the Eighteenth Century and Ballet at the Court of Mannheim." In *Ballet Music from the Mannheim Court*, ed. Paul Corneilson and Eugene K. Wolf, Part I, pp. ix–xxiii. Recent Researches in the Music of the Classical Era, 45. Madison, Wisc.: A-R Editions, 1996.
Denkmäler der Tonkunst in Bayern [**DTB**]. (*Denkmäler deutscher Tonkunst, zweite Folge*.) Jg. III/1, VII/2, VIII/2: *Sinfonien der pfalzbayerischen Schule (Mannheimer Symphoniker)*; Jg. XVI: *Mannheimer Kammermusik des 18. Jahrhunderts, II. Teil: Trios und Duos*. Ed. Hugo Riemann. Leipzig: Breitkopf & Härtel, 1902–15.

———. See also Cannabich, Christian; Schmitt, Eduard, ed.

Dray, William. *Laws and Explanations in History*. London: Oxford University Press, 1957.
Dunning, Albert. "Official Court Music: Means and Symbol of Might." In *Société internationale de musicologie: Actes du XIIIe congrès, Strasbourg, 1982*, vol. 1, ed. Marc Honegger and Christian Meyer, pp. 17–21. Strasbourg: Association des publications près des Universités de Strasbourg, 1986.
Ebersold, Günther. *Rokoko, Reform und Revolution: ein politisches Lebensbild des Kurfürsten Karl Theodor*. Frankfurt am Main: Peter Lang, 1985.
Edge, Dexter. "The Fragmentary Minuet in E-flat, K. deest, in the Palácio Nacional da Ajuda in Lisbon." Paper delivered at study session of Mozart Society of America, Toronto, 3 November 2000.
——————. *Mozart's Viennese Copyists*. Ph.D. diss., University of Southern California, 2001.
Eineder, Georg. *The Ancient Paper-Mills of the Former Austro-Hungarian Empire and Their Watermarks*. Hilversum: Paper Publications Society, 1960.
Eisen, Cliff. "The Scoring of the Orchestral Bass Part in Mozart's Salzburg Keyboard Concertos: The Evidence of the Authentic Copies." In *Mozart's Piano Concertos: Text, Context, Interpretation*, ed. Neal Zaslaw, 411–25. Ann Arbor: University of Michigan Press, 1996.
Eitner, Robert. *Biographisch-bibliographisches Quellen-Lexikon der Musiker und Musikgelehrten*. 10 vols. Leipzig: Breitkopf & Härtel, 1898–1904.
Emery, Walter. Review of *Festschrift für Friedrich Smend zum 70. Geburtstag*. In *Music and Letters* 45 (1964): 168–70.
Enßlin, Wolfram. *Niccolò Piccinni*, Catone in Utica: *Quellenüberlieferung, Aufführungsgeschichte und Analyse*. Quellen und Studien zur Geschichte der Mannheimer Hofkapelle, 4. Frankfurt am Main: Peter Lang, 1996.
Fava, Domenico. *La Biblioteca Estense nel suo sviluppo storico*. Modena: Vincenzi, 1925.
Feder, Georg. *Musikphilologie: eine Einführung in die musikalische Textkritik, Hermeneutik und Editionstechnik*. Darmstadt: Wissenschaftliche Buchgesellschaft, 1987.
Finscher, Ludwig, ed. *Die Mannheimer Hofkapelle im Zeitalter Carl Theodors*. Mannheim: Palatium Verlag im J & J Verlag, 1992.
Finscher, Ludwig, Bärbel Pelker, and Jochen Reutter, eds. *Mozart und Mannheim: Kongreßbericht 1991*. Quellen und Studien zur Geschichte der Mannheimer Hofkapelle, 2. Frankfurt am Main: Peter Lang, 1994.
Freitäger, Andreas. "Carlo Luigi Pietragrua d. Ältere (ca. 1665–1726): Studien zur Biographie eines 'Vor-Mannheimer.'" *Musik in Bayern* 44 (1992): 7–41.
Fruehwald, Scott. *Authenticity Problems in Joseph Haydn's Early Instrumental Works: A Stylistic Investigation*. New York: Pendragon Press, 1988.
Fuchs, Peter. "Karl (IV.) Theodor." *Neue deutsche Biographie*, vol. 11, pp. 252–58. Berlin: Duncker & Hublot, 1977.
Gaskell, Philip. *A New Introduction to Bibliography*. Oxford: Oxford University Press, 1972.
Geertz, Clifford. "Centers, Kings, and Charisma: Reflections on the Symbolics of Power." In his *Local Knowledge: Further Essays in Interpretive Anthropology*, 121–46. New York: Basic Books, 1983.
Gericke, Hannelore. *Der Wiener Musikalienhandel von 1700 bis 1778*. Wiener musikwissenschaftliche Beiträge, 5. Graz: Hermann Böhlaus Nachfolger, 1960.

Goy, François-Pierre. "Bilan de l'inventaire des fonds musicaux anciens: Région Champagne-Ardenne." *Revue de musicologie* 81 (1995): 275–80.
Goy, François-Pierre, and Marc Desmet. *Catalogue des fonds musicaux anciens conservés en Champagne-Ardenne, 1500–1800*. Paris: Minkoff, 2000.
Gradenwitz, Peter. "Johann Stamitz als Kirchenkomponist." *Die Musikforschung* 11 (1958): 2–15.
———. *Johann Stamitz: Leben – Umwelt – Werke*. Wilhelmshaven: Heinrichshofen's Verlag, 1984.
———. "The Stamitz Family: Some Errors, Omissions, and Falsifications Corrected." *Notes* 7 (1749/50): 54–64.
Grave, Floyd K., ed. *Ballet Music from the Mannheim Court*. Part I: Christian Cannabich, *Le rendes-vous, ballet de chasse*; Georg Joseph Vogler, *Le rendez-vous de chasse*. Recent Researches in the Music of the Classical Era, 45. Madison, Wisc.: A-R Editions, 1996.
Grave, Floyd K., and Margaret G. Grave. *In Praise of Harmony: The Teachings of Abbé Georg Joseph Vogler*. Lincoln, Neb.: University of Nebraska Press, 1987.
Gravell, Thomas L. "A New Method of Reproducing Watermarks for Study." *Restaurator* 2 (1975): 94–104.
Gravell, Thomas L., and George Miller. *A Catalogue of American Watermarks, 1690–1835*. New York: Garland Publishing, 1979.
Grout, Donald Jay. "Current Historiography and Music History." In *Studies in Music History: Essays for Oliver Strunk*, ed. Harold Powers, 23-40. Princeton, N.J.: Princeton University Press, 1968.
Haberkamp, Gertraut. *Thematischer Katalog der Musikhandschriften der Fürstlich Oettingen-Wallerstein'schen Bibliothek Schloß Harburg*. Kataloge bayerischer Musiksammlungen, 3. Munich: G. Henle, 1976.
Haberkamp, Gertraut, and Hugo Angerer, eds. *Die Musikhandschriften der Fürst Thurn und Taxis Hofbibliothek Regensburg: thematischer Katalog*. Kataloge bayerischer Musiksammlungen, 6. Munich: G. Henle, 1981.
Haberkamp, Gertraut, and Robert Münster. *Die ehemaligen Musikhandschriftensammlungen der Königlichen Hofkapelle und der Kurfürstin Maria Anna in München: thematischer Katalog*. Kataloge bayerischer Musiksammlungen, 9. Munich: G. Henle, 1982.
Harrison, Wilson R. *Suspect Documents: Their Scientific Examination*. Repr. of the 1st ed. of 1956. Chicago: Nelson-Hall, 1981.
Haydn, Joseph. *Il mondo della luna*. Ser. XXV, vol. 7 of *Joseph Haydn Werke*, ed. Günter Thomas. 3 vols. Munich: G. Henle, 1979–82.
Heartz, Daniel. "The Genesis of Mozart's *Idomeneo*." *The Musical Quarterly* 55 (1969): 1–19.
———. *Haydn, Mozart and the Viennese School, 1740–1780*. New York: W. W. Norton, 1995.
———. "Traetta, Tommaso." *New Grove*, 1st ed., vol. 19, pp. 111–14.
Heawood, Edward. *Watermarks, Mainly of the 17th and 18th Centuries*. Hilversum: Paper Publications Society, 1950.
Heitz, Paul. *Les filigranes avec la crosse de Bâle*. Strasbourg: J. H. Ed. Heitz, 1904.
Hell, Helmut. *Die neapolitanische Opernsinfonie in der ersten Hälfte des 18. Jahrhunderts*. Münchner Veröffentlichungen zur Musikgeschichte, 19. Tutzing: Hans Schneider, 1971.

Hieckel, Hans Otto. *Katalog der Rastrierungen in den Originalhandschriften J. S. Bachs*. 1963; unpubl.

Hirsch, Paul. "Über die Vorlage zum Klavierkonzert in d-moll." *Bach-Jahrbuch* 26 (1929): 153–74.

Hofer, Heinrich. *Christian Cannabich: Biographie und vergleichende Analyse seiner Sinfonien*. Diss., University of Munich, 1921.

Holzbauer, Ignaz. *Günther von Schwarzburg: Singspiel in drei Aufzügen*. Ed. Bärbel Pelker. Quellen zur Musikgeschichte in Baden-Württemberg, 1. Facs. ed. 2 vols. Munich: Strube Verlag, 2000.

———. "Kurzer Lebensbegrif des Herrn Ignaz Holzbauer, kurpfälzischen Kapellmeisters." In *Pfälzisches Museum* 1 (Mannheim, 1783): 460–77. Reprinted, inter alia, in Friedrich Walter, *Geschichte des Theaters und der Musik am kurpfälzischen Hofe*, 356–61.

———. *Missa in C*. Ed. Jochen Reutter. Musik der Mannheimer Hofkapelle, 1. Stuttgart: Carus-Verlag, 1995.

———. See also Pelker, Bärbel, ed.

Horn, Wolfgang. "Die wichtigsten Schreiber im Umkreis Jan Dismas Zelenkas: Überlegungen zur Methode ihrer Bestimmung und Entwurf einer Gruppierung der Quellen." In *Zelenka-Studien I*, ed. Thomas Kohlhase and Hubert Unverricht, vol. 14 of *Musik des Ostens*, 141–210. Kassel: Bärenreiter, 1993.

Hortschansky, Klaus. "Autographe Stimmen zu Mozarts Klavierkonzert KV 175 im Archiv André zu Offenbach." *Mozart-Jahrbuch*, 1989/90, pp. 37–54.

———. "Ignaz Holzbauers *Ippolito ed Aricia* (1759): zur Einführung der Tragédie lyrique in Mannheim." In Wolfgang Birtel and Christoph-Hellmut Mahling, eds., *Aufklärungen: Studien zur deutsch-französischen Musikgeschichte im 18. Jahrhundert*, vol. 2, pp. 105–16. Heidelberg: Carl Winter, 1986.

Hössle, Friedrich von. *Württembergische Papiergeschichte*. Biberach/Riss: Karl Höhn, 1914.

Hudson, Frederick. "The Study of Watermarks As a Research Factor in Undated Manuscripts and Prints: Beta-Radiography with Carbon-14 Sources." In *International Musicological Society: Report of the Eighth Congress, Copenhagen 1972*, ed. Henrik Glahn et al., 447–53. Copenhagen: Wilhelm Hansen, 1974.

Hunt, Lynn A. *Politics, Culture, and Class in the French Revolution*. Berkeley: University of California Press, 1984.

Jaenecke, Joachim [Jaenecke]. *Die Musikbibliothek des Ludwig Freiherrn von Pretlack (1716–1781)*. Neue musikgeschichtliche Forschungen, 8. Wiesbaden: Breitkopf & Härtel, 1973.

Jaffé, Albert. *Die Papierindustrie in den kurpfälzischen Stammlanden unter Kurfürst Carl Theodor*. Schotten: Wilhelm Engel, 1935.

Jander, Owen. "Staff-Liner Identification, a Technique for the Age of Microfilm." *JAMS* 20 (1967): 112–16.

Jeffery, Peter. *The Autograph Manuscripts of Francesco Cavalli*. Ph.D. diss., Princeton University, 1980.

Johansson, Cari. *French Music Publishers' Catalogues of the Second Half of the Eighteenth Century* [*FMPC*]. Publications of the Royal Swedish Academy of Music, 2. 2 vols. Stockholm: Almqvist & Wiksells, 1955.

Johnson, Douglas P. *Beethoven's Early Sketches in the "Fischhof Miscellany."* Ann Arbor, Mich.: UMI Research Press, 1988.
Johnson, Douglas, Alan Tyson, and Robert Winter. *The Beethoven Sketchbooks: History, Reconstruction, Inventory.* Berkeley: University of California Press, 1985.
Jung, Hermann. "Mannheim nach 1777: Ausprägung einer bürgerlichen Musikkultur bis zur Mitte des 19. Jahrhunderts." In Ludwig Finscher, ed., *Die Mannheimer Hofkapelle im Zeitalter Carl Theodors,* 197–218.
Kade, Otto. *Die Musikalien-Sammlung des Grossherzoglich Mecklenburg-Schweriner Fürstenhauses aus den letzten zwei Jahrhunderten.* 2 vols. Schwerin: Sandmeyersche Hofbuchdruckerei, 1893.
Kallberg, Jeffrey. *The Chopin Sources: Variants and Versions in Later Manuscripts and Printed Editions.* Ph.D. diss., University of Chicago, 1982.
Kataloge bayerischer Musiksammlungen **[KBM]**. See Haberkamp, Gertraut; Münster, Robert.
Kerman, Joseph, ed. *Ludwig van Beethoven: Autograph Miscellany from circa 1786 to 1799 . . . (the "Kafka Sketchbook").* Facs. ed. 2 vols. London: Trustees of the British Museum, 1970.
Kleeberger, Karl. "Urkundliches über die Papiermühle in Mosbach." *Mannheimer Geschichtsblätter* 26 (1925): 10–15.
Kloiber, Rudolf. *Die dramatischen Ballette von Christian Cannabich.* Munich: H. Kutzner, 1928.
Kobayashi, Yoshitake. *Die Notenschrift Johann Sebastian Bachs: Dokumente seiner Entwicklung.* Neue Bach-Ausgabe, ser. 9, vol. 2. Kassel: Bärenreiter, 1989.
Kramer, Richard A. *The Sketches for Beethoven's Violin Sonatas, Opus 30: History, Transcription, Analysis.* Ph.D. diss., Princeton University, 1973.
Kreutz, Jörg. "Aufklärung und französische Hofkultur im Zeitalter Carl Theodors in Mannheim." In Ludwig Finscher, ed., *Die Mannheimer Hofkapelle im Zeitalter Carl Theodors,* 1–19.
Kusko, Bruce. "Proton Milliprobe Analysis of the Hand-Penned Annotations in Bach's Calov Bible." In *The Calov Bible of J. S. Bach,* ed. Howard H. Cox, 31–106. Ann Arbor, Mich.: UMI Research Press, 1985.
Labarre, E. J., ed. *The Nostitz Papers.* Hilversum: Paper Publications Society, 1955.
La Che[s]naye-Desbois, [François-Alexandre Aubert] de, and ———— Badier (given names not known). *Dictionnaire de la noblesse.* 3d ed. Paris: [Schlesinger frères], 1863–77.
LaRue, Jan. "Abbreviated Description for Watermarks." *Fontes artis musicae* 4 (1957): 26–28.
———— [LaRue]. *A Catalogue of 18th-Century Symphonies.* Vol. 1: *Thematic Identifier.* Bloomington, Ind.: Indiana University Press, 1988.
————. "Symphonie, B." *MGG,* 1st ed., 12 (1965): 1807–32.
————. "Watermarks and Musicology." *Acta musicologica* 33 (1961): 120–46.
————. "Watermarks Are Singles, Too: A Miscellany of Research Notes." In *Haydn, Mozart, and Beethoven: Studies in the Music of the Classical Period. Essays in Honour of Alan Tyson,* ed. Sieghard Brandenburg, 1–12. Oxford: Clarendon Press, 1998.
Lepsius, B. "Sickingen, Karl Heinrich Joseph Reichsgraf von S." *Allgemeine deutsche Biographie,* vol. 34, pp. 158–60. Leipzig: Duncker & Humblot, 1892.
Majo, Gian Francesco de. *Ifigenia in Tauride.* Ed. Paul Corneilson. Recent Researches in the Music of the Classical Era, 46. Madison, Wisc.: A-R Editions, 1996.

Mannlich, Johann Christian von. *Rokoko und Revolution: Lebenserinnerungen*. Ed. Friedrich Matthaesius. Stuttgart: K. F. Koehler, 1966.
Marshall, Robert Lewis. *The Compositional Process of J. S. Bach: A Study of the Autograph Scores of the Vocal Works*. 2 vols. Princeton, N.J.: Princeton University Press, 1972.
McClymonds, Marita P. "Mattia Verazi and the Opera at Mannheim, Stuttgart, and Ludwigsburg." *Studies in Music from the University of Western Ontario* 7 (1982): 99–136.
Méguin, A. B. *Art de la réglure des registres et des papiers de musique*. Paris: Augot, 1828.
Mercure de France [*MdF*]. Paris, 1749–92.
Mörz, Stefan. *Aufgeklärter Absolutismus in der Kurpfalz während der Regierungszeit des Kurfürsten Karl Theodor (1742–1777)*. Stuttgart: W. Kohlhammer, 1991.
Münster, Robert. "Johann Cramer und andere Hofmusik-Kopisten in Mannheim und München zwischen 1770 und 1810." *Die Musikforschung* 22 (1969): 475–77.
——— [Münster]. *Die Sinfonien Toeschis: ein Beitrag zur Geschichte der Mannheimer Sinfonie*. Diss., University of Munich, 1956.
Münster, Robert, und Robert Machold. *Die Musikhandschriften der ehemaligen Klosterkirchen Weyarn, Tegernsee und Benediktbeuern*. Kataloge bayerischer Musiksammlungen, 1. Munich: G. Henle, 1971.
Münster, Robert, Ursula Bockholdt, Robert Machold, and Lisbet Thew, eds. *Thematischer Katalog der Musikhandschriften der Benediktinerabtei Frauenwörth und der Pfarrkirchen Indersdorf, Wasserburg am Inn und Bad Tölz*. Kataloge bayerischer Musiksammlungen, 2. Munich: G. Henle, 1975.
Die Musik in Geschichte und Gegenwart [*MGG*]. 1st ed. by Friedrich Blume. 17 vols. Kassel: Bärenreiter, 1949–86. 2d ed. by Ludwig Finscher. [Part I:] *Sachteil*. 10 vols. Ibid., 1994–99. [Part II:] *Personenteil*. Ibid., 1999– .
The New Grove Dictionary of Music and Musicians [*New Grove*]. 1st ed. by Stanley Sadie. 20 vols. London: Macmillan, 1980. 2d ed. by Stanley Sadie and John Tyrrell. 29 vols. Ibid., 2001.
The New Grove Dictionary of Opera. Ed. Stanley Sadie and Christine Bashford. 4 vols. London: Macmillan, 1992.
Obser, Karl. "Aufzeichnungen des Staatskanzlers Fürsten von Hardenberg über seinen Aufenthalt am Oberrhein im Jahre 1772." *Zeitschrift für die Geschichte des Oberrheins*, Neue Folge, 22 (1907): 145–67.
Osborne, Albert S. *Questioned Documents*. Repr. of the 2d ed. of 1929. Montclair, N.J.: Patterson Smith Publishing, 1973. Orig. ed., 1910.
Paymer, Marvin. *The Instrumental Music Attributed to Giovanni Battista Pergolesi: A Study in Authenticity*. Ph.D. diss., City University of New York, 1977.
Pelker, Bärbel. "Musikalische Akademien am Hof Carl Theodors in Mannheim." In Ludwig Finscher, ed., *Die Mannheimer Hofkapelle im Zeitalter Carl Theodors*, 49–58.
———. "Theateraufführungen und musikalische Akademien am Hof Carl Theodors in Mannheim: eine Chronik der Jahre 1742–1777." In Ludwig Finscher, ed., *Die Mannheimer Hofkapelle im Zeitalter Carl Theodors*, 113–21.
———. "Zur Struktur des Musiklebens am Hof Carl Theodors in Mannheim." In Ludwig Finscher et al., eds., *Mozart und Mannheim*, 29–40.
———, ed. *Ignaz Holzbauer / Franz Beck: Solowerke für Sopran und Orchester*. Musik der Mannheimer Hofkapelle, 2. Stuttgart: Carus-Verlag, 1999.

Pelker, Bärbel, and Rüdiger Thomsen-Fürst. *Georg Joseph Vogler (1749–1814): Materialen zu Leben und Werk unter besonderer Berücksichtigung der pfalzbayerischen Dienstjahre*. Quellen und Studien zur Geschichte der Mannheimer Hofkapelle, 6. Frankfurt am Main: Peter Lang; in press.

Piccinni, Niccolò. *Catone in Utica*. Vol. 50 of *Italian Opera, 1640–1770*, ed. Howard Mayer Brown. Facs. ed. New York: Garland Publishing, 1978.

Pierre, Constant. *Histoire du Concert spirituel 1725–1790*. Paris: Société française de musicologie, Heugel, 1975.

Pinto, Edward H. *Treen and Other Wooden Bygones: An Encyclopædia and Social History*. London: G. Bell & Sons, 1969.

Plath, Wolfgang. "Beiträge zur Mozart-Autographie II: Schriftchronologie 1770–1780." *Mozart-Jahrbuch*, 1976/77, pp. 131–73.

Platoff, John. "Writing about Influences: *Idomeneo*, a Case Study." In *Explorations in Music, the Arts, and Ideas: Essays in Honor of Leonard B. Meyer*, ed. Eugene Narmour and Ruth A. Solie, 43–65. Stuyvesant, N.Y.: Pendragon Press, 1988.

Prevost, M. "Cossé (Lousi-Hercule-Timoléon de), VIIIe duc de Brissac." *Dictionnaire de biographie française*, vol. 9, cols. 769–70. Paris: Letouzey et Ané, 1961.

The Public Advertiser [PA]. London, 1752–94.

Recent Researches in the Music of the Classical Era [RRMCE]. See Baker, Nicole, ed.; Cannabich, Christian; Cauthen, Paul, ed.; Grave, Floyd K., ed.; Majo, Gian Francesco de.

Répertoire International des Sources Musicales [RISM]. Series A/I: *Einzeldrucke vor 1800*. Ed. Karlheinz Schlager et al. 9 vols. Kassel: Bärenreiter, 1971–81.

Reutter, Jochen. "Die Kirchenmusik am Mannheimer Hof." In Ludwig Finscher, ed., *Die Mannheimer Hofkapelle im Zeitalter Carl Theodors*, 97–112.

——— [Reutter]. *Studien zur Kirchenmusik Franz Xaver Richters (1709–1789)*. Quellen und Studien zur Geschichte der Mannheimer Hofkapelle, 1. 2 vols. Frankfurt am Main: Peter Lang, 1993.

Riemann, Hugo, ed. See *Denkmäler der Tonkunst in Bayern*.

Rosenlehner, August. "Zur Lebensgeschichte des kurpfalzbayrischen Bibliothekars und Hofhistoriographen Karl Theodor von Traitteur (1756–1830). *Mannheimer Geschichtsblätter* 9 (1908): 170–76.

Rotenstein, Gottfried von. Letter of 11 May 1785. In *Lustreise in die Rheingegenden, in Briefen an Fr. J. v. Pf.*, pp. 102–6. Frankfurt and Leipzig, 1791. Reprinted in Friedrich Walter, "Ein Akademiekonzert im Rittersaale des Mannheimer Schlosses," 210–11, and Eugene K. Wolf, "On the Composition of the Mannheim Orchestra," 127–30 (the latter article with Engl. trans.).

Sandberger, Adolf. "Aus der Korrespondenz des pfalzbayerischen Kurfürsten Karl Theodor mit seinem römischen Ministerresidenten." In *Adolf Sandberger: Ausgewählte Aufsätze*, vol. 1, pp. 218–20. Munich: Drei Masken Verlag, 1921. Originally published in the Kretzschmar Festschrift, 1918.

Schaal, Richard. "Die Autographen der Wiener Musiksammlung von Aloys Fuchs." *Haydn Yearbook* 6 (1969): 5–191.

Schafhäutl, Karl Emil von. *Abt Georg Joseph Vogler: sein Leben, Charakter und musikalisches System, seine Werke, seine Schule, Bildnisse &c*. Augsburg: M. Huttler, 1888.

Schiedermair, Ludwig. "Die Blütezeit der Öttingen-Wallerstein'schen Hofkapelle." *Sammelbände der Internationalen Musikgesellschaft* 9 (1907/8): 83–130.

Schmid, Manfred Hermann, Ursula Menzel, and Christian Segebade. "Trompeten als Zeichen der Representation am Mannheimer Hof." In Ludwig Finscher et al., eds., *Mozart und Mannheim*, 41–64.
Schmidt, Hans. "Karl (III.) Philipp." *Neue deutsche Biographie*, vol. 11, pp. 250–52. Berlin: Duncker & Humblot, 1977.
Schmitt, Eduard. *Die kurpfälzische Kirchenmusik im 18. Jahrhundert*. Diss., University of Heidelberg, 1958.
―――――, ed. [Schmitt]. *Kirchenmusik der Mannheimer Schule, 1. Auswahl*. DTB, Neue Folge, 2. Wiesbaden: Breitkopf & Härtel, 1982.
Schmitt, Eduard, and Josef Troller. "Mannheim." *MGG*, 1st ed., 8 (1960): 1594–1601.
Schneider, Hans. *Der Musikverleger Johann Michael Götz (1740–1810) und seine kurfürstlich privilegirte Notenfabrique*. 2 vols. Tutzing: Hans Schneider, 1989.
Schoonover, David. "Techniques of Reproducing Watermarks: A Practical Introduction." In Stephen Spector, ed., *Essays in Paper Analysis*, 154–67. Washington, D.C.: Folger Books, 1987.
Schubart, Carl Friedrich Daniel. *Leben und Gesinnungen*. Stuttgart: Gebrüder Mäntler, 1791–93.
Scriven, Michael. "Truisms As the Grounds for Historical Explanations." In Patrick Gardiner, ed., *Theories of History*, 443–75. New York: The Free Press, 1959.
Sherman, Charles H. *The Masses of Johann Michael Haydn: A Critical Survey of Sources*. Ph.D. diss., University of Michigan, 1967.
Sherman, Charles H., and T. Donley Thomas. *Johann Michael Haydn (1737–1806): A Chronological Thematic Catalogue of His Works*. Stuyvesant, N.Y.: Pendragon Press, 1993.
"Sickingen, auch Freiherren und Grafen." In *Neues allgemeines deutsches Adels-Lexikon*, ed. Ernst Heinrich Kneschke, vol. 8, pp. 485–86. Leipzig: Friedrich Voigt, 1868.
Siebmacher, J. *Grosses Wappenbuch*. Vol. 24: *Die Wappen des Adels in Baden, Elsaß-Lothringen und Luxemburg*. Repr. ed. Neustadt an der Aisch: Bauer & Raspe, 1974. Orig. ed., Nürnberg: Bauer & Raspe, 1878.
Smither, Howard E. *A History of the Oratorio*. Vol. 3: *The Oratorio in the Classical Era*. Chapel Hill, N.C.: University of North Carolina Press, 1987.
Sonneck, Oscar George Theodore. *Catalogue of Opera Librettos Printed before 1800*. Vol. 1: *Title Catalogue*. Washington, D.C.: Government Printing Office, 1914.
Sprague, Cheryl R. *A Comparison of Five Musical Settings of Metastasio's* Artaserse. Ph.D. diss., University of California, Los Angeles, 1979.
Stevenson, Alan H. "Watermarks Are Twins." *Studies in Bibliography: Papers of the Bibliographical Society of the University of Virginia* 4 (1951–52): 57–91.
Strohm, Reinhard. *Die italienische Oper im 18. Jahrhundert*. Wilhelmshaven: Heinrichshofen's Verlag, 1979.
Tanselle, G. Thomas. "The Bibliographical Description of Paper." *Studies in Bibliography* 24 (1971): 27–67.
Terry, Miriam. "C. P. E. Bach and J. J. H. Westphal—A Clarification." *JAMS* 22 (1969): 106–15.
Thoor, Alf. "Hugo Riemann, Mannheimskolan och 'Denkmälerstriden.'" *Svensk Tidskrift för Musikforskning* 34 (1952): 5–27.
Thouret, Georg. *Katalog der Musiksammlung aus der Königlichen Hausbibliothek im Schloße zu Berlin*. Leipzig: Breitkopf & Härtel, 1895.

Toeschi, Carl Joseph. *Céphale et Procris* and *L'Enlèvement de Proserpine*. Part III of *Ballet Music from the Mannheim Court*, ed. Paul Cauthen. Recent Researches in the Music of the Classical Era, 52. Madison, Wisc.: A-R Editions, 1998.

―――. See also Baker, Nicole, ed.

Traetta, Tommaso. *Ippolito ed Aricia*. Ed. Eric Weimer. Vol. 78 of *Italian Opera, 1640–1770*, ed. Howard Mayer Brown. Facs. ed. New York: Garland Publishing, 1982.

Tschudin, W. Fr. *The Ancient Paper-Mills of Basle and Their Marks*. Hilversum: Paper Publications Society, 1958.

Tyson, Alan. *Mozart: Studies of the Autograph Scores*. Cambridge, Mass.: Harvard University Press, 1987.

―――. "The Problem of Beethoven's 'First' *Leonore* Overture." *JAMS* 28 (1975): 292–334.

―――. "A Reconstruction of the Pastoral Symphony Sketchbook (British Museum Add. MS. 31766)." In *Beethoven Studies*, ed. Alan Tyson, 67–96. New York: W. W. Norton, 1973.

――― [Tyson, NMA]. *Wolfgang Amadeus Mozart: Neue Ausgabe sämtlicher Werke*. Vol. X/33/2: *Wasserzeichen-Katalog*. [Part 1:] *Textband*. [Part 2:] *Abbildungen*. Kassel: Bärenreiter, 1992.

Unverricht, Hubert. "Johann Anton Fils (1733–1760): zur Herkunft und Bedeutung des Komponisten." In Hermann Holzbauer, ed., *Johann Anton Fils (1733–1760): ein Eichstätter Komponist der Mannheimer Klassik*, 11–32. Tutzing: Hans Schneider, 1983.

Vander Meulen, David L. "The Identification of Paper without Watermarks: The Example of Pope's *Dunciad*." *Studies in Bibliography* 37 (1984): 58–81.

Veit, Joachim. *Der junge Carl Maria von Weber: Untersuchungen zum Einfluß Franz Danzis und Abbé Georg Joseph Voglers*. Mainz: Schott, 1990.

Veit, Joachim, and Frank Ziegler. *Carl Maria von Weber in Darmstadt*. Tutzing: Hans Schneider, 1997.

Vogler, Georg Joseph. *Betrachtungen der Mannheimer Tonschule*. 3 vols. [Mannheim: Götz,] 1778–81. Repr. ed., with the *Gegenstände der Betrachtungen* as vol. 4. Hildesheim: Georg Olms, 1974.

―――. *Der Kaufmann von Smyrna*. Vol. 21 of *German Opera, 1770–1800*, ed. Thomas Bauman. Facs. ed. New York: Garland Publishing, 1986.

―――. *Utile Dulci: A. Voglers belehrende musikalische Herausgaben. Deutsche Kirchenmusik mit einer Zergliederung . . . .* Munich: Senefelder & Gleissner, 1808.

―――. See also Grave, Floyd K., ed.

Walter, Friedrich. "Ein Akademiekonzert im Rittersaale des Mannheimer Schlosses 1785." *Mannheimer Geschichtsblätter* 10 (1909): 210–11.

―――. *Archiv und Bibliothek des Grossh. Hof- und Nationaltheaters in Mannheim 1779–1839*. Vol. 1: *Das Theater-Archiv*. Vol. 2: *Die Theater-Bibliothek*. Leipzig: S. Hirzel, 1899.

―――. *Geschichte des Theaters und der Musik am kurpfälzischen Hofe*. Leipzig: Breitkopf & Härtel, 1898.

―――. "Die Hof- und Kirchenfeste am kurfürstlichen Hof zu Mannheim." *Mannheimer Geschichtsblätter* 14 (1913): 253–59.

―――. "Ein Mannheimer Trompeter-Lehrbrief vom Jahr 1749." *Mannheimer Geschichtsblätter* 2 [1901]: 91-92.

Wolf, Eugene K. "Authenticity and Stylistic Evidence in the Early Symphony: A Conflict in Attribution between Richter and Stamitz." In *A Musical Offering: Essays in Honor of Martin Bernstein*, ed. Edward H. Clinkscale and Claire Brook, 275–94. New York: Pendragon Press, 1977.

———. "The 'Concert' in Munich under Elector Carl Theodor." In Theodor Göllner and Stephan Hörner, eds., *Mozarts Idomeneo und die Musik in München zur Zeit Karl Theodors*, 223–36. Bayerische Akademie der Wissenschaften, Philosophisch-historische Klasse, Abhandlungen, Neue Folge, vol. 119. Munich: Verlag der Bayerischen Akademie der Wissenschaften, 2001.

———. "Driving a Hard Bargain: Johann Stamitz's Correspondence with Stuttgart (1748)." In *Festschrift Christoph-Hellmut Mahling zum 65. Geburtstag*, ed. Axel Beer, Kristina Pfarr, and Wolfgang Ruf, 1553–70. Mainzer Studien zur Musikwissenschaft, 37. Tutzing: Hans Schneider, 1997.

———. "Fulda, Frankfurt, and the Library of Congress: A Recent Discovery." *JAMS* 24 (1971): 286–91. See also the "Communication," *JAMS* 25 (1972): 122–23.

———. "The Mannheim Court." In *The Classical Era*, ed. Neal Zaslaw, vol. 5 of *Man and Music* [new title *Music and Society*], ed. Stanley Sadie, 213–39. Englewood Cliffs, N.J.: Prentice Hall, 1989.

———. "The Music Collection of the Hessische Landesbibliothek Fulda and Its Relationship with Collections in Frankfurt, Washington, and Elsewhere." In *Von der Klosterbibliothek zur Landesbibliothek: Beiträge zum zweihundertjährigen Bestehen der Hessischen Landesbibliothek Fulda*, ed. Artur Brall, 361–70. Stuttgart: Anton Hiersemann, 1978.

———. "On the Composition of the Mannheim Orchestra, ca. 1740–1778." *Basler Jahrbuch für historische Musikpraxis* 17 (1993): 113–38.

———. "The Path to *Manuscripts from Mannheim*: A 'Pre-Preface.'" In Ludwig Finscher, Bärbel Pelker, and Rüdiger Thomsen-Fürst, eds., *Mannheim – "Ein Paradies der Tonkünstler"? Kongreßbericht Mannheim 1999*, 171–81. Quellen und Studien zur Geschichte der Mannheimer Hofkapelle, 8. Frankfurt am Main: Peter Lang, 2002.

———. Review of *Studien zur Kirchenmusik Franz Xaver Richters*, by Jochen Reutter. *Notes* 51 (1994): 127–31.

———. [**Wolf**]. *The Symphonies of Johann Stamitz: A Study in the Formation of the Classic Style*. Utrecht: Bohn, Scheltema & Holkema, 1981.

Wolf, Eugene K., and Jean K. Wolf. "A Newly Identified Complex of Manuscripts from Mannheim." *JAMS* 27 (1974): 379–437.

———, eds. *The Symphony at Mannheim: Johann Stamitz, Christian Cannabich*. Vol. C/III of *The Symphony, 1720–1840*, ed. Barry S. Brook and Barbara B. Heyman. New York: Garland Publishing, 1984.

Wolf, Jean K. "(Johann) Christian Cannabich." *New Grove*, 2d ed., vol. 2, pp. 934–36.

———. *The Orchestral Works of Christian Cannabich: A Documentary Study*. M.A. thesis, New York University, 1968.

Wolf, Jean K., and Eugene K. Wolf. "Rastrology and Its Use in Eighteenth-Century Manuscript Studies." In *Studies in Musical Sources and Style: Essays in Honor of Jan LaRue*, ed. Eugene K. Wolf and Edward H. Roesner, 237–95. Madison, Wisc.: A-R Editions, 1990.

Wolff, Christoph. "Die Rastrierungen in den Originalhandschriften Joh. Seb. Bachs und ihre Bedeutung für die diplomatische Quellenkritik." In *Festschrift für Friedrich Smend zum 70. Geburtstag*, 80–92. Berlin: Merseburger, 1963.

Würtz, Roland. *Ignaz Fränzl: ein Beitrag zur Musikgeschichte der Stadt Mannheim*. Beiträge zur mittelrheinischen Musikgeschichte, 12. Mainz: B. Schott's Söhne, 1970.

―――――. *Verzeichnis und Ikonographie der kurpfälzischen Hofmusiker zu Mannheim nebst darstellendem Theaterpersonal 1723–1803*. Quellenkataloge zur Musikgeschichte, 8. Wilhelmshaven: Heinrichshofen's Verlag, 1975.

―――――, ed. *Mannheim und Italien: zur Vorgeschichte der Mannheimer*. Beiträge zur mittelrheinischen Musikgeschichte, 25. Mainz: Schott, 1984.

Zobeley, Fritz. "Aus Alt-Mannheimer Musikerbriefen." *Neue Mannheimer Zeitung*, 9 May 1931.

Index

Note: The following index is generally comprehensive as regards the main text of this book. However, works of minor significance are not indexed individually but only by their composers' names, and works with generic titles (Symphony, Mass) are lumped together by genre. Copyists and Blum and Heusler papers are listed separately (i.e., are given separate subheadings), but other, less important papers are referred to only by manufacturer. Likewise, rastra mentioned in the main text are indexed only by type (single, double, five-stave, etc.). The appendices are treated more selectively. Here the introductions and footnotes are fully indexed, as are composers and titles of works in Appendix A (using the principles outlined above). The page numbers of the main listing of each paper, type of staving, and copyist in Appendices B–D, respectively, are also given. However, those portions of the appendices that are themselves indices—the paper, staving, and copyists columns of Appendix A, the "Found in" rubrics of Appendices B–D—are *not* indexed. Following standard practice, in both the main text and appendices, items that are part of a bibliographical citation are not generally indexed, and libraries are not cited unless there has been a substantive reference to their collections. Throughout, particular references take precedence over general ones. Accordingly, a page reference to a discussion of Mozart's *Idomeneo*, for example, will appear under the subheading *"Idomeneo"* rather than under the main heading, "Mozart," and one to the palace at Mannheim will appear only under "palace." As an aid to the reader, references to footnotes are indicated by the letter *n* appended to the page number; to avoid fussiness, however, only the page number (i.e., without the *n*) will be given in the case of references that appear in both the text and footnotes of a given page. Finally, under each composer's name, individual works and genres appear in a separate alphabetical list after the other subheadings.

Abelshauser, Joseph, 96–97, 100
academies. *See* Mannheim.
Accessisten (*Akzessisten*; accessists, supernumeraries), 108n
Adobe Photoshop, 94, 335
almanacs, incl. *Calender*, 24n, 27–28, 95–96, 100, 108, 194n
Alston, Robin, 59
"Amadori." *See* Tedeschi, Giovanni.
André, Johann, 37n, 164, 167
André-Archiv. *See* Offenbach am Main.
Appendix A: organization of, 12, 45, 47, 164–65, 173, 223; relation to Appendix C and table 2:1, 83
Appendix B, organization of, 293–95
Appendix C: organization of, 76, 83, 317–18; relation to table 2:1, 83

Appendix D, organization of, 94, 335
aria forms, as indicators of chronology, 124n
arias. *See* insertion arias; manuscripts.
Asam, Cosmas Damian, 28, 105
Asam, Egid Quirin, 105
Augsburg, 218–19
authentic copies, 39, 159
authentication, 90n–91n, 102
autographs, 35–36, 38–39, 45, 47, 55, 64–65, 67, 74, 91–92, 95, 105–10, 123, 125–26, 128–30, 138, 154, 156, 159–63, 167–68, 173, 176–77, 178n, 191n, 204, 207–8, 210, 215–17, 220, 223, 228, 234, 247, 252, 254, 261n, 280, 308–9, 314, 336–41, 343, 348–49, 352. *See also* manuscripts; parts; scores.

Babenhausen, 205
Bach, Johann Christian, 174, 193; *Amor vincitore*, 175–76, 179, 280; *Endimione*, 175–76, 178n, 179, 280; *Lucio Silla*, 169, 176, 179, 193, 194n, 280; *Temistocle*, 176, 177n–178n, 179–80, 191, 193, 208, 219n, 263, 266, 274, 279; *La tempesta*, 193n
Bach, Johann Michael, paper, 119, 309–11
Bach, Johann Sebastian, 50, 65–67, 69, 102
Baden, 57, 63n, 144, 154n, 303, 305, 308
Baden-Durlach, 209
Badische Landesbibliothek. *See* Karlsruhe.
ballet. *See* Mannheim; manuscripts.
Bartenstein (Schloss), 125
Basel, 57, 63–64, 106, 138, 144, 154n, 176, 295–96, 302–3, 305, 308
Bavaria, 11, 34, 154–55, 314
Bayerische Staatsbibliothek. *See* Munich.
Beethoven, Ludwig van, 55n, 67, 76n, 203n, 293
Bengtsson, Ingmar, 89–90
Bentheim-Tecklenburg. *See* Rheda.
Benzien, Christina Caritas Schneider, 70
Bergen op Zoom, 64n, 115n, 312
Berlin, 36, 52, 64, 88, 91, 92n, 95, 126, 170, 174, 180, 184, 191n, 192, 194, 198, 201, 205–9, 220, 300, 352, 371; Königliche Hausbibliothek, 205, 207. *See also* Pretlack collection.
Bern, 191n
beta-radiography, 58
Bibiena, Alessandro Galli da, 24, 105
Biblioteca Estense. *See* Modena.
bindings. *See* heraldry, heraldic devices; "Mannheim" bindings; manuscripts.
Birmingham (UK) Museum and Art Gallery, 68n
Blauw, D. & C., paper, 185
Blum family, paper, 63, 106, 108, 111, 138, 166, 295–303; Blum 1, 117–18, 121–22, 138, 161, 206, 211, 295–99; Blum 2, 210n, 211–12, 298–99; Blum 3, 117–18, 121, 123, 202, 206–7, 210n, 211–12, 214–16, 219, 299–300; Blum 4, 300, 302;

Blum 5, 115, 117–20, 138, 141, 143, 145–46, 150, 168, 204, 217–19, 300–303; Blum 6, 123n, 143, 208, 295, 300, 302–3; Blum 7, 261n, 300, 302–3; ?Blum or Heusler 1, 303, 309
Blum, Hieronymus III, 138, 295–96, 300, 302
Bohrer, Caspar, 97, 100, 261n, 357, 360. *See also* copyists, anonymous: Mannheim 4.
Bohrer, Johann Philipp, 97, 100
Bologna, 208, 275
Bonn, 203–4. *See also* Cologne.
Bouqueton, François André, 108, 226
Braun, Georg Lorenz, 69–70
Breitkopf Catalogue, 269
British Library. *See* London.
Brno: Staré Brno monastery, 202; St. Thomas monastery, 123n, 202, 263
Brunner, Franz Anton, 95–96, 98, 101
Brussels, 161, 191n, 216
Buchsbaum (Buxbaum), Andreas, 97
Burg Echzell, 205
Burney, Charles, 26–27
Burrows, Donald, 49n, 67
Bush, Deanna, 202–3, 228, 262

Cabin Light Panel, 60
Caldara, Antonio, 252
Calender. *See* almanacs.
calligraphy. *See* handwriting.
Calov bible, 50
Cannabich, Carl, 127n
Cannabich, Christian, 27, 32, 34–37, 40–41, 45, 47–48, 52, 67, 79, 95, 101–2, 114, 127–57, 160, 162, 174–75, 210, 213, 223, 228, 234–50 (Appendix A/III), 253, 261n, 262, 288, 340, 360; beginning of Munich period, 153–56; hand, handwriting, 74, 128–29, 133, 340, 342–45; numbering in Munich symphony series, 128–31, 134, 142, 144–48, 150–51, 153n, 213–14, 234–35, 239, 244–49; publication of orchestral works, 128, 140–41, 144, 147–49, 151–52, 215; ballets, 42, 105, 108–9, 115, 117, 219n, 226,

314; concertos, 127, 128n, 141, 148, 211, 234, 247–49, 304; *Electra*, 219n; *Les fêtes du seraïlles*, 210, 214–15, 283–84, 288; *Médée et Jason*, 219n, 357; "miscellaneous" works (M1–7), 127, 136–37, 139, 141, 145–46, 148, 150–51, 234, 248–49; music for church, 140–41, 235–36, 247–49, 340; orchestral trios, 144, 238; pastorales, 127, 128n, 141, 150, 234, 248–49; *Renaud et Armide*, 207, 264, 354; symphonies, 35n, 39n, 65, 73–74, 82–85, 99–100, 106, 124, 127–57, 160, 162, 165–66, 168, 206–10, 212–15, 219–20, 234–47, 249, 265, 282–83, 300, 310, 340, 342, 344–45, 352, 354, 356–61, 370; *symphonies concertantes*, 127–28, 148, 149n, 152, 210, 214, 240–41, 265, 283, 314
Cannabich, Marie Elisabeth, 32
cantatas, 24, 28, 33
Carbari (?), ———, 195n
Carl Philipp, Elector Palatine, 23, 26–27, 208, 210
Carl Theodor, Elector Palatine, 11, 26–27, 29, 32, 34, 40, 44, 64, 87n, 101, 106, 109, 113, 115, 136, 149, 156n, 163, 169, 174, 180, 184, 192, 194, 199n, 207, 210, 309, 312, 336, 348; Enlightenment influences on, 26
Cauthen, Paul, 176, 291n
chain-lines. *See* paper.
Châlons-en-Champagne (formerly Châlons-sur-Marne), 220–21
Chanel, Coco, 296
Charlottenburg (palace), 207
Chiara, S., paper, 161n
Chiarini, Pietro, 270
Chopin, Fryderyk, 67
chronology, incl. dating, 36, 39, 49, 55–56, 65–66, 84, 88, 91, 102, 108–9, 111, 115–17, 121–26, 128–33, 138–52, 156–57, 159–62, 164–66, 168–71, 173, 179, 205–7, 211–17, 234, 254, 295, 317–18, 335, 338. *See also* dates.
Clemens August, elector/archbishop of Cologne, 203n

Cocchi, Gioacchino, 270
codicology, 12, 47
Colla, Giuseppe, 44, 176, 181, 190, 275, 290. *See also* Jommelli, Niccolò, *Cajo Fabrizio.*
Collini, Cosimo Alessandro, 28
Cologne, electors/archbishops of (at Bonn), 202–3
concert programs, 31
Concert spirituel (Paris),
connoisseurship, 90n
copying style: at Mannheim, 51, 83, 94–95, 203, 218–19; at Munich, 143, 154; Italian, 181, 208, 372. *See also* copyists; handwriting.
copying, cost of, 40
copyists (general), 40, 44, 48–49, 51–52, 56, 83, 88, 91, 94–103, 106–7, 130–31, 133, 147, 153, 155, 159, 165, 168, 173, 177, 178n, 179, 180n, 181, 184, 193, 202–6, 209–10, 213, 216–21, 223, 233n, 291n, 318, 335–82 (Appendix D); anonymous, 352–82; labeling of, 94, 335, 371; named, 336–52. *See also the following entry, and names of individual composers and copyists.*
copyists, anonymous (by siglum): Bln./Mh. 1, 372; Bln./Mh. 2 (Innocenz Danzi?), 336, 372; Bln./Mh. 3 (Anton Fils?), 336, 372–73; BP/Mh. 1, 373; BP/Mh. 2, 367, 374; Dres./Mh. 1, 374; DS/Mh. 1, 168, 374; DS/Mh. 2, 168, 375; DS/Mh. 3, 97, 168, 375; DS/Mh. 4–5, 168, 375; DS/Mh. 6, 376; KA/Mh.(?) 1–2, 376; KN/Mh. 1, 376; Mannheim 1 (probably Jacob Cramer), 82, 95–96, 99, 103, 115, 117–19, 121, 123, 137, 140, 146–48, 150, 179, 216, 232n–233n, 305, 335, 347–48, 352–54, 356; Mannheim 2 (?Johann Lochner), 96, 103, 115, 117–22, 137, 160, 169, 202, 215, 335, 354–56; Mannheim 3 (?Wilhelm Sepp), 39n, 82, 85, 97, 100, 102, 119, 121, 133–34, 137–40, 142–44, 146–48, 150–51, 153, 155, 213–14, 283–4, 335, 356–59; Mannheim 4

(Caspar Bohrer?), 39n, 100, 102, 130–33, 135, 139, 142–44, 146–47, 150–51, 153, 155n, 335, 357, 360–61; Mannheim 5, 65n, 88, 96n, 97, 100, 103, 118, 123, 168–70, 179–80, 203–4, 313, 321–22, 324, 335, 360, 362–63; Mannheim 6, 88, 100-101, 103, 107, 111, 115, 117–21, 123n, 168, 179–80, 208, 335, 356, 362, 364–65; Mannheim 7, 117–18, 204, 364; Mannheim 8, 96n, 118–19, 121, 366; Mannheim 9, 117–18, 366–67, 374; Mannheim 10, 137, 138n, 323, 367; Mannheim 11, 137, 141, 367; Mannheim 12, 144–48, 150, 367; Mannheim 13, 144–48, 150–51, 368; Mannheim 14, 144–48, 150, 214–15, 368–69; Mannheim 15, 145–46, 148, 369; Mannheim 16, 146, 150, 369; Mannheim 17, 153, 168, 369–70; Mannheim 18–20, 370; Mannheim 21, 92, 207, 371; Mf/Mh. 1–2, 376; MH/Jk. 1–2, 377; Munich 1, 139, 142, 153, 154n, 156, 239; Munich 2, 142, 153; Munich 3, 239; Munich 4, 153; Munich 5, 154, 156; Munich 6, 239; RH/Mh. 1, 82, 377; Rtt/Mh. 1, 97, 213–15, 335, 377–79; Rtt/Mh. 2, 213–14, 378, 380; Rtt/Mh. 3, 97, 213–14, 335, 377–79, 380; Rtt/Mh. 4, 381; Rtt/Mh. 5, 82, 381; Stanf./?Mh. 1, 217–19, 381; Strasb./Mh. 1, 253n, 382
"core" group. *See* manuscripts.
Corneilson, Paul, 173, 184, 191, 262, 273, 291n
Cossé, duchesse de (probably Adélaïde-Diane-Hortense-Délie Mancini de Nevers de Cossé), 194–95
Cossé, Louis-Hercule-Timoléon, duc de, 194n–195n
countermarks (in paper). *See* watermarks.
Cramer, Jacob, 95–98, 115, 123, 137, 150, 216n, 347–48, 352–54, 362. *See also* copyists, anonymous: Mannheim 1.
Cramer, Johann, 95, 97, 100, 114n, 115, 117–21, 123, 125, 154n, 168, 216, 347–48, 354; hand, handwriting, 346–48

Dadelsen, Georg von, 102
Dalberg, Wolfgang Heribert von, 116
Danielson, Ruben, 89–90
Danner, Johann Georg, 261n
Danzi, Innocenz, 27, 34n, 39n, 95, 207–9, 266, 336, 372
Darmstadt, incl. Hessische Landes- und Hochschulbibliothek, 37–39, 47, 94, 133, 163–67, 169, 177n–178n, 194n, 199–200, 205, 208n, 219n, 244, 254–61, 371
dates, conventions for specifying, 223–24, 335–36
dating. *See* chronology.
digital photography (of watermarks), 58
distance between lines (DL), distance between spaces (DS). *See* staving, analytical specifications.
Donaueschingen, incl. Fürstenberg family, 108, 209
Dragonetti, Domenico, 184n
Dresden, incl. Sächsische Landesbibliothek, 37, 58, 88, 91, 143n, 174, 206, 208–9, 271, 371
Dus(s)art, Maria Anna, 267
Düsseldorf, 24
Dylux paper (Dupont), 59

Eastman School of Music. *See* Rochester, N.Y.
Edge, Dexter, 91, 93
Egk, Friedrich, 249n
Ehreshoven (Schloss), 35, 199–200
Eichner, Ernst, 152n
electors, of Holy Roman Empire, 23
"elephant" paper, 54, 64, 106, 109, 202, 204, 208, 309–10. *See also* Knöckel, Wolfgang Adam.
Elisabeth Auguste, electress of the Palatinate, 32, 34, 149, 174, 336
Elisabeth von Pfalz-Neuburg, 24
Elssler family, 96
endpapers. *See* manuscripts.
Ettal, 160

Falgera, Sigismund, 95, 105, 108–9, 111, 115, 117, 144, 147, 161, 226, 346; hand, handwriting, 346
fascicle structure. *See* manuscripts.
Faulheitsstriche, 223
feature analysis. *See* handwriting.
Ferdinand von Österreich, governor of Lombardy, 203n
Ferrari, Domenico, 106, 220, 327
Fétis, François-Joseph, 216
Fiber Optic Lightsheet, 61
Fils, Anton, 27, 39n, 95, 207–8, 210, 220–21, 266, 284, 327, 336, 372
flyleaves (i.e., free endpapers of a manuscript). *See* manuscripts: endpapers.
forgery (of handwriting), 89, 92
format (of manuscripts), 40, 49, 51–54, 62, 80, 167, 223, 318; oblong (quarto), 40, 51–53, 62, 106, 127, 167, 203, 209, 223, 318, 332; of title pages at Mannheim, 95; upright (folio), 40, 51–53, 54n, 62, 106, 114, 167–68, 220, 223, 323, 325, 333–34
Fotoscientifica (Parma), 58
Fränkisch-Crumbach, 205
Fränzl, Ferdinand Rudolph, 87, 100–101, 155n, 362, 364
Fränzl, Ignaz, 35, 87, 100–101
Frederick II, King of Prussia, 26, 184, 207
Freising, 159
Friedel, Ferdinand, 261n
Friedrich Wilhelm II, King of Prussia, 207
Froimont, Johann Clemens, 25
Fuchs, Aloys, 64, 125, 232
Fürstenberg family. *See* Donaueschingen.
Fulda, 132, 153, 357

gala days. *See* Mannheim.
Galuppi, Baldassare, 139, 174, 199, 270–71; *L'amante di tutti*, 192; *Antigona*, 206, 270; *Antigono*, 206n, 269; *Il filosofo di campagna*, 199; *Le nozze*, 199; *Siroe*, 208, 220, 266
Gargan, ———, 221
Gassmann, Florian Leopold, *L'amore artigiano*, 176, 180, 182, 190, 199, 266

Geerevink, Lubertus (or Lucas) van, paper, 312
Geertz, Clifford, 33n
genetic order, 117
Gesellenbrief. See Lehrbrief.
Giorgetti, Silvio, 232n, 261n
Gluck, Christoph Willibald, 179n, 190–91, 269; *Alceste*, 185, 190–93, 198; *Le feste d'Apollo*, 185n, 190–91, 198n; *Orfeo ed Euridice*, 185n, 190–91
Göttweig (monastery), 123, 202
Götz, Johann Michael, 152, 242–43, 249n
Gradenwitz, Peter, 91
grapheme, grapheme principle, 89–90, 93, 131–33, 343, 357, 360
graphography, 89
graphology. *See* handwriting.
Gravell, Thomas L., 59
Grimm, Baron Friedrich Melchior von, 197
Grout, Donald Jay, 48n
Grua, Carlo Luigi, 38, 105, 107–8, 113n, 133, 138, 167, 201, 251, 336, 338; hand, handwriting, 95, 111, 159, 336–38; *Littanie della beata vergine*, 107, 225, 337; masses, 39n, 41, 107, 121n, 159–60, 204, 206, 212, 225, 251, 269; *Memento Domine David*, 39n, 41, 126, 204, 225, 280
Grua, Franz Paul, 38, 107–8

Handel, George Frideric, 36n, 67
hands, identification of, 88–94, 102
handwriting, 12, 36, 49, 51, 57, 83, 88–103, 111, 114–15, 123, 128, 130–33, 135, 139, 150–51, 159, 161, 165–66, 203, 207–8, 213; and chronology, 102–3, 338; comparative analysis of, 89–94; feature analysis of, 90–93, 102; forensic approaches to, 89, 92–93; parameters for analysis of, 93–94. *See also* copying style; copyists.
Harburg (Schloss). *See* Oettingen-Wallerstein.
Hardenberg, Karl August von, 174
Hartig, Franz, 261n

Hasse, Johann Adolf, 265, 269, 272; *Demofoonte*, 92n, 206, 269–72
Haydn, Joseph, 67, 96, 142n, 239, 249n
Haydn, Michael, 154n–155n, 314
Heartz, Daniel, 192n
Heidelberg, 124n, 125, 166, 208; transfer of Mannheim court from, 23
Henkel, Heinrich, 218
heraldry, heraldic devices, 54, 181n, 195–96, 197n, 290, 305, 309
Herzogenburg Catalogue, 232n
Heusler family, paper, 57, 63, 106, 108, 111, 144, 177, 203n, 295–96, 303–8; ?Blum or Heusler 1, 303, 309; Heusler 1, 161n, 303–5; Heusler 2, 119, 121, 123, 141, 210n, 211–12, 303–5; Heusler 3, 206, 305; Heusler 4, 206, 303, 305; Heusler 5, 57, 63n, 82, 110, 115, 117–20, 125, 138–39, 147, 150, 154, 162, 165–66, 168, 170n, 204, 206, 213, 217–18, 245, 300, 305–6, 308; Heusler 6, 119, 203, 206, 214, 220, 306–7; Heusler 7, 63n, 82, 109, 117–18, 125, 144, 147, 154n, 162, 168–69, 177, 202, 204, 206, 211–13, 219, 307–8; Heusler 8, 57, 63n, 153–56, 305, 308, 314; ?J. J. Heusler 1, 308
Heusler, Johann Jakob IV, 308
Heusler, Niklaus (Nicolaus), 57, 303
Heymann, Johann Gerhard, 210, 219, 284
Hieckel, Hans Otto, 67n
Hilser, Johann Georg, ?310
Hilser, Josef Anton, paper, 202n–203n, ?310
Hirsch, Paul, 65
Hirsvogl, Sixtus, 150, 156, 180n, 245–46
Hofer, Heinrich, 128–29
Hoffstetter, Roman(?), 225
Holešov (Holleschau), 113, 202
Holland, 64
holographs, 38, 210, 215–16. *See also* manuscripts; parts.
Holy Roman Empire, 23
Holzbauer, Ignaz, 27, 36–38, 41, 45, 47–48, 52n, 113–26, 128, 134, 160, 174, 191, 194, 220n, 223, 228–33 (Appendix A/II), 262, 267, 273–74, ?282, 309, 338, 340, 348, 355; hand, handwriting, 95, 176–77, 180, 216, 340–41; *Adriano in Siria*, 185, 187, 190–93, 198n, 199, 264, 267, 272; *Adulatrice corde sonore*, 123, 173n, 232; *Betulia liberata*, 35n, 65n, 100, 123–24, 151, 185, 190, 191n, 198n, 201n, 220, 231; *La clemenza di Tito*, 272; concertos, 82, 84, 86, 209–10, 212, 216, 281, 285; *Il giudizio di Salomone*, 106, 123–25, 139, 143n, 185, 190, 191n, 198n, 231–32, 249; *Günther von Schwarzburg*, 32, 41, 65n, 116, 123, 125, 176, 179, 232, 233n, 267, 341; *Ippolito ed Aricia*, 192; *Issipile*, 208–9, 266–67, 273, 356; masses, 38, 41, 55, 113–23, 134, 144, 201–4, 211–12, 216, 219n, 228–31, 262–64, 280, 289, 304, 347, 352, 354, 356; *La morte di Didone* (incl. *Der Tod der Dido*), 100, 123n, 173, 175–76, 178n, 179, 267, 362; *La Nitteti*, 185, 190–91, 198n, 219n; symphonies, 109, 207, 210, 215–17, 220, 263, 265, 282, 284, 288; *La tempesta*, 173n, 267
Holzbauer, Rosalie Andreides, 38, 116n
Honig, C & I [Cornelis and Jan Adriaan], paper, 312
Honig, J[an], & Zoon(en), paper, 171, 312
Hönisch, Georg Anton, 87n
Horn, Wolfgang, 91
Hortschansky, Klaus, 162, 192n
Huberty, Antoine, 214
hunt, music for, 28

ink, 40, 50, 89, 137, 175, 180–81
Innsbruck, 24, 208
insertion arias, 173, 177, 180, 273–74, 281–82, 362
instrumental music, sources, 40, 42
intertextuality, 13

Jaenecke, Joachim, 177, 184, 205, 206n, 367, 371, 373–74
Jaffé, Albert, 63
Jesuitenkirche. *See* Mannheim.
Jesuits, 24, 26, 121–22

Johann Wilhelm, Elector Palatine, 24
Johnson, Douglas, 67
Jommelli, Niccolò, 44, 52n, 140, 174, 178n, 220, 274, 276; *Artaserse*, 174, 176, 179–80, 274; *Caio Mario*, 269, 275–76; *Cajo Fabrizio* (with Giuseppe Colla), 176, 179–81, 184, 190, 194–97, 275, 290, 362; *Demetrio*, 273; *Salmo L*, 185, 190
Joseph II, Holy Roman Emperor, 26

Kabinettsmusik, 28, 97
Kallberg, Jeffrey, 67
Kandern, 63n, 144, 154n, 308
Karlsruhe, incl. Badische Landesbibliothek, 91n, 107–8, 160, 209
Kassel, 107
Kempten, 160
Kerman, Joseph, 67
Klosterneuburg (monastery), 202, 371
Knöckel, Wolfgang Adam, paper, 64, 106, 109, 115, 204, 206, 208, 309–11
Königliche Hausbibliothek. *See* Berlin.
Kramer, Richard, 67
Kurpfalz. *See* Palatinate.
Kusko, Bruce, 50
Kutter, Elias, paper, 142, 234, 314

La Chevardière, Louis-Balthasar de, 144n, 148, 149n, 220n
laid-lines. *See* paper.
LaRue, Jan, 59–61, 293
Lauchery, Etienne, 108n
Lebrun, Alexander, 27
Lehrbrief (*Gesellenbrief*) for Franz Anton Brunner, 95–96, 98, 101, 364
Leiden, 64n, 115n, 312
Leipzig, Deutsches Buch- und Schriftmuseum, 63
Ley, Pieter van der, paper, 115, 117–18, 313
Library of Congress. *See* Washington.
Liebhaberkonzerte (Concert des Amateurs). *See* Mannheim; Munich.
Lindbergh case, 89
Link, Johann Sebastian Albrecht, 202n
Lisbon, 191n

Lite-a-Page Insertable Viewer, 60
Lochner, Johann, 96–97, 100, 115, 137, 169, 230, 354–56, 362. *See also* copyists, anonymous: Mannheim 2.
logical order, 116
London, 87; The British Library, 180, 184
loupe (comparator), use in rastrology, 81
Ludewig I, Grand Duke of Hesse, 164n

machines for lining paper, 68, 71n, 88n
Macklem, Mary S., 291n
Madrid, 270
Mainz, 197
Majo, Gian Francesco de, 174; *Alessandro nell'Indie*, 176, 179, 199, 265, 268; *Ifigenia in Tauride*, 176, 179–80, 183, 190, 196, 268–69, 363, 365; *Semiramide*, 276, 300
Malherbe, Charles, 125
Mannheim 1–21. *See* copyists.
Mannheim: academies (concerts), 28–32, 109, 218; academies (of fine arts, sciences, etc.), 26; ballet at, 27–29, 32–33, 95, 108, 226, 346; ball house, 25; balls, 28–29, 32; carnival, 29, 192; chamber music at, 24, 28; Concert des Amateurs (Liebhaberkonzerte), 35; court chapel, 25, 29, 32, 105–6; court ritual, 32–34; cultural year at, 29–34; depot for writing materials ("Schreibmaterialen Magazin"), 40–41, 45, 56, 87, 111, 321; economic and political aspects, 23, 26; galas, gala days, 31–33, 109, 180; Jesuitenkirche, 39–40, 64, 105–7, 109, 115, 224–25, 371; Kapelle, 24, 27, 29, 34–35, 39, 115, 133, 136, 149, 157, 163n; Lenten season, 33–34; manuscripts left in, 35–36, 105–7, 175, 199–200, 223–25; military music, 28, 33; musical life at, 24, 26, 27–34; music collection (performance library), 11, 40, 44, 65n, 114, 136, 149, 173, 194, 223, 234, 335; music collection, destruction of, 11, 35, 41–43, 175, 194; music collection, extant manuscripts from, 39–41, 45, 173; Nationaltheater, 35, 41–42,

401

116, 123n, 175–76, 199; opera at, 26–29, 32–33, 174–75, 206–7; opera house, 24–25, 29, 40–42, 174; orchestra, size of, 133–35, 160, 167, 204, 251, 261n, 280 (*see also* roman numerals); palace, 23–25, 28–30, 32, 41–42, 174; Reiss-Museum, 95, 124n, 178n, 184; sacred music at, 24, 28, 32–34, 141, 159–60, 165, 167, 338; secular vocal music at, 24, 28, 33; Seminarium musicum, 40, 106–7, 168n, 204, 224; social conditions, 26, 29; spoken drama at, 26, 28–29, 32, 40; Theaterbibliothek, 35n, 39, 42, 124n, 199–200. *See also* copyists; Heidelberg, transfer of Mannheim court from; "Mannheim" bindings; Munich, transfer of Mannheim court to.

"Mannheim" bindings, 176–79, 181–84, 191–94, 196–97, 198n, 262, 266, 268–69, 289–90

Mannheimer Tonschule, 191n

manuscripts: bindings, 49, 54, 178n, 179, 181–84, 191n, 196, 310; "core" group, 47, 105–11, 115, 223–27; covers (wrappers) of, 54, 57, 64, 106, 111, 117, 119, 127, 142n, 151, 167, 202, 204, 206, 208, 309–10; endpapers, flyleaves, 180, 184, 296, 303, 309; fascicle structure, 49, 54–55, 180; for external use (i.e., other than at Mannheim), 44–45, 51–52, 155, 173, 201–14; French, 185; grouping of, 50–51, 66, 67n, 79–80, 116–17, 129–30, 136–37, 210–14, 217–19, 228; initial examination of, 50–55; "integral," defined, 234; Italian, 177, 180–81, 320; left in Mannheim, 35–36, 105–7, 175, 199–200, 223; *not* from Mannheim, 64–65, 177n–178n, 191n, 202–4, 219–21, 357; of arias, 38, 52, 125, 169, 176, 201, 205–9, 219n, 220, 305, 351–52, 367; of ballets, 40, 42, 105, 108–9, 115, 117, 144, 147, 207; of operas, 35n, 37–38, 41–42, 44–45, 54, 65n, 88, 100, 107, 173–200, 205, 207, 223, 321, 360, 362; of sacred music, 40–41, 52, 64, 106–7, 113–25, 167, 201–4, 208–9, 362; physical characteristics of, 40, 51–55; size of, 51–52, 54, 57; title pages, 49–51, 54, 90, 95, 106, 114, 128n, 129, 135–36, 139–40, 142–44, 147, 150–51, 155, 171, 202, 213, 216–17, 223, 239; types of, 38–45; *See also* autographs; chronology; format; "Mannheim" bindings; Munich; parts; paste-overs; scores.

Martini, Padre Giovanni Battista, 208, 343

Mattei, Saverio, 185n

Maximilian Franz, elector/archbishop of Cologne, 203n

Maximilian Friedrich, elector/archbishop of Cologne, 203n

Maximilian III Joseph, elector of Bavaria, 34

Mayer, Manfred, 61

Mecklenburg-Schwerin. *See* Schwerin.

Méguin, A. B., 71–72, 84

Metastasio, Pietro, 269–71, 273–74

Milan, 140, 192n

Modena, 203; Biblioteca Estense, 202–4

Molter, Johann Melchior, 209

Mosbach, 106, 115, 310–11

Mozart, Leopold, 149, 155n, 199, 219

Mozart, Maria Anna, 31–32, 109, 149, 197

Mozart, Wolfgang Amadeus, 31–32, 34, 38–40, 67, 88n, 91, 95, 101, 105, 109–11, 149, 155n, 159, 194n, 195–99, 217–19, 226–27, 251, 293, 352; "Aer tranquillo" (from *Il rè pastore*), 101, 204n, 268, 351; Concerto for Piano, K. 175, 162, 253; Concerto for Three Pianos, K. 242, 201, 217–19, 290, 292n; *Idomeneo*, 38, 65, 95, 143n, 154, 198–99, 308, 314; Kyrie, K. 322/296a, 227n; "Paris" Symphony, 197, 306; "Popoli di Tessaglia," 198; Sonatas for Violin and Piano, K. 296 and 301–6, 110–11, 197, 198n, 226–27

Munich, 11, 36, 39–41, 47–48, 52, 55, 57, 63–65, 73, 83, 87, 95, 100–102, 109, 127, 130, 136, 142, 154, 156–57, 163n, 166, 174, 179, 180n, 209, 218, 342, 354, 356; academies (concerts) in, 31n, 157n,

241, 246; Bayerische Staatsbibliothek, 41, 63, 94, 107, 113–23, 127–57, 159–60, 162, 180n, 191n, 204, 209–11, 213, 220, 228–31, 234–50, 335, 371; Concert des Amateurs (Liebhaberkonzerte), 157, 239, 246, 250n; Frauenkirche (Munich cathedral), 39, 41, 107, 133, 159, 167, 204; *Hofmusikintendanz*, 40, 107, 114, 127, 134, 160; Hof- und Nationaltheater, 127n, 249n; manuscripts from, 37n, 131–37, 139–40, 142–44, 147, 150–51, 153–57, 168, 234, 243–47, 314, 342, 357, 370; Musikinstrumentenmuseum, 28n, 66n; paper used in, 57, 64–65, 153–56, 293, 305, 308, 314–15; rastra used in, 326, 328, 330–31; Residenztheater (Cuvilliés-Theater), 127n; transfer of Mannheim court to, 11, 34–37, 48, 73, 87, 97, 100–101, 113, 115–16, 136, 140, 142–43, 151–53, 156–57, 163, 164n, 166, 173, 179, 199n, 234, 243, 293, 296, 300, 314, 319, 340, 346, 348, 350, 360, 370. *See also* copyists.

Münster (Westfalen), 209

Münster, Robert, 97, 114n, 143n, 215n, 262, 348

musicology, as discipline, 13

Naples, 180n

Nassau-Weilburg, Princess Caroline von, 101

Neuenstein, Hohenlohe Zentralarchiv, 125

Neustadt/Pfalz, 64, 106, 115, 310

New Haven, Ct., Yale University, 178n, 219n

Nürnberg, 69–70

Oettingen-Wallerstein, incl. Schloss Harburg, 121, 126n, 202, 212n, 219, 220n

Offenbach am Main, Verlagsarchiv André, 37n, 47, 162n, 164–65, 167–68, 171, 254–61

Oggersheim, 34, 149, 178n

Olomouc, 229–30

opera. *See* Mannheim, opera at; manuscripts.

oratorio, 34, 185. *See also* Holzbauer, Ignaz; Ritschel, Johannes.

orchestra, size of. *See* Mannheim.

Ordonez, Carlo d', 143n

Padua, 270

Pagnozzi, Joseph Maria von, 174

Palatinate (*Kurpfalz*), 11, 23, 34, 63

Palm, Joseph, 97n, 154n, 348

pantomime (harlequinade), 28–29

paper, 12, 39–40, 48–49, 51–65, 83, 111, 117, 123, 126, 128, 132–33, 137, 144–45, 148, 153, 159–60, 162, 165, 168, 175, 177, 179–81, 184, 202n, 203–7, 209, 211, 212n, 215–18, 220–21, 223, 293–315 (Appendix B); chain-lines of, 56n, 58, 62, 211–12, 293, 299, 305, 308–9; characteristics of, 56–57; cost of, 40, 126n, 220n; division of original sheet, 53; felt side of, 56–57, 62, 293; identification of, 63; laid-lines of, 56n, 58; manufacturing process, 56–57, 293; mold side of, 56–57, 62, 293; orientation of, 318; post paper, 305, 309, 313; printed, 79; size of, 51–52, 54, 57, 126n, 154, 210, 314; without watermarks, 55n, 82, 138, 141, 206, 209, 210n, 211–12, 309; with penciled verticals, 143, 145–46, 148. *See also* Munich; watermarks.

paper, by origin: Alsatian, 65, 293, 309, 313; Auvergnese, 162; Bavarian, 133, 142; Dutch, 64, 111, 115, 117, 171, 185, 206, 211, 293–94, 312–13; French, 65, 178n, 221, 313; German, 57, 87, 106, 156, 210, 218, 220, 293, 309–11, 314–15; Italian, 62, 64–65, 153–55, 181, 184, 218, 234, 293–94, 314; Palatine, 63–64, 106, 111, 121, 206, 293, 309–11, 313; Swiss, 51, 55n, 57, 62–64, 82, 87, 106, 108, 111, 115, 117, 138, 141, 176, 184, 206, 209–13, 293–309. *See also names of individual papermakers, especially* Blum family, Heusler family; watermarks.

403

Paper Publications Society (Hilversum), 63
Paris, 71, 87, 101, 110, 125, 136, 140–41, 147–49, 152, 160–62, 194–95, 197–98, 207, 214–15, 220, 241, 253, 265; Concert spirituel, 161, 253; Conservatory, 125
Parma, 58, 185n, 190, 192
particle-induced X-ray emission (PIXE), 50
parts, 49, 52, 54–55, 59, 62, 65, 83, 106–7, 135–36, 163, 165–68, 203, 223, 234; added, 50–52, 116–17, 121–22, 129, 135, 137–40, 142, 150–51, 156, 167, 204, 220, 228, 234, 280, 336, 342; autograph, 39n, 74, 95, 114, 128–29, 159–62, 210, 215–16, 340, 344–45, 348; duplicate, 51–52, 114, 129–30, 133–34, 136–37, 140, 160, 167, 210, 220, 246, 261n; for sacred music, 52–54, 167; number of, 49, 51, 133–35, 160, 167, 204, 251, 261n, 280, 344, 361 (*see also* roman numerals); original, 129–33; replacement, 116, 129–33, 135–40, 142n, 143–45, 150, 153, 155–56, 210, 234
Pasquai, Joseph, paper, 65n, 313
paste-overs (paste-ons), 55, 65, 106, 115–17, 119, 124–25, 177, 179, 217, 233n, 309
pastorales, 24, 28, 33, 141
Pelker, Bärbel, 101, 125, 350
Pergolesi, Giovanni Battista, 180n, 224
Pescetti, Giovanni Battista, 52n, 271, 277
Pfalzbayern, 34
Pfeffinger, Ph. J., 252
Photoshop. *See* Adobe.
Piccinni, Niccolò, 174; *La buona figliuola*, 200; *Catone in Utica*, 44, 177, 178n, 179, 190, 198n, 200, 281, 289; *Le contadine bizzarre*, 190–91, 198n
Pierron, Therese, 227
Pigage, Nicolas de, 28
Pinto, Edward H., 68n
piracy, 44–45, 179, 192
Pokorny, Franz Xaver, 126, 138n, 139, 212, 220n, 300, 304, 328

positivism, 13
Potsdam, 207
Prati, Alessio, 154
Pretlack collection (D-B), 37, 44, 52, 64, 88, 92n, 126, 205–9, 220, 269–77, 291n, 300, 305–6, 352, 367, 371
Pretlack, Johann Ludwig, Freiherr von, 44, 205, 291n
programs (of academies), 31
provenance, 36, 45, 48–49, 55, 65, 84, 88, 91, 105, 115, 154–55, 159, 161–62, 164, 167, 173, 176, 178n, 185, 195–97, 199, 213–14, 219–21, 223, 227n, 251, 262, 290, 292n, 295, 317
"puzzle" paradigm, 48, 130

Quaglio, Lorenzo, 42
quills, quill pens, 40

Raaff, Anton, 110, 180n, 195, 197, 227
rastra (singular "rastrum"), 44–45, 48–49, 68–80, 83, 111, 140, 145, 151, 162, 203n, 223; construction of, 68–72, 79; variations in, 317, 319, 322, 330. *See also* staving; staving, analytical specifications.
rastra, by type: simple (single, one-stave), 44, 66–70, 73–74, 76–77, 80, 88, 101, 106–7, 109, 117–19, 123, 139–40, 142n, 143, 145–46, 148, 150–51, 155, 161n, 165, 167–68, 178n, 179, 206, 208, 213, 216, 218–19, 236, 240, 261n, 317–20; compound (multi-stave), 44–45, 67, 69, 71–73, 75–77, 80–83, 88, 138, 145, 148, 155, 206, 317–34 (Appendix C); double (two-stave), 69–71, 73, 77, 80–81, 88, 107, 133, 143, 155–56, 179, 202, 213, 217, 318–20; triple, 75, 80, 133, 155; four-stave, 161n, 320; five-stave, 73, 76, 80, 88, 124n, 138, 144, 148, 156, 161n–162n, 206, 217, 318, 320–24; six-stave, 118, 122, 325; seven-stave, 325; ten-stave, 71n, 73, 76–77, 80–83, 109, 124–26, 138–39, 141–48, 150–51, 155–56, 161–62, 165–66, 168–69, 170n, 179, 203, 204n, 208–9, 213,

216–18, 220, 245, 317, 325–31; twelve-stave, 73, 110, 114, 117–21, 124, 167–68, 179, 204, 227n, 317, 332–34; fourteen-stave, 111
rastrology, 12, 36, 49, 65, 73, 83, 123, 135, 140, 161, 215. *See also* rastra; stafflining; staving.
Ravensburg, 314
Regensburg, incl. Thurn und Taxis family, 36, 39n, 44, 51–52, 54n, 83, 87–88, 138, 191n, 206, 210–16, 218–19, 291n, 299–300, 304, 318, 352, 354, 356, 371
registers, lining of, 68, 71
Reinhard, ——— (copyist), 96–97, 377
Répertoire International des Sources Musicales (RISM), 63, 223, 269, 371
Research Libraries Information Network (RLIN), 63
Reutter, Jochen, 102, 161, 251, 338
Rheda (Schloss), incl. Bentheim-Tecklenburg family, 87, 209
Riaucour, Count Andreas von, 109n, 178n, 191–92, 194n
Richter, Franz Xaver, 27, 38, 39n, 64, 95, 102, 109, 159–62, 251–53, 338–39; hand, handwriting, 161–62, 338–39; *Harmonische Belehrungen* (manuscript treatise, ca. 1767), 161–62, 252; *Messa à 4: voci concert:* (F-Pc, Ms. 20140), 161–62; *Super flumina Babylonis*, 147, 161, 253; symphonies, 214n, 215, 220–21, 287
Riemann, Hugo, 35, 127n
Rigel, Henri-Joseph(?), 224
RISM. *See* Répertoire International des Sources Musicales.
Ritschel, Franz (Dresden), 208–9
Ritschel, Franz (Mannheim), 209n
Ritschel, Johannes, 37–38, 88, 143n, 208–10, 215, 220, 277–79, 285, 343; hand, handwriting, 95, 111, 343; *Gioas, rè di Giuda*, 37, 208–9, 277; masses, 37–38, 106–7, 138–39, 141, 208, 224, 249, 277; motets, 208, 278–79
Rittersaal (Knights' Hall, in Mannheim palace), 25, 29–30

Rochester, N.Y., Eastman School of Music, 181
Roeder, Jobst (Johann?) Friedrich, paper, 106, ?311
Roeser, Valentin, 377
Rogge, Adriaan, paper, 312
roman numerals, in parts, 133–34, 137, 140, 236–38, 240–42, 246, 334, 344, 348–49, 351, 358, 361. *See also* Mannheim: orchestra, size of; parts, number of.
Roman, Johan Helmich, 89
Rome, 140, 174, 176, 180, 190, 206, 275–76
Roncaglio, Francesco, 261n
Ronish, Martha J., 49n, 67
Rottal, Count (Holešov), 202

Sächsische Landesbibliothek. *See* Dresden.
Sacchini, Antonio, 177, 180n, 281; *L'isola d'amore*, 200
sacred music. *See* Mannheim; manuscripts.
Salieri, Antonio, 44n, 125, 143n, 174; *La fiera di Venezia*, 177, 179–80, 190, 198n, 208, 263, 279; *La secchia rapita*, 177, 179–80, 184, 190, 282, 289
Salzburg, 88n, 154n–155n, 217–18, 314
Sans Souci (palace, Potsdam), 207
scanners: potential use in rastrology, 76n; use in handwriting studies, 94
Schmitt, Eduard, 159, 227n, 228, 251, 262
Schönborn-Wiesentheid. *See* Wiesentheid.
Schubart, Christian Friedrich Daniel, 26, 34
Schwan, Christian Friedrich, 168
Schweitzer, Anton: *Alceste*, 177, 179, 185n, 190, 193, 200, 290, 362; *Rosamunde*, 42, 200
Schwerin, incl. Mecklenburg-Schwerin, 215n, 216–17
Schwetzingen, 29, 34, 108, 149, 174–76, 223–24
scores, 36, 38–39, 44–45, 49, 54–55, 59–60, 92n, 105–9, 117, 123–26, 128, 130, 138,

405

144, 147, 154, 156, 159–61, 163, 165–71, 173–200, 203–5, 207, 208n, 218. 228, 233n, 234, 247, 252, 262, 280, 308–9, 336–37, 339–41, 348–49, 360, 362. *See also* autographs.
Sedlmayr, Philipp, 242
Seeau, Count Joseph Anton von, 87n, 116
Seiffert, Max, 36n
selenometry, 62
Sepp, Wilhelm, 96–97, 356–59. *See also* copyists, anonymous: Mannheim 3.
serenatas, 24, 28, 33
sets (of parts), replacement, 135–36, 155
Seyler troupe, 199
Sickingen, Count Carl Heinrich Joseph von, 194–98, 362; coat of arms, 195–97, 290; music collection, 65n, 100, 193–95, 197–98, 207, 266, 268–69, 289–90, 360; thematic catalogue, 177, 184–95, 197–98
Siegmund-Schultze, Walther, 36n
Slimlight, 60–61
Sonneck, Oscar George Theodore, 168
staff-liners. *See* rastra.
staff-lining (process of), 68, 71, 79n, 80, 84, 87–88; at Mannheim, 71, 79n, 84, 87–88; in Italy, 80, 88; in Salzburg, 88n; in Vienna, 71, 88. *See also* machines for lining paper; staving.
Stamitz, Carl, 336
Stamitz, Johann, 24, 27, 36, 51–52, 54n, 113, 127, 138, 140, 201, 209, 262, 281; hand, handwriting, 91–92; Mass in D, 64, 91–92, 156, 201–2, 203n, 206–7, 265, 272, 311, 338, 340; symphonies, 206, 210–14, 219–20, 285–88, 299, 304–5, 308, 379–80; symphonies, printed vs. manuscript versions, 214
Stanford, Cal., Stanford University, 201, 217, 371
Starck, Johann Friedrich, 224
staving, 12, 36, 49, 55, 65–88, 106, 109, 111, 117, 121, 123, 132, 135, 138–41, 143–48, 150, 153n, 155–56, 159, 161, 166, 179–81, 203–4, 206–9, 213, 215, 217, 219, 223, 261n, 317; analysis of,

79–87; determination of type, 80; measurement of, 66–67, 73, 76n, 81. *See also* rastra; rastrology; staff-lining.
staving, analytical specifications, 73–79; characteristics of lines (CL), 66, 75, 77, 78n, 84, 318; distance between lines (DL), 66, 75, 77, 84, 318; distance between staves (DS), 67, 75, 77, 80n, 83–84, 316; irregularities (IR), 75, 77–78, 80, 84, 87, 318; irregularities at beginning and end of staff, 66n, 78–79; length of staff (LS), 75, 78n, 79; stave span (SS), 66, 75–76; thickness of lines (TL), 75, 77; total span (TS), 65–67, 73, 75–76, 83–84, 110n, 317
Stockholm, 89, 164n
Strasbourg, 109, 160, 162n, 252, 338, 371
Strasser, Barbara, 169–70
Strasser, Sebastian, 311
Strohm, Reinhard, 178n
Stuckle, Franz Carl, 143n
Stuttgart, 91, 113n, 124, 140, 174, 201
Swabia, 24

Tafelmusik, 28
Tanselle, G. Thomas, 58
Tedeschi, Giovanni ("Amadori"), 269
Thuma. *See* Tuma.
Thurn und Taxis, Countess Violanta Therese, 210
Thurn und Taxis family. *See* Regensburg.
title pages. *See* manuscripts.
Toeschi, Johann, 34n, 64, 261n(?), 336
Toeschi, Joseph, 34, 156n, 213, 219, 262, 336; *L'enlèvement de Proserpine*, 108–9, 226; *Mars et Venus*, 144, 148, 151, 207, 265; symphonies, 82, 84, 209–10, 213–16, 219, 282, 286–88; symphonies, publication of, 215–16
total span (TS). *See* staving, analytical specifications.
tracing: of handwriting, 93–94, 335; of staving, 75–76; of watermarks, 59–62, 295
Traetta, Tommaso, 44n, 174, 181n, 191; *Ippolito ed Aricia*, 177, 180–81, 184, 190,

192; *Sofonisba*, 177, 179–82, 190, 192, 200, 269, 290, 352; *I Tintaridi*, 177, 179, 180n, 181, 184, 190–92
Traitteur, Theodor von, 42–43
trumpets, 28n
Tuma, Franz, 224
Turckheim, 65n, 313
Turner, Victor, 33n
Tyrol, 24
Tyson, Alan, 49n, 62, 67, 110, 217, 227n, 293

Unold, Joseph Anton, paper, 218, 234, 315
Uttini, Francesco, 275

Venier, Jean-Baptiste, 152
Verazi, Mattia, 178n
Vienna, 49, 71, 87, 88n, 91, 101, 113, 124, 128, 174, 177, 178n, 180, 191n, 201n, 202, 218, 232, 234, 282, 314, 320, 350
Vivaldi, Antonio, 58
Vogler, Georg Joseph, 34n, 36n, 37–39, 45, 47, 95, 97, 111, 117, 121, 133, 153, 163–71, 194, 199, 204, 223, 225, 230, 254–61 (Appendix A/V), 280, 328, 348–49, 370; hand, handwriting, 348–50; *Verzeichniß* (auction catalogue of Vogler's estate), 164–65, 167, 254; arias, 169–70, 223, 258; *Die Auferstehung Jesu*, 164n, 257, 261n, 348; *Deutsche Kirchenmusik*, 139, 165–67, 258, 348; *Der Kaufmann von Smyrna*, 163, 164n, 167–71, 173n, 254, 258, 348, 362; *Le rendez-vous de chasse*, 124, 151, 163, 164n, 167, 254–55, 348
Voltaire (François Marie Arouet), 26, 28

Waldkirch (Breisgau), 310
Waldmichelbach, 311
Walter, Friedrich, 35, 41, 116, 170
Washington, D.C., Library of Congress, 44, 132, 155n, 180, 181n, 195, 250n, 357
Wasselonne (Alsace), 65n, 313
watermark readers, 57–61
watermarks, 12, 36, 49, 55–65, 88, 109, 111, 135, 138–40, 144–45, 147, 150, 161–62, 166, 169, 170n, 185, 204, 212, 223, 293–315 (Appendix B); countermarks, 61, 64, 293–95, 300, 303, 305; identification of, 63; labeling of (incl. "abbreviated descriptions"), 57n, 62n, 64n, 293–95; measurement of, 62; mirror type, 62n, 294, 303; placement within sheet, 61–62, 293; principal watermark, 293–94; recording and reproduction of, 57–63, 293, 295; transposition type, 62n, 293–94; twin forms of, 56, 62, 293–95, 298–300, 303–5; variant forms of, 57, 308; variation type, 62n, 294, 304. *See also names of individual papermakers, especially* Blum family, Heusler family; paper.
Weber, Aloysia, 101, 110–11, 169n, 198, 218, 226, 268, 350
Weber, Carl Maria von, 101
Weber, Constanze, 111, 218, 350
Weber, Fridolin, 39n, 95, 101, 111, 169n, 204n, 218–19, 350; hand, handwriting, 350–51
Wendling, Dorothea, 110n
Wendling, Johann Baptist, 27, 178n, 195, 209, 281
Westphal, Johann Jacob Heinrich, 216
Weyh(e)r family, paper, 65n, 313
Wieland, Christoph Martin, 42
Wiesentheid, Musiksammlung des Grafen von Schönborn-Wiesentheid, 132, 153, 155n, 250n, 357
Winston-Salem, North Carolina, 69–70
Winter, Peter, 261n
Winter, Robert, 67
Wodiczka, Wenceslaus, 209, 281
Wolf, Jean K., 36, 68, 127, 136n–137n, 234, 262, 340
Wolfegg, 218, 315
Wormerveer, 313
Württemberg, 91, 113, 205, 218, 311, 314
Würzburg, 163

Xerography, use in rastrology, 76n, 78

Yale University. *See* New Haven, Ct.

Zaandam, 312
Zaandyk, 312–13
Zach, Johann, 224
Zweibrücken, Duke and Duchess of, 32
Zweibrücken, Maria Anna von, 109n

**QUELLEN UND STUDIEN ZUR GESCHICHTE
DER MANNHEIMER HOFKAPELLE**

Herausgegeben von der Forschungsstelle *Mannheimer Hofkapelle*
der Heidelberger Akademie der Wissenschaften unter Leitung von Silke Leopold

Band 1   Jochen Reutter: Studien zur Kirchenmusik Franz Xaver Richters (1709-1789). 1993.

Band 2   Ludwig Finscher / Bärbel Pelker / Jochen Reutter (Hrsg.): Mozart und Mannheim. Kongreßbericht Mannheim 1991. 1994.

Band 3   Ludwig Finscher (Hrsg.): J.C.F. Fischer in seiner Zeit. Tagungsbericht Rastatt 1988. 1994.

Band 4   Wolfram Enßlin: Niccolò Piccinni: *Catone in Utica*. Quellenüberlieferung, Aufführungsgeschichte und Analyse. 1996.

Band 5   Wilhelm Herrmann: Hoftheater – Volkstheater – Nationaltheater. Die Wanderbühnen im Mannheim des 18. Jahrhunderts und ihr Beitrag zur Gründung des Nationaltheaters. 1999.

Band 6   Bärbel Pelker / Rüdiger Thomsen-Fürst (Hrsg.): Georg Joseph Vogler (1749-1814). Materialien zu Leben und Werk unter besonderer Berücksichtigung der pfalz-bayerischen Dienstjahre. Teil I und II. 2002.

Band 7   Thomas Betzwieser / Silke Leopold (Hrsg.): Abbé Vogler. Ein Mannheimer im europäischen Kontext. Internationales Colloquium Heidelberg, 3.–5. Juni 1999. 2002.

Band 8   Ludwig Finscher / Bärbel Pelker / Rüdiger Thomsen-Fürst (Hrsg.): Mannheim – Ein *Paradies der Tonkünstler?* Kongressbericht Mannheim 1999. 2002.

Band 9   Eugene K. Wolf: Manuscripts from Mannheim, ca. 1730–1778. A Study in the Methodology of Musical Source Research. 2002.

Hans Keller

Functional Analysis: The Unity of Contrasting Themes
Funktionsanalyse: Die Einheit kontrastierender Themen

Complete Edition of the Analytical Scores
Gesamtausgabe der analytischen Partituren
Edited by / Herausgegeben von Gerold W. Gruber

Frankfurt/M., Berlin, Bern, Bruxelles, New York, Oxford, Wien, 2001.
496 S., zahlr. Notenbeisp.Publikationen des Instituts für Musikanalyse Wien.
Herausgegeben von Gottfried Scholz. Bd.5
ISBN 3-631-36129-7 · Geb. € 70.60*
US-ISBN 0-8204-5350-1

Der in Wien geborene britische Musiker und Musiktheoretiker Hans Keller (1919-1985) verfasste neben Büchern über Igor Strawinsky, Benjamin Britten und Joseph Haydn auch zahlreiche Artikel über Mozart, Beethoven, Schönberg sowie über Filmmusik oder zu methodischen Fragen der Musikanalyse und -theorie. 1957 erfand Keller eine nonverbale Analysemethode („Funktionsanalyse"): durch Verknüpfung einzelner Elemente aus der Originalkomposition wird der logische Zusammenhang der Komposition unmittelbar während der Aufführung gehört (eine neue Methode, die verbale Analyse auf kreative und künstlerische Weise ergänzt).

The British musician and music theorist Hans Keller (1919-1985) who was born in Vienna/Austria, wrote several books about Igor Strawinsky, Benjamin Britten und Joseph Haydn as well as articles about Mozart, Beethoven, Schönberg, about film music and about methods in music analysis and music theory. In 1957 Keller invented a nonverbal method of music analysis („functional analysis"): Analytical results are presented as interludes during the performance of a musical piece and the logical network within a composition can easily be heard.

Frankfurt/M · Berlin · Bern · Bruxelles · New York · Oxford · Wien
Distribution: Verlag Peter Lang AG
Moosstr. 1, CH-2542 Pieterlen
Telefax 00 41 (0) 32 / 376 17 27

*The €-price includes German tax rate
Prices are subject to change without notice
Homepage http://www.peterlang.de